Publisher
MIKE RICHARDSON

Series Editor
JAMIE S. RICH

Collection Editor
CHRIS WARNER

Collection Designer
KRISTEN BURDA

USAGI YOJIMBO™ (BOOK 12): GRASSCUTTER
© 1997, 1998, 1999 Stan Sakai. Introduction © 1999 Will Eisner. Usagi Yojimbo and all other
prominently featured characters are trademarks of Stan Sakai. All rights reserved. No portion of this
publication may be reproduced or transmitted, in any form or by any means, without the express written
permission of the copyright holder(s). Names, characters, places, and incidents featured in this publication
either are the product of the author's imagination or are used fictitiously. Any resemblance to actual persons
(living or dead), events, institutions, or locales, without satiric intent, is coincidental. Dark Horse Maverick™
is a trademark of Dark Horse Comics, Inc. Dark Horse Comics® and the Dark Horse logo are trademarks
of Dark Horse Comics, Inc., registered in various categories and countries. All rights reserved.

This book collects issues 13–22
of the Dark Horse comic-book series *Usagi Yojimbo™ Volume III*

Visit the Usagi Dojo website
www.usagiyojimbo.com

Published by
Dark Horse Comics, Inc.
10956 SE Main Street
Milwaukie, OR 97222

www.darkhorse.com

To find a comics shop in your area,
call the Comic Shop Locator Service toll-free at 1-888-266-4226

First edition: August 1999
ISBN: 1-56971-413-4

3 5 7 9 10 8 6 4
Printed in Canada

USAGI

YOJIMBO™

— GRASSCUTTER —

Created, Written,
and Illustrated by
STAN SAKAI

Introduction by
WILL EISNER

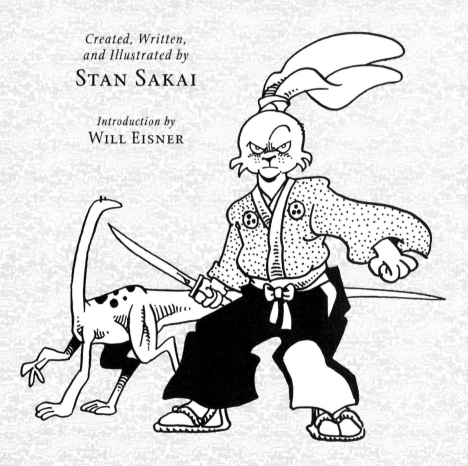

DARK HORSE
MAVERICK™

Usagi Yojimbo

An American Komikkusu

WHILE I HAVE KNOWN about Stan Sakai's work for some time, I came upon *Usagi Yojimbo* only recently. This is because my attention over the years has been centered on what I regarded as the expansion of the medium as literature, and I look for those works that seem to be "pushing the envelope." From time to time I make a "discovery" such as *Bone* or encourage what I believe is a promising new self-published work. More often my attention is centered on trends, a focus that seemed so necessary during my years of teaching.

While I have always been a staunch apostle of the internationalization of our medium, I confess that I really assumed the form emanated from American comics. Oh, yes, as a student I studied early Japanese prints like the narrative work of Hiroshige, and I used a Japanese brush myself for a long time. I have admired modern Japanese graphic storytelling. But I believed it to be insular and even untranslatable. I never anticipated an integration such as that demonstrated by *Usagi*.

In the Autumn of 1994 I was shepherded through Japan by Fred Schodt, a leading American scholar and expert on Japanese comics, in the company of a group of American artists and writers. I was stunned by what I found. I saw a booming industry, an enormous readership, and a pervasive social presence of the medium beyond any of my fondest dreams, for the medium to which I've devoted my life. There are obvious cultural reasons for this but the fact remains that *manga*, or *komikkusu* as the Japanese also call it, is a very singular form of the art of sequentially arranged images and text to narrate a story or dramatize an idea. As in America, manga occupies a place somewhere between films, literature, and "fine" art. The range of an American comic's subject matter, however, is limited mostly to the interest of young males. They are the best sellers, and the outer margins are left to the foraging of those who address children, women, and adults. In Japan, comic books occupy nearly the same public acceptance as novels and films. The medium has a legitimacy not yet attained anywhere else. But perhaps the most significant characteristic of manga is their range of readership and subject matter. There are komikkusu specifically addressed to expectant mothers, little children, pre-teens, boys, girls, adults, and seniors male and female. Many are centered on sports and games.

However enviable is this lateral coverage, the fact remains that Japanese publishers make little effort to reach beyond what is "commercial." The art is designed to shock, titillate, or emulate animation. Style and surface technique dominate art and content. Like the American superhero and horror comics, their plots are generally simple.

As far as I could see, the Japanese comics are reluctant to introduce stories or ideas of another culture. Save for a surface fascination with American names and certain Western physical characteristics, it is hard to find manga that undertake subjects with realistic problems of the human condition. Work by other nationals that introduce foreign cultures such as those that appear in European and American comic books is rarely seen.

Yet for all of that, the Japanese comics have an undeniable fascination and have succeeded in invading the American and European markets. There is little doubt that they deliver exciting graphics. The trouble is that they have provided us with very little insight into Japanese life, culture, or history such as in the work of Tezuka or the classic *Gen*.

So, it was with this prejudice that I began to read the *Usagi Yojimbo* books Stan Sakai sent me. My first reaction was dismissive. I shrugged at his use of anthropomorphic characters as a way of avoiding the demands of realistic art, which made Frank Miller's *Ronin* so compelling. Gradually, however, as the story absorbed me I changed my opinion. I felt I was somehow *reading* a komikkusu in *Japanese*! Stan's animal-people faces allow the reader to imagine and insert "real" faces out of their own memory. After I finished several stories, the accomplishment was obvious. I was transported into the fascinating world of Japanese folklore.

This is an important event in the progress of this medium because Stan Sakai has successfully brought to American comics a collection of Japanese fables well told in the American style. He has a good control of sequential art, and his compositions have the ability to create powerful understatements.

Usagi Yojimbo is an enduring work. *Bravo*.

WILL EISNER

CONTENTS

FOR SCOTT, JUDY,
AND KIRBY SHAW!

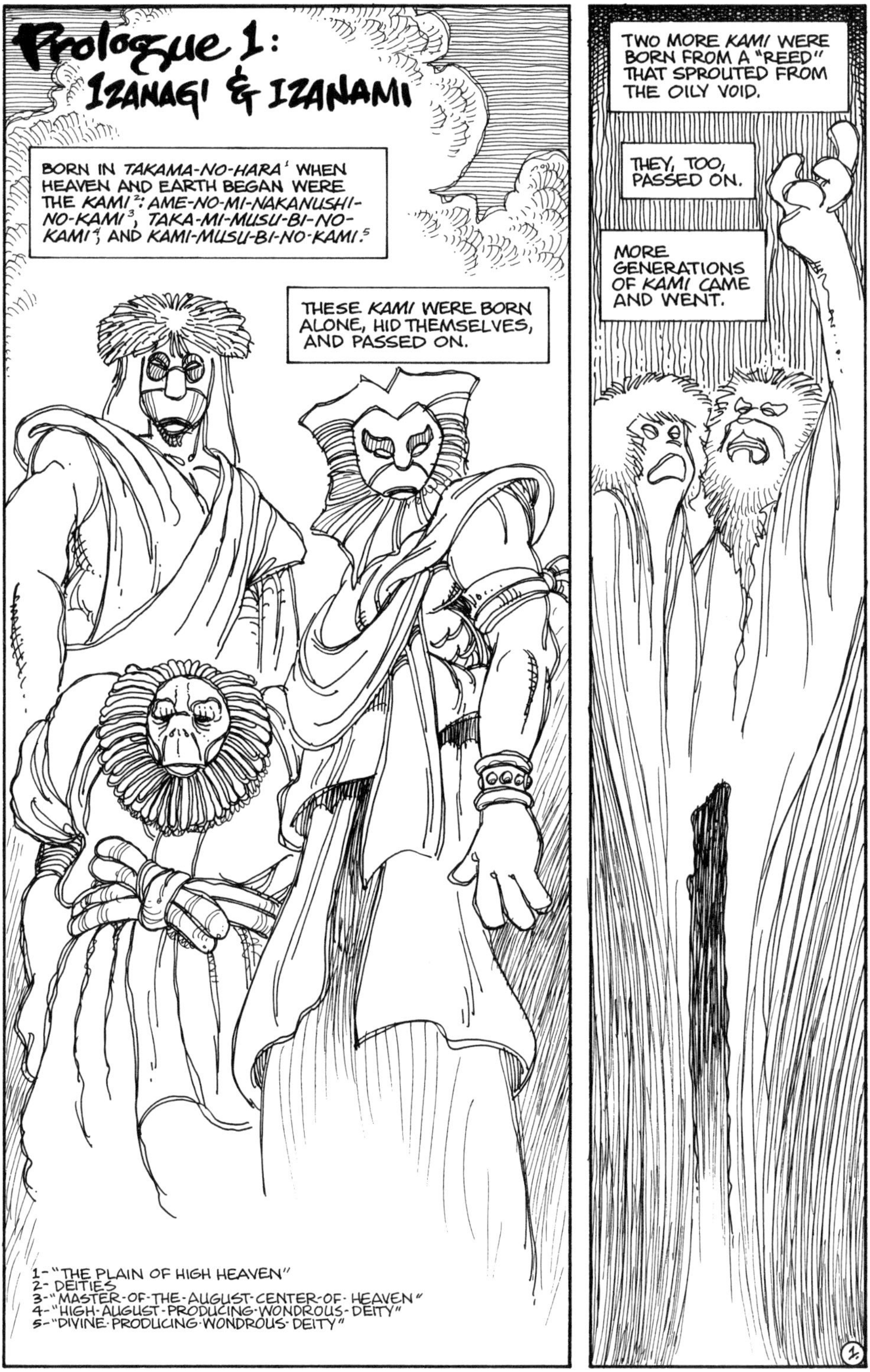
Prologue 1:
IZANAGI & IZANAMI
BORN IN TAKAMA-NO-HARA[1] WHEN HEAVEN AND EARTH BEGAN WERE THE KAMI[2]: AME-NO-MI-NAKANUSHI-NO-KAMI[3], TAKA-MI-MUSU-BI-NO-KAMI[4], AND KAMI-MUSU-BI-NO-KAMI.[5]
THESE KAMI WERE BORN ALONE, HID THEMSELVES, AND PASSED ON.
1- "THE PLAIN OF HIGH HEAVEN"
2- DEITIES
3- "MASTER-OF-THE-AUGUST-CENTER-OF-HEAVEN"
4- "HIGH-AUGUST-PRODUCING-WONDROUS-DEITY"
5- "DIVINE-PRODUCING-WONDROUS-DEITY"
TWO MORE KAMI WERE BORN FROM A "REED" THAT SPROUTED FROM THE OILY VOID.
THEY, TOO, PASSED ON.
MORE GENERATIONS OF KAMI CAME AND WENT.
1

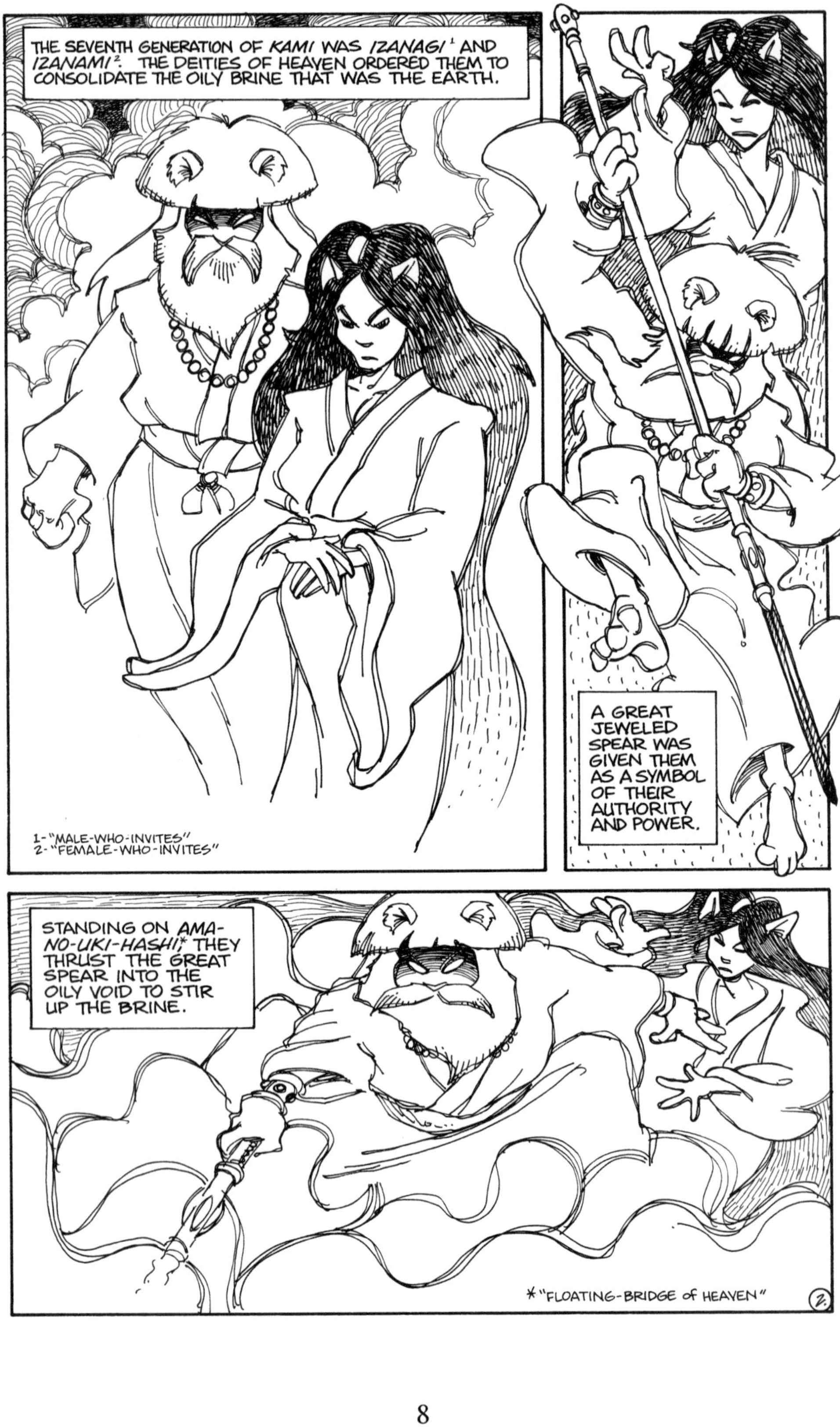
THE SEVENTH GENERATION OF *KAMI* WAS *IZANAGI*[1] AND *IZANAMI*[2]. THE DEITIES OF HEAVEN ORDERED THEM TO CONSOLIDATE THE OILY BRINE THAT WAS THE EARTH.
1- "MALE-WHO-INVITES"
2- "FEMALE-WHO-INVITES"
A GREAT JEWELED SPEAR WAS GIVEN THEM AS A SYMBOL OF THEIR AUTHORITY AND POWER.
STANDING ON *AMA-NO-UKI-HASHI*,* THEY THRUST THE GREAT SPEAR INTO THE OILY VOID TO STIR UP THE BRINE.
* "FLOATING-BRIDGE of HEAVEN"

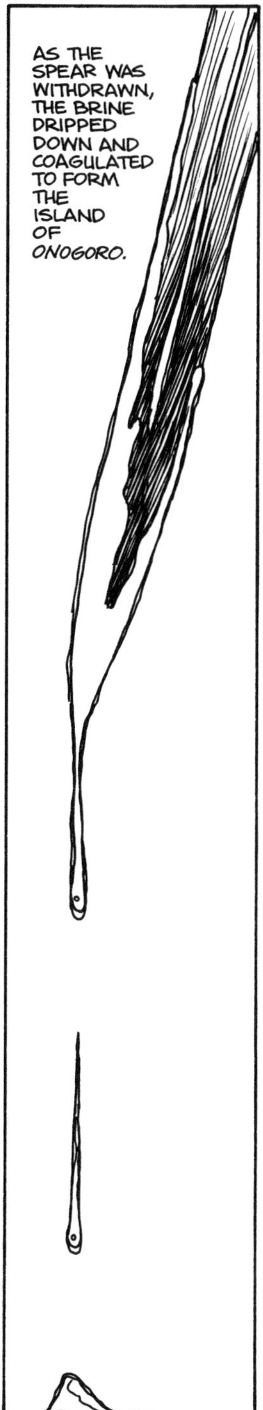
AS THE
SPEAR WAS
WITHDRAWN,
THE BRINE
DRIPPED
DOWN AND
COAGULATED
TO FORM
THE
ISLAND
OF
ONOGORO.

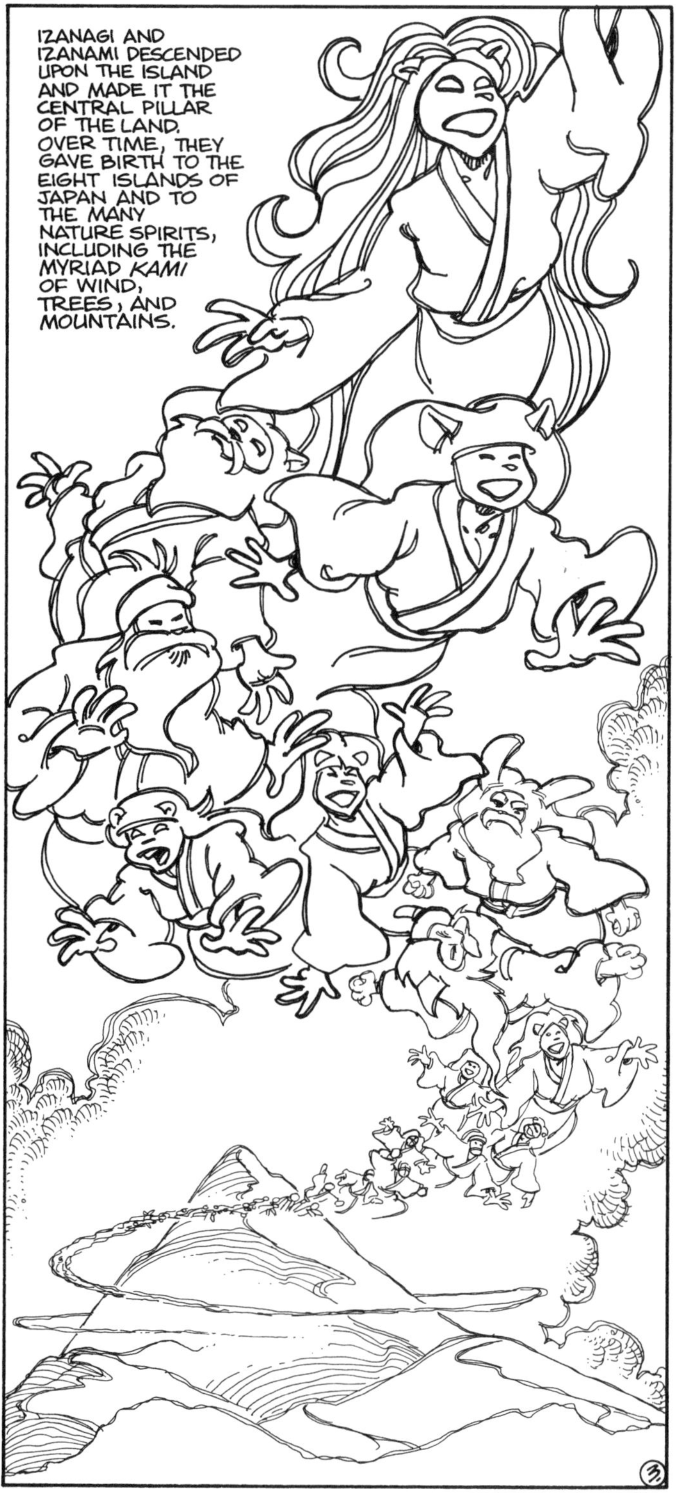
IZANAGI AND
IZANAMI DESCENDED
UPON THE ISLAND
AND MADE IT THE
CENTRAL PILLAR
OF THE LAND.
OVER TIME, THEY
GAVE BIRTH TO THE
EIGHT ISLANDS OF
JAPAN AND TO
THE MANY
NATURE SPIRITS,
INCLUDING THE
MYRIAD *KAMI*
OF WIND,
TREES, AND
MOUNTAINS.

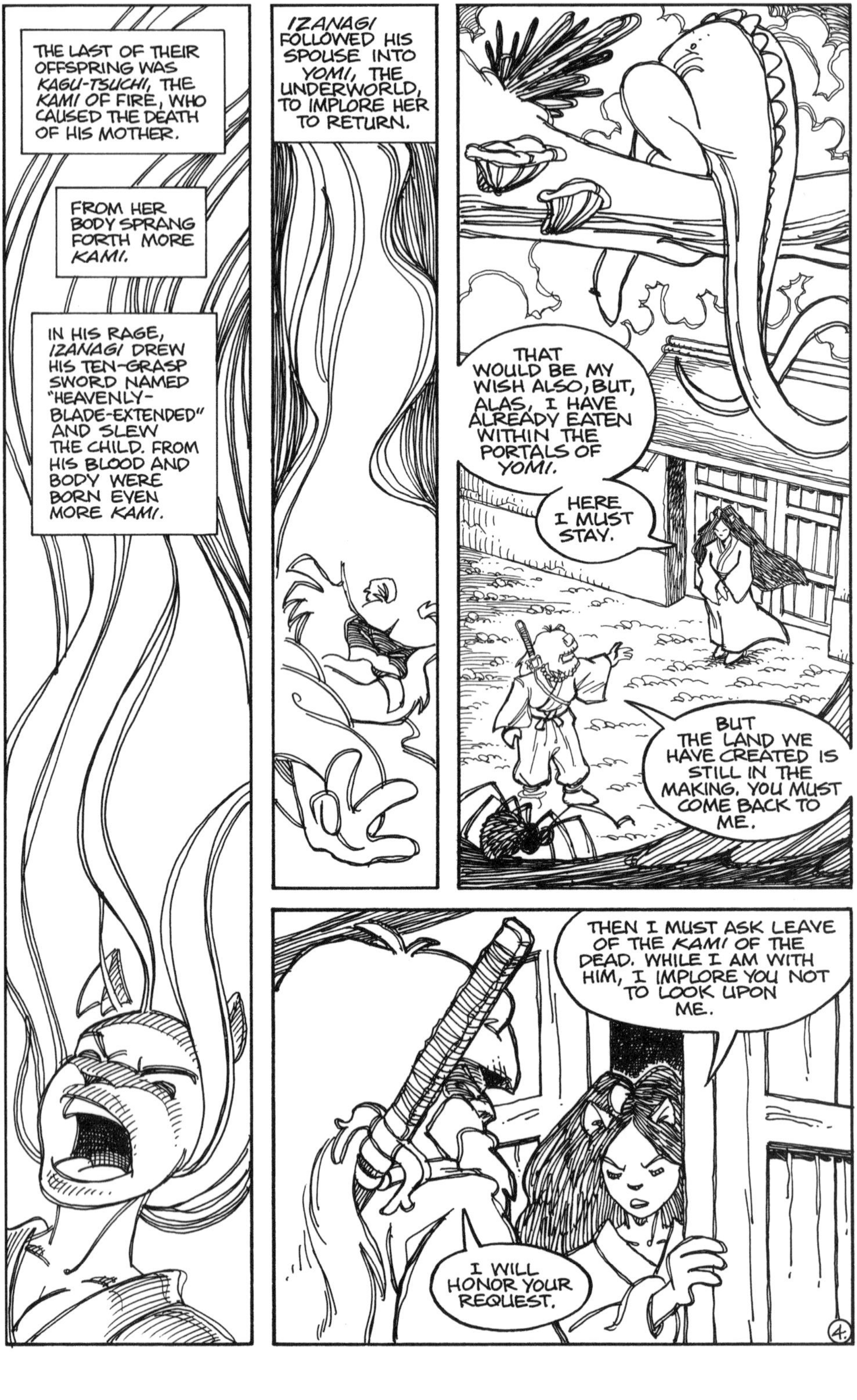
THE LAST OF THEIR OFFSPRING WAS *KAGU-TSUCHI*, THE *KAMI* OF FIRE, WHO CAUSED THE DEATH OF HIS MOTHER.
FROM HER BODY SPRANG FORTH MORE *KAMI*.
IN HIS RAGE, *IZANAGI* DREW HIS TEN-GRASP SWORD NAMED "HEAVENLY-BLADE-EXTENDED" AND SLEW THE CHILD. FROM HIS BLOOD AND BODY WERE BORN EVEN MORE *KAMI*.
IZANAGI FOLLOWED HIS SPOUSE INTO *YOMI*, THE UNDERWORLD, TO IMPLORE HER TO RETURN.
THAT WOULD BE MY WISH ALSO, BUT, ALAS, I HAVE ALREADY EATEN WITHIN THE PORTALS OF *YOMI*.
HERE I MUST STAY.
BUT THE LAND WE HAVE CREATED IS STILL IN THE MAKING. YOU MUST COME BACK TO ME.
THEN I MUST ASK LEAVE OF THE *KAMI* OF THE DEAD. WHILE I AM WITH HIM, I IMPLORE YOU NOT TO LOOK UPON ME.
I WILL HONOR YOUR REQUEST.
4.

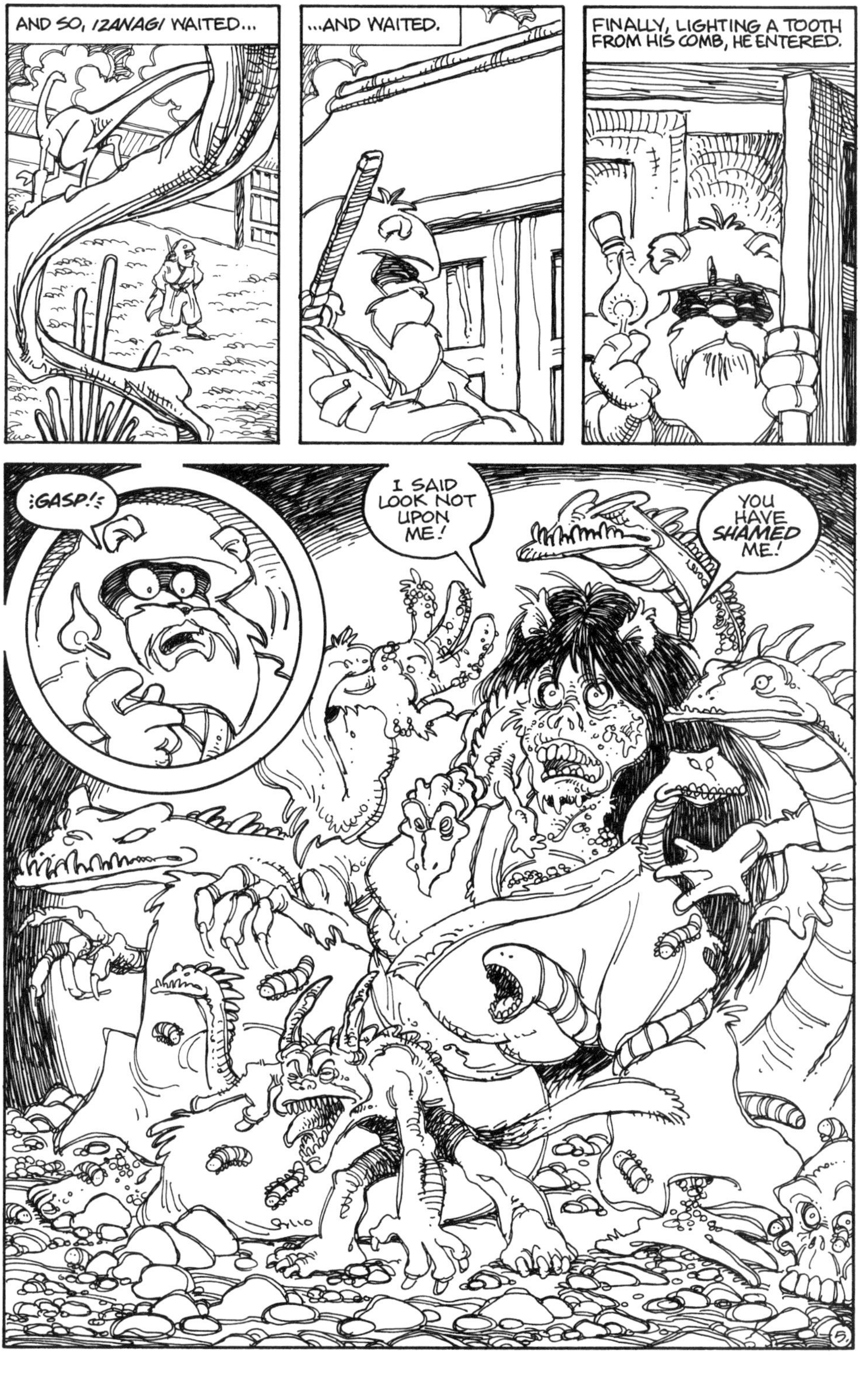
AND SO, IZANAGI WAITED...
...AND WAITED.
FINALLY, LIGHTING A TOOTH FROM HIS COMB, HE ENTERED.
¡GASP!¡
I SAID LOOK NOT UPON ME!
YOU HAVE SHAMED ME!
5

ENRAGED BY THE INSULT, *IZANAMI* SENT THE HAGS OF HELL, THE EIGHT *KAMI* OF THUNDER, AND FIFTEEN HUNDRED WARRIORS OF HELL TO PURSUE HER HUSBAND.

IZANAGI MANAGED TO ELUDE HIS PURSUERS, AND *IZANAMI*, IN HER RAGE, GAVE CHASE HERSELF ...

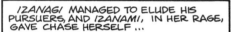

...ONLY TO FIND THE FINAL PATH BLOCKED BY AN ENORMOUS ROCK PLACED THERE BY HER HUSBAND.

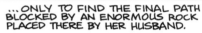

A CURSE I PLACE UPON YOU-- EACH DAY I WILL KILL A THOUSAND IN YOUR LAND!

DO SO AND EACH DAY I WILL CAUSE FIFTEEN HUNDRED TO BE BORN!

FROM THIS DAY I TAKE MY LEAVE OF YOU...

...FOREVER!

6.

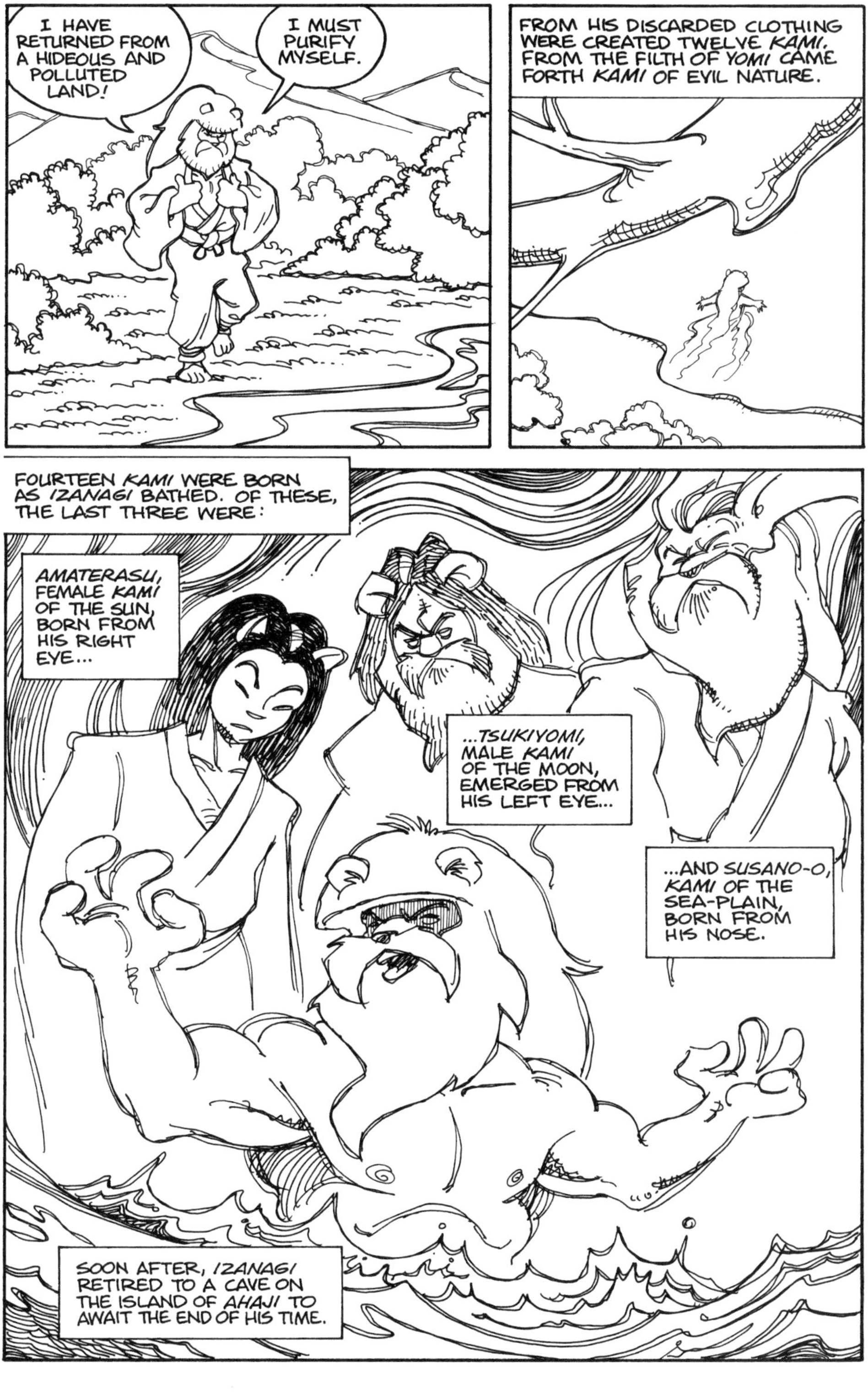
I HAVE RETURNED FROM A HIDEOUS AND POLLUTED LAND!
I MUST PURIFY MYSELF.
FROM HIS DISCARDED CLOTHING WERE CREATED TWELVE *KAMI*. FROM THE FILTH OF *YOMI* CAME FORTH *KAMI* OF EVIL NATURE.
FOURTEEN *KAMI* WERE BORN AS *IZANAGI* BATHED. OF THESE, THE LAST THREE WERE:
AMATERASU, FEMALE *KAMI* OF THE SUN, BORN FROM HIS RIGHT EYE...
...*TSUKIYOMI*, MALE *KAMI* OF THE MOON, EMERGED FROM HIS LEFT EYE...
...AND *SUSANO-O*, *KAMI* OF THE SEA-PLAIN, BORN FROM HIS NOSE.
SOON AFTER, *IZANAGI* RETIRED TO A CAVE ON THE ISLAND OF *AHAJI* TO AWAIT THE END OF HIS TIME.

PROLOGUE 2: SUSANO-O

HAVING BEEN EXPELLED FROM HEAVEN BY THE EIGHT HUNDRED MYRIAD DEITIES FOR AN INSULT UPON *AMATERASU* THAT, FOR A TIME, BROUGHT DARKNESS UPON THE WORLD, *SUSANO-O* WANDERED THE LAND OF *IZUMO* AT THE HEADWATERS OF THE RIVER *HI*.

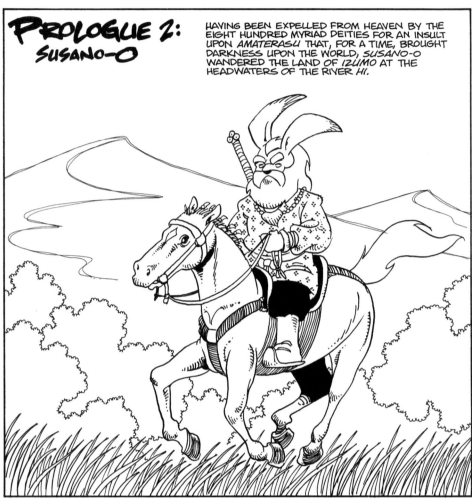

EH? WHAT'S THIS FLOATING ON THE WATER?

CHOPSTICKS! THERE ARE PEOPLE HIGHER UP THE RIVER.

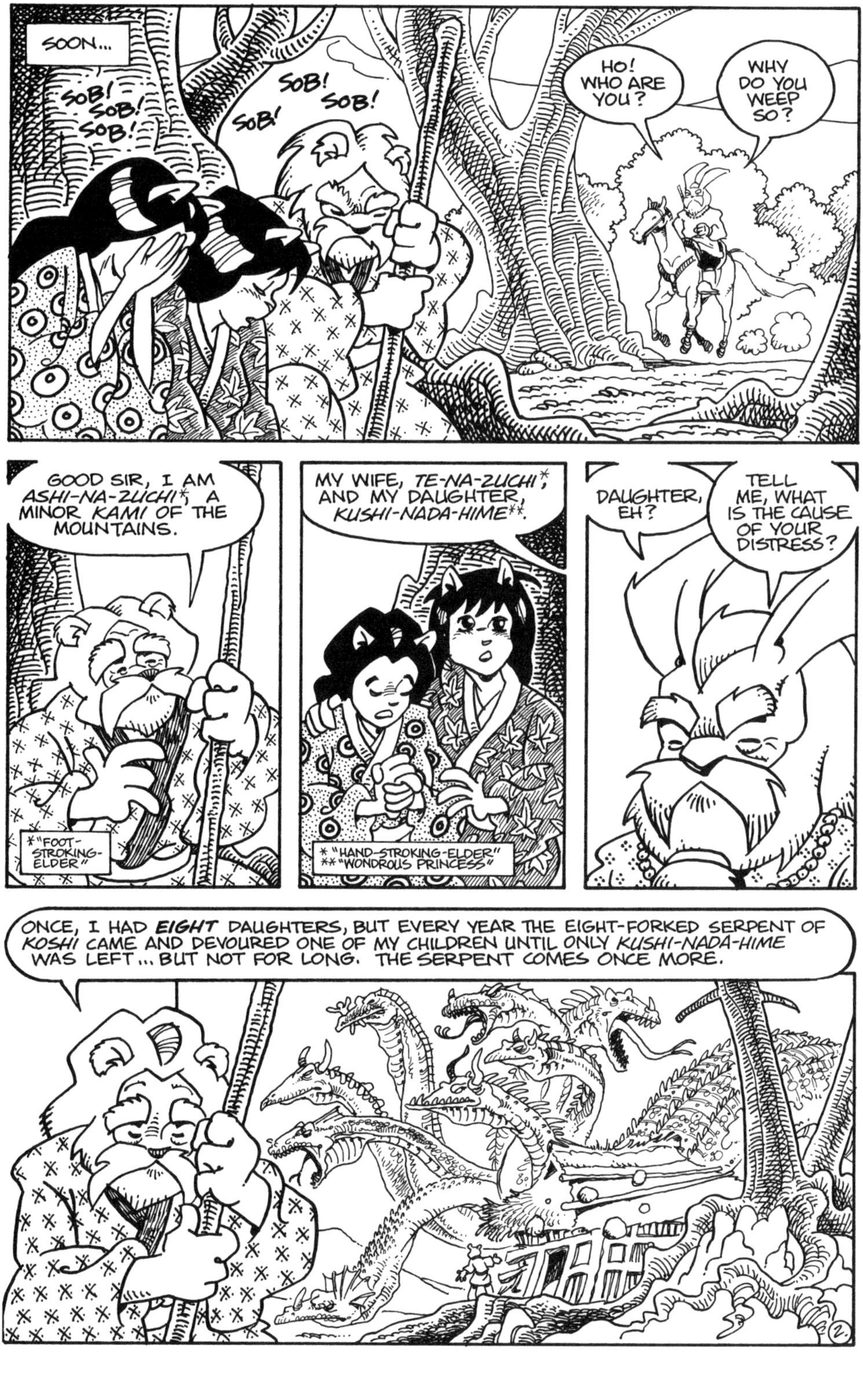
SOON...
SOB! SOB! SOB!
SOB! SOB! SOB!
HO! WHO ARE YOU?
WHY DO YOU WEEP SO?
GOOD SIR, I AM *ASHI-NA-ZUCHI**, A MINOR *KAMI* OF THE MOUNTAINS.
*"FOOT-STROKING-ELDER"
MY WIFE, *TE-NA-ZUCHI**, AND MY DAUGHTER, *KUSHI-NADA-HIME***.
* "HAND-STROKING-ELDER"
** "WONDROUS PRINCESS"
DAUGHTER, EH?
TELL ME, WHAT IS THE CAUSE OF YOUR DISTRESS?
ONCE, I HAD **EIGHT** DAUGHTERS, BUT EVERY YEAR THE EIGHT-FORKED SERPENT OF *KOSHI* CAME AND DEVOURED ONE OF MY CHILDREN UNTIL ONLY *KUSHI-NADA-HIME* WAS LEFT... BUT NOT FOR LONG. THE SERPENT COMES ONCE MORE.
2.

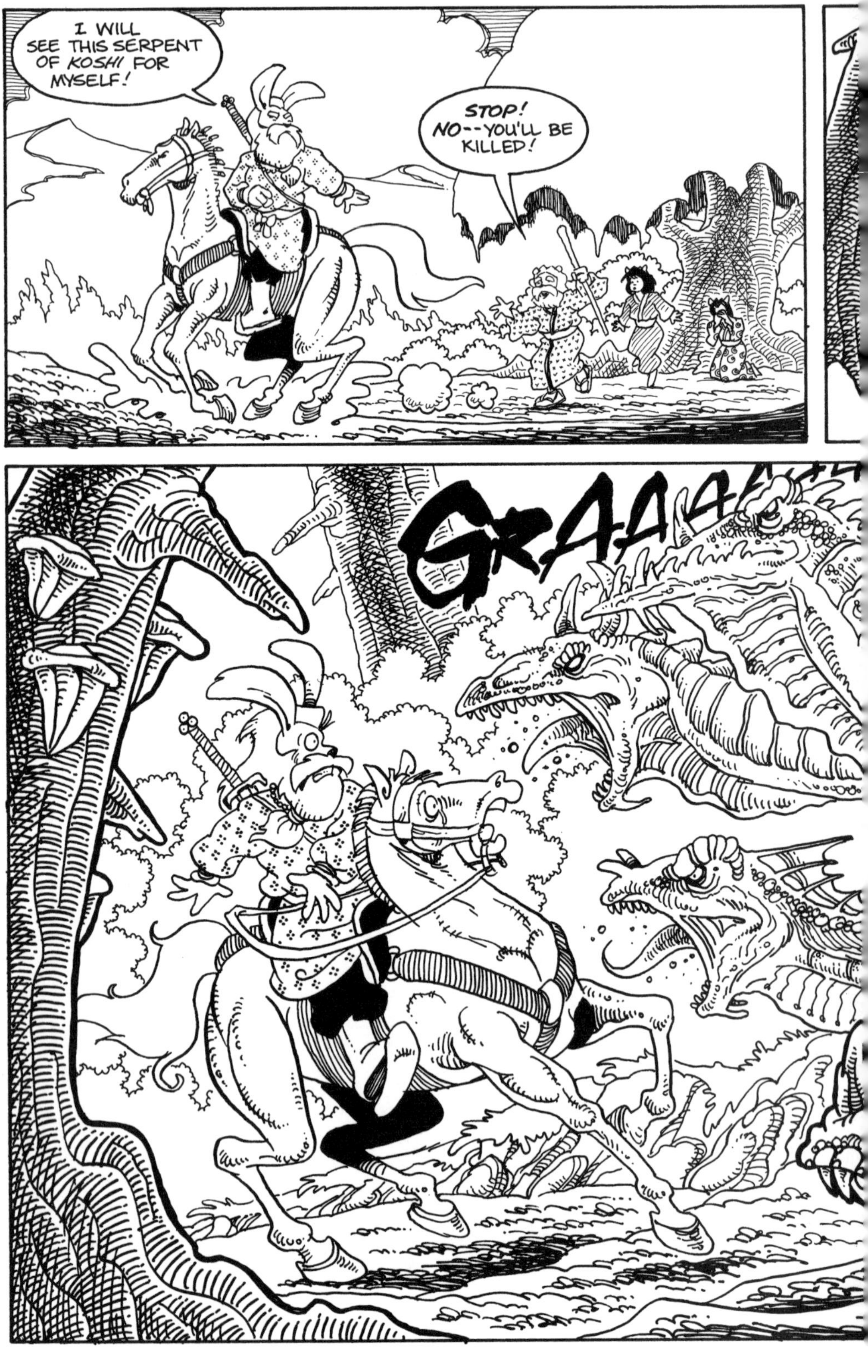
I WILL SEE THIS SERPENT OF *KOSHI* FOR MYSELF!
STOP! NO--YOU'LL BE KILLED!
GRAAAA

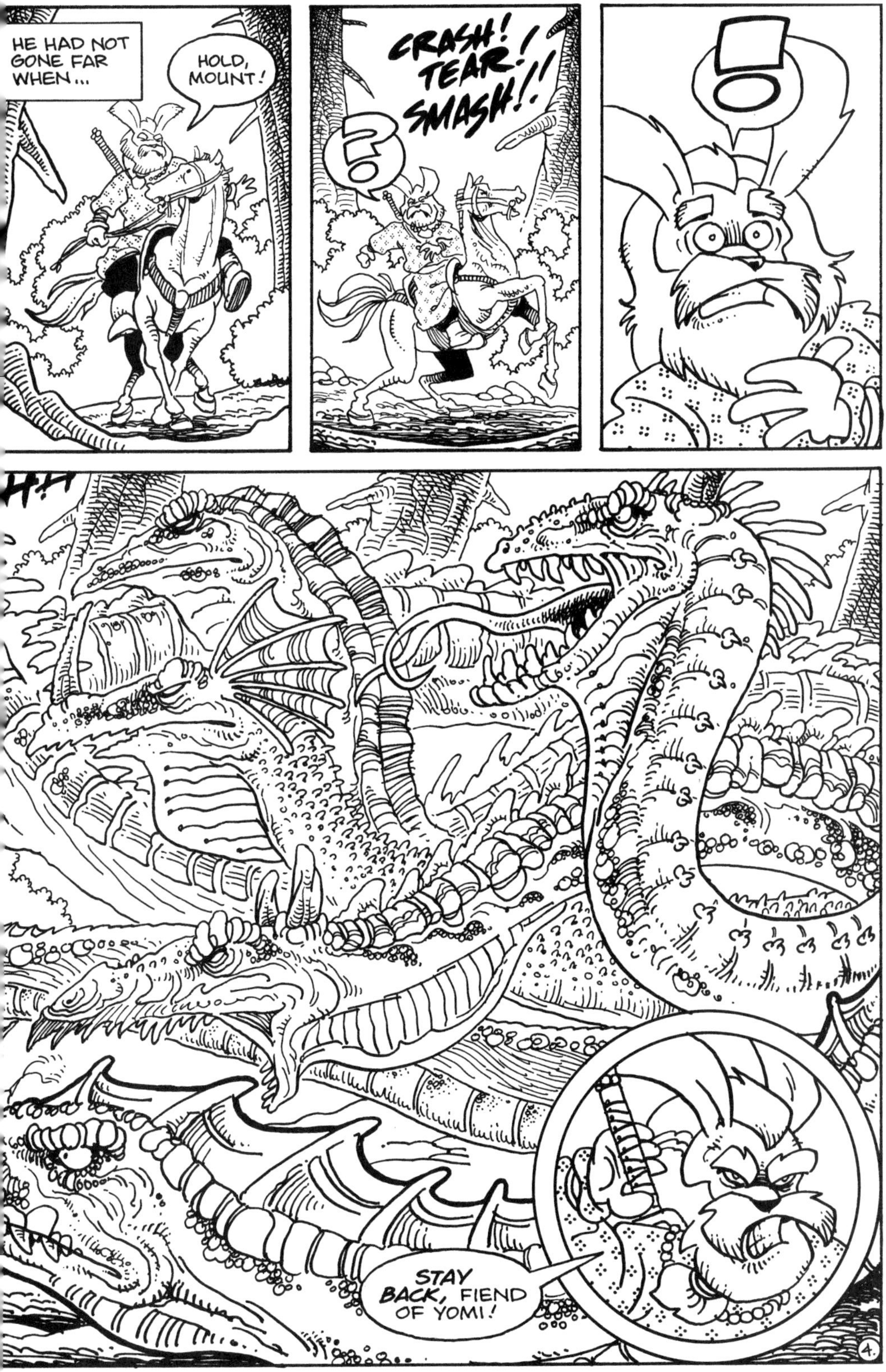
HE HAD NOT GONE FAR WHEN...
HOLD, MOUNT!
CRASH! TEAR! SMASH!!
?!
!
STAY BACK, FIEND OF YOMI!
4.

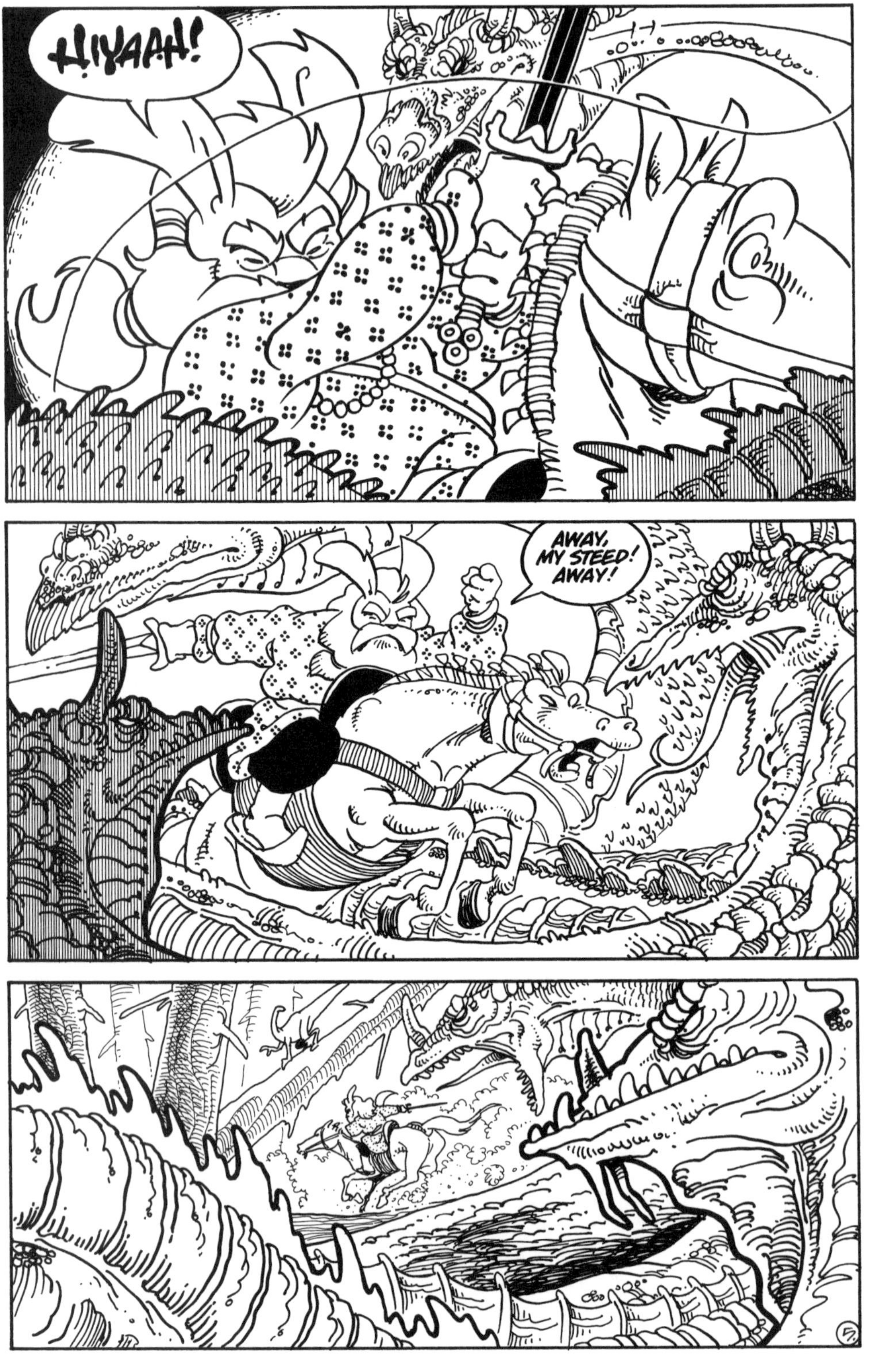
HIYAAH!
AWAY, MY STEED! AWAY!

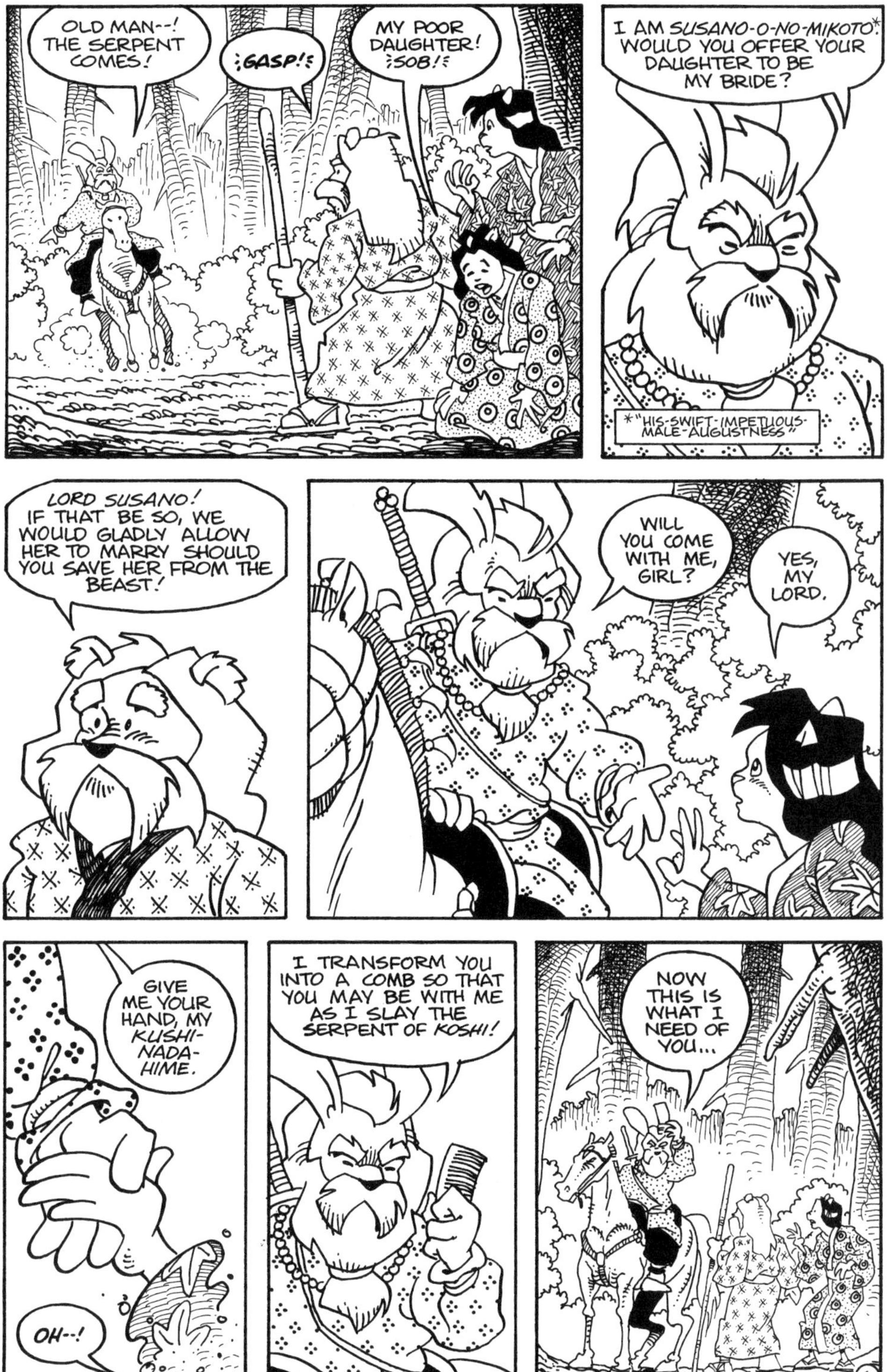

OLD MAN--! THE SERPENT COMES!
GASP!
MY POOR DAUGHTER! SOB!
I AM SUSANO-O-NO-MIKOTO* WOULD YOU OFFER YOUR DAUGHTER TO BE MY BRIDE?
*"HIS-SWIFT-IMPETUOUS-MALE-AUGUSTNESS"
LORD SUSANO! IF THAT BE SO, WE WOULD GLADLY ALLOW HER TO MARRY SHOULD YOU SAVE HER FROM THE BEAST!
WILL YOU COME WITH ME, GIRL?
YES, MY LORD.
GIVE ME YOUR HAND, MY KUSHI-NADA-HIME.
OH--!
I TRANSFORM YOU INTO A COMB SO THAT YOU MAY BE WITH ME AS I SLAY THE SERPENT OF KOSHI!
NOW THIS IS WHAT I NEED OF YOU...
6.

Panel 1:
"RICE-BEER MUST BE REFINED EIGHT TIMES.

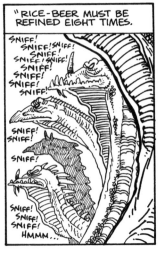

SNIFF!
SNIFF! SNIFF!
SNIFF!
SNIFF! SNIFF!
SNIFF!
SNIFF!
SNIFF!

SNIFF!
SNIFF!

SNIFF!

SNIFF!
SNIFF!
SNIFF!
HMMM...

Panel 2:
"THEN BUILD A FENCE WITH EIGHT GATES.

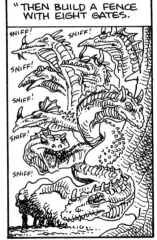

SNIFF!   SNIFF!

SNIFF!

SNIFF!

SNIFF!

Panel 3:
"BEYOND EACH GATE, BUILD A PLATFORM.

Panel 4:
"ON EACH PLATFORM, PLACE A VAT OF RICE-BEER."

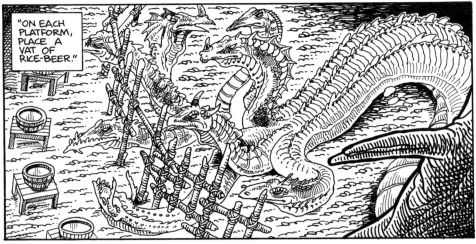

Panel 5:
SLURP! SLURP!

Panel 6:
AHHH... BELCH!

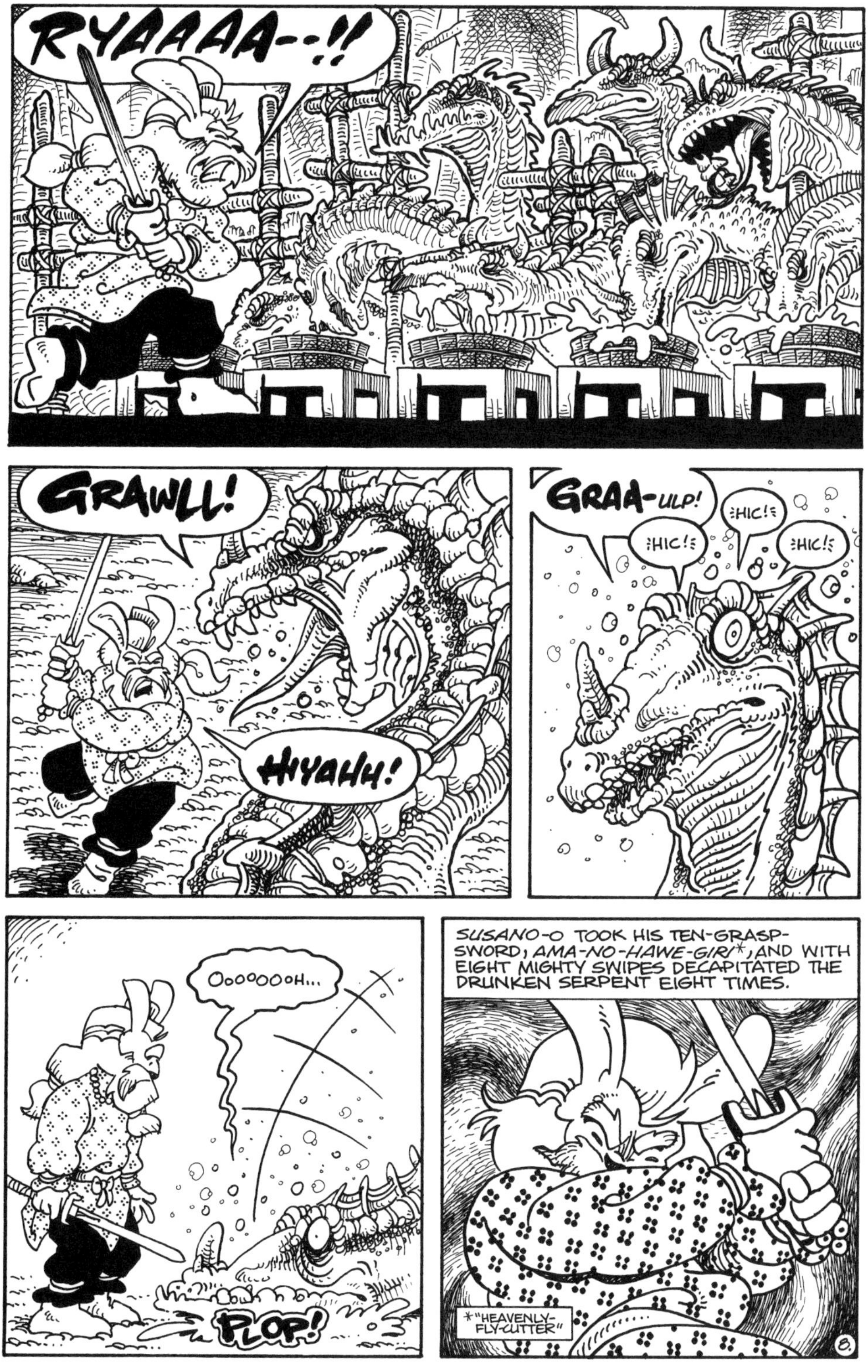
RYAAAA--!!
GRAWLL!
HIYAHH!
GRAA-ULP!
HIC!
HIC!
HIC!
OOOOOOOH...
PLOP!
SUSANO-O TOOK HIS TEN-GRASP-SWORD, AMA-NO-HAWE-GIRI*, AND WITH EIGHT MIGHTY SWIPES DECAPITATED THE DRUNKEN SERPENT EIGHT TIMES.
*"HEAVENLY-FLY-CUTTER"
8.

AS HE WAS CHOPPING OFF THE FOURTH TAIL...
EH?
CLANG!
WHAT COULD IT BE?
SLIIIITT!
A SPLENDOROUS SWORD!
SUSANO-O PRESENTED THE SWORD, CALLED MURAKUMO-NO-TSURUGI*, TO AMATERASU TO APPEASE HER ANGER.
*"SWORD-OF-THE-VILLAGE-OF-THE-CLUSTERING-CLOUDS"
SUSANO-O AND KUSHI-NADA-HIME WERE MARRIED AND DWELLED IN A MAGNIFICENT PALACE IN IZUMO.

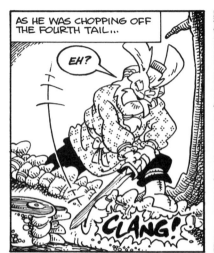

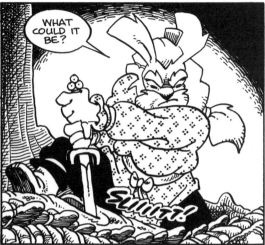

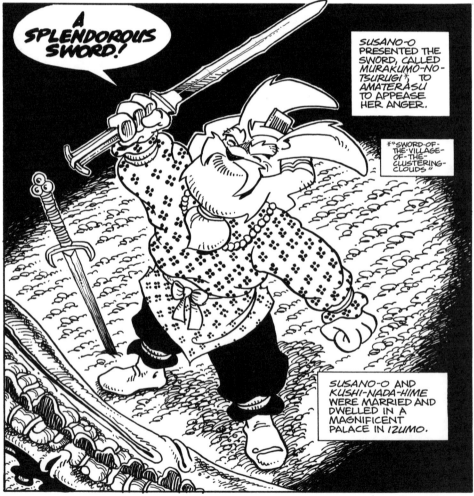

END of PROLOGUE 2

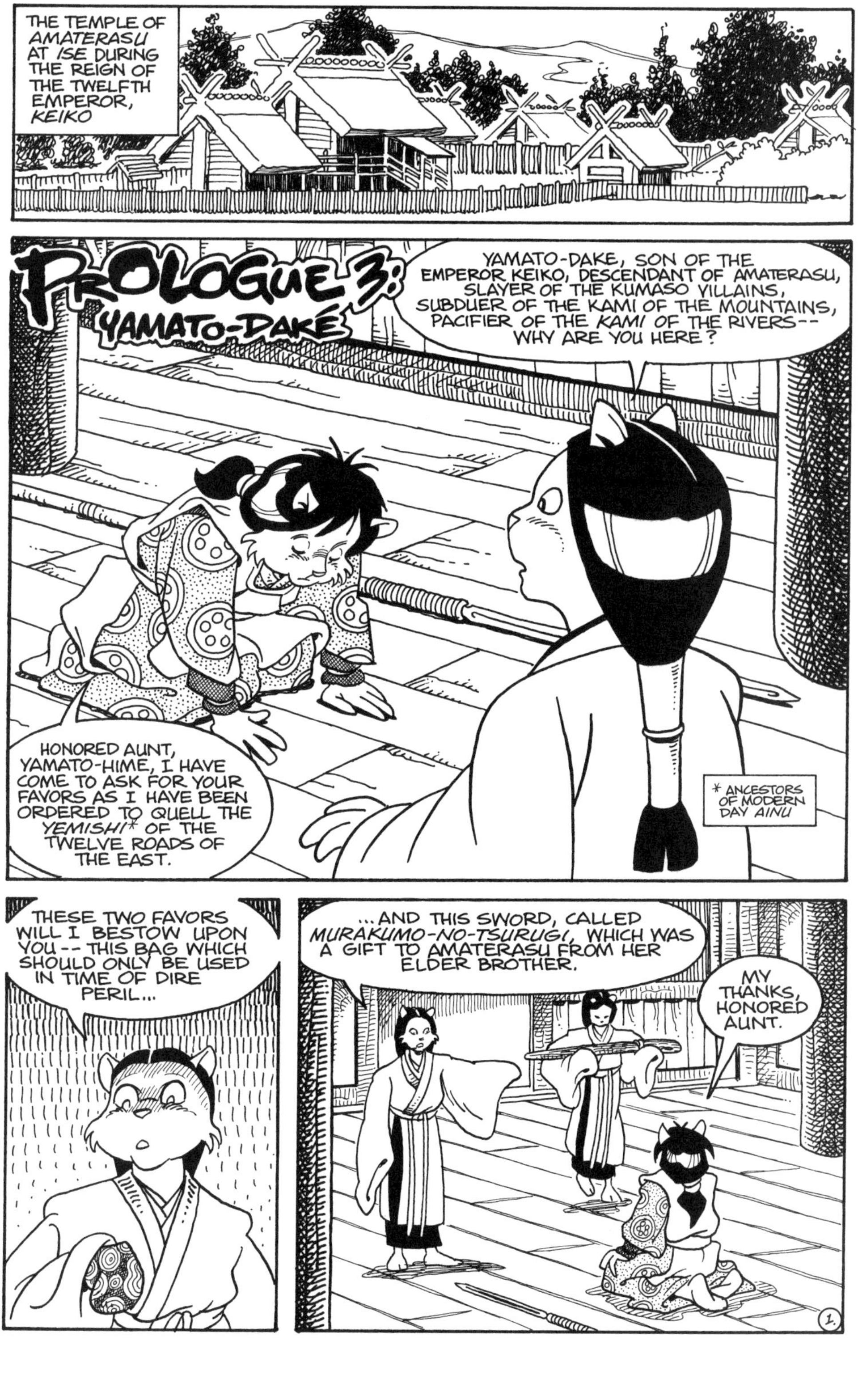
THE TEMPLE OF AMATERASU AT ISE DURING THE REIGN OF THE TWELFTH EMPEROR, KEIKO
PROLOGUE 3: YAMATO-DAKÉ
YAMATO-DAKE, SON OF THE EMPEROR KEIKO, DESCENDANT OF AMATERASU, SLAYER OF THE KUMASO VILLAINS, SUBDUER OF THE KAMI OF THE MOUNTAINS, PACIFIER OF THE KAMI OF THE RIVERS-- WHY ARE YOU HERE?
HONORED AUNT, YAMATO-HIME, I HAVE COME TO ASK FOR YOUR FAVORS AS I HAVE BEEN ORDERED TO QUELL THE YEMISHI* OF THE TWELVE ROADS OF THE EAST.
* ANCESTORS OF MODERN DAY AINU
THESE TWO FAVORS WILL I BESTOW UPON YOU -- THIS BAG WHICH SHOULD ONLY BE USED IN TIME OF DIRE PERIL...
...AND THIS SWORD, CALLED MURAKUMO-NO-TSURUGI, WHICH WAS A GIFT TO AMATERASU FROM HER ELDER BROTHER.
MY THANKS, HONORED AUNT.
1.

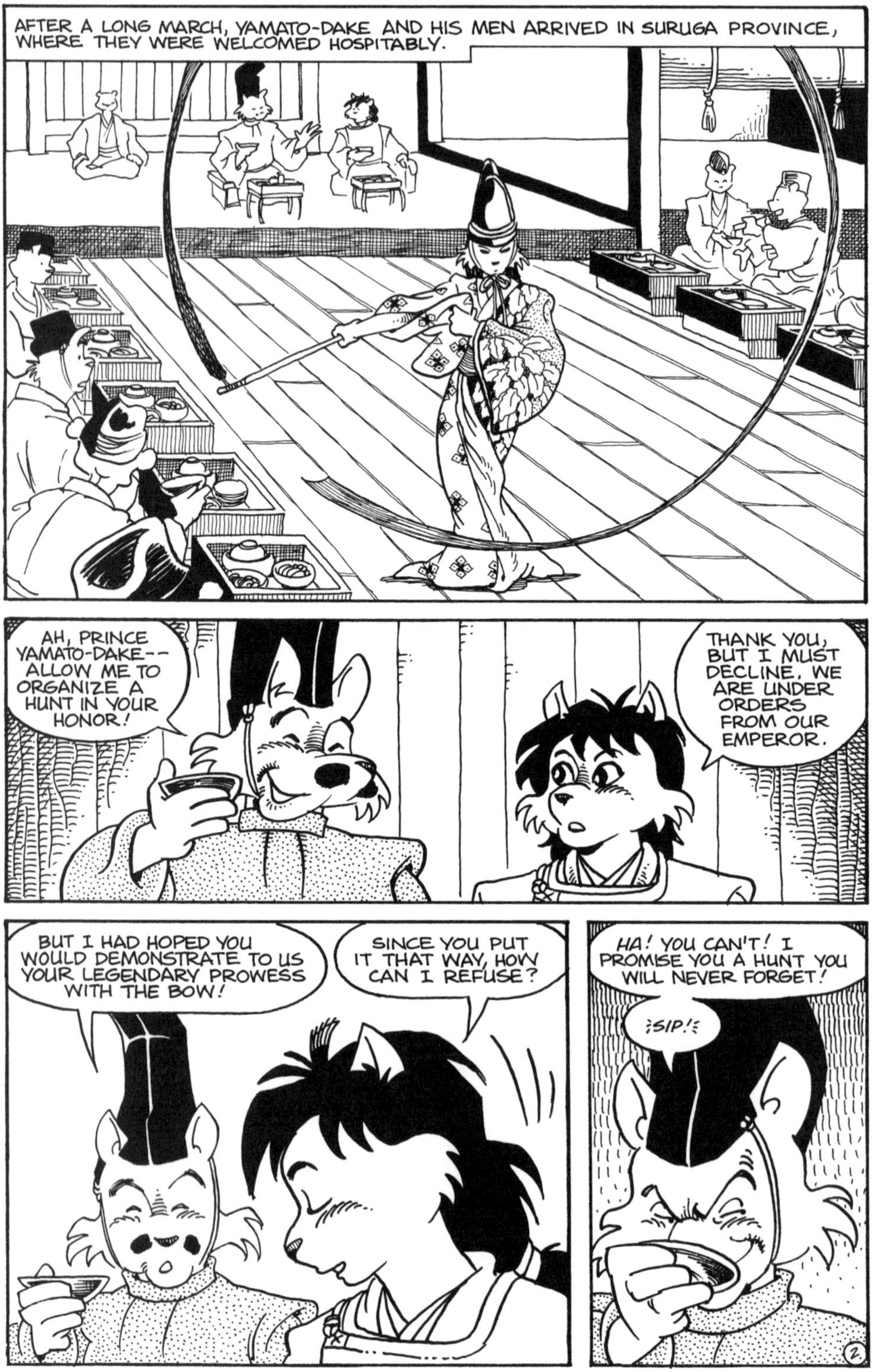
AFTER A LONG MARCH, YAMATO-DAKE AND HIS MEN ARRIVED IN SURUGA PROVINCE, WHERE THEY WERE WELCOMED HOSPITABLY.
AH, PRINCE YAMATO-DAKE-- ALLOW ME TO ORGANIZE A HUNT IN YOUR HONOR!
THANK YOU, BUT I MUST DECLINE. WE ARE UNDER ORDERS FROM OUR EMPEROR.
BUT I HAD HOPED YOU WOULD DEMONSTRATE TO US YOUR LEGENDARY PROWESS WITH THE BOW!
SINCE YOU PUT IT THAT WAY, HOW CAN I REFUSE?
HA! YOU CAN'T! I PROMISE YOU A HUNT YOU WILL NEVER FORGET!
SIP!
2

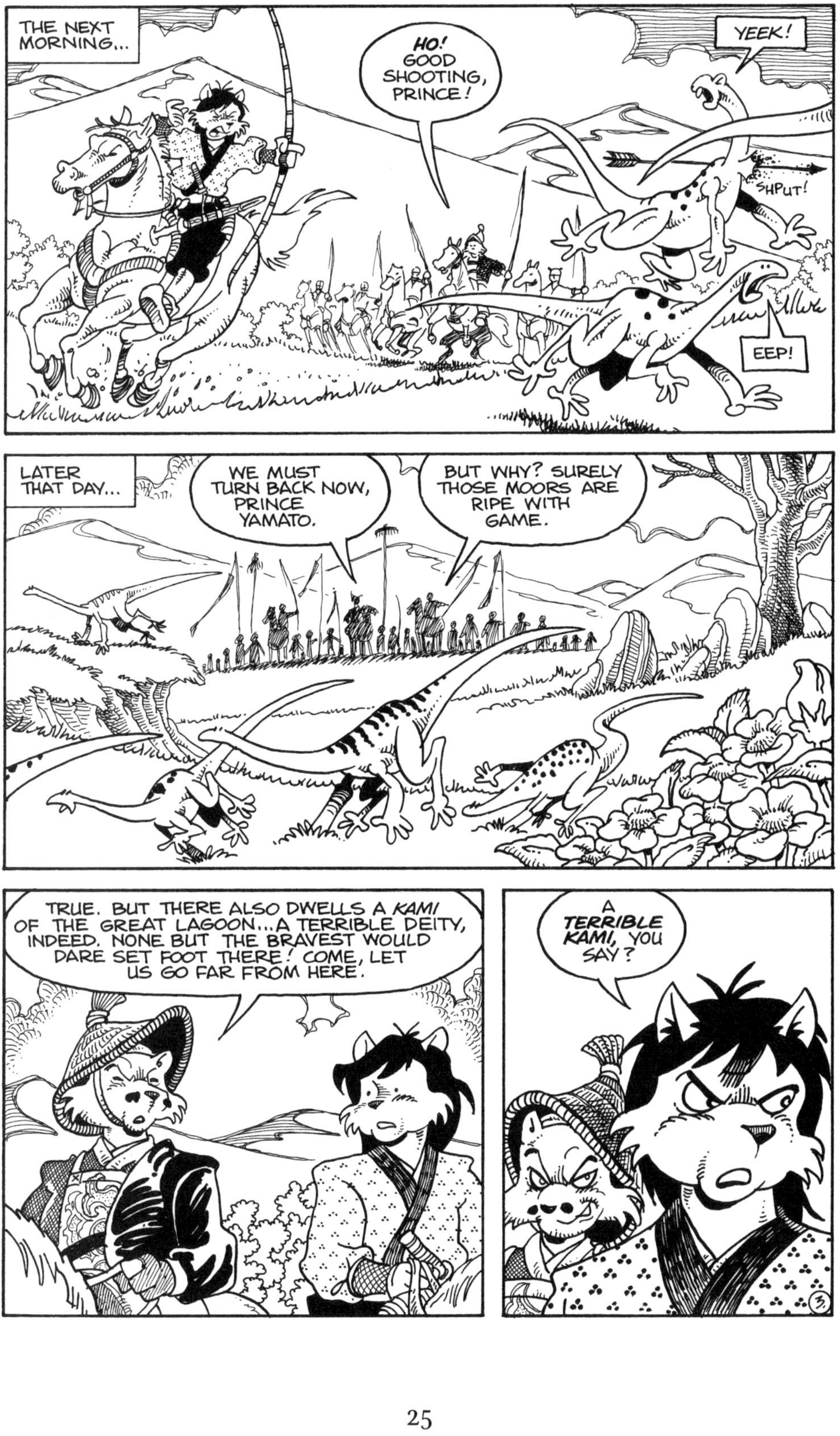
THE NEXT MORNING...
HO! GOOD SHOOTING, PRINCE!
YEEK!
SHPUT!
EEP!
LATER THAT DAY...
WE MUST TURN BACK NOW, PRINCE YAMATO.
BUT WHY? SURELY THOSE MOORS ARE RIPE WITH GAME.
TRUE. BUT THERE ALSO DWELLS A KAMI OF THE GREAT LAGOON...A TERRIBLE DEITY, INDEED. NONE BUT THE BRAVEST WOULD DARE SET FOOT THERE! COME, LET US GO FAR FROM HERE.
A TERRIBLE KAMI, YOU SAY?
3.

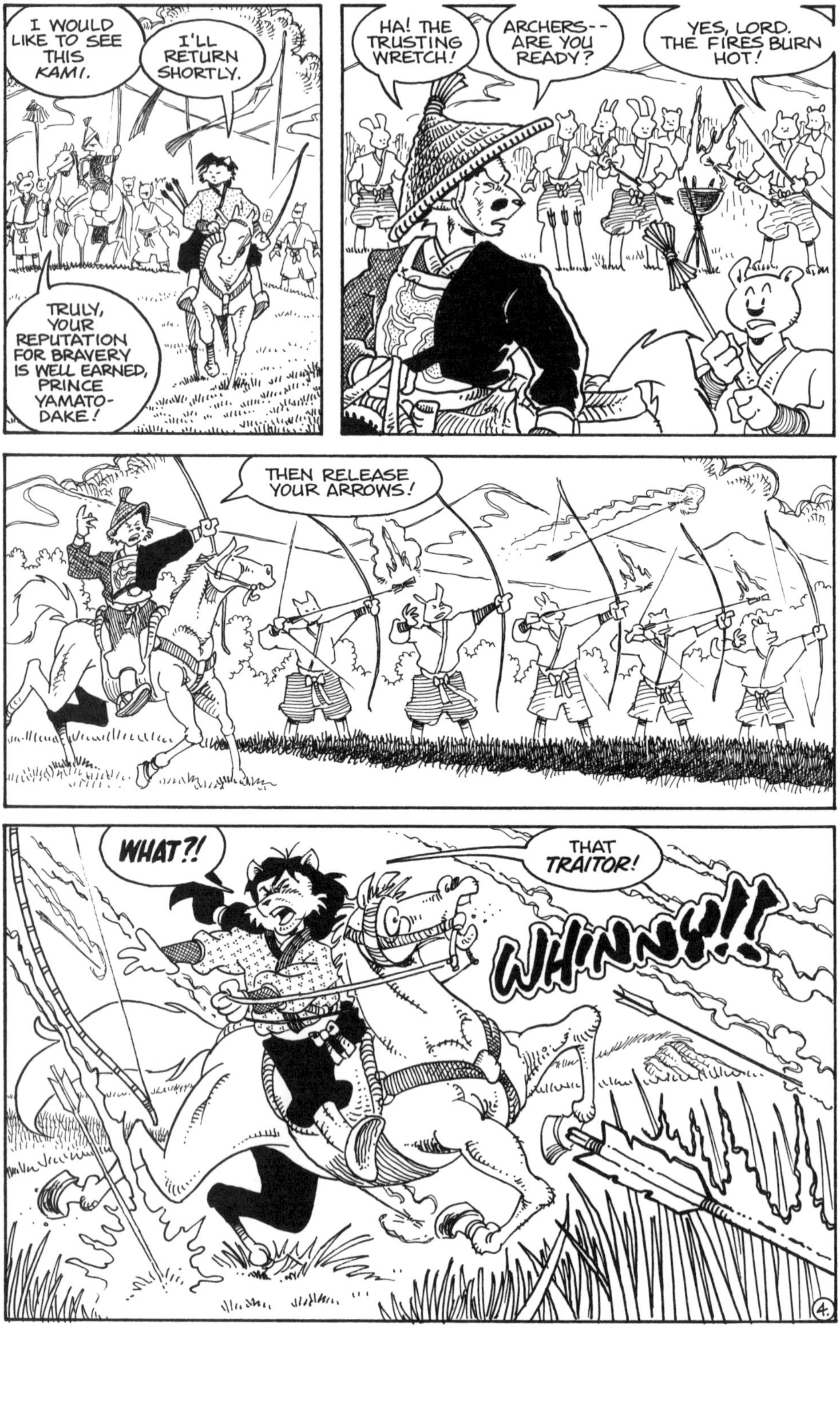
I WOULD LIKE TO SEE THIS *KAMI.*
I'LL RETURN SHORTLY.
TRULY, YOUR REPUTATION FOR BRAVERY IS WELL EARNED, PRINCE YAMATO-DAKE!
HA! THE TRUSTING WRETCH!
ARCHERS-- ARE YOU READY?
YES, LORD. THE FIRES BURN HOT!
THEN RELEASE YOUR ARROWS!
WHAT?!
THAT *TRAITOR!*
WHINNY!!
4.

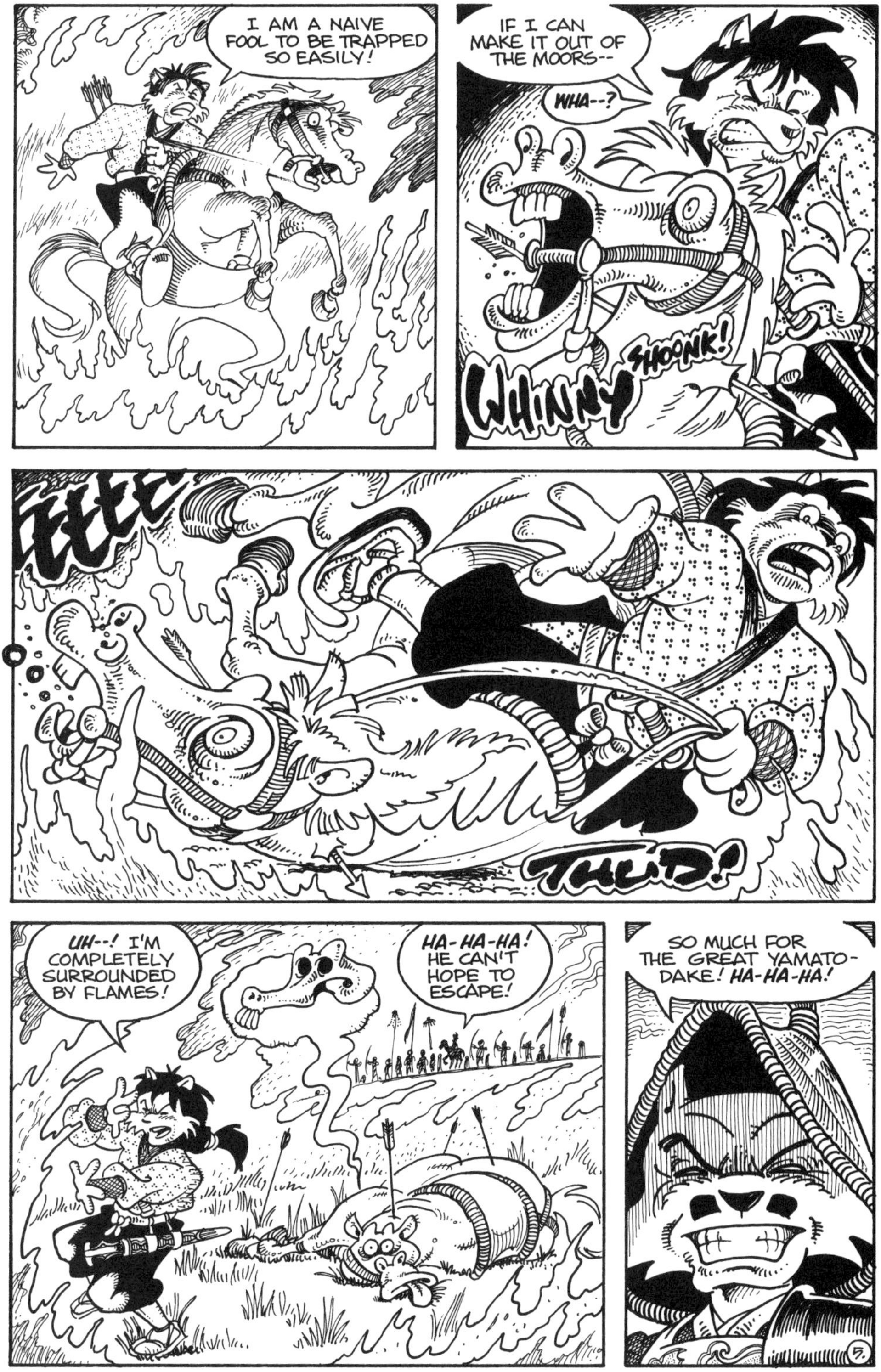
I AM A NAIVE FOOL TO BE TRAPPED SO EASILY!
IF I CAN MAKE IT OUT OF THE MOORS--
WHA--?
WHINNY
SHOONK!
EEEEE
THUD!
UH--! I'M COMPLETELY SURROUNDED BY FLAMES!
HA-HA-HA! HE CAN'T HOPE TO ESCAPE!
SO MUCH FOR THE GREAT YAMATO-DAKE! HA-HA-HA!
5.

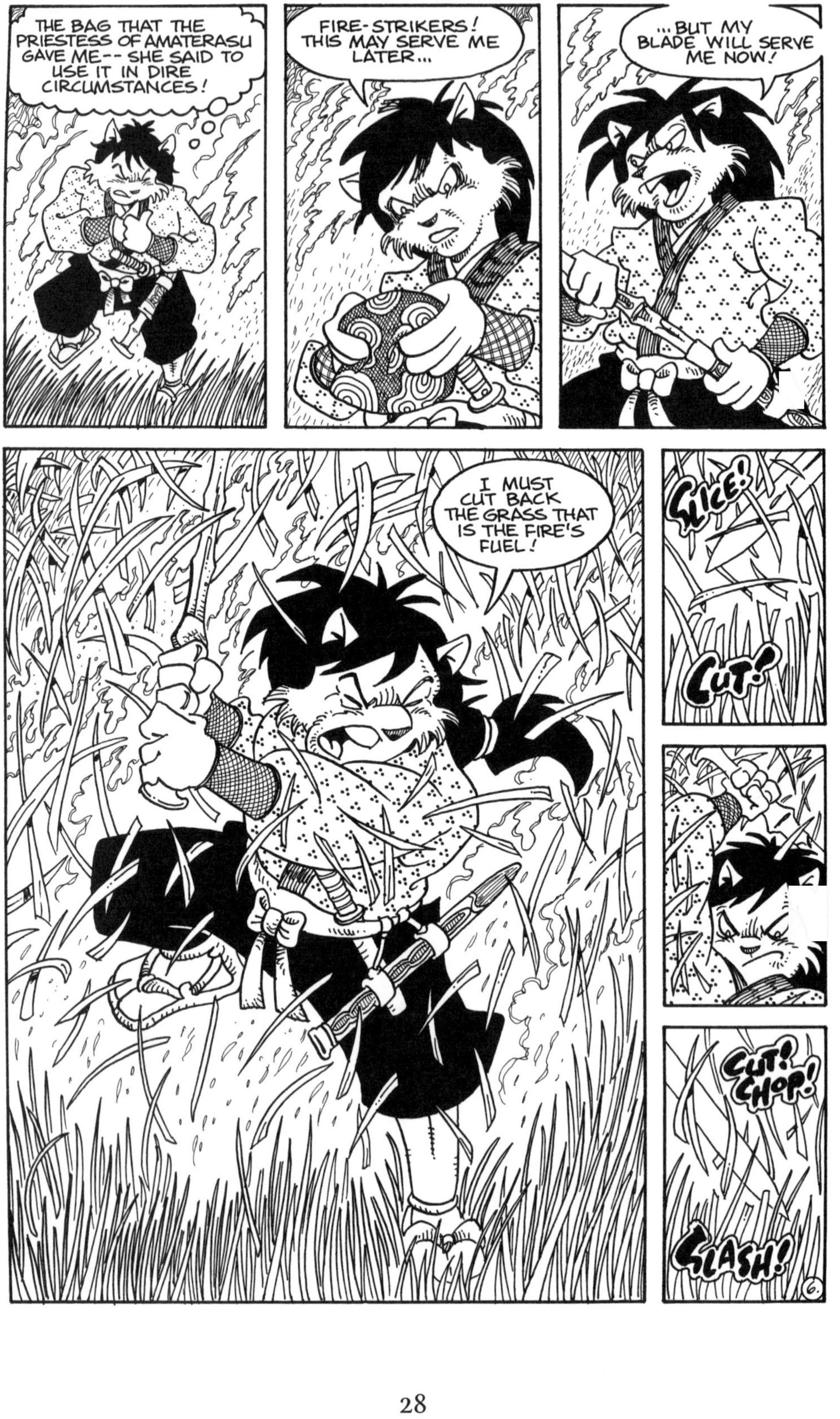
THE BAG THAT THE PRIESTESS OF AMATERASU GAVE ME-- SHE SAID TO USE IT IN DIRE CIRCUMSTANCES!
FIRE-STRIKERS! THIS MAY SERVE ME LATER...
...BUT MY BLADE WILL SERVE ME NOW!
I MUST CUT BACK THE GRASS THAT IS THE FIRE'S FUEL!
SLICE!
CUT!
CUT!
CHOP!
SLASH!
6.

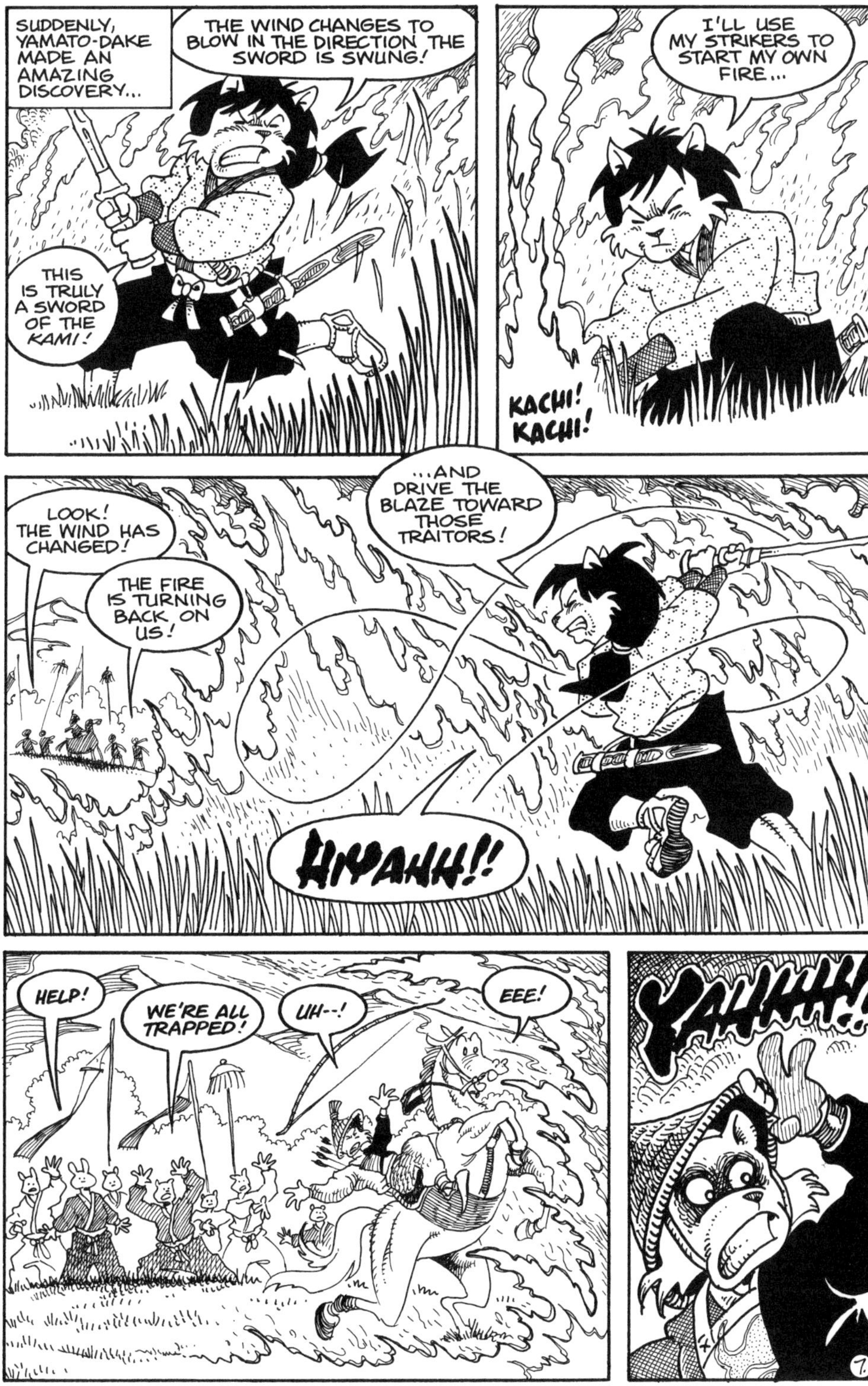

SUDDENLY, YAMATO-DAKE MADE AN AMAZING DISCOVERY...
THE WIND CHANGES TO BLOW IN THE DIRECTION THE SWORD IS SWUNG!
THIS IS TRULY A SWORD OF THE *KAMI*!
I'LL USE MY STRIKERS TO START MY OWN FIRE...
KACHI! KACHI!
LOOK! THE WIND HAS CHANGED!
THE FIRE IS TURNING BACK ON US!
...AND DRIVE THE BLAZE TOWARD THOSE TRAITORS!
HIYAHH!!
HELP!
WE'RE ALL TRAPPED!
UH--!
EEE!
YAHHH!!
7.

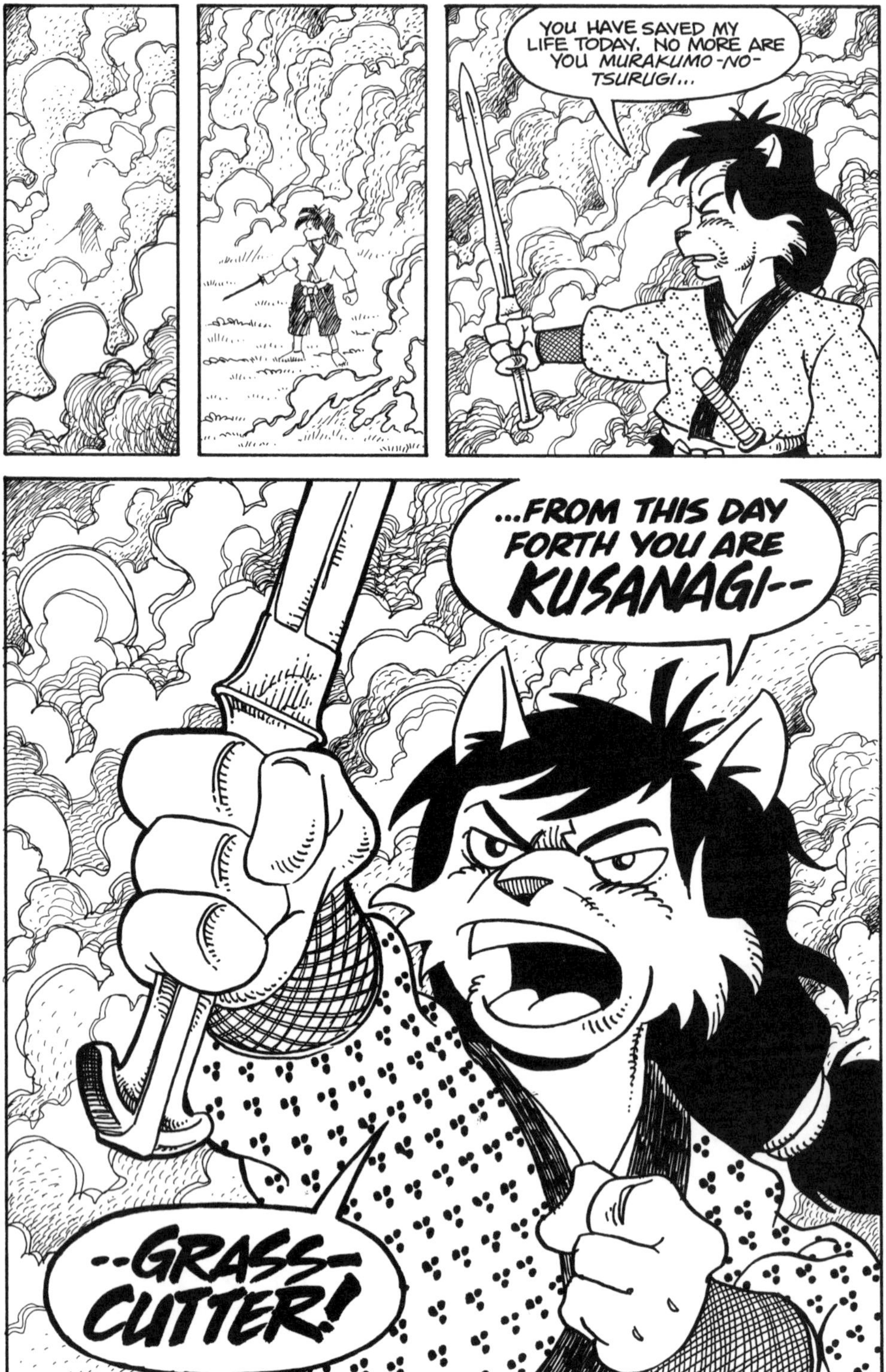
YOU HAVE SAVED MY LIFE TODAY. NO MORE ARE YOU MURAKUMO-NO-TSURUGI...
...FROM THIS DAY FORTH YOU ARE KUSANAGI--
--GRASS-CUTTER!

END of PROLOGUE 3

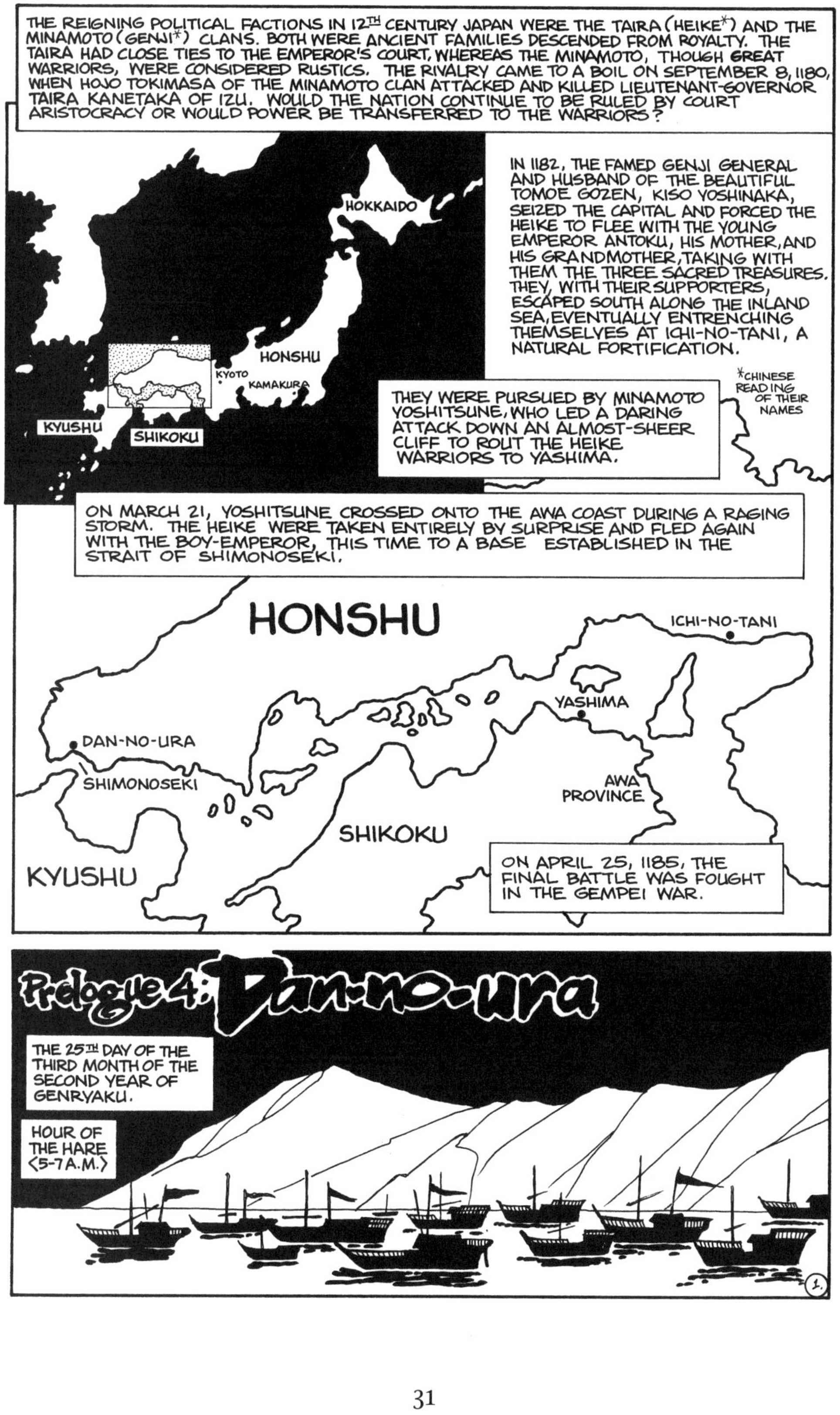
THE REIGNING POLITICAL FACTIONS IN 12TH CENTURY JAPAN WERE THE TAIRA (HEIKE*) AND THE MINAMOTO (GENJI*) CLANS. BOTH WERE ANCIENT FAMILIES DESCENDED FROM ROYALTY. THE TAIRA HAD CLOSE TIES TO THE EMPEROR'S COURT, WHEREAS THE MINAMOTO, THOUGH GREAT WARRIORS, WERE CONSIDERED RUSTICS. THE RIVALRY CAME TO A BOIL ON SEPTEMBER 8, 1180, WHEN HOJO TOKIMASA OF THE MINAMOTO CLAN ATTACKED AND KILLED LIEUTENANT-GOVERNOR TAIRA KANETAKA OF IZU. WOULD THE NATION CONTINUE TO BE RULED BY COURT ARISTOCRACY OR WOULD POWER BE TRANSFERRED TO THE WARRIORS?
HOKKAIDO
HONSHU
KYOTO
KAMAKURA
KYUSHU
SHIKOKU
IN 1182, THE FAMED GENJI GENERAL AND HUSBAND OF THE BEAUTIFUL TOMOE GOZEN, KISO YOSHINAKA, SEIZED THE CAPITAL AND FORCED THE HEIKE TO FLEE WITH THE YOUNG EMPEROR ANTOKU, HIS MOTHER, AND HIS GRANDMOTHER, TAKING WITH THEM THE THREE SACRED TREASURES. THEY, WITH THEIR SUPPORTERS, ESCAPED SOUTH ALONG THE INLAND SEA, EVENTUALLY ENTRENCHING THEMSELVES AT ICHI-NO-TANI, A NATURAL FORTIFICATION.
THEY WERE PURSUED BY MINAMOTO YOSHITSUNE, WHO LED A DARING ATTACK DOWN AN ALMOST-SHEER CLIFF TO ROUT THE HEIKE WARRIORS TO YASHIMA.
*CHINESE READING OF THEIR NAMES
ON MARCH 21, YOSHITSUNE CROSSED ONTO THE AWA COAST DURING A RAGING STORM. THE HEIKE WERE TAKEN ENTIRELY BY SURPRISE AND FLED AGAIN WITH THE BOY-EMPEROR, THIS TIME TO A BASE ESTABLISHED IN THE STRAIT OF SHIMONOSEKI.
HONSHU
ICHI-NO-TANI
YASHIMA
DAN-NO-URA
SHIMONOSEKI
AWA PROVINCE
SHIKOKU
KYUSHU
ON APRIL 25, 1185, THE FINAL BATTLE WAS FOUGHT IN THE GEMPEI WAR.
Prologue 4: Dan-no-ura
THE 25TH DAY OF THE THIRD MONTH OF THE SECOND YEAR OF GENRYAKU.
HOUR OF THE HARE <5-7 A.M.>
1.

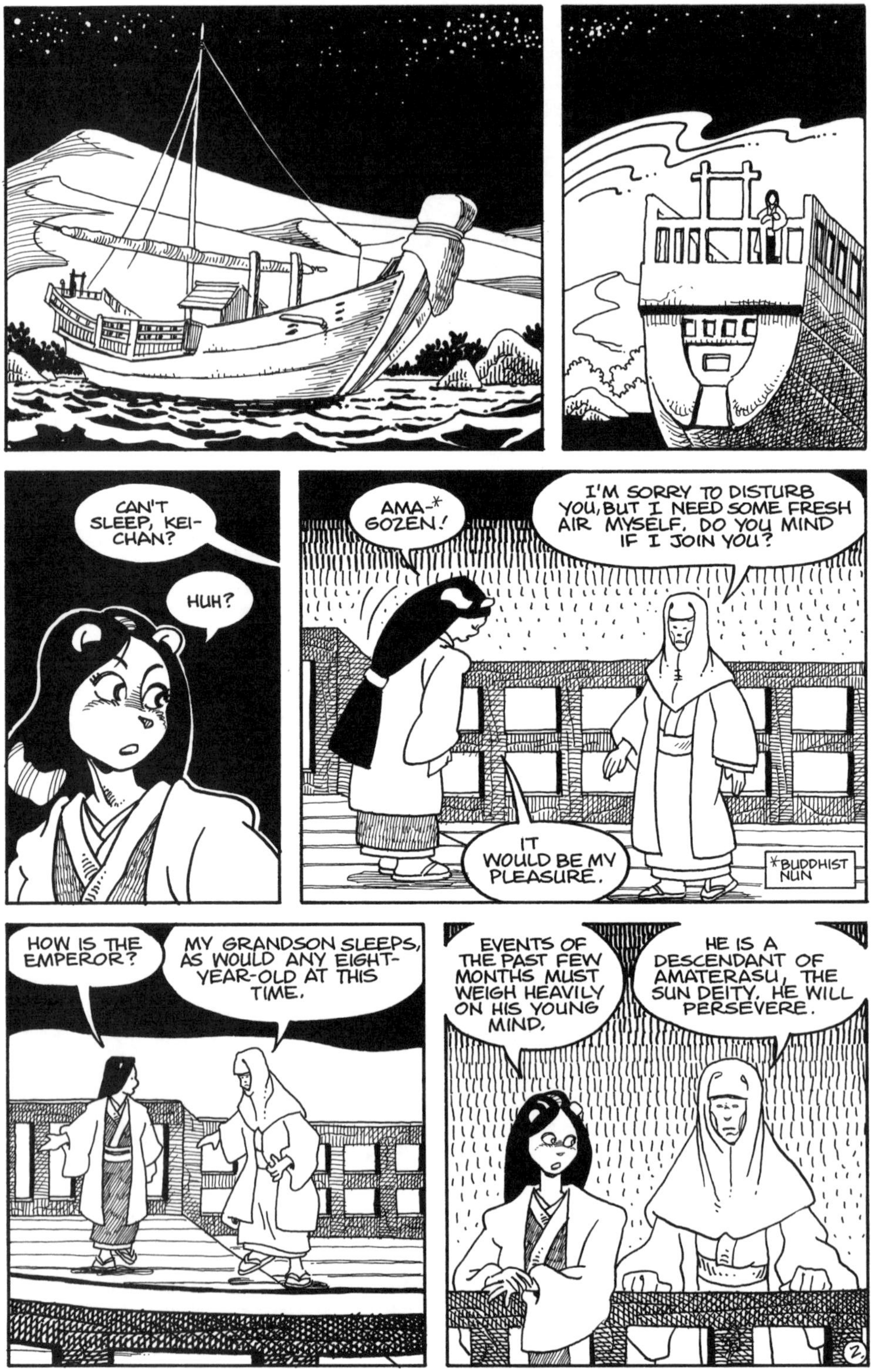

CAN'T SLEEP, KEI-CHAN?
HUH?
AMA-* GOZEN!
I'M SORRY TO DISTURB YOU, BUT I NEED SOME FRESH AIR MYSELF. DO YOU MIND IF I JOIN YOU?
IT WOULD BE MY PLEASURE.
*BUDDHIST NUN
HOW IS THE EMPEROR?
MY GRANDSON SLEEPS, AS WOULD ANY EIGHT-YEAR-OLD AT THIS TIME.
EVENTS OF THE PAST FEW MONTHS MUST WEIGH HEAVILY ON HIS YOUNG MIND.
HE IS A DESCENDANT OF AMATERASU, THE SUN DEITY. HE WILL PERSEVERE.
2

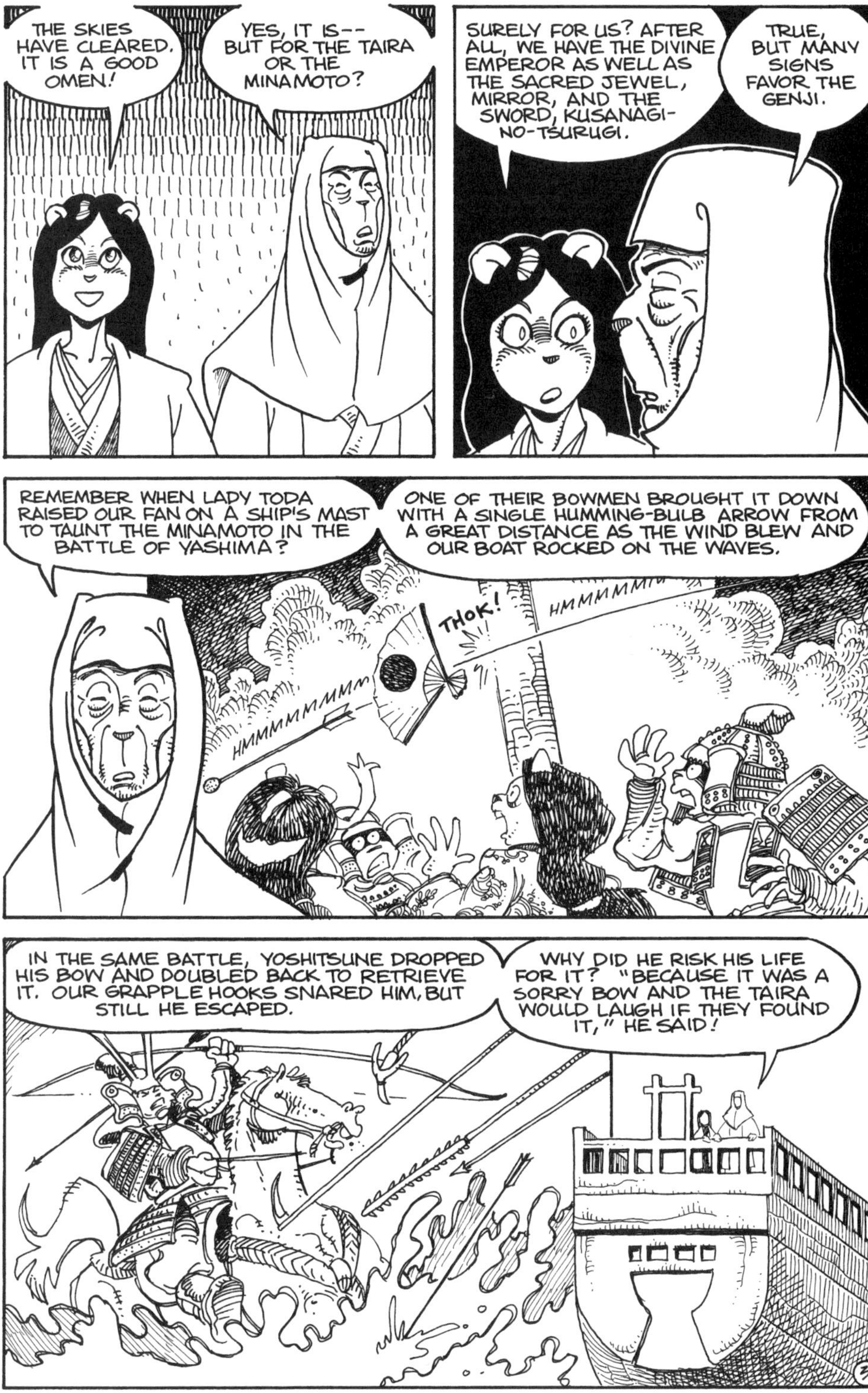
THE SKIES HAVE CLEARED. IT IS A GOOD OMEN!
YES, IT IS-- BUT FOR THE TAIRA OR THE MINAMOTO?
SURELY FOR US? AFTER ALL, WE HAVE THE DIVINE EMPEROR AS WELL AS THE SACRED JEWEL, MIRROR, AND THE SWORD, KUSANAGI-NO-TSURUGI.
TRUE, BUT MANY SIGNS FAVOR THE GENJI.
REMEMBER WHEN LADY TODA RAISED OUR FAN ON A SHIP'S MAST TO TAUNT THE MINAMOTO IN THE BATTLE OF YASHIMA?
ONE OF THEIR BOWMEN BROUGHT IT DOWN WITH A SINGLE HUMMING-BULB ARROW FROM A GREAT DISTANCE AS THE WIND BLEW AND OUR BOAT ROCKED ON THE WAVES.
HMMMMMMMMM
THOK!
HMMMMMMMMMM
IN THE SAME BATTLE, YOSHITSUNE DROPPED HIS BOW AND DOUBLED BACK TO RETRIEVE IT. OUR GRAPPLE HOOKS SNARED HIM, BUT STILL HE ESCAPED.
WHY DID HE RISK HIS LIFE FOR IT? "BECAUSE IT WAS A SORRY BOW AND THE TAIRA WOULD LAUGH IF THEY FOUND IT," HE SAID!
3.

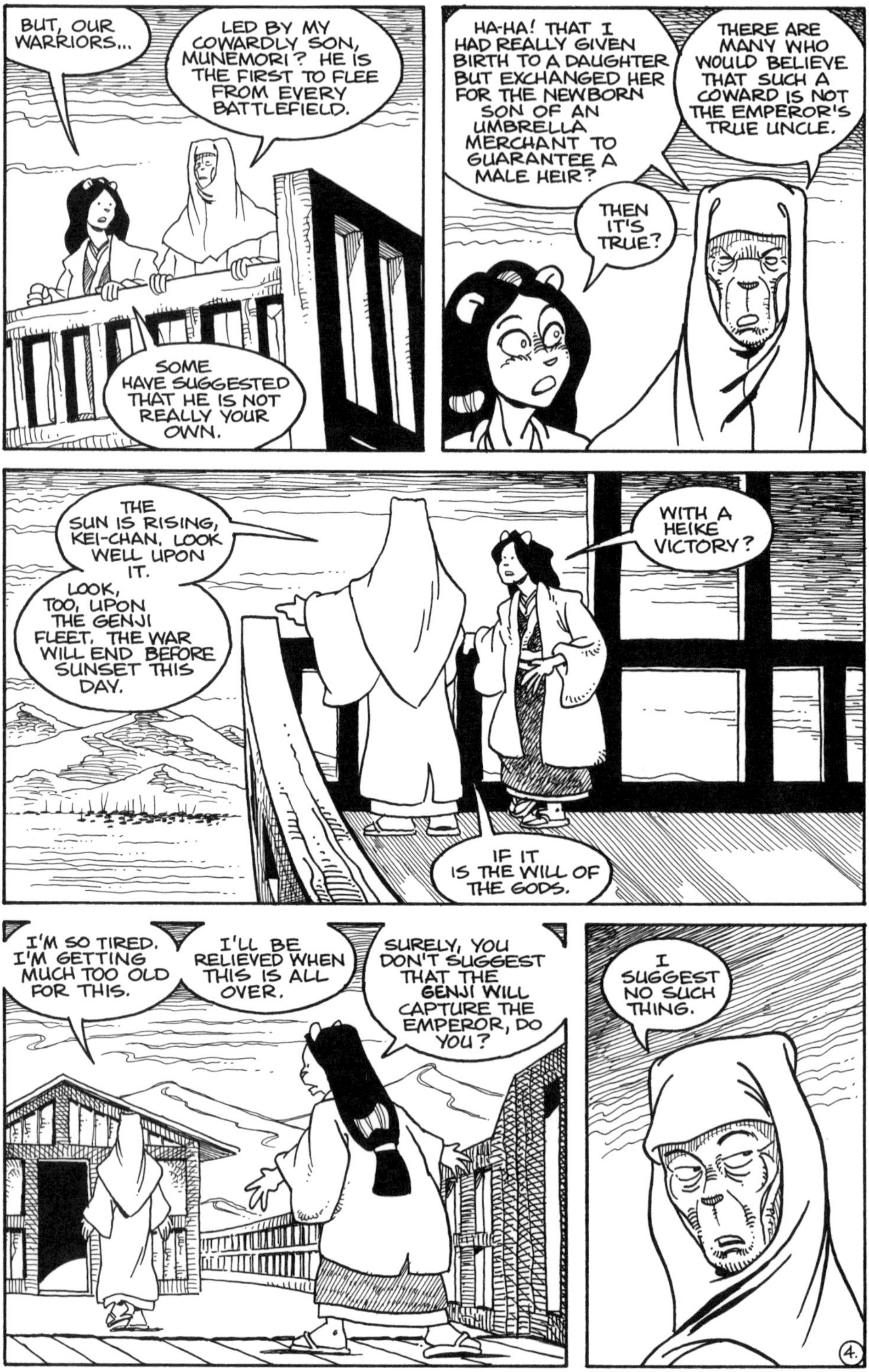
BUT, OUR WARRIORS...
LED BY MY COWARDLY SON, MUNEMORI? HE IS THE FIRST TO FLEE FROM EVERY BATTLEFIELD.
SOME HAVE SUGGESTED THAT HE IS NOT REALLY YOUR OWN.
HA-HA! THAT I HAD REALLY GIVEN BIRTH TO A DAUGHTER BUT EXCHANGED HER FOR THE NEWBORN SON OF AN UMBRELLA MERCHANT TO GUARANTEE A MALE HEIR?
THERE ARE MANY WHO WOULD BELIEVE THAT SUCH A COWARD IS NOT THE EMPEROR'S TRUE UNCLE.
THEN IT'S TRUE?
THE SUN IS RISING, KEI-CHAN. LOOK WELL UPON IT.
LOOK, TOO, UPON THE GENJI FLEET. THE WAR WILL END BEFORE SUNSET THIS DAY.
WITH A HEIKE VICTORY?
IF IT IS THE WILL OF THE GODS.
I'M SO TIRED. I'M GETTING MUCH TOO OLD FOR THIS.
I'LL BE RELIEVED WHEN THIS IS ALL OVER.
SURELY, YOU DON'T SUGGEST THAT THE GENJI WILL CAPTURE THE EMPEROR, DO YOU?
I SUGGEST NO SUCH THING.
4.

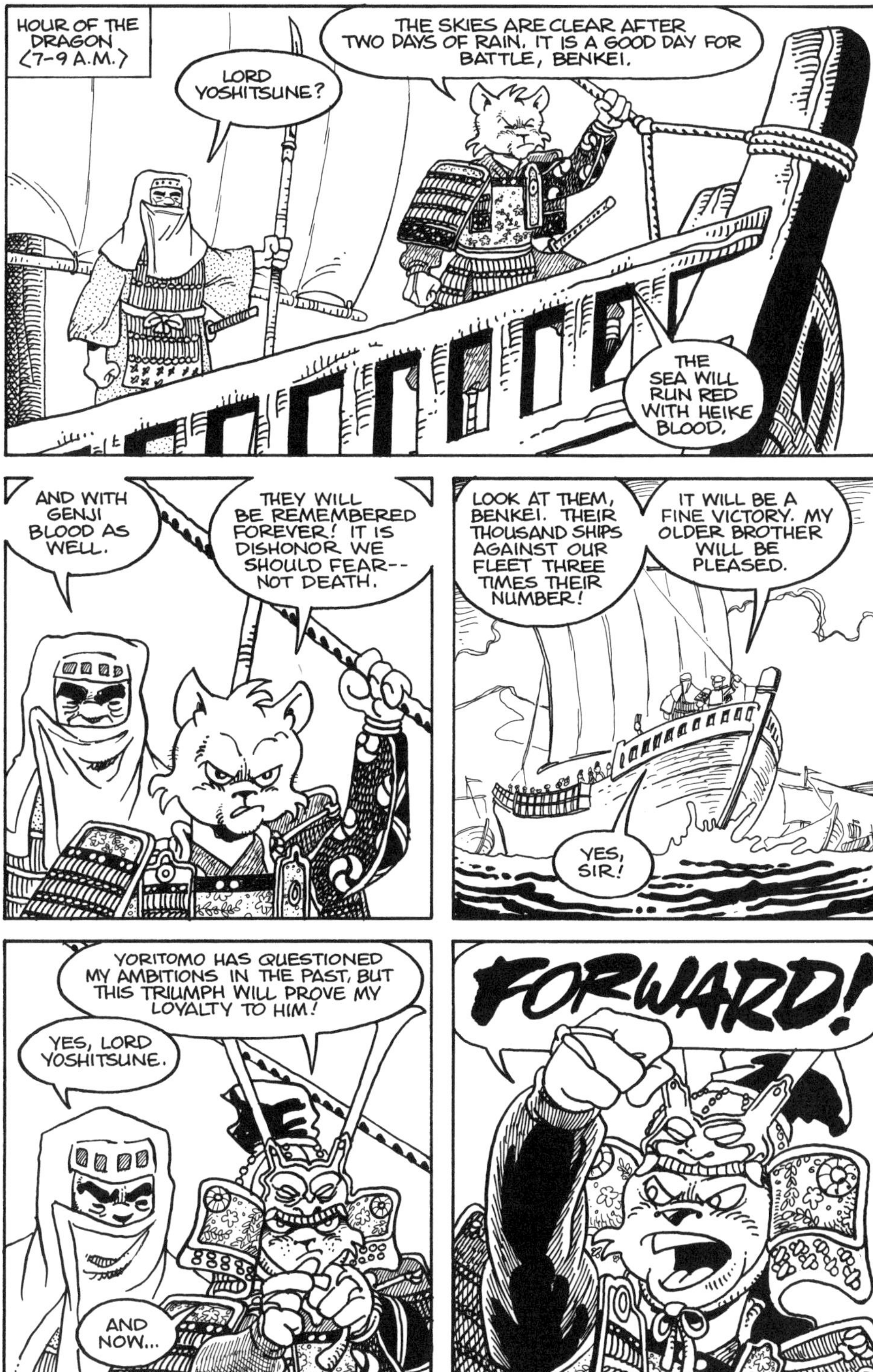
HOUR OF THE DRAGON <7-9 A.M.>
LORD YOSHITSUNE?
THE SKIES ARE CLEAR AFTER TWO DAYS OF RAIN. IT IS A GOOD DAY FOR BATTLE, BENKEI.
THE SEA WILL RUN RED WITH HEIKE BLOOD.
AND WITH GENJI BLOOD AS WELL.
THEY WILL BE REMEMBERED FOREVER! IT IS DISHONOR WE SHOULD FEAR-- NOT DEATH.
LOOK AT THEM, BENKEI. THEIR THOUSAND SHIPS AGAINST OUR FLEET THREE TIMES THEIR NUMBER!
IT WILL BE A FINE VICTORY. MY OLDER BROTHER WILL BE PLEASED.
YES, SIR!
YORITOMO HAS QUESTIONED MY AMBITIONS IN THE PAST, BUT THIS TRIUMPH WILL PROVE MY LOYALTY TO HIM!
YES, LORD YOSHITSUNE.
AND NOW...
FORWARD!
5.

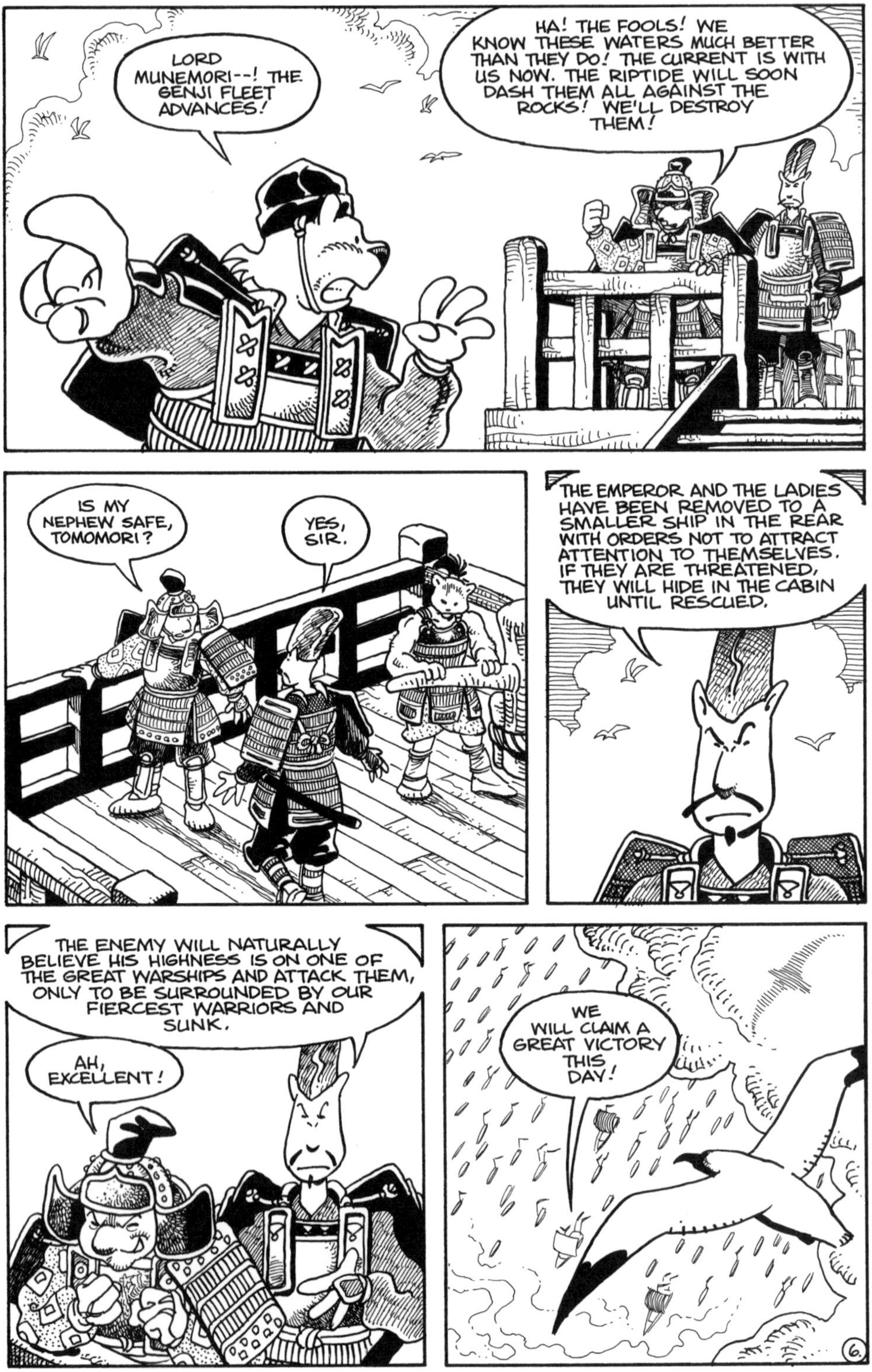
LORD MUNEMORI--! THE GENJI FLEET ADVANCES!
HA! THE FOOLS! WE KNOW THESE WATERS MUCH BETTER THAN THEY DO! THE CURRENT IS WITH US NOW. THE RIPTIDE WILL SOON DASH THEM ALL AGAINST THE ROCKS! WE'LL DESTROY THEM!
IS MY NEPHEW SAFE, TOMOMORI?
YES, SIR.
THE EMPEROR AND THE LADIES HAVE BEEN REMOVED TO A SMALLER SHIP IN THE REAR WITH ORDERS NOT TO ATTRACT ATTENTION TO THEMSELVES. IF THEY ARE THREATENED, THEY WILL HIDE IN THE CABIN UNTIL RESCUED.
THE ENEMY WILL NATURALLY BELIEVE HIS HIGHNESS IS ON ONE OF THE GREAT WARSHIPS AND ATTACK THEM, ONLY TO BE SURROUNDED BY OUR FIERCEST WARRIORS AND SUNK.
AH, EXCELLENT!
WE WILL CLAIM A GREAT VICTORY THIS DAY!
6

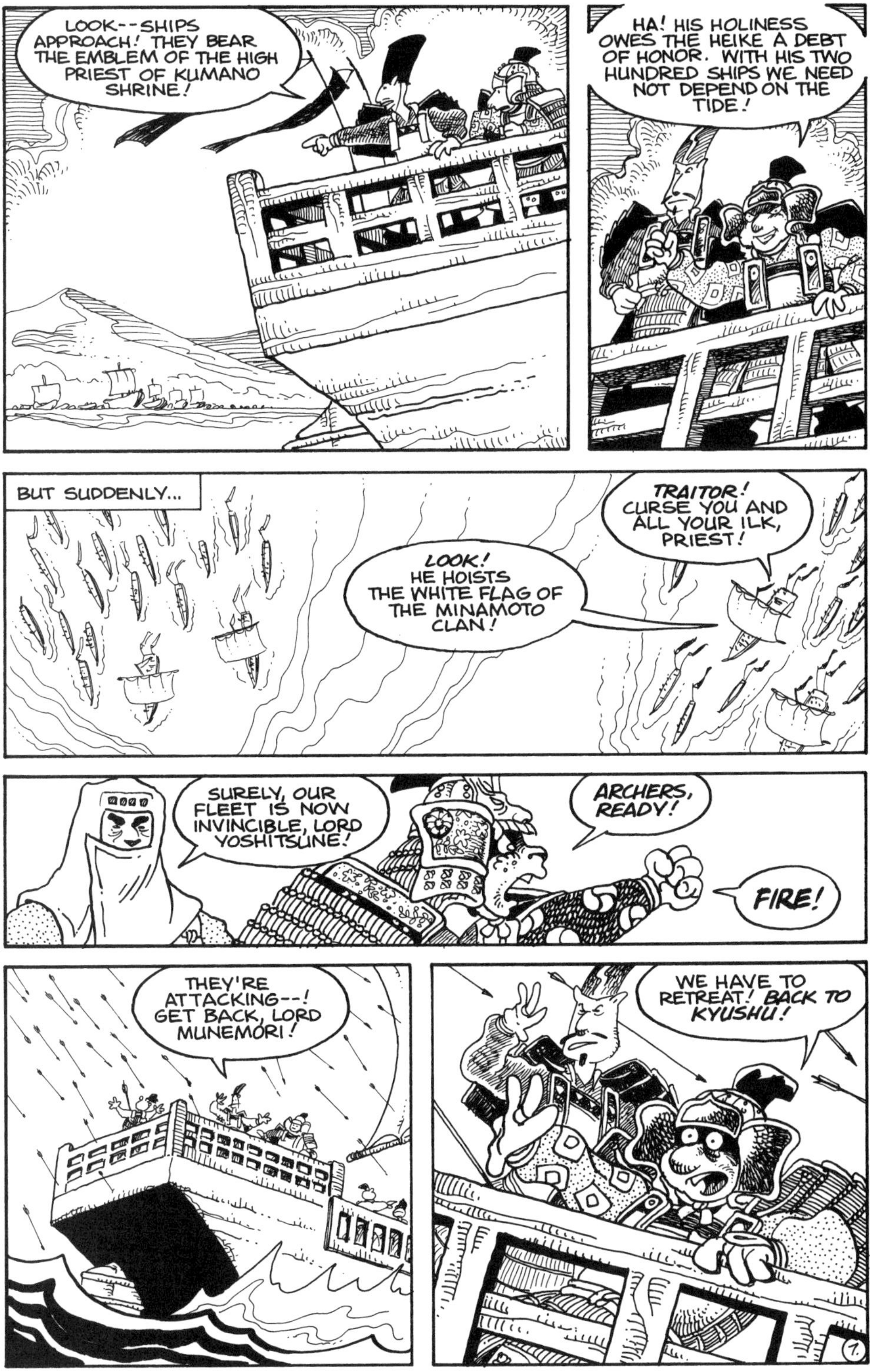
LOOK--SHIPS APPROACH! THEY BEAR THE EMBLEM OF THE HIGH PRIEST OF KUMANO SHRINE!
HA! HIS HOLINESS OWES THE HEIKE A DEBT OF HONOR. WITH HIS TWO HUNDRED SHIPS WE NEED NOT DEPEND ON THE TIDE!
BUT SUDDENLY...
LOOK! HE HOISTS THE WHITE FLAG OF THE MINAMOTO CLAN!
TRAITOR! CURSE YOU AND ALL YOUR ILK, PRIEST!
SURELY, OUR FLEET IS NOW INVINCIBLE, LORD YOSHITSUNE!
ARCHERS, READY!
FIRE!
THEY'RE ATTACKING--! GET BACK, LORD MUNEMORI!
WE HAVE TO RETREAT! BACK TO KYUSHU!
7.

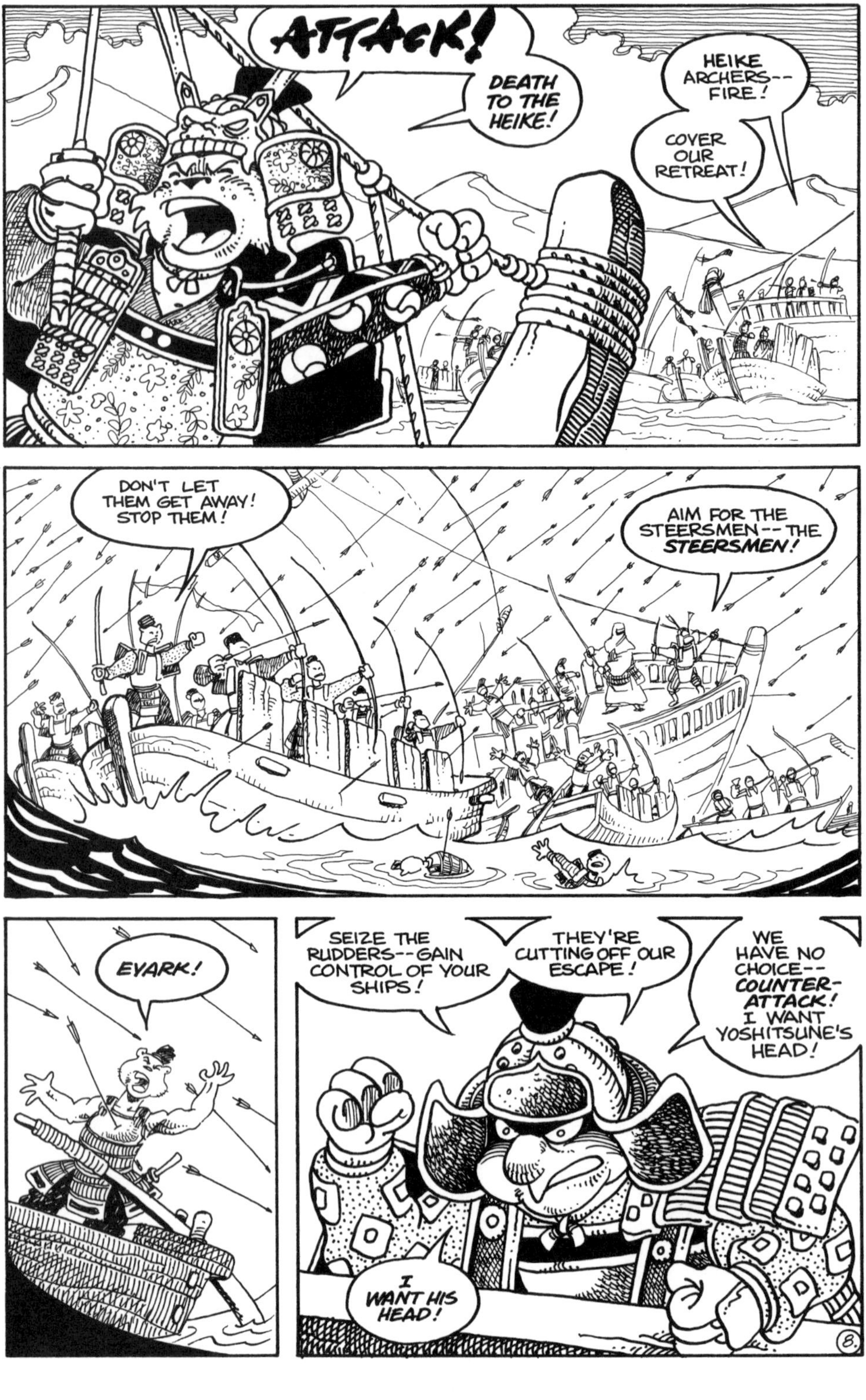
ATTACK!
DEATH TO THE HEIKE!
HEIKE ARCHERS-- FIRE!
COVER OUR RETREAT!
DON'T LET THEM GET AWAY! STOP THEM!
AIM FOR THE STEERSMEN -- THE STEERSMEN!
EYARK!
SEIZE THE RUDDERS--GAIN CONTROL OF YOUR SHIPS!
THEY'RE CUTTING OFF OUR ESCAPE!
WE HAVE NO CHOICE-- COUNTER-ATTACK! I WANT YOSHITSUNE'S HEAD!
I WANT HIS HEAD!
8.

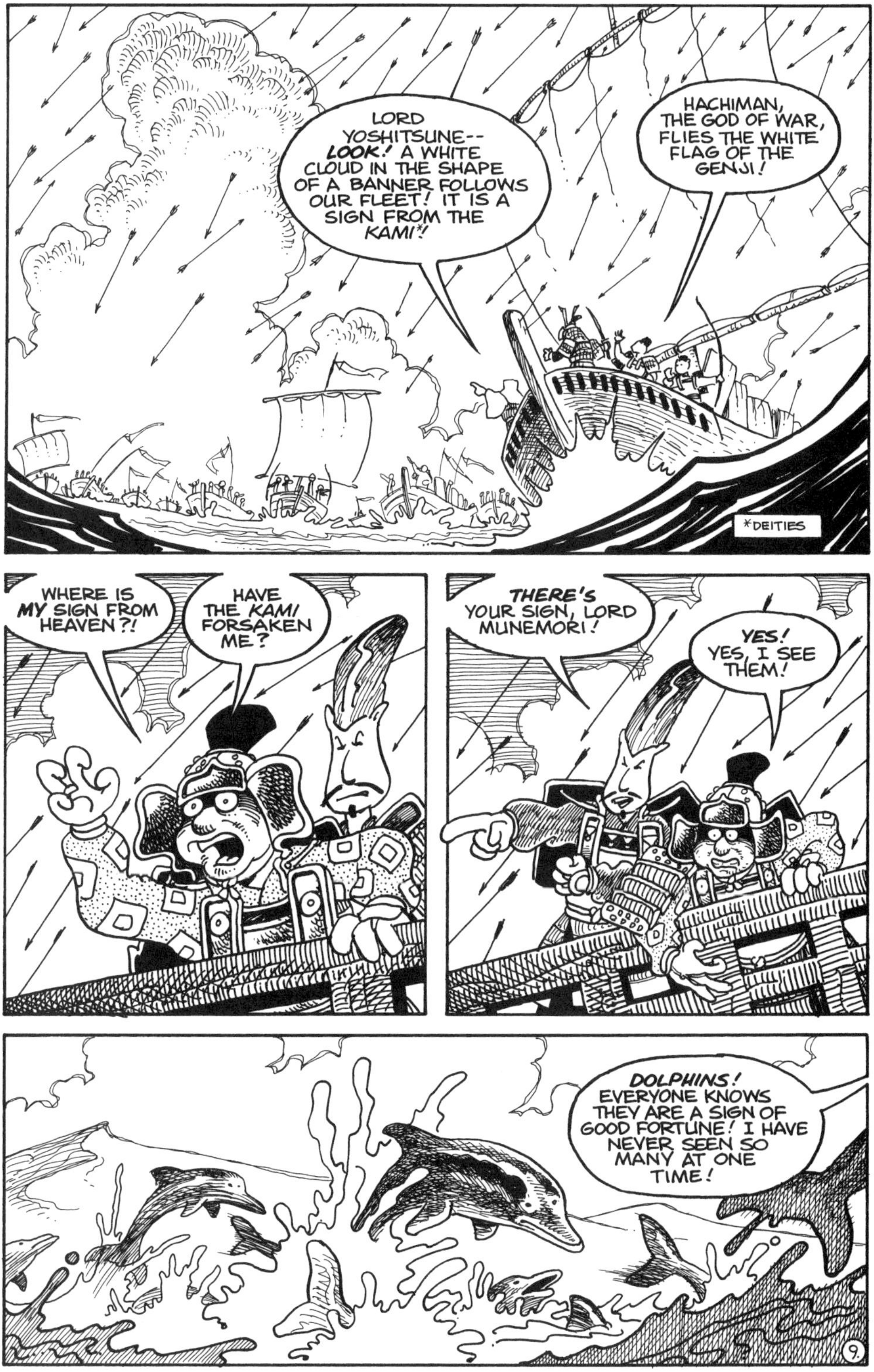
LORD YOSHITSUNE-- LOOK! A WHITE CLOUD IN THE SHAPE OF A BANNER FOLLOWS OUR FLEET! IT IS A SIGN FROM THE KAMI*!
HACHIMAN, THE GOD OF WAR, FLIES THE WHITE FLAG OF THE GENJI!
*DEITIES
WHERE IS MY SIGN FROM HEAVEN?!
HAVE THE KAMI FORSAKEN ME?
THERE'S YOUR SIGN, LORD MUNEMORI!
YES! YES, I SEE THEM!
DOLPHINS! EVERYONE KNOWS THEY ARE A SIGN OF GOOD FORTUNE! I HAVE NEVER SEEN SO MANY AT ONE TIME!
9.

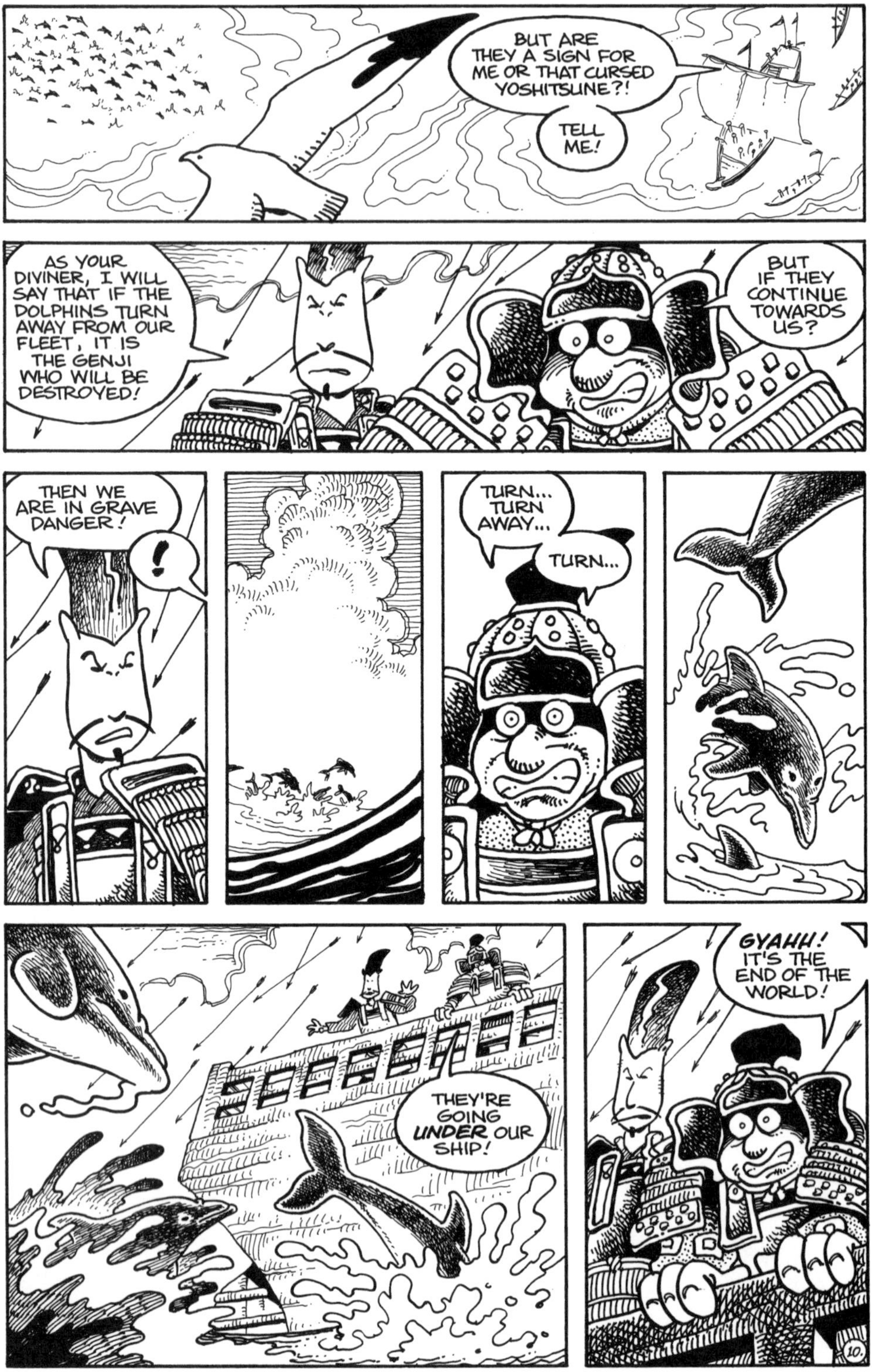

BUT ARE THEY A SIGN FOR ME OR THAT CURSED YOSHITSUNE?!
TELL ME!
AS YOUR DIVINER, I WILL SAY THAT IF THE DOLPHINS TURN AWAY FROM OUR FLEET, IT IS THE GENJI WHO WILL BE DESTROYED!
BUT IF THEY CONTINUE TOWARDS US?
THEN WE ARE IN GRAVE DANGER!
!
TURN... TURN AWAY...
TURN...
THEY'RE GOING **UNDER** OUR SHIP!
GYAHH! IT'S THE END OF THE WORLD!
10.

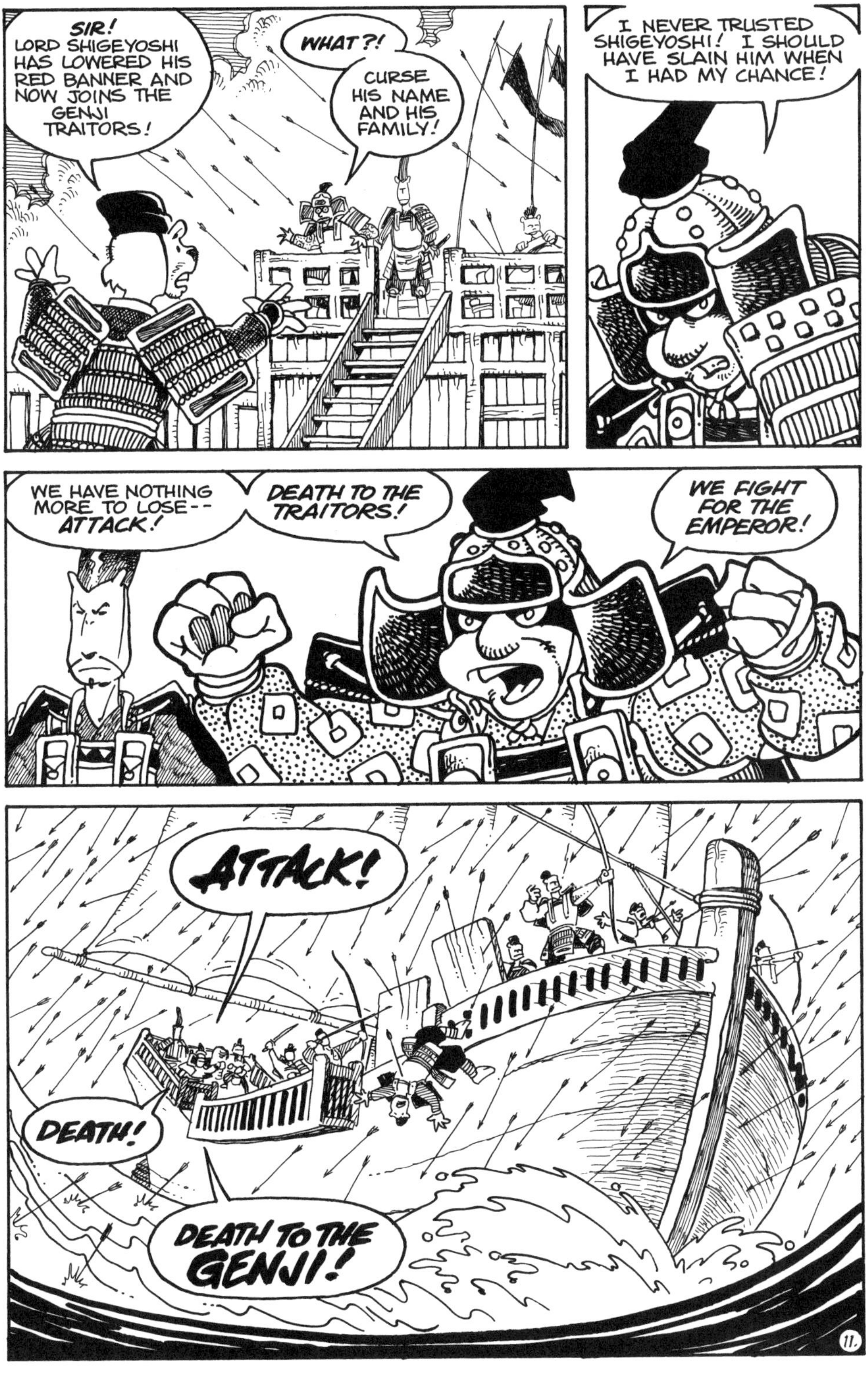
SIR! LORD SHIGEYOSHI HAS LOWERED HIS RED BANNER AND NOW JOINS THE GENJI TRAITORS!
WHAT?!
CURSE HIS NAME AND HIS FAMILY!
I NEVER TRUSTED SHIGEYOSHI! I SHOULD HAVE SLAIN HIM WHEN I HAD MY CHANCE!
WE HAVE NOTHING MORE TO LOSE-- ATTACK!
DEATH TO THE TRAITORS!
WE FIGHT FOR THE EMPEROR!
ATTACK!
DEATH!
DEATH TO THE GENJI!
11.

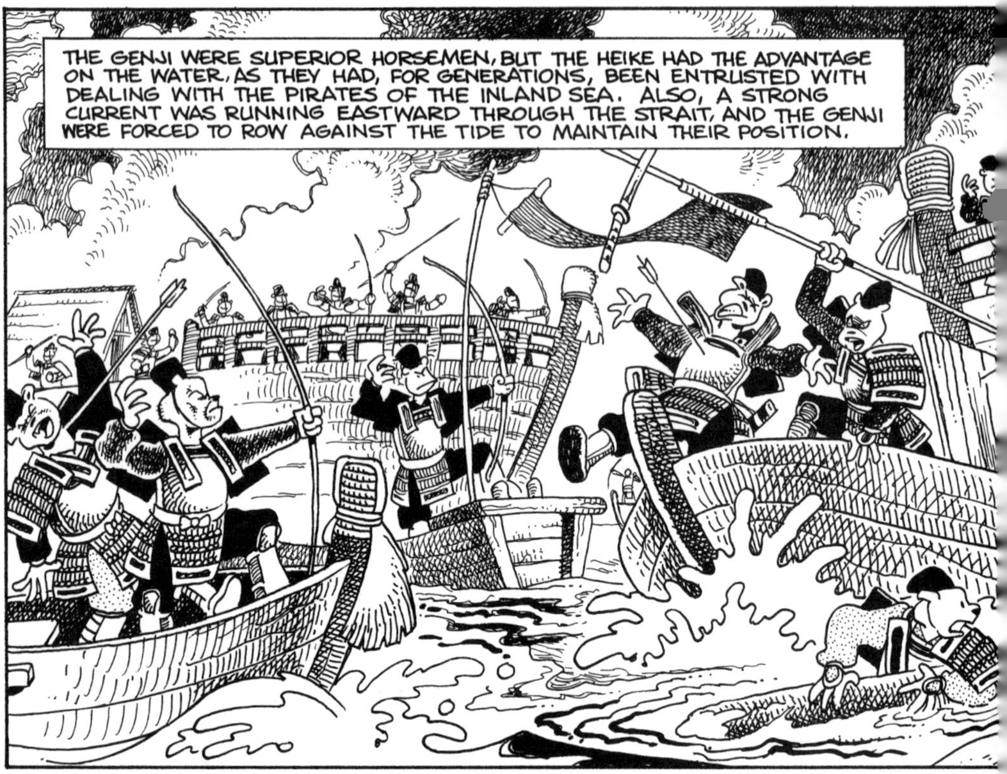
THE GENJI WERE SUPERIOR HORSEMEN, BUT THE HEIKE HAD THE ADVANTAGE ON THE WATER, AS THEY HAD, FOR GENERATIONS, BEEN ENTRUSTED WITH DEALING WITH THE PIRATES OF THE INLAND SEA. ALSO, A STRONG CURRENT WAS RUNNING EASTWARD THROUGH THE STRAIT, AND THE GENJI WERE FORCED TO ROW AGAINST THE TIDE TO MAINTAIN THEIR POSITION.
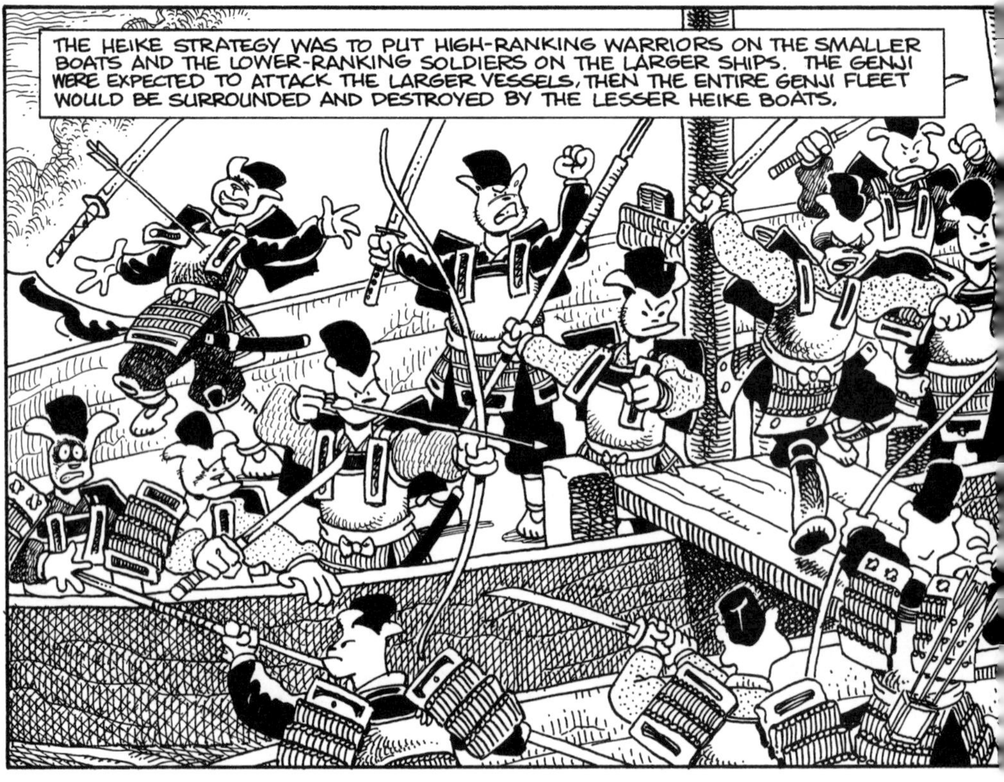
THE HEIKE STRATEGY WAS TO PUT HIGH-RANKING WARRIORS ON THE SMALLER BOATS AND THE LOWER-RANKING SOLDIERS ON THE LARGER SHIPS. THE GENJI WERE EXPECTED TO ATTACK THE LARGER VESSELS, THEN THE ENTIRE GENJI FLEET WOULD BE SURROUNDED AND DESTROYED BY THE LESSER HEIKE BOATS.

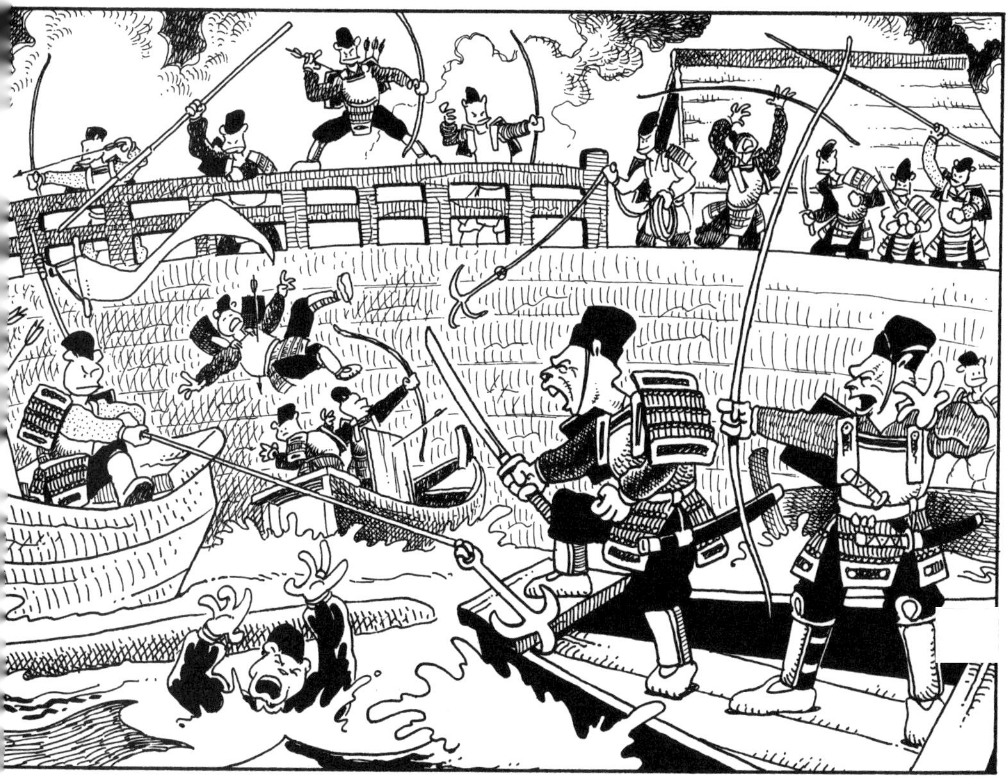

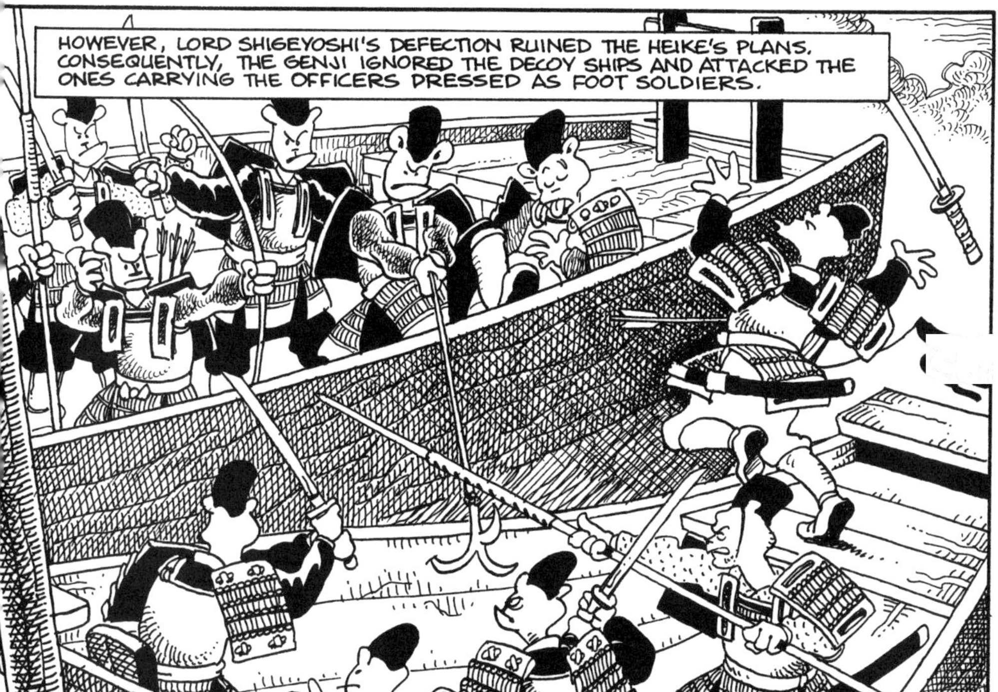
HOWEVER, LORD SHIGEYOSHI'S DEFECTION RUINED THE HEIKE'S PLANS. CONSEQUENTLY, THE GENJI IGNORED THE DECOY SHIPS AND ATTACKED THE ONES CARRYING THE OFFICERS DRESSED AS FOOT SOLDIERS.
13.

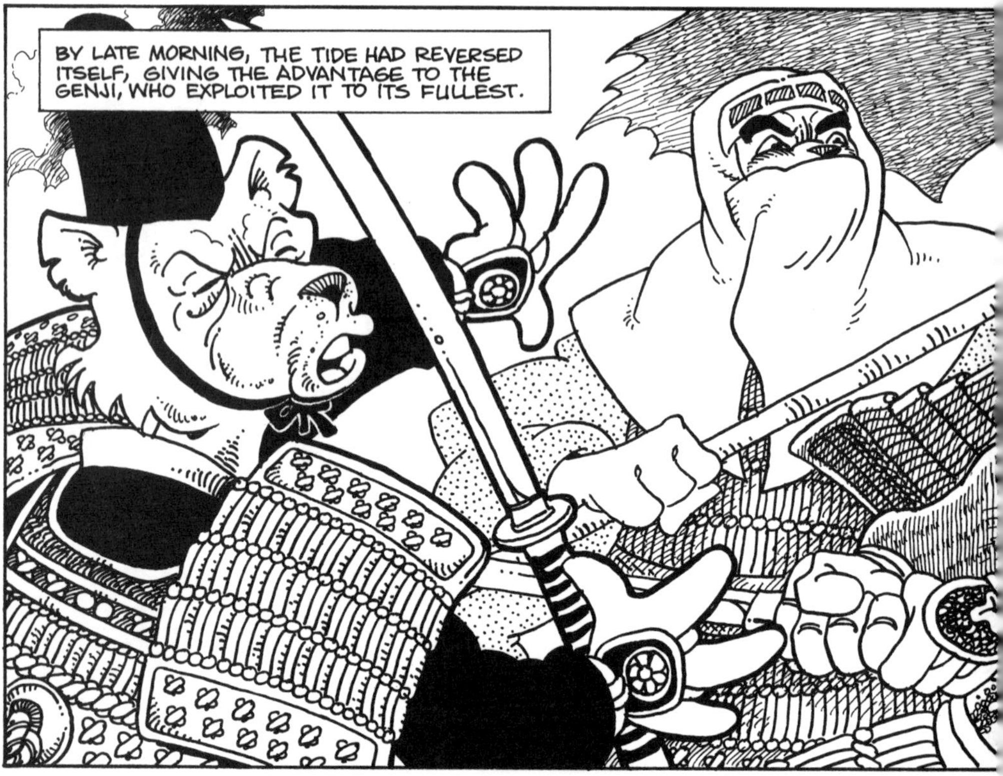
BY LATE MORNING, THE TIDE HAD REVERSED ITSELF, GIVING THE ADVANTAGE TO THE GENJI, WHO EXPLOITED IT TO ITS FULLEST.

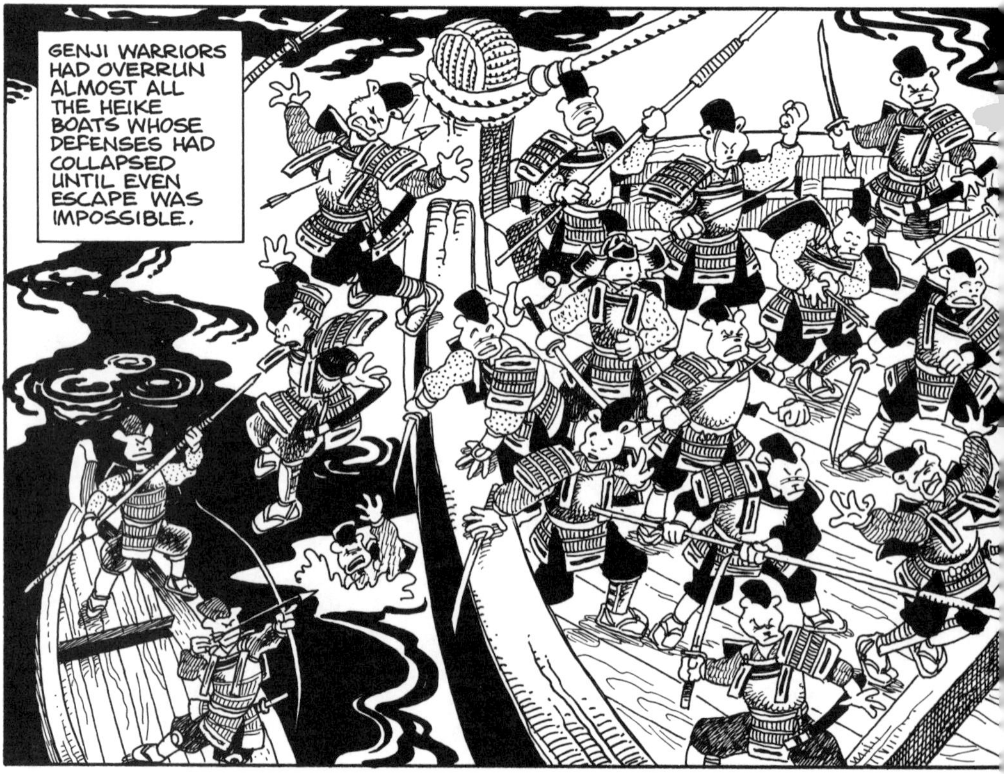
GENJI WARRIORS HAD OVERRUN ALMOST ALL THE HEIKE BOATS WHOSE DEFENSES HAD COLLAPSED UNTIL EVEN ESCAPE WAS IMPOSSIBLE.

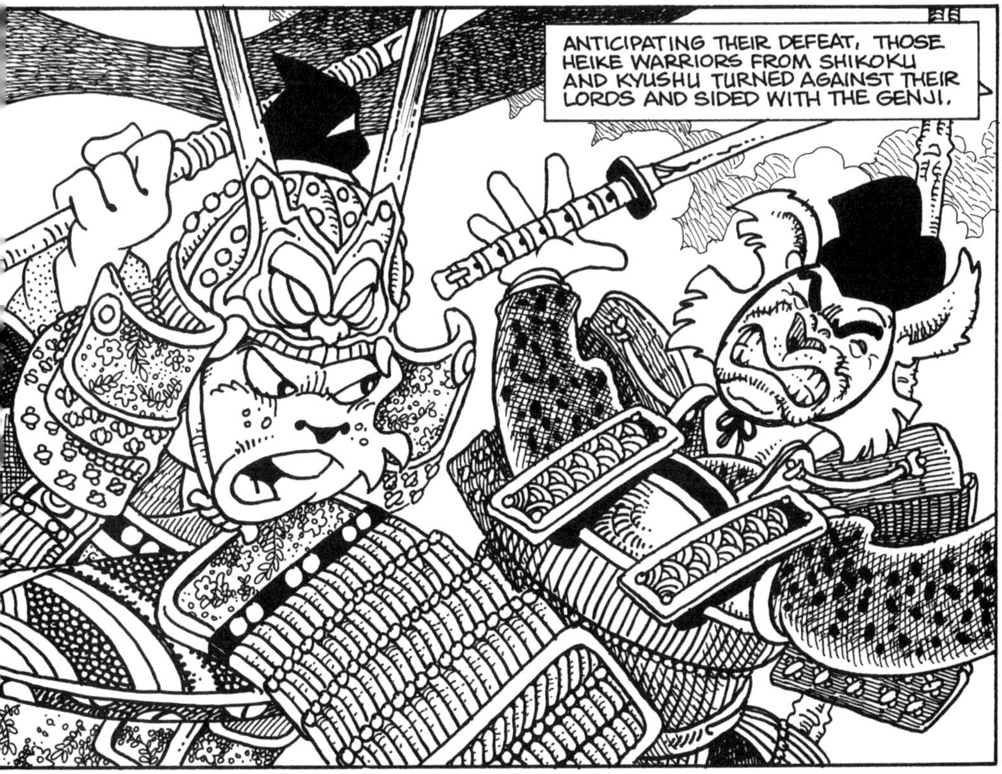
ANTICIPATING THEIR DEFEAT, THOSE HEIKE WARRIORS FROM SHIKOKU AND KYUSHU TURNED AGAINST THEIR LORDS AND SIDED WITH THE GENJI.
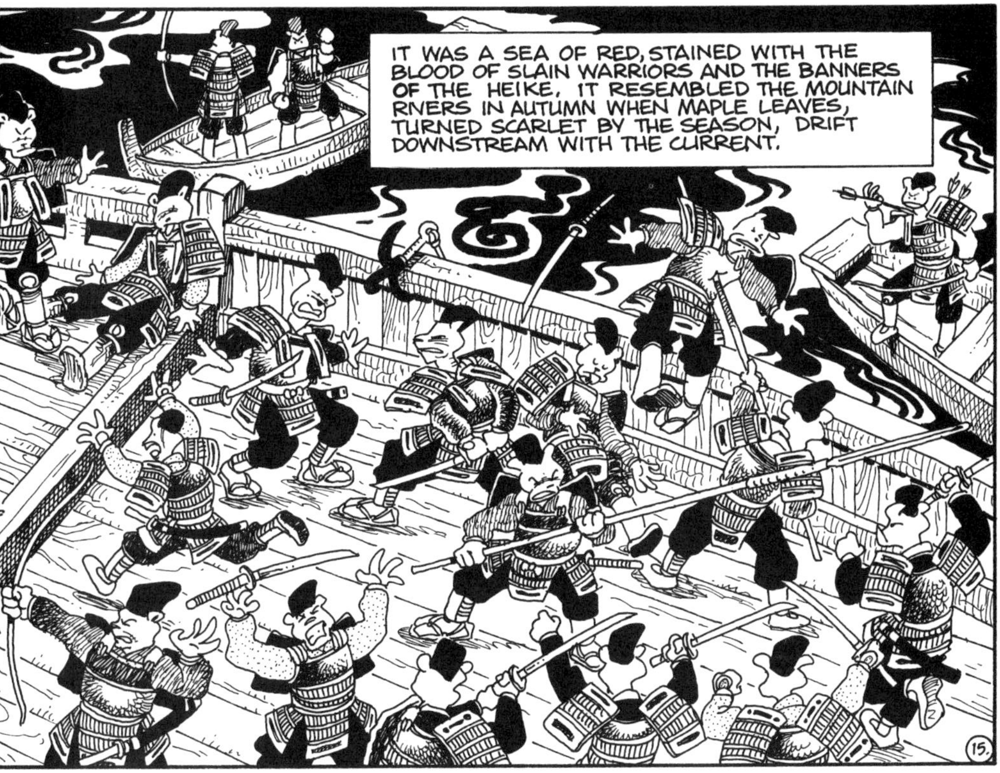
IT WAS A SEA OF RED, STAINED WITH THE BLOOD OF SLAIN WARRIORS AND THE BANNERS OF THE HEIKE. IT RESEMBLED THE MOUNTAIN RIVERS IN AUTUMN WHEN MAPLE LEAVES, TURNED SCARLET BY THE SEASON, DRIFT DOWNSTREAM WITH THE CURRENT.
15.

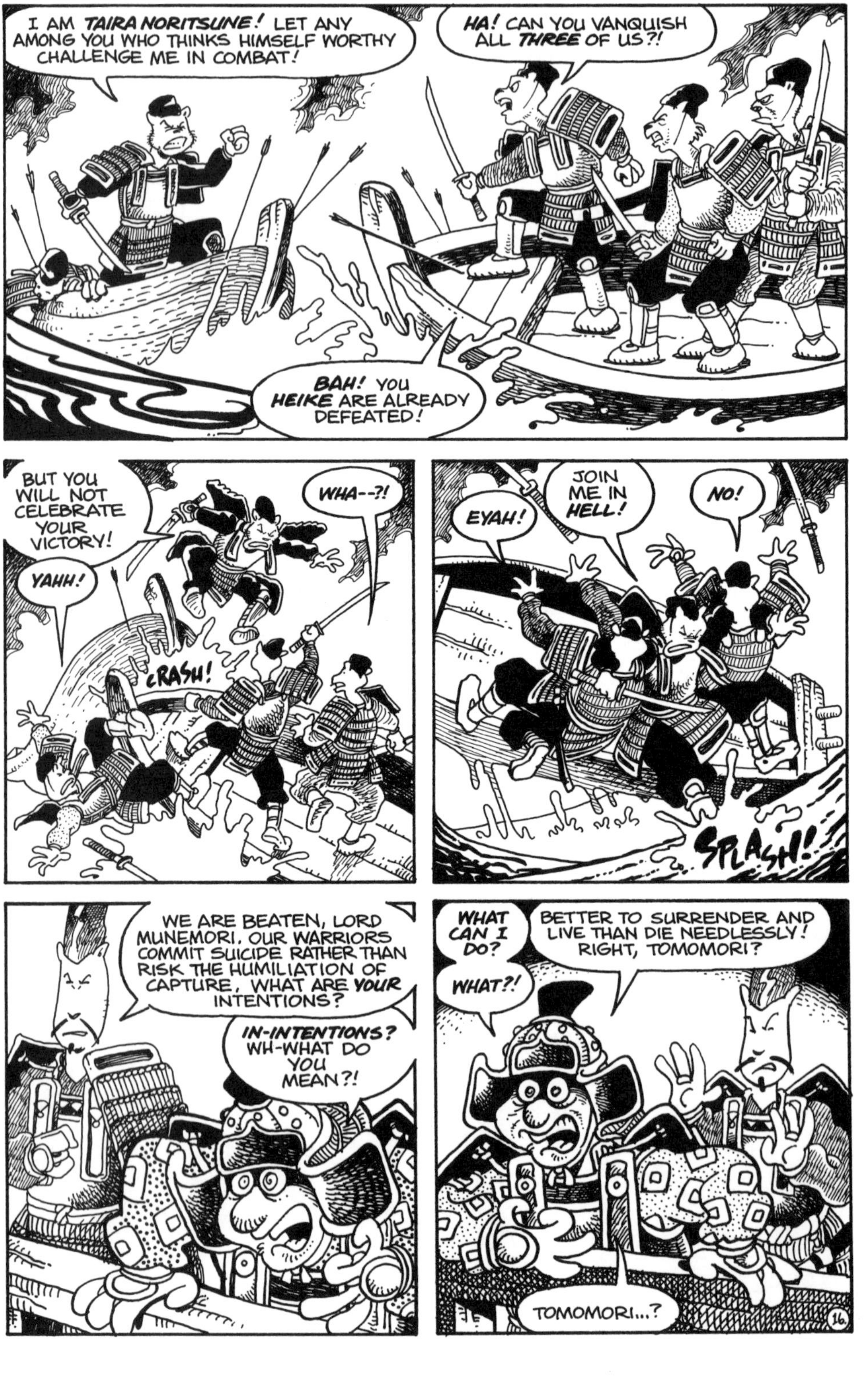
I AM TAIRA NORITSUNE! LET ANY AMONG YOU WHO THINKS HIMSELF WORTHY CHALLENGE ME IN COMBAT!
HA! CAN YOU VANQUISH ALL THREE OF US?!
BAH! YOU HEIKE ARE ALREADY DEFEATED!
BUT YOU WILL NOT CELEBRATE YOUR VICTORY!
YAHH!
WHA--?!
CRASH!
EYAH!
JOIN ME IN HELL!
NO!
SPLASH!!
WE ARE BEATEN, LORD MUNEMORI. OUR WARRIORS COMMIT SUICIDE RATHER THAN RISK THE HUMILIATION OF CAPTURE. WHAT ARE YOUR INTENTIONS?
IN-INTENTIONS? WH-WHAT DO YOU MEAN?!
WHAT CAN I DO?
WHAT?!
BETTER TO SURRENDER AND LIVE THAN DIE NEEDLESSLY! RIGHT, TOMOMORI?
TOMOMORI...?
16.

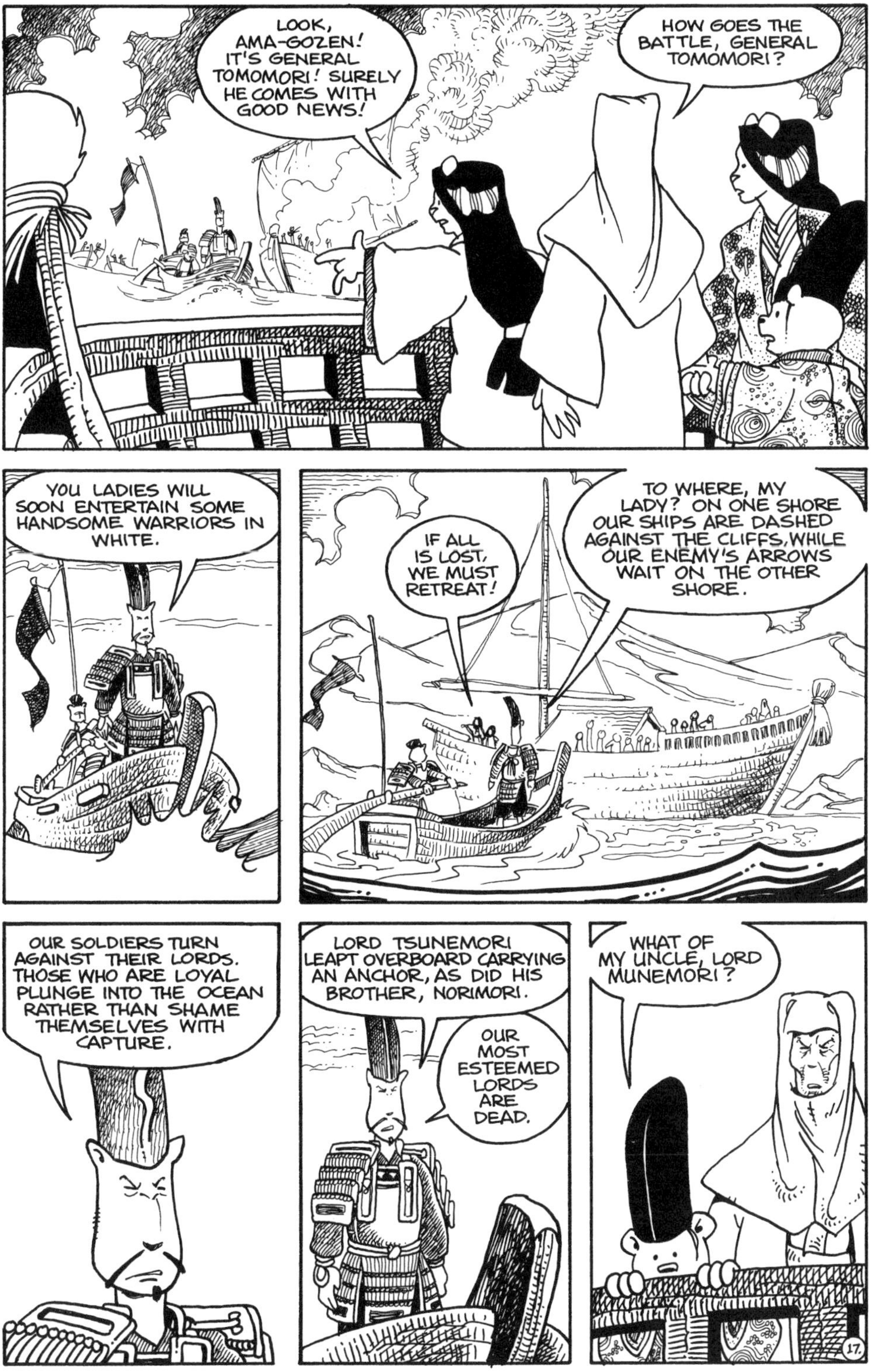
LOOK, AMA-GOZEN! IT'S GENERAL TOMOMORI! SURELY HE COMES WITH GOOD NEWS!
HOW GOES THE BATTLE, GENERAL TOMOMORI?
YOU LADIES WILL SOON ENTERTAIN SOME HANDSOME WARRIORS IN WHITE.
IF ALL IS LOST, WE MUST RETREAT!
TO WHERE, MY LADY? ON ONE SHORE OUR SHIPS ARE DASHED AGAINST THE CLIFFS, WHILE OUR ENEMY'S ARROWS WAIT ON THE OTHER SHORE.
OUR SOLDIERS TURN AGAINST THEIR LORDS. THOSE WHO ARE LOYAL PLUNGE INTO THE OCEAN RATHER THAN SHAME THEMSELVES WITH CAPTURE.
LORD TSUNEMORI LEAPT OVERBOARD CARRYING AN ANCHOR, AS DID HIS BROTHER, NORIMORI.
OUR MOST ESTEEMED LORDS ARE DEAD.
WHAT OF MY UNCLE, LORD MUNEMORI?
17.

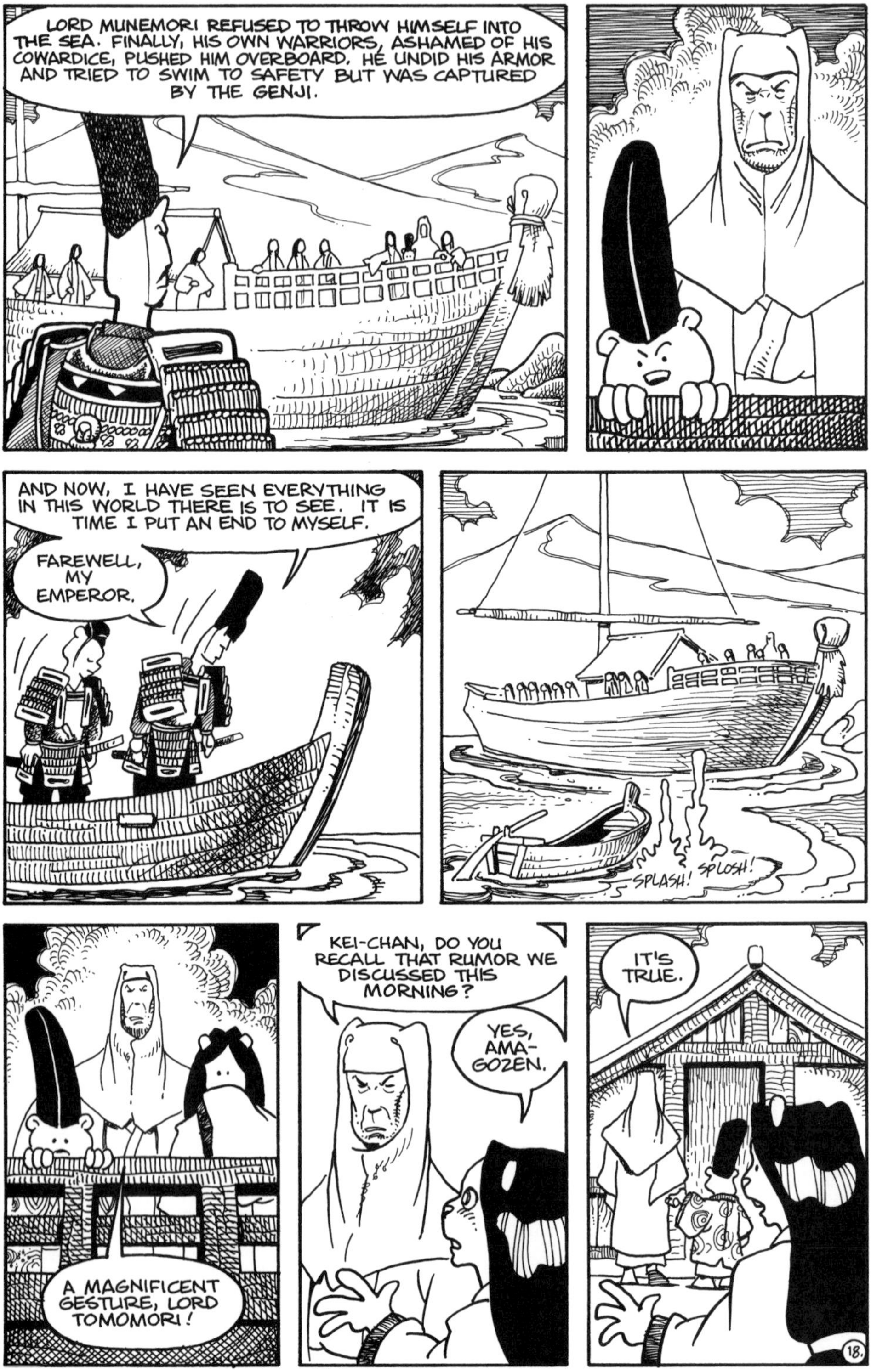
LORD MUNEMORI REFUSED TO THROW HIMSELF INTO THE SEA. FINALLY, HIS OWN WARRIORS, ASHAMED OF HIS COWARDICE, PUSHED HIM OVERBOARD. HE UNDID HIS ARMOR AND TRIED TO SWIM TO SAFETY BUT WAS CAPTURED BY THE GENJI.
AND NOW, I HAVE SEEN EVERYTHING IN THIS WORLD THERE IS TO SEE. IT IS TIME I PUT AN END TO MYSELF.
FAREWELL, MY EMPEROR.
SPLASH!
SPLOSH!
A MAGNIFICENT GESTURE, LORD TOMOMORI!
KEI-CHAN, DO YOU RECALL THAT RUMOR WE DISCUSSED THIS MORNING?
YES, AMA-GOZEN.
IT'S TRUE.
18.

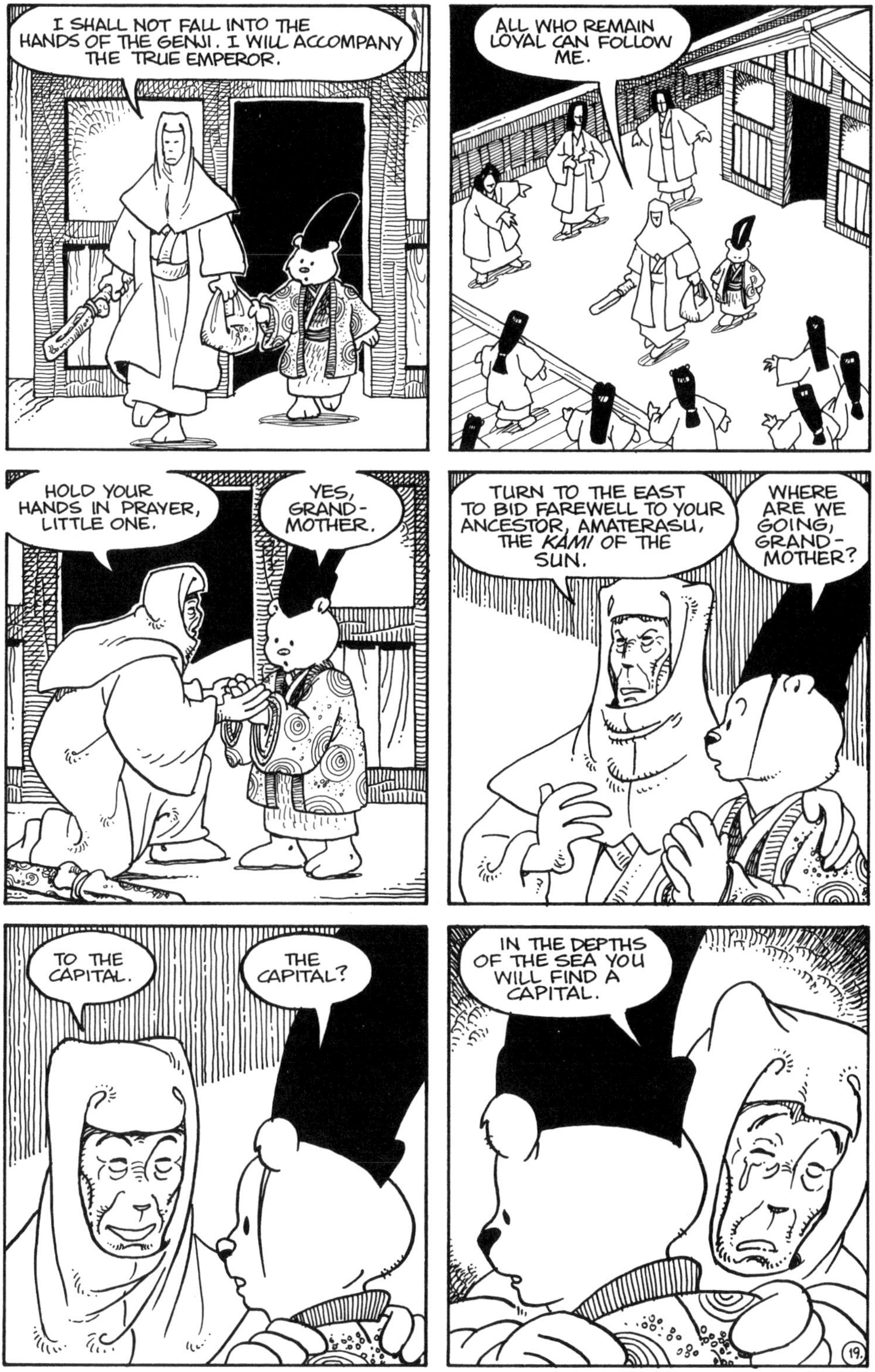
I SHALL NOT FALL INTO THE HANDS OF THE GENJI. I WILL ACCOMPANY THE TRUE EMPEROR.
ALL WHO REMAIN LOYAL CAN FOLLOW ME.
HOLD YOUR HANDS IN PRAYER, LITTLE ONE.
YES, GRAND-MOTHER.
TURN TO THE EAST TO BID FAREWELL TO YOUR ANCESTOR, AMATERASU, THE *KAMI* OF THE SUN.
WHERE ARE WE GOING, GRAND-MOTHER?
TO THE CAPITAL.
THE CAPITAL?
IN THE DEPTHS OF THE SEA YOU WILL FIND A CAPITAL.
19.

I WILL TAKE THE SWORD, *KUSANAGI-NO-TSURUGI*, AND THE SACRED JEWEL, *YASAKANI-NO-MAGATAMA.*

I TRUST *YATA-NO-KAGAMI*, THE STAR-HAND MIRROR, WILL NOT BE LEFT FOR THE MINAMOTO RABBLE.

HAIL, AMIDA BUDDHA!

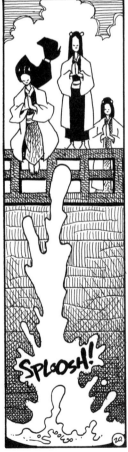

SPLOOSH!

50

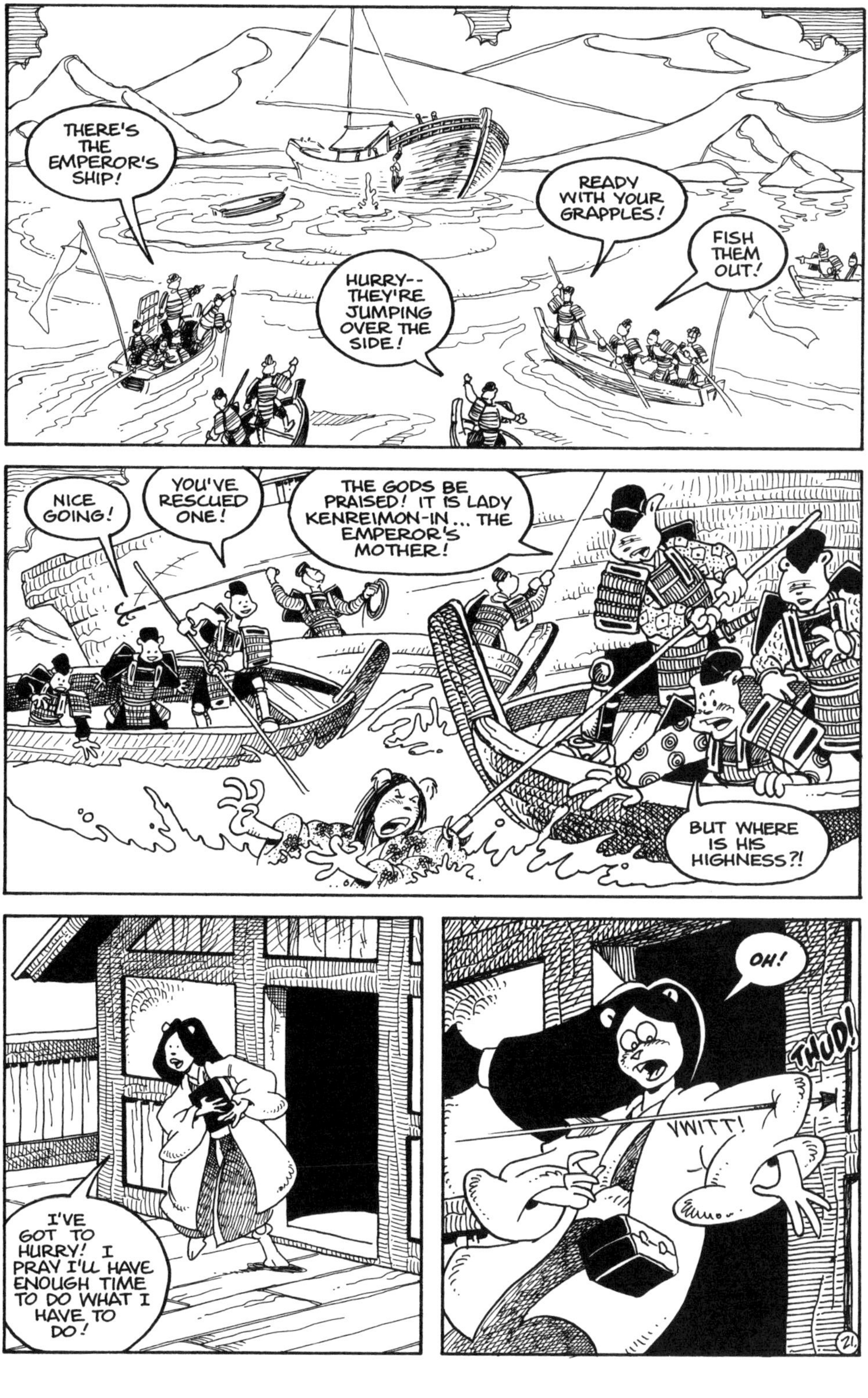
THERE'S THE EMPEROR'S SHIP!
HURRY-- THEY'RE JUMPING OVER THE SIDE!
READY WITH YOUR GRAPPLES!
FISH THEM OUT!
NICE GOING!
YOU'VE RESCUED ONE!
THE GODS BE PRAISED! IT IS LADY KENREIMON-IN... THE EMPEROR'S MOTHER!
BUT WHERE IS HIS HIGHNESS?!
I'VE GOT TO HURRY! I PRAY I'LL HAVE ENOUGH TIME TO DO WHAT I HAVE TO DO!
OH!
THUD!
VWITT!
21.

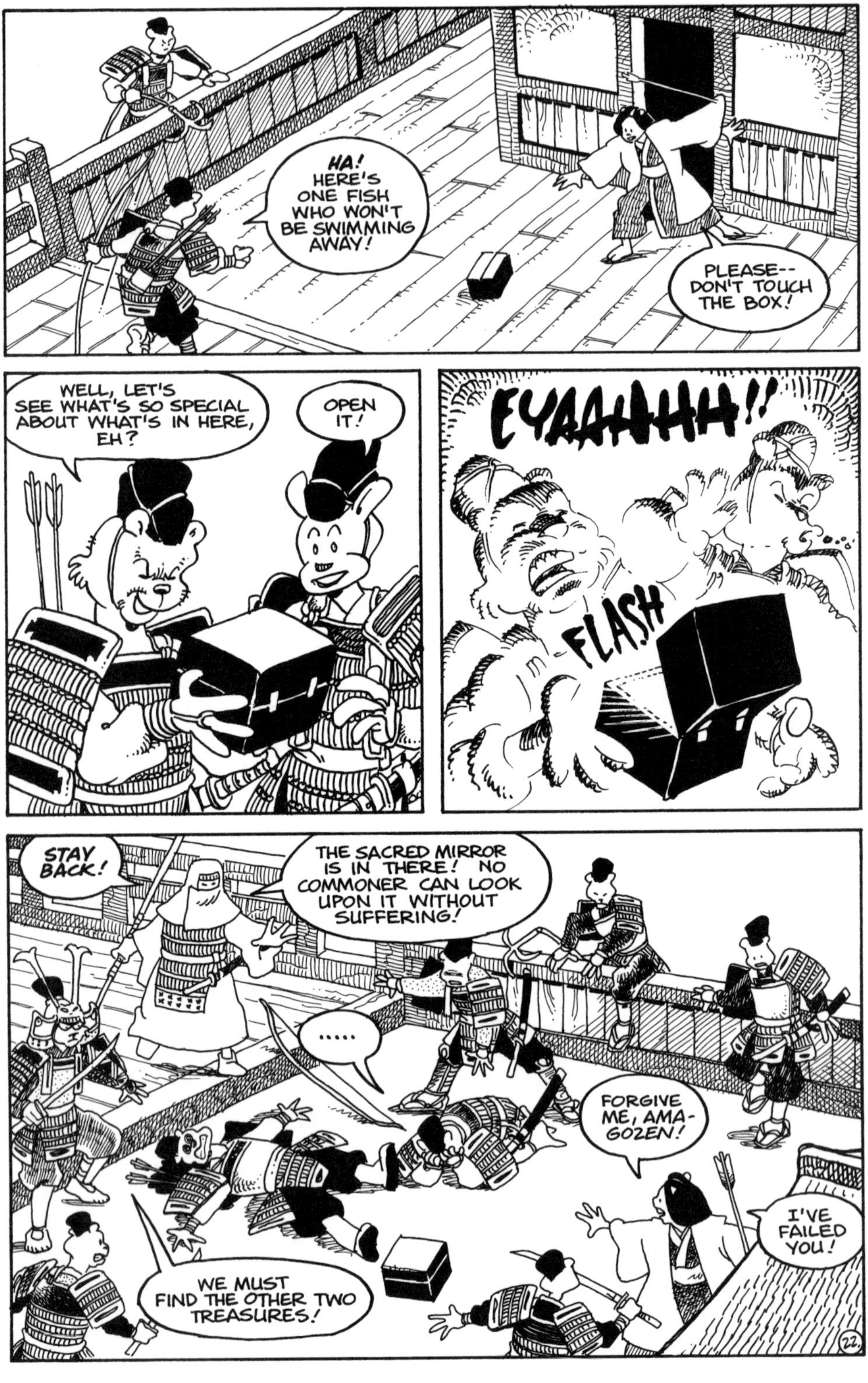
HA! HERE'S ONE FISH WHO WON'T BE SWIMMING AWAY!
PLEASE-- DON'T TOUCH THE BOX!
WELL, LET'S SEE WHAT'S SO SPECIAL ABOUT WHAT'S IN HERE, EH?
OPEN IT!
EYAAHHH!!
FLASH
STAY BACK!
THE SACRED MIRROR IS IN THERE! NO COMMONER CAN LOOK UPON IT WITHOUT SUFFERING!
.....
FORGIVE ME, AMA-GOZEN!
I'VE FAILED YOU!
WE MUST FIND THE OTHER TWO TREASURES!
22.

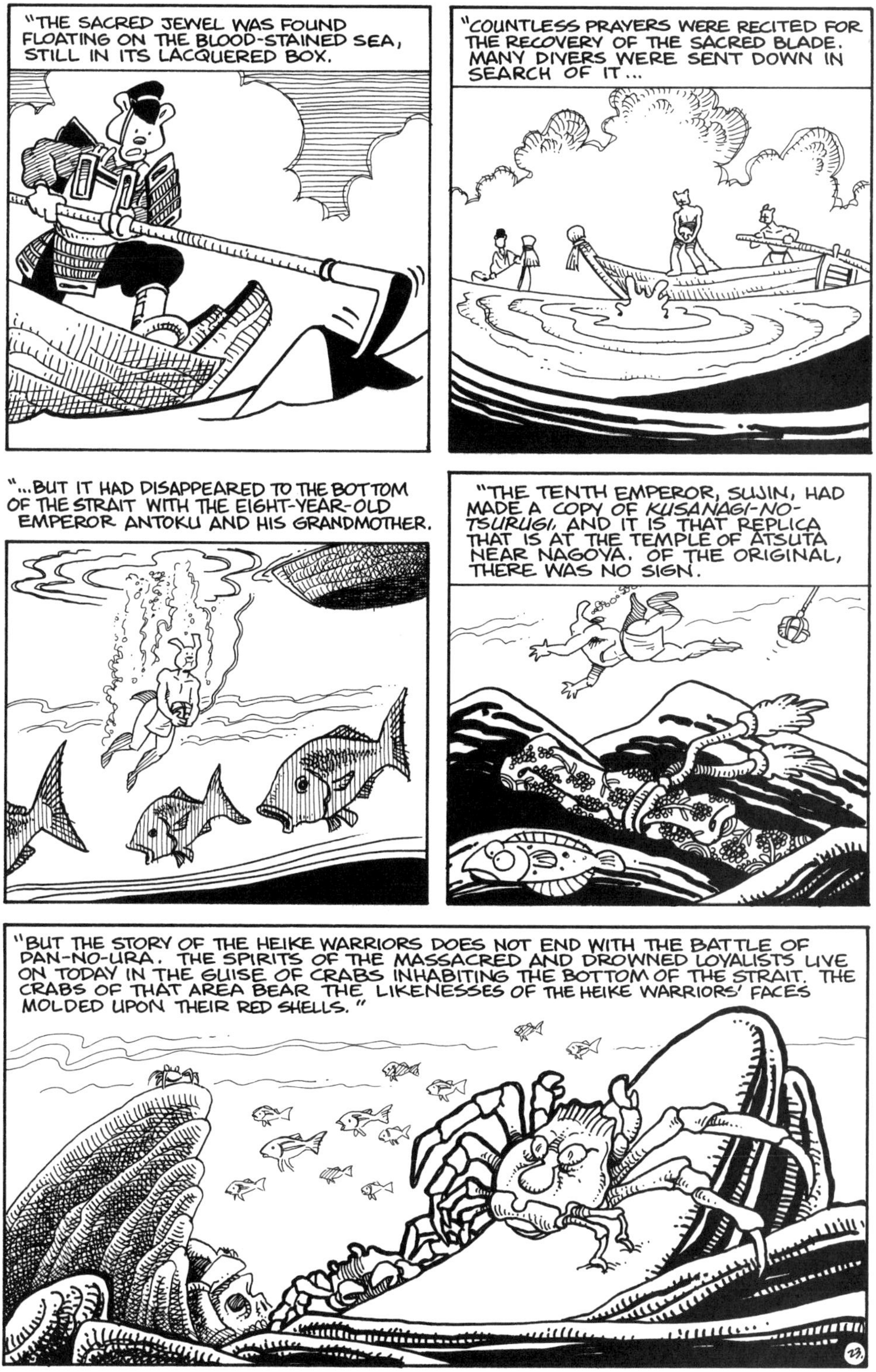
"THE SACRED JEWEL WAS FOUND FLOATING ON THE BLOOD-STAINED SEA, STILL IN ITS LACQUERED BOX.
"COUNTLESS PRAYERS WERE RECITED FOR THE RECOVERY OF THE SACRED BLADE. MANY DIVERS WERE SENT DOWN IN SEARCH OF IT...
"...BUT IT HAD DISAPPEARED TO THE BOTTOM OF THE STRAIT WITH THE EIGHT-YEAR-OLD EMPEROR ANTOKU AND HIS GRANDMOTHER.
"THE TENTH EMPEROR, SUJIN, HAD MADE A COPY OF *KUSANAGI-NO-TSURUGI,* AND IT IS THAT REPLICA THAT IS AT THE TEMPLE OF ATSUTA NEAR NAGOYA. OF THE ORIGINAL, THERE WAS NO SIGN.
"BUT THE STORY OF THE HEIKE WARRIORS DOES NOT END WITH THE BATTLE OF DAN-NO-URA. THE SPIRITS OF THE MASSACRED AND DROWNED LOYALISTS LIVE ON TODAY IN THE GUISE OF CRABS INHABITING THE BOTTOM OF THE STRAIT. THE CRABS OF THAT AREA BEAR THE LIKENESSES OF THE HEIKE WARRIORS' FACES MOLDED UPON THEIR RED SHELLS."
23.

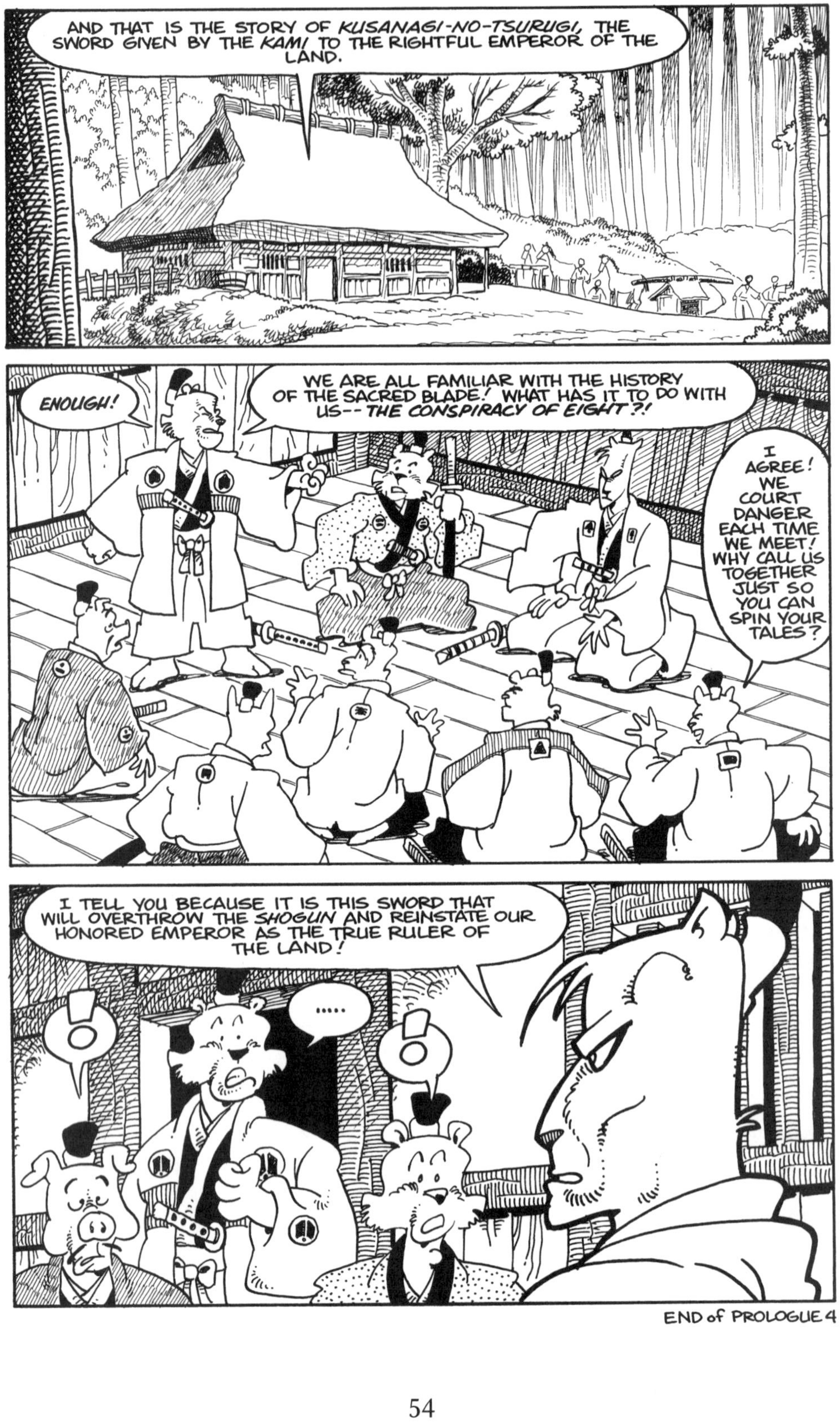
AND THAT IS THE STORY OF *KUSANAGI-NO-TSURUGI*, THE SWORD GIVEN BY THE *KAMI* TO THE RIGHTFUL EMPEROR OF THE LAND.
ENOUGH!
WE ARE ALL FAMILIAR WITH THE HISTORY OF THE SACRED BLADE! WHAT HAS IT TO DO WITH US-- *THE CONSPIRACY OF EIGHT*?!
I AGREE! WE COURT DANGER EACH TIME WE MEET! WHY CALL US TOGETHER JUST SO YOU CAN SPIN YOUR TALES?
I TELL YOU BECAUSE IT IS THIS SWORD THAT WILL OVERTHROW THE *SHOGUN* AND REINSTATE OUR HONORED EMPEROR AS THE TRUE RULER OF THE LAND!
!
......
!

END of PROLOGUE 4

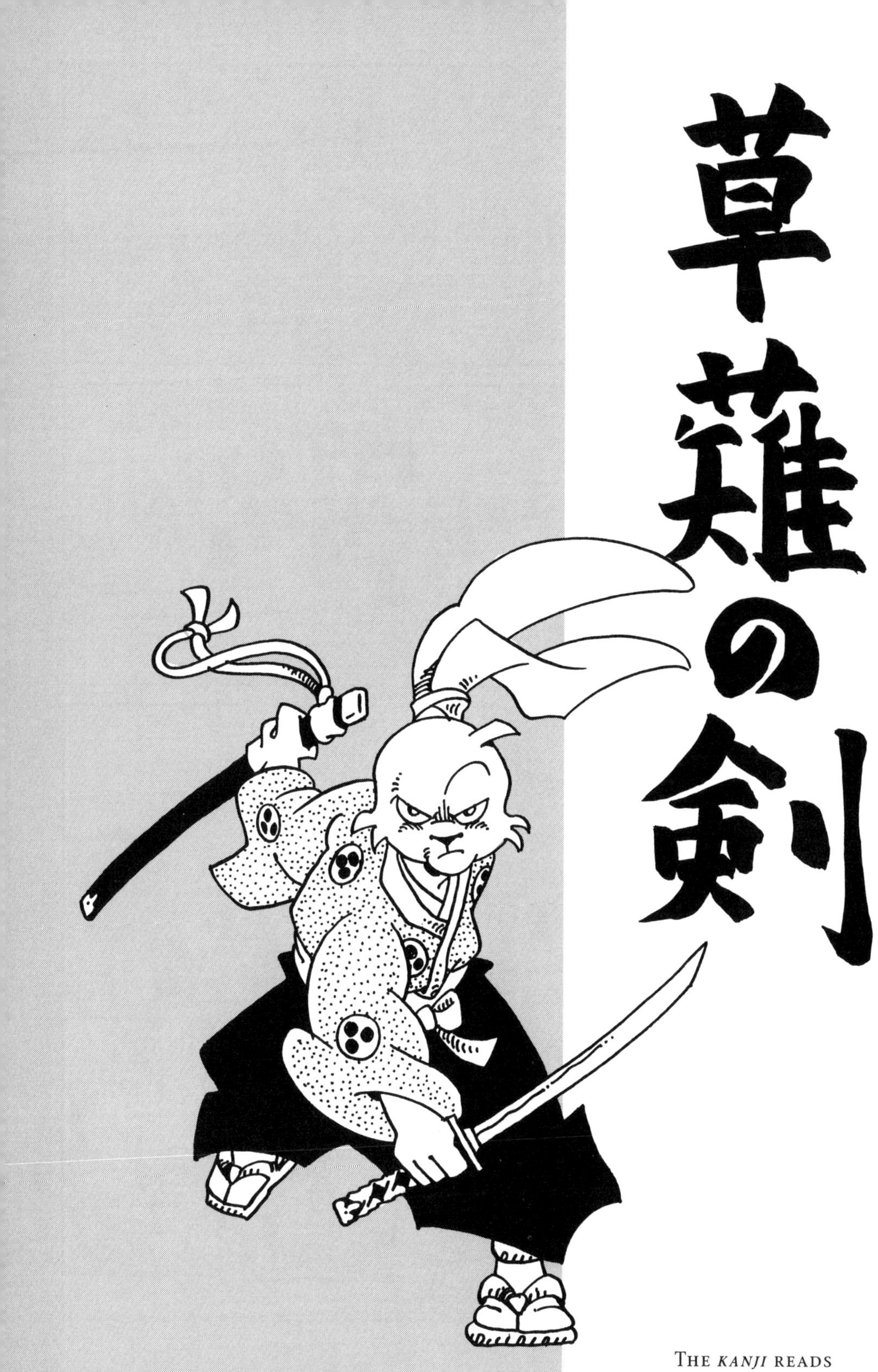
草薙の剣

THE *KANJI* READS
"*KUSANAGI-NO-TSURUGI*" —
"THE GRASSCUTTING SWORD."

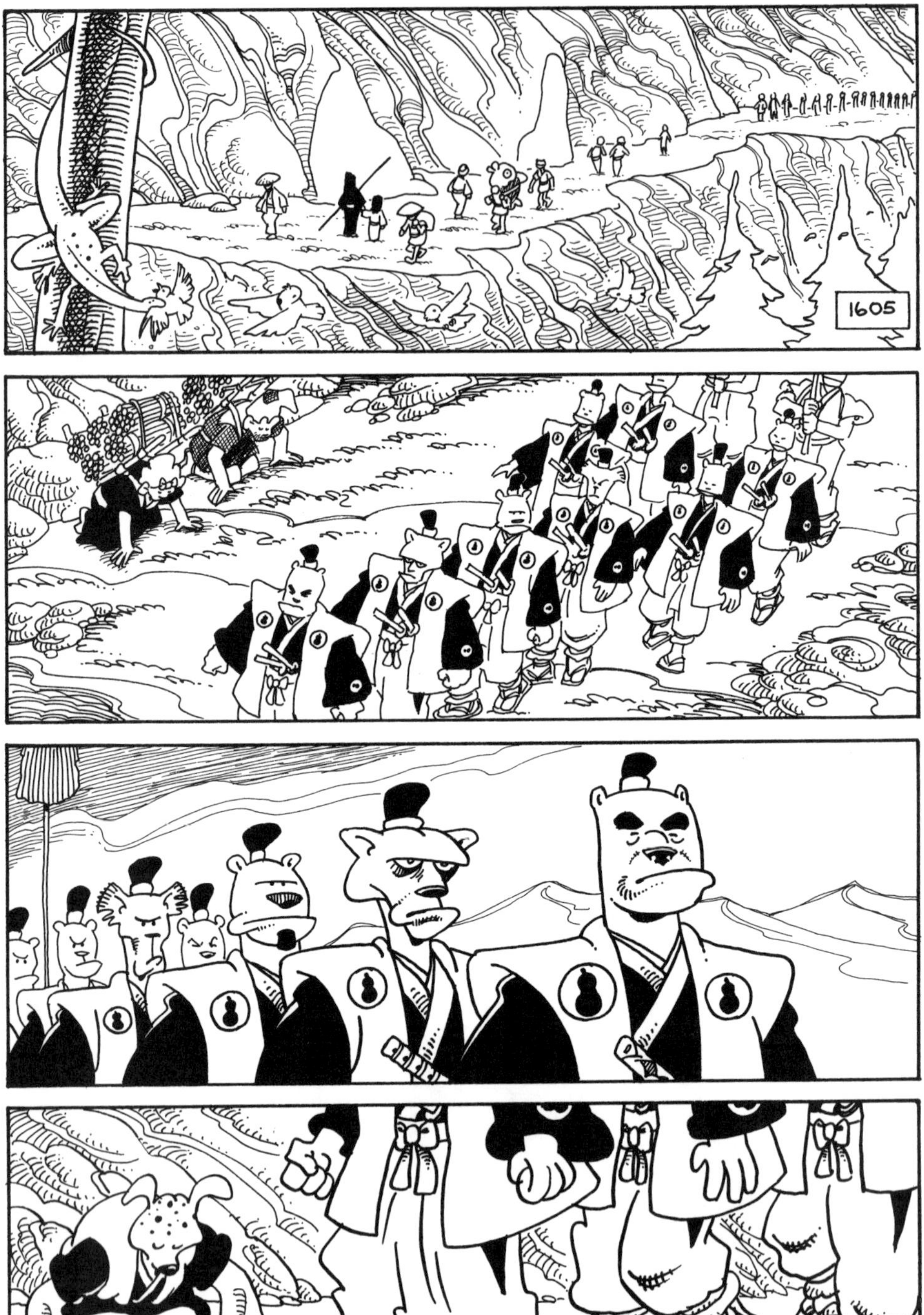
1605

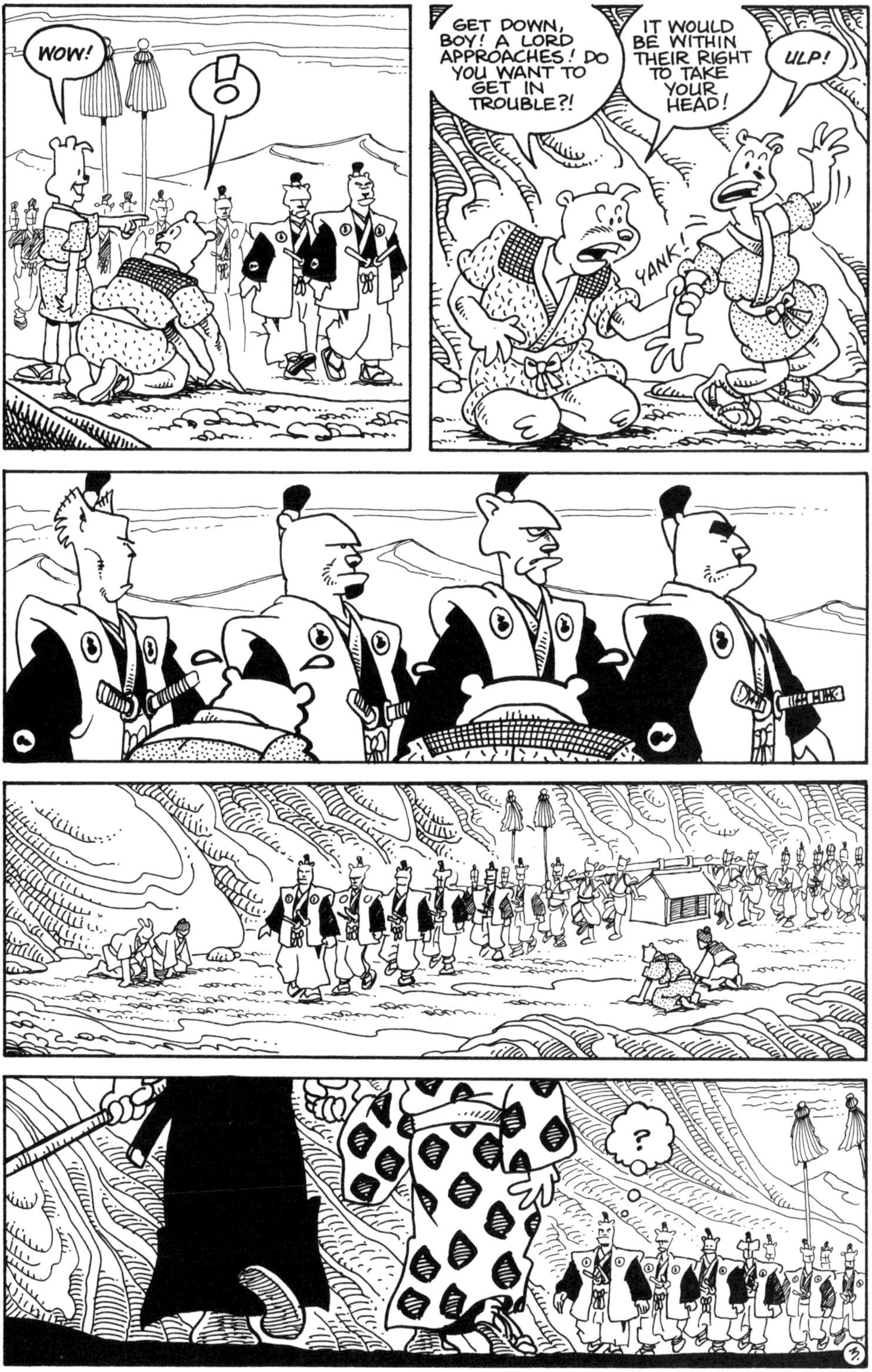
WOW!
!
GET DOWN, BOY! A LORD APPROACHES! DO YOU WANT TO GET IN TROUBLE?!
IT WOULD BE WITHIN THEIR RIGHT TO TAKE YOUR HEAD!
ULP!
YANK!
?

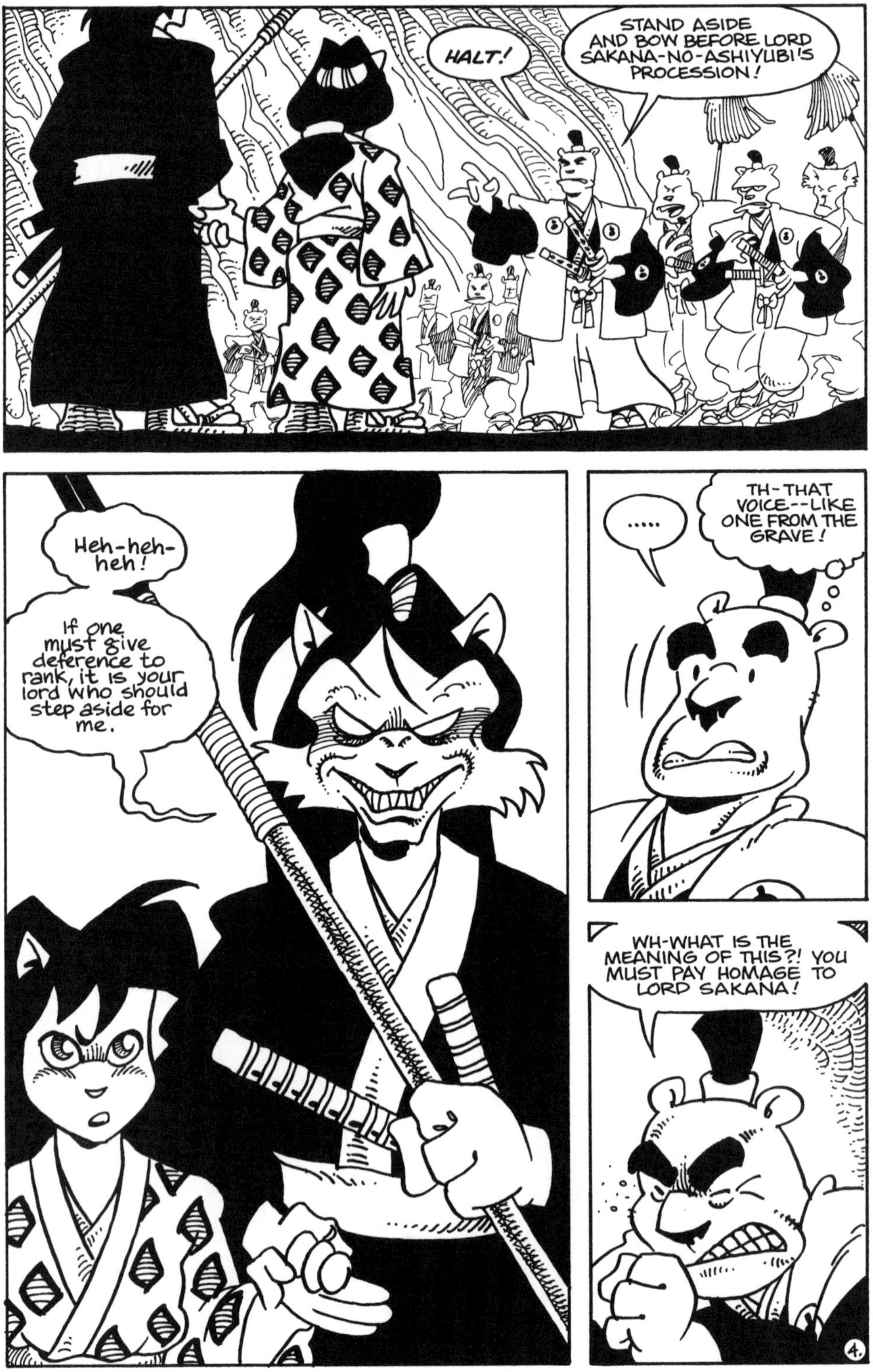
HALT!
STAND ASIDE AND BOW BEFORE LORD SAKANA-NO-ASHIYUBI'S PROCESSION!
Heh-heh-heh!
If one must give deference to rank, it is your lord who should step aside for me.
.....
TH-THAT VOICE--LIKE ONE FROM THE GRAVE!
WH-WHAT IS THE MEANING OF THIS?! YOU MUST PAY HOMAGE TO LORD SAKANA!
4.

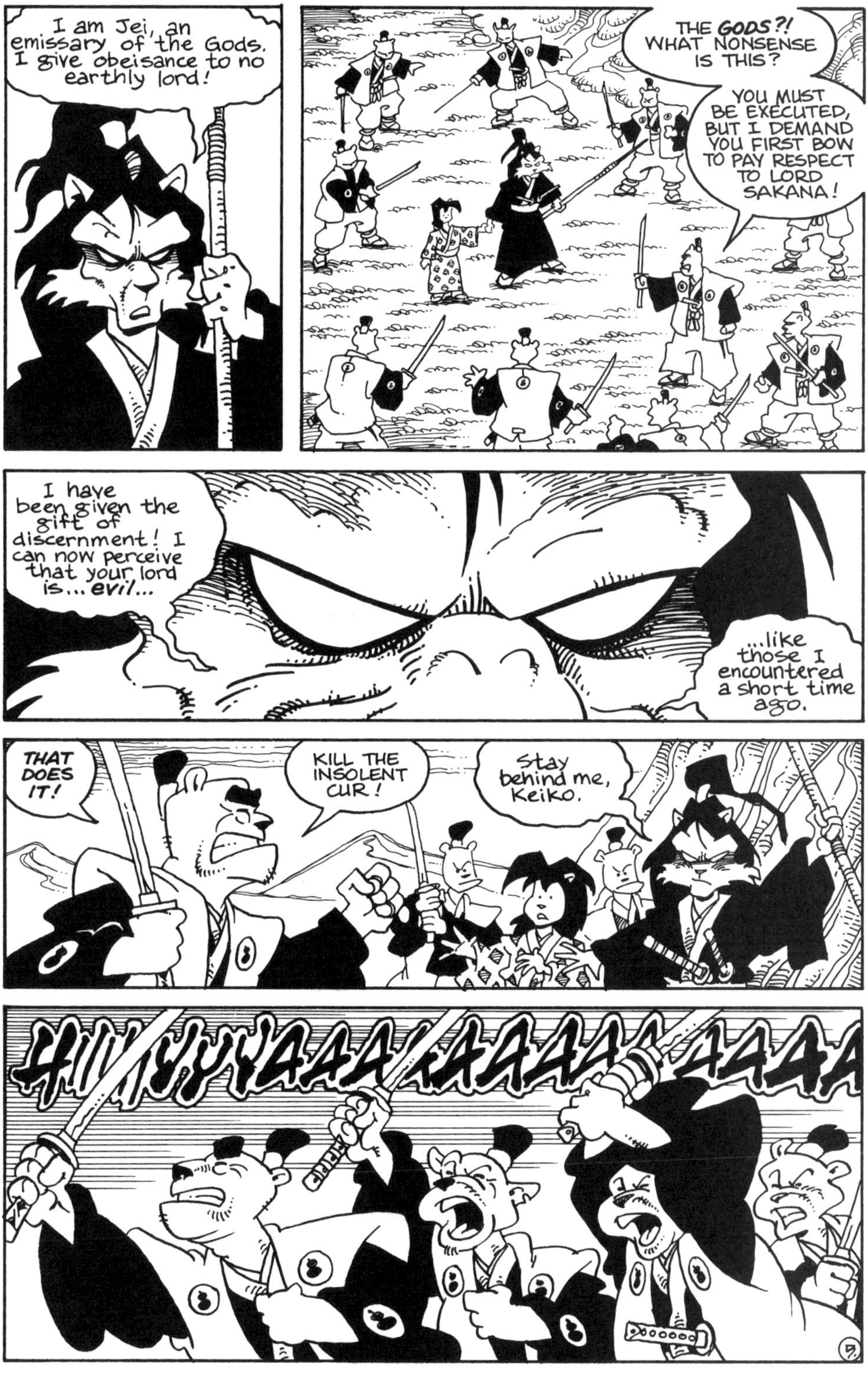
I am Jei, an emissary of the Gods. I give obeisance to no earthly lord!
THE GODS?! WHAT NONSENSE IS THIS?
YOU MUST BE EXECUTED, BUT I DEMAND YOU FIRST BOW TO PAY RESPECT TO LORD SAKANA!
I have been given the gift of discernment! I can now perceive that your lord is... evil...
...like those I encountered a short time ago.
THAT DOES IT!
KILL THE INSOLENT CUR!
Stay behind me, Keiko.
HIIIYYYAAAAAAAAAAAAA

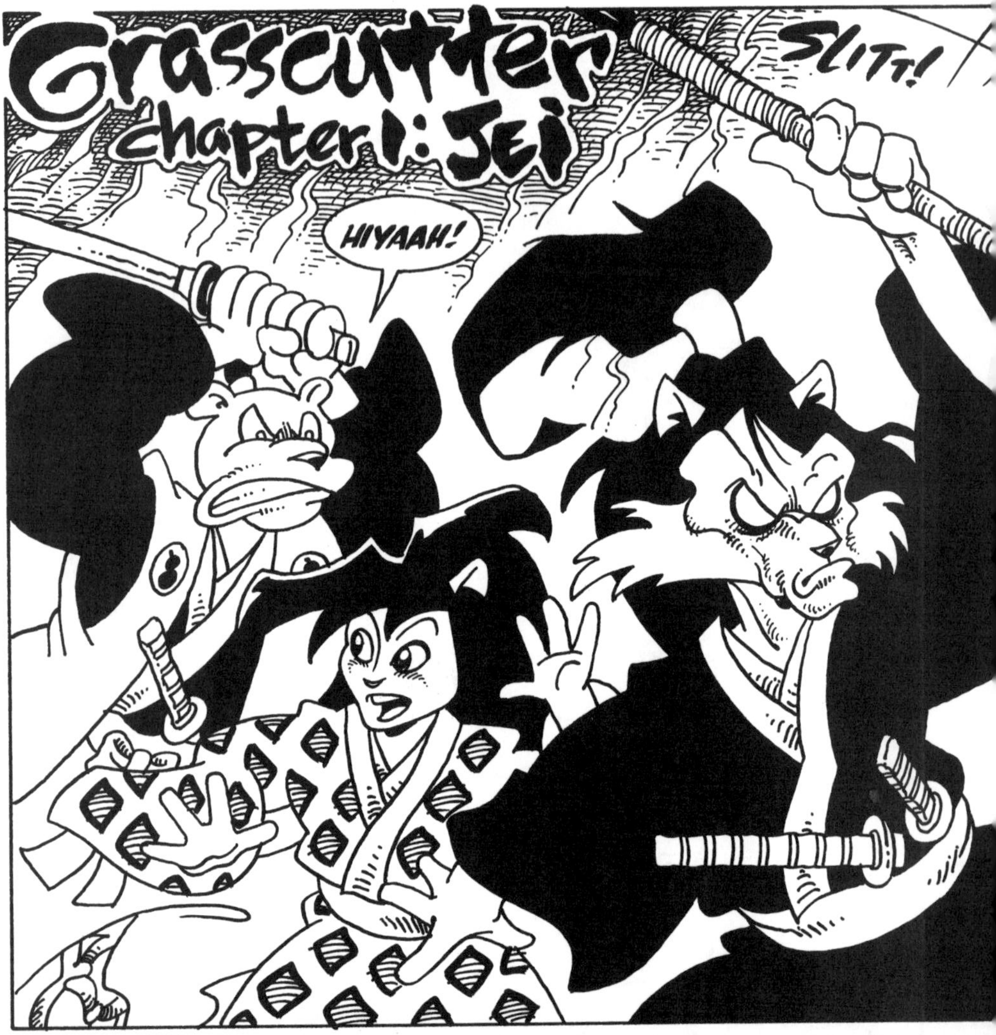
Grasscutter
chapter 1: Jei
SLITT!
HIYAAH!

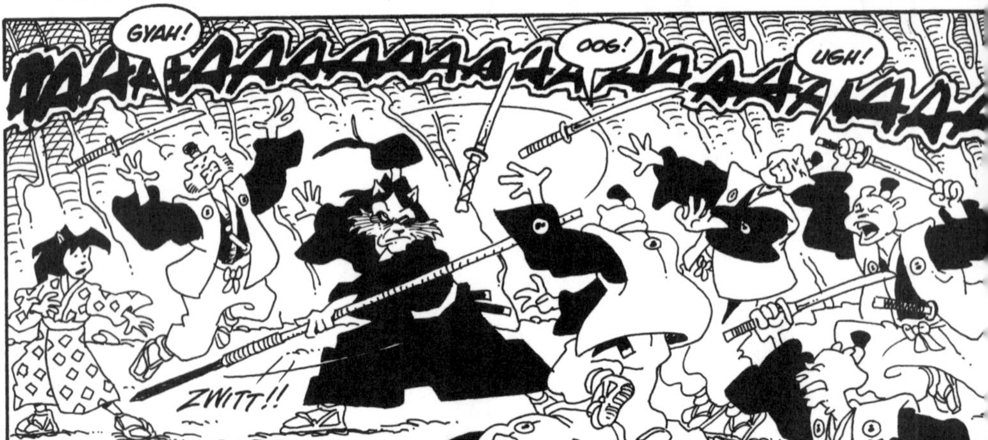
GYAH!
OOG!
UGH!
ZWITT!!

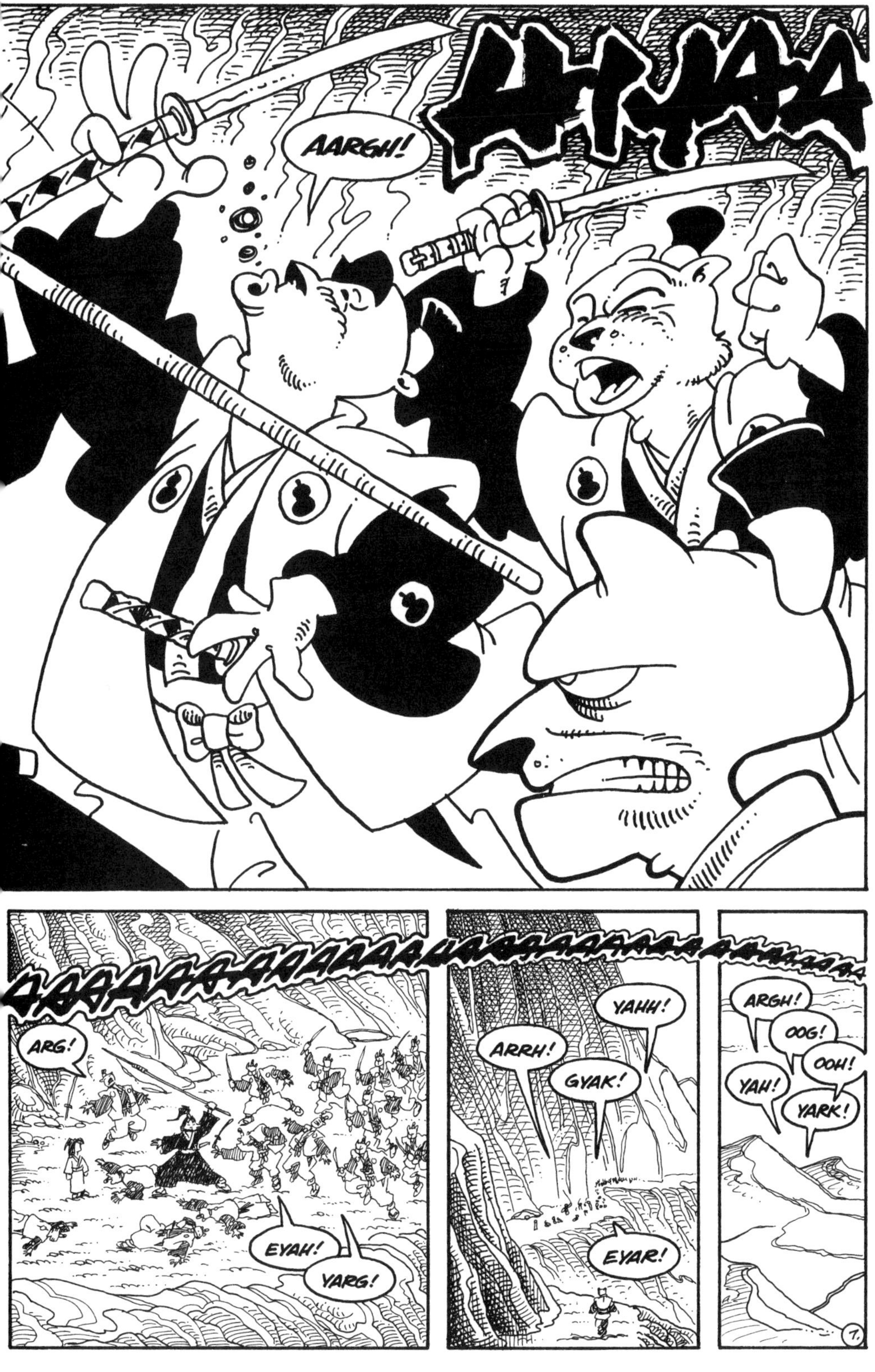
AARGH!
HI-YAA
AAAAAAAAAAAAAAAAAAAAAAAAAAAAAAAAAAAAAAAAAA
ARG!
EYAH!
YARG!
ARRH!
YAHH!
GYAK!
EYAR!
ARGH!
OOG!
YAH!
OOH!
YARK!
7.

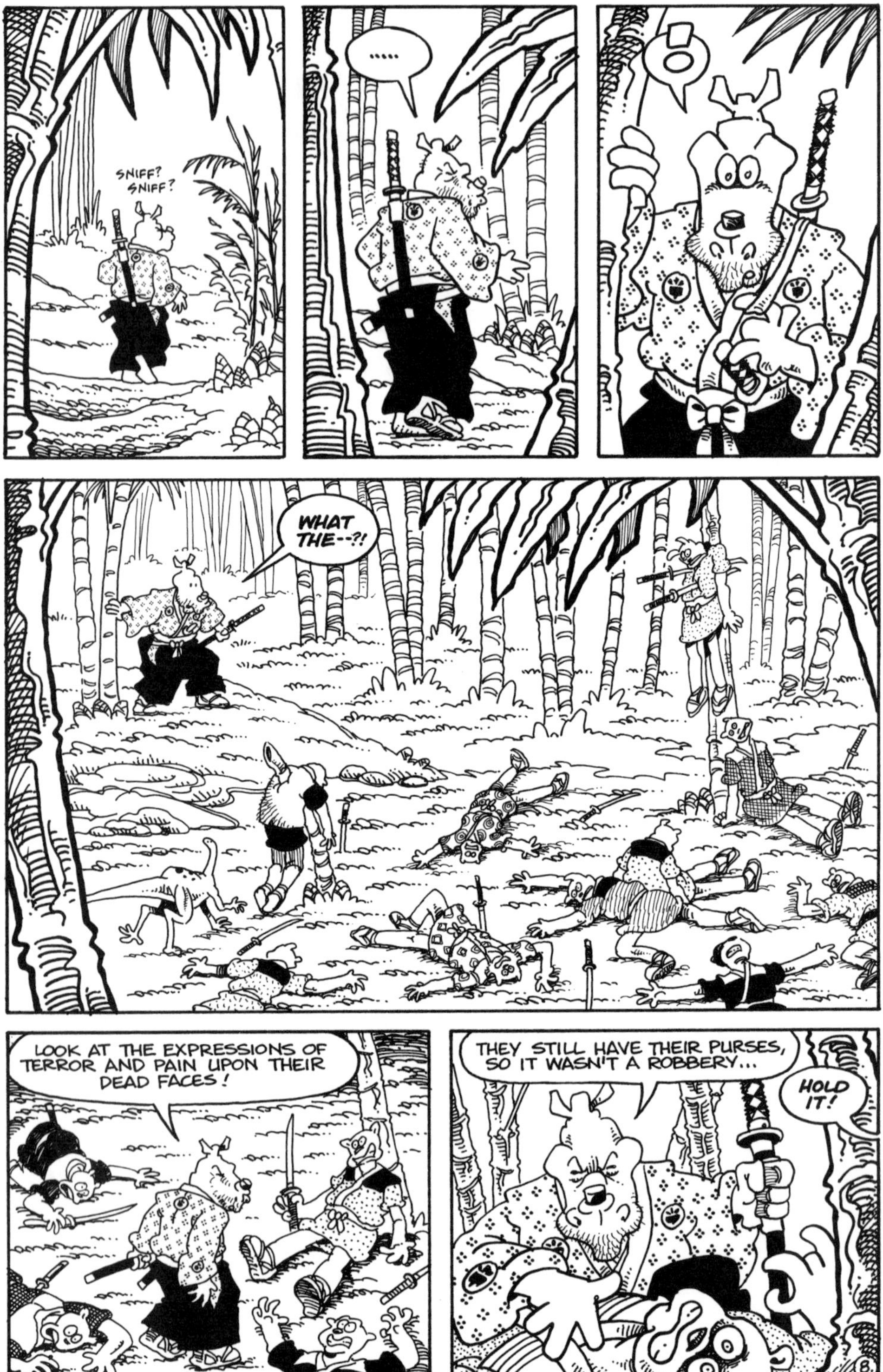
SNIFF?
SNIFF?
......
!
WHAT THE--?!
LOOK AT THE EXPRESSIONS OF TERROR AND PAIN UPON THEIR DEAD FACES!
THEY STILL HAVE THEIR PURSES, SO IT WASN'T A ROBBERY...
HOLD IT!
8.

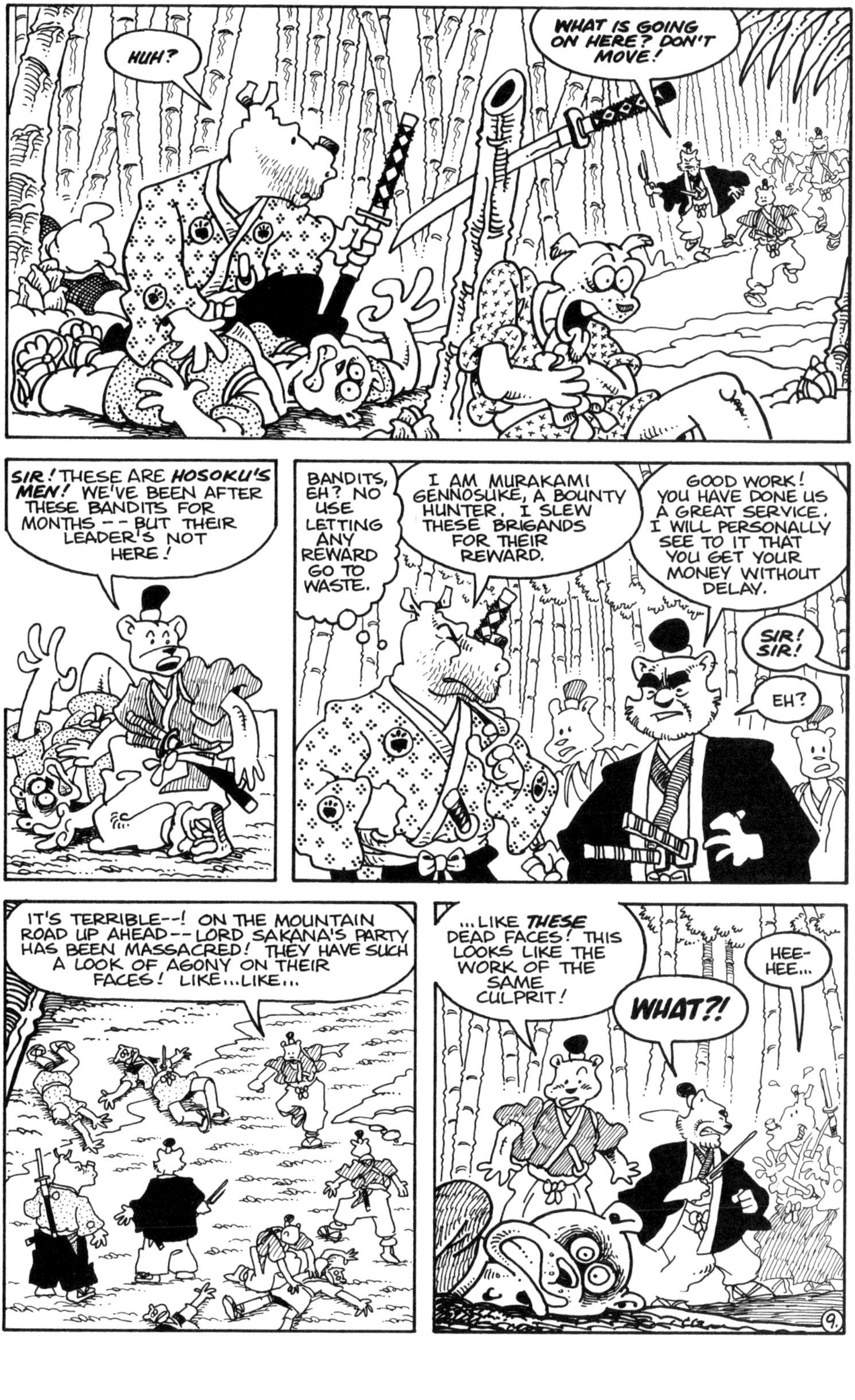
HUH?
WHAT IS GOING ON HERE? DON'T MOVE!
SIR! THESE ARE HOSOKU'S MEN! WE'VE BEEN AFTER THESE BANDITS FOR MONTHS -- BUT THEIR LEADER'S NOT HERE!
BANDITS, EH? NO USE LETTING ANY REWARD GO TO WASTE.
I AM MURAKAMI GENNOSUKE, A BOUNTY HUNTER. I SLEW THESE BRIGANDS FOR THEIR REWARD.
GOOD WORK! YOU HAVE DONE US A GREAT SERVICE. I WILL PERSONALLY SEE TO IT THAT YOU GET YOUR MONEY WITHOUT DELAY.
SIR! SIR!
EH?
IT'S TERRIBLE--! ON THE MOUNTAIN ROAD UP AHEAD--LORD SAKANA'S PARTY HAS BEEN MASSACRED! THEY HAVE SUCH A LOOK OF AGONY ON THEIR FACES! LIKE...LIKE...
...LIKE THESE DEAD FACES! THIS LOOKS LIKE THE WORK OF THE SAME CULPRIT!
WHAT?!
HEE-HEE...
9.

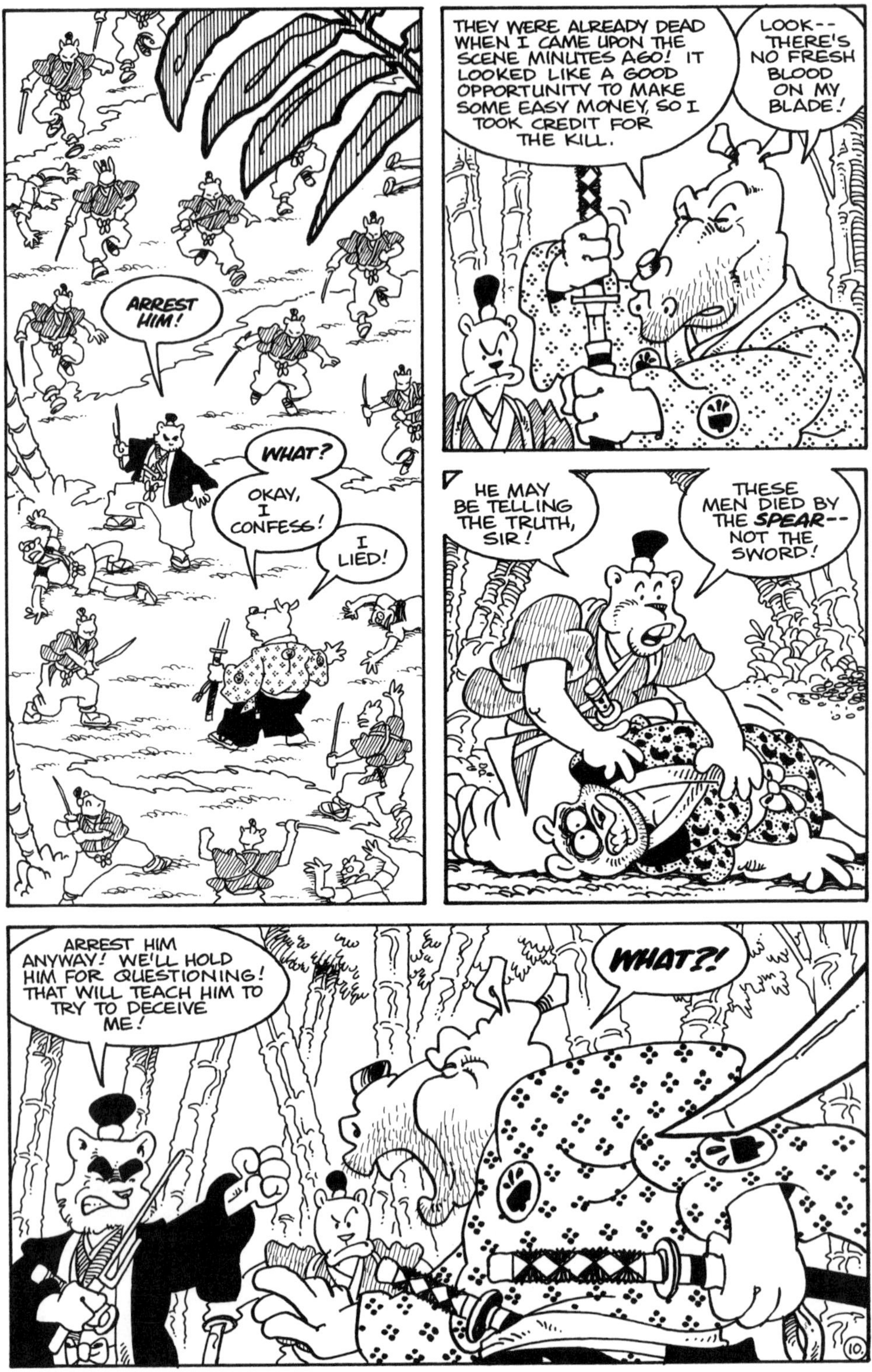

ARREST HIM!
WHAT?
OKAY, I CONFESS!
I LIED!
THEY WERE ALREADY DEAD WHEN I CAME UPON THE SCENE MINUTES AGO! IT LOOKED LIKE A GOOD OPPORTUNITY TO MAKE SOME EASY MONEY, SO I TOOK CREDIT FOR THE KILL.
LOOK-- THERE'S NO FRESH BLOOD ON MY BLADE!
HE MAY BE TELLING THE TRUTH, SIR!
THESE MEN DIED BY THE SPEAR-- NOT THE SWORD!
ARREST HIM ANYWAY! WE'LL HOLD HIM FOR QUESTIONING! THAT WILL TEACH HIM TO TRY TO DECEIVE ME!
WHAT?!
10.

HERE'S YOUR TEA, MA'AM. DRINK IT WHILE IT'S STILL HOT.

GO ON, DRINK IT.

GO ON!

IT'S GOOD!

YUMMY.

ZZZZ...

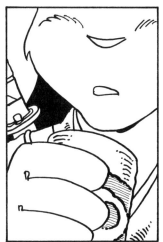

HERE, INNKEEPER, YOU DRINK IT.

WHAT? ME? UH... UH...

N-NO! I CAN'T! I-I MEAN, I'M ALLERGIC TO TEA. IT DOESN'T AGREE WITH ME....ER...I'LL SWELL UP...BREAK OUT IN A RASH... AND...UH...AND...

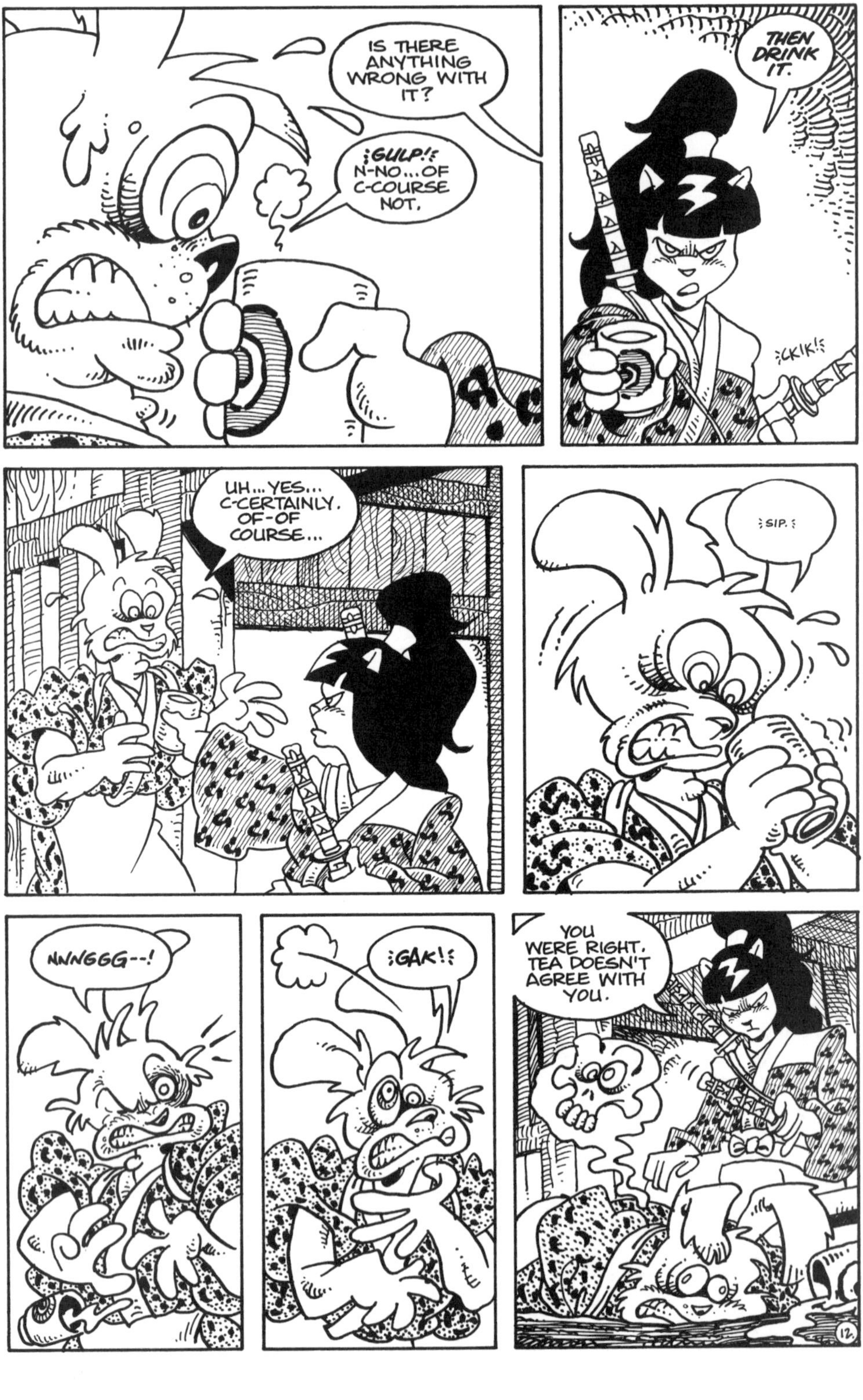
IS THERE ANYTHING WRONG WITH IT?
GULP!
N-NO...OF C-COURSE NOT.
THEN DRINK IT.
CKIK!
UH...YES... C-CERTAINLY. OF-OF COURSE...
SIP.
NNNGGG--!
GAK!
YOU WERE RIGHT. TEA DOESN'T AGREE WITH YOU.

ASSASSINATION IS A DANGEROUS GAME--ESPECIALLY FOR AN AMATEUR!

YOU SHOULD HAVE STUCK TO RUNNING YOUR INN.

¡YAWN!¿ INNKEEPER! MORE SAKE!

I SAID, *MORE SAKE!*

HEY, YOU HEARD ME?!

YOU WANT ME TO COME BACK WITH MY GANG?

WHERE IS MY SAKE?!

¡ULP!¿

TH-THAT'S *INAZUMA!*

THEY SAY SHE'S UNMATCHED WITH THE SWORD!

BOSS BAKUCHI PUT A PRICE ON HER HEAD. THERE ARE MANY WHO WOULD LIKE TO CLAIM IT!

MAYBE I SHOULD GATHER THE GANG AND GO AFTER HER.

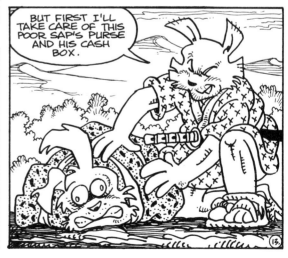

BUT FIRST I'LL TAKE CARE OF THIS POOR SAP'S PURSE AND HIS CASH BOX.

13

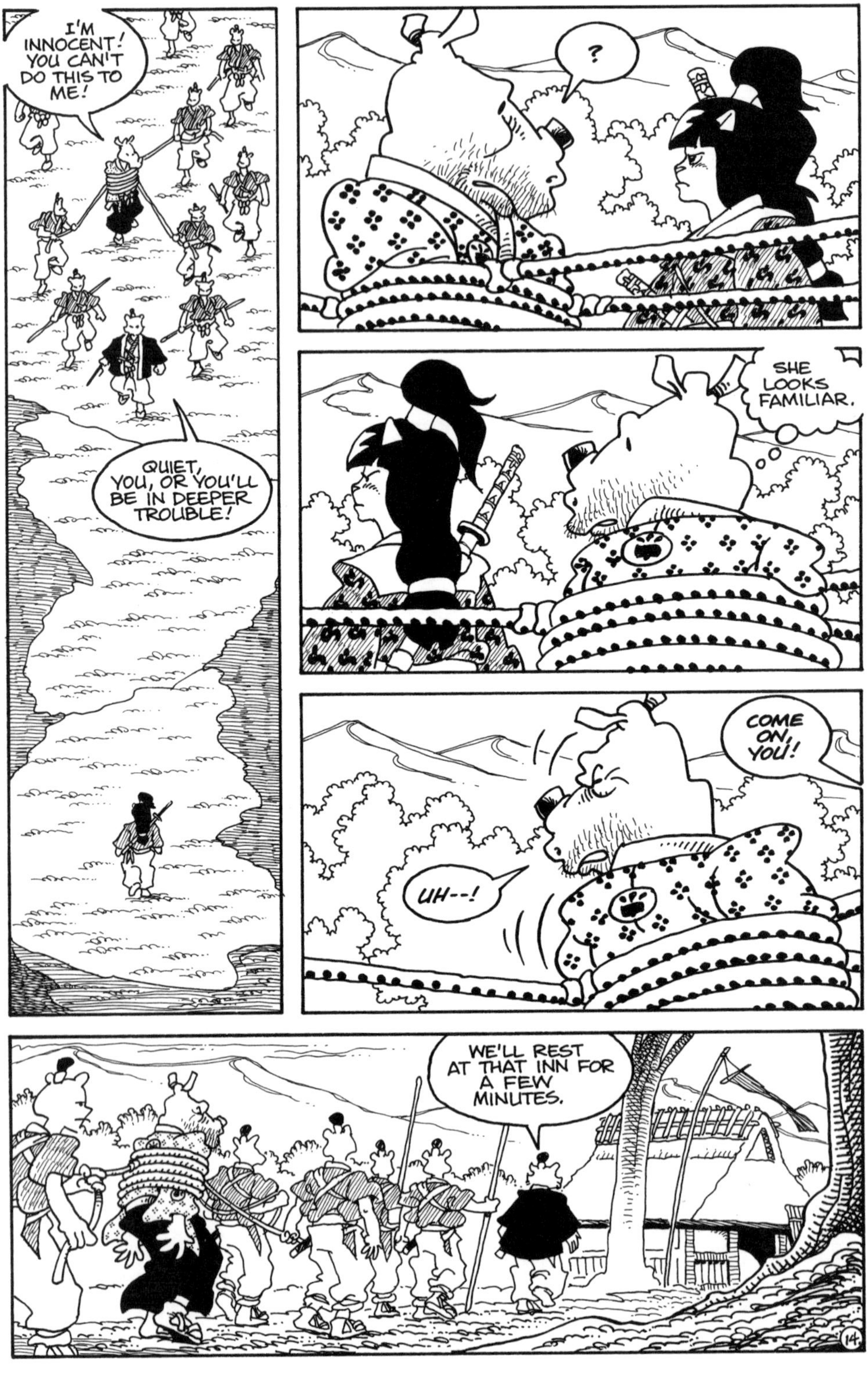
I'M INNOCENT! YOU CAN'T DO THIS TO ME!
QUIET, YOU, OR YOU'LL BE IN DEEPER TROUBLE!
?
SHE LOOKS FAMILIAR.
COME ON, YOU!
UH--!
WE'LL REST AT THAT INN FOR A FEW MINUTES.
14

LOOK! IT'S TOZA THE INNKEEPER! HE'S DEAD!
THERE'S THE MURDERER-- WITH THE CASH BOX!
IT'S HOSOKU THE BANDIT!
NO! I DIDN'T KILL HIM! I'M INNOCENT!
AND SO...
I'M INNOCENT! INNOCENT!
SAVE YOUR BREATH!
BUT IT'S TRUE! I DIDN'T KILL THE INNKEEPER! IT WAS INAZUMA!
INAZUMA?!
THAT'S WHO THAT WAS! I WOULD LOVE TO GET BAKUCHI'S REWARD FOR HER!
INNOCENT!
COME ON, YOU TWO! STOP DAWDLING!
15

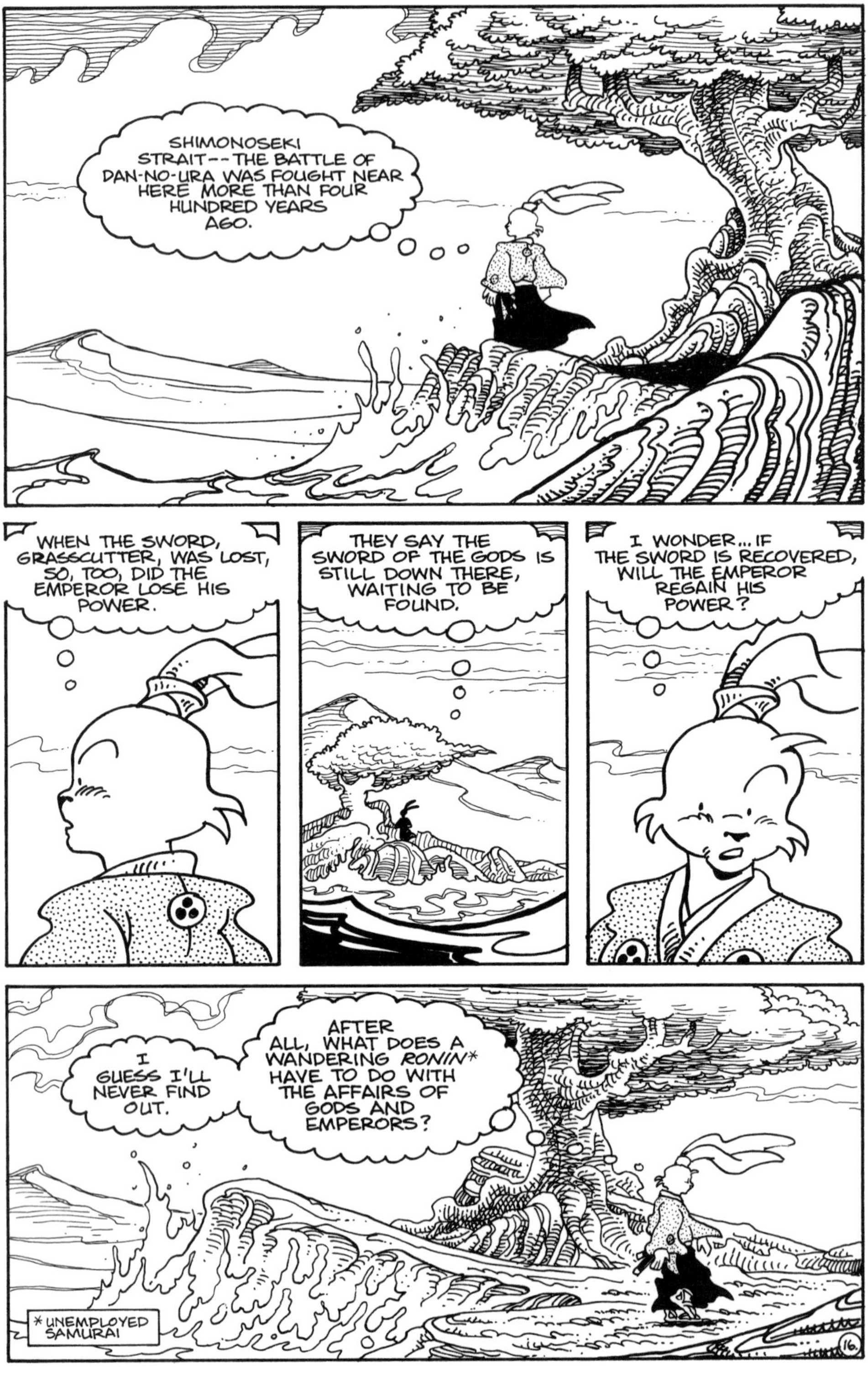
SHIMONOSEKI STRAIT--THE BATTLE OF DAN-NO-URA WAS FOUGHT NEAR HERE MORE THAN FOUR HUNDRED YEARS AGO.
WHEN THE SWORD, GRASSCUTTER, WAS LOST, SO, TOO, DID THE EMPEROR LOSE HIS POWER.
THEY SAY THE SWORD OF THE GODS IS STILL DOWN THERE, WAITING TO BE FOUND.
I WONDER... IF THE SWORD IS RECOVERED, WILL THE EMPEROR REGAIN HIS POWER?
I GUESS I'LL NEVER FIND OUT.
AFTER ALL, WHAT DOES A WANDERING *RONIN** HAVE TO DO WITH THE AFFAIRS OF GODS AND EMPERORS?
*UNEMPLOYED SAMURAI
16.

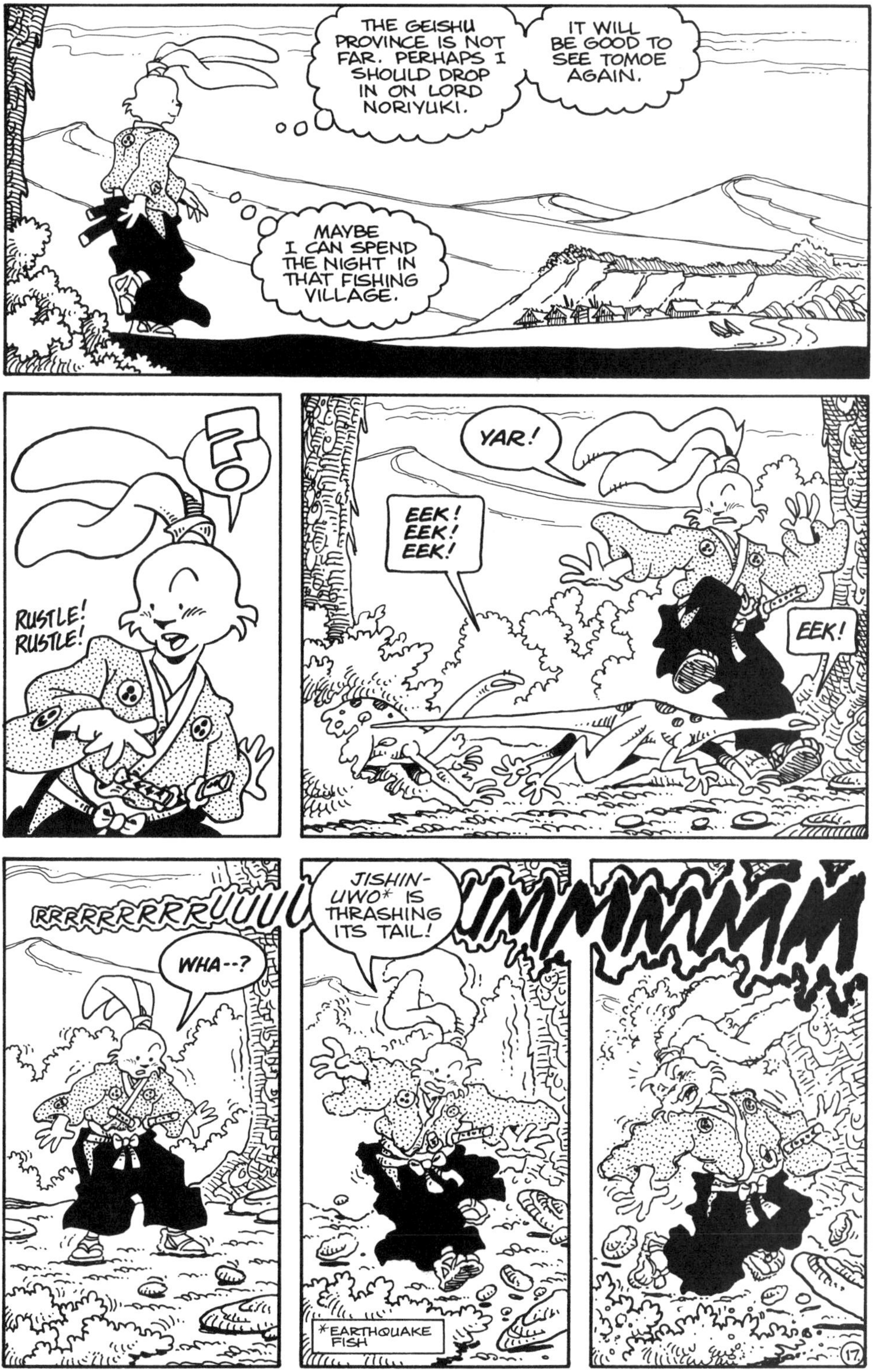
THE GEISHU PROVINCE IS NOT FAR. PERHAPS I SHOULD DROP IN ON LORD NORIYUKI.
IT WILL BE GOOD TO SEE TOMOE AGAIN.
MAYBE I CAN SPEND THE NIGHT IN THAT FISHING VILLAGE.
?
RUSTLE! RUSTLE!
YAR!
EEK! EEK! EEK!
EEK!
RRRRRRRRRRUUUUUMMMMMM
WHA--?
JISHIN-UWO* IS THRASHING ITS TAIL!
*EARTHQUAKE FISH
17

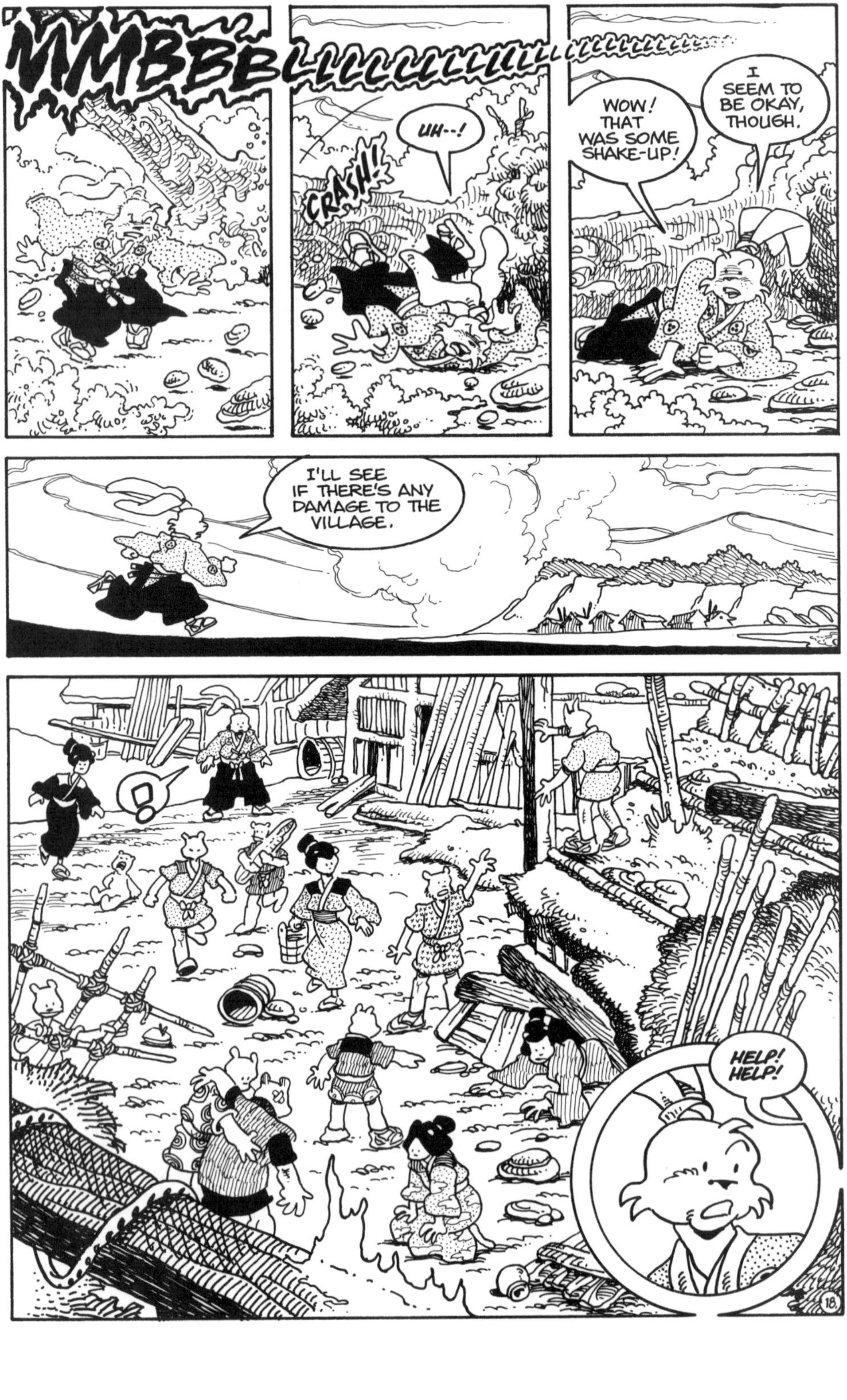
MMBBBLLLLLLLLLLLLLLLLLLLLLL
CRASH!
UH--!
WOW! THAT WAS SOME SHAKE-UP!
I SEEM TO BE OKAY, THOUGH.
I'LL SEE IF THERE'S ANY DAMAGE TO THE VILLAGE.
!
HELP! HELP!
18

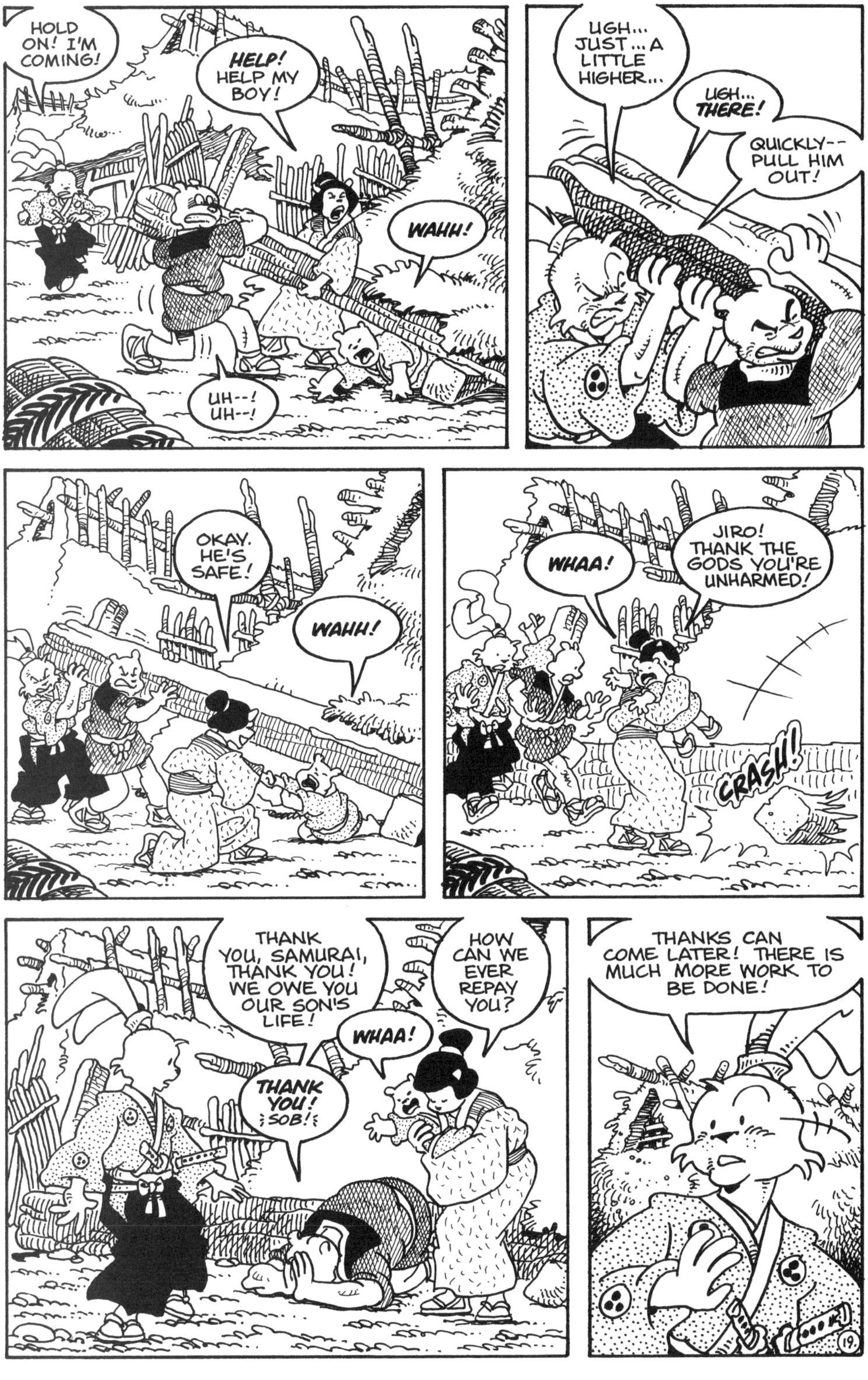
HOLD ON! I'M COMING!
HELP! HELP MY BOY!
WAHH!
UH--! UH--!
UGH... JUST... A LITTLE HIGHER...
UGH... THERE!
QUICKLY-- PULL HIM OUT!
OKAY. HE'S SAFE!
WAHH!
WHAA!
JIRO! THANK THE GODS YOU'RE UNHARMED!
CRASH!
THANK YOU, SAMURAI, THANK YOU! WE OWE YOU OUR SON'S LIFE!
HOW CAN WE EVER REPAY YOU?
WHAA!
THANK YOU! SOB!
THANKS CAN COME LATER! THERE IS MUCH MORE WORK TO BE DONE!
19.

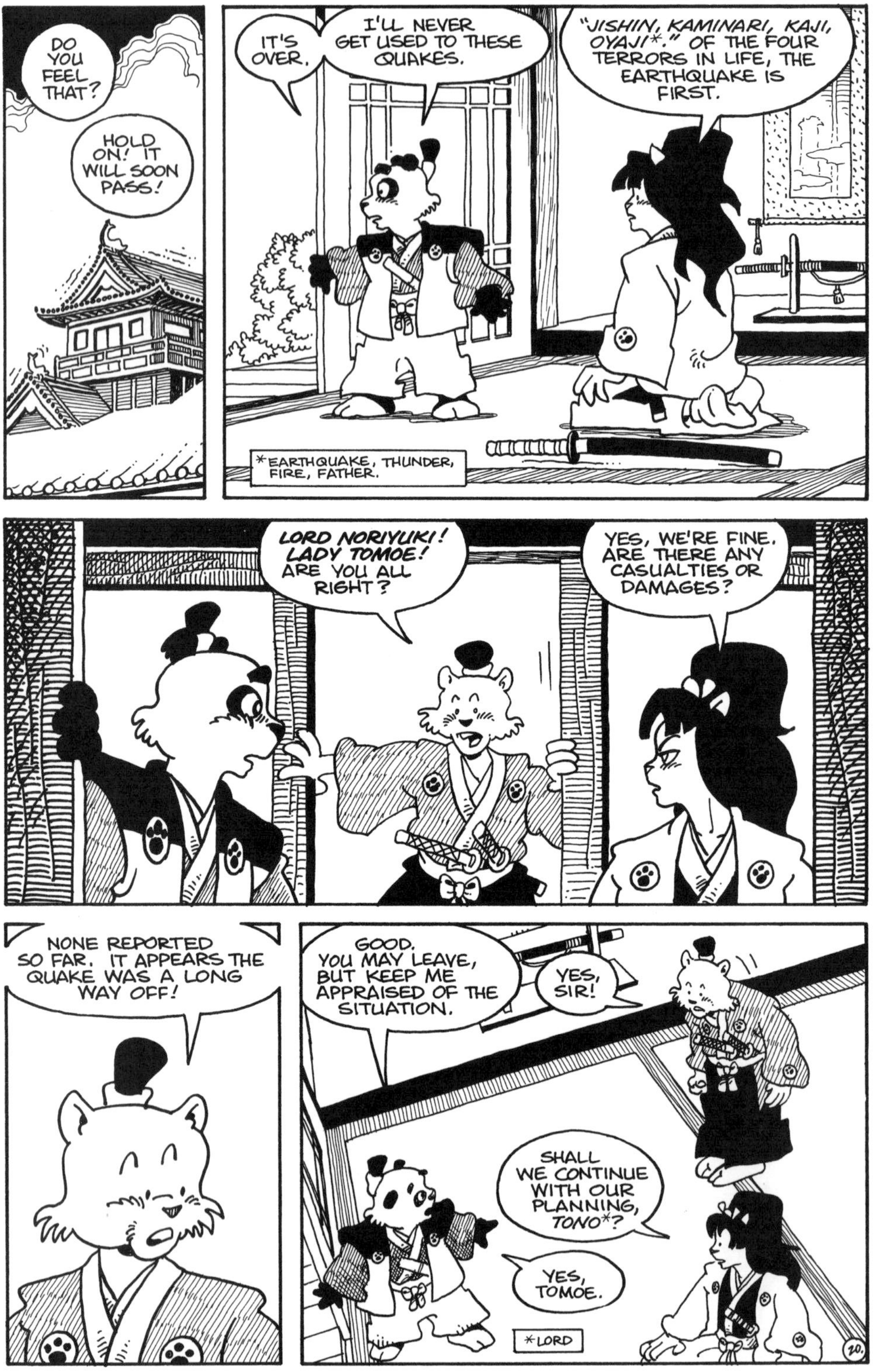
DO YOU FEEL THAT?
HOLD ON! IT WILL SOON PASS!
IT'S OVER.
I'LL NEVER GET USED TO THESE QUAKES.
"JISHIN, KAMINARI, KAJI, OYAJI*." OF THE FOUR TERRORS IN LIFE, THE EARTHQUAKE IS FIRST.
*EARTHQUAKE, THUNDER, FIRE, FATHER.
LORD NORIYUKI! LADY TOMOE! ARE YOU ALL RIGHT?
YES, WE'RE FINE. ARE THERE ANY CASUALTIES OR DAMAGES?
NONE REPORTED SO FAR. IT APPEARS THE QUAKE WAS A LONG WAY OFF!
GOOD. YOU MAY LEAVE, BUT KEEP ME APPRAISED OF THE SITUATION.
YES, SIR!
SHALL WE CONTINUE WITH OUR PLANNING, TONO*?
YES, TOMOE.
*LORD
20.

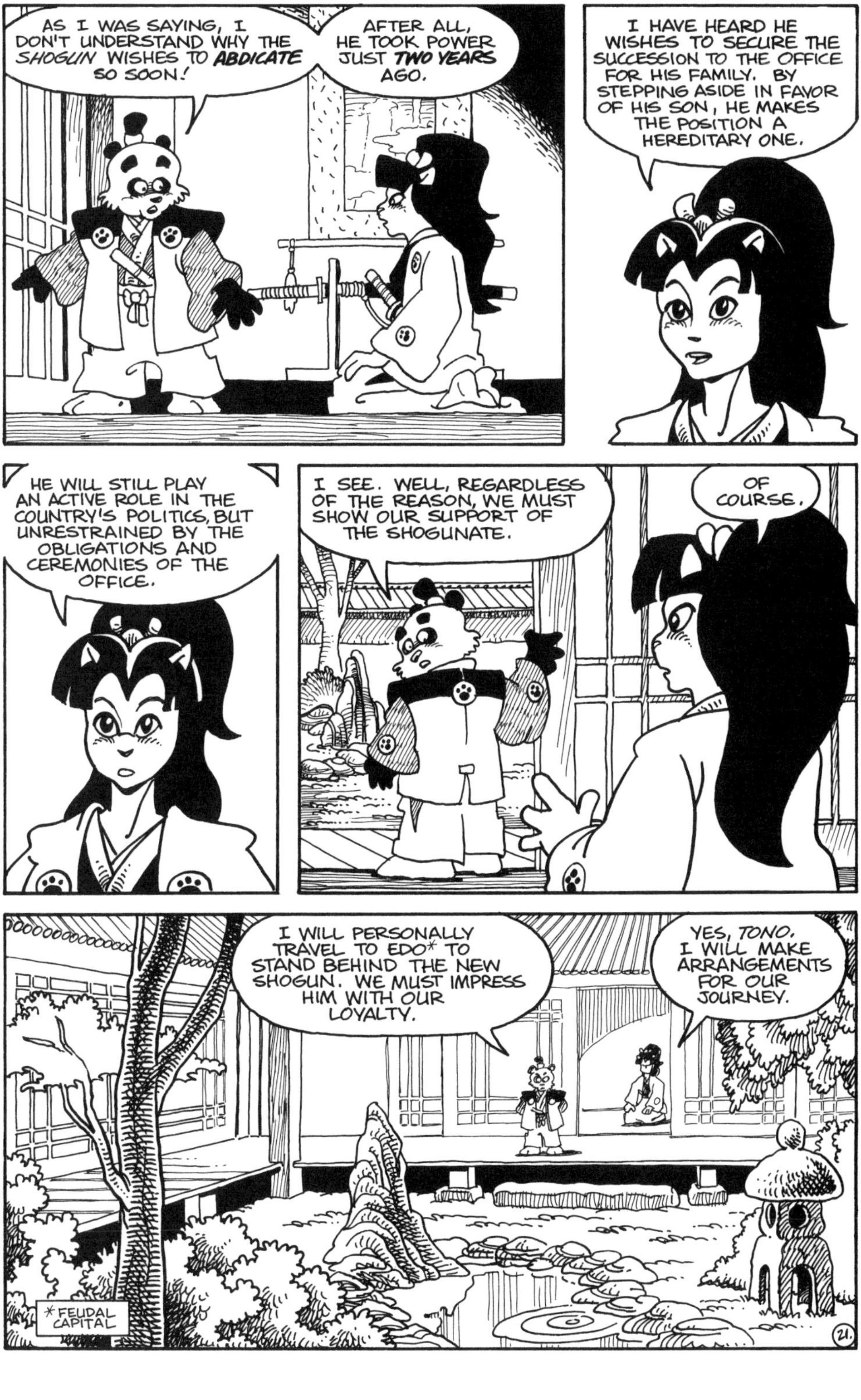
AS I WAS SAYING, I DON'T UNDERSTAND WHY THE SHOGUN WISHES TO ABDICATE SO SOON!
AFTER ALL, HE TOOK POWER JUST TWO YEARS AGO.
I HAVE HEARD HE WISHES TO SECURE THE SUCCESSION TO THE OFFICE FOR HIS FAMILY. BY STEPPING ASIDE IN FAVOR OF HIS SON, HE MAKES THE POSITION A HEREDITARY ONE.
HE WILL STILL PLAY AN ACTIVE ROLE IN THE COUNTRY'S POLITICS, BUT UNRESTRAINED BY THE OBLIGATIONS AND CEREMONIES OF THE OFFICE.
I SEE. WELL, REGARDLESS OF THE REASON, WE MUST SHOW OUR SUPPORT OF THE SHOGUNATE.
OF COURSE.
I WILL PERSONALLY TRAVEL TO EDO* TO STAND BEHIND THE NEW SHOGUN. WE MUST IMPRESS HIM WITH OUR LOYALTY.
YES, TONO. I WILL MAKE ARRANGEMENTS FOR OUR JOURNEY.
*FEUDAL CAPITAL
21.

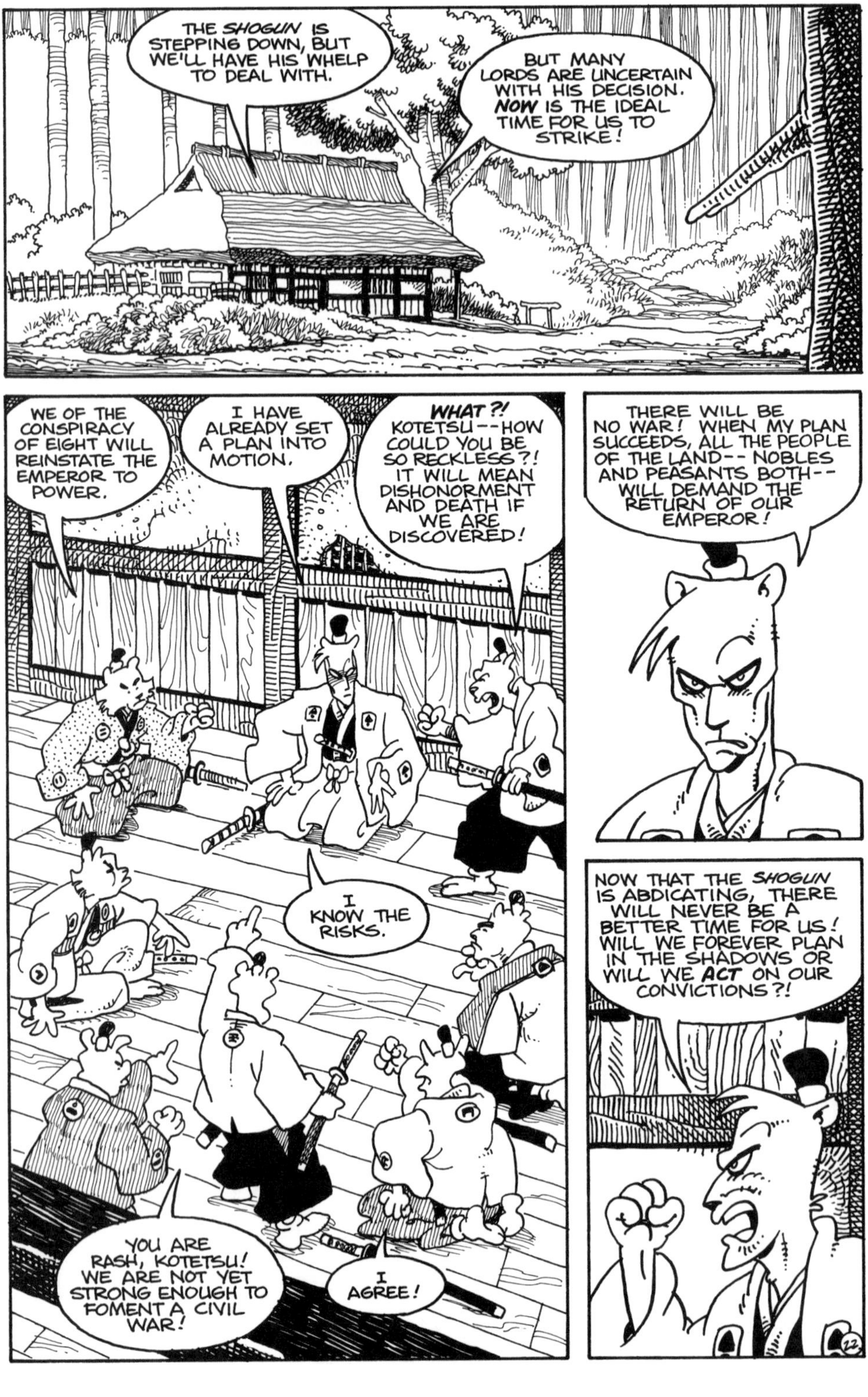
THE SHOGUN IS STEPPING DOWN, BUT WE'LL HAVE HIS WHELP TO DEAL WITH.
BUT MANY LORDS ARE UNCERTAIN WITH HIS DECISION. NOW IS THE IDEAL TIME FOR US TO STRIKE!
WE OF THE CONSPIRACY OF EIGHT WILL REINSTATE THE EMPEROR TO POWER.
I HAVE ALREADY SET A PLAN INTO MOTION.
WHAT?! KOTETSU--HOW COULD YOU BE SO RECKLESS?! IT WILL MEAN DISHONORMENT AND DEATH IF WE ARE DISCOVERED!
I KNOW THE RISKS.
YOU ARE RASH, KOTETSU! WE ARE NOT YET STRONG ENOUGH TO FOMENT A CIVIL WAR!
I AGREE!
THERE WILL BE NO WAR! WHEN MY PLAN SUCCEEDS, ALL THE PEOPLE OF THE LAND-- NOBLES AND PEASANTS BOTH-- WILL DEMAND THE RETURN OF OUR EMPEROR!
NOW THAT THE SHOGUN IS ABDICATING, THERE WILL NEVER BE A BETTER TIME FOR US! WILL WE FOREVER PLAN IN THE SHADOWS OR WILL WE ACT ON OUR CONVICTIONS?!
22

WELL... KOTETSU DOES HAVE A POINT.

VERY WELL, WHAT IS THIS PLAN OF YOURS?

CALM, YOURSELF, LORD OKU. I WILL TELL YOU.

WE WILL RECOVER KUSANAGI-NO-TSURUGI, THE LOST SWORD OF THE GODS!

MILITARY DOMINANCE OF OUR LAND CAME ABOUT WITH THE LOSS OF THE SACRED SWORD.

WHEN THE EMPEROR ONCE MORE HAS POSSESSION OF ALL THREE OF THE DIVINE TREASURES, THE PEOPLE WILL LOOK UPON IT AS A SIGN THAT THE GODS WISH THE RETURN OF THE EMPEROR TO POWER!

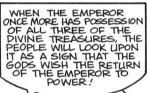

BAH! THE EMPEROR HAS THE SACRED JEWEL AND MIRROR, BUT THE SWORD WAS LOST AT SEA! PEOPLE HAVE TRIED FOR CENTURIES TO RECOVER IT... ALL IN VAIN!

I HAVE FOUND SOMEONE WHO CAN FIND IT.

MY LORD--?

AH, HERE SHE IS NOW.

YOU WOULD DARE REVEAL OUR EXISTENCE TO AN OUTSIDER?!

THE STAKES ARE HIGH. I WOULD DARE ANYTHING!

ENTER!

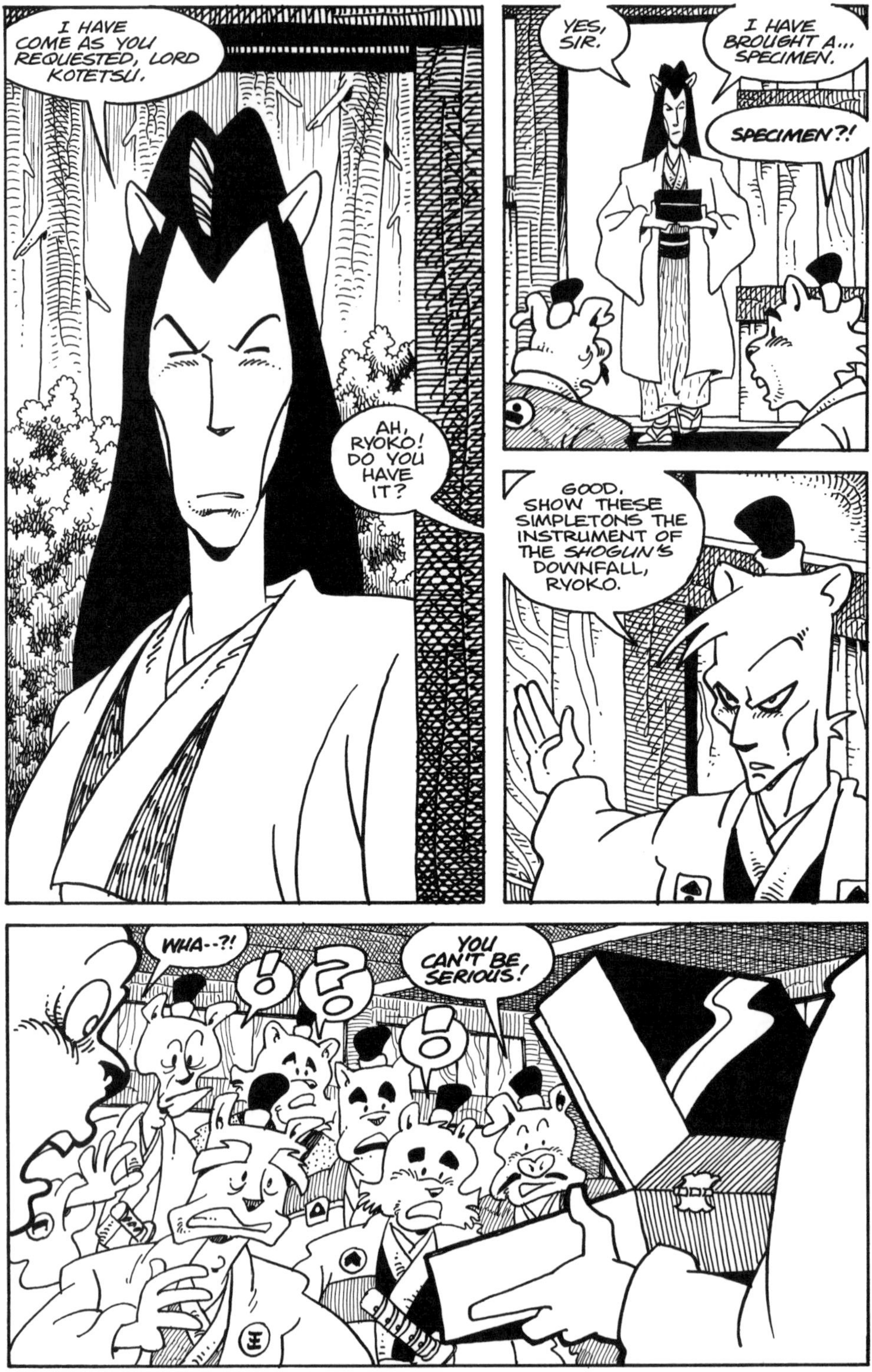
I HAVE COME AS YOU REQUESTED, LORD KOTETSU.
AH, RYOKO! DO YOU HAVE IT?
YES, SIR.
I HAVE BROUGHT A... SPECIMEN.
SPECIMEN?!
GOOD. SHOW THESE SIMPLETONS THE INSTRUMENT OF THE SHOGUN'S DOWNFALL, RYOKO.
WHA--?!
!
?
YOU CAN'T BE SERIOUS!
!

END OF CHAPTER 1

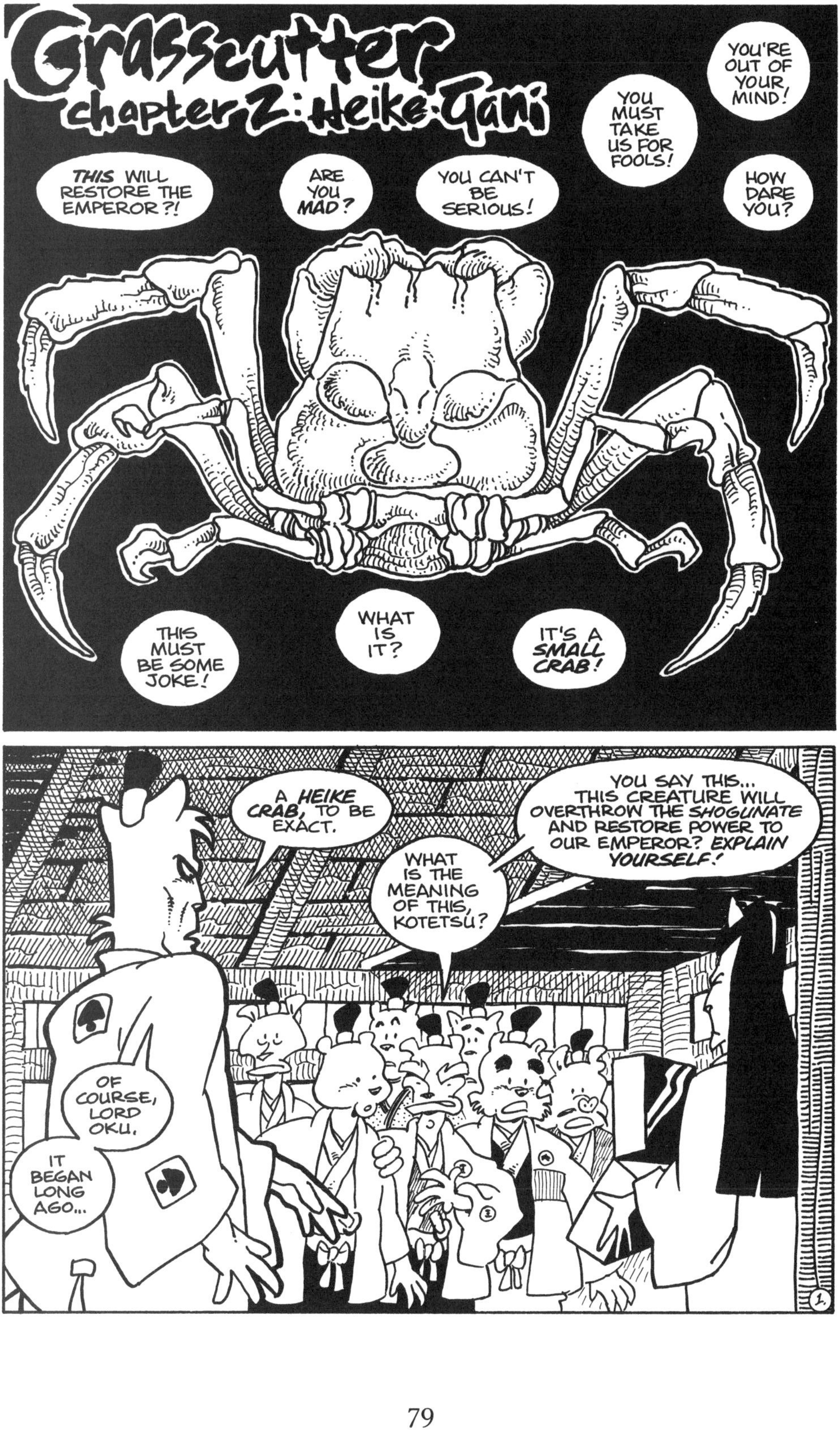
Grasscutter
chapter 2: Heike Gani
YOU'RE OUT OF YOUR MIND!
YOU MUST TAKE US FOR FOOLS!
THIS WILL RESTORE THE EMPEROR?!
ARE YOU MAD?
YOU CAN'T BE SERIOUS!
HOW DARE YOU?
THIS MUST BE SOME JOKE!
WHAT IS IT?
IT'S A SMALL CRAB!
A HEIKE CRAB, TO BE EXACT.
YOU SAY THIS... THIS CREATURE WILL OVERTHROW THE SHOGUNATE AND RESTORE POWER TO OUR EMPEROR? EXPLAIN YOURSELF!
WHAT IS THE MEANING OF THIS, KOTETSU?
OF COURSE, LORD OKU.
IT BEGAN LONG AGO...
1.

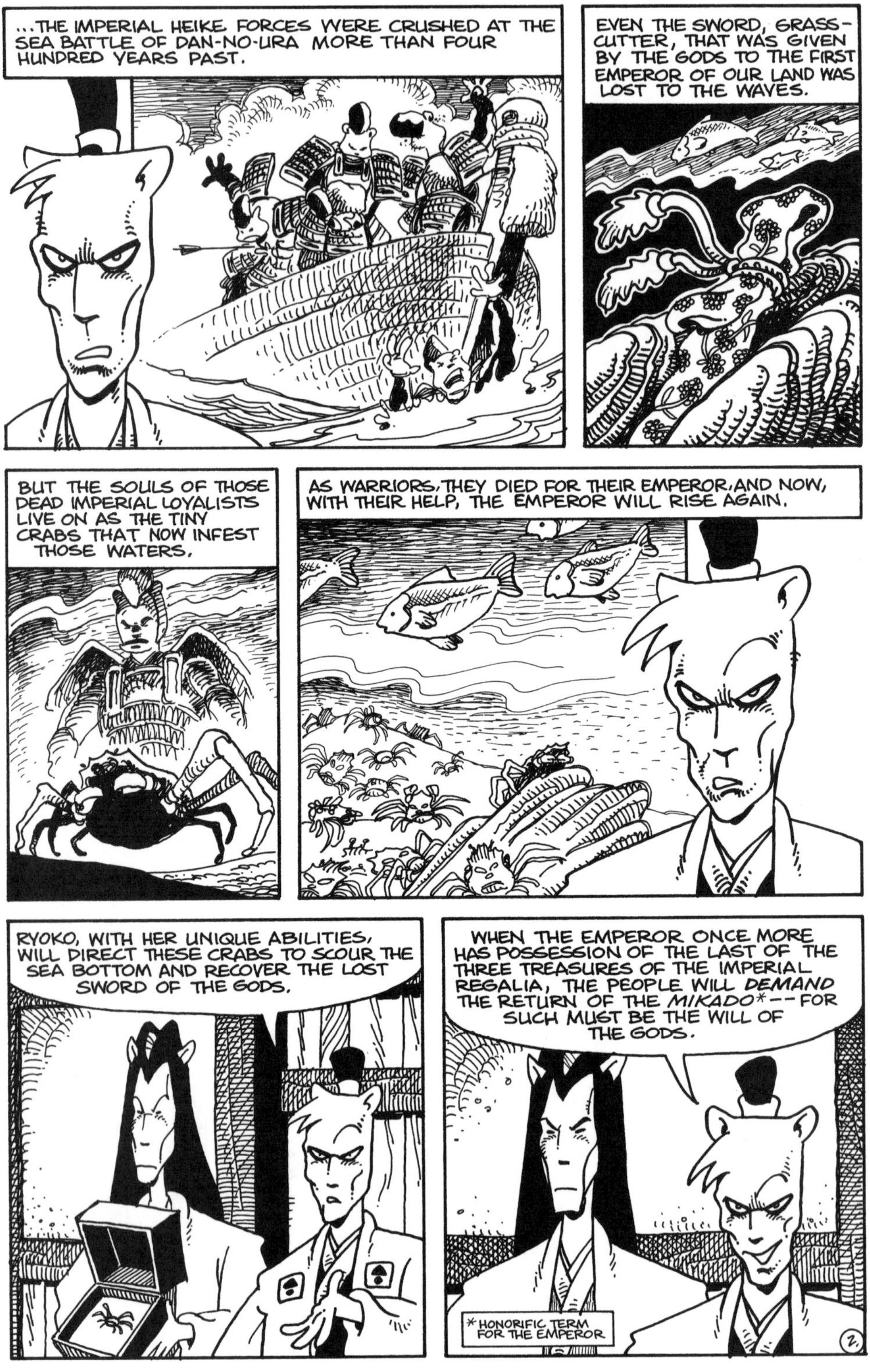
...THE IMPERIAL HEIKE FORCES WERE CRUSHED AT THE SEA BATTLE OF DAN-NO-URA MORE THAN FOUR HUNDRED YEARS PAST.
EVEN THE SWORD, GRASS-CUTTER, THAT WAS GIVEN BY THE GODS TO THE FIRST EMPEROR OF OUR LAND WAS LOST TO THE WAVES.
BUT THE SOULS OF THOSE DEAD IMPERIAL LOYALISTS LIVE ON AS THE TINY CRABS THAT NOW INFEST THOSE WATERS.
AS WARRIORS, THEY DIED FOR THEIR EMPEROR, AND NOW, WITH THEIR HELP, THE EMPEROR WILL RISE AGAIN.
RYOKO, WITH HER UNIQUE ABILITIES, WILL DIRECT THESE CRABS TO SCOUR THE SEA BOTTOM AND RECOVER THE LOST SWORD OF THE GODS.
WHEN THE EMPEROR ONCE MORE HAS POSSESSION OF THE LAST OF THE THREE TREASURES OF THE IMPERIAL REGALIA, THE PEOPLE WILL *DEMAND* THE RETURN OF THE *MIKADO**-- FOR SUCH MUST BE THE WILL OF THE GODS.
*HONORIFIC TERM FOR THE EMPEROR
2.

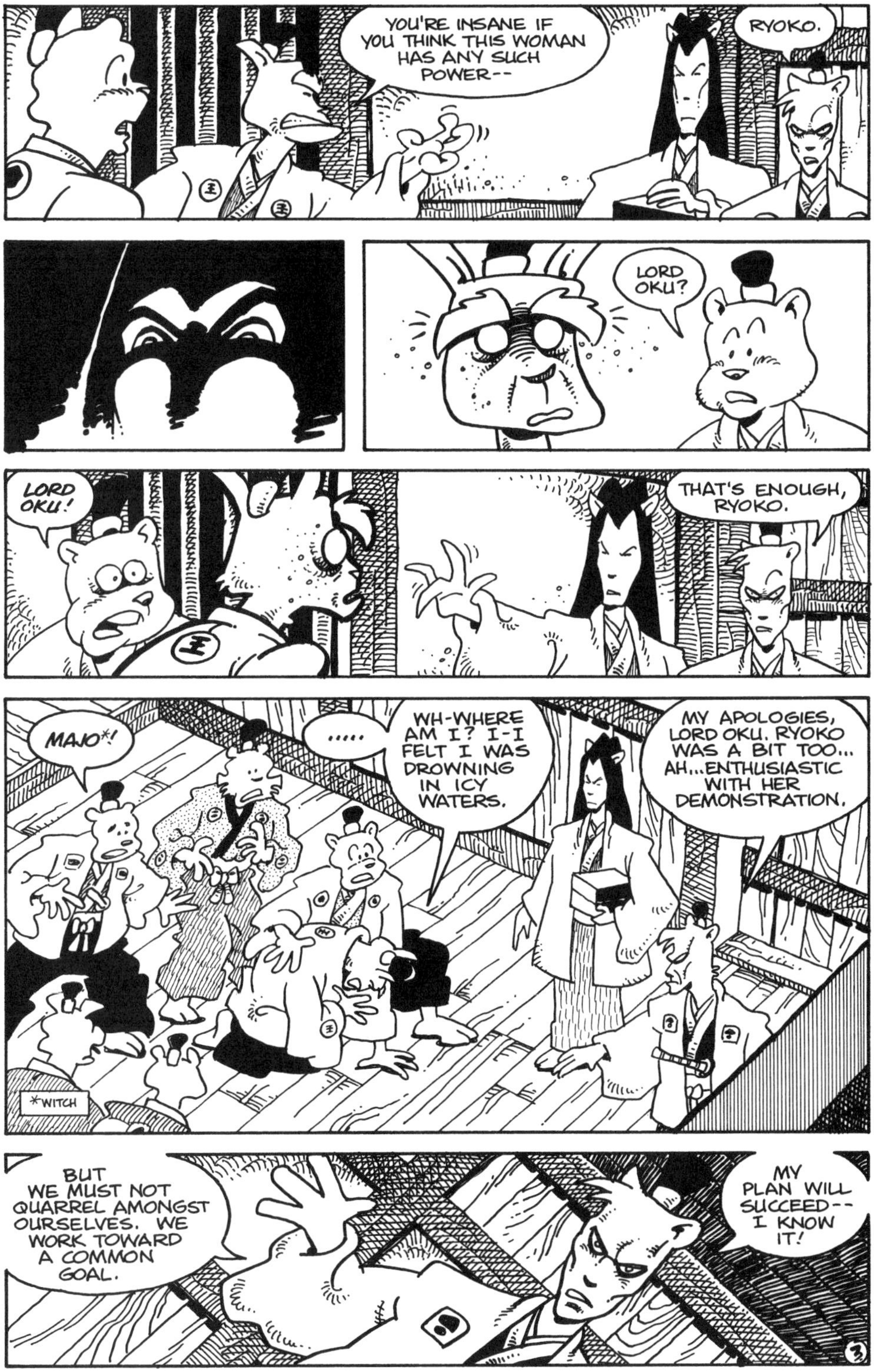
YOU'RE INSANE IF YOU THINK THIS WOMAN HAS ANY SUCH POWER--
RYOKO.
LORD OKU?
LORD OKU!
THAT'S ENOUGH, RYOKO.
MAJO*!
.....
WH-WHERE AM I? I-I FELT I WAS DROWNING IN ICY WATERS.
MY APOLOGIES, LORD OKU. RYOKO WAS A BIT TOO... AH...ENTHUSIASTIC WITH HER DEMONSTRATION.
*WITCH
BUT WE MUST NOT QUARREL AMONGST OURSELVES. WE WORK TOWARD A COMMON GOAL.
MY PLAN WILL SUCCEED-- I KNOW IT!
3

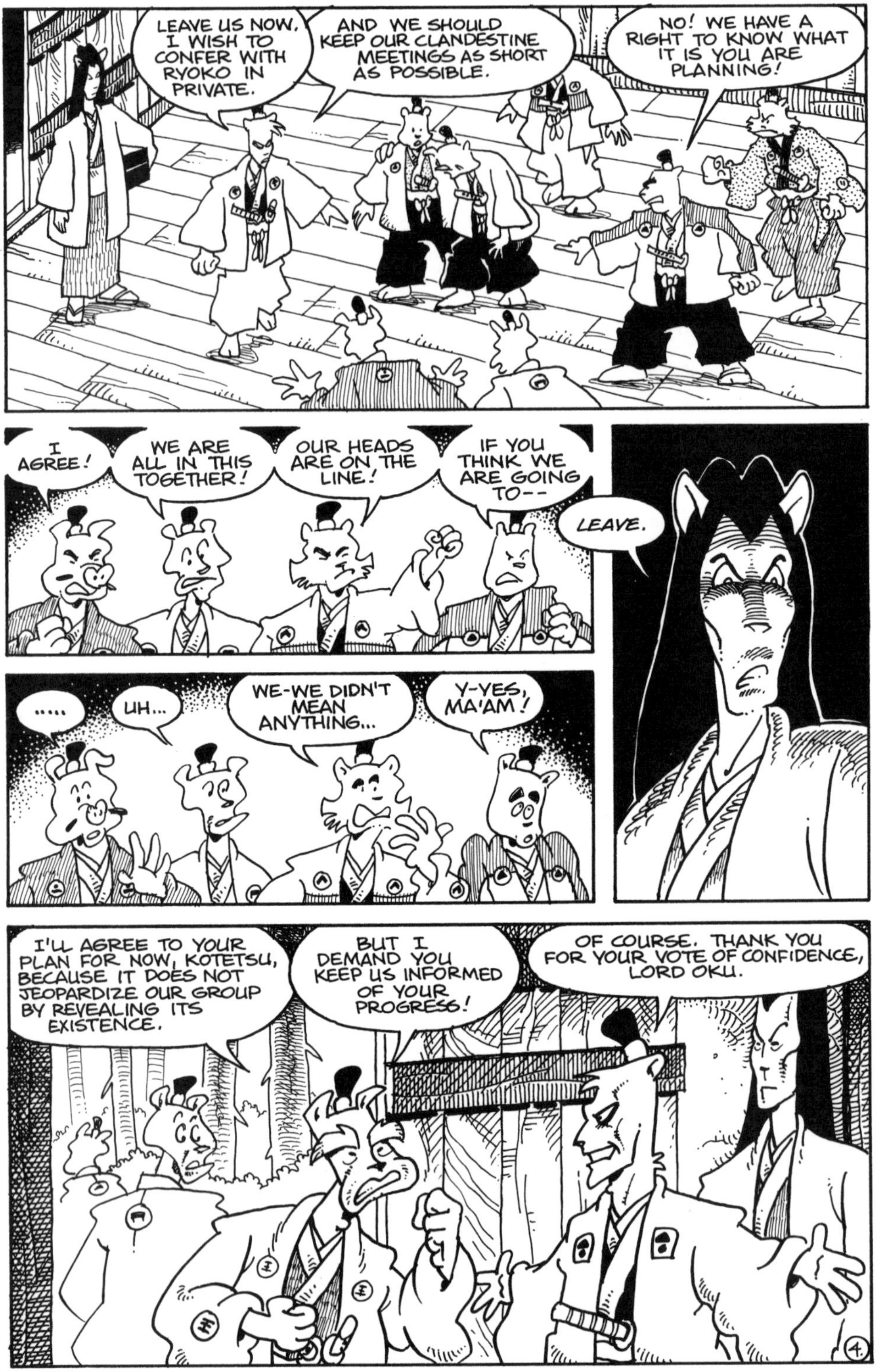
LEAVE US NOW. I WISH TO CONFER WITH RYOKO IN PRIVATE.
AND WE SHOULD KEEP OUR CLANDESTINE MEETINGS AS SHORT AS POSSIBLE.
NO! WE HAVE A RIGHT TO KNOW WHAT IT IS YOU ARE PLANNING!
I AGREE!
WE ARE ALL IN THIS TOGETHER!
OUR HEADS ARE ON THE LINE!
IF YOU THINK WE ARE GOING TO--
.....
UH...
WE-WE DIDN'T MEAN ANYTHING...
Y-YES, MA'AM!
LEAVE.
I'LL AGREE TO YOUR PLAN FOR NOW, KOTETSU, BECAUSE IT DOES NOT JEOPARDIZE OUR GROUP BY REVEALING ITS EXISTENCE.
BUT I DEMAND YOU KEEP US INFORMED OF YOUR PROGRESS!
OF COURSE. THANK YOU FOR YOUR VOTE OF CONFIDENCE, LORD OKU.
4.

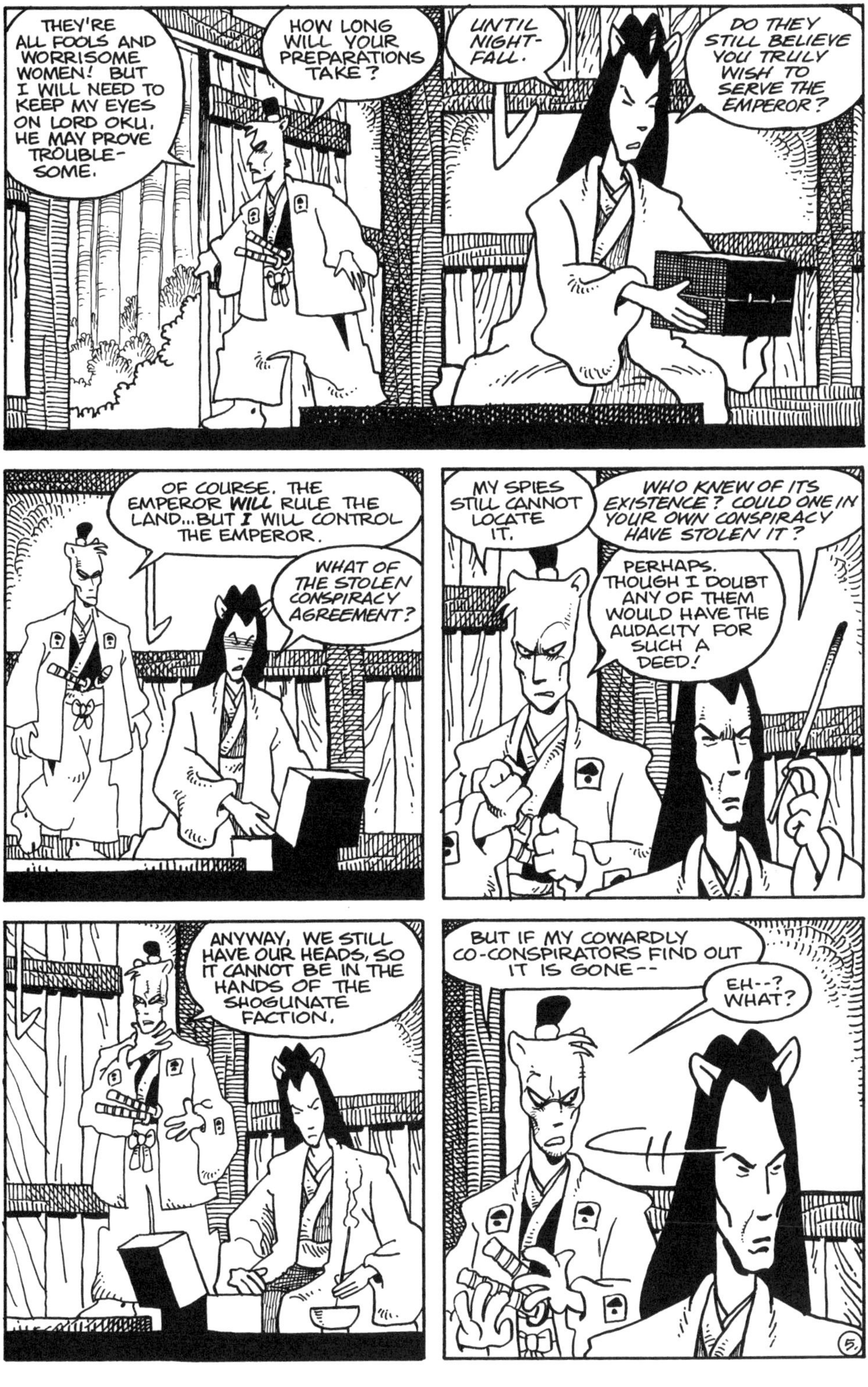
THEY'RE ALL FOOLS AND WORRISOME WOMEN! BUT I WILL NEED TO KEEP MY EYES ON LORD OKU. HE MAY PROVE TROUBLE-SOME.
HOW LONG WILL YOUR PREPARATIONS TAKE?
UNTIL NIGHT-FALL.
DO THEY STILL BELIEVE YOU TRULY WISH TO SERVE THE EMPEROR?
OF COURSE. THE EMPEROR WILL RULE THE LAND...BUT I WILL CONTROL THE EMPEROR.
WHAT OF THE STOLEN CONSPIRACY AGREEMENT?
MY SPIES STILL CANNOT LOCATE IT.
WHO KNEW OF ITS EXISTENCE? COULD ONE IN YOUR OWN CONSPIRACY HAVE STOLEN IT?
PERHAPS. THOUGH I DOUBT ANY OF THEM WOULD HAVE THE AUDACITY FOR SUCH A DEED!
ANYWAY, WE STILL HAVE OUR HEADS, SO IT CANNOT BE IN THE HANDS OF THE SHOGUNATE FACTION.
BUT IF MY COWARDLY CO-CONSPIRATORS FIND OUT IT IS GONE--
EH--? WHAT?
5.

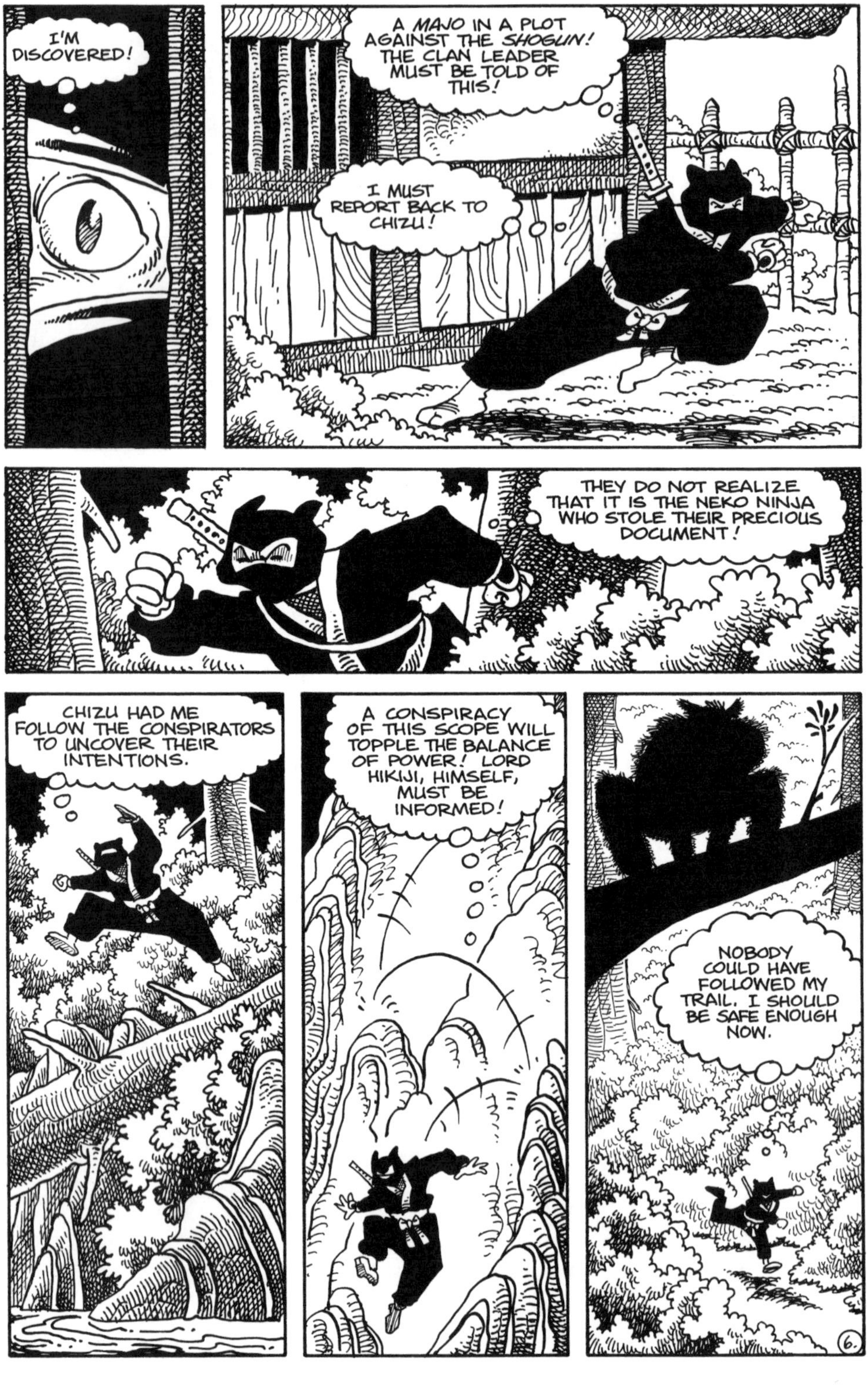
I'M DISCOVERED!
A *MAJO* IN A PLOT AGAINST THE *SHOGUN*! THE CLAN LEADER MUST BE TOLD OF THIS!
I MUST REPORT BACK TO CHIZU!
THEY DO NOT REALIZE THAT IT IS THE NEKO NINJA WHO STOLE THEIR PRECIOUS DOCUMENT!
CHIZU HAD ME FOLLOW THE CONSPIRATORS TO UNCOVER THEIR INTENTIONS.
A CONSPIRACY OF THIS SCOPE WILL TOPPLE THE BALANCE OF POWER! LORD HIKIJI, HIMSELF, MUST BE INFORMED!
NOBODY COULD HAVE FOLLOWED MY TRAIL. I SHOULD BE SAFE ENOUGH NOW.
6.

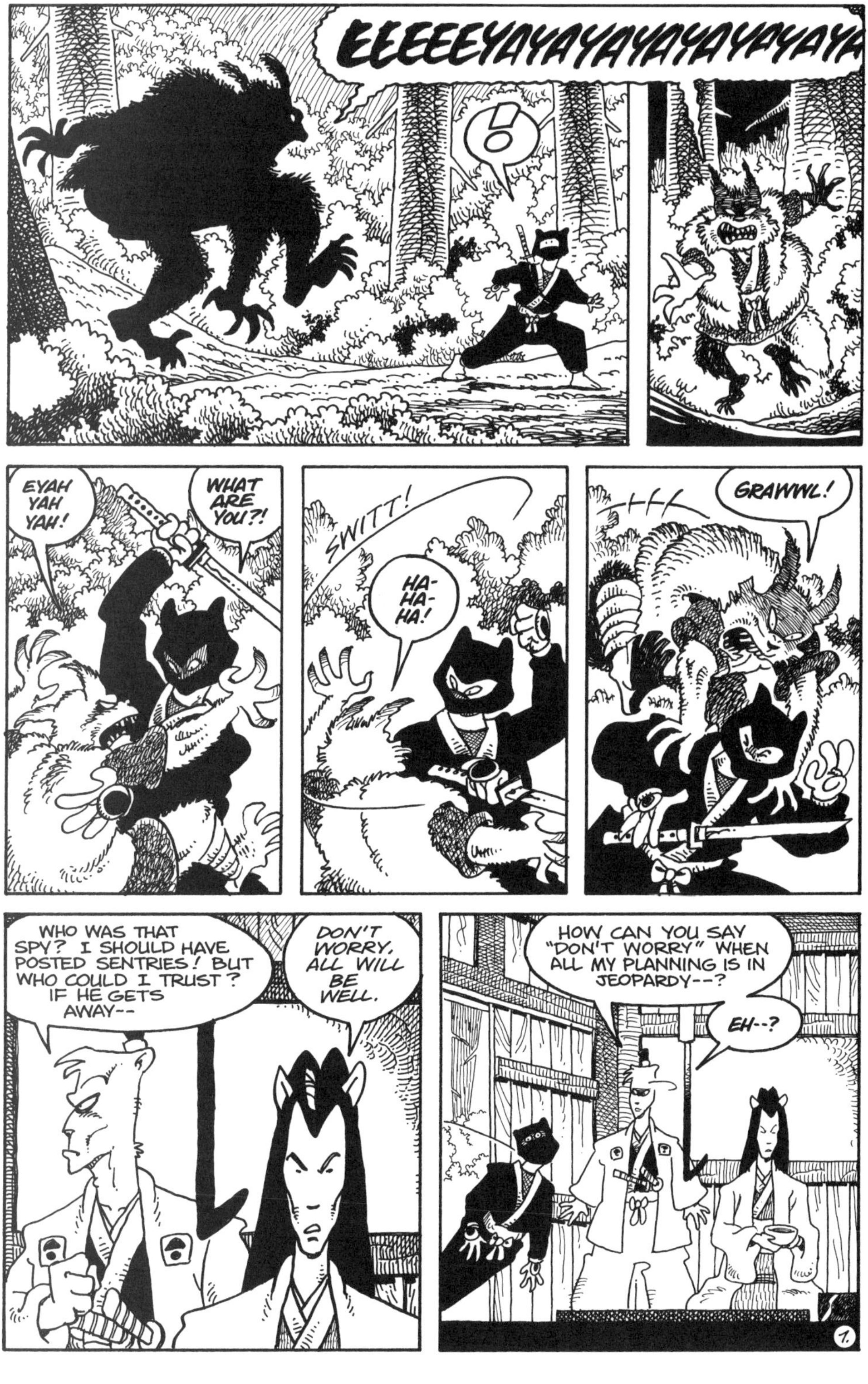
EEEEEEYAYAYAYAYAYAYAYAYA
!
EYAH YAH YAH!
WHAT ARE YOU?!
SWITT!
HA-HA-HA!
GRAWWL!
WHO WAS THAT SPY? I SHOULD HAVE POSTED SENTRIES! BUT WHO COULD I TRUST? IF HE GETS AWAY--
DON'T WORRY. ALL WILL BE WELL.
HOW CAN YOU SAY "DON'T WORRY" WHEN ALL MY PLANNING IS IN JEOPARDY--?
EH--?
1.

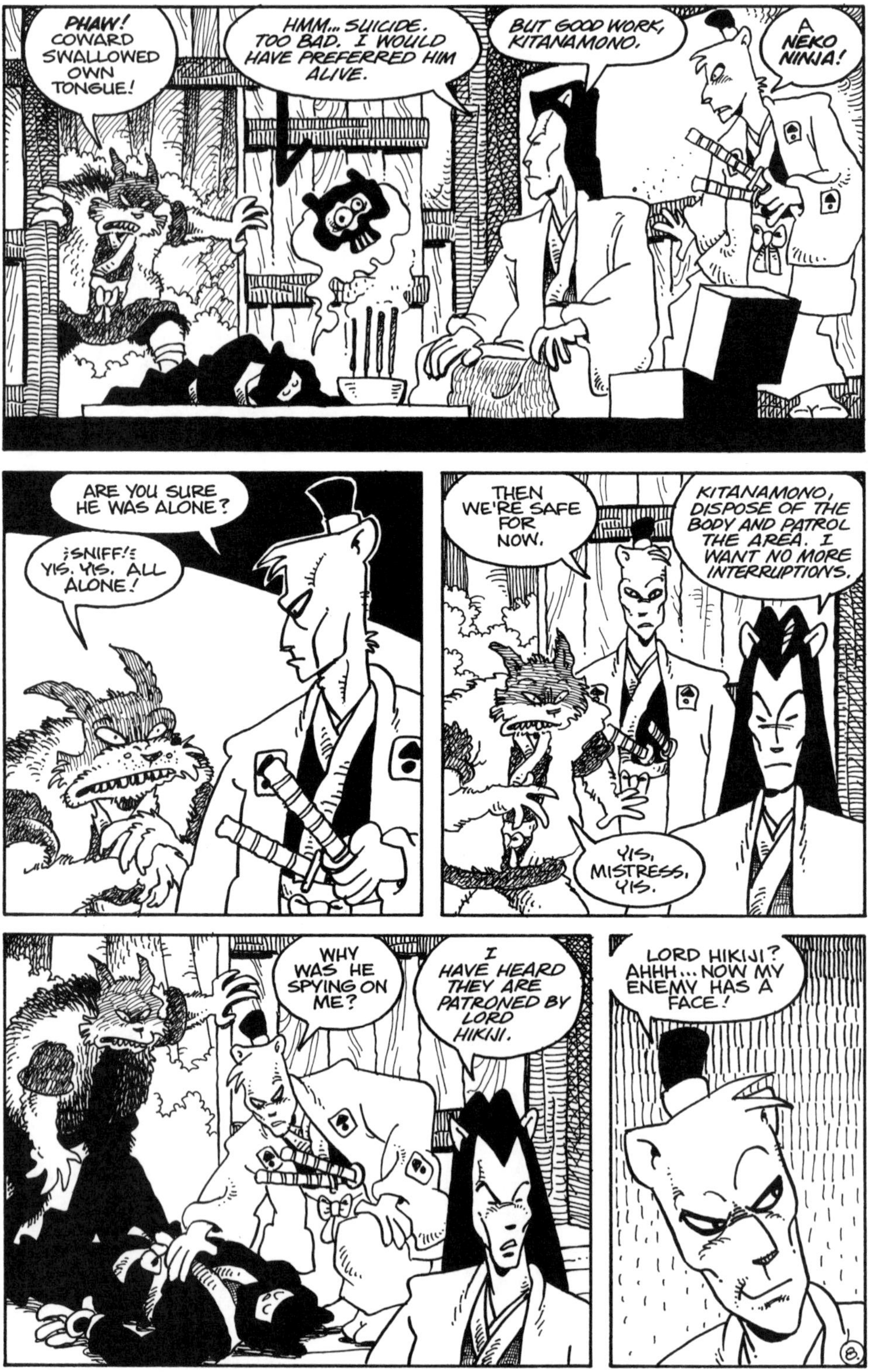
PHAW! COWARD SWALLOWED OWN TONGUE!
HMM... SUICIDE. TOO BAD. I WOULD HAVE PREFERRED HIM ALIVE.
BUT GOOD WORK, KITANAMONO.
A NEKO NINJA!
ARE YOU SURE HE WAS ALONE?
SNIFF! YIS. YIS. ALL ALONE!
THEN WE'RE SAFE FOR NOW.
KITANAMONO, DISPOSE OF THE BODY AND PATROL THE AREA. I WANT NO MORE INTERRUPTIONS.
YIS, MISTRESS, YIS.
WHY WAS HE SPYING ON ME?
I HAVE HEARD THEY ARE PATRONED BY LORD HIKIJI.
LORD HIKIJI? AHHH... NOW MY ENEMY HAS A FACE!
8

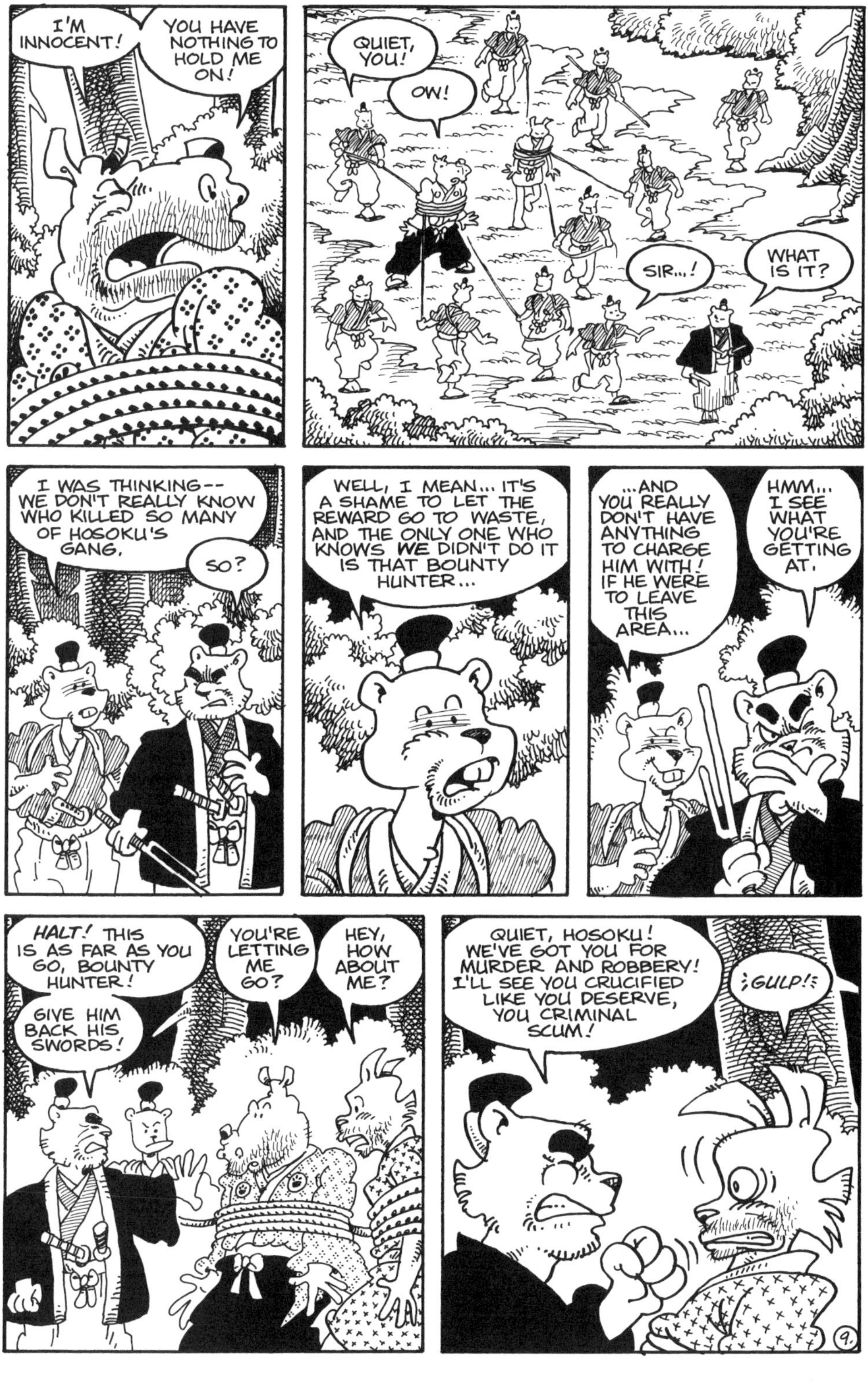
I'M INNOCENT!
YOU HAVE NOTHING TO HOLD ME ON!
QUIET, YOU!
OW!
SIR...!
WHAT IS IT?
I WAS THINKING-- WE DON'T REALLY KNOW WHO KILLED SO MANY OF HOSOKU'S GANG.
SO?
WELL, I MEAN... IT'S A SHAME TO LET THE REWARD GO TO WASTE, AND THE ONLY ONE WHO KNOWS **WE** DIDN'T DO IT IS THAT BOUNTY HUNTER...
...AND YOU REALLY DON'T HAVE ANYTHING TO CHARGE HIM WITH! IF HE WERE TO LEAVE THIS AREA...
HMM... I SEE WHAT YOU'RE GETTING AT.
HALT! THIS IS AS FAR AS YOU GO, BOUNTY HUNTER!
GIVE HIM BACK HIS SWORDS!
YOU'RE LETTING ME GO?
HEY, HOW ABOUT ME?
QUIET, HOSOKU! WE'VE GOT YOU FOR MURDER AND ROBBERY! I'LL SEE YOU CRUCIFIED LIKE YOU DESERVE, YOU CRIMINAL SCUM!
GULP!
9.

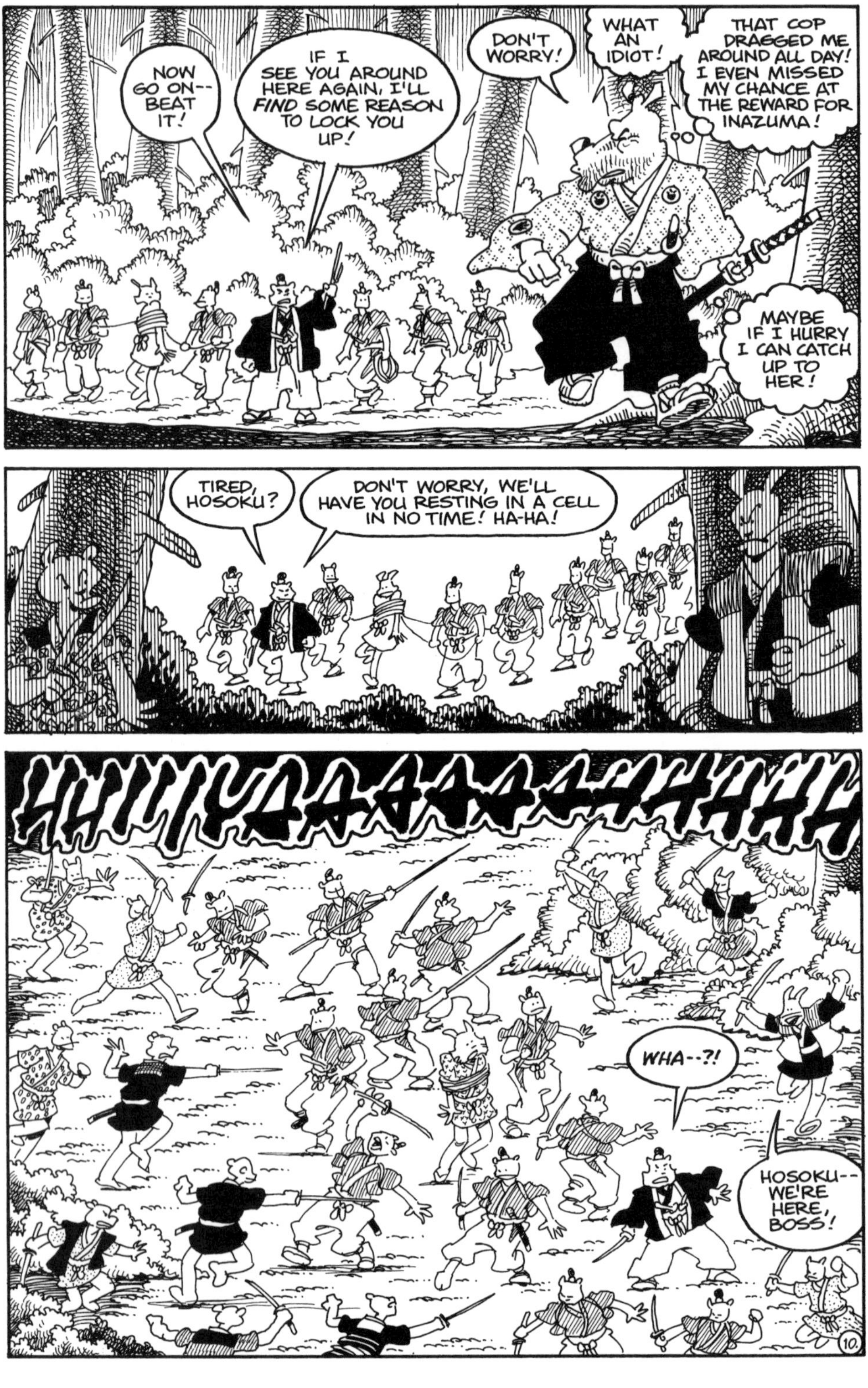
NOW GO ON-- BEAT IT!
IF I SEE YOU AROUND HERE AGAIN, I'LL FIND SOME REASON TO LOCK YOU UP!
DON'T WORRY!
WHAT AN IDIOT!
THAT COP DRAGGED ME AROUND ALL DAY! I EVEN MISSED MY CHANCE AT THE REWARD FOR INAZUMA!
MAYBE IF I HURRY I CAN CATCH UP TO HER!
TIRED, HOSOKU?
DON'T WORRY, WE'LL HAVE YOU RESTING IN A CELL IN NO TIME! HA-HA!
HHIIYAAAAAAHHHHH
WHA--?!
HOSOKU-- WE'RE HERE, BOSS!
10.

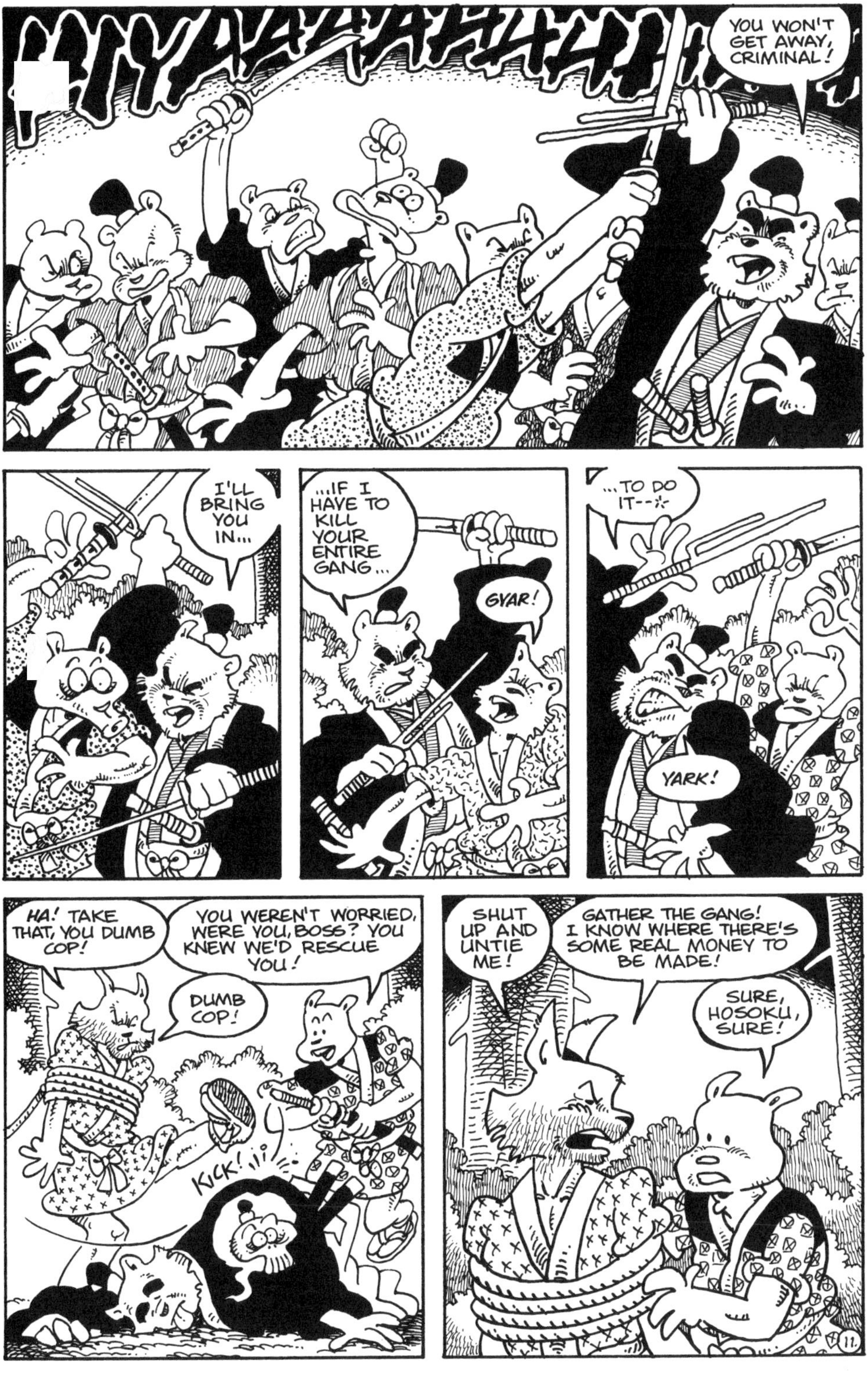
HIYAAAAAAAAH
YOU WON'T GET AWAY, CRIMINAL!
I'LL BRING YOU IN...
...IF I HAVE TO KILL YOUR ENTIRE GANG...
GYAR!
...TO DO IT--
YARK!
HA! TAKE THAT, YOU DUMB COP!
YOU WEREN'T WORRIED, WERE YOU, BOSS? YOU KNEW WE'D RESCUE YOU!
DUMB COP!
KICK!
SHUT UP AND UNTIE ME!
GATHER THE GANG! I KNOW WHERE THERE'S SOME REAL MONEY TO BE MADE!
SURE, HOSOKU, SURE!
11.

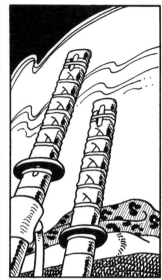

SPLASH!
SPLASH!!

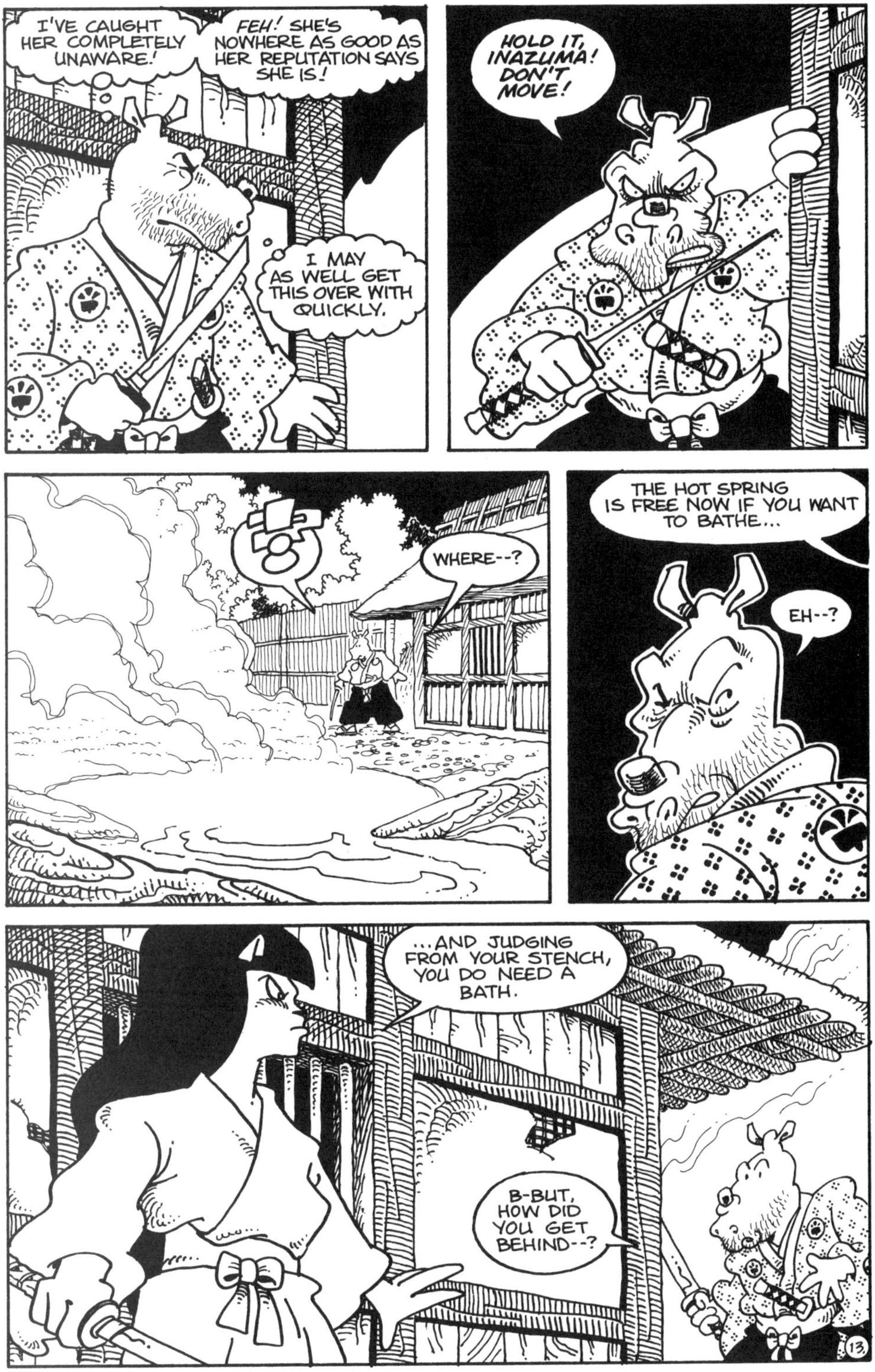
I'VE CAUGHT HER COMPLETELY UNAWARE!
FEH! SHE'S NOWHERE AS GOOD AS HER REPUTATION SAYS SHE IS!
I MAY AS WELL GET THIS OVER WITH QUICKLY.
HOLD IT, INAZUMA! DON'T MOVE!
WHERE--?
THE HOT SPRING IS FREE NOW IF YOU WANT TO BATHE...
EH--?
...AND JUDGING FROM YOUR STENCH, YOU DO NEED A BATH.
B-BUT, HOW DID YOU GET BEHIND--?
13

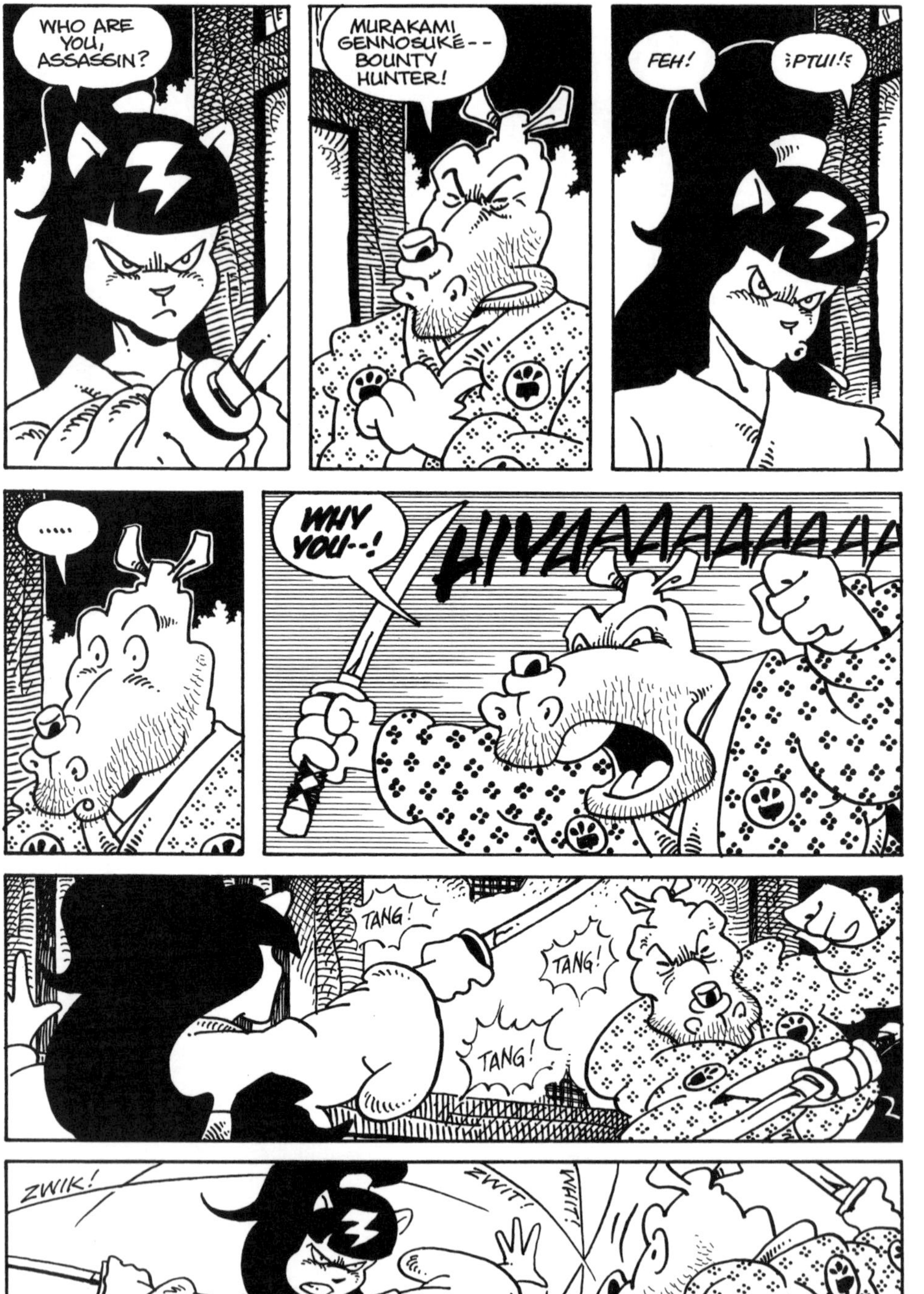
WHO ARE YOU, ASSASSIN?
MURAKAMI GENNOSUKE--BOUNTY HUNTER!
FEH!
PTUI!
.....
WHY YOU--!
HIYAAAAAAAAAA
TANG!
TANG!
TANG!
ZWIK!
ZWIT!
WHIT!
ZWIPT!
ZWIM!
14.

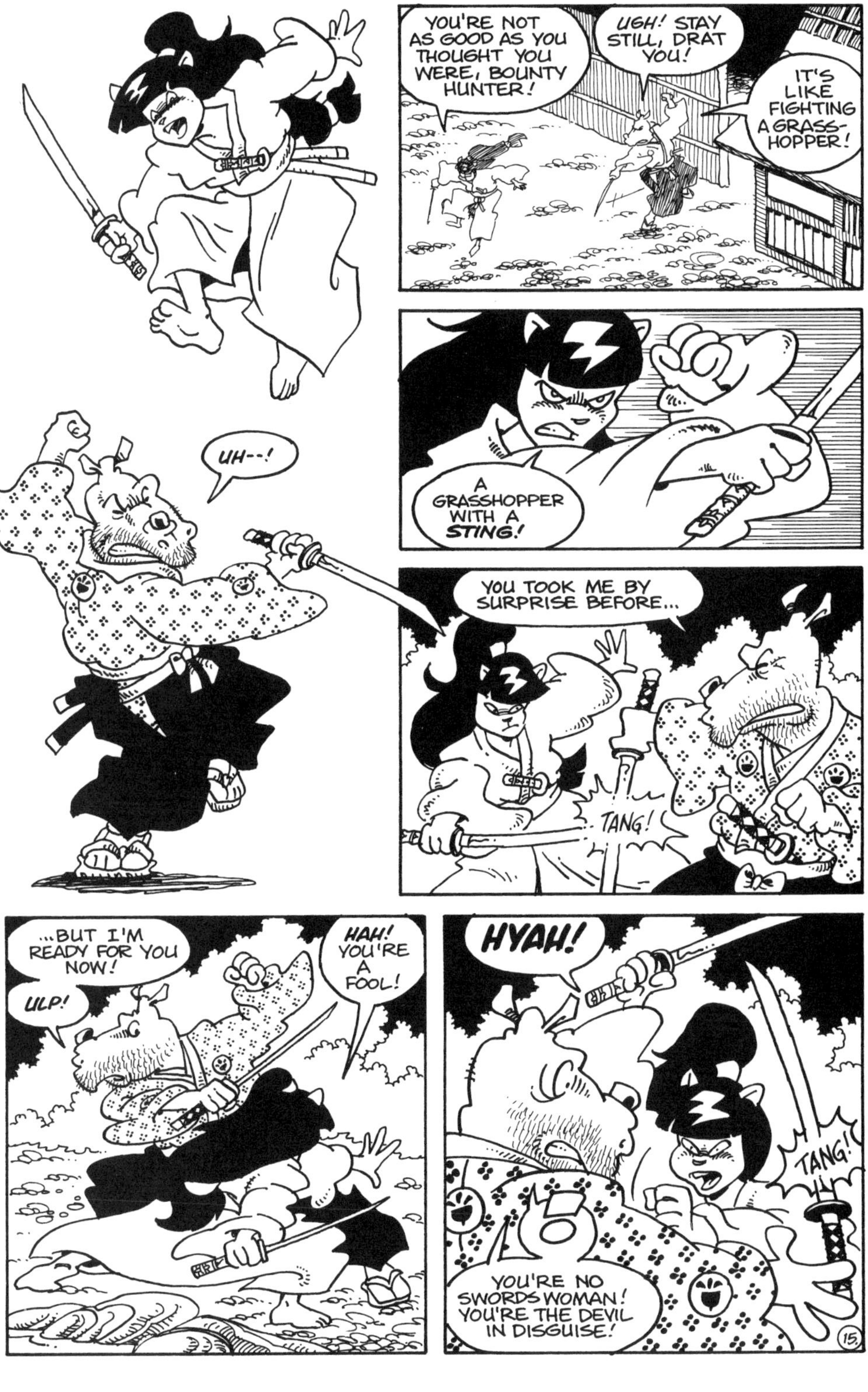
UH--!
YOU'RE NOT AS GOOD AS YOU THOUGHT YOU WERE, BOUNTY HUNTER!
UGH! STAY STILL, DRAT YOU!
IT'S LIKE FIGHTING A GRASS-HOPPER!
A GRASSHOPPER WITH A STING!
YOU TOOK ME BY SURPRISE BEFORE...
TANG!
...BUT I'M READY FOR YOU NOW!
ULP!
HAH! YOU'RE A FOOL!
HYAH!
TANG!
YOU'RE NO SWORDSWOMAN! YOU'RE THE DEVIL IN DISGUISE!
15

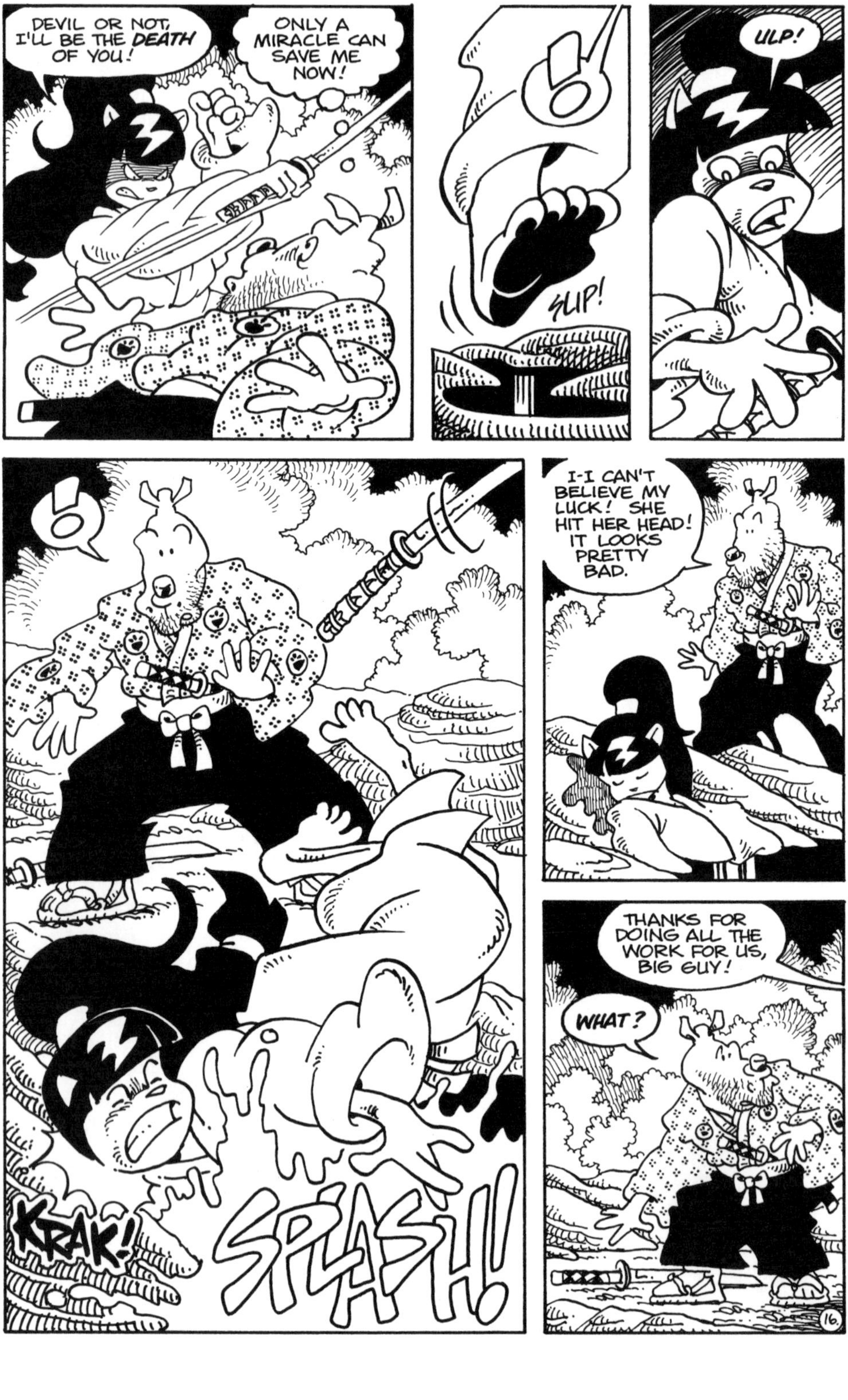
DEVIL OR NOT, I'LL BE THE *DEATH* OF YOU!
ONLY A MIRACLE CAN SAVE ME NOW!
!
SLIP!
ULP!
!
KRAK!
SPLASH!
I-I CAN'T BELIEVE MY LUCK! SHE HIT HER HEAD! IT LOOKS PRETTY BAD.
THANKS FOR DOING ALL THE WORK FOR US, BIG GUY!
WHAT?
16.

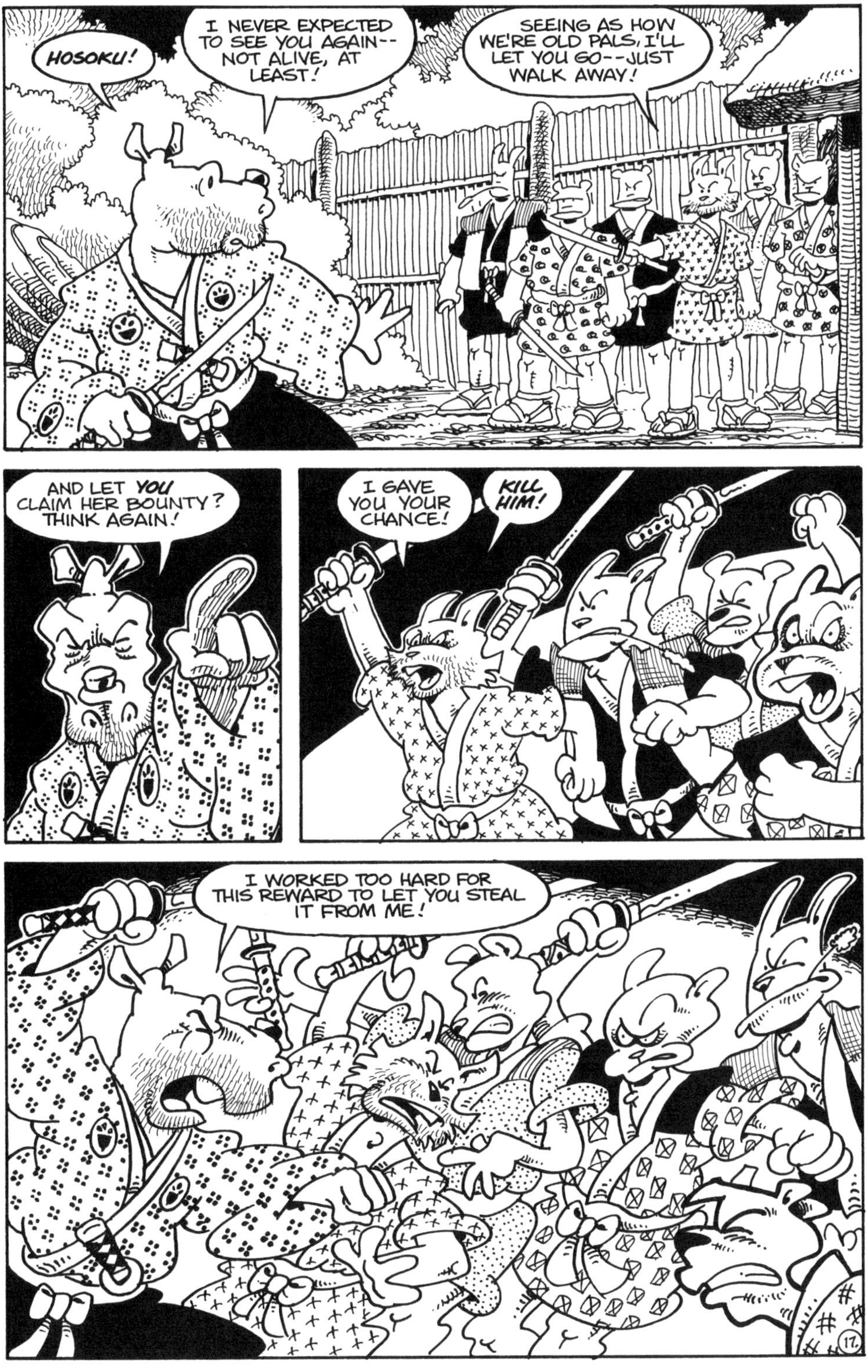
HOSOKU!
I NEVER EXPECTED TO SEE YOU AGAIN-- NOT ALIVE, AT LEAST!
SEEING AS HOW WE'RE OLD PALS, I'LL LET YOU GO--JUST WALK AWAY!
AND LET YOU CLAIM HER BOUNTY? THINK AGAIN!
I GAVE YOU YOUR CHANCE!
KILL HIM!
I WORKED TOO HARD FOR THIS REWARD TO LET YOU STEAL IT FROM ME!
17.

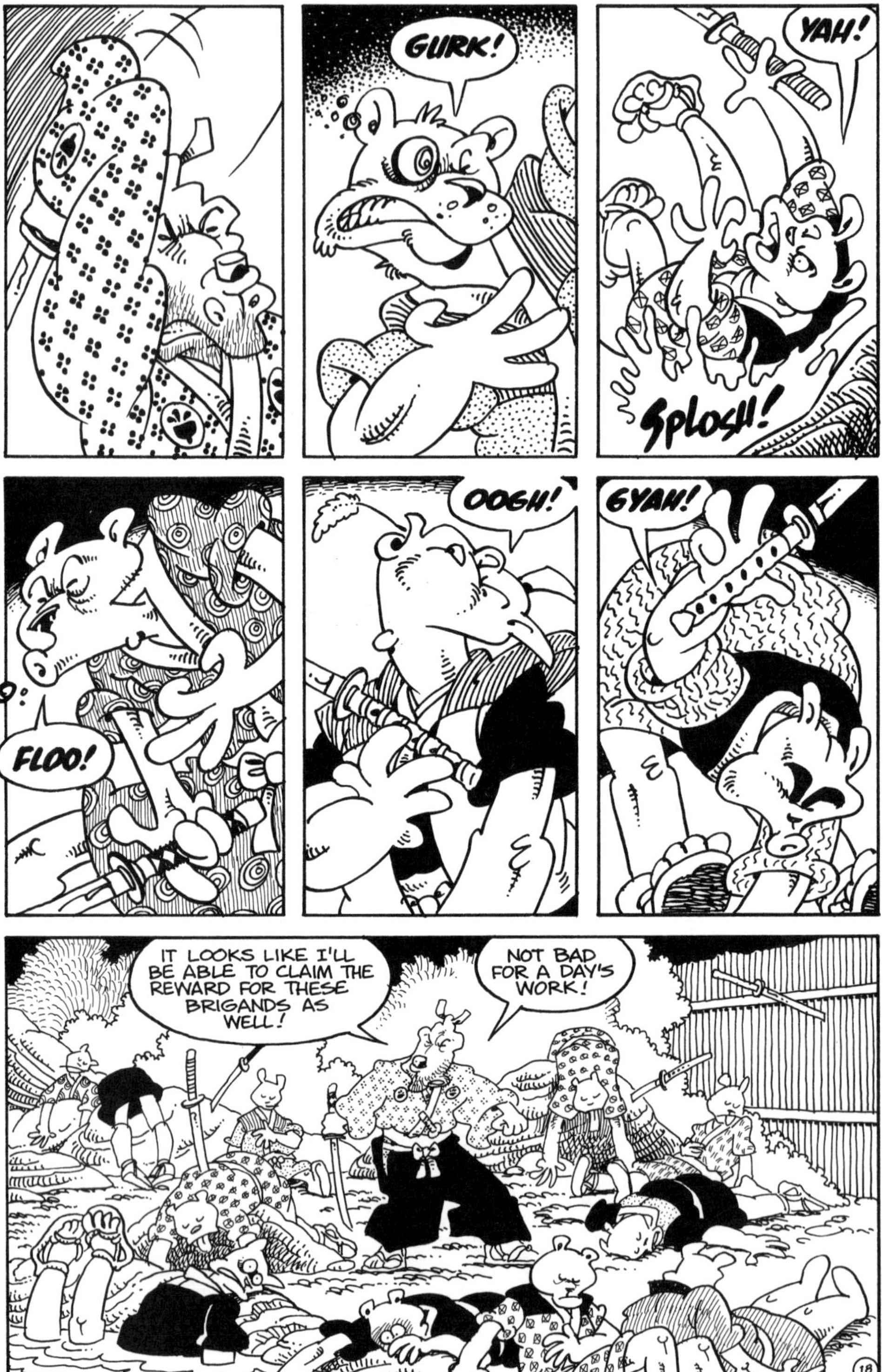
GURK!
YAH!
SPLOSH!
FLOO!
OOGH!
GYAH!
IT LOOKS LIKE I'LL BE ABLE TO CLAIM THE REWARD FOR THESE BRIGANDS AS WELL!
NOT BAD FOR A DAY'S WORK!
18.

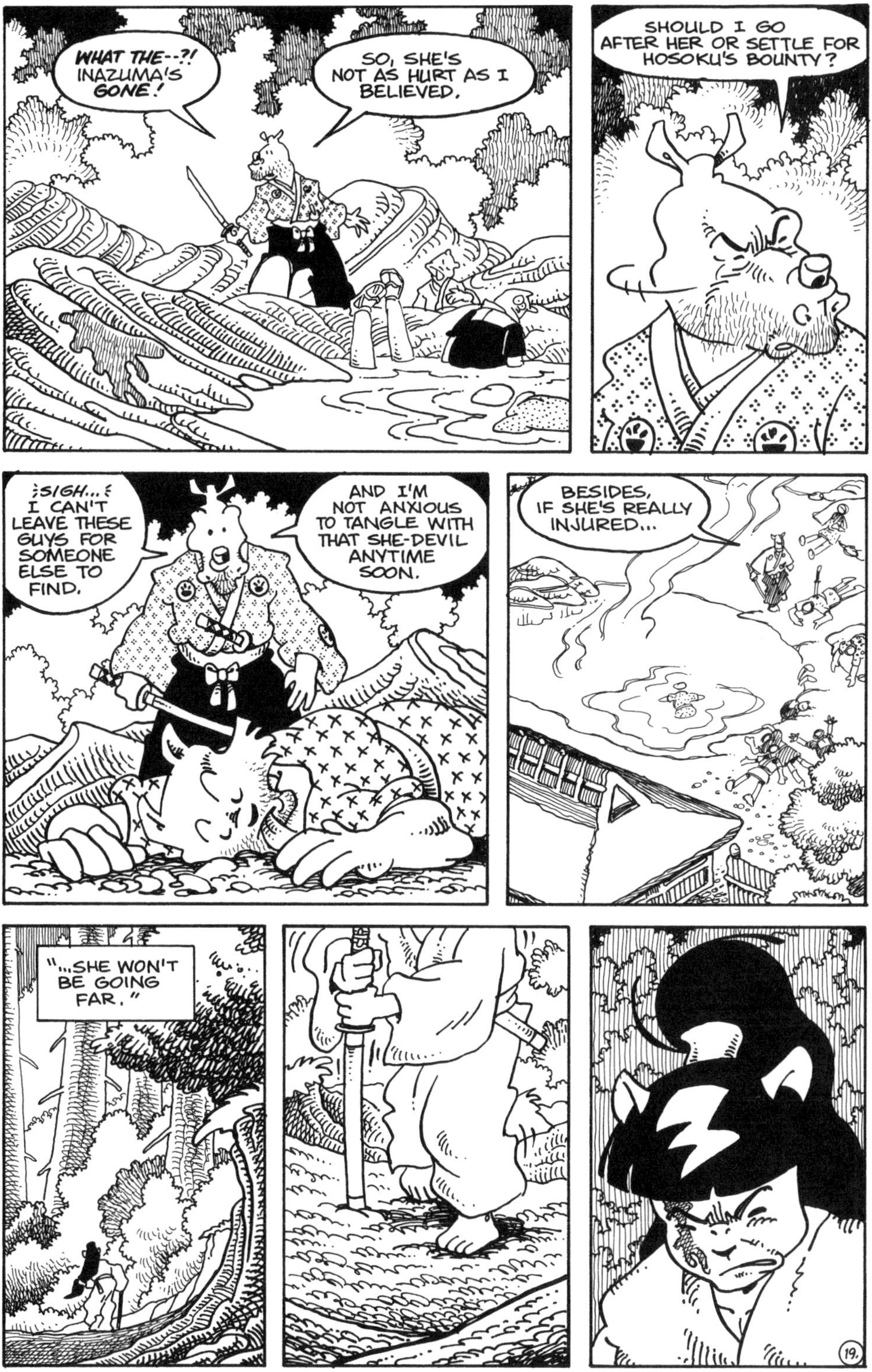
WHAT THE--?! INAZUMA'S GONE!
SO, SHE'S NOT AS HURT AS I BELIEVED.
SHOULD I GO AFTER HER OR SETTLE FOR HOSOKU'S BOUNTY?
SIGH... I CAN'T LEAVE THESE GUYS FOR SOMEONE ELSE TO FIND.
AND I'M NOT ANXIOUS TO TANGLE WITH THAT SHE-DEVIL ANYTIME SOON.
BESIDES, IF SHE'S REALLY INJURED...
"...SHE WON'T BE GOING FAR."
19.

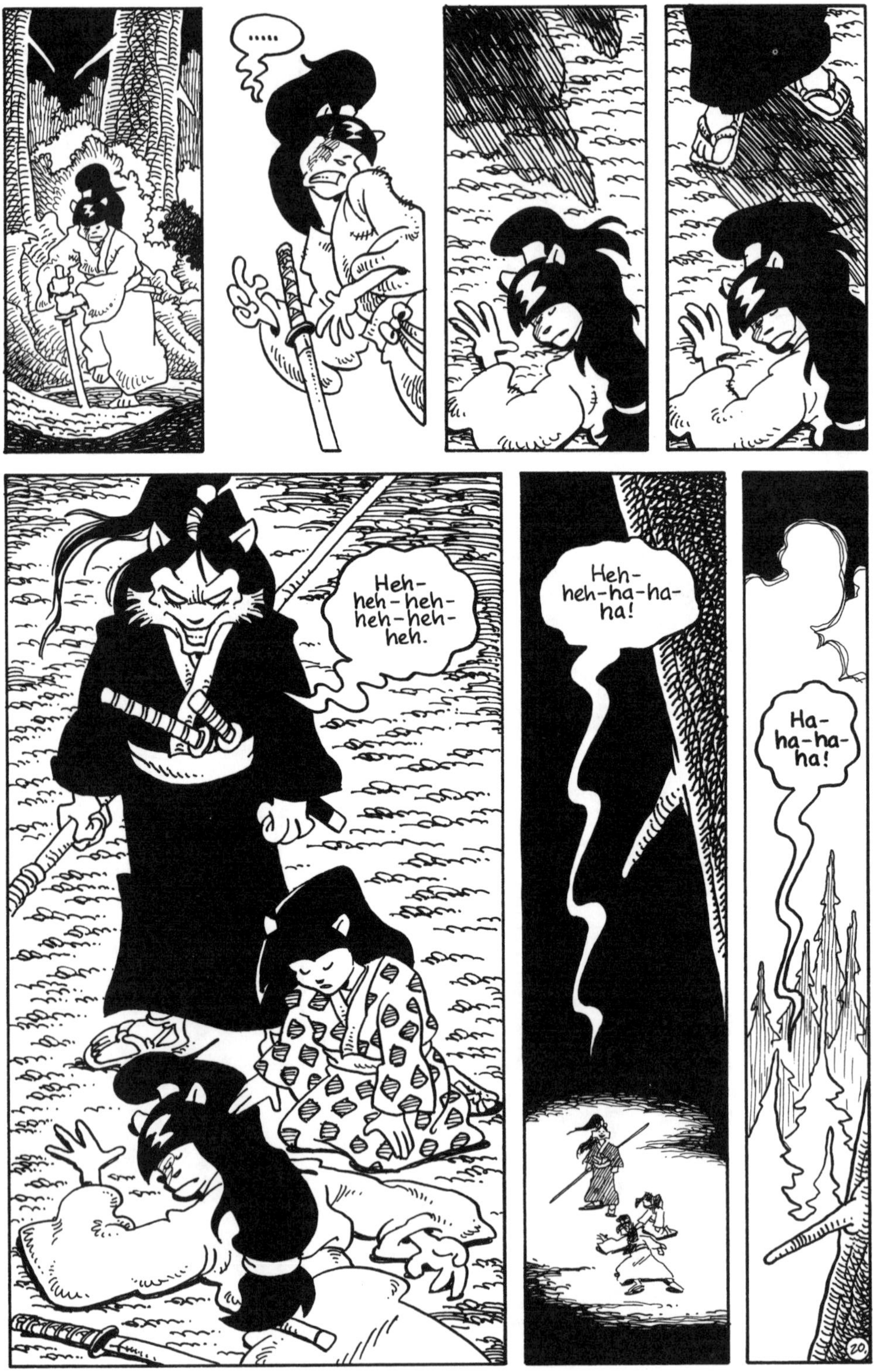
......
Heh-heh-heh-heh-heh-heh.
Heh-heh-ha-ha-ha!
Ha-ha-ha-ha!
20.

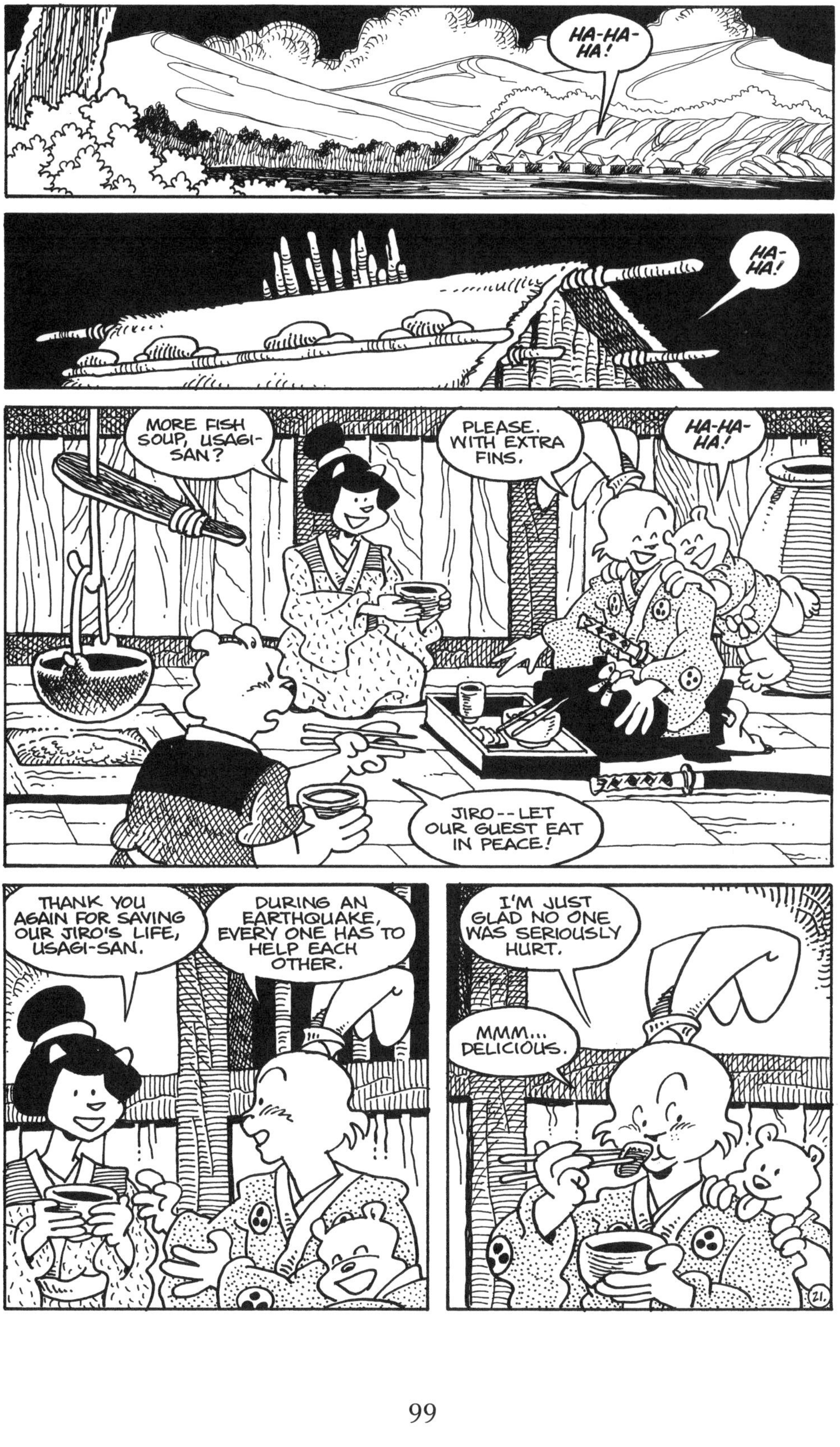
HA-HA-HA!
HA-HA!
MORE FISH SOUP, USAGI-SAN?
PLEASE. WITH EXTRA FINS.
HA-HA-HA!
JIRO--LET OUR GUEST EAT IN PEACE!
THANK YOU AGAIN FOR SAVING OUR JIRO'S LIFE, USAGI-SAN.
DURING AN EARTHQUAKE, EVERY ONE HAS TO HELP EACH OTHER.
I'M JUST GLAD NO ONE WAS SERIOUSLY HURT.
MMM... DELICIOUS.
21.

BUT THAT'S ENOUGH TALK OF EARTHQUAKES.

I UNDERSTAND THE BATTLE OF DAN-NO-URA WAS FOUGHT NOT FAR FROM HERE.

¡YAWN!¡

REALLY?

YES. ALMOST FIVE HUNDRED YEARS AGO.

OUR VILLAGE WAS STARTED BY DIVERS SEARCHING FOR GRASS-CUTTER.

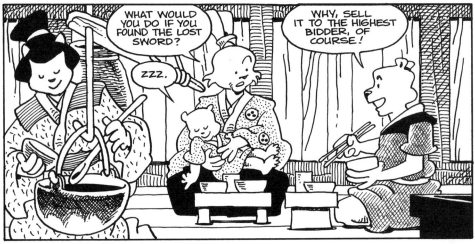

WHAT WOULD YOU DO IF YOU FOUND THE LOST SWORD?

ZZZ.

WHY, SELL IT TO THE HIGHEST BIDDER, OF COURSE!

BUT DON'T YOU HAVE ANY LOYALTY TO THE EMPEROR OR THE SHOGUN?

BAH! WHAT HAVE THEY TO DO WITH POOR PEASANTS LIKE US? TO US, ONE RULER IS JUST AS BAD AS ANOTHER!

NO OFFENSE MEANT TO YOU, USAGI-SAN.

SNORE! SNORK!

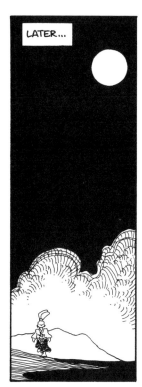

SPLASH!

SPLASH!

IT'S UNDER THERE SOMEWHERE.

AND NO DOUBT IT WILL STAY THERE FOR ANOTHER FIVE HUNDRED YEARS.

PREPARATIONS ARE COMPLETED.

FINALLY!

WHAT OF *YOUR* PREPARATIONS?

DON'T WORRY ABOUT ME. I'VE ALREADY DISPATCHED MY SAMURAI TO THE AREA.

WHAT TOKENS DO YOU HAVE?

HAIR AND FINGERNAIL CLIPPINGS FROM TWO OF THEM.

GOOD. I WILL NEED THEM LATER.

23.

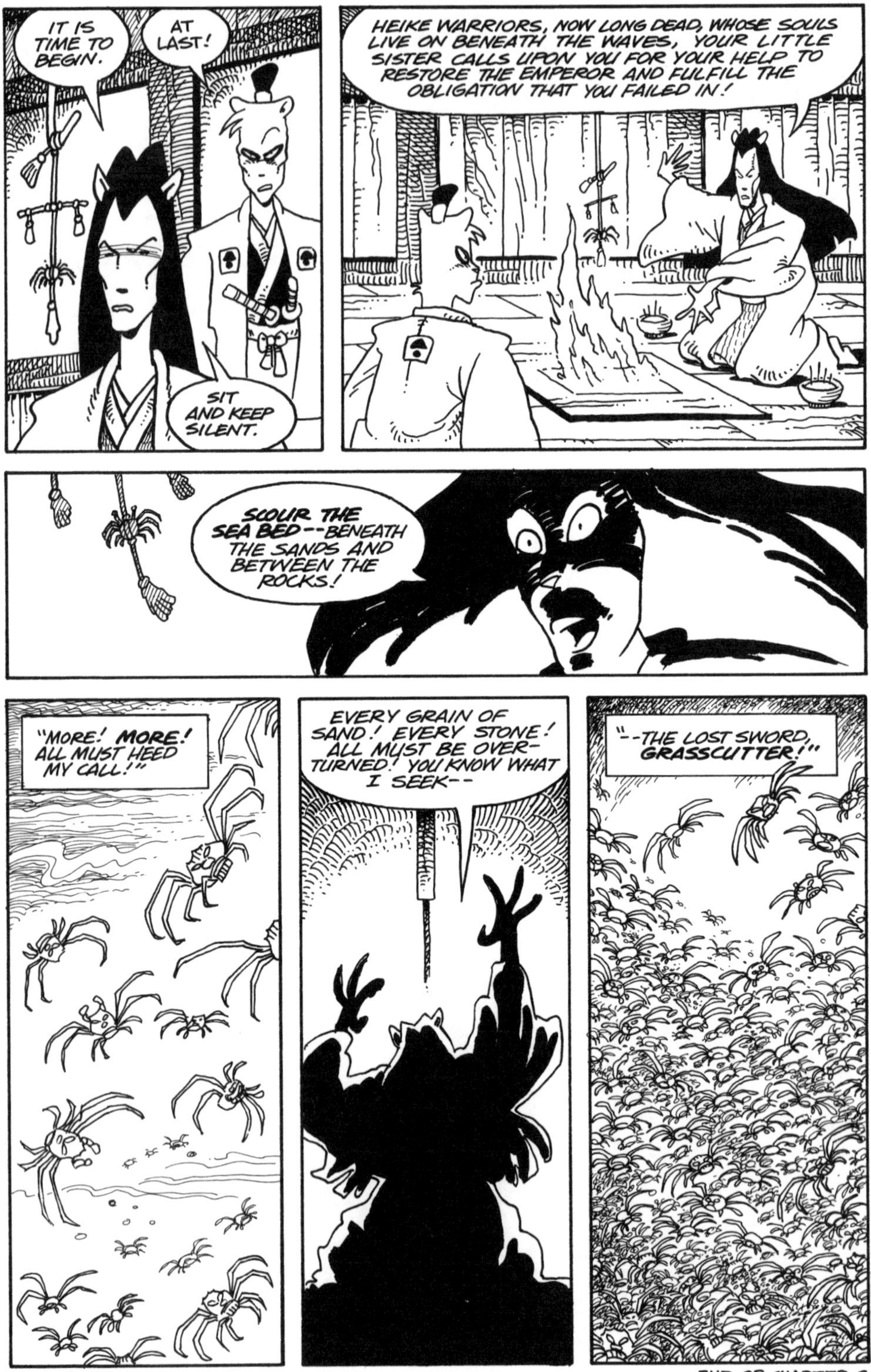
IT IS TIME TO BEGIN.
AT LAST!
SIT AND KEEP SILENT.
HEIKE WARRIORS, NOW LONG DEAD, WHOSE SOULS LIVE ON BENEATH THE WAVES, YOUR LITTLE SISTER CALLS UPON YOU FOR YOUR HELP TO RESTORE THE EMPEROR AND FULFILL THE OBLIGATION THAT YOU FAILED IN!
SCOUR THE SEA BED--BENEATH THE SANDS AND BETWEEN THE ROCKS!
"MORE! **MORE!** ALL MUST HEED MY CALL!"
EVERY GRAIN OF SAND! EVERY STONE! ALL MUST BE OVER-TURNED! YOU KNOW WHAT I SEEK--
"--THE LOST SWORD, **GRASSCUTTER!**"

END OF CHAPTER 2

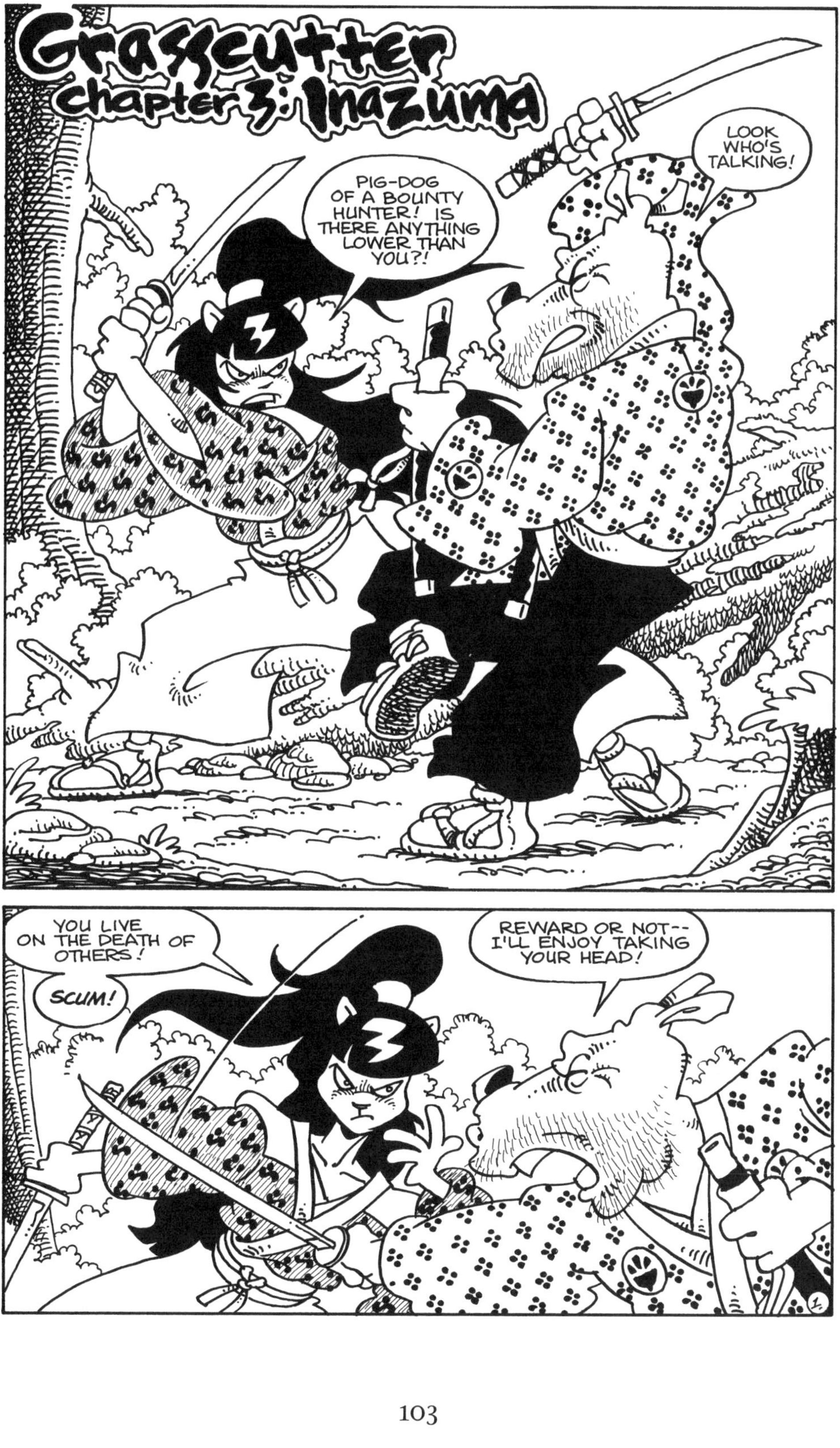
Grasscutter
Chapter 3: Inazuma
PIG-DOG OF A BOUNTY HUNTER! IS THERE ANYTHING LOWER THAN YOU?!
LOOK WHO'S TALKING!
YOU LIVE ON THE DEATH OF OTHERS!
SCUM!
REWARD OR NOT-- I'LL ENJOY TAKING YOUR HEAD!

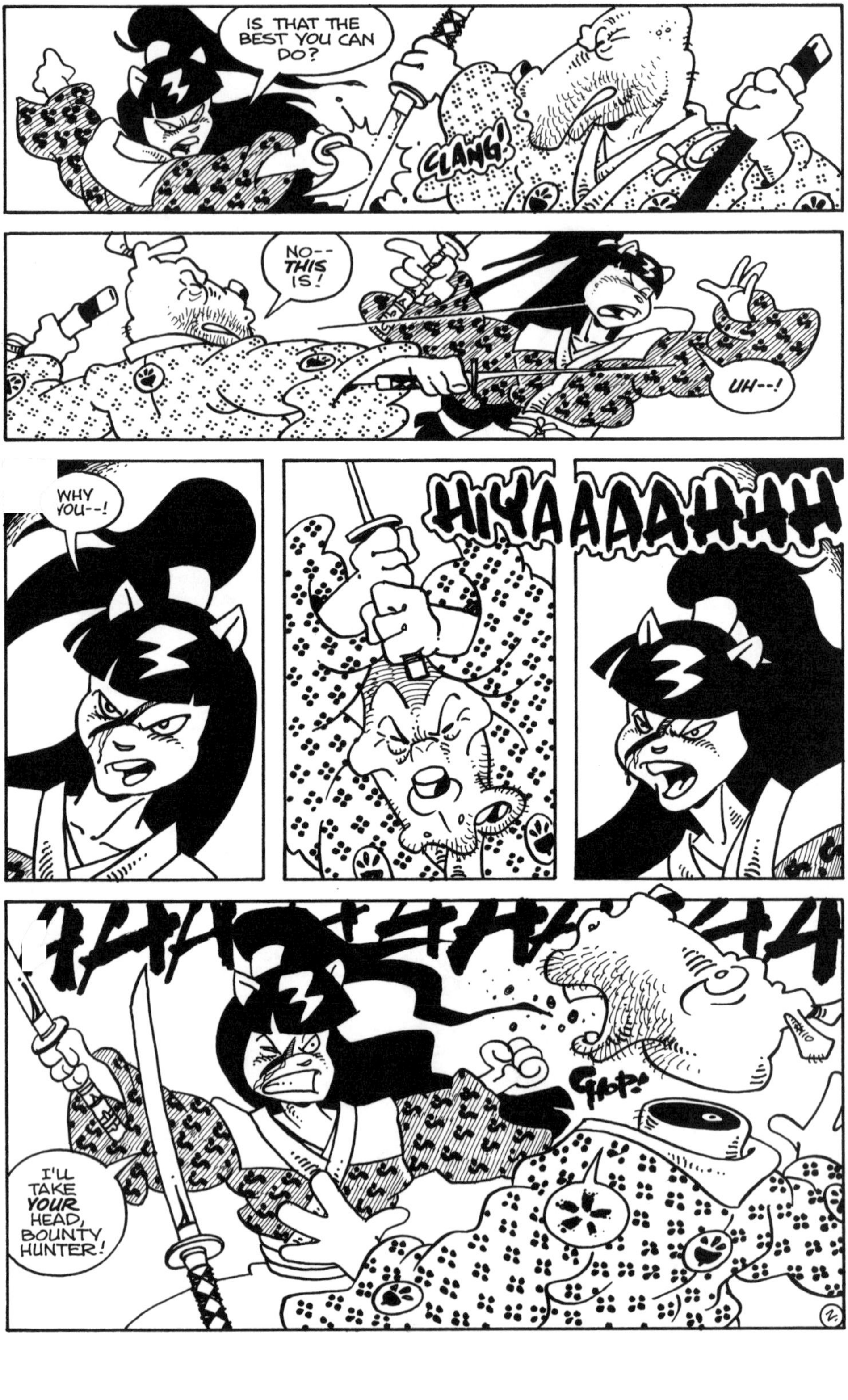

IS THAT THE BEST YOU CAN DO?
CLANG!
NO-- THIS IS!
UH--!
WHY YOU--!
HIYAAAAHHH
I'LL TAKE YOUR HEAD, BOUNTY HUNTER!
CHOP!

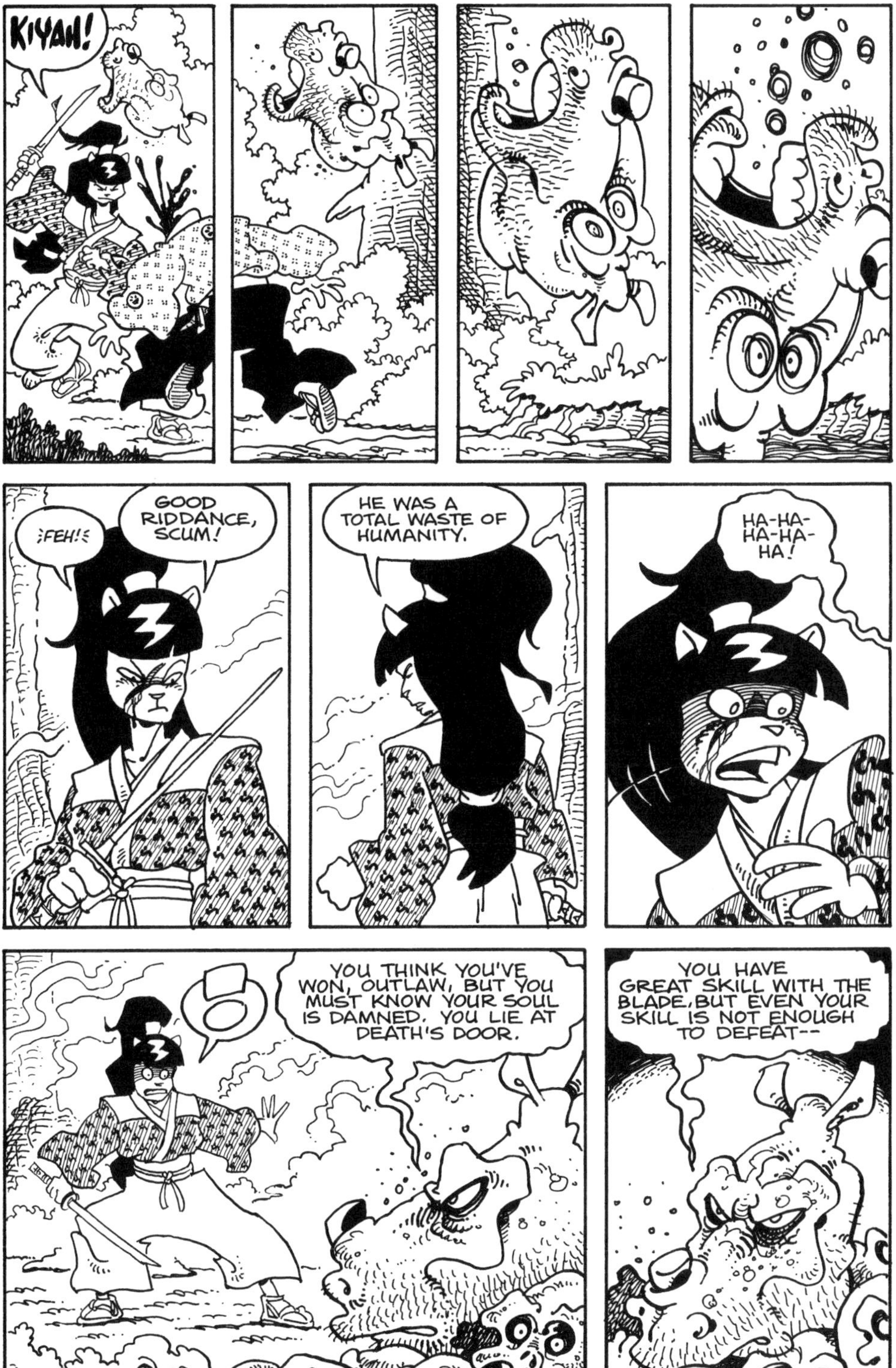
KIYAH!
;FEH!;
GOOD RIDDANCE, SCUM!
HE WAS A TOTAL WASTE OF HUMANITY.
HA-HA-HA-HA-HA!
YOU THINK YOU'VE WON, OUTLAW, BUT YOU MUST KNOW YOUR SOUL IS DAMNED. YOU LIE AT DEATH'S DOOR.
YOU HAVE GREAT SKILL WITH THE BLADE, BUT EVEN YOUR SKILL IS NOT ENOUGH TO DEFEAT--

--THE FORCES OF YOMI*!
THAT BLACK FIGURE--!
HA-HA-HA-HA!
LORD ENMA** HIMSELF?!
*HELL
**LORD OF HELL
NO. THAT IS YOUR SAVIOR!
THAT IS, IF YOU CAN GET TO HIM!
WHO IS HE?!
GO TO HIM IF YOU CAN--AND DARE!
HAHAHAHAHAHAHAHA
EEYAHH!
HAHA HAHAHA
HAHAHAHAHAHAHAHAHAHAHAHAHAHAHAHA
HAHAHA HAHAHAHAHAHAHAHAHAHAHAHAHAHA
SHUT UP, BOUNTY HUNTER!
HAHAHA
4.

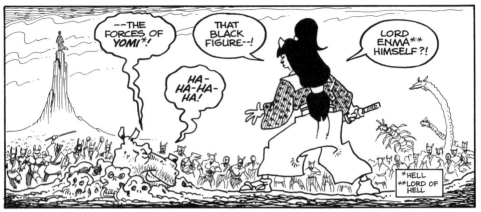

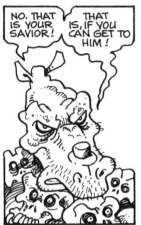

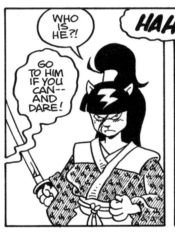

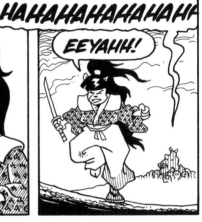

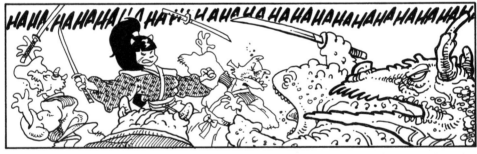

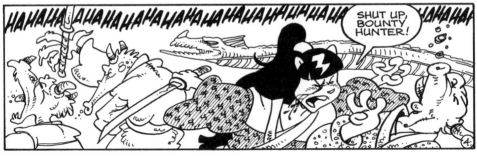

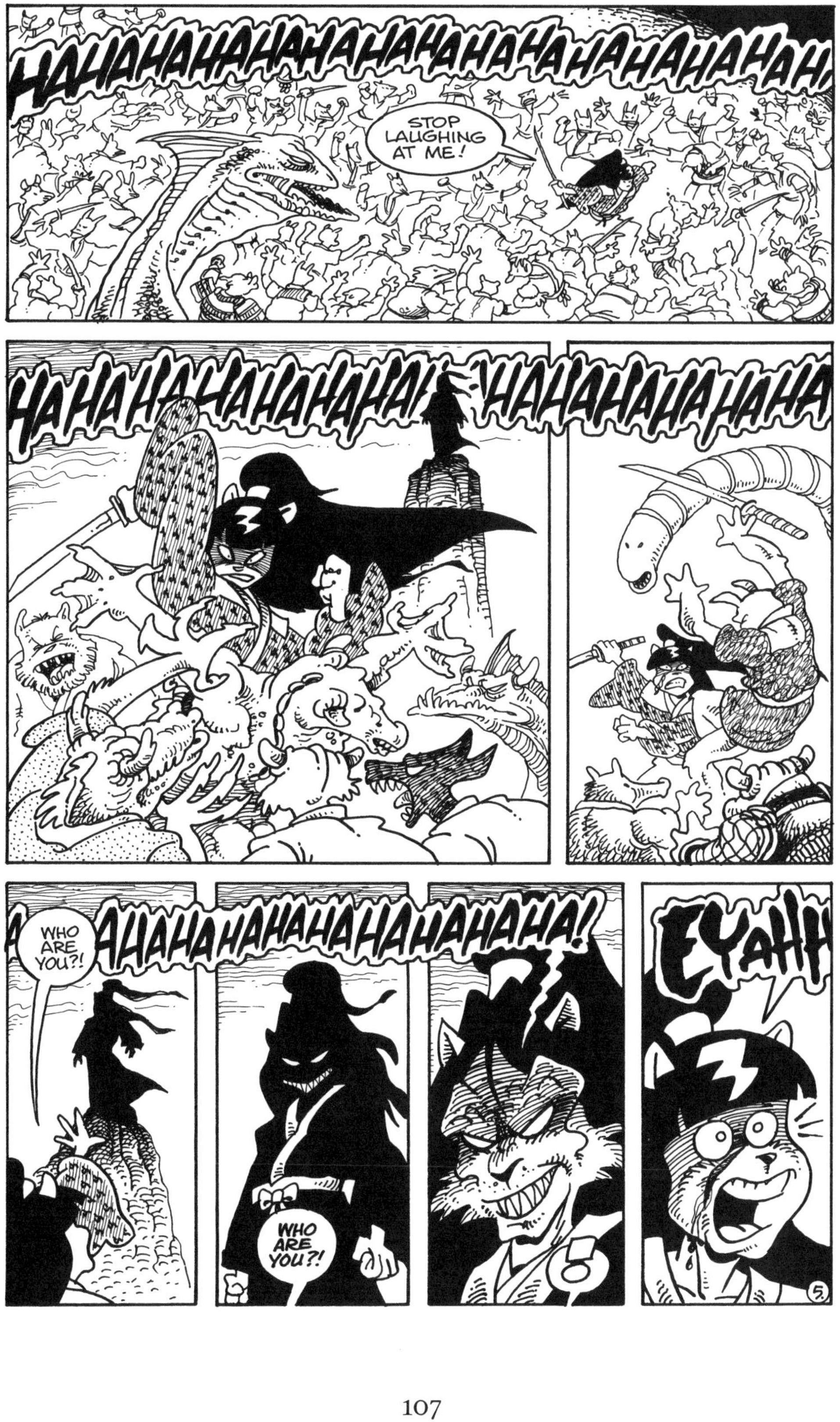
HAHAHAHAHAHAHAHAHAHAHAHAHAHAHAHAHAH
STOP LAUGHING AT ME!
HAHAHAHAHAHAHAHAHA!
HAHAHAHAHAHAHAHA
WHO ARE YOU?!
AHAHAHAHAHAHAHAHAHAHAHAHA!
WHO ARE YOU?!
EYAHH
5.

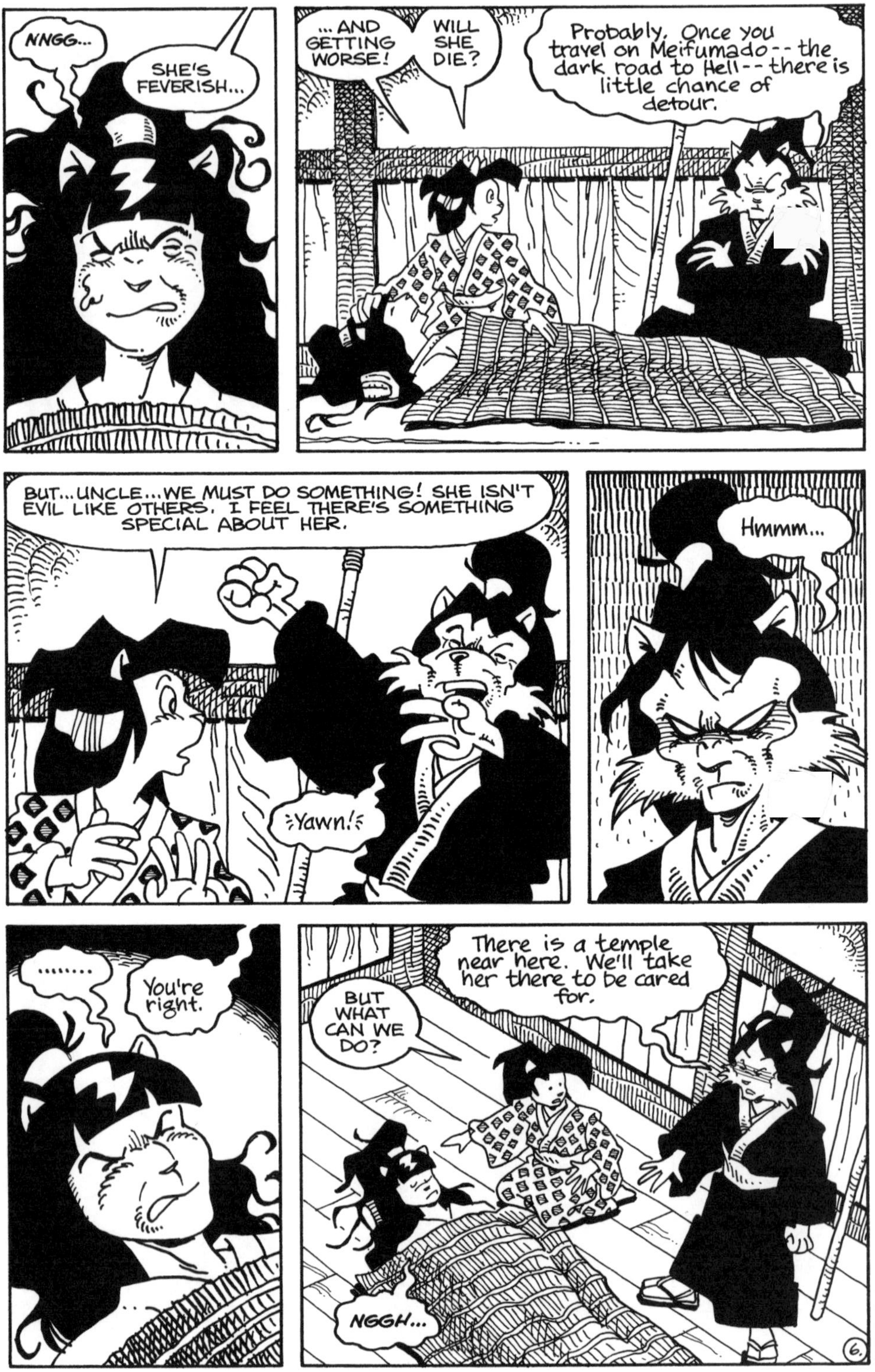
NNGG...
SHE'S FEVERISH...
...AND GETTING WORSE!
WILL SHE DIE?
Probably. Once you travel on Meifumado--the dark road to Hell--there is little chance of detour.
BUT...UNCLE...WE MUST DO SOMETHING! SHE ISN'T EVIL LIKE OTHERS. I FEEL THERE'S SOMETHING SPECIAL ABOUT HER.
Yawn!
Hmmm...
....
You're right.
BUT WHAT CAN WE DO?
There is a temple near here. We'll take her there to be cared for.
NGGH...
6.

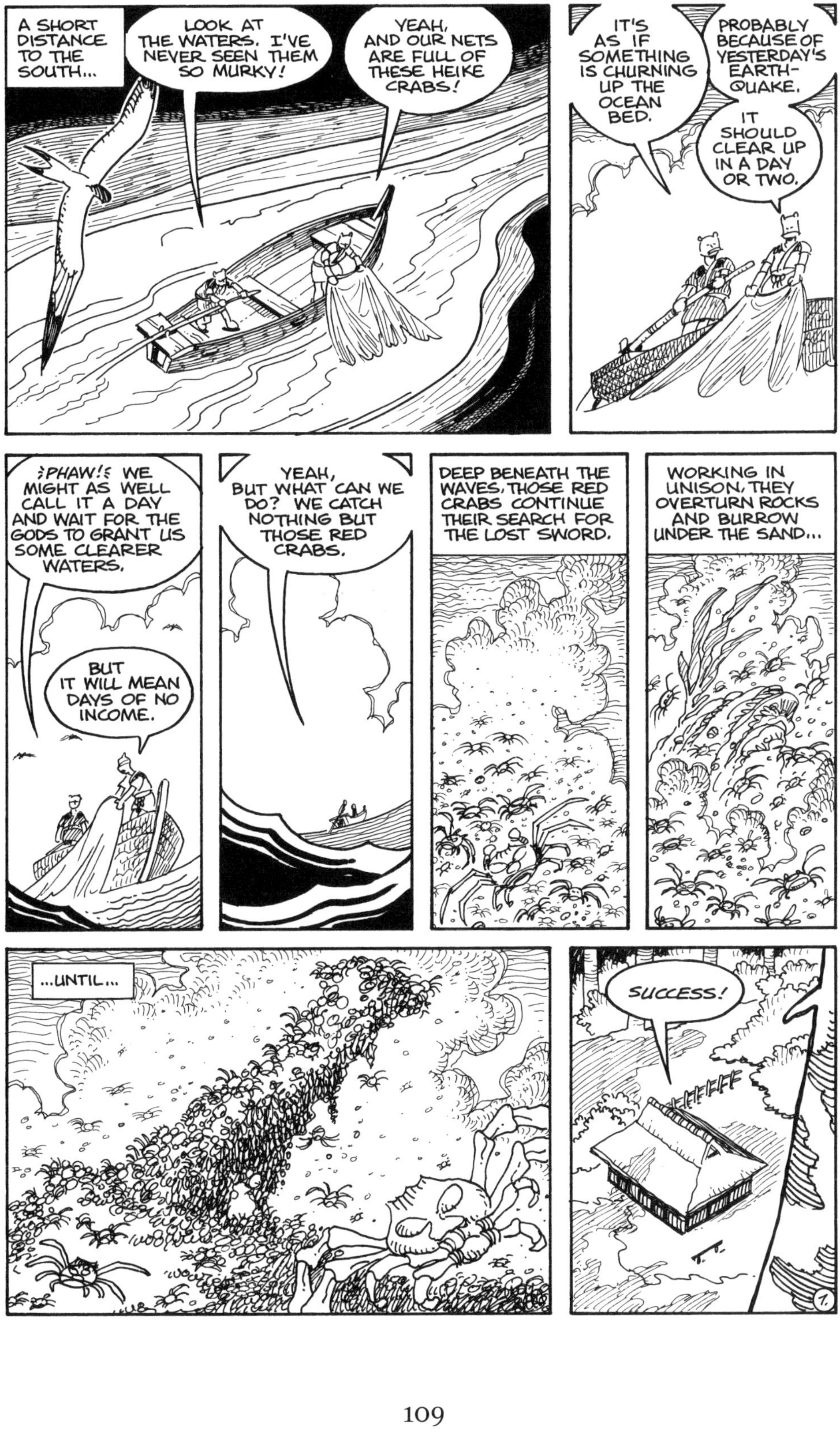
A SHORT DISTANCE TO THE SOUTH...
LOOK AT THE WATERS. I'VE NEVER SEEN THEM SO MURKY!
YEAH, AND OUR NETS ARE FULL OF THESE HEIKE CRABS!
IT'S AS IF SOMETHING IS CHURNING UP THE OCEAN BED.
PROBABLY BECAUSE OF YESTERDAY'S EARTH-QUAKE.
IT SHOULD CLEAR UP IN A DAY OR TWO.
PHAW! WE MIGHT AS WELL CALL IT A DAY AND WAIT FOR THE GODS TO GRANT US SOME CLEARER WATERS.
BUT IT WILL MEAN DAYS OF NO INCOME.
YEAH, BUT WHAT CAN WE DO? WE CATCH NOTHING BUT THOSE RED CRABS.
DEEP BENEATH THE WAVES, THOSE RED CRABS CONTINUE THEIR SEARCH FOR THE LOST SWORD.
WORKING IN UNISON, THEY OVERTURN ROCKS AND BURROW UNDER THE SAND...
...UNTIL...
SUCCESS!
7.

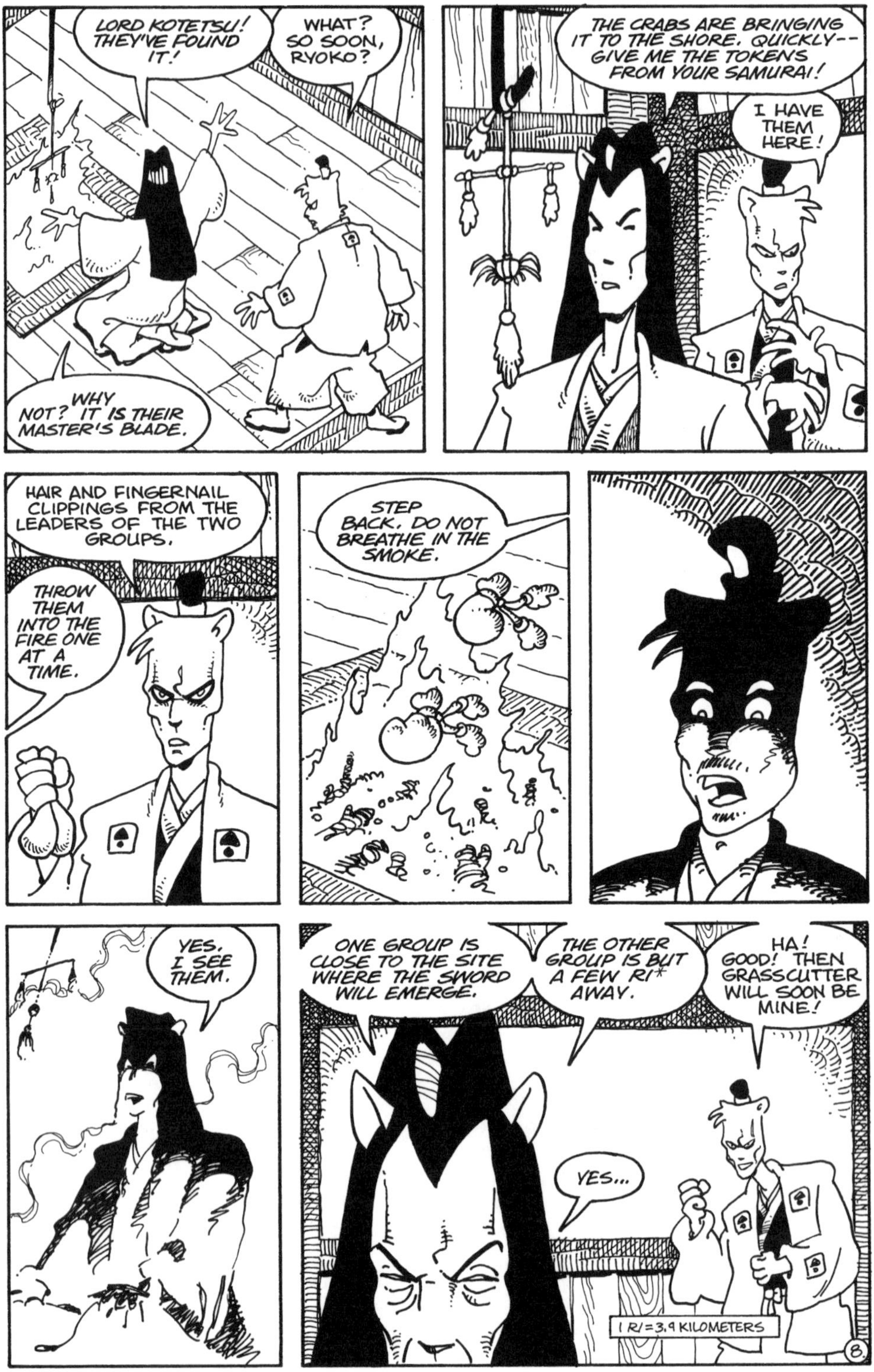
LORD KOTETSU! THEY'VE FOUND IT!
WHAT? SO SOON, RYOKO?
WHY NOT? IT IS THEIR MASTER'S BLADE.
THE CRABS ARE BRINGING IT TO THE SHORE. QUICKLY-- GIVE ME THE TOKENS FROM YOUR SAMURAI!
I HAVE THEM HERE!
HAIR AND FINGERNAIL CLIPPINGS FROM THE LEADERS OF THE TWO GROUPS.
THROW THEM INTO THE FIRE ONE AT A TIME.
STEP BACK. DO NOT BREATHE IN THE SMOKE.
YES. I SEE THEM.
ONE GROUP IS CLOSE TO THE SITE WHERE THE SWORD WILL EMERGE.
THE OTHER GROUP IS BUT A FEW RI* AWAY.
HA! GOOD! THEN GRASSCUTTER WILL SOON BE MINE!
YES...
1 RI = 3.9 KILOMETERS
8

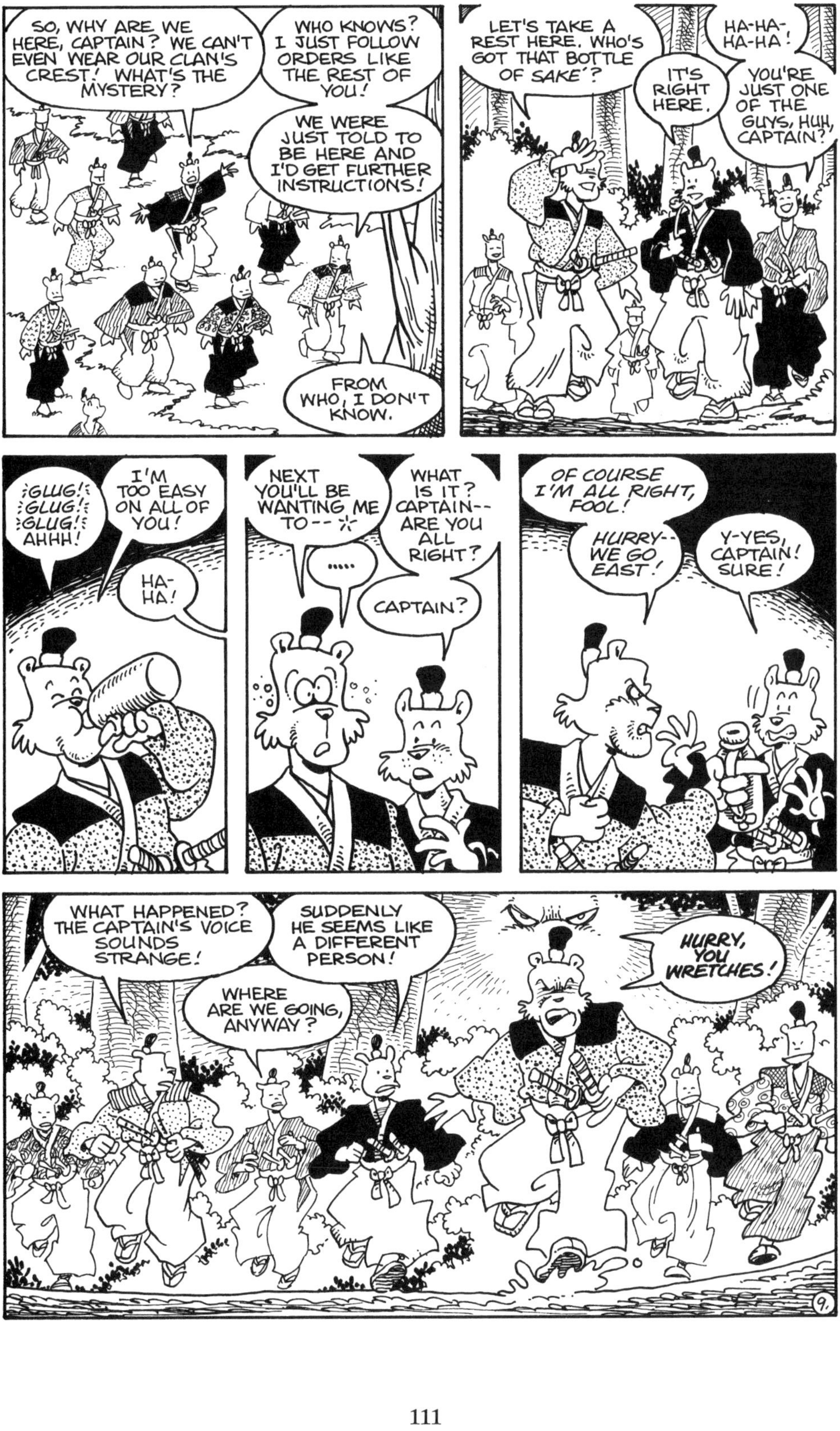
SO, WHY ARE WE HERE, CAPTAIN? WE CAN'T EVEN WEAR OUR CLAN'S CREST! WHAT'S THE MYSTERY?
WHO KNOWS? I JUST FOLLOW ORDERS LIKE THE REST OF YOU!
WE WERE JUST TOLD TO BE HERE AND I'D GET FURTHER INSTRUCTIONS!
FROM WHO, I DON'T KNOW.
LET'S TAKE A REST HERE. WHO'S GOT THAT BOTTLE OF *SAKE*?
IT'S RIGHT HERE.
HA-HA-HA-HA!
YOU'RE JUST ONE OF THE GUYS, HUH, CAPTAIN?
GLUG! GLUG! GLUG! AHHH!
I'M TOO EASY ON ALL OF YOU!
HA-HA!
NEXT YOU'LL BE WANTING ME TO--
.....
WHAT IS IT? CAPTAIN-- ARE YOU ALL RIGHT?
CAPTAIN?
OF COURSE I'M ALL RIGHT, FOOL!
HURRY-- WE GO EAST!
Y-YES, CAPTAIN! SURE!
WHAT HAPPENED? THE CAPTAIN'S VOICE SOUNDS STRANGE!
SUDDENLY HE SEEMS LIKE A DIFFERENT PERSON!
WHERE ARE WE GOING, ANYWAY?
HURRY, YOU WRETCHES!
9.

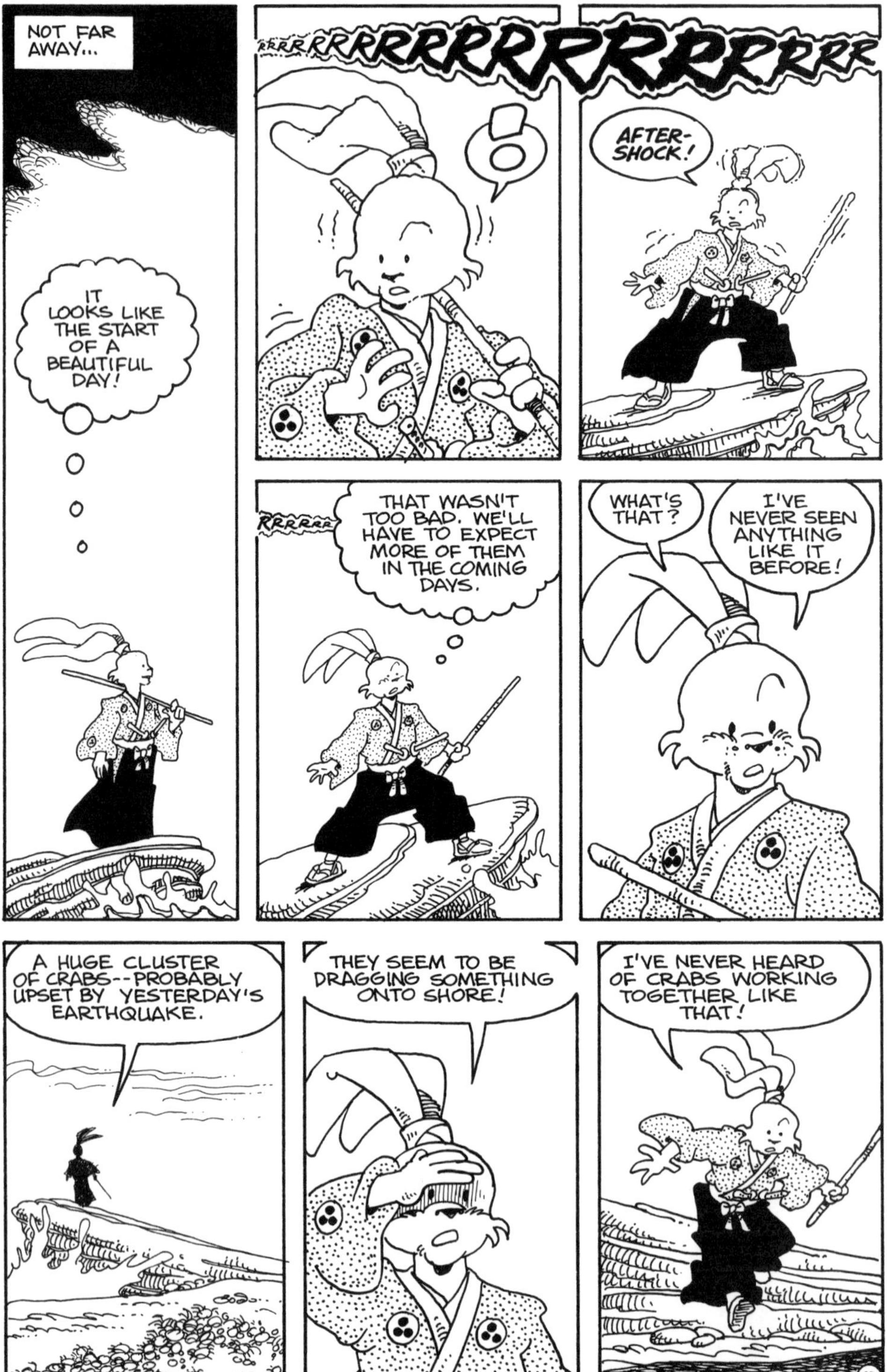
NOT FAR AWAY...
IT LOOKS LIKE THE START OF A BEAUTIFUL DAY!
RRRRRRRRRRRRRRRRRRRRRRRRR
!
AFTER-SHOCK!
RRRRRR
THAT WASN'T TOO BAD. WE'LL HAVE TO EXPECT MORE OF THEM IN THE COMING DAYS.
WHAT'S THAT?
I'VE NEVER SEEN ANYTHING LIKE IT BEFORE!
A HUGE CLUSTER OF CRABS--PROBABLY UPSET BY YESTERDAY'S EARTHQUAKE.
THEY SEEM TO BE DRAGGING SOMETHING ONTO SHORE!
I'VE NEVER HEARD OF CRABS WORKING TOGETHER LIKE THAT!
10.

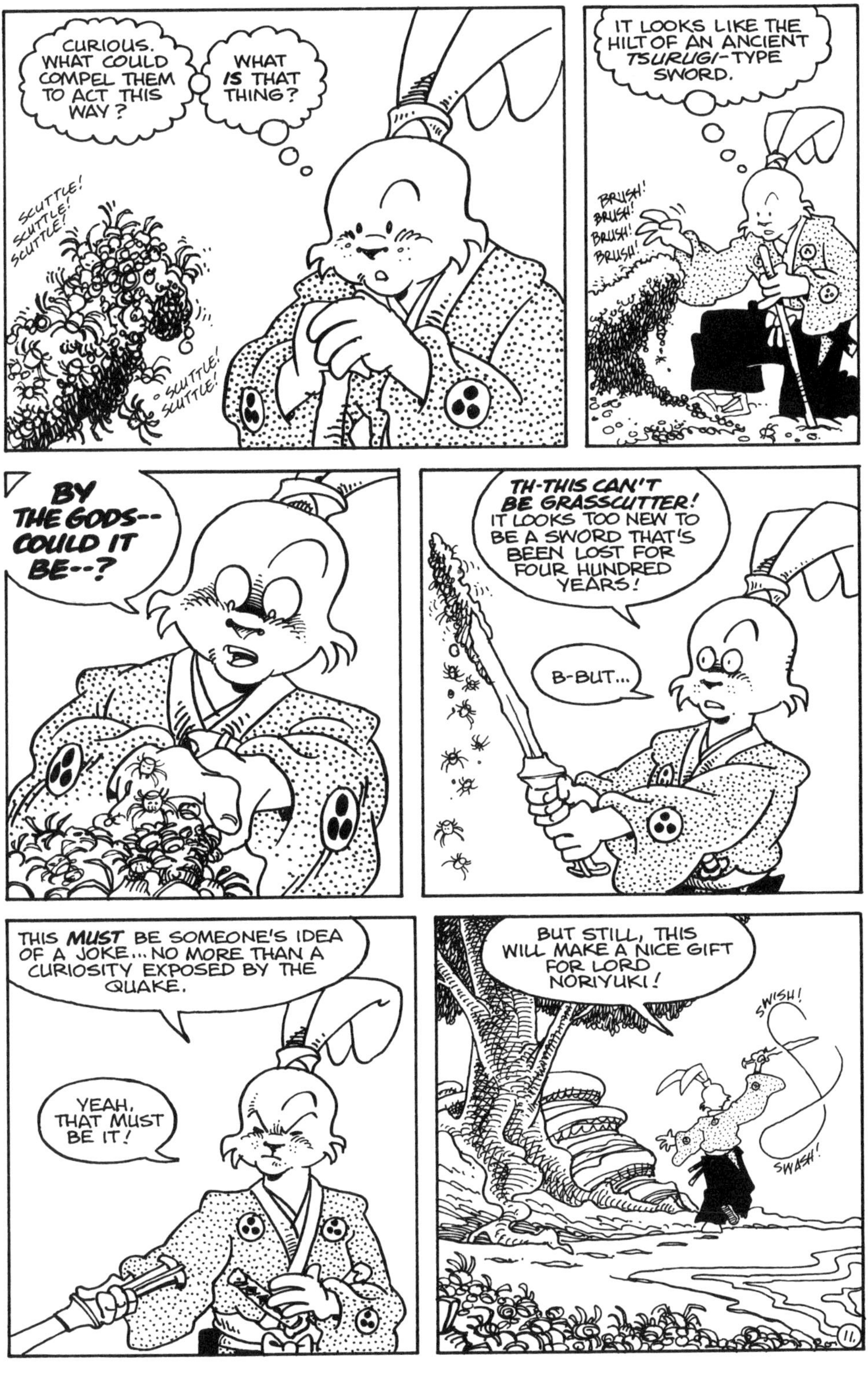

CURIOUS. WHAT COULD COMPEL THEM TO ACT THIS WAY?
WHAT IS THAT THING?
SCUTTLE! SCUTTLE! SCUTTLE!
SCUTTLE! SCUTTLE!
IT LOOKS LIKE THE HILT OF AN ANCIENT TSURUGI-TYPE SWORD.
BRUSH! BRUSH! BRUSH! BRUSH!
BY THE GODS-- COULD IT BE--?
TH-THIS CAN'T BE GRASSCUTTER! IT LOOKS TOO NEW TO BE A SWORD THAT'S BEEN LOST FOR FOUR HUNDRED YEARS!
B-BUT...
THIS MUST BE SOMEONE'S IDEA OF A JOKE... NO MORE THAN A CURIOSITY EXPOSED BY THE QUAKE.
YEAH, THAT MUST BE IT!
BUT STILL, THIS WILL MAKE A NICE GIFT FOR LORD NORIYUKI!
SWISH!
SWASH!
11.

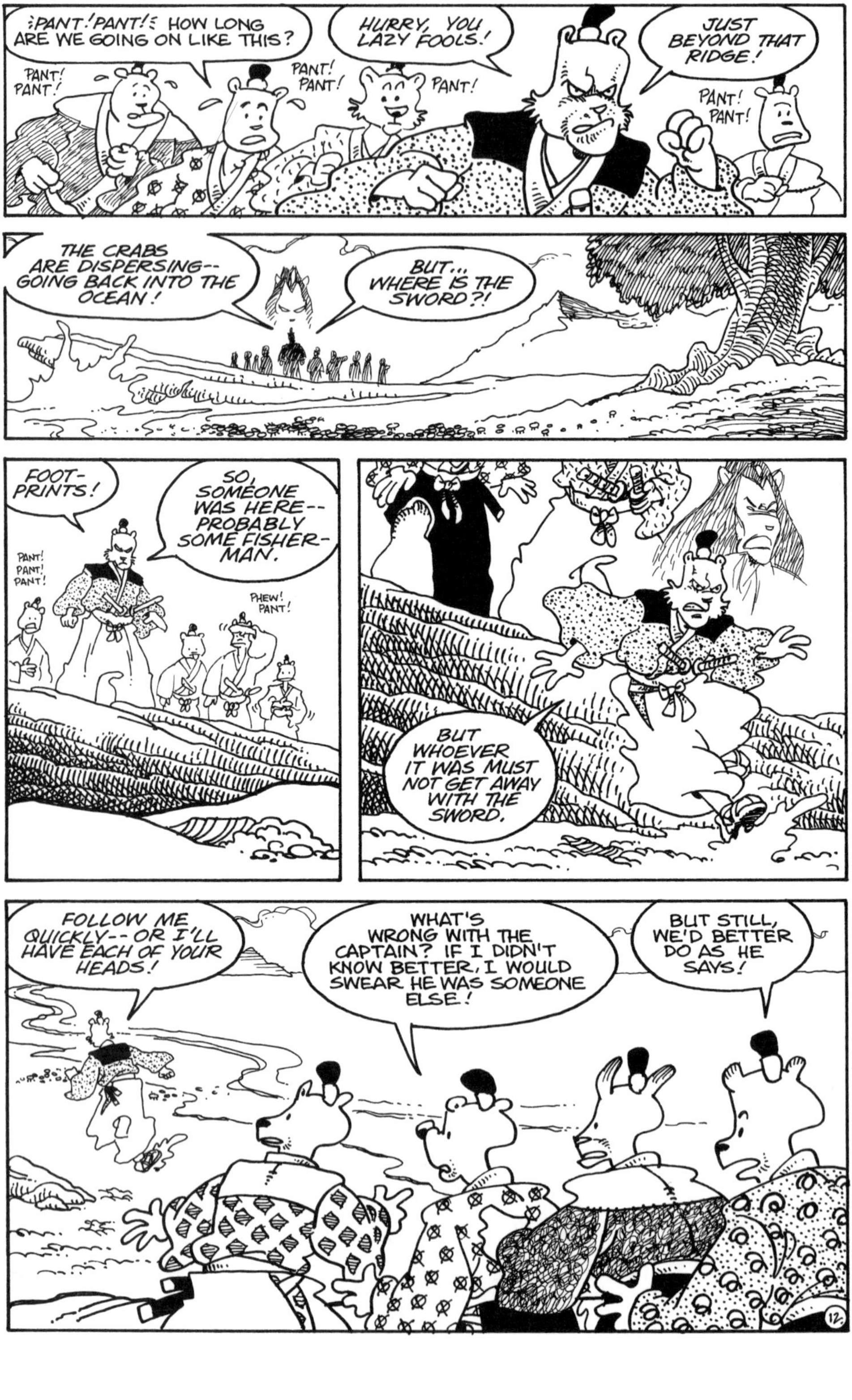

PANT! PANT! HOW LONG ARE WE GOING ON LIKE THIS?
PANT! PANT!
PANT! PANT!
HURRY, YOU LAZY FOOLS!
PANT!
JUST BEYOND THAT RIDGE!
PANT! PANT!
THE CRABS ARE DISPERSING-- GOING BACK INTO THE OCEAN!
BUT... WHERE IS THE SWORD?!
FOOT-PRINTS!
SO, SOMEONE WAS HERE-- PROBABLY SOME FISHER-MAN.
PANT! PANT! PANT!
PHEW! PANT!
BUT WHOEVER IT WAS MUST NOT GET AWAY WITH THE SWORD.
FOLLOW ME QUICKLY-- OR I'LL HAVE EACH OF YOUR HEADS!
WHAT'S WRONG WITH THE CAPTAIN? IF I DIDN'T KNOW BETTER, I WOULD SWEAR HE WAS SOMEONE ELSE!
BUT STILL, WE'D BETTER DO AS HE SAYS!
12.

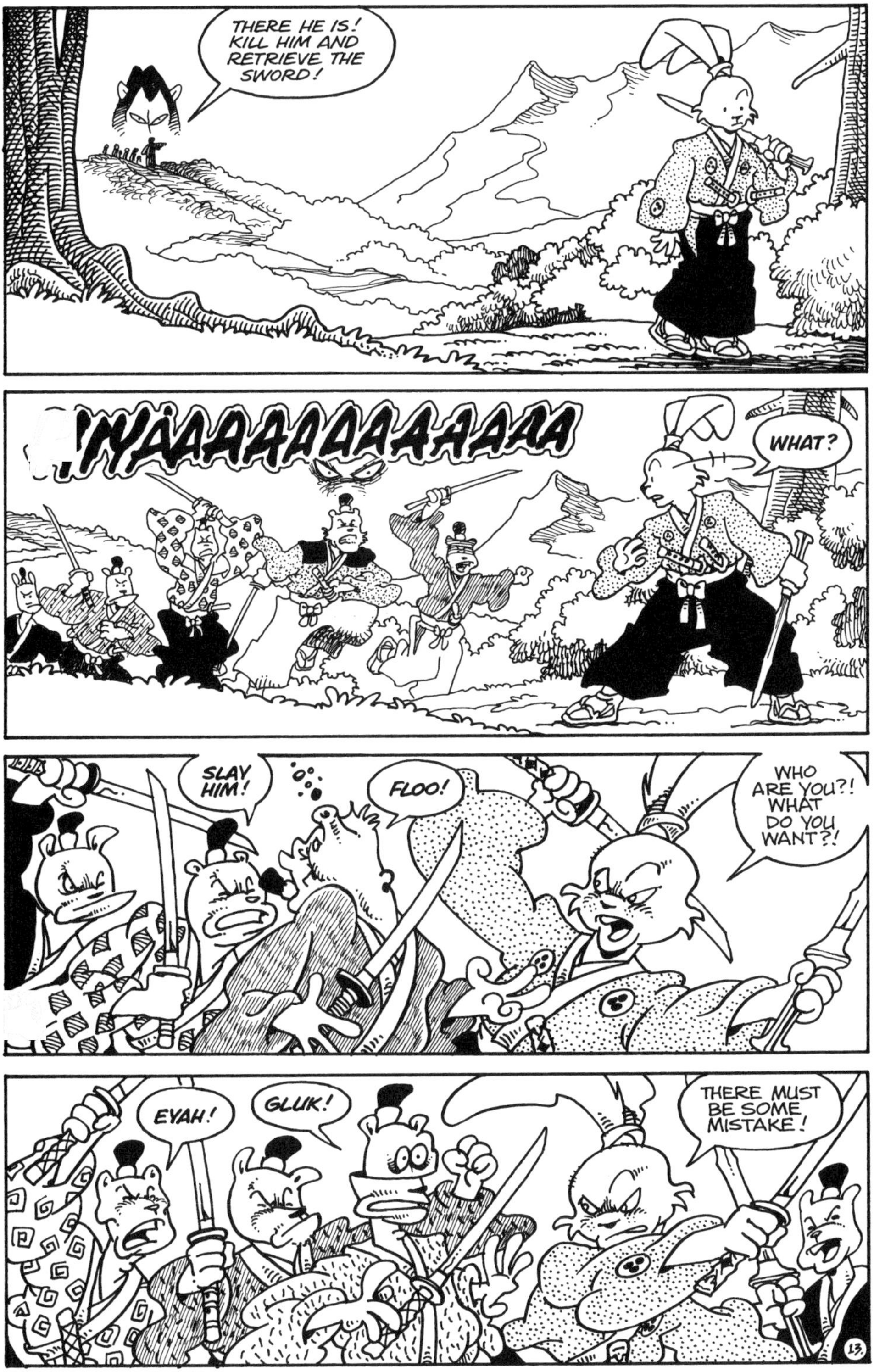
THERE HE IS! KILL HIM AND RETRIEVE THE SWORD!
WAAAAAAAAAAAA
WHAT?
SLAY HIM!
FLOO!
WHO ARE YOU?! WHAT DO YOU WANT?!
EYAH!
GLUK!
THERE MUST BE SOME MISTAKE!
13.

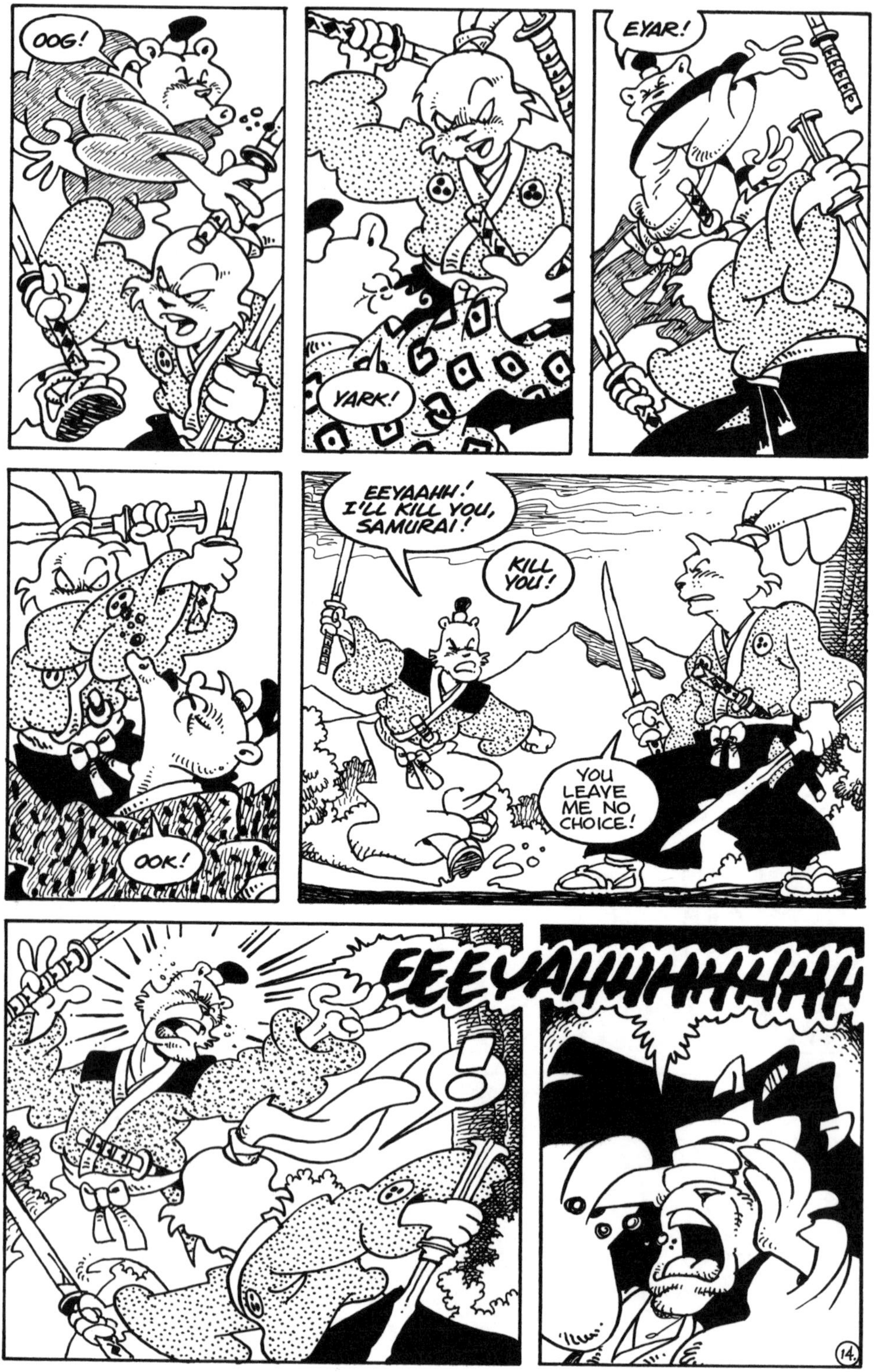

OOG!
YARK!
EYAR!
OOK!
EEYAAHH! I'LL KILL YOU, SAMURAI!
KILL YOU!
YOU LEAVE ME NO CHOICE!
EEEYAHHHHHHHH
14

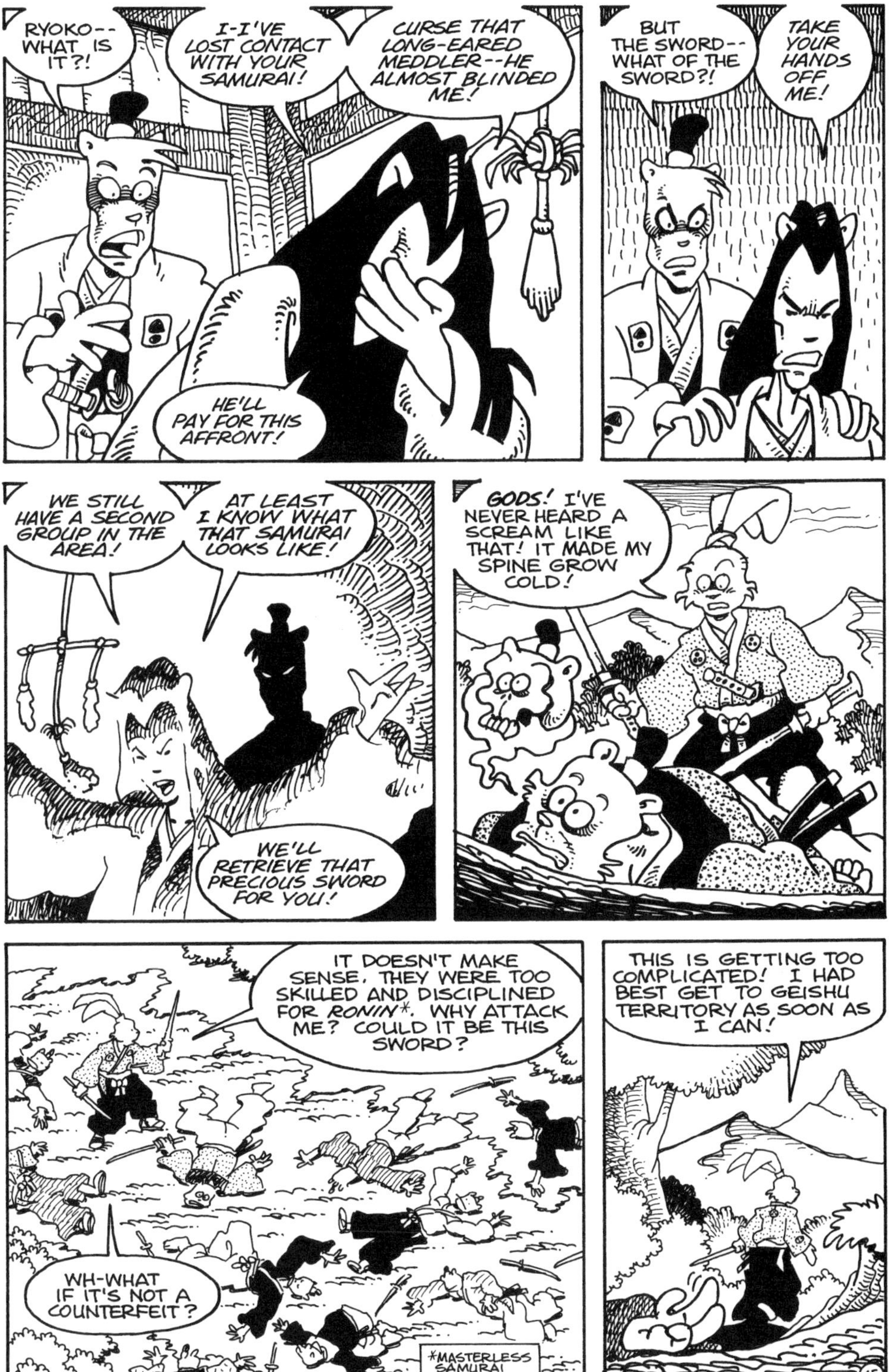
RYOKO-- WHAT IS IT?!
I-I'VE LOST CONTACT WITH YOUR SAMURAI!
CURSE THAT LONG-EARED MEDDLER--HE ALMOST BLINDED ME!
HE'LL PAY FOR THIS AFFRONT!
BUT THE SWORD-- WHAT OF THE SWORD?!
TAKE YOUR HANDS OFF ME!
WE STILL HAVE A SECOND GROUP IN THE AREA!
AT LEAST I KNOW WHAT THAT SAMURAI LOOKS LIKE!
WE'LL RETRIEVE THAT PRECIOUS SWORD FOR YOU!
GODS! I'VE NEVER HEARD A SCREAM LIKE THAT! IT MADE MY SPINE GROW COLD!
IT DOESN'T MAKE SENSE. THEY WERE TOO SKILLED AND DISCIPLINED FOR RONIN*. WHY ATTACK ME? COULD IT BE THIS SWORD?
WH-WHAT IF IT'S NOT A COUNTERFEIT?
*MASTERLESS SAMURAI
THIS IS GETTING TOO COMPLICATED! I HAD BEST GET TO GEISHU TERRITORY AS SOON AS I CAN!
15

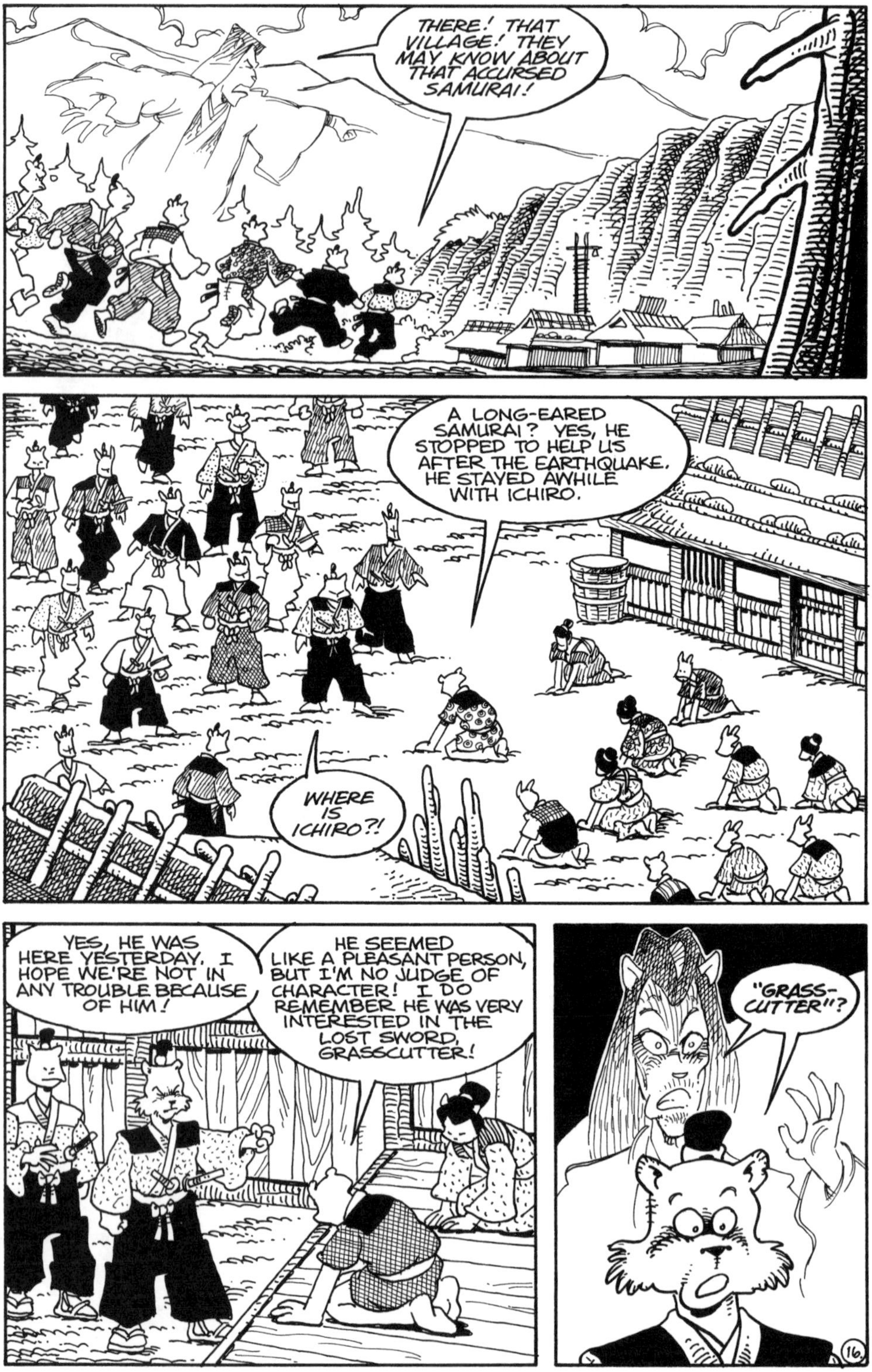
THERE! THAT VILLAGE! THEY MAY KNOW ABOUT THAT ACCURSED SAMURAI!
A LONG-EARED SAMURAI? YES, HE STOPPED TO HELP US AFTER THE EARTHQUAKE. HE STAYED AWHILE WITH ICHIRO.
WHERE IS ICHIRO?!
YES, HE WAS HERE YESTERDAY. I HOPE WE'RE NOT IN ANY TROUBLE BECAUSE OF HIM!
HE SEEMED LIKE A PLEASANT PERSON, BUT I'M NO JUDGE OF CHARACTER! I DO REMEMBER HE WAS VERY INTERESTED IN THE LOST SWORD, GRASSCUTTER!
"GRASS-CUTTER"?
16

FORGIVE US ANY WRONGDOING. WE WOULDN'T HAVE HAD ANYTHING TO DO WITH HIM, BUT HE DID SAVE OUR SON...

WHAT ELSE DID HE SAY? WHICH WAY DID HE GO?

HE WENT TO THE NORTH-EAST.

TOWARD THE GEISHU PROVINCE. I UNDERSTAND HE IS TRAVELING TO SEE LORD NORIYUKI HIMSELF!

IS HE A FUGITIVE? IS THERE A REWARD?

LORD NORIYUKI?! ARE YOU SURE?!

I JUST REPORT WHAT I HEAR.

NORIYUKI IS A SUPPORTER OF THE *SHOGUN*. IF HE GETS HIS HANDS ON GRASSCUTTER, MY PLAN IS *RUINED!*

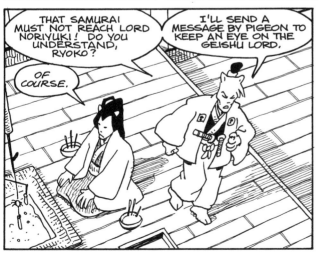

THAT SAMURAI MUST NOT REACH LORD NORIYUKI! DO YOU UNDERSTAND, RYOKO?

OF COURSE.

I'LL SEND A MESSAGE BY PIGEON TO KEEP AN EYE ON THE GEISHU LORD.

AND DESTROY THAT FISHING VILLAGE. I WANT NO ONE TO KNOW WE ARE AFTER THAT SAMURAI!

17.

119

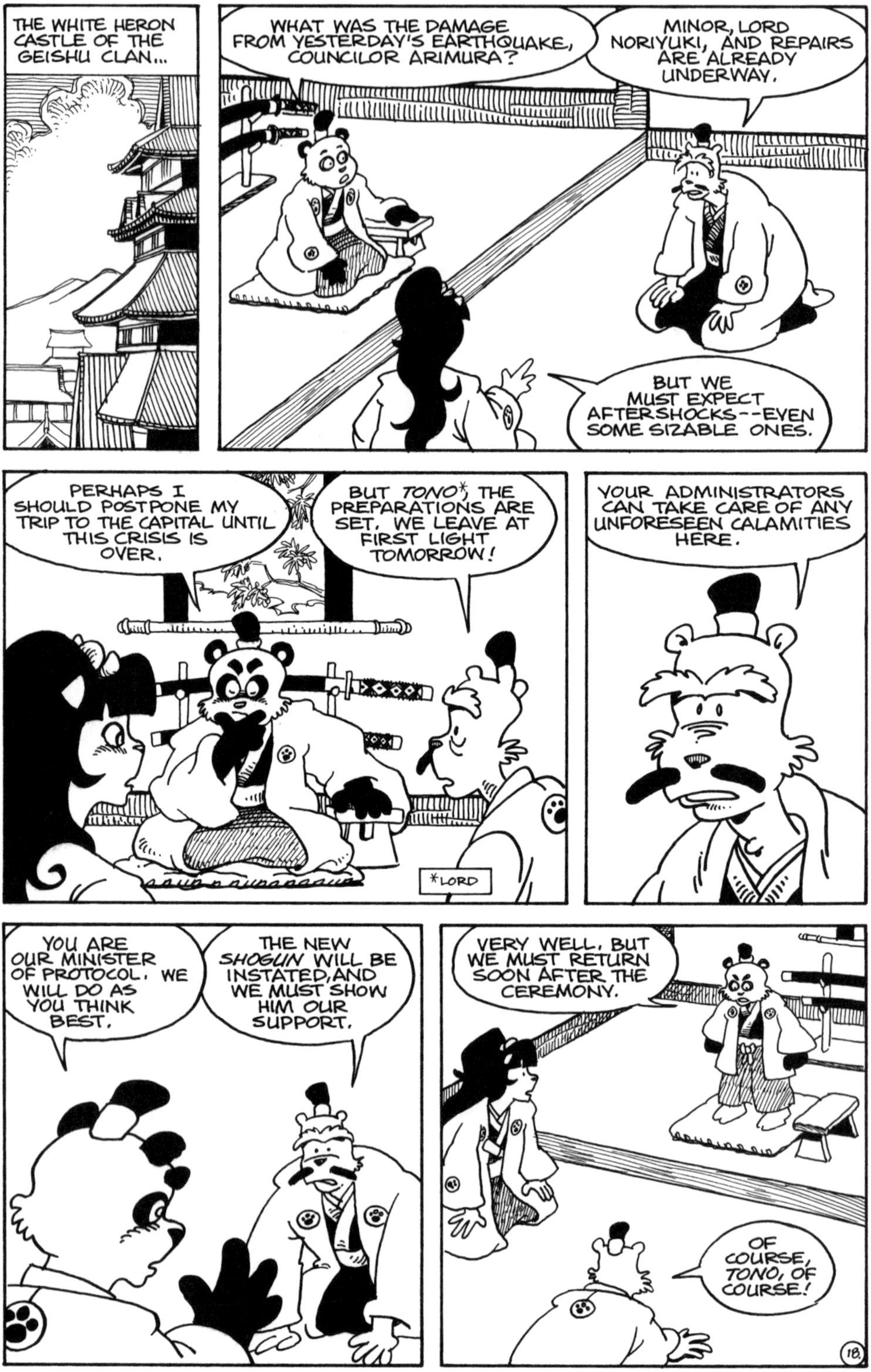
THE WHITE HERON CASTLE OF THE GEISHU CLAN...
WHAT WAS THE DAMAGE FROM YESTERDAY'S EARTHQUAKE, COUNCILOR ARIMURA?
MINOR, LORD NORIYUKI, AND REPAIRS ARE ALREADY UNDERWAY.
BUT WE MUST EXPECT AFTERSHOCKS--EVEN SOME SIZABLE ONES.
PERHAPS I SHOULD POSTPONE MY TRIP TO THE CAPITAL UNTIL THIS CRISIS IS OVER.
BUT *TONO**, THE PREPARATIONS ARE SET. WE LEAVE AT FIRST LIGHT TOMORROW!
*LORD
YOUR ADMINISTRATORS CAN TAKE CARE OF ANY UNFORESEEN CALAMITIES HERE.
YOU ARE OUR MINISTER OF PROTOCOL. WE WILL DO AS YOU THINK BEST.
THE NEW *SHOGUN* WILL BE INSTATED, AND WE MUST SHOW HIM OUR SUPPORT.
VERY WELL. BUT WE MUST RETURN SOON AFTER THE CEREMONY.
OF COURSE, *TONO*, OF COURSE!
18

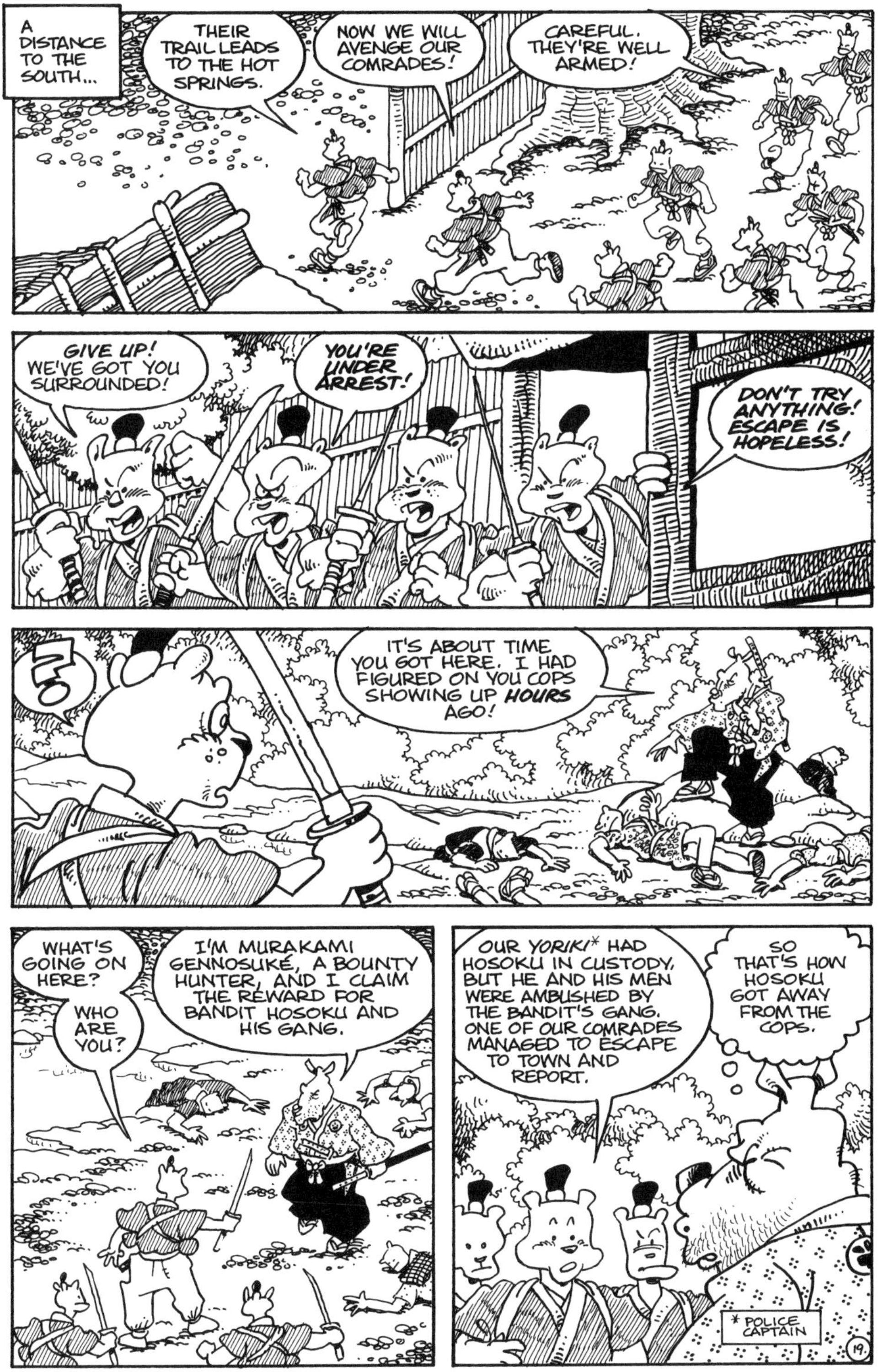
A DISTANCE TO THE SOUTH...
THEIR TRAIL LEADS TO THE HOT SPRINGS.
NOW WE WILL AVENGE OUR COMRADES!
CAREFUL. THEY'RE WELL ARMED!
GIVE UP! WE'VE GOT YOU SURROUNDED!
YOU'RE UNDER ARREST!
DON'T TRY ANYTHING! ESCAPE IS HOPELESS!
?!
IT'S ABOUT TIME YOU GOT HERE. I HAD FIGURED ON YOU COPS SHOWING UP HOURS AGO!
WHAT'S GOING ON HERE?
WHO ARE YOU?
I'M MURAKAMI GENNOSUKÉ, A BOUNTY HUNTER, AND I CLAIM THE REWARD FOR BANDIT HOSOKU AND HIS GANG.
OUR YORIKI* HAD HOSOKU IN CUSTODY, BUT HE AND HIS MEN WERE AMBUSHED BY THE BANDIT'S GANG. ONE OF OUR COMRADES MANAGED TO ESCAPE TO TOWN AND REPORT.
SO THAT'S HOW HOSOKU GOT AWAY FROM THE COPS.
*POLICE CAPTAIN
19.

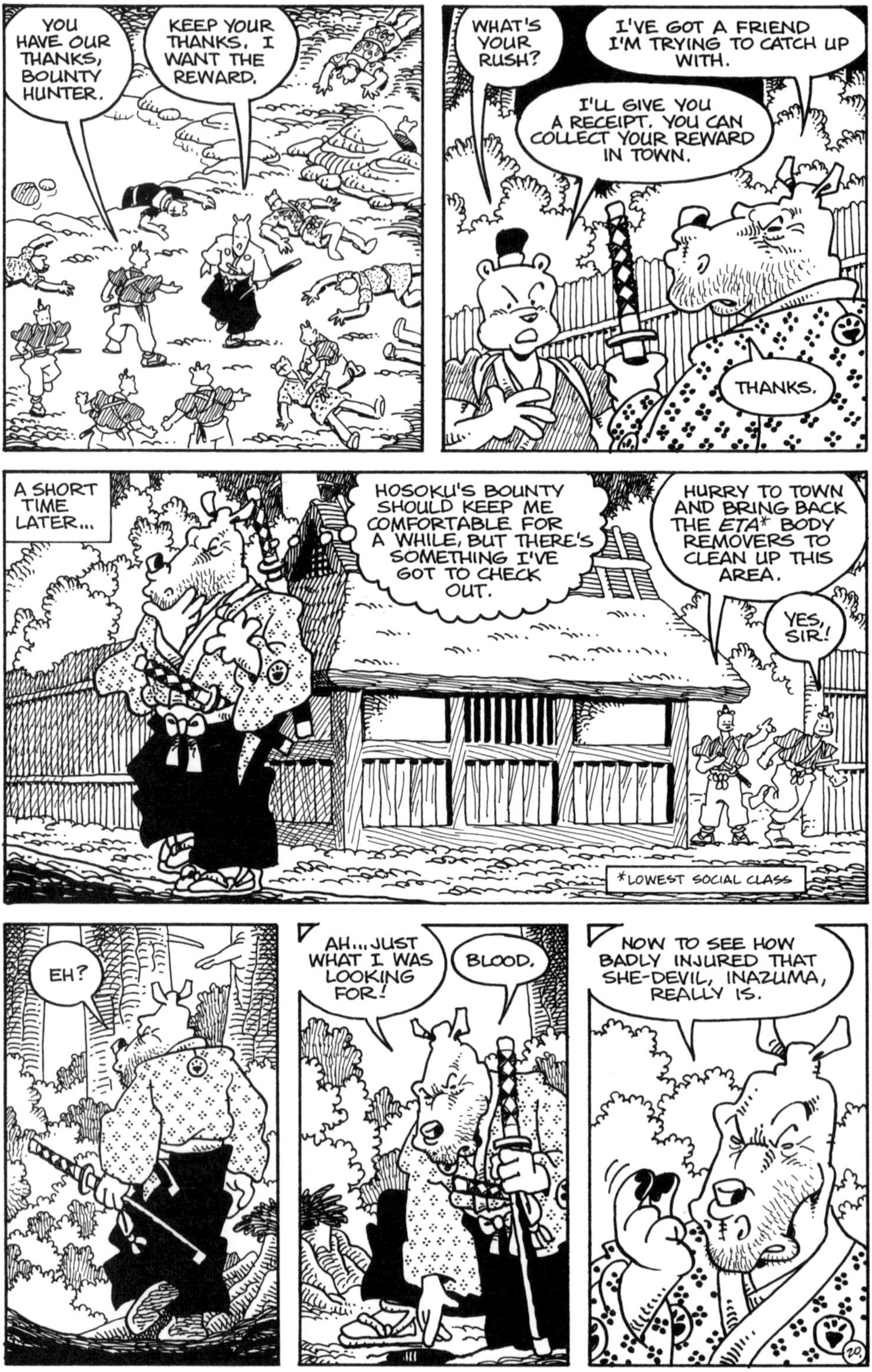
YOU HAVE OUR THANKS, BOUNTY HUNTER.
KEEP YOUR THANKS. I WANT THE REWARD.
WHAT'S YOUR RUSH?
I'VE GOT A FRIEND I'M TRYING TO CATCH UP WITH.
I'LL GIVE YOU A RECEIPT. YOU CAN COLLECT YOUR REWARD IN TOWN.
THANKS.
A SHORT TIME LATER...
HOSOKU'S BOUNTY SHOULD KEEP ME COMFORTABLE FOR A WHILE, BUT THERE'S SOMETHING I'VE GOT TO CHECK OUT.
HURRY TO TOWN AND BRING BACK THE *ETA** BODY REMOVERS TO CLEAN UP THIS AREA.
YES, SIR!
*LOWEST SOCIAL CLASS
EH?
AH...JUST WHAT I WAS LOOKING FOR!
BLOOD.
NOW TO SEE HOW BADLY INJURED THAT SHE-DEVIL, INAZUMA, REALLY IS.
20.

SHE'S STAGGERING HERE. I SHOULD COME ACROSS HER BODY SOON.
WHAT'S THIS?
TWO NEW SETS OF FOOTPRINTS-- AN ADULT AND A CHILD. SHE WAS DISCOVERED, CARRIED AWAY.
MAYBE I CAN TALK THEM INTO SPLITTING THE REWARD WITH ME.
EH?
SOUNDS LIKE FIGHTING!
COULD BE SOMEONE ELSE IS AFTER MY REWARD!
!
STOP! WHAT DO YOU WANT WITH ME?
21.

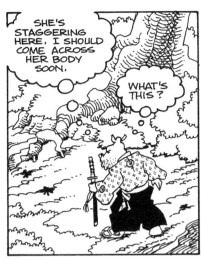

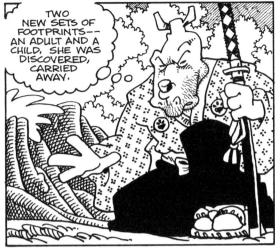

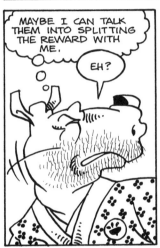

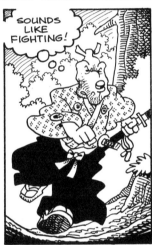

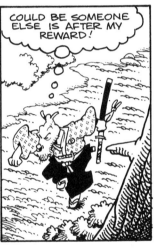

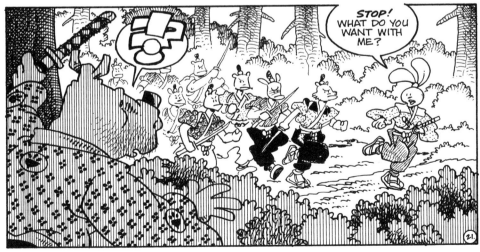

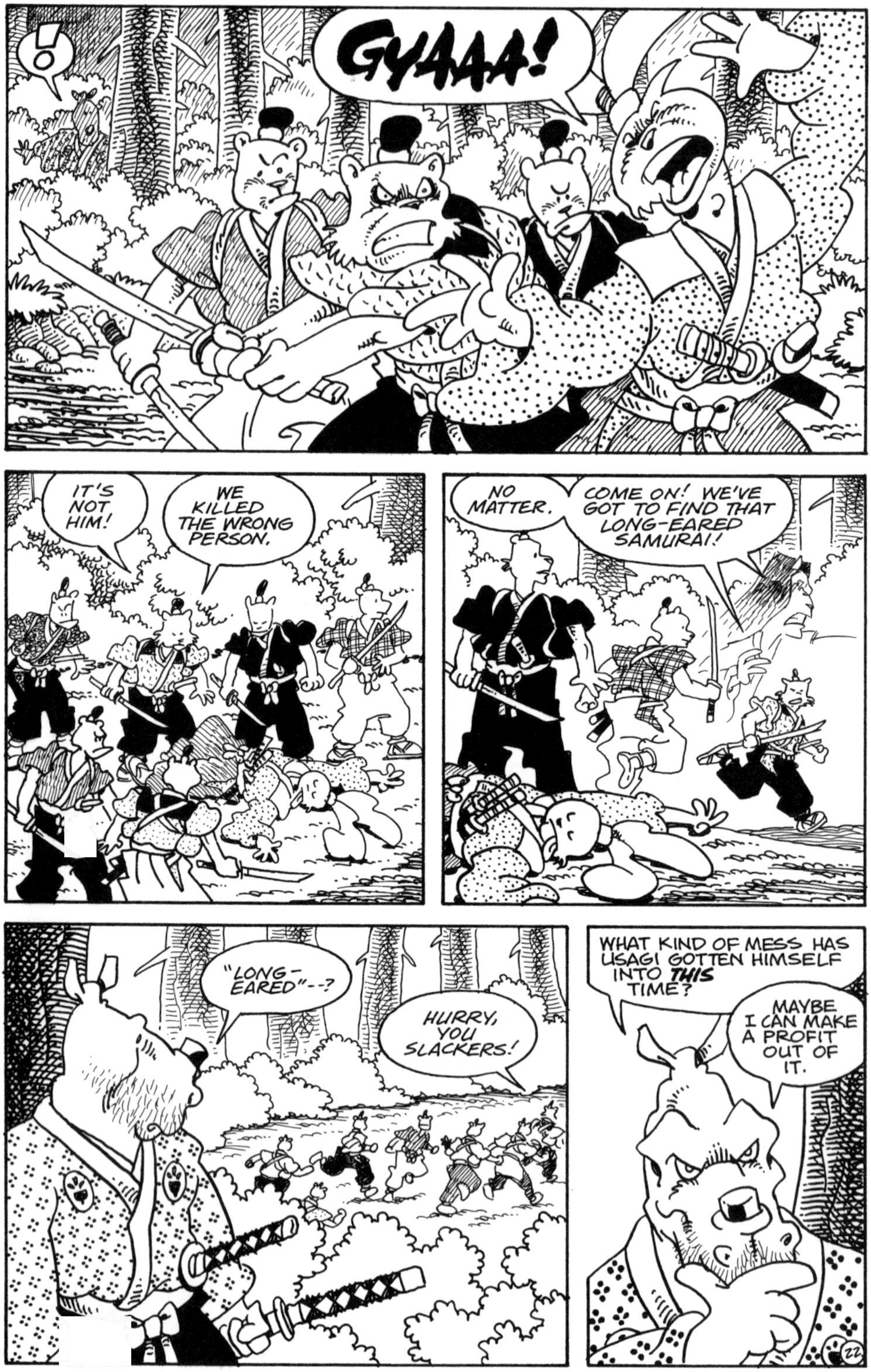
!
GYAAA!
IT'S NOT HIM!
WE KILLED THE WRONG PERSON.
NO MATTER.
COME ON! WE'VE GOT TO FIND THAT LONG-EARED SAMURAI!
"LONG-EARED"--?
HURRY, YOU SLACKERS!
WHAT KIND OF MESS HAS USAGI GOTTEN HIMSELF INTO THIS TIME?
MAYBE I CAN MAKE A PROFIT OUT OF IT.
22

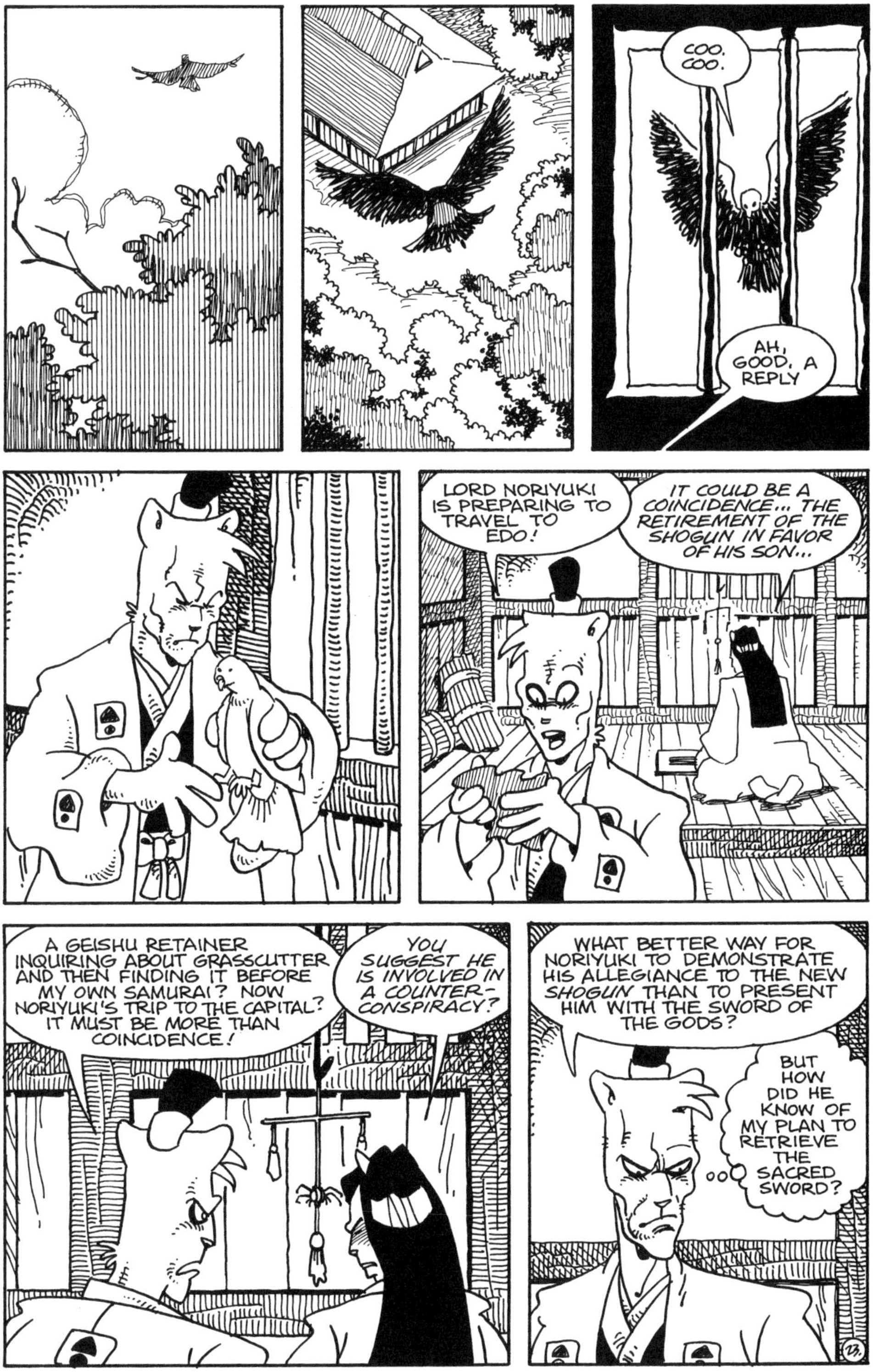

COO. COO.
AH, GOOD, A REPLY
LORD NORIYUKI IS PREPARING TO TRAVEL TO EDO!
IT COULD BE A COINCIDENCE... THE RETIREMENT OF THE SHOGUN IN FAVOR OF HIS SON...
A GEISHU RETAINER INQUIRING ABOUT GRASSCUTTER AND THEN FINDING IT BEFORE MY OWN SAMURAI? NOW NORIYUKI'S TRIP TO THE CAPITAL? IT MUST BE MORE THAN COINCIDENCE!
YOU SUGGEST HE IS INVOLVED IN A COUNTER-CONSPIRACY?
WHAT BETTER WAY FOR NORIYUKI TO DEMONSTRATE HIS ALLEGIANCE TO THE NEW SHOGUN THAN TO PRESENT HIM WITH THE SWORD OF THE GODS?
BUT HOW DID HE KNOW OF MY PLAN TO RETRIEVE THE SACRED SWORD?
23.

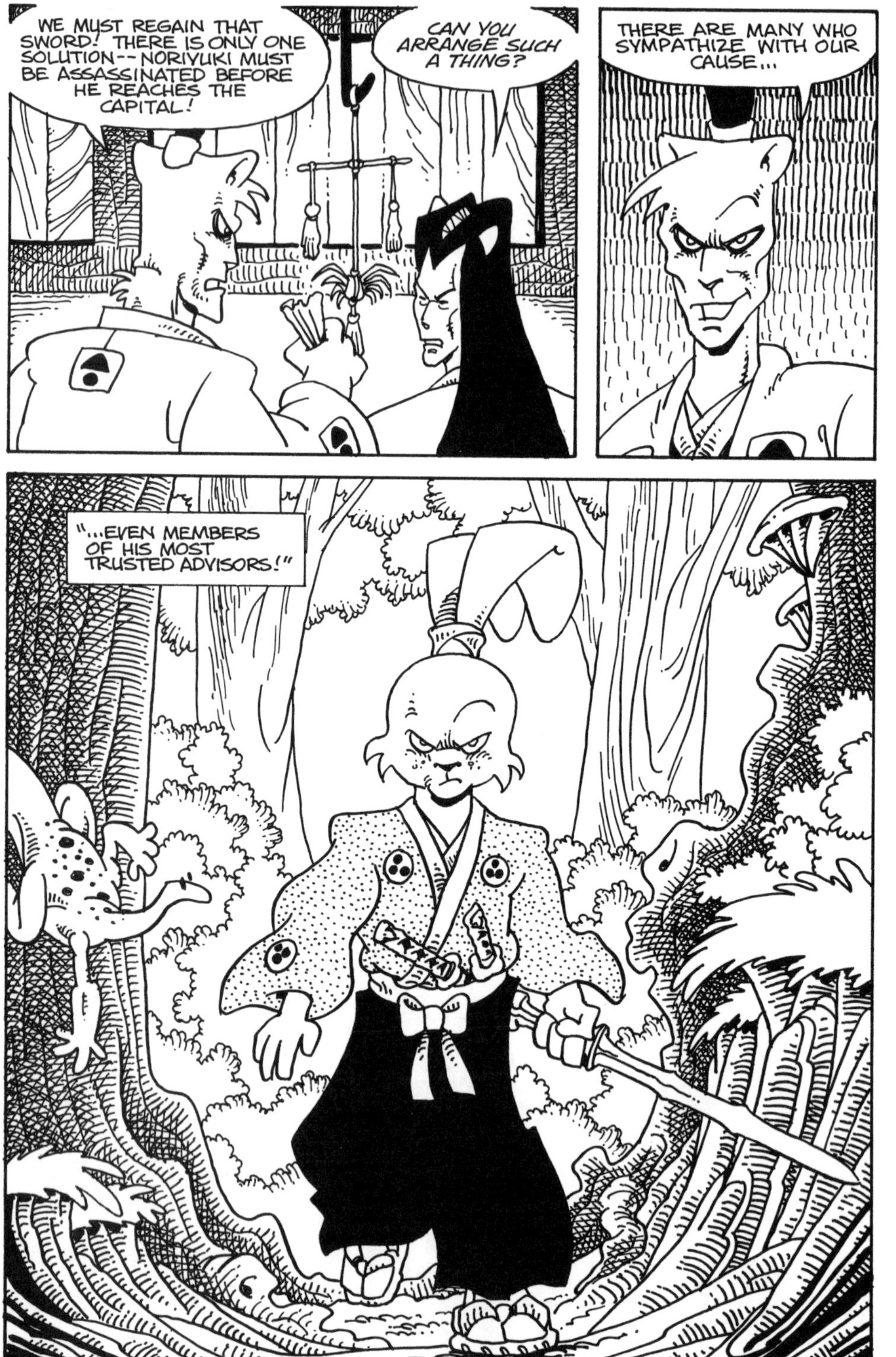
WE MUST REGAIN THAT SWORD! THERE IS ONLY ONE SOLUTION-- NORIYUKI MUST BE ASSASSINATED BEFORE HE REACHES THE CAPITAL!
CAN YOU ARRANGE SUCH A THING?
THERE ARE MANY WHO SYMPATHIZE WITH OUR CAUSE...
"...EVEN MEMBERS OF HIS MOST TRUSTED ADVISORS!"

END OF CHAPTER 3

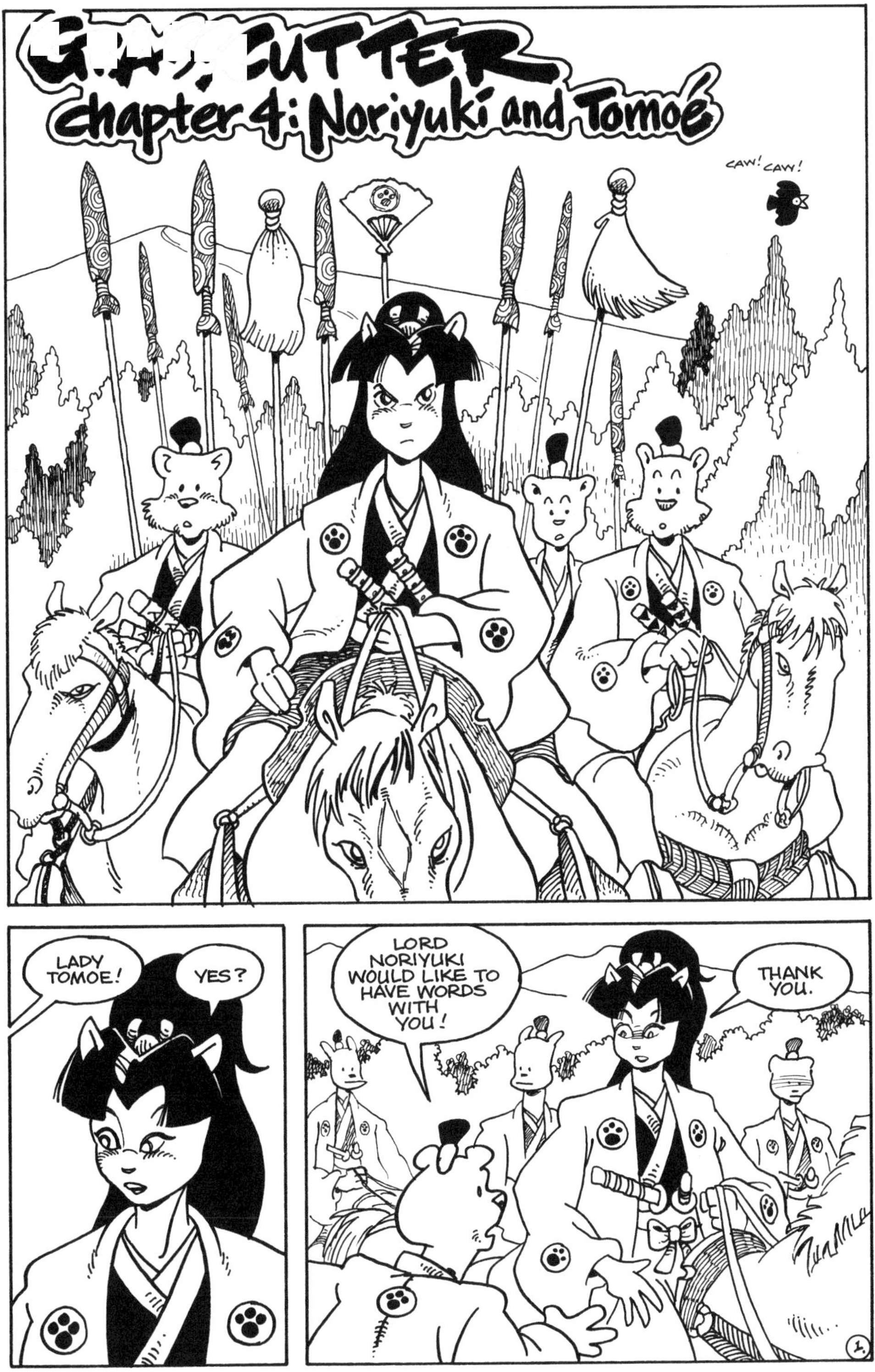
CUTTER
chapter 4: Noriyuki and Tomoé
CAW! CAW!
LADY TOMOE!
YES?
LORD NORIYUKI WOULD LIKE TO HAVE WORDS WITH YOU!
THANK YOU.
1.

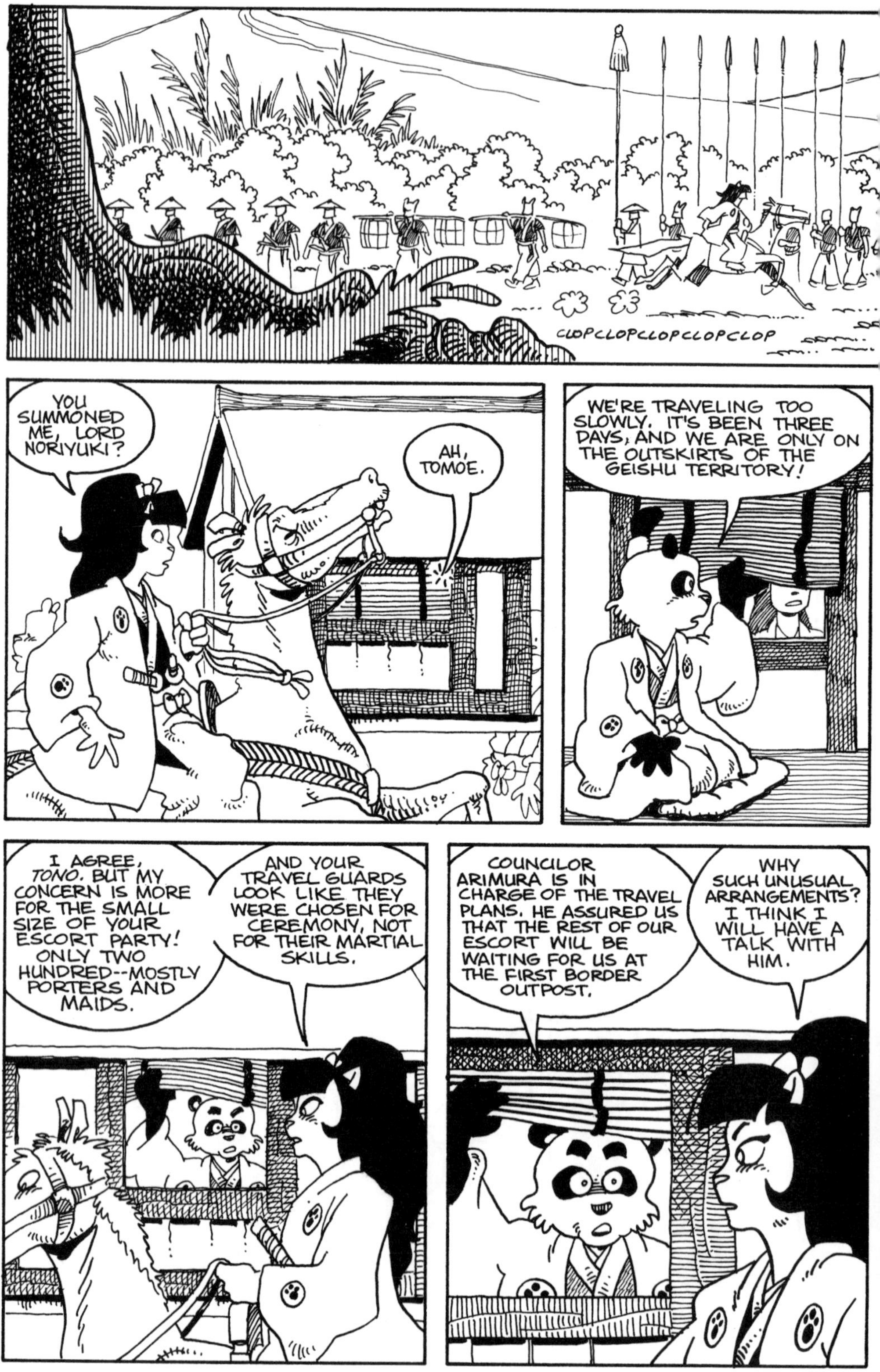
CLOPCLOPCLOPCLOPCLOP
YOU SUMMONED ME, LORD NORIYUKI?
AH, TOMOE.
WE'RE TRAVELING TOO SLOWLY. IT'S BEEN THREE DAYS, AND WE ARE ONLY ON THE OUTSKIRTS OF THE GEISHU TERRITORY!
I AGREE, *TONO*. BUT MY CONCERN IS MORE FOR THE SMALL SIZE OF YOUR ESCORT PARTY! ONLY TWO HUNDRED--MOSTLY PORTERS AND MAIDS.
AND YOUR TRAVEL GUARDS LOOK LIKE THEY WERE CHOSEN FOR CEREMONY, NOT FOR THEIR MARTIAL SKILLS.
COUNCILOR ARIMURA IS IN CHARGE OF THE TRAVEL PLANS. HE ASSURED US THAT THE REST OF OUR ESCORT WILL BE WAITING FOR US AT THE FIRST BORDER OUTPOST.
WHY SUCH UNUSUAL ARRANGEMENTS? I THINK I WILL HAVE A TALK WITH HIM.

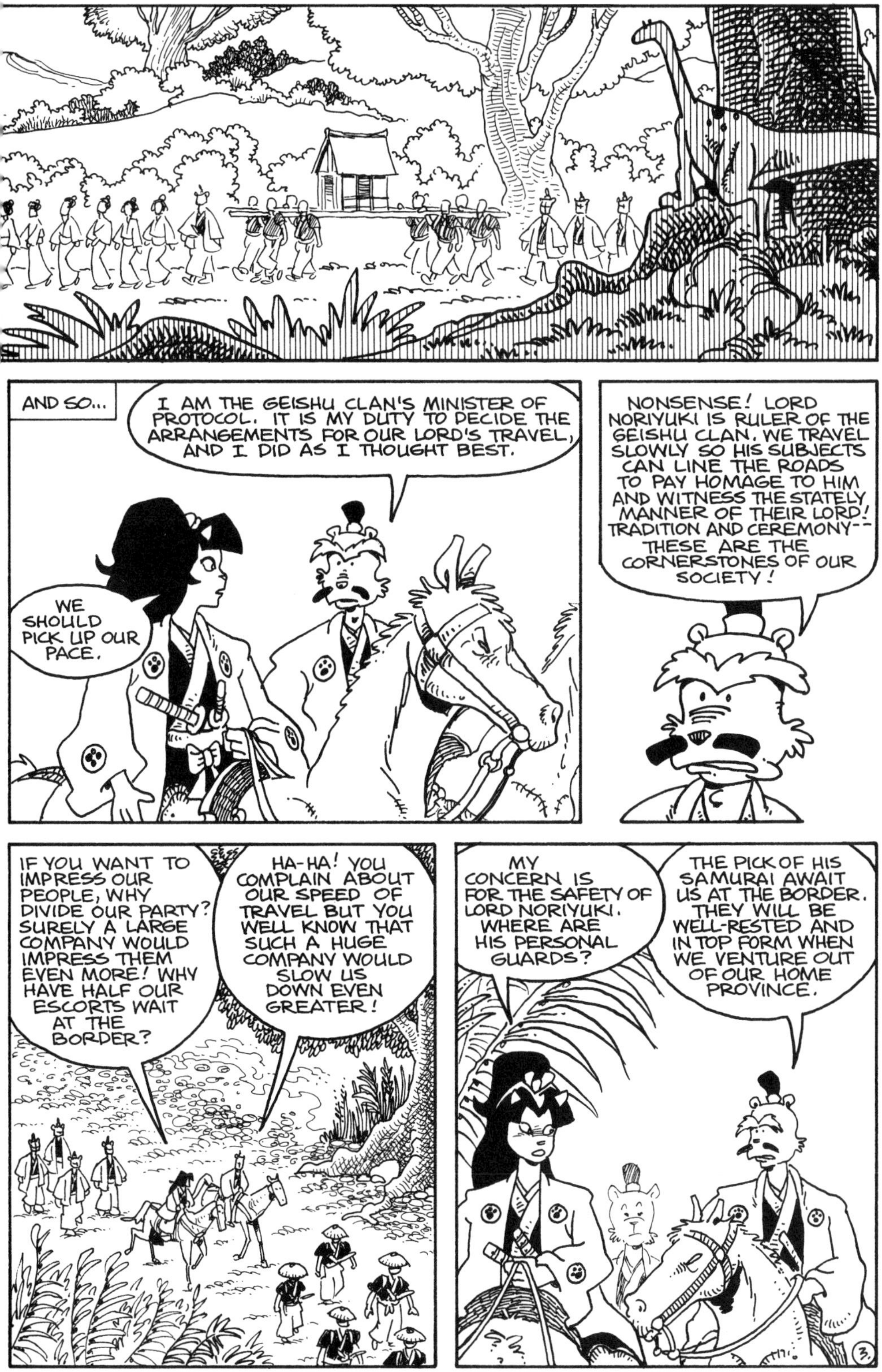
AND SO...
I AM THE GEISHU CLAN'S MINISTER OF PROTOCOL. IT IS MY DUTY TO DECIDE THE ARRANGEMENTS FOR OUR LORD'S TRAVEL, AND I DID AS I THOUGHT BEST.
WE SHOULD PICK UP OUR PACE.
NONSENSE! LORD NORIYUKI IS RULER OF THE GEISHU CLAN. WE TRAVEL SLOWLY SO HIS SUBJECTS CAN LINE THE ROADS TO PAY HOMAGE TO HIM AND WITNESS THE STATELY MANNER OF THEIR LORD! TRADITION AND CEREMONY-- THESE ARE THE CORNERSTONES OF OUR SOCIETY!
IF YOU WANT TO IMPRESS OUR PEOPLE, WHY DIVIDE OUR PARTY? SURELY A LARGE COMPANY WOULD IMPRESS THEM EVEN MORE! WHY HAVE HALF OUR ESCORTS WAIT AT THE BORDER?
HA-HA! YOU COMPLAIN ABOUT OUR SPEED OF TRAVEL BUT YOU WELL KNOW THAT SUCH A HUGE COMPANY WOULD SLOW US DOWN EVEN GREATER!
MY CONCERN IS FOR THE SAFETY OF LORD NORIYUKI. WHERE ARE HIS PERSONAL GUARDS?
THE PICK OF HIS SAMURAI AWAIT US AT THE BORDER. THEY WILL BE WELL-RESTED AND IN TOP FORM WHEN WE VENTURE OUT OF OUR HOME PROVINCE.
3.

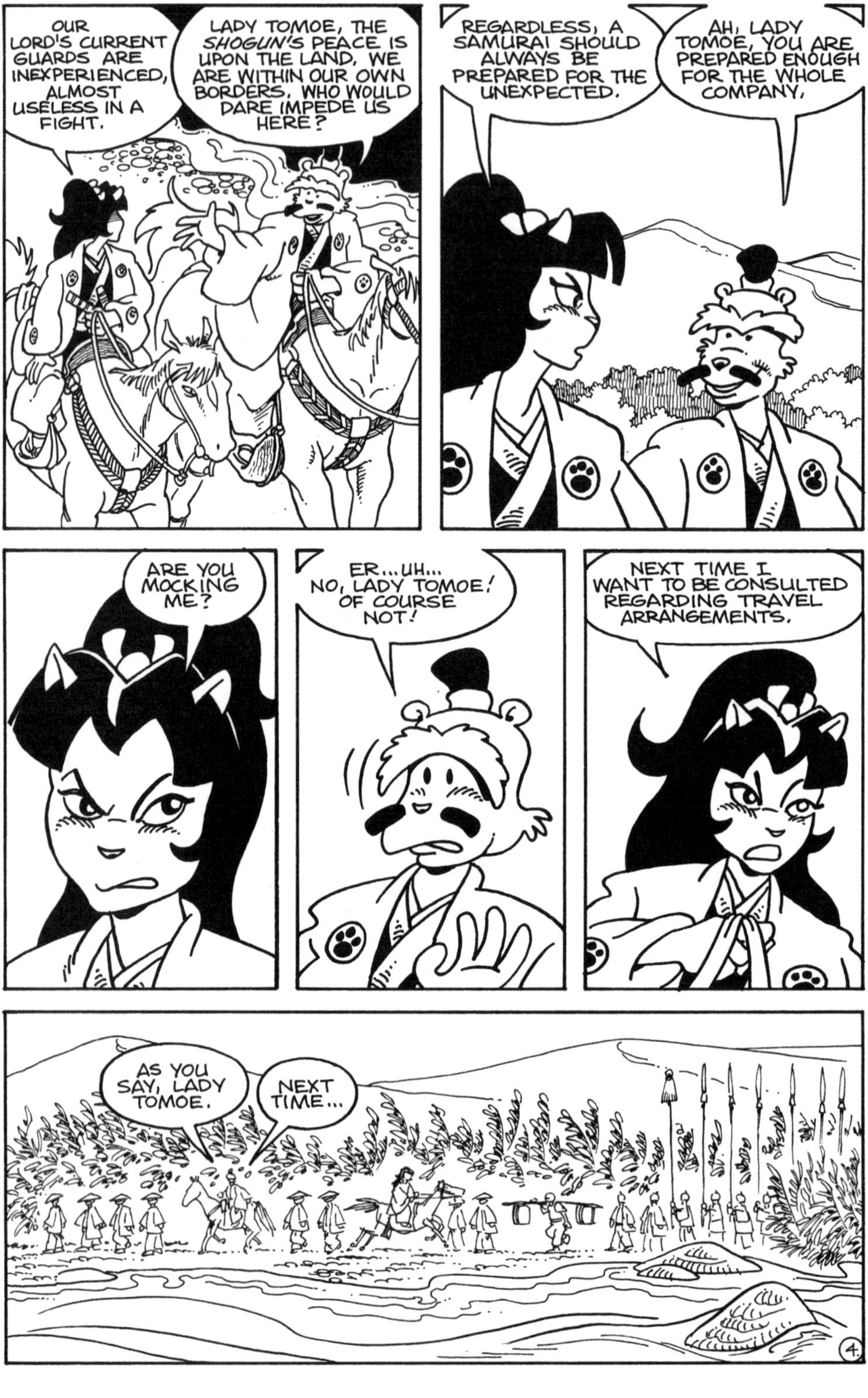
OUR LORD'S CURRENT GUARDS ARE INEXPERIENCED, ALMOST USELESS IN A FIGHT.
LADY TOMOE, THE *SHOGUN'S* PEACE IS UPON THE LAND. WE ARE WITHIN OUR OWN BORDERS. WHO WOULD DARE IMPEDE US HERE?
REGARDLESS, A SAMURAI SHOULD ALWAYS BE PREPARED FOR THE UNEXPECTED.
AH, LADY TOMOE, YOU ARE PREPARED ENOUGH FOR THE WHOLE COMPANY.
ARE YOU MOCKING ME?
ER...UH... NO, LADY TOMOE! OF COURSE NOT!
NEXT TIME I WANT TO BE CONSULTED REGARDING TRAVEL ARRANGEMENTS.
AS YOU SAY, LADY TOMOE.
NEXT TIME...
4.

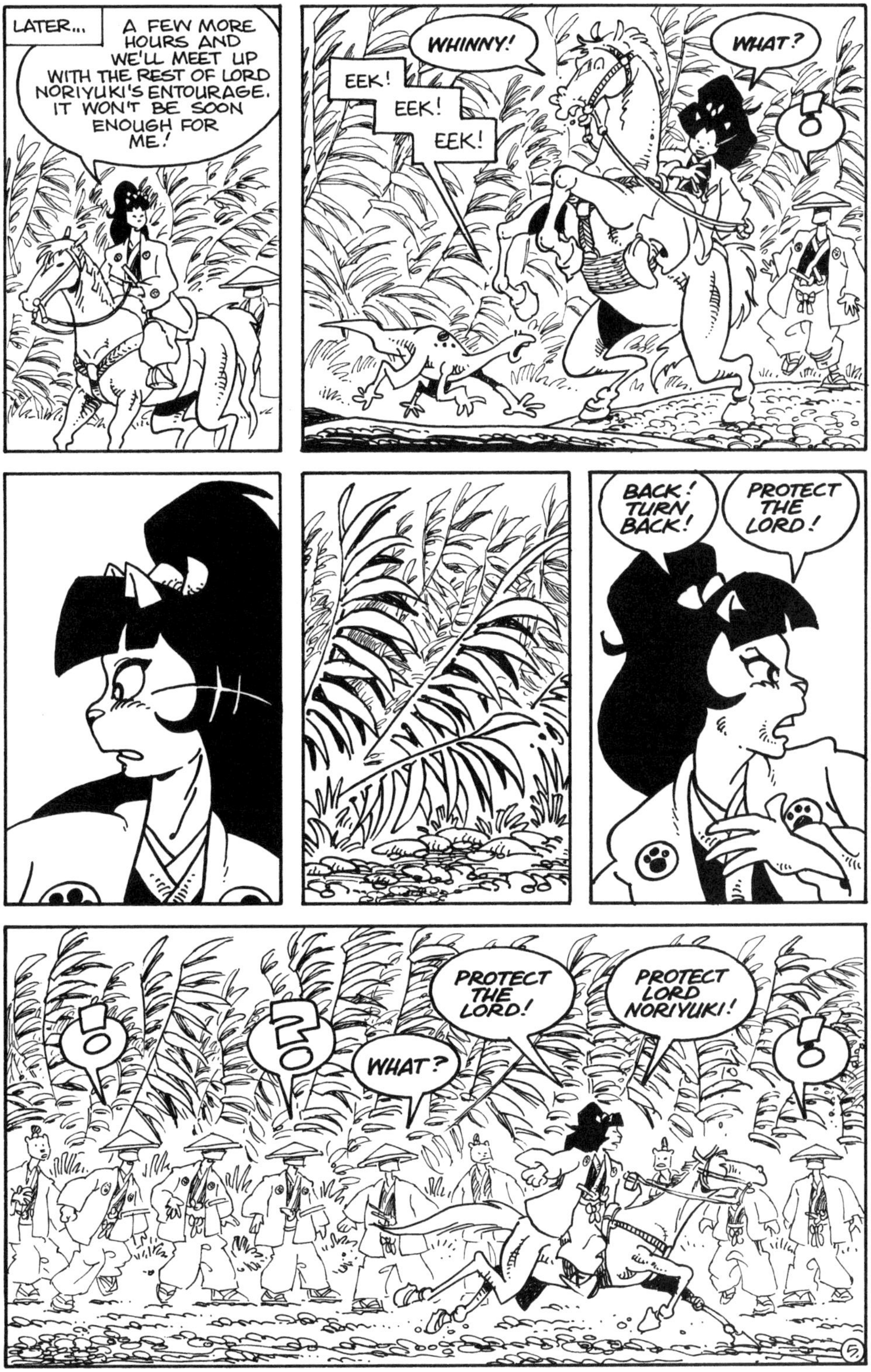
LATER...
A FEW MORE HOURS AND WE'LL MEET UP WITH THE REST OF LORD NORIYUKI'S ENTOURAGE. IT WON'T BE SOON ENOUGH FOR ME!
EEK! EEK! EEK!
WHINNY!
WHAT?
!
BACK! TURN BACK!
PROTECT THE LORD!
!
?!
WHAT?
PROTECT THE LORD!
PROTECT LORD NORIYUKI!
!
5

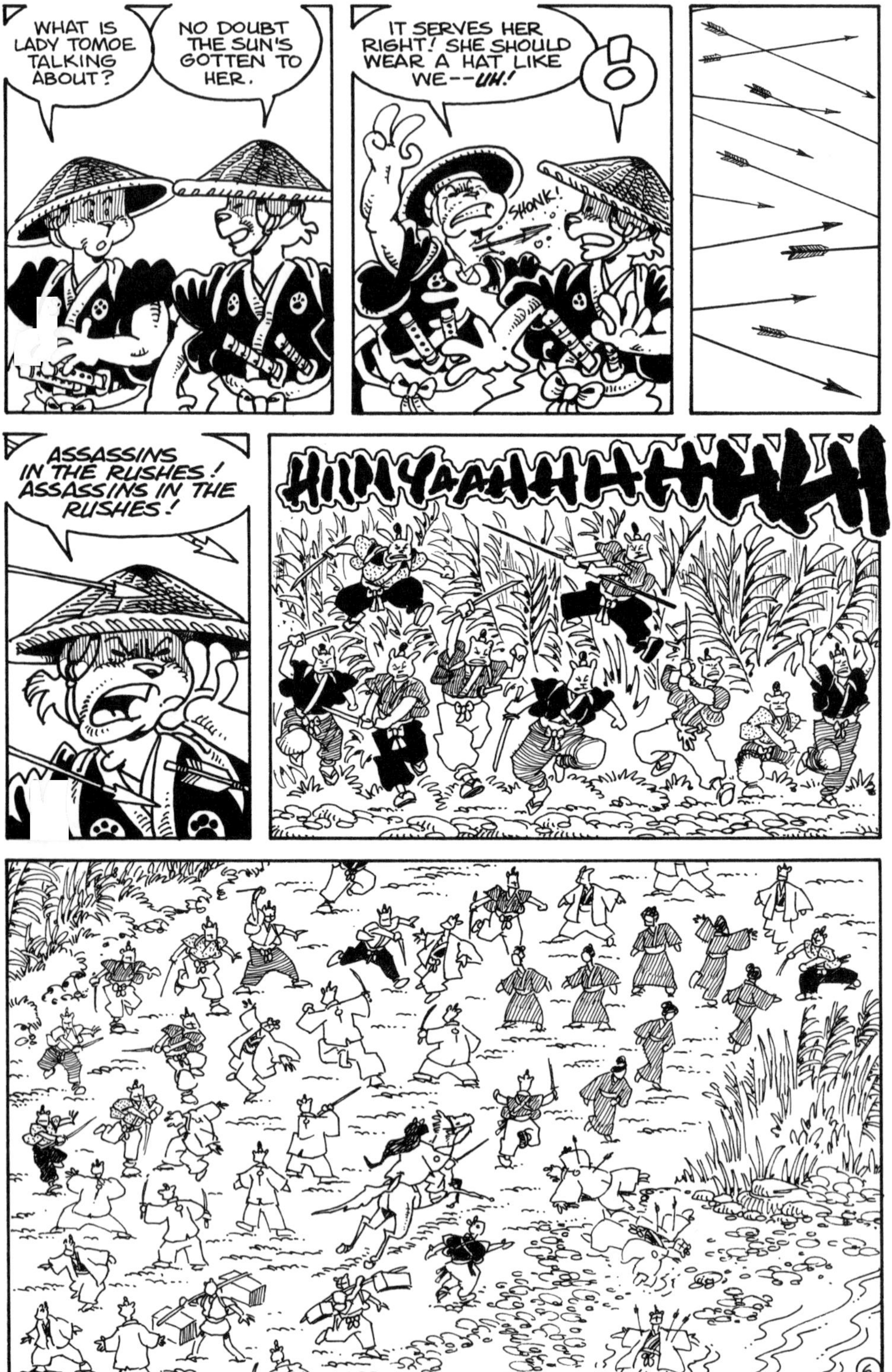
WHAT IS LADY TOMOE TALKING ABOUT?
NO DOUBT THE SUN'S GOTTEN TO HER.
IT SERVES HER RIGHT! SHE SHOULD WEAR A HAT LIKE WE--UH!
SHONK!
!
ASSASSINS IN THE RUSHES! ASSASSINS IN THE RUSHES!
HIIIYAAHHHHHHHH!
6.

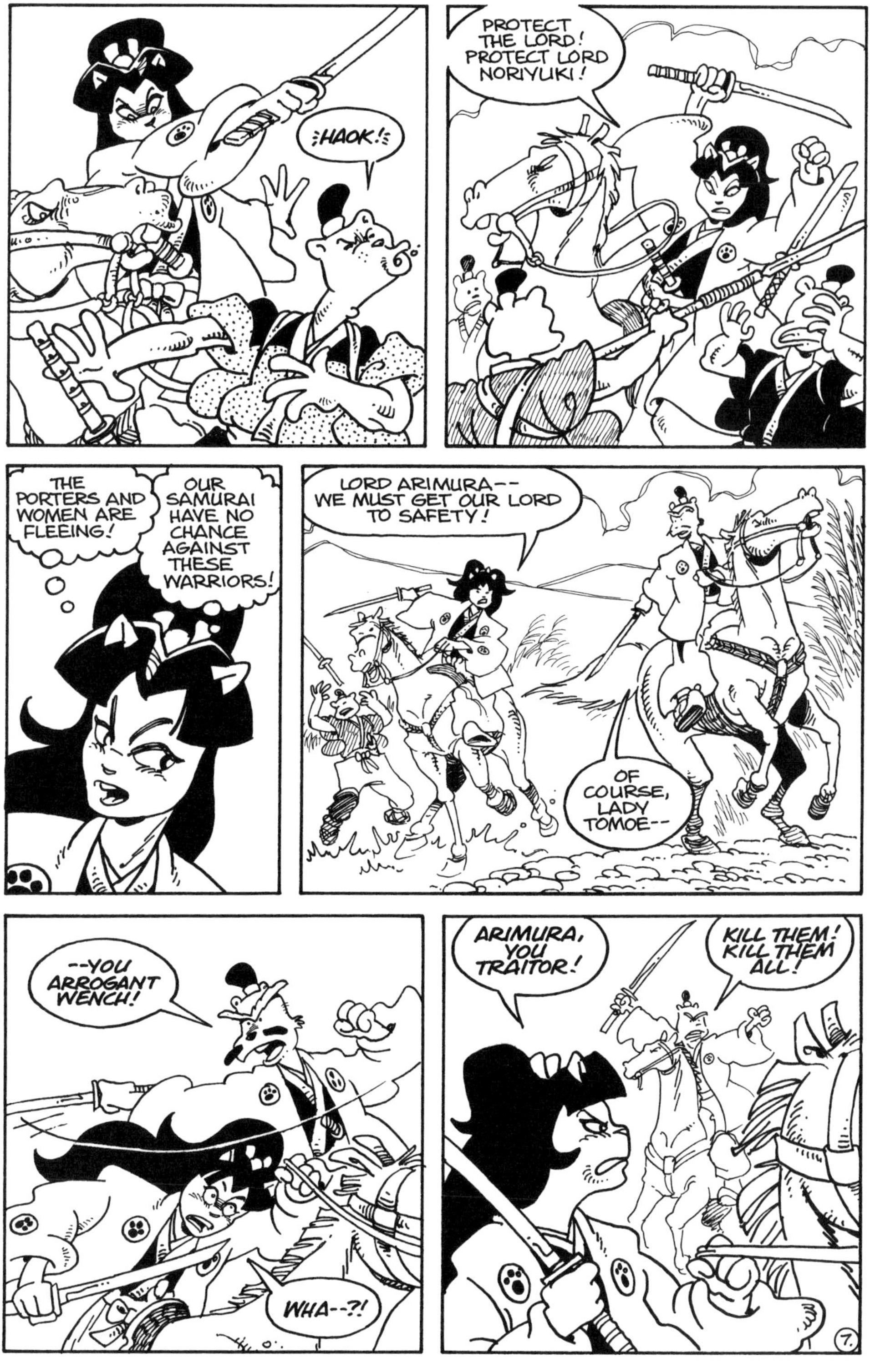

¡HAOK!¡
PROTECT THE LORD! PROTECT LORD NORIYUKI!
THE PORTERS AND WOMEN ARE FLEEING!
OUR SAMURAI HAVE NO CHANCE AGAINST THESE WARRIORS!
LORD ARIMURA-- WE MUST GET OUR LORD TO SAFETY!
OF COURSE, LADY TOMOE--
--YOU ARROGANT WENCH!
WHA--?!
ARIMURA, YOU TRAITOR!
KILL THEM! KILL THEM ALL!
7.

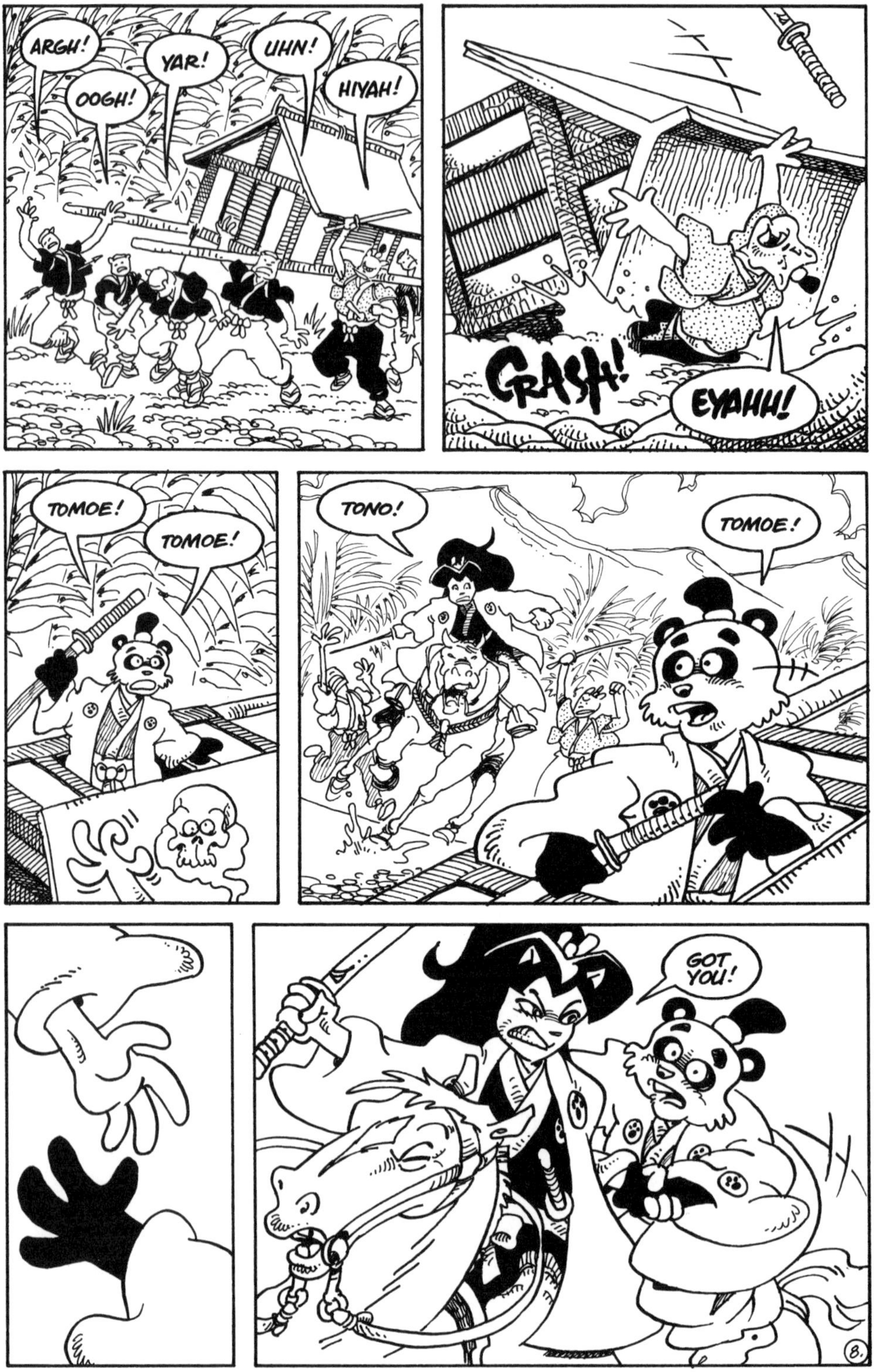
ARGH!
OOGH!
YAR!
UHN!
HIYAH!
CRASH!
EYAHH!
TOMOE!
TOMOE!
TONO!
TOMOE!
GOT YOU!
8.

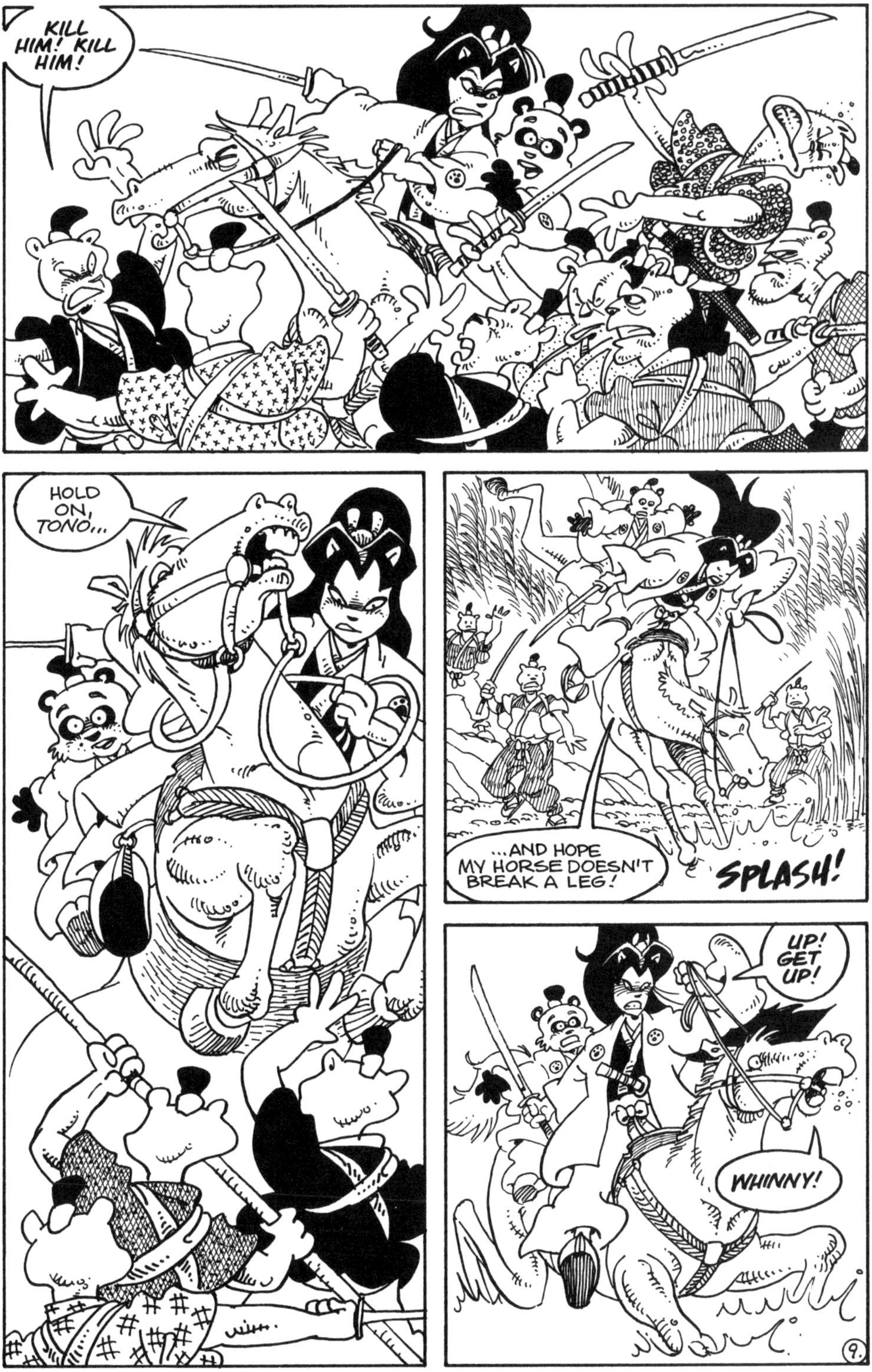
KILL HIM! KILL HIM!
HOLD ON, TONO...
...AND HOPE MY HORSE DOESN'T BREAK A LEG!
SPLASH!
UP! GET UP!
WHINNY!

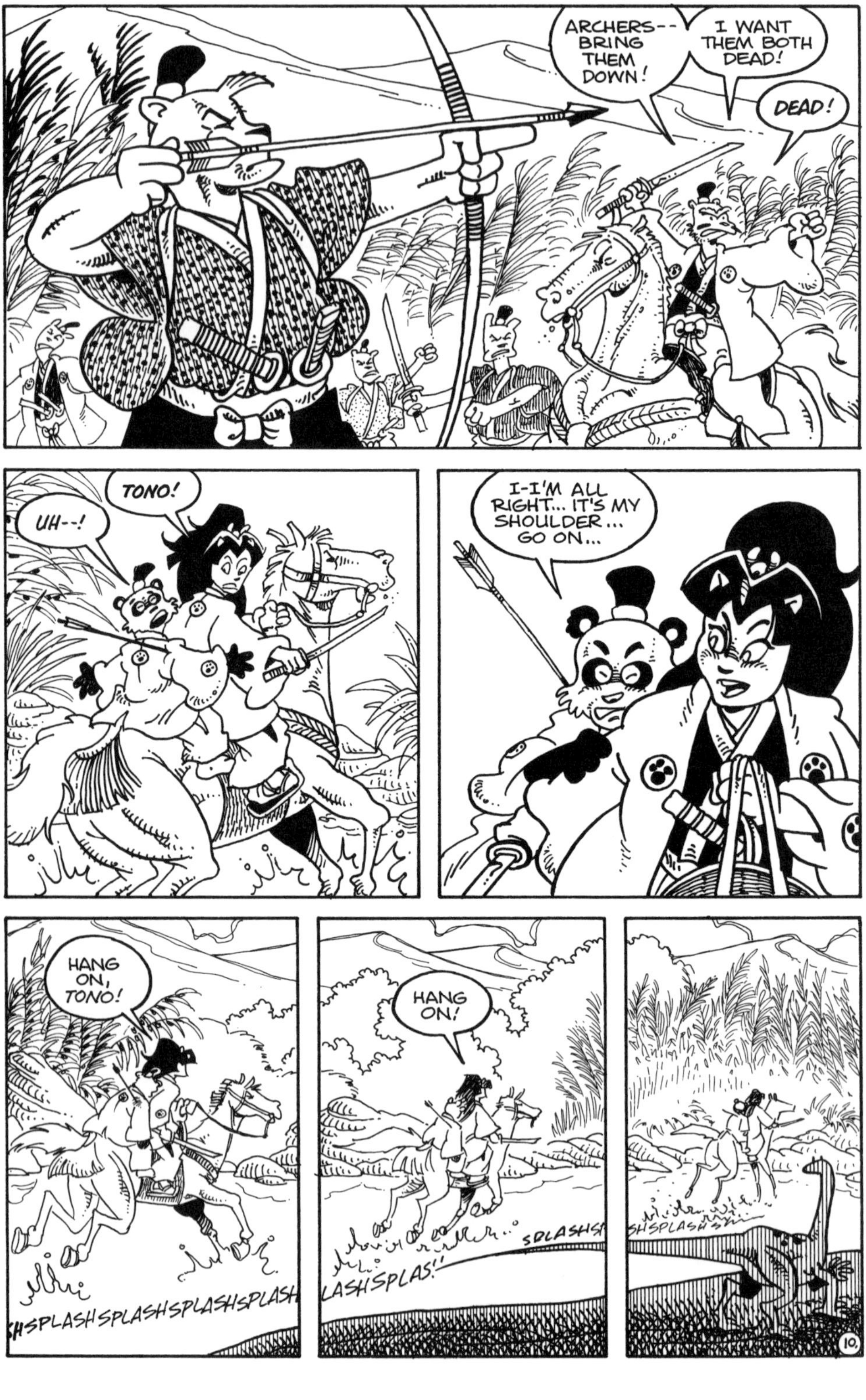
ARCHERS-- BRING THEM DOWN!
I WANT THEM BOTH DEAD!
DEAD!
UH--!
TONO!
I-I'M ALL RIGHT... IT'S MY SHOULDER... GO ON...
HANG ON, TONO!
SHSPLASHSPLASHSPLASHSPLASH
HANG ON!
LASHSPLAS!
SPLASHSP
SHSPLASHSP
10

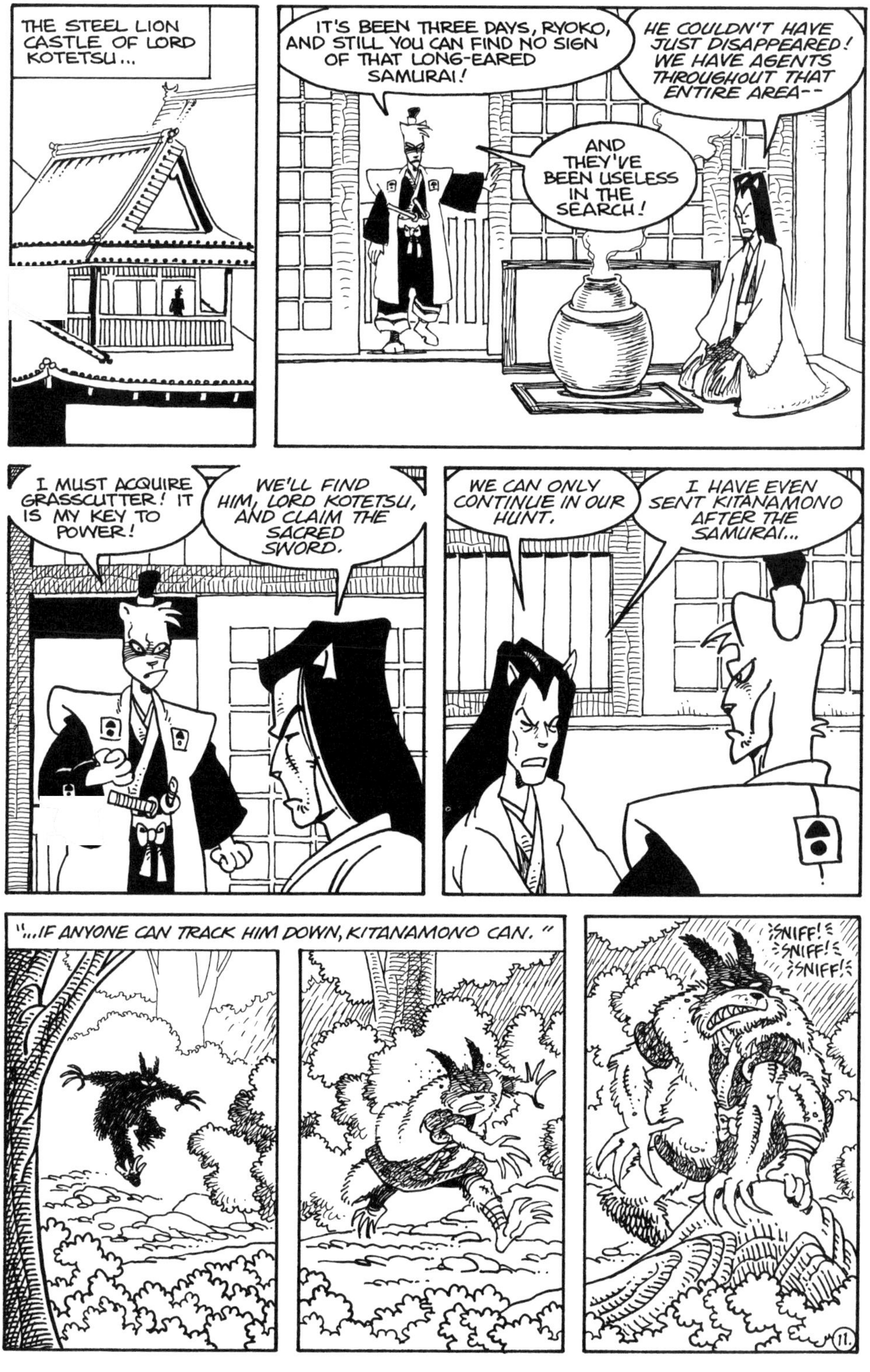

THE STEEL LION CASTLE OF LORD KOTETSU...
IT'S BEEN THREE DAYS, RYOKO, AND STILL YOU CAN FIND NO SIGN OF THAT LONG-EARED SAMURAI!
HE COULDN'T HAVE JUST DISAPPEARED! WE HAVE AGENTS THROUGHOUT THAT ENTIRE AREA--
AND THEY'VE BEEN USELESS IN THE SEARCH!
I MUST ACQUIRE GRASSCUTTER! IT IS MY KEY TO POWER!
WE'LL FIND HIM, LORD KOTETSU, AND CLAIM THE SACRED SWORD.
WE CAN ONLY CONTINUE IN OUR HUNT.
I HAVE EVEN SENT KITANAMONO AFTER THE SAMURAI...
"...IF ANYONE CAN TRACK HIM DOWN, KITANAMONO CAN."
SNIFF! SNIFF! SNIFF!
11.

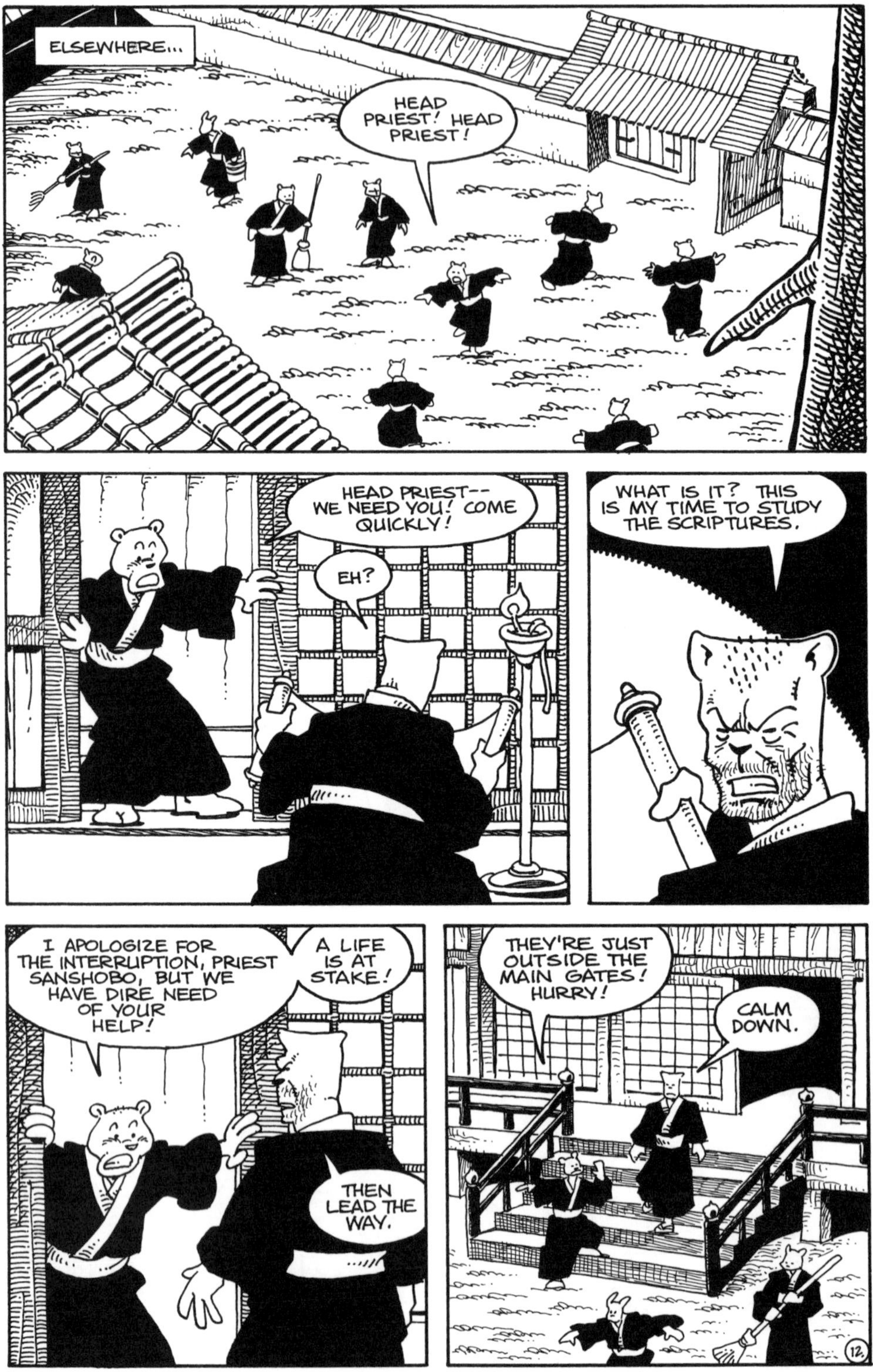
ELSEWHERE...
HEAD PRIEST! HEAD PRIEST!
HEAD PRIEST-- WE NEED YOU! COME QUICKLY!
EH?
WHAT IS IT? THIS IS MY TIME TO STUDY THE SCRIPTURES.
I APOLOGIZE FOR THE INTERRUPTION, PRIEST SANSHOBO, BUT WE HAVE DIRE NEED OF YOUR HELP!
A LIFE IS AT STAKE!
THEN LEAD THE WAY.
THEY'RE JUST OUTSIDE THE MAIN GATES! HURRY!
CALM DOWN.
12

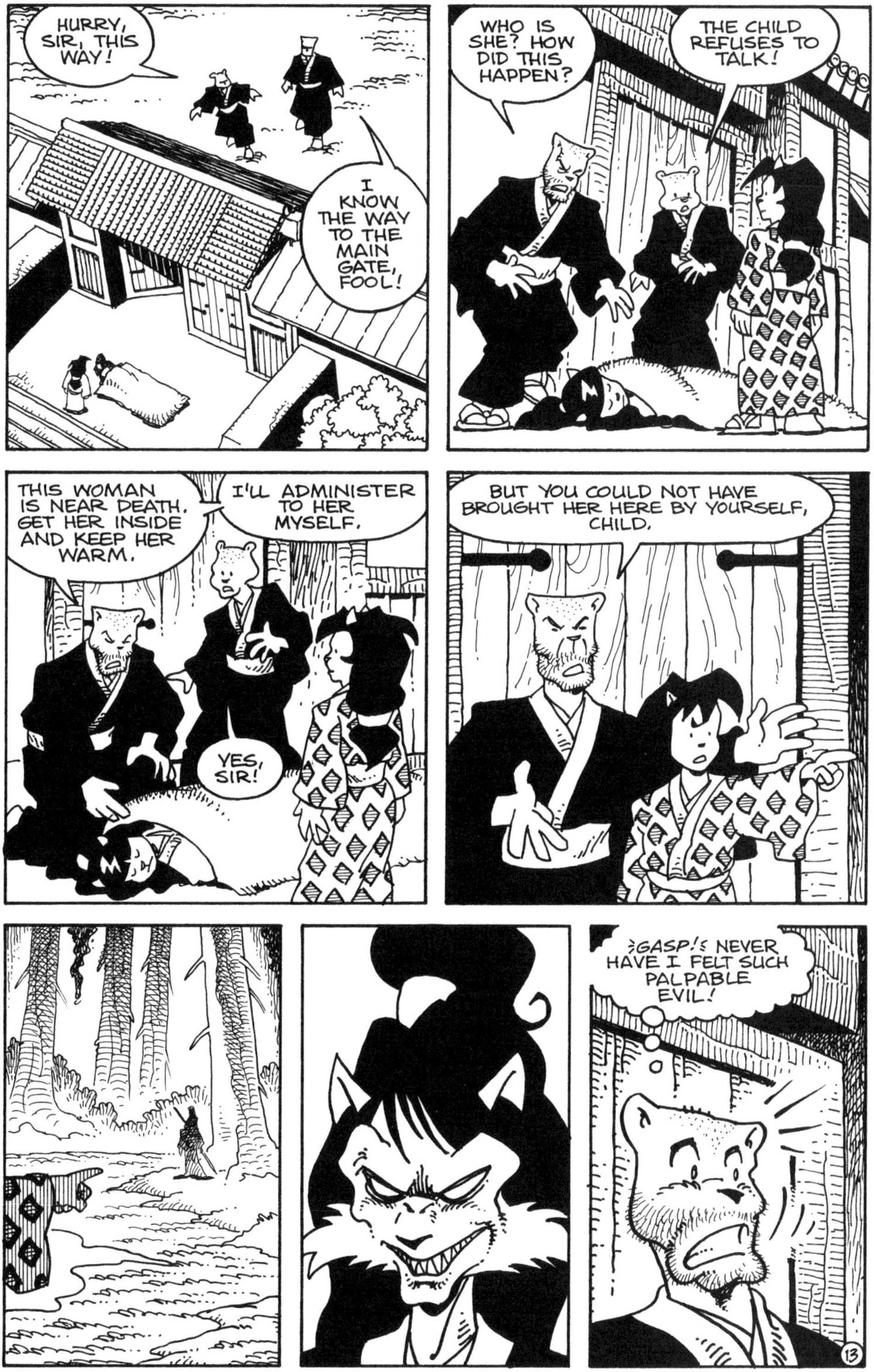
HURRY, SIR, THIS WAY!
I KNOW THE WAY TO THE MAIN GATE, FOOL!
WHO IS SHE? HOW DID THIS HAPPEN?
THE CHILD REFUSES TO TALK!
THIS WOMAN IS NEAR DEATH. GET HER INSIDE AND KEEP HER WARM.
I'LL ADMINISTER TO HER MYSELF.
YES, SIR!
BUT YOU COULD NOT HAVE BROUGHT HER HERE BY YOURSELF, CHILD.
GASP! NEVER HAVE I FELT SUCH PALPABLE EVIL!
13

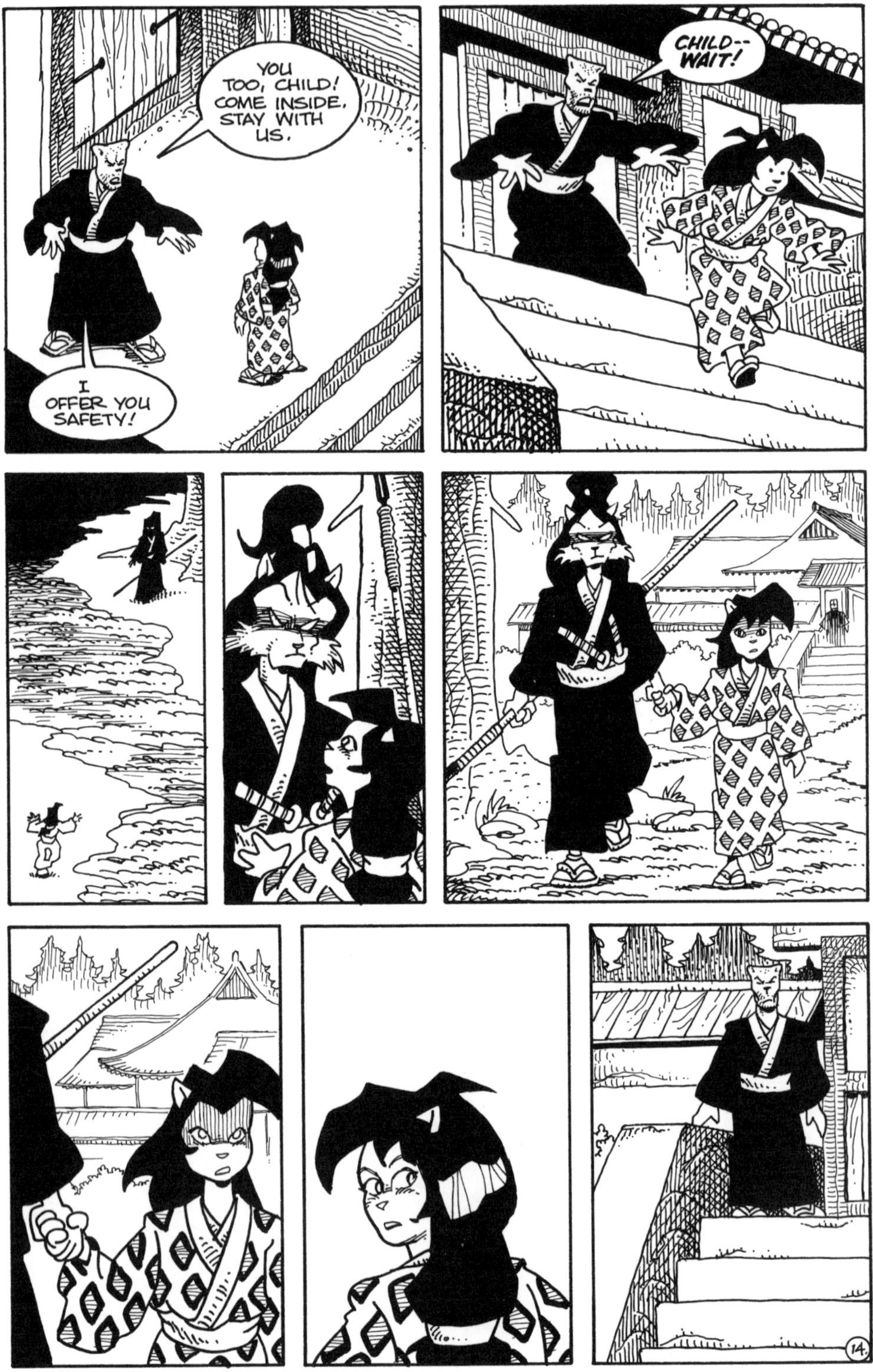
YOU TOO, CHILD! COME INSIDE, STAY WITH US.
I OFFER YOU SAFETY!
CHILD-- WAIT!
14.

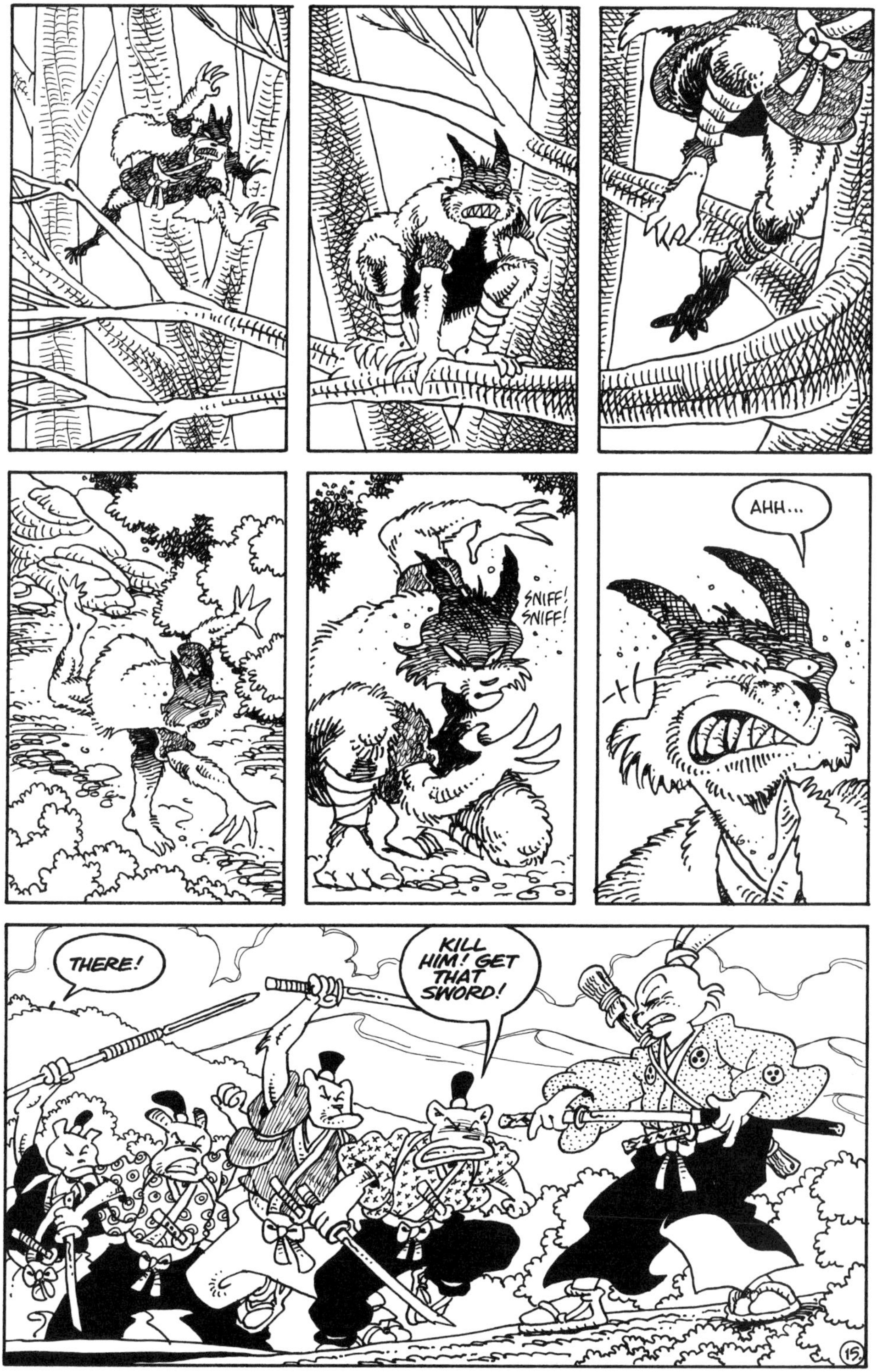
SNIFF! SNIFF!
AHH...
THERE!
KILL HIM! GET THAT SWORD!
15

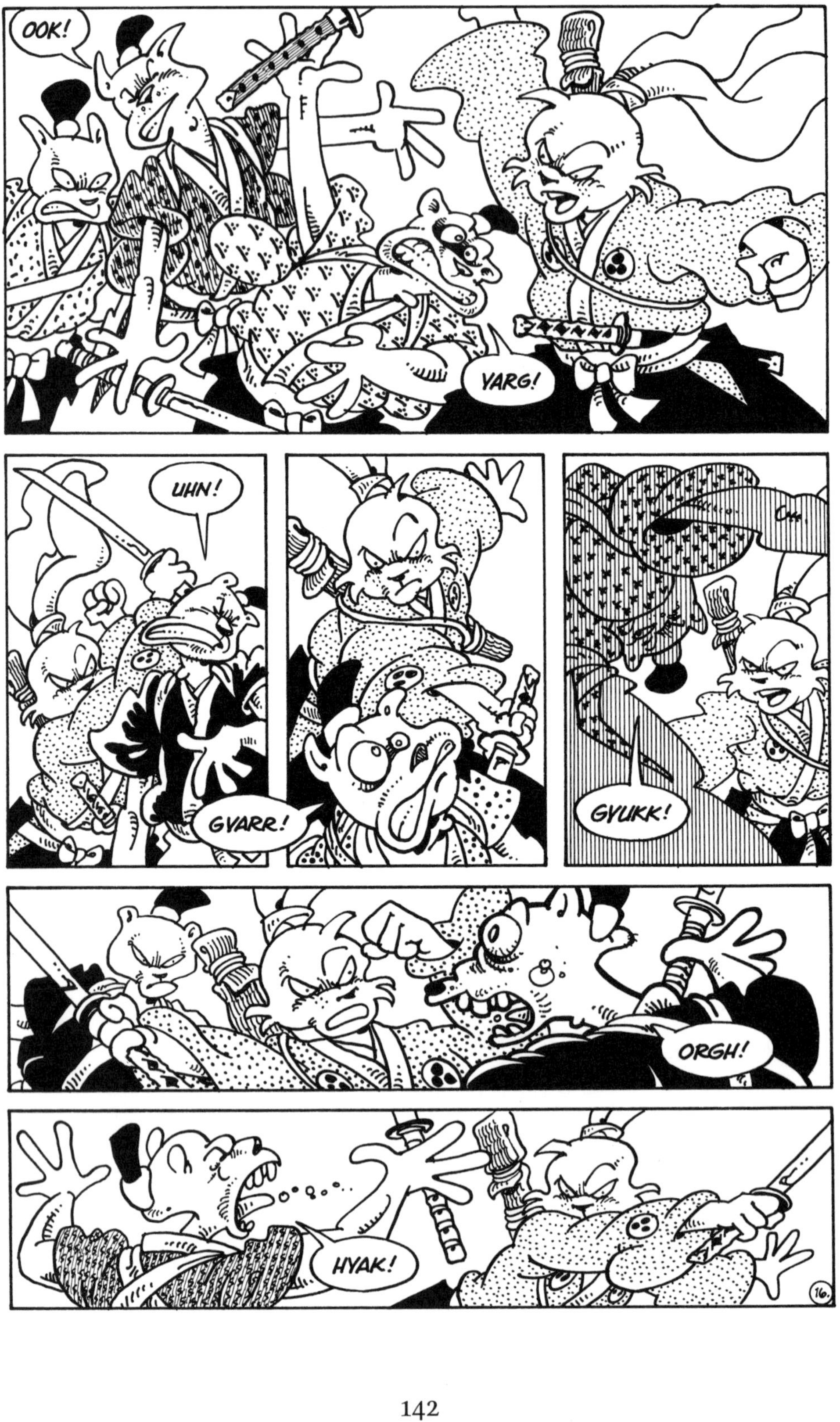
OOK!
YARG!
UHN!
GVARR!
GYUKK!
ORGH!
HYAK!
16.

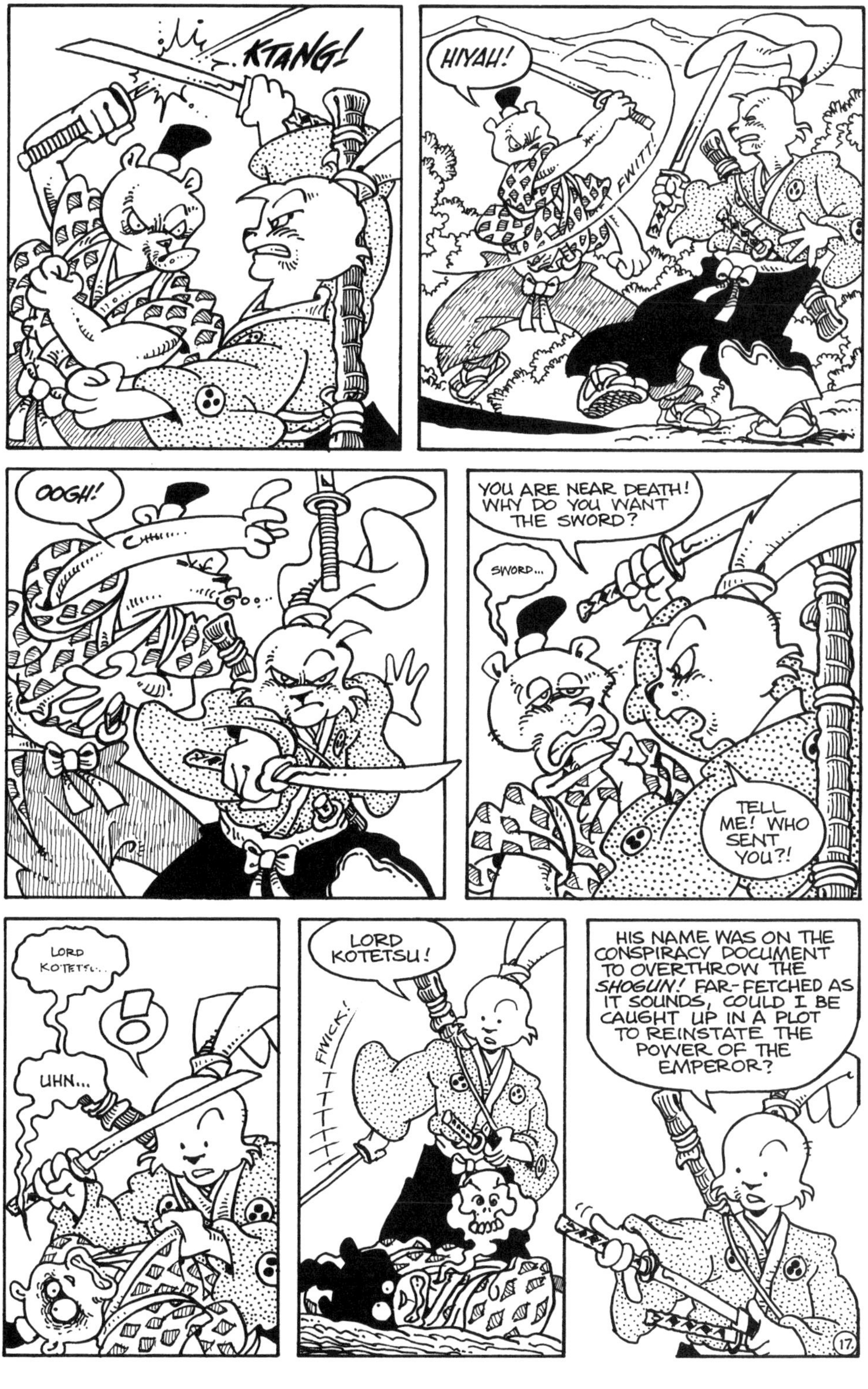

KTANG!
HIYAH!
FWITT!
OOGH!
YOU ARE NEAR DEATH! WHY DO YOU WANT THE SWORD?
SWORD...
TELL ME! WHO SENT YOU?!
LORD KOTETSU...
UHN...
LORD KOTETSU!
FWICK!
HIS NAME WAS ON THE CONSPIRACY DOCUMENT TO OVERTHROW THE *SHOGUN!* FAR-FETCHED AS IT SOUNDS, COULD I BE CAUGHT UP IN A PLOT TO REINSTATE THE POWER OF THE EMPEROR?
17

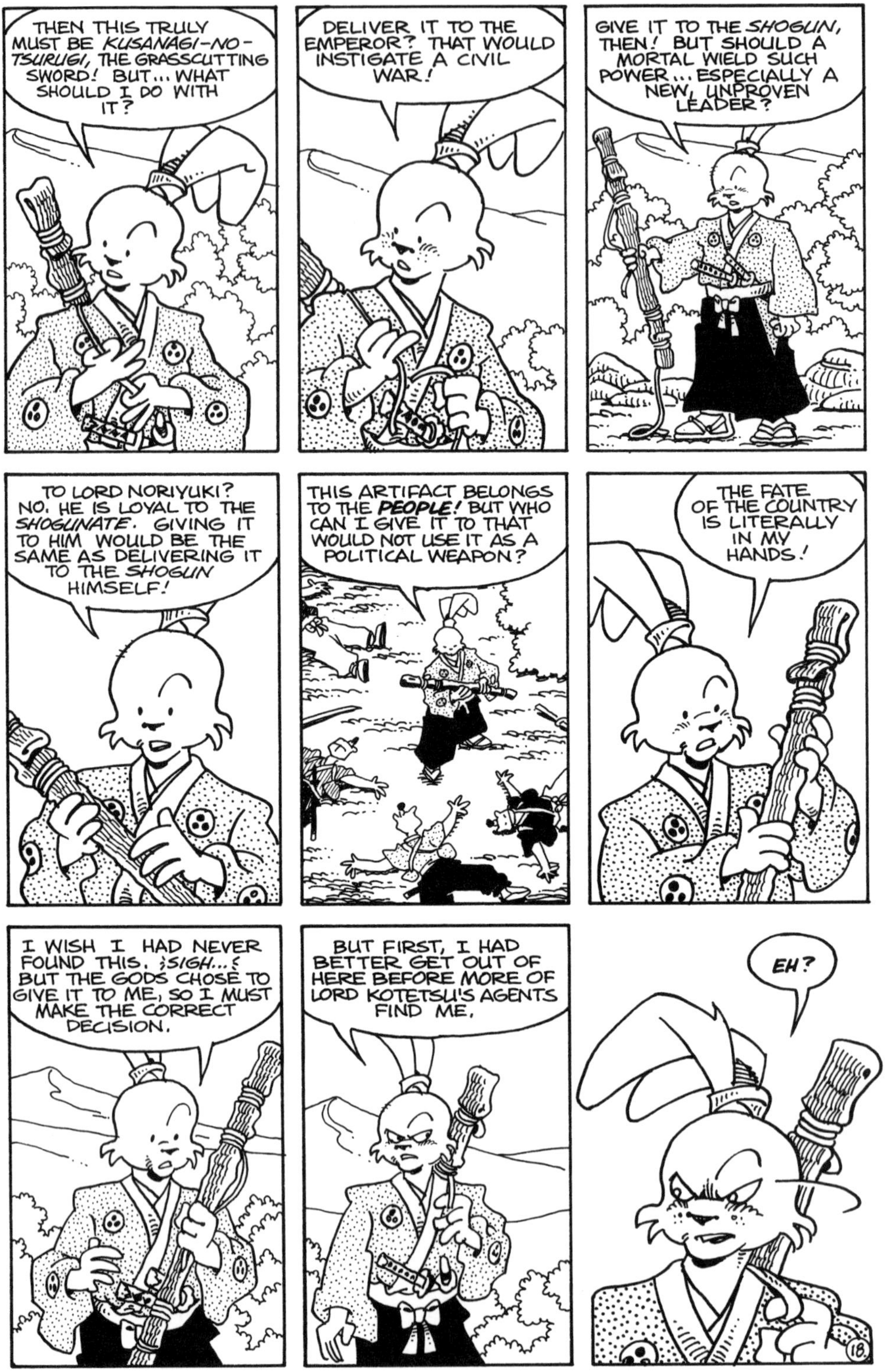
THEN THIS TRULY MUST BE KUSANAGI-NO-TSURUGI, THE GRASSCUTTING SWORD! BUT... WHAT SHOULD I DO WITH IT?
DELIVER IT TO THE EMPEROR? THAT WOULD INSTIGATE A CIVIL WAR!
GIVE IT TO THE SHOGUN, THEN! BUT SHOULD A MORTAL WIELD SUCH POWER... ESPECIALLY A NEW, UNPROVEN LEADER?
TO LORD NORIYUKI? NO. HE IS LOYAL TO THE SHOGUNATE. GIVING IT TO HIM WOULD BE THE SAME AS DELIVERING IT TO THE SHOGUN HIMSELF!
THIS ARTIFACT BELONGS TO THE PEOPLE! BUT WHO CAN I GIVE IT TO THAT WOULD NOT USE IT AS A POLITICAL WEAPON?
THE FATE OF THE COUNTRY IS LITERALLY IN MY HANDS!
I WISH I HAD NEVER FOUND THIS. ;SIGH...; BUT THE GODS CHOSE TO GIVE IT TO ME, SO I MUST MAKE THE CORRECT DECISION.
BUT FIRST, I HAD BETTER GET OUT OF HERE BEFORE MORE OF LORD KOTETSU'S AGENTS FIND ME.
EH?
18.

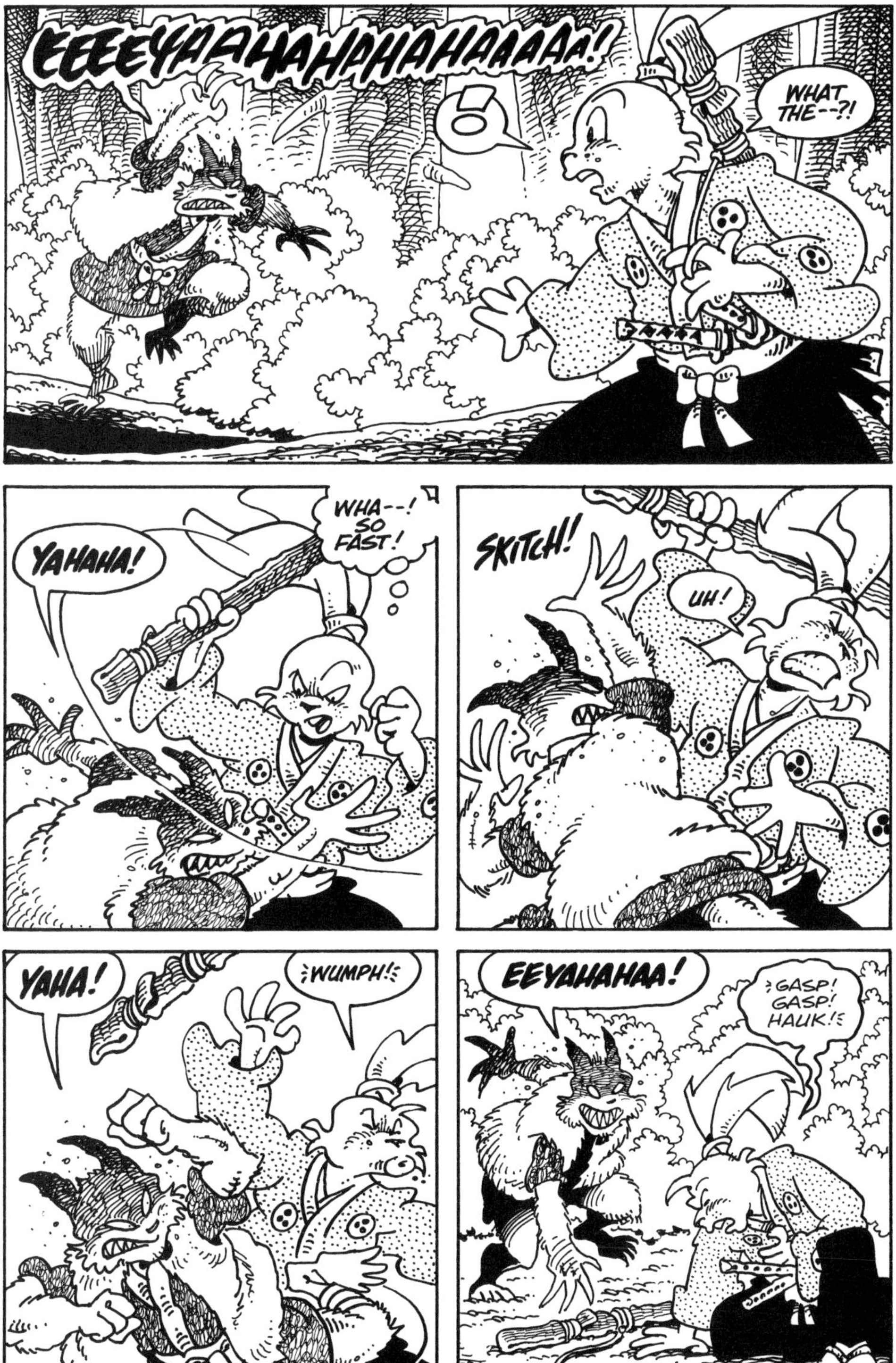
EEEEYAAHAHAHAHAAAAAA!
!
WHAT THE--?!
YAHAHA!
WHA--! SO FAST!
SKITCH!
UH!
YAHA!
WUMPH!
EEYAHAHAA!
GASP! GASP! HAUK!
19.

WHOEVER--OR **WHAT**EVER--HE IS, HE'S GETTING AWAY WITH THE SWORD!

EEEYAHAAHAHA!

A MINUTE AGO I WISHED I HAD NEVER LAID EYES ON THAT SWORD...

...BUT NOW...

...I'VE GOT TO GET IT BACK!

SUCCESS! KITANAMONO HAS THE SWORD! HE WILL DELIVER IT HERE DIRECTLY.

ARE YOU SURE? HOW CAN YOU BE SO CONFIDENT?

KITANAMONO IS MY FAMILIAR. HE IS PART OF ME JUST AS I AM A PART OF HIM. HE WOULD NOT FAIL ME... NO MORE THAN I WOULD FAIL YOU, LORD KOTETSU.

20.

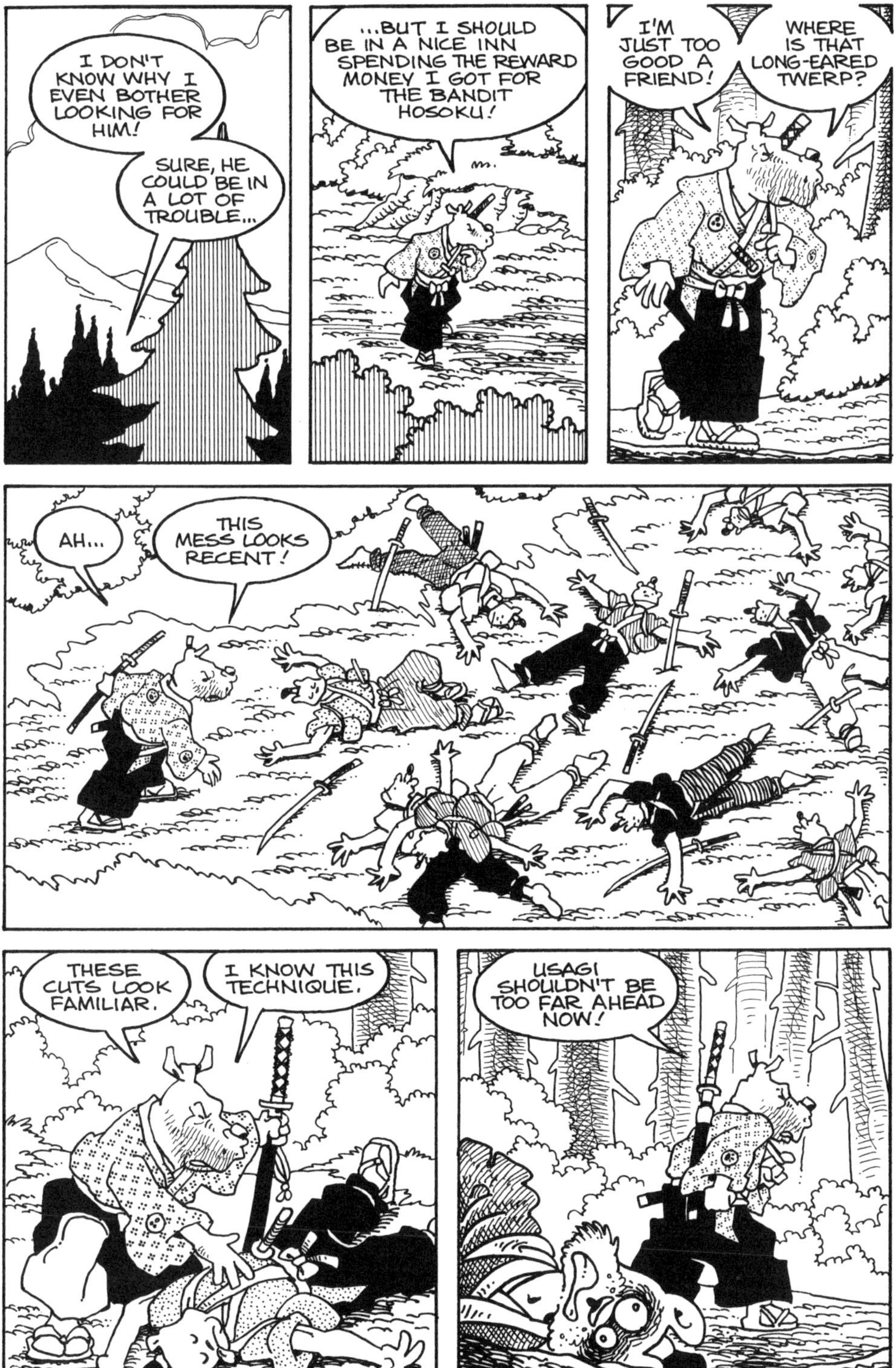
I DON'T KNOW WHY I EVEN BOTHER LOOKING FOR HIM!
SURE, HE COULD BE IN A LOT OF TROUBLE...
...BUT I SHOULD BE IN A NICE INN SPENDING THE REWARD MONEY I GOT FOR THE BANDIT HOSOKU!
I'M JUST TOO GOOD A FRIEND!
WHERE IS THAT LONG-EARED TWERP?
AH...
THIS MESS LOOKS RECENT!
THESE CUTS LOOK FAMILIAR.
I KNOW THIS TECHNIQUE.
USAGI SHOULDN'T BE TOO FAR AHEAD NOW!
21.

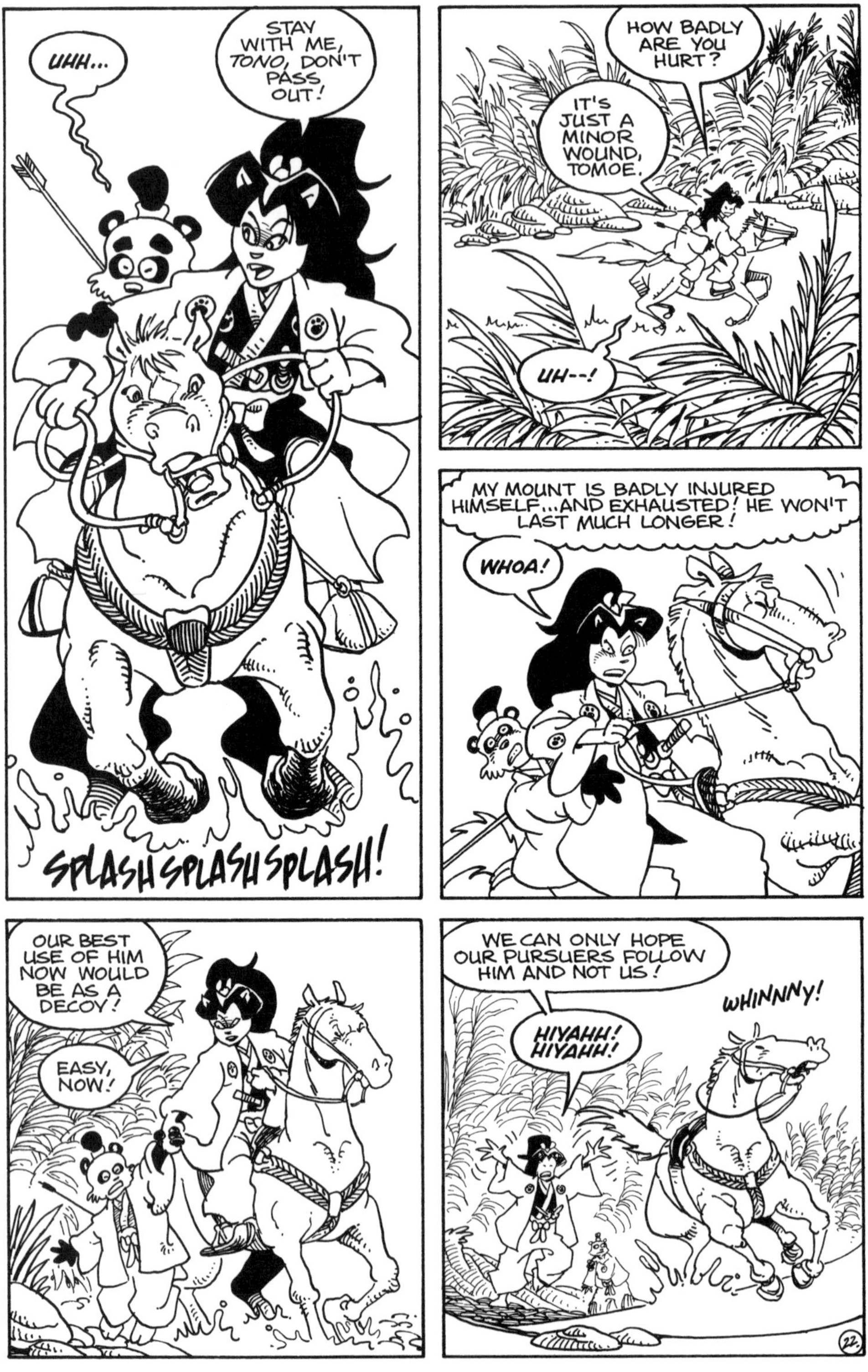
UHH...
STAY WITH ME, TONO, DON'T PASS OUT!
SPLASH SPLASH SPLASH!
HOW BADLY ARE YOU HURT?
IT'S JUST A MINOR WOUND, TOMOE.
UH--!
MY MOUNT IS BADLY INJURED HIMSELF...AND EXHAUSTED! HE WON'T LAST MUCH LONGER!
WHOA!
OUR BEST USE OF HIM NOW WOULD BE AS A DECOY!
EASY, NOW!
WE CAN ONLY HOPE OUR PURSUERS FOLLOW HIM AND NOT US!
HIYAHH! HIYAHH!
WHINNNY!
22.

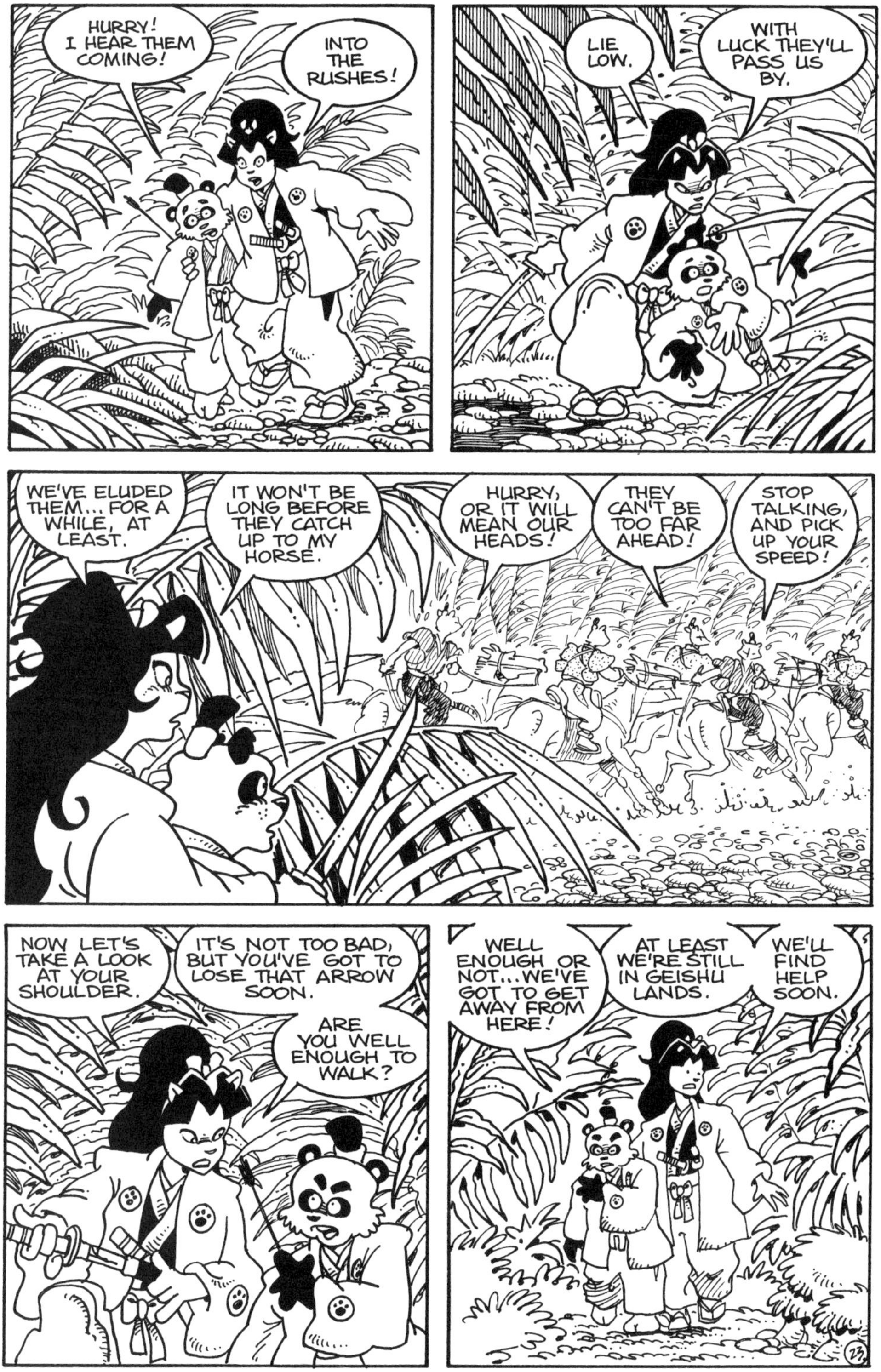
HURRY! I HEAR THEM COMING!
INTO THE RUSHES!
LIE LOW.
WITH LUCK THEY'LL PASS US BY.
WE'VE ELUDED THEM... FOR A WHILE, AT LEAST.
IT WON'T BE LONG BEFORE THEY CATCH UP TO MY HORSE.
HURRY, OR IT WILL MEAN OUR HEADS!
THEY CAN'T BE TOO FAR AHEAD!
STOP TALKING, AND PICK UP YOUR SPEED!
NOW LET'S TAKE A LOOK AT YOUR SHOULDER.
IT'S NOT TOO BAD, BUT YOU'VE GOT TO LOSE THAT ARROW SOON.
ARE YOU WELL ENOUGH TO WALK?
WELL ENOUGH OR NOT... WE'VE GOT TO GET AWAY FROM HERE!
AT LEAST WE'RE STILL IN GEISHU LANDS.
WE'LL FIND HELP SOON.
23

LATER...

TOMOE... I'VE GOT TO REST FOR A WHILE.

FORGIVE ME, *TONO*, I'VE BEEN INCONSIDERATE OF YOUR INJURY.

THERE'S A FARMHOUSE. WE CAN SEEK HELP THERE!

PEASANT-- YOUR LORD NEEDS YOUR HELP!

YOU WILL BE WELL REWARDED FOR YOUR AID.

DIDN'T YOU HEAR ME? I SAID LORD NORIYUKI NEEDS YOUR HELP!

I HEARD. I HEARD.

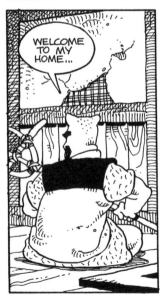

WELCOME TO MY HOME...

...LORD NORIYUKI.

END OF CHAPTER 4

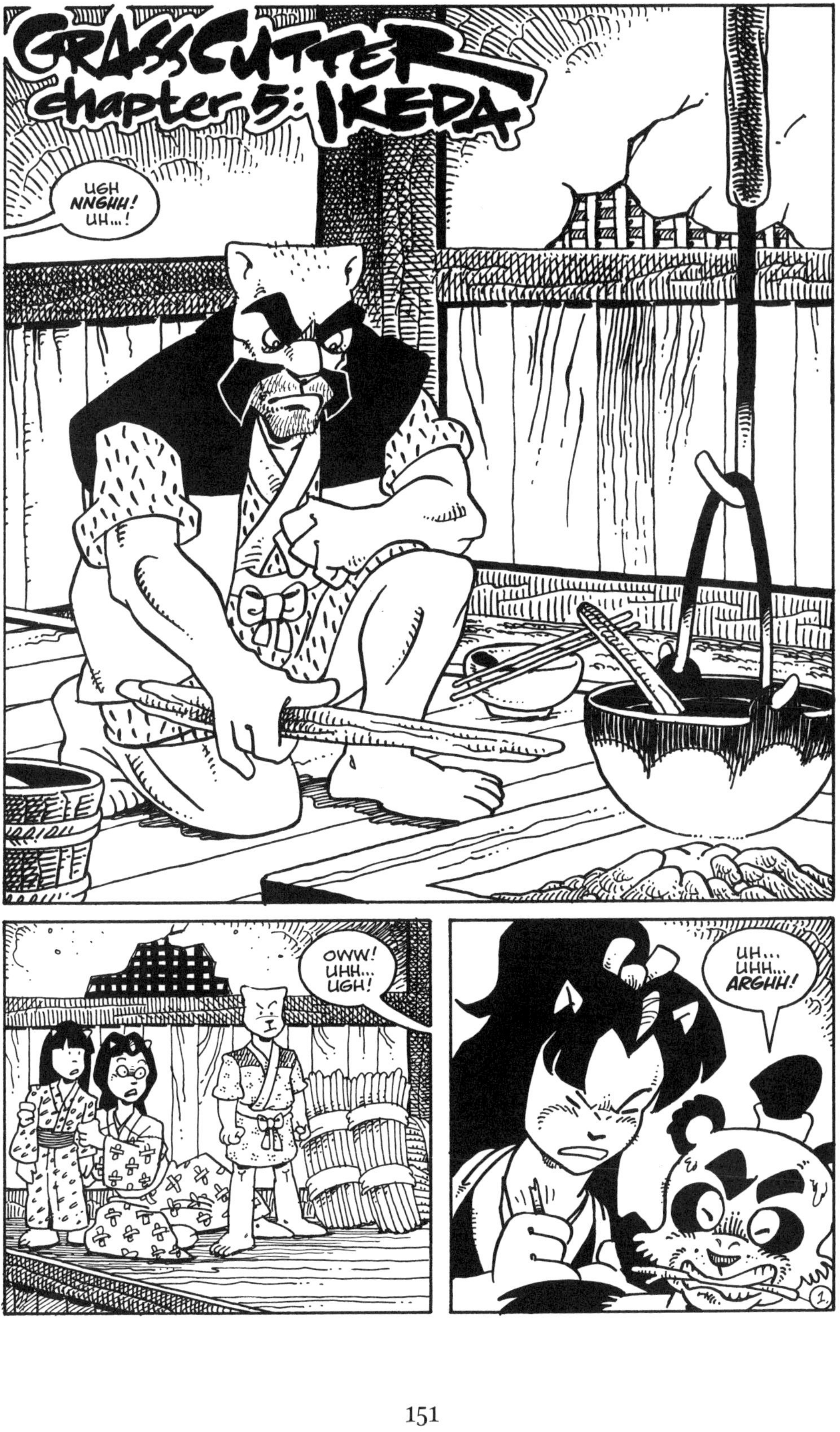
GRASSCUTTER
chapter 5: IKEDA
UGH NNGHH! UH...!
OWW! UHH... UGH!
UH... UHH... ARGHH!

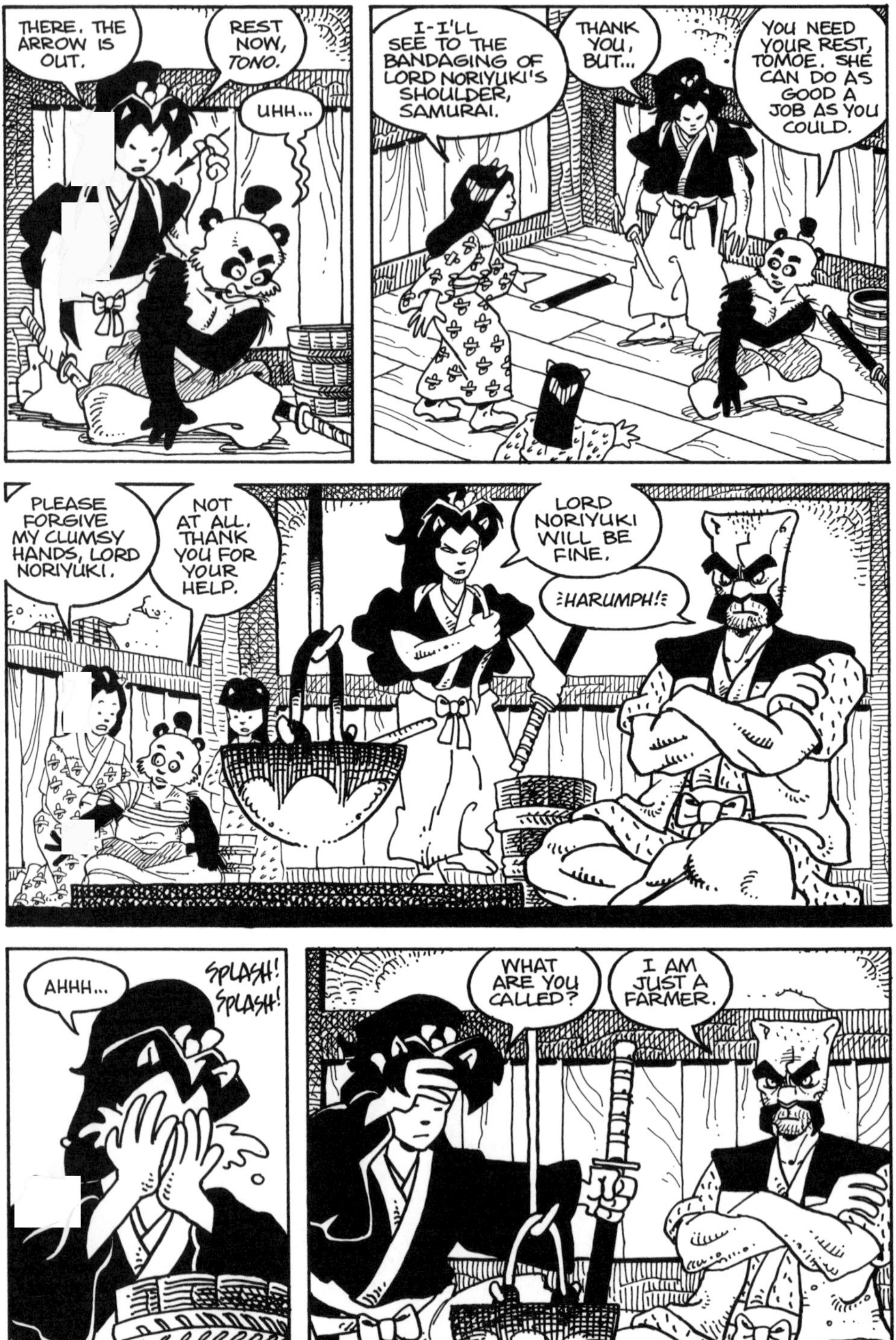
THERE. THE ARROW IS OUT.
REST NOW, *TONO.*
UHH...
I-I'LL SEE TO THE BANDAGING OF LORD NORIYUKI'S SHOULDER, SAMURAI.
THANK YOU, BUT...
YOU NEED YOUR REST, TOMOE. SHE CAN DO AS GOOD A JOB AS YOU COULD.
PLEASE FORGIVE MY CLUMSY HANDS, LORD NORIYUKI.
NOT AT ALL. THANK YOU FOR YOUR HELP.
LORD NORIYUKI WILL BE FINE.
HARUMPH!
AHHH...
SPLASH! SPLASH!
WHAT ARE YOU CALLED?
I AM JUST A FARMER.
2.

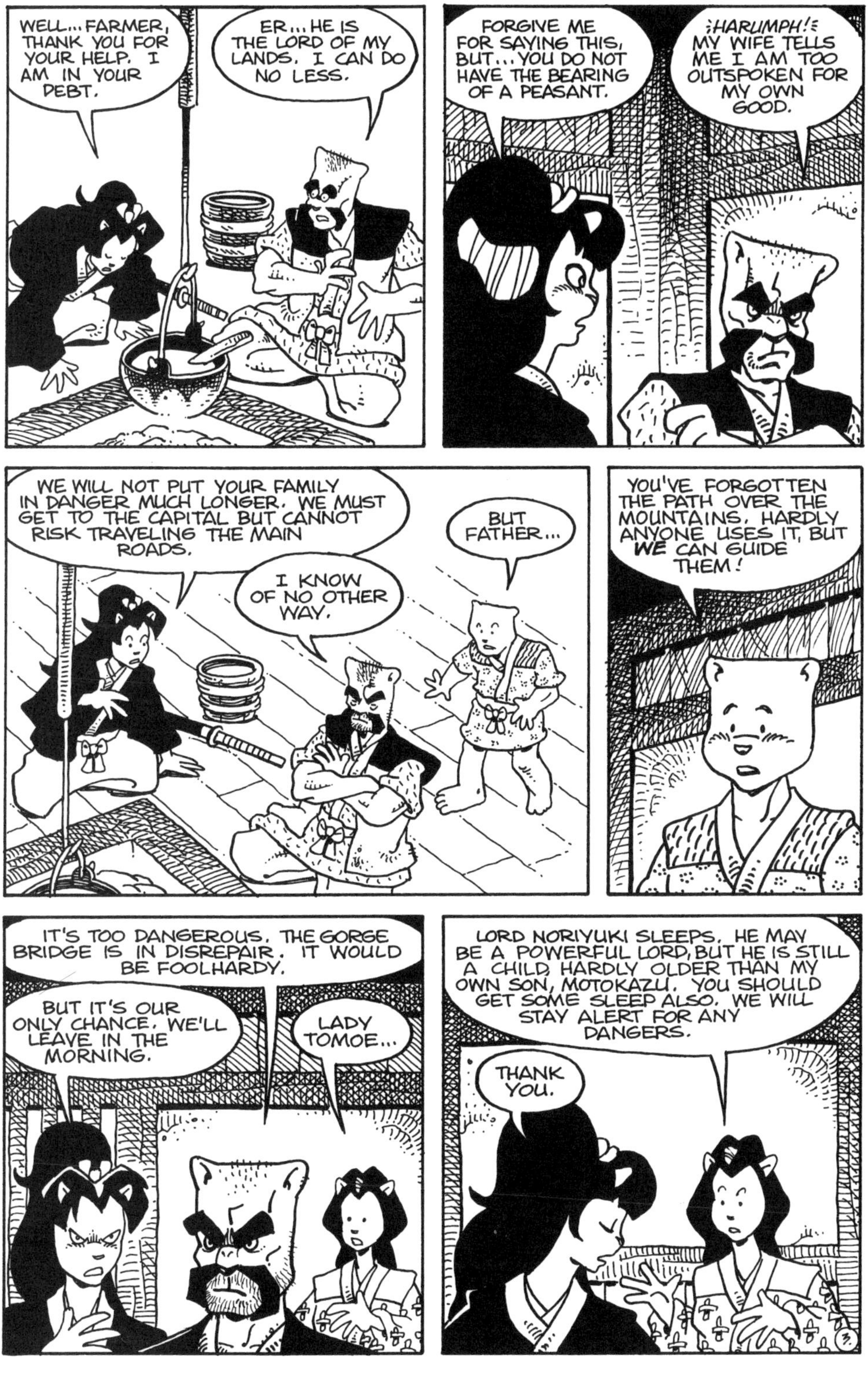
WELL... FARMER, THANK YOU FOR YOUR HELP. I AM IN YOUR DEBT.
ER... HE IS THE LORD OF MY LANDS. I CAN DO NO LESS.
FORGIVE ME FOR SAYING THIS, BUT... YOU DO NOT HAVE THE BEARING OF A PEASANT.
¡HARUMPH!¡ MY WIFE TELLS ME I AM TOO OUTSPOKEN FOR MY OWN GOOD.
WE WILL NOT PUT YOUR FAMILY IN DANGER MUCH LONGER. WE MUST GET TO THE CAPITAL BUT CANNOT RISK TRAVELING THE MAIN ROADS.
I KNOW OF NO OTHER WAY.
BUT FATHER...
YOU'VE FORGOTTEN THE PATH OVER THE MOUNTAINS. HARDLY ANYONE USES IT, BUT WE CAN GUIDE THEM!
IT'S TOO DANGEROUS. THE GORGE BRIDGE IS IN DISREPAIR. IT WOULD BE FOOLHARDY.
BUT IT'S OUR ONLY CHANCE. WE'LL LEAVE IN THE MORNING.
LADY TOMOE...
LORD NORIYUKI SLEEPS. HE MAY BE A POWERFUL LORD, BUT HE IS STILL A CHILD, HARDLY OLDER THAN MY OWN SON, MOTOKAZU. YOU SHOULD GET SOME SLEEP ALSO. WE WILL STAY ALERT FOR ANY DANGERS.
THANK YOU.
3.

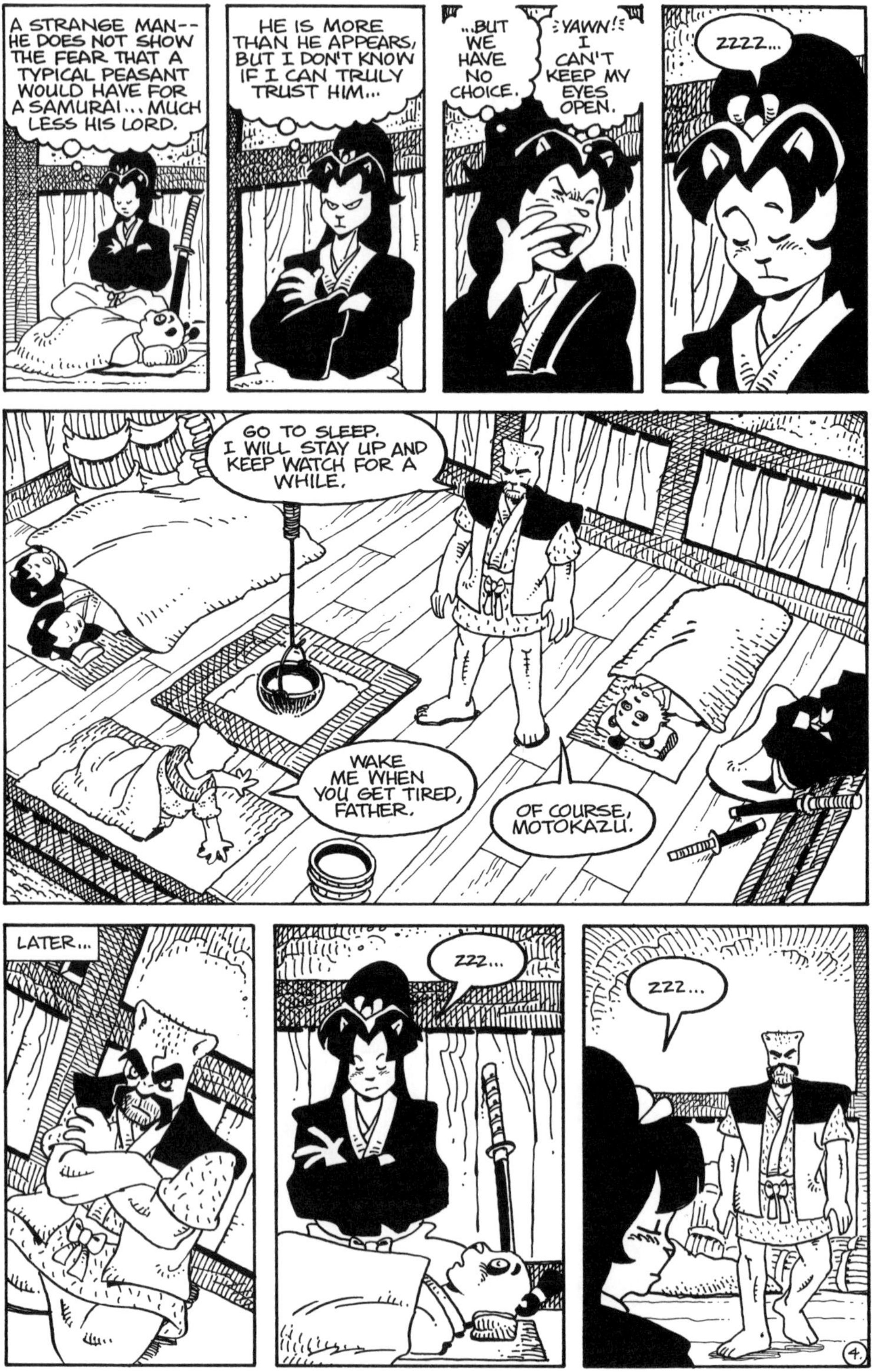
A STRANGE MAN-- HE DOES NOT SHOW THE FEAR THAT A TYPICAL PEASANT WOULD HAVE FOR A SAMURAI... MUCH LESS HIS LORD.
HE IS MORE THAN HE APPEARS, BUT I DON'T KNOW IF I CAN TRULY TRUST HIM...
...BUT WE HAVE NO CHOICE.
YAWN! I CAN'T KEEP MY EYES OPEN.
ZZZZ...
GO TO SLEEP. I WILL STAY UP AND KEEP WATCH FOR A WHILE.
WAKE ME WHEN YOU GET TIRED, FATHER.
OF COURSE, MOTOKAZU.
LATER...
ZZZ...
ZZZ...
4.

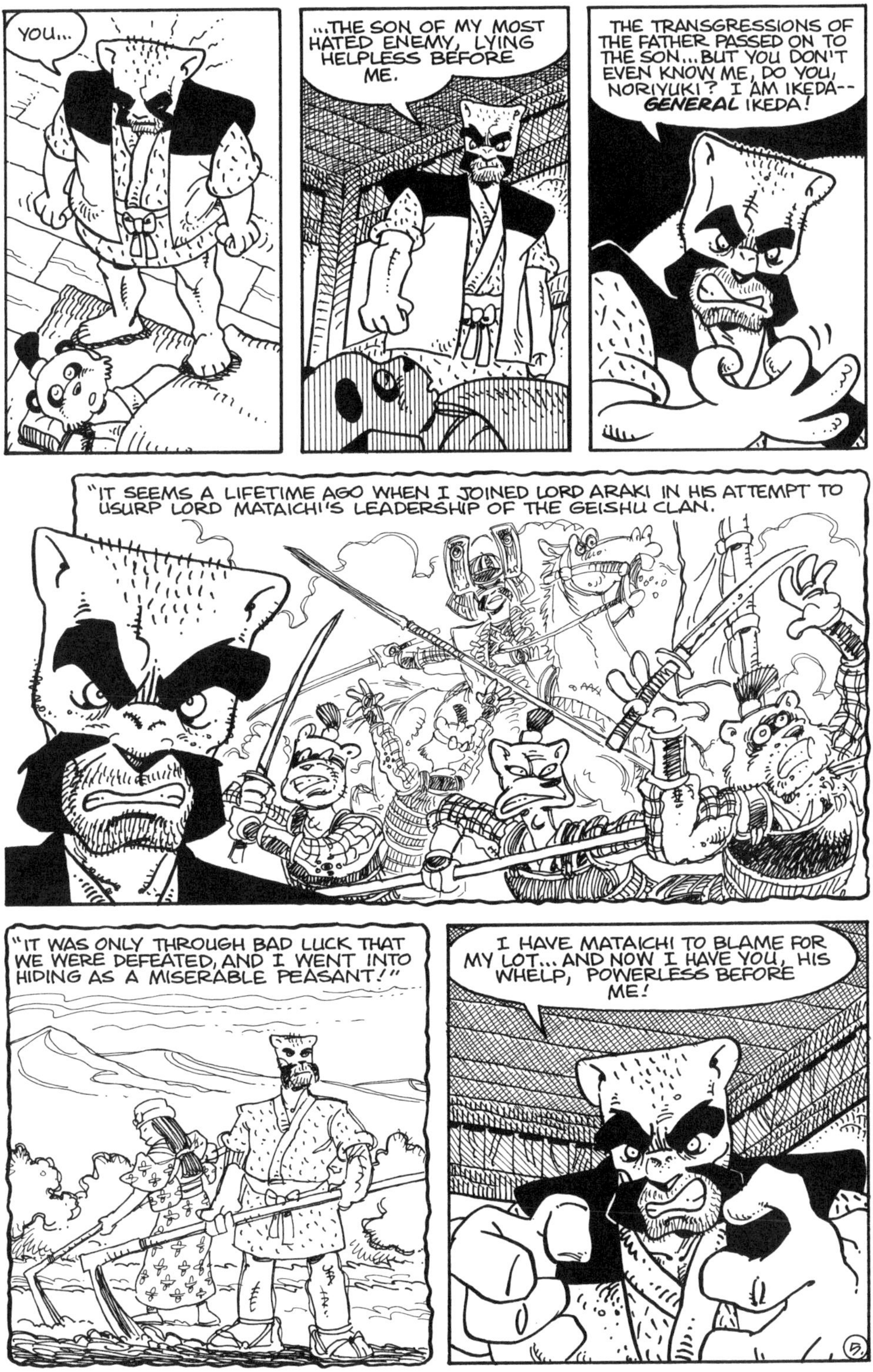
YOU...
...THE SON OF MY MOST HATED ENEMY, LYING HELPLESS BEFORE ME.
THE TRANSGRESSIONS OF THE FATHER PASSED ON TO THE SON... BUT YOU DON'T EVEN KNOW ME, DO YOU, NORIYUKI? I AM IKEDA-- **GENERAL** IKEDA!
"IT SEEMS A LIFETIME AGO WHEN I JOINED LORD ARAKI IN HIS ATTEMPT TO USURP LORD MATAICHI'S LEADERSHIP OF THE GEISHU CLAN.
"IT WAS ONLY THROUGH BAD LUCK THAT WE WERE DEFEATED, AND I WENT INTO HIDING AS A MISERABLE PEASANT!"
I HAVE MATAICHI TO BLAME FOR MY LOT... AND NOW I HAVE YOU, HIS WHELP, POWERLESS BEFORE ME!
5

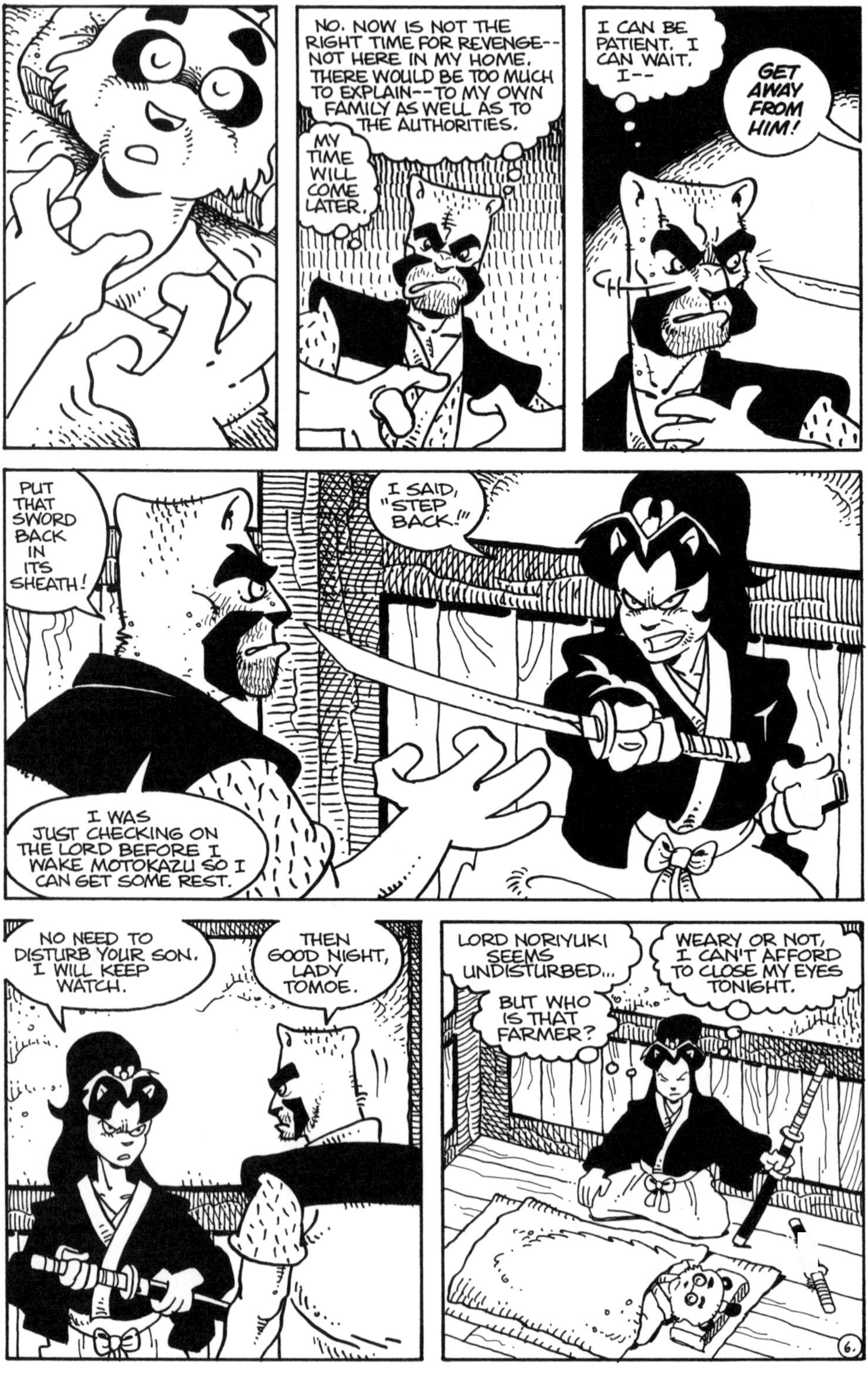
NO. NOW IS NOT THE RIGHT TIME FOR REVENGE--NOT HERE IN MY HOME. THERE WOULD BE TOO MUCH TO EXPLAIN--TO MY OWN FAMILY AS WELL AS TO THE AUTHORITIES.
MY TIME WILL COME LATER.
I CAN BE PATIENT. I CAN WAIT. I--
GET AWAY FROM HIM!
PUT THAT SWORD BACK IN ITS SHEATH!
I SAID, "STEP BACK!"
I WAS JUST CHECKING ON THE LORD BEFORE I WAKE MOTOKAZU SO I CAN GET SOME REST.
NO NEED TO DISTURB YOUR SON. I WILL KEEP WATCH.
THEN GOOD NIGHT, LADY TOMOE.
LORD NORIYUKI SEEMS UNDISTURBED...
BUT WHO IS THAT FARMER?
WEARY OR NOT, I CAN'T AFFORD TO CLOSE MY EYES TONIGHT.
6.

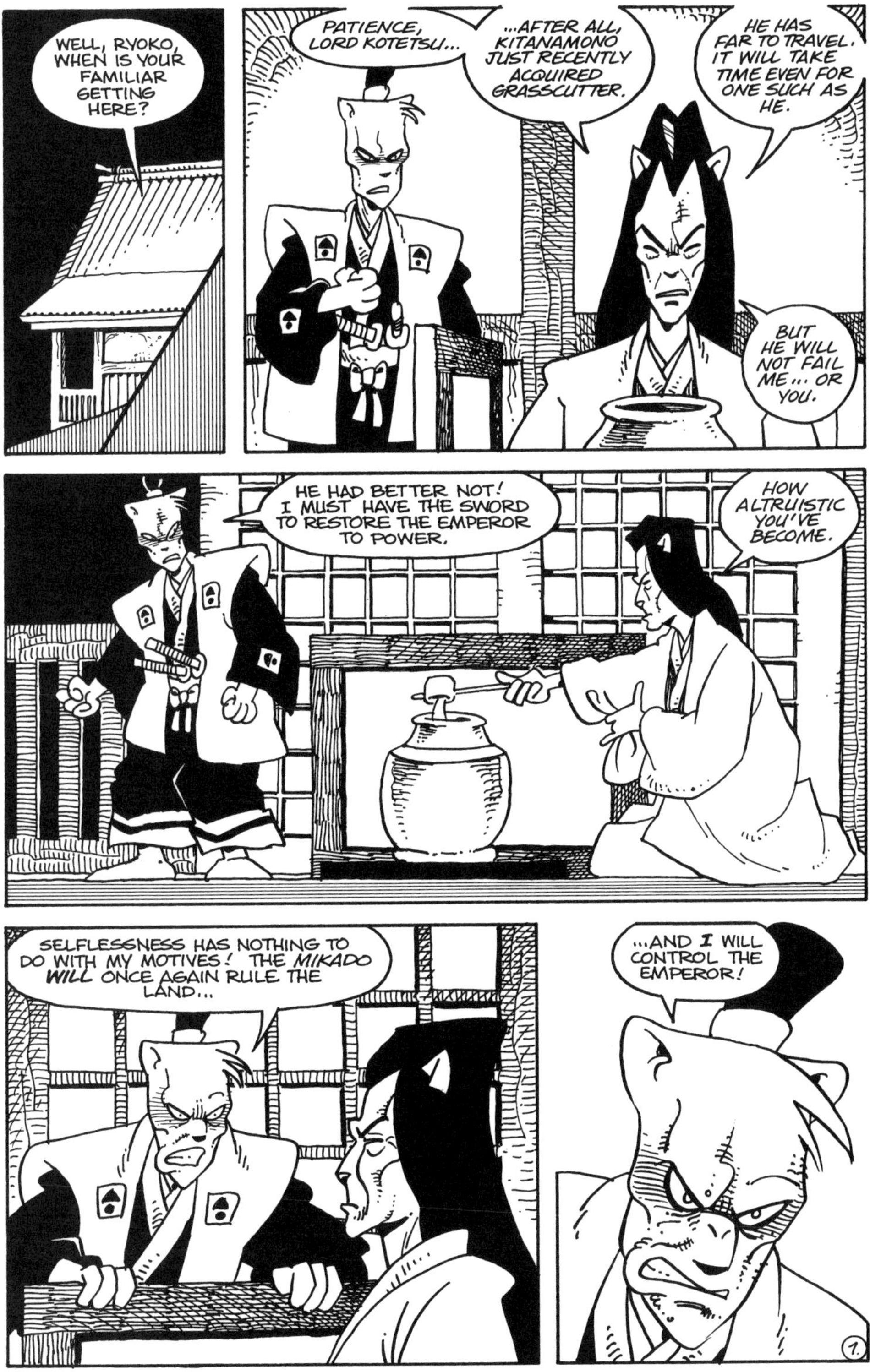
WELL, RYOKO, WHEN IS YOUR FAMILIAR GETTING HERE?
PATIENCE, LORD KOTETSU...
...AFTER ALL, KITANAMONO JUST RECENTLY ACQUIRED GRASSCUTTER.
HE HAS FAR TO TRAVEL. IT WILL TAKE TIME EVEN FOR ONE SUCH AS HE.
BUT HE WILL NOT FAIL ME... OR YOU.
HE HAD BETTER NOT! I MUST HAVE THE SWORD TO RESTORE THE EMPEROR TO POWER.
HOW ALTRUISTIC YOU'VE BECOME.
SELFLESSNESS HAS NOTHING TO DO WITH MY MOTIVES! THE MIKADO WILL ONCE AGAIN RULE THE LAND...
...AND I WILL CONTROL THE EMPEROR!
7.

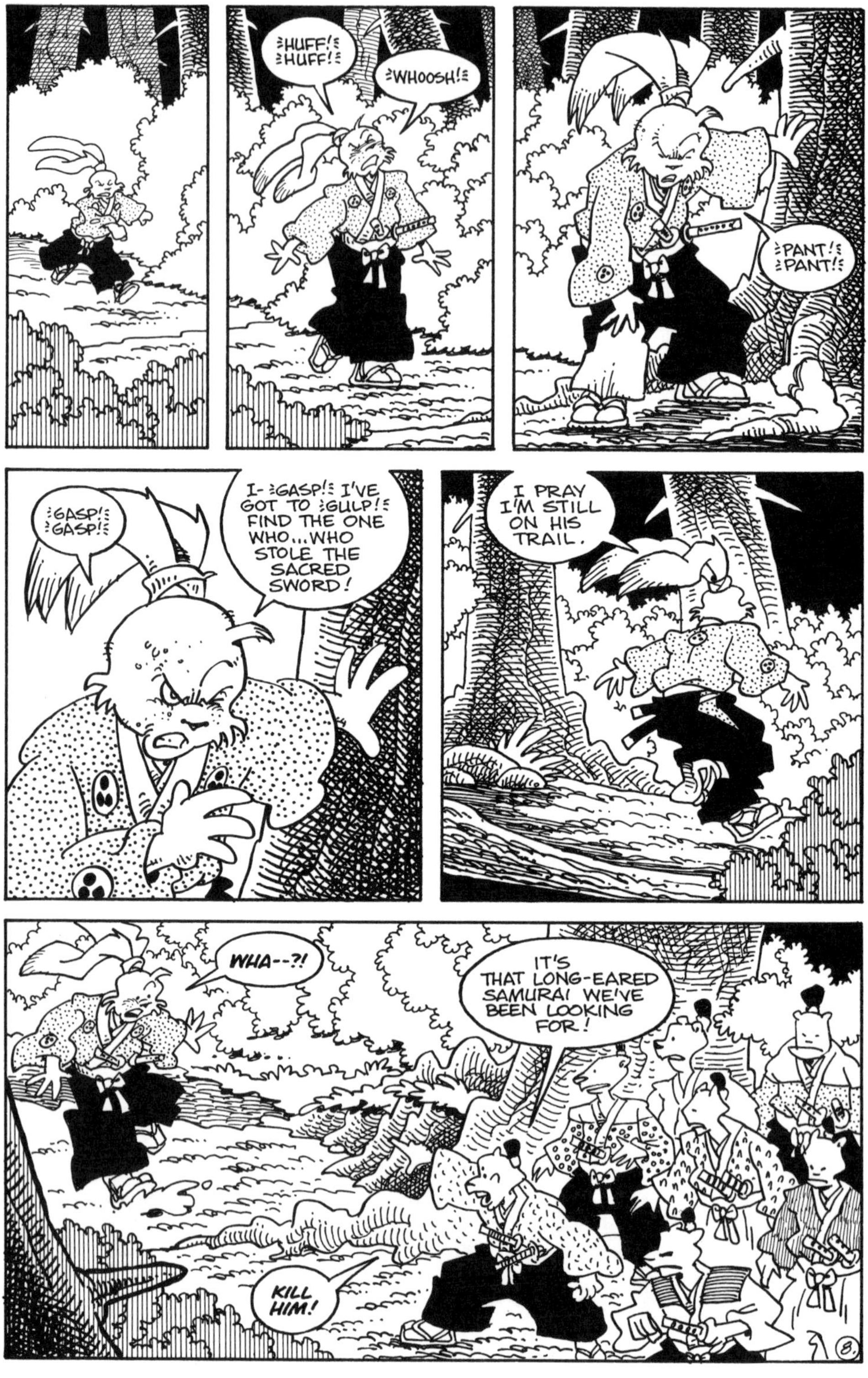
HUFF! HUFF!
WHOOSH!
PANT! PANT!
GASP! GASP!
I- GASP! I'VE GOT TO GULP! FIND THE ONE WHO...WHO STOLE THE SACRED SWORD!
I PRAY I'M STILL ON HIS TRAIL.
WHA--?!
IT'S THAT LONG-EARED SAMURAI WE'VE BEEN LOOKING FOR!
KILL HIM!
8

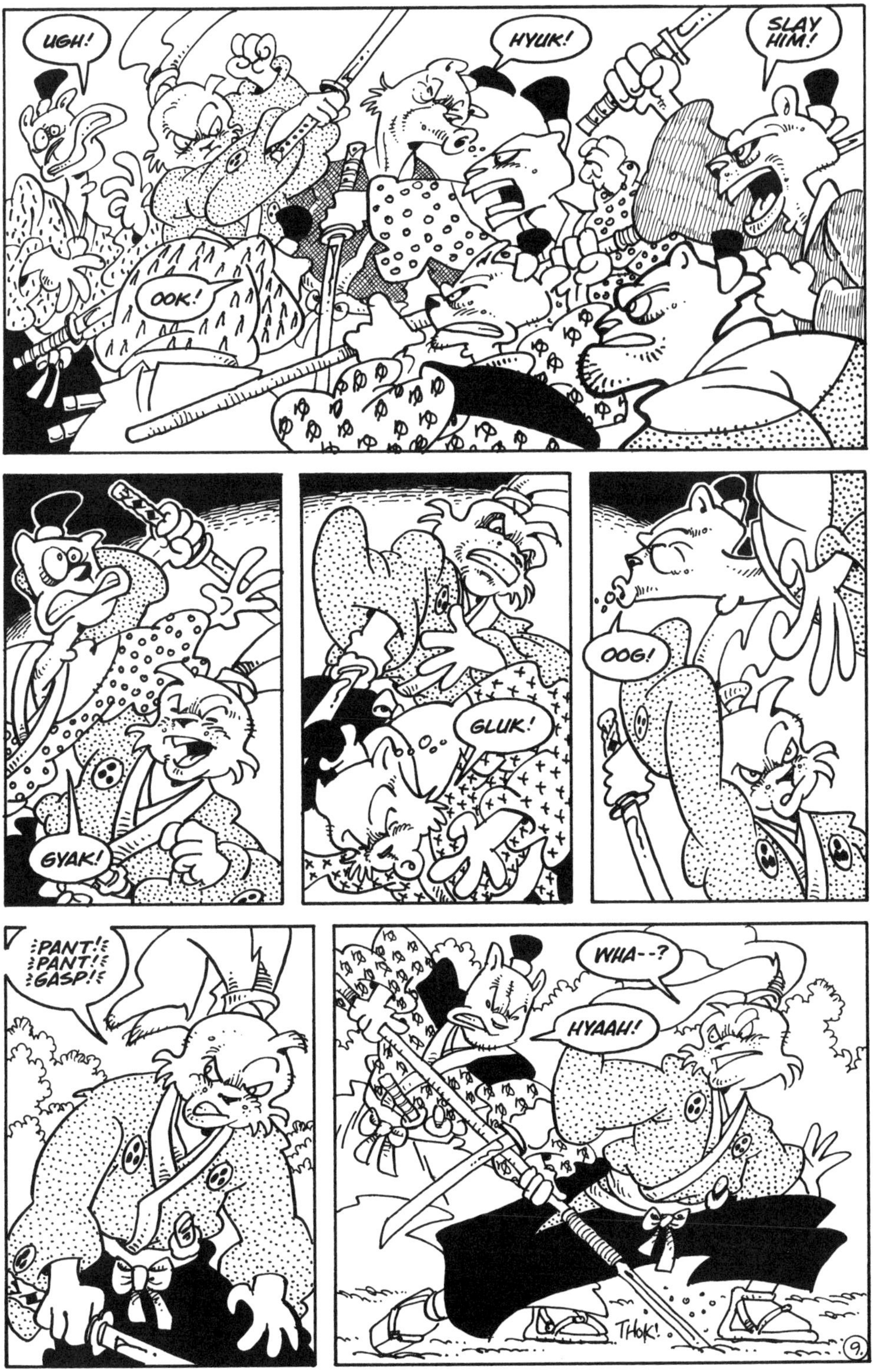
UGH!
HYUK!
SLAY HIM!
OOK!
GYAK!
GLUK!
OOG!
PANT! PANT! GASP!
WHA--?
HYAAH!
THOK!
9

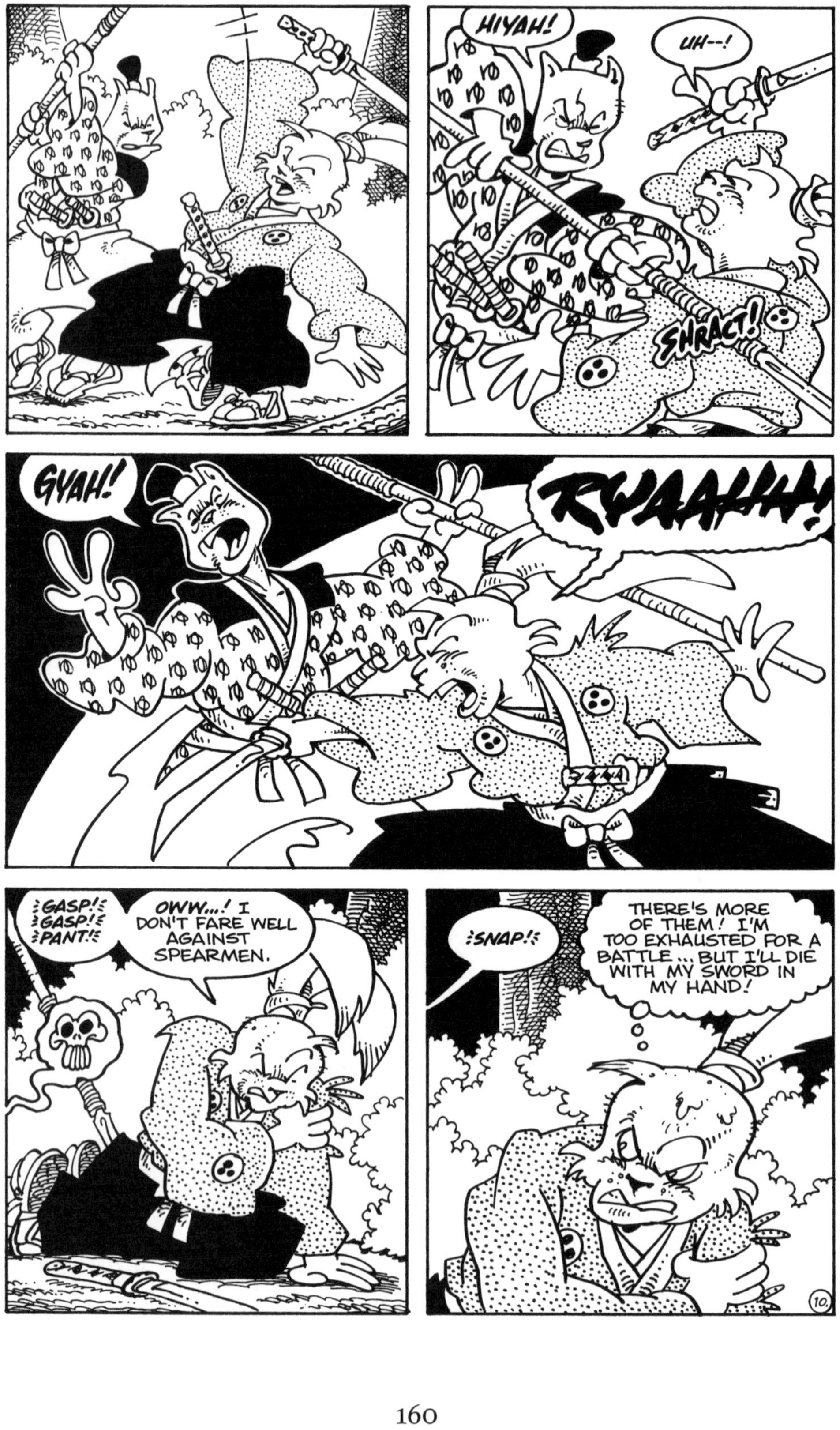

HIYAH!
UH--!
EHRACT!
GYAH!
RWAAHH!
GASP! GASP! PANT!
OWW...! I DON'T FARE WELL AGAINST SPEARMEN.
SNAP!
THERE'S MORE OF THEM! I'M TOO EXHAUSTED FOR A BATTLE... BUT I'LL DIE WITH MY SWORD IN MY HAND!
10.

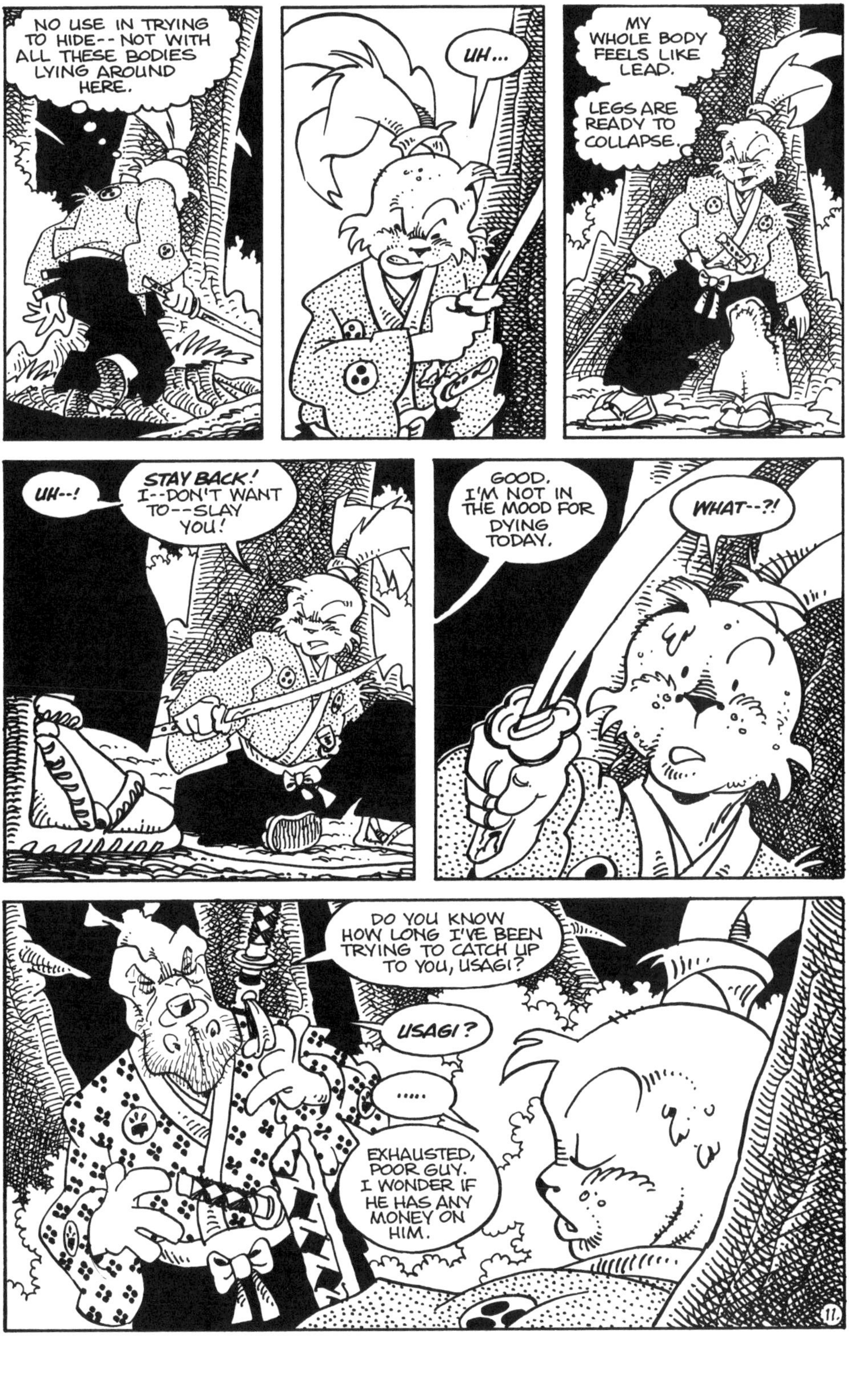

NO USE IN TRYING TO HIDE--NOT WITH ALL THESE BODIES LYING AROUND HERE.
UH...
MY WHOLE BODY FEELS LIKE LEAD.
LEGS ARE READY TO COLLAPSE.
UH--!
STAY BACK! I--DON'T WANT TO--SLAY YOU!
GOOD. I'M NOT IN THE MOOD FOR DYING TODAY.
WHAT--?!
DO YOU KNOW HOW LONG I'VE BEEN TRYING TO CATCH UP TO YOU, USAGI?
USAGI?
.....
EXHAUSTED, POOR GUY. I WONDER IF HE HAS ANY MONEY ON HIM.
11.

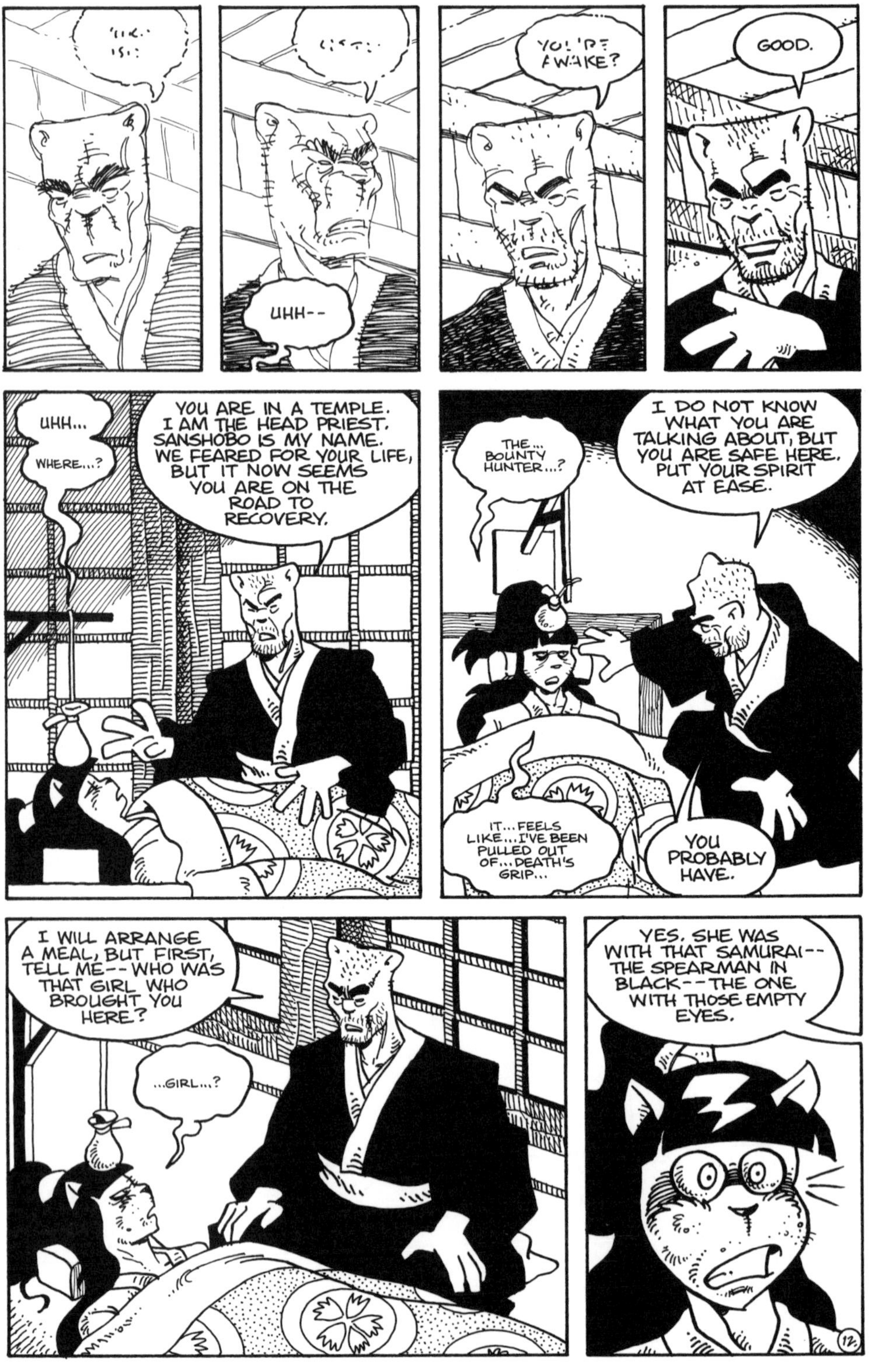
UHH--
YOU'RE AWAKE?
GOOD.
UHH... WHERE...?
YOU ARE IN A TEMPLE. I AM THE HEAD PRIEST. SANSHOBO IS MY NAME. WE FEARED FOR YOUR LIFE, BUT IT NOW SEEMS YOU ARE ON THE ROAD TO RECOVERY.
THE... BOUNTY HUNTER...?
I DO NOT KNOW WHAT YOU ARE TALKING ABOUT, BUT YOU ARE SAFE HERE. PUT YOUR SPIRIT AT EASE.
IT... FEELS LIKE... I'VE BEEN PULLED OUT OF... DEATH'S GRIP...
YOU PROBABLY HAVE.
I WILL ARRANGE A MEAL, BUT FIRST, TELL ME-- WHO WAS THAT GIRL WHO BROUGHT YOU HERE?
...GIRL...?
YES. SHE WAS WITH THAT SAMURAI-- THE SPEARMAN IN BLACK-- THE ONE WITH THOSE EMPTY EYES.
12

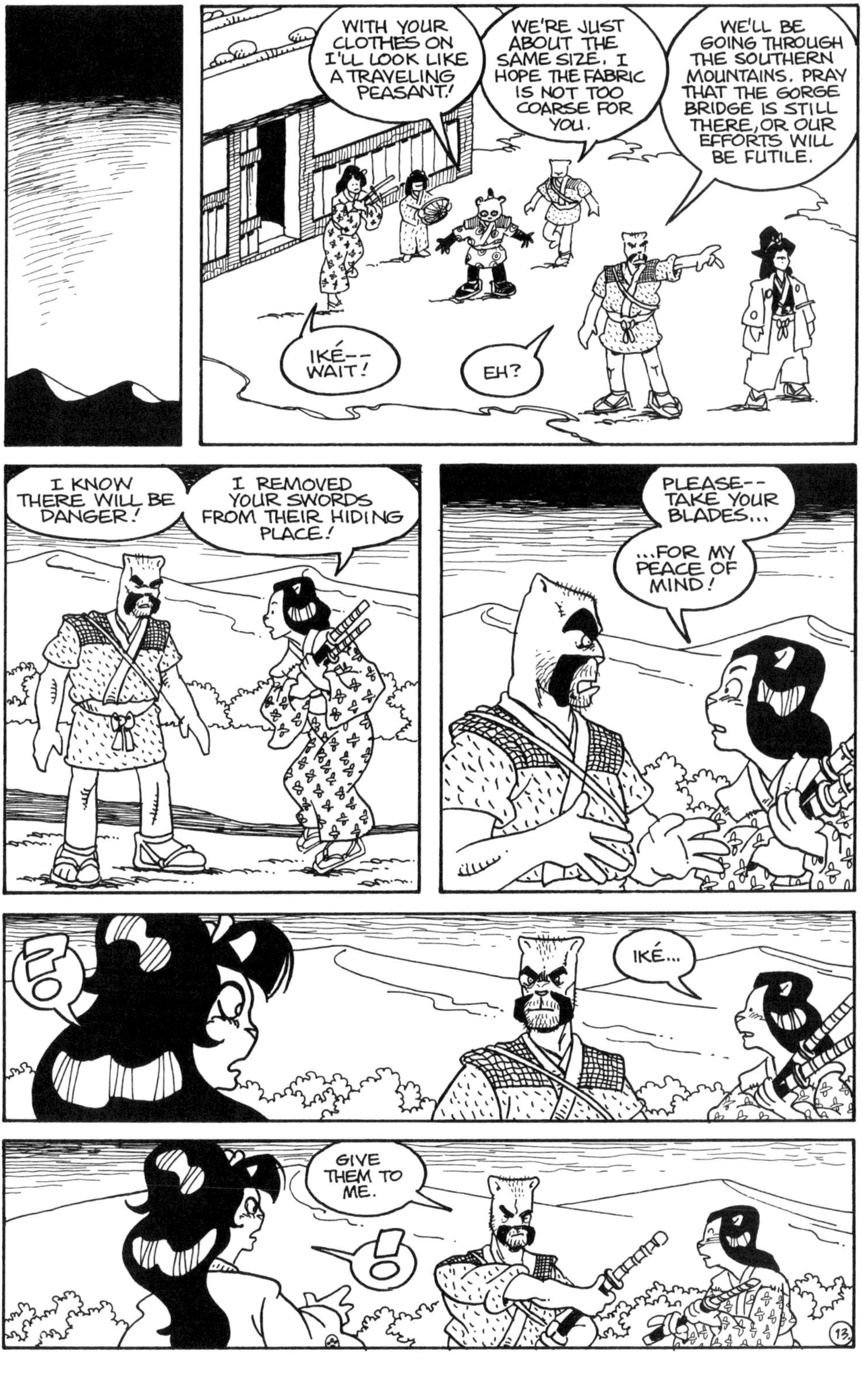
WITH YOUR CLOTHES ON I'LL LOOK LIKE A TRAVELING PEASANT!
WE'RE JUST ABOUT THE SAME SIZE. I HOPE THE FABRIC IS NOT TOO COARSE FOR YOU.
WE'LL BE GOING THROUGH THE SOUTHERN MOUNTAINS. PRAY THAT THE GORGE BRIDGE IS STILL THERE, OR OUR EFFORTS WILL BE FUTILE.
IKÉ-- WAIT!
EH?
I KNOW THERE WILL BE DANGER!
I REMOVED YOUR SWORDS FROM THEIR HIDING PLACE!
PLEASE-- TAKE YOUR BLADES...
...FOR MY PEACE OF MIND!
?!
IKÉ...
GIVE THEM TO ME.
!
13

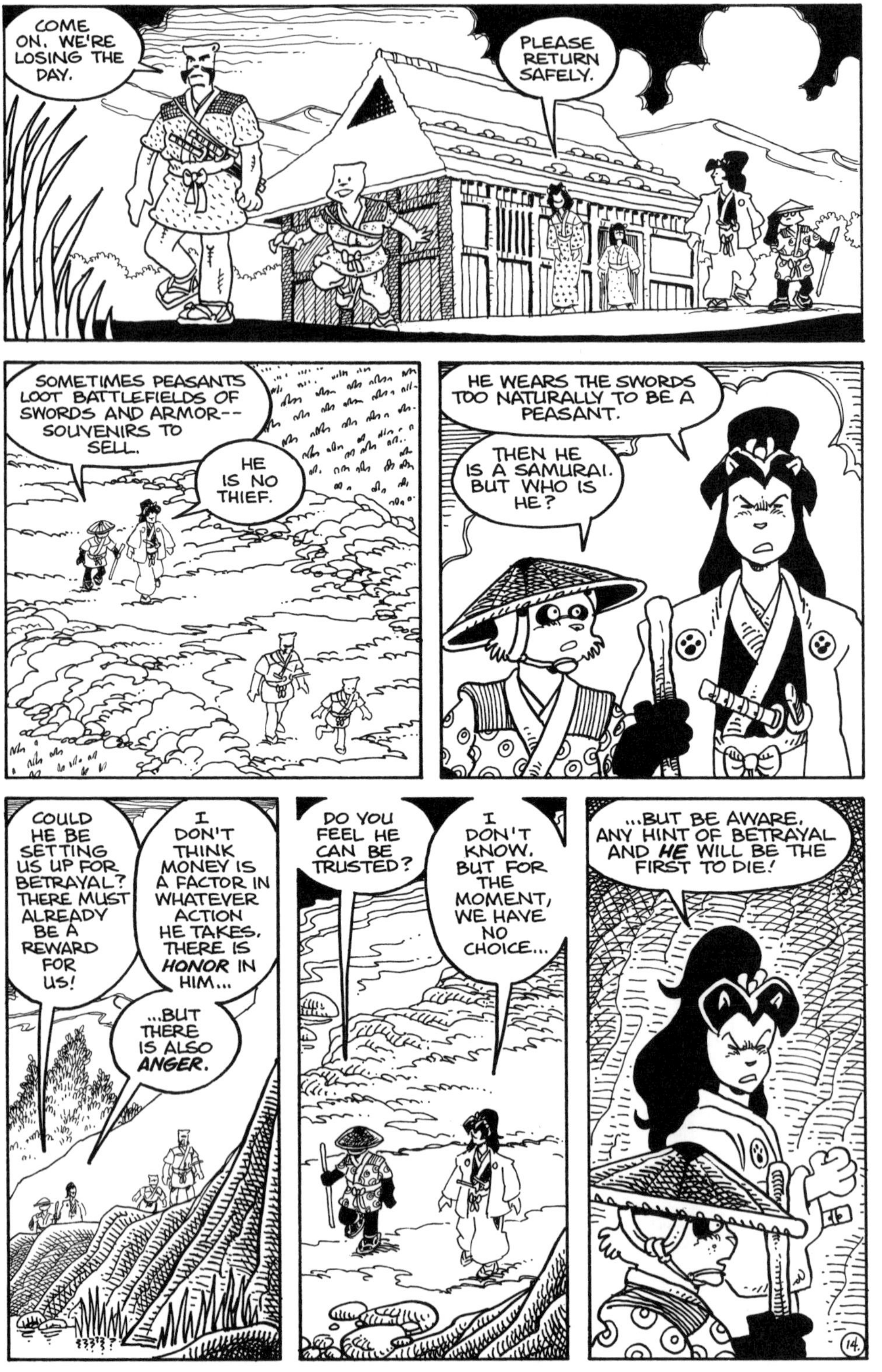
COME ON. WE'RE LOSING THE DAY.
PLEASE RETURN SAFELY.
SOMETIMES PEASANTS LOOT BATTLEFIELDS OF SWORDS AND ARMOR-- SOUVENIRS TO SELL.
HE IS NO THIEF.
HE WEARS THE SWORDS TOO NATURALLY TO BE A PEASANT.
THEN HE IS A SAMURAI. BUT WHO IS HE?
COULD HE BE SETTING US UP FOR BETRAYAL? THERE MUST ALREADY BE A REWARD FOR US!
I DON'T THINK MONEY IS A FACTOR IN WHATEVER ACTION HE TAKES. THERE IS HONOR IN HIM...
...BUT THERE IS ALSO ANGER.
DO YOU FEEL HE CAN BE TRUSTED?
I DON'T KNOW. BUT FOR THE MOMENT, WE HAVE NO CHOICE...
...BUT BE AWARE. ANY HINT OF BETRAYAL AND HE WILL BE THE FIRST TO DIE!
14.

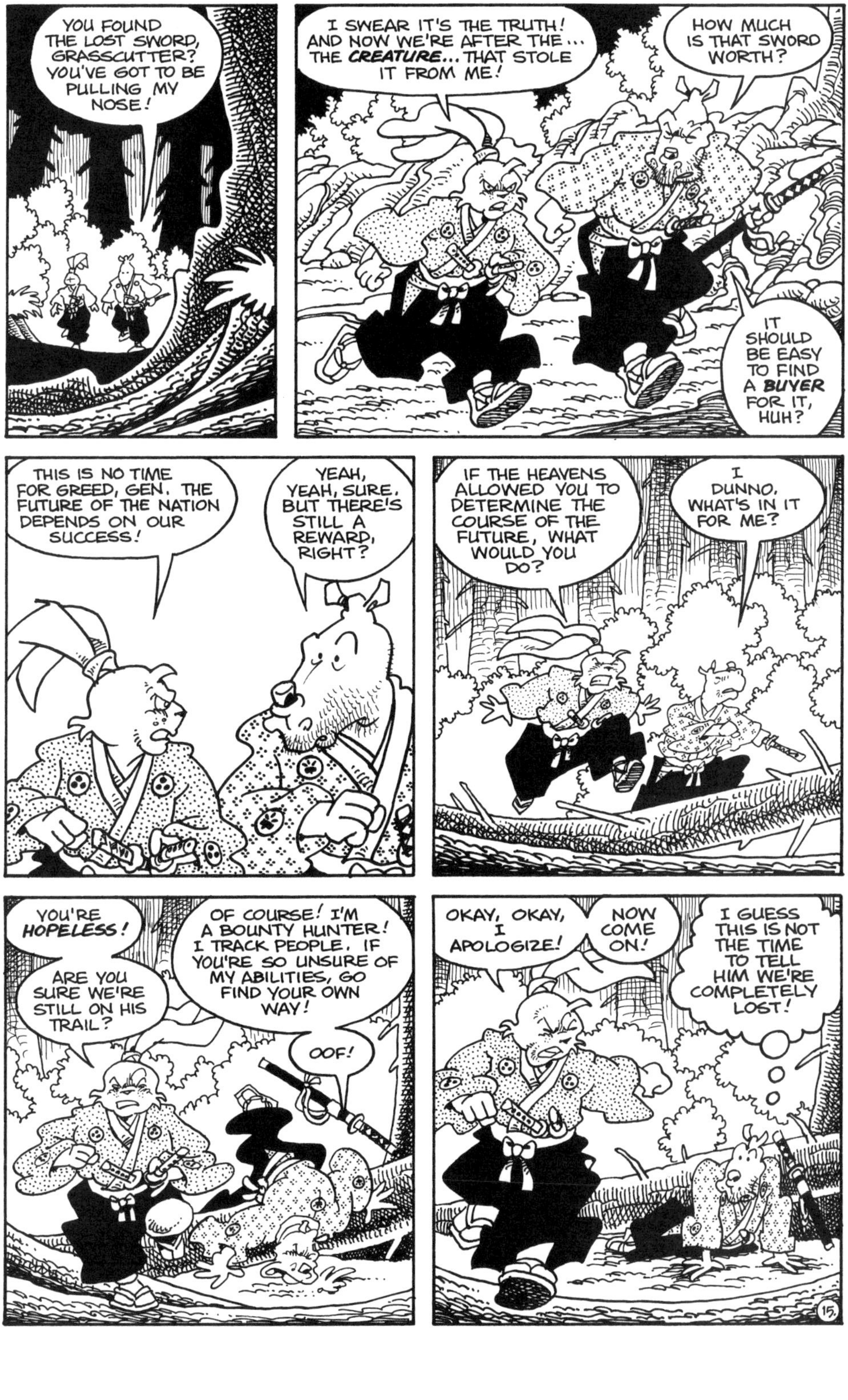
YOU FOUND THE LOST SWORD, GRASSCUTTER? YOU'VE GOT TO BE PULLING MY NOSE!
I SWEAR IT'S THE TRUTH! AND NOW WE'RE AFTER THE... THE CREATURE... THAT STOLE IT FROM ME!
HOW MUCH IS THAT SWORD WORTH?
IT SHOULD BE EASY TO FIND A BUYER FOR IT, HUH?
THIS IS NO TIME FOR GREED, GEN. THE FUTURE OF THE NATION DEPENDS ON OUR SUCCESS!
YEAH, YEAH, SURE. BUT THERE'S STILL A REWARD, RIGHT?
IF THE HEAVENS ALLOWED YOU TO DETERMINE THE COURSE OF THE FUTURE, WHAT WOULD YOU DO?
I DUNNO. WHAT'S IN IT FOR ME?
YOU'RE HOPELESS!
ARE YOU SURE WE'RE STILL ON HIS TRAIL?
OF COURSE! I'M A BOUNTY HUNTER! I TRACK PEOPLE. IF YOU'RE SO UNSURE OF MY ABILITIES, GO FIND YOUR OWN WAY!
OOF!
OKAY, OKAY, I APOLOGIZE!
NOW COME ON!
I GUESS THIS IS NOT THE TIME TO TELL HIM WE'RE COMPLETELY LOST!
15.

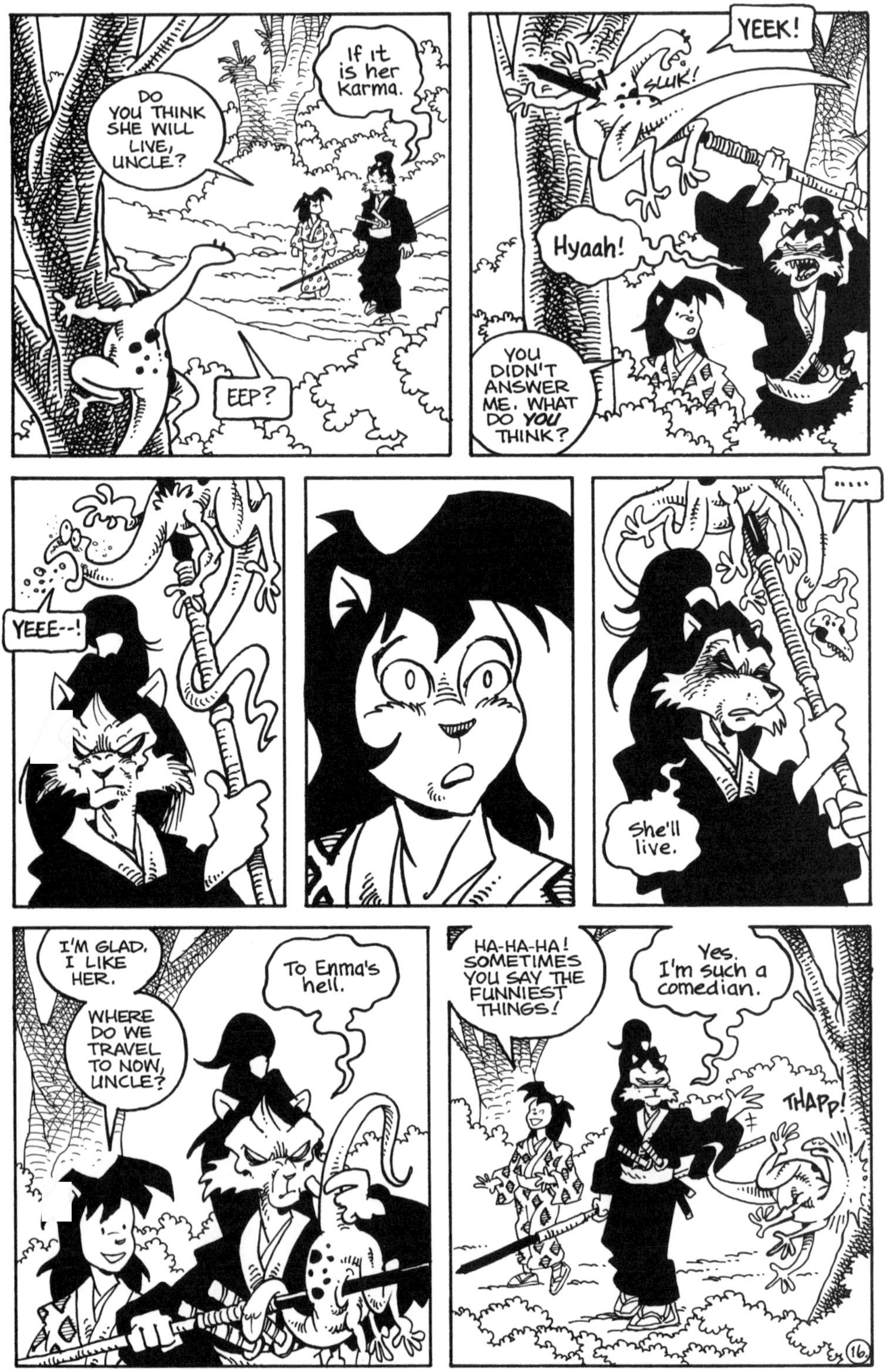
DO YOU THINK SHE WILL LIVE, UNCLE?
If it is her karma.
EEP?
YEEK!
SLUK!
Hyaah!
YOU DIDN'T ANSWER ME. WHAT DO YOU THINK?
YEEE--!
.....
She'll live.
I'M GLAD. I LIKE HER.
WHERE DO WE TRAVEL TO NOW, UNCLE?
To Enma's hell.
HA-HA-HA! SOMETIMES YOU SAY THE FUNNIEST THINGS!
Yes. I'm such a comedian.
THAPP!
16.

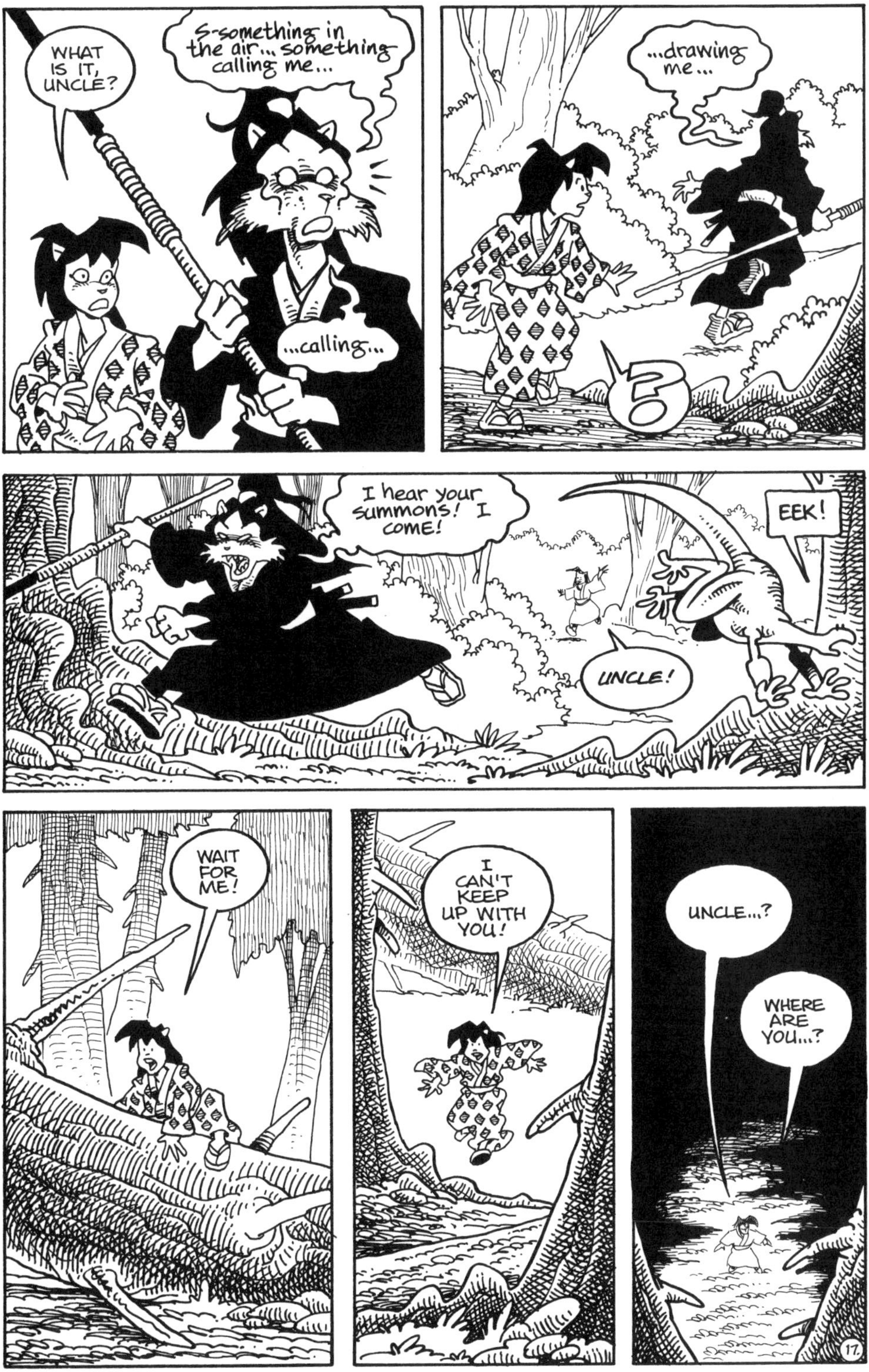
WHAT IS IT, UNCLE?
S-something in the air... something calling me...
...calling...
...drawing me...
?
I hear your summons! I come!
EEK!
UNCLE!
WAIT FOR ME!
I CAN'T KEEP UP WITH YOU!
UNCLE...?
WHERE ARE YOU...?
17.

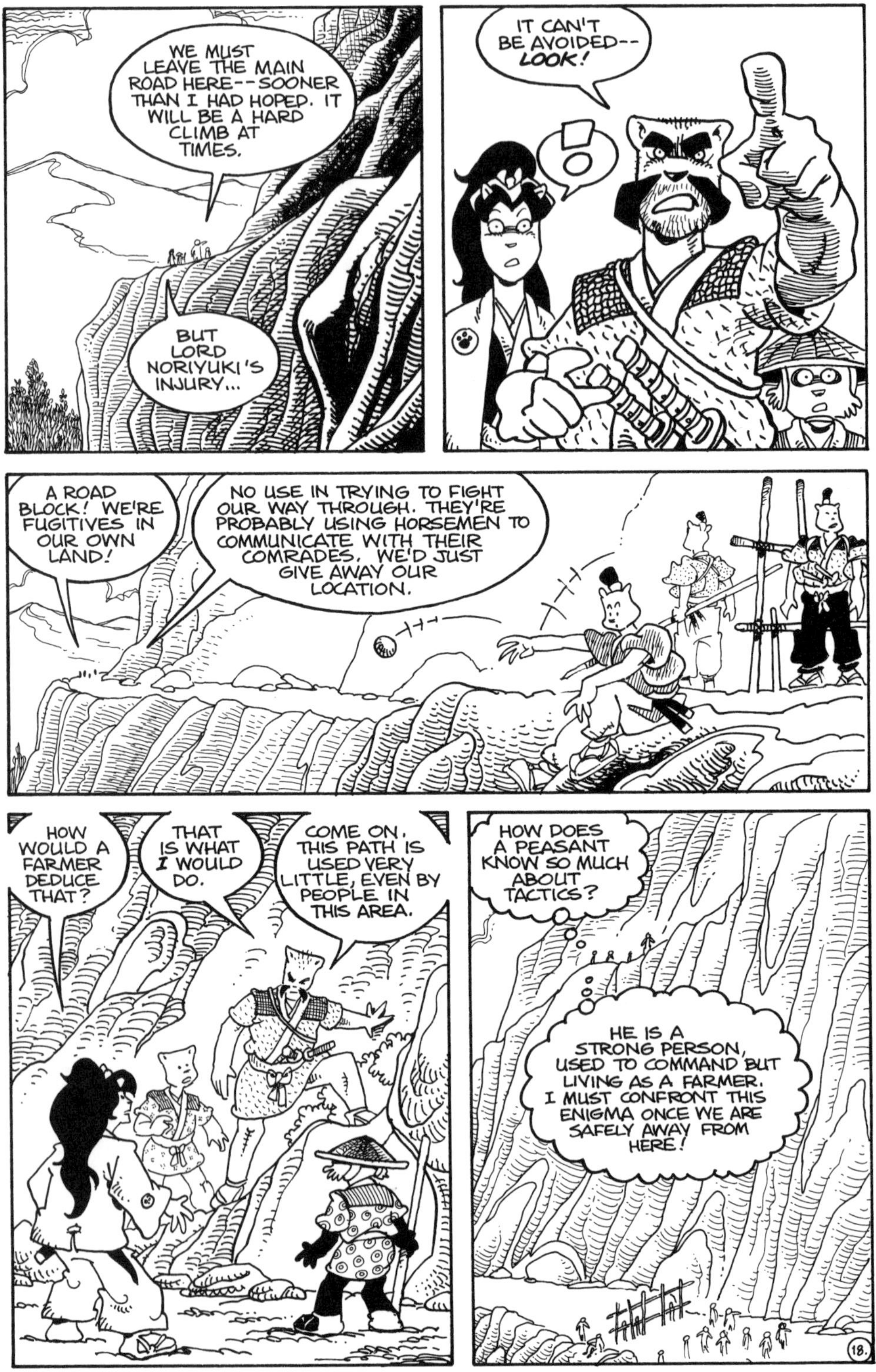
WE MUST LEAVE THE MAIN ROAD HERE--SOONER THAN I HAD HOPED. IT WILL BE A HARD CLIMB AT TIMES.
BUT LORD NORIYUKI'S INJURY...
IT CAN'T BE AVOIDED-- *LOOK*!
!
A ROAD BLOCK! WE'RE FUGITIVES IN OUR OWN LAND!
NO USE IN TRYING TO FIGHT OUR WAY THROUGH. THEY'RE PROBABLY USING HORSEMEN TO COMMUNICATE WITH THEIR COMRADES. WE'D JUST GIVE AWAY OUR LOCATION.
HOW WOULD A FARMER DEDUCE THAT?
THAT IS WHAT *I* WOULD DO.
COME ON. THIS PATH IS USED VERY LITTLE, EVEN BY PEOPLE IN THIS AREA.
HOW DOES A PEASANT KNOW SO MUCH ABOUT TACTICS?
HE IS A STRONG PERSON, USED TO COMMAND BUT LIVING AS A FARMER. I MUST CONFRONT THIS ENIGMA ONCE WE ARE SAFELY AWAY FROM HERE!
18.

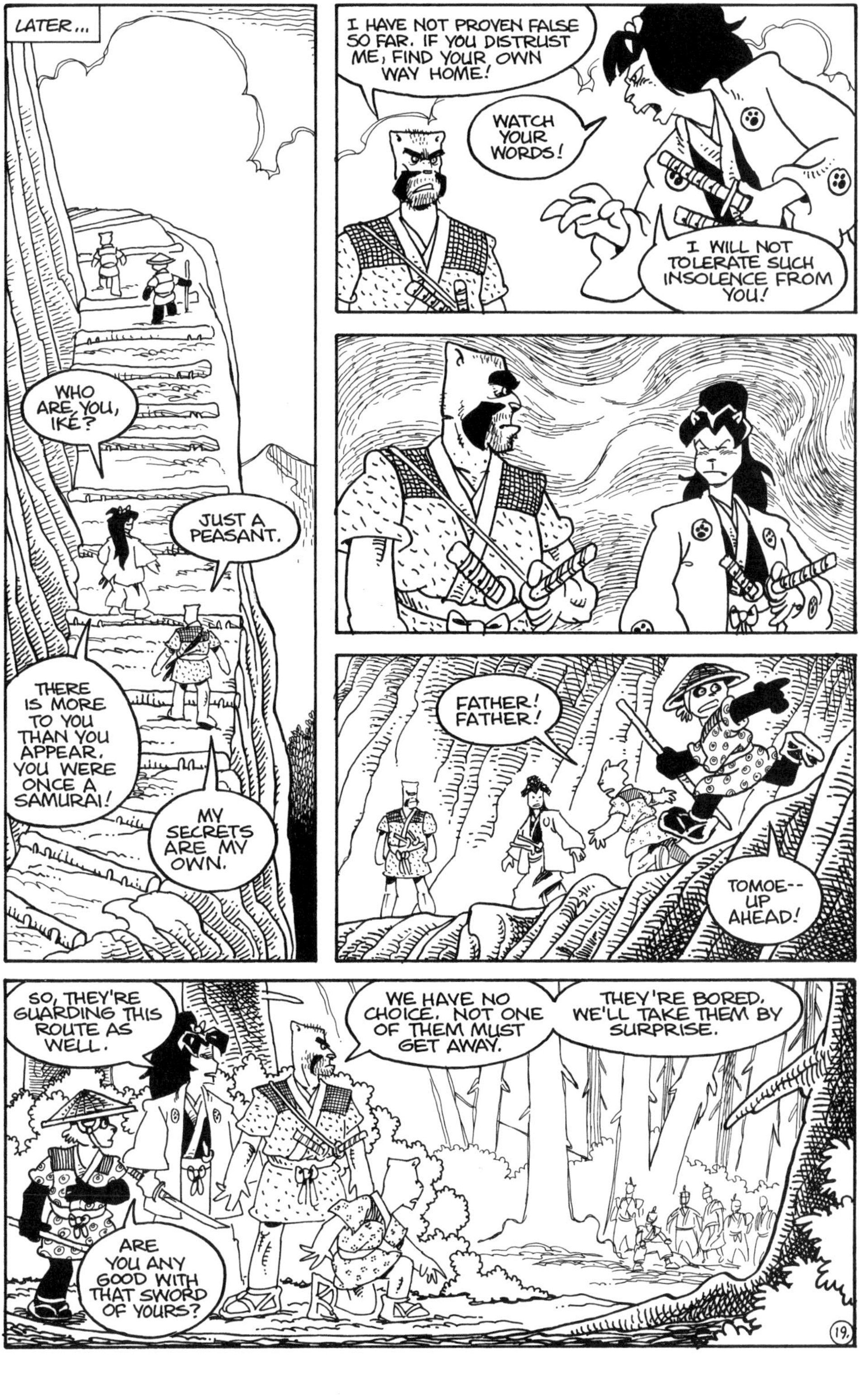
LATER...
WHO ARE YOU, IKÉ?
JUST A PEASANT.
THERE IS MORE TO YOU THAN YOU APPEAR. YOU WERE ONCE A SAMURAI!
MY SECRETS ARE MY OWN.
I HAVE NOT PROVEN FALSE SO FAR. IF YOU DISTRUST ME, FIND YOUR OWN WAY HOME!
WATCH YOUR WORDS!
I WILL NOT TOLERATE SUCH INSOLENCE FROM YOU!
FATHER! FATHER!
TOMOE-- UP AHEAD!
SO, THEY'RE GUARDING THIS ROUTE AS WELL.
WE HAVE NO CHOICE. NOT ONE OF THEM MUST GET AWAY.
THEY'RE BORED. WE'LL TAKE THEM BY SURPRISE.
ARE YOU ANY GOOD WITH THAT SWORD OF YOURS?
19

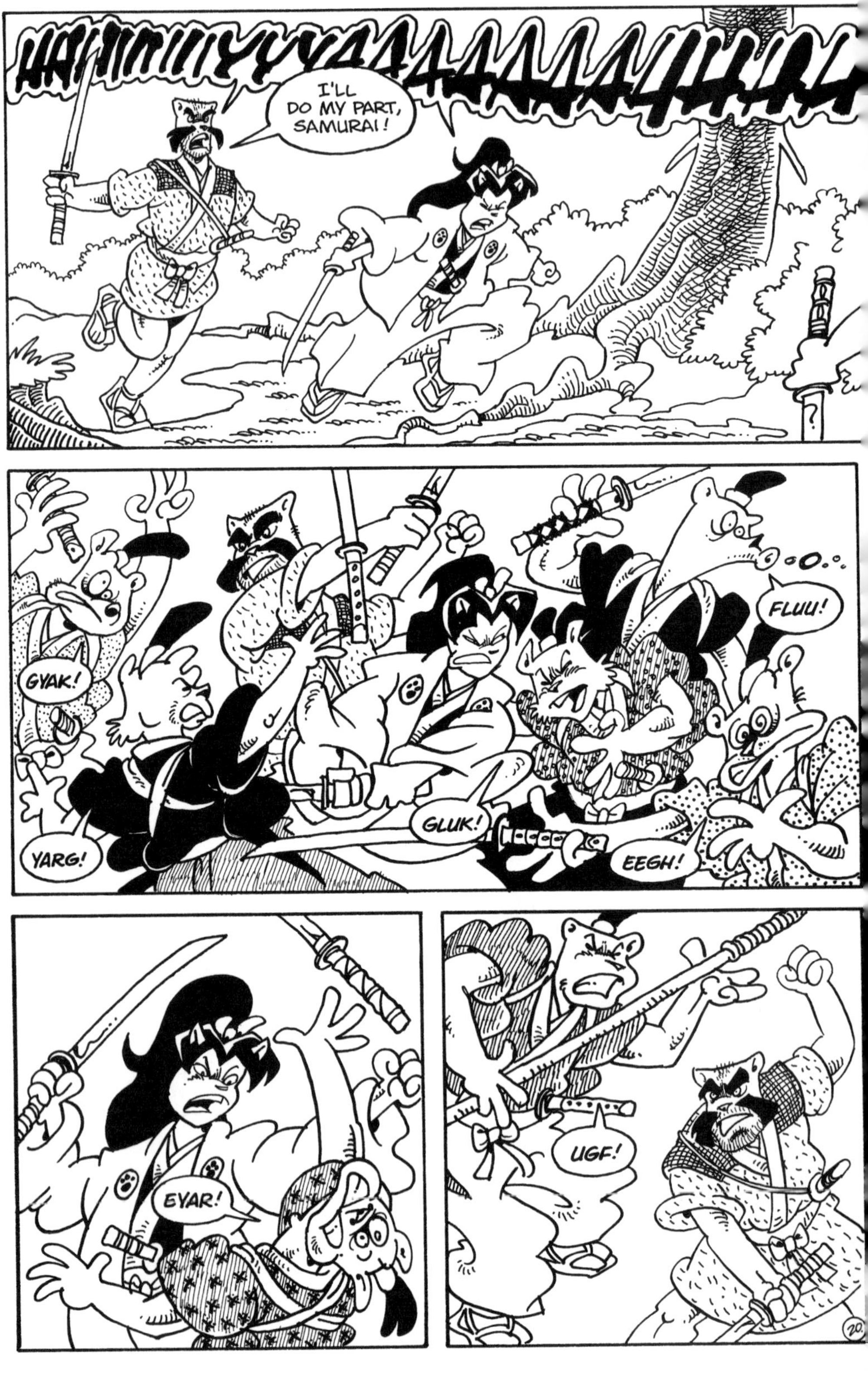
HAIIIIIIYYYAAAAAAAAAAIIIII
I'LL DO MY PART, SAMURAI!
GYAK!
YARG!
GLUK!
EEGH!
FLUU!
EYAR!
UGF!
20.

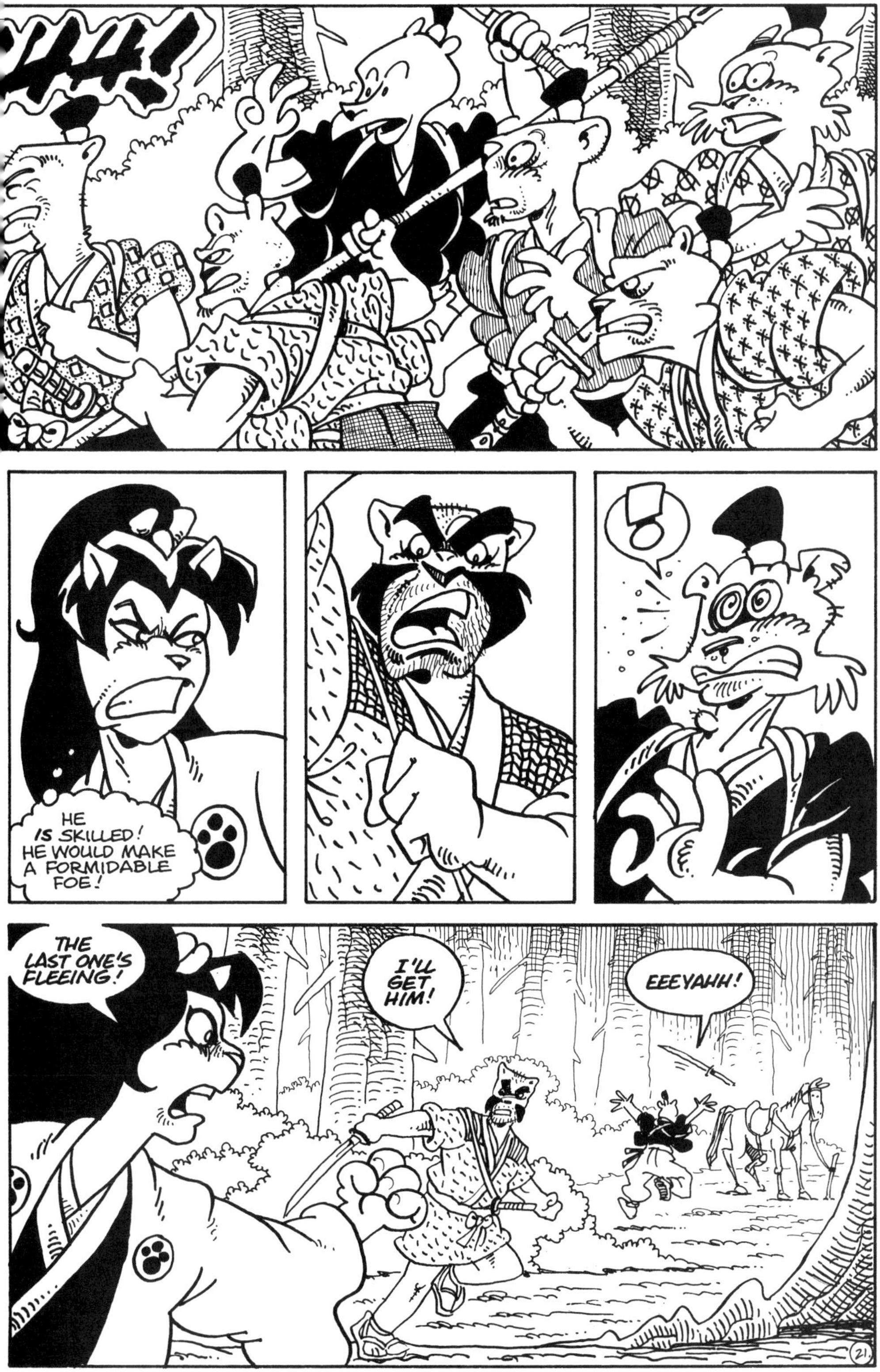
HE IS SKILLED! HE WOULD MAKE A FORMIDABLE FOE!
!
THE LAST ONE'S FLEEING!
I'LL GET HIM!
EEEYAHH!
21.

STOP HIM!
DON'T WORRY! HE WON'T ESCAPE!
EEVAHH!
UH--!
MY LEG!
UH!
THUD!
HE GOT AWAY!
IT'S MY FAULT--AN OLD INJURY.
IT'S NOT THE FIRST TIME MY LEGS HAVE FAILED ME.
THEY'RE ALERTED! THE DANGER IS GREATER NOW. TELL US THE ROUTE AND WE'LL TRY TO MAKE IT ON OUR OWN!
NO. WE OFFERED TO GUIDE YOU, AND WE'LL SEE IT THROUGH TO THE END!
22

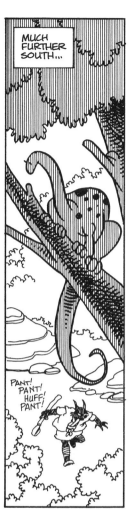

MUCH FURTHER SOUTH...

PANT! PANT! HUFF! PANT!

:PANT! HUFF! PUFF!:

REST.

:SNIFF! SNIFF!: AHH....ALL ALONE.

SAFE.

TAKE LOOK, WON'T HURT.

WON'T HURT AT ALL.

.....

:CRUNCH!: :MUNCH!: :SLURP!:

HMM....

:SNIFF!: :SNIFF!: BAH! NOTHING SPECIAL ABOUT BLADE.

SO MUCH TROUBLE FOR WORTHLESS SWORD!

KITANAMONO!

WHIMPER...

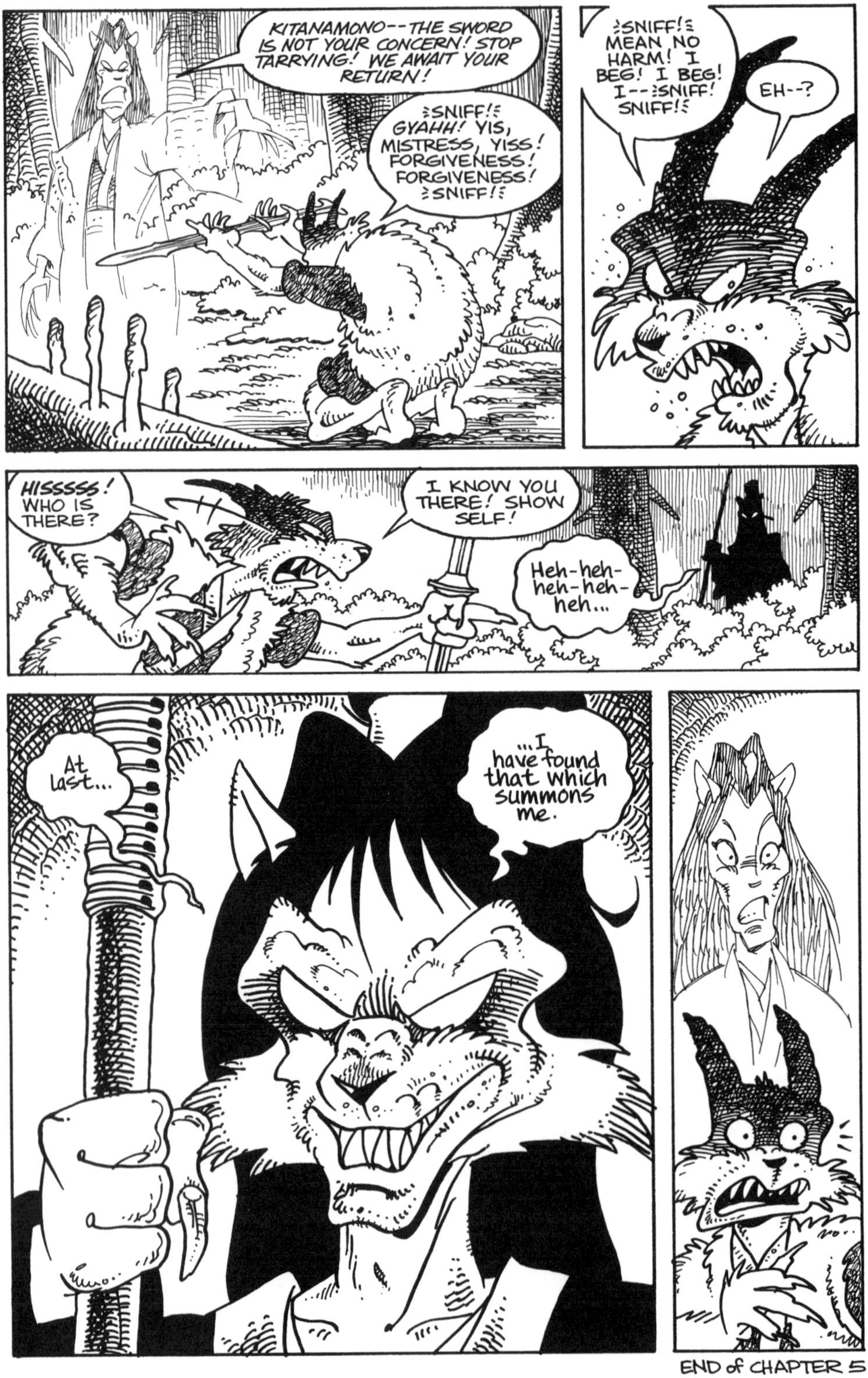
KITANAMONO--THE SWORD IS NOT YOUR CONCERN! STOP TARRYING! WE AWAIT YOUR RETURN!
SNIFF! GYAHH! YIS, MISTRESS, YISS! FORGIVENESS! FORGIVENESS! SNIFF!
SNIFF! MEAN NO HARM! I BEG! I BEG! I--SNIFF! SNIFF!
EH--?
HISSSSS! WHO IS THERE?
I KNOW YOU THERE! SHOW SELF!
Heh-heh-heh-heh-heh...
At last...
...I have found that which summons me.
END of CHAPTER 5

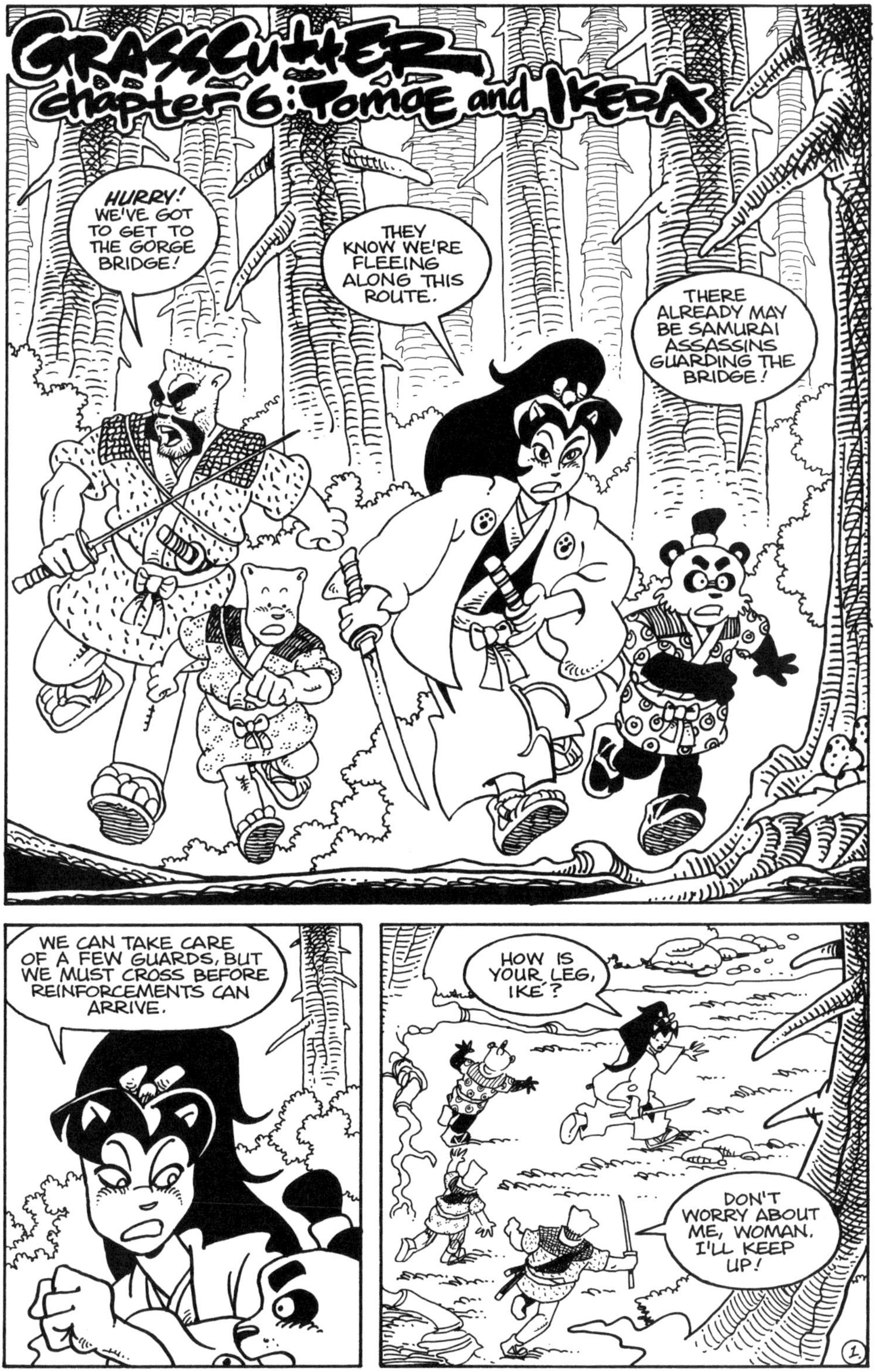
GRASSCUTTER
chapter 6: TOMOE and IKEDA
HURRY! WE'VE GOT TO GET TO THE GORGE BRIDGE!
THEY KNOW WE'RE FLEEING ALONG THIS ROUTE.
THERE ALREADY MAY BE SAMURAI ASSASSINS GUARDING THE BRIDGE!
WE CAN TAKE CARE OF A FEW GUARDS, BUT WE MUST CROSS BEFORE REINFORCEMENTS CAN ARRIVE.
HOW IS YOUR LEG, IKE?
DON'T WORRY ABOUT ME, WOMAN. I'LL KEEP UP!
1.

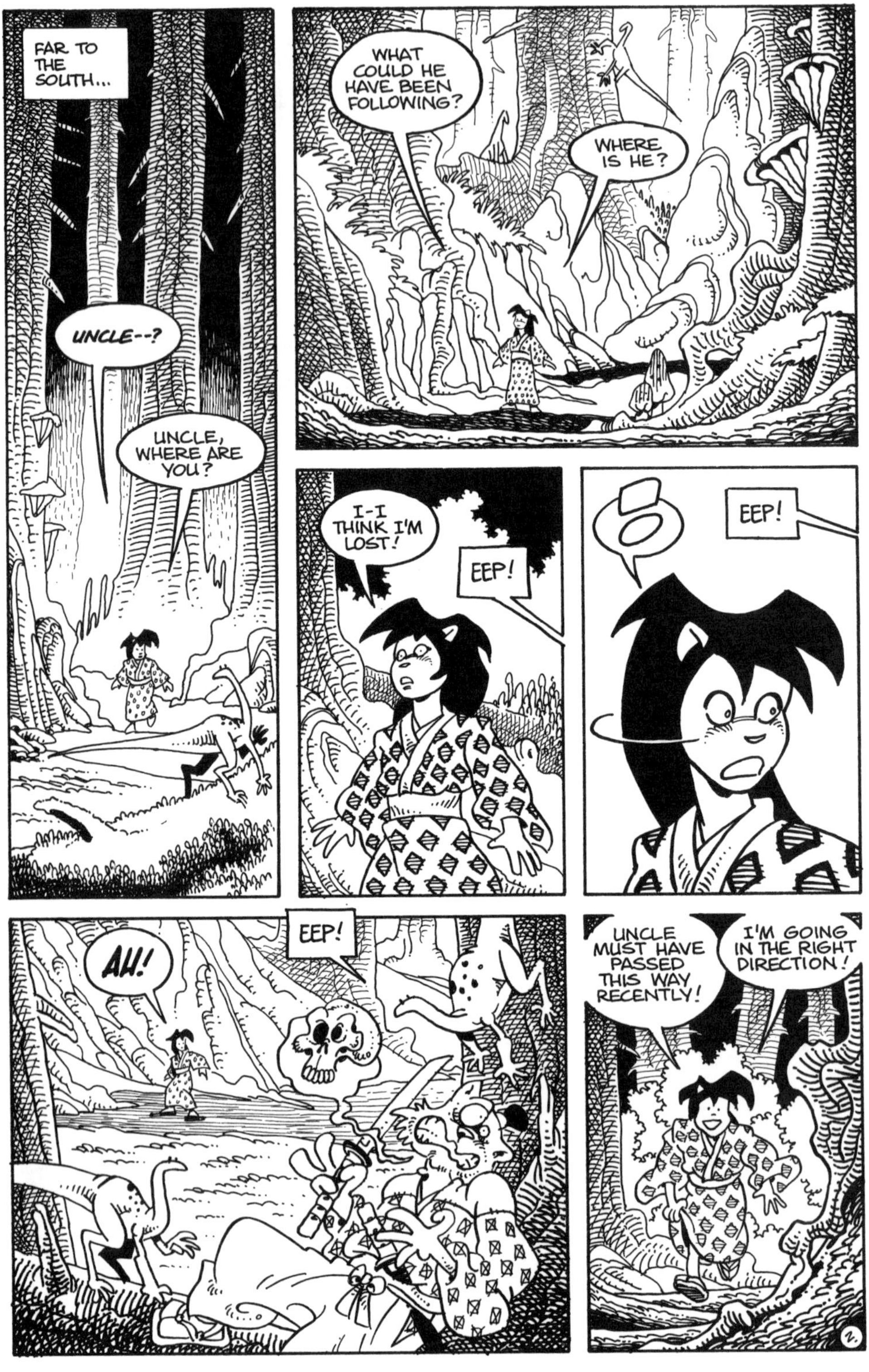
FAR TO THE SOUTH...
UNCLE--?
UNCLE, WHERE ARE YOU?
WHAT COULD HE HAVE BEEN FOLLOWING?
WHERE IS HE?
I-I THINK I'M LOST!
EEP!
EEP!
AH!
EEP!
UNCLE MUST HAVE PASSED THIS WAY RECENTLY!
I'M GOING IN THE RIGHT DIRECTION!
2.

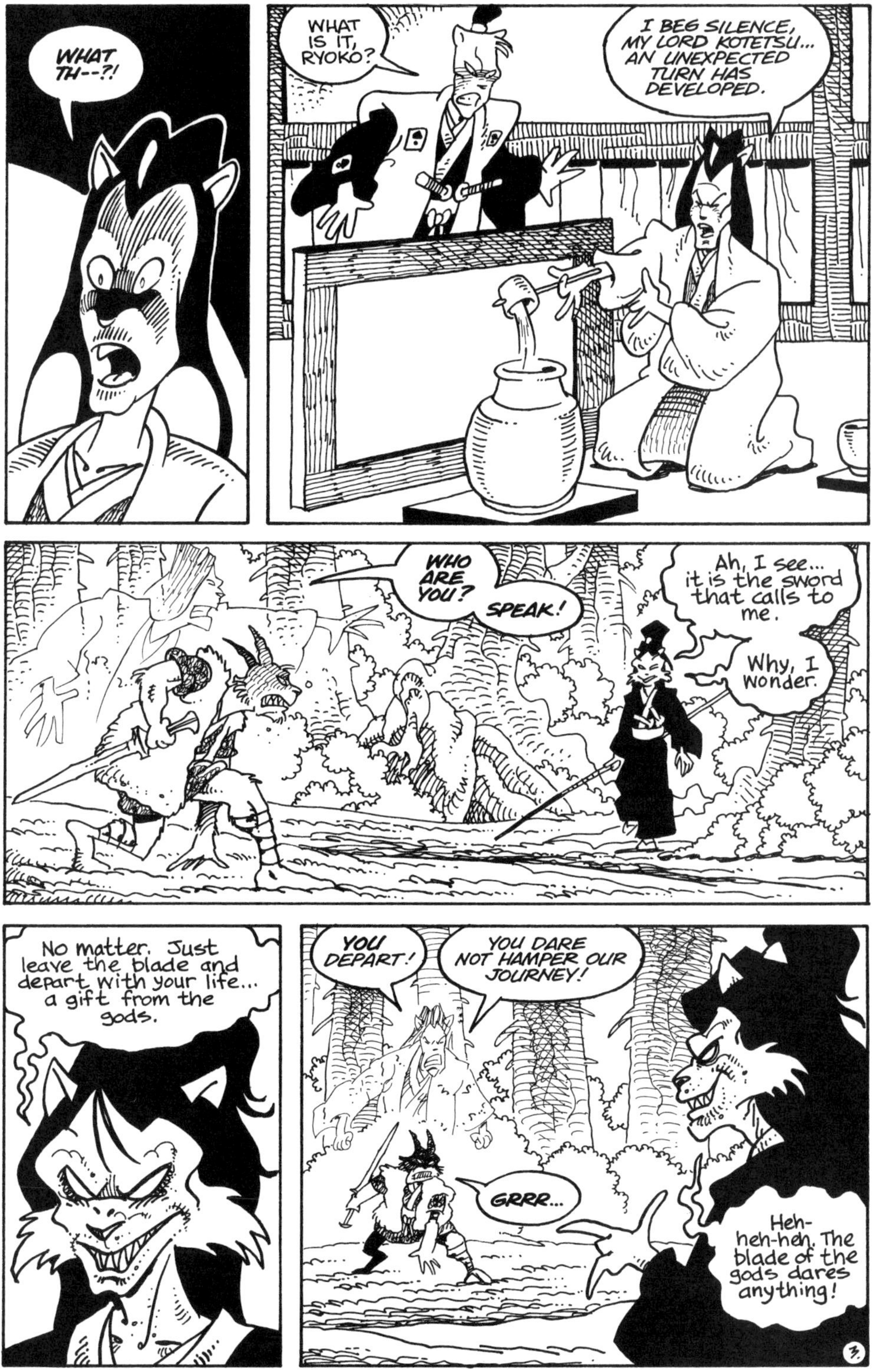
WHAT TH--?!
WHAT IS IT, RYOKO?
I BEG SILENCE, MY LORD KOTETSU... AN UNEXPECTED TURN HAS DEVELOPED.
WHO ARE YOU?
SPEAK!
Ah, I see... it is the sword that calls to me.
Why, I wonder.
No matter. Just leave the blade and depart with your life... a gift from the gods.
YOU DEPART!
YOU DARE NOT HAMPER OUR JOURNEY!
GRRR...
Heh-heh-heh. The blade of the gods dares anything!
3.

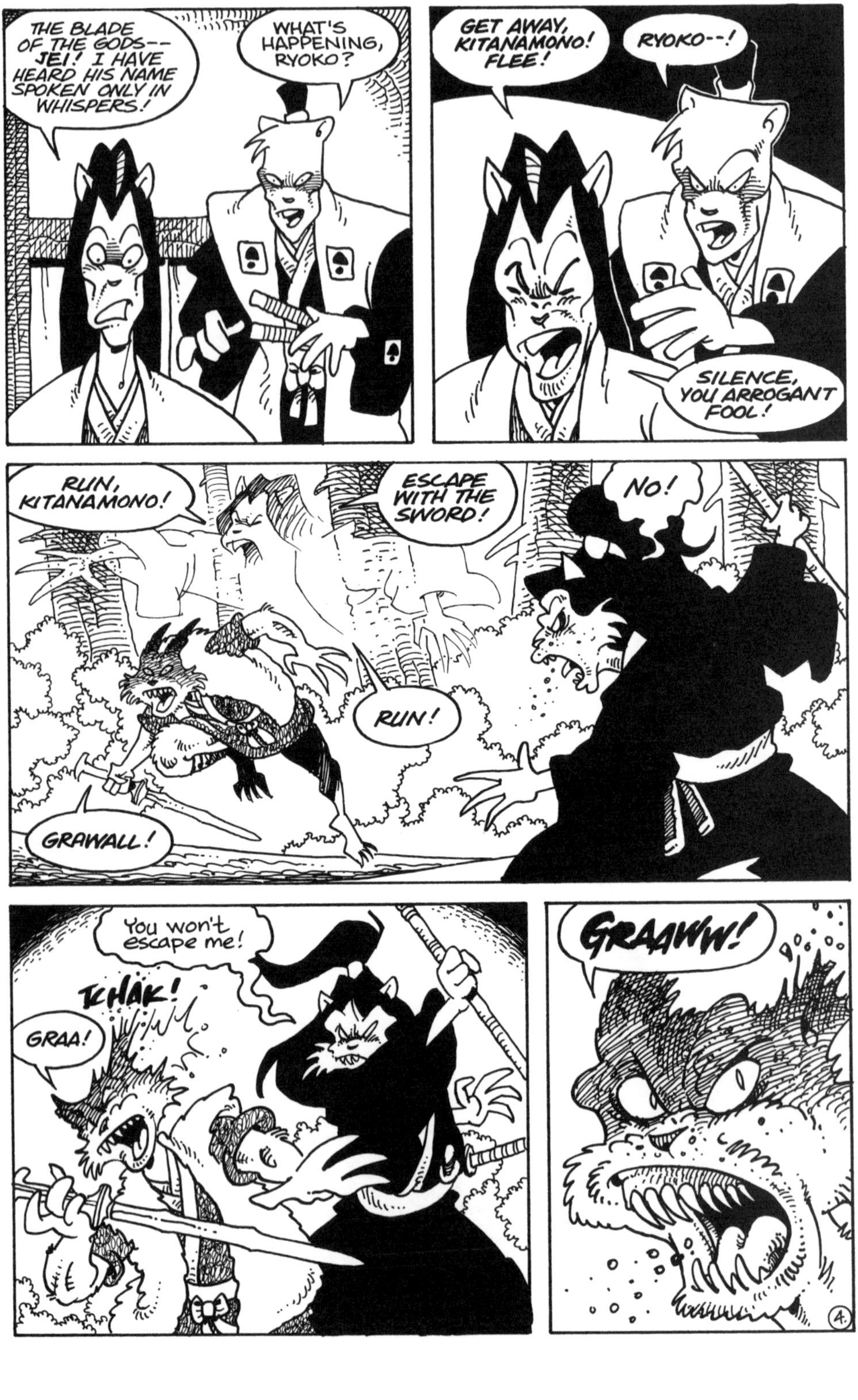
THE BLADE OF THE GODS-- JEI! I HAVE HEARD HIS NAME SPOKEN ONLY IN WHISPERS!
WHAT'S HAPPENING, RYOKO?
GET AWAY, KITANAMONO! FLEE!
RYOKO--!
SILENCE, YOU ARROGANT FOOL!
RUN, KITANAMONO!
ESCAPE WITH THE SWORD!
NO!
RUN!
GRAWLL!
You won't escape me!
KHAK!
GRAA!
GRAAWW!
4.

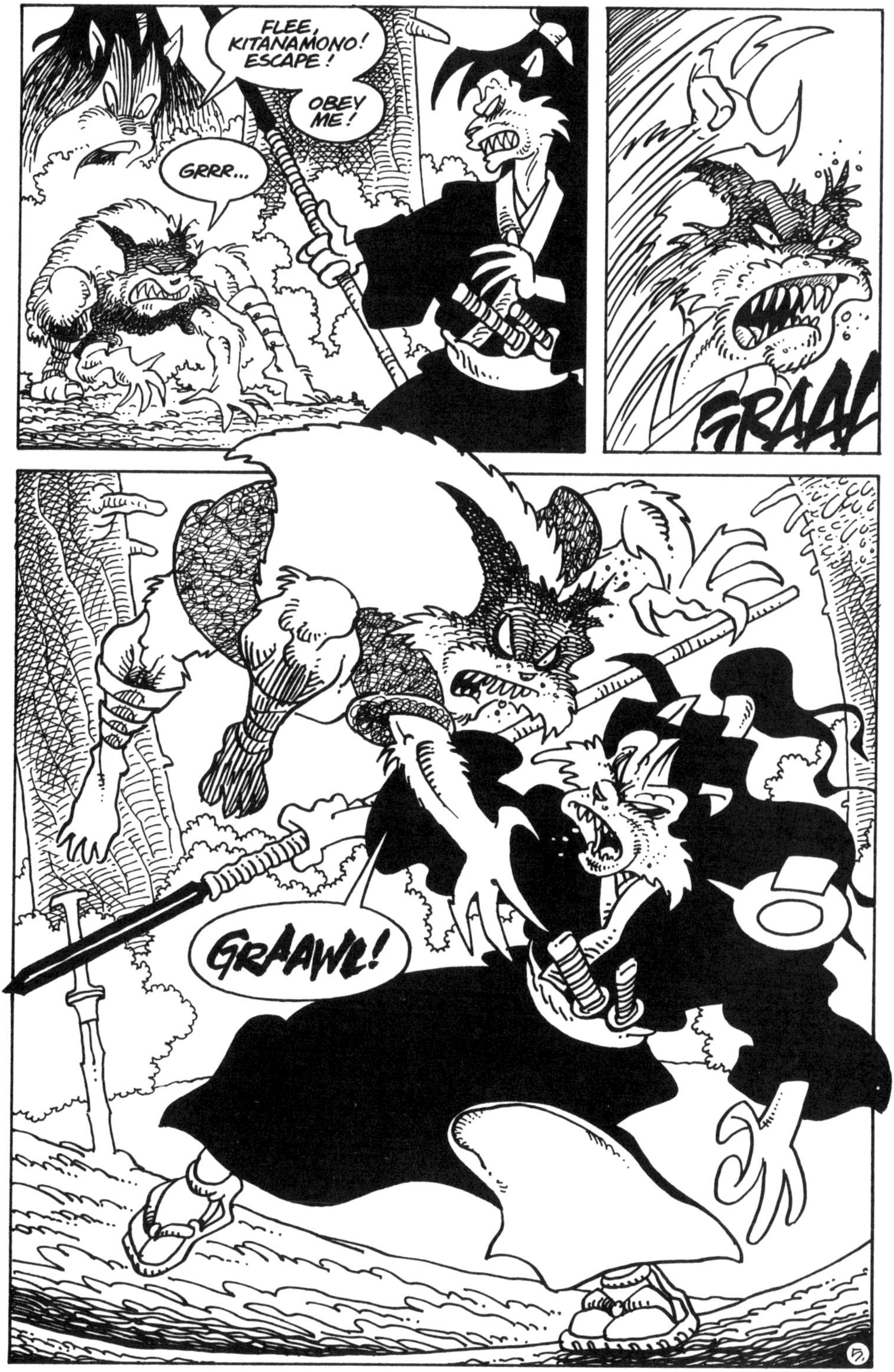
FLEE, KITANAMONO! ESCAPE!
OBEY ME!
GRRR...
GRAAA
GRAAWL!

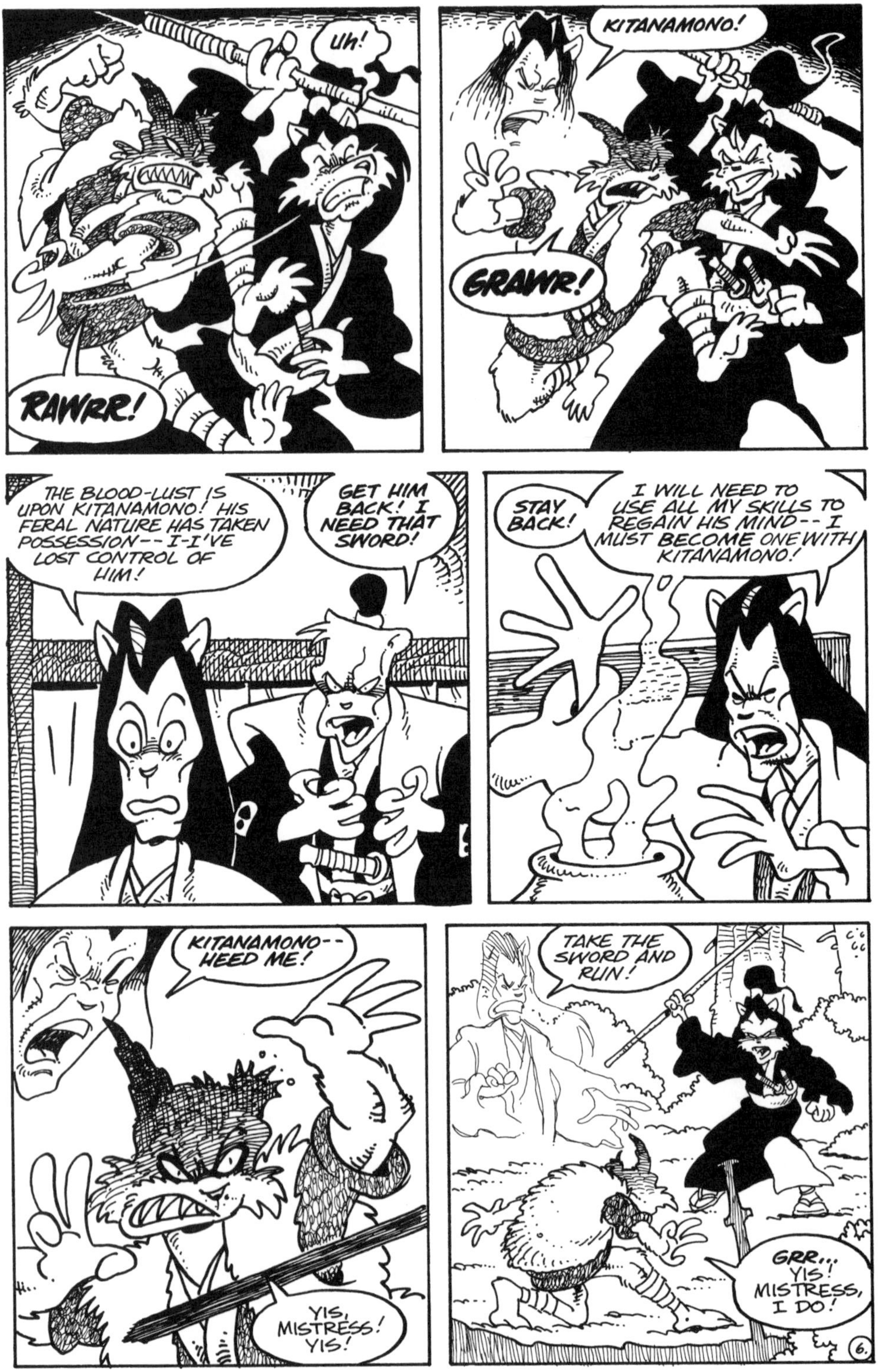

UH!
RAWRR!
KITANAMONO!
GRAWR!
THE BLOOD-LUST IS UPON KITANAMONO! HIS FERAL NATURE HAS TAKEN POSSESSION-- I-I'VE LOST CONTROL OF HIM!
GET HIM BACK! I NEED THAT SWORD!
STAY BACK!
I WILL NEED TO USE ALL MY SKILLS TO REGAIN HIS MIND-- I MUST BECOME ONE WITH KITANAMONO!
KITANAMONO-- HEED ME!
YIS, MISTRESS! YIS!
TAKE THE SWORD AND RUN!
GRR... YIS! MISTRESS, I DO!
6.

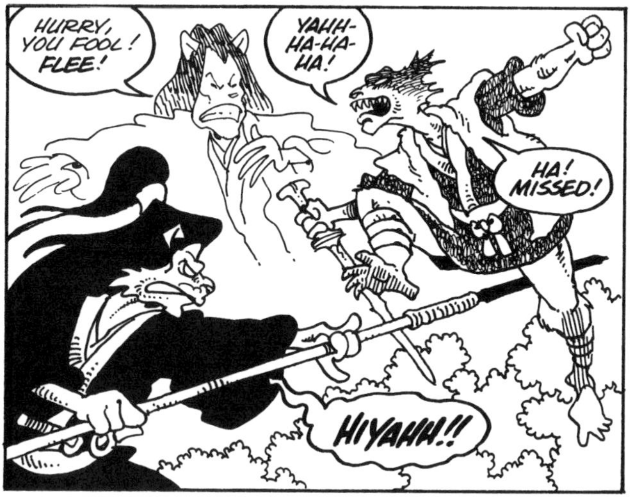
HURRY, YOU FOOL! FLEE!
YAHH-HA-HA-HA!
HA! MISSED!
HIYAHH!!

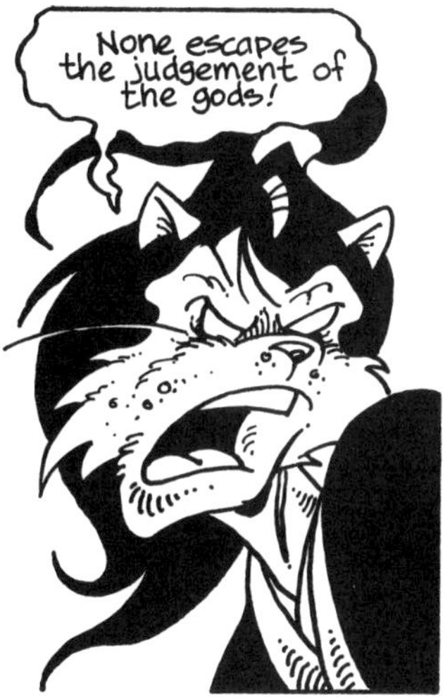
None escapes the judgement of the gods!

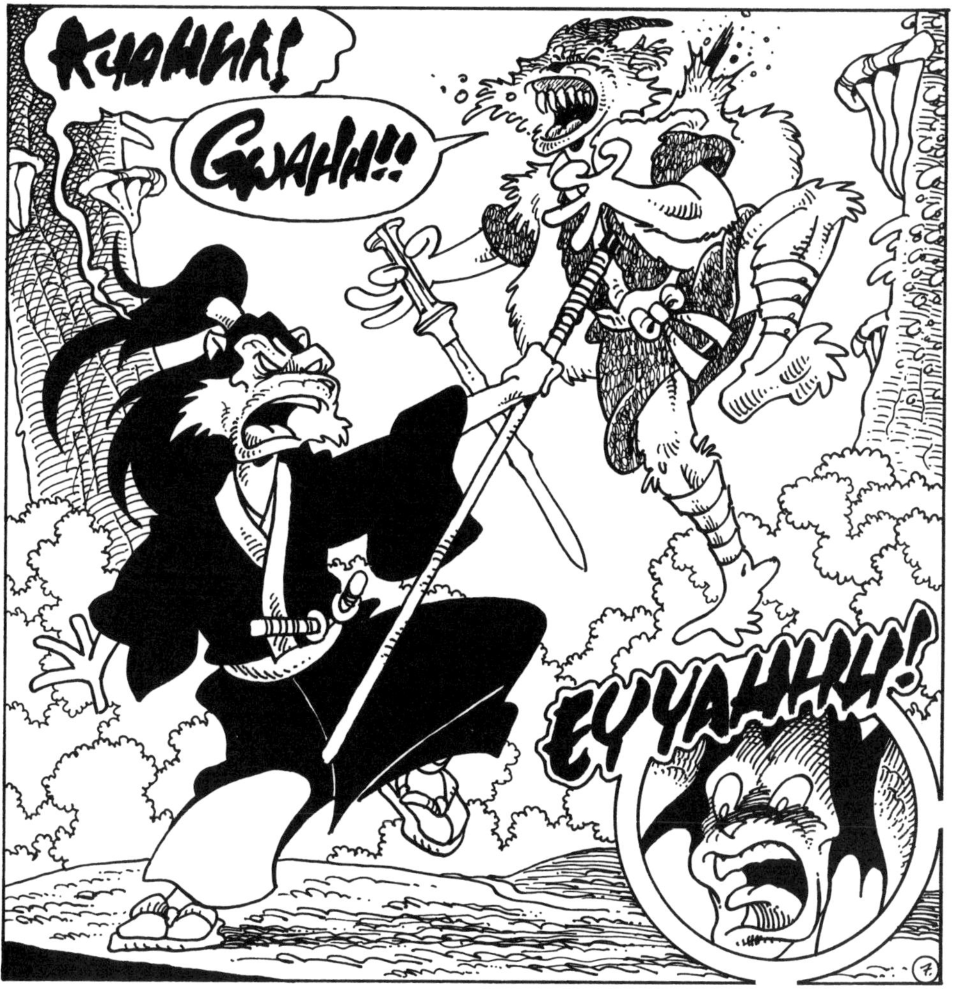
KYAHHH!
GWAHH!!
EY YAHHH!

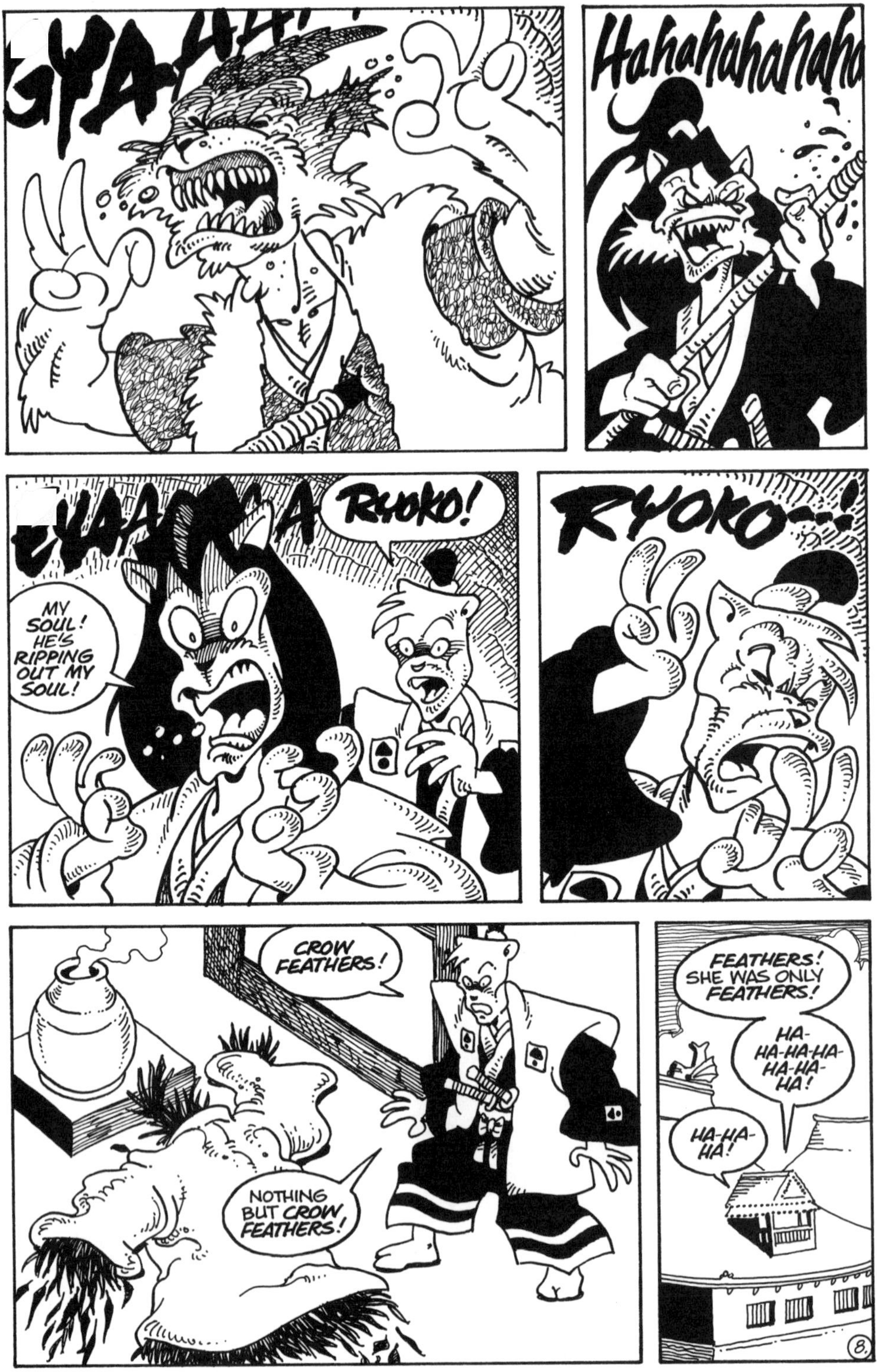
GYAAAH!
Hahahahahahaha
RYOKO!
MY SOUL! HE'S RIPPING OUT MY SOUL!
RYOKO--!
CROW FEATHERS!
NOTHING BUT CROW FEATHERS!
FEATHERS! SHE WAS ONLY FEATHERS!
HA-HA-HA-HA HA-HA-HA HA!
HA-HA-HA!
8.

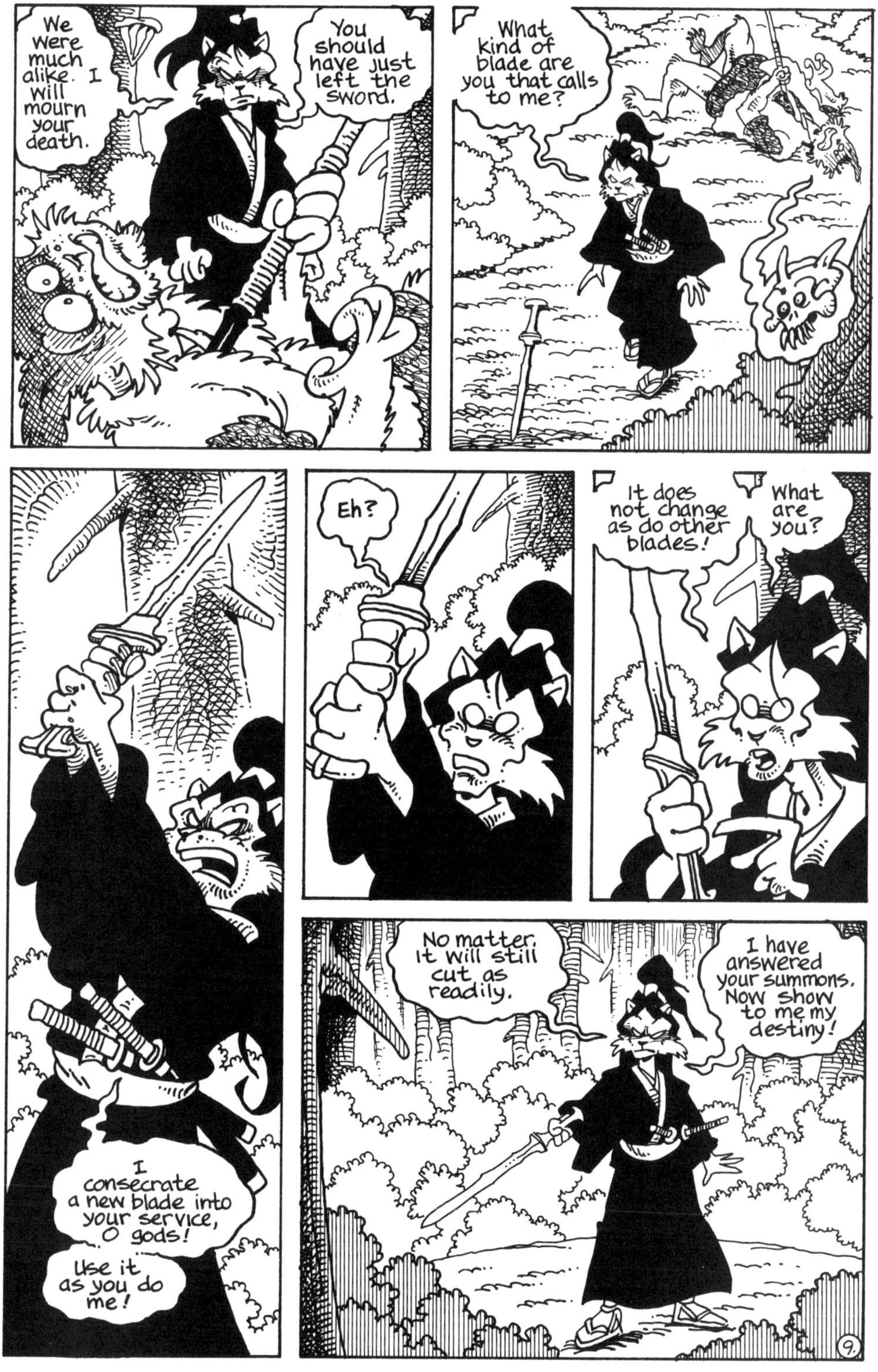
We were much alike. I will mourn your death.
You should have just left the sword.
What kind of blade are you that calls to me?
Eh?
I consecrate a new blade into your service, O gods!
Use it as you do me!
It does not change as do other blades!
What are you?
No matter. It will still cut as readily.
I have answered your summons. Now show to me my destiny!
9.

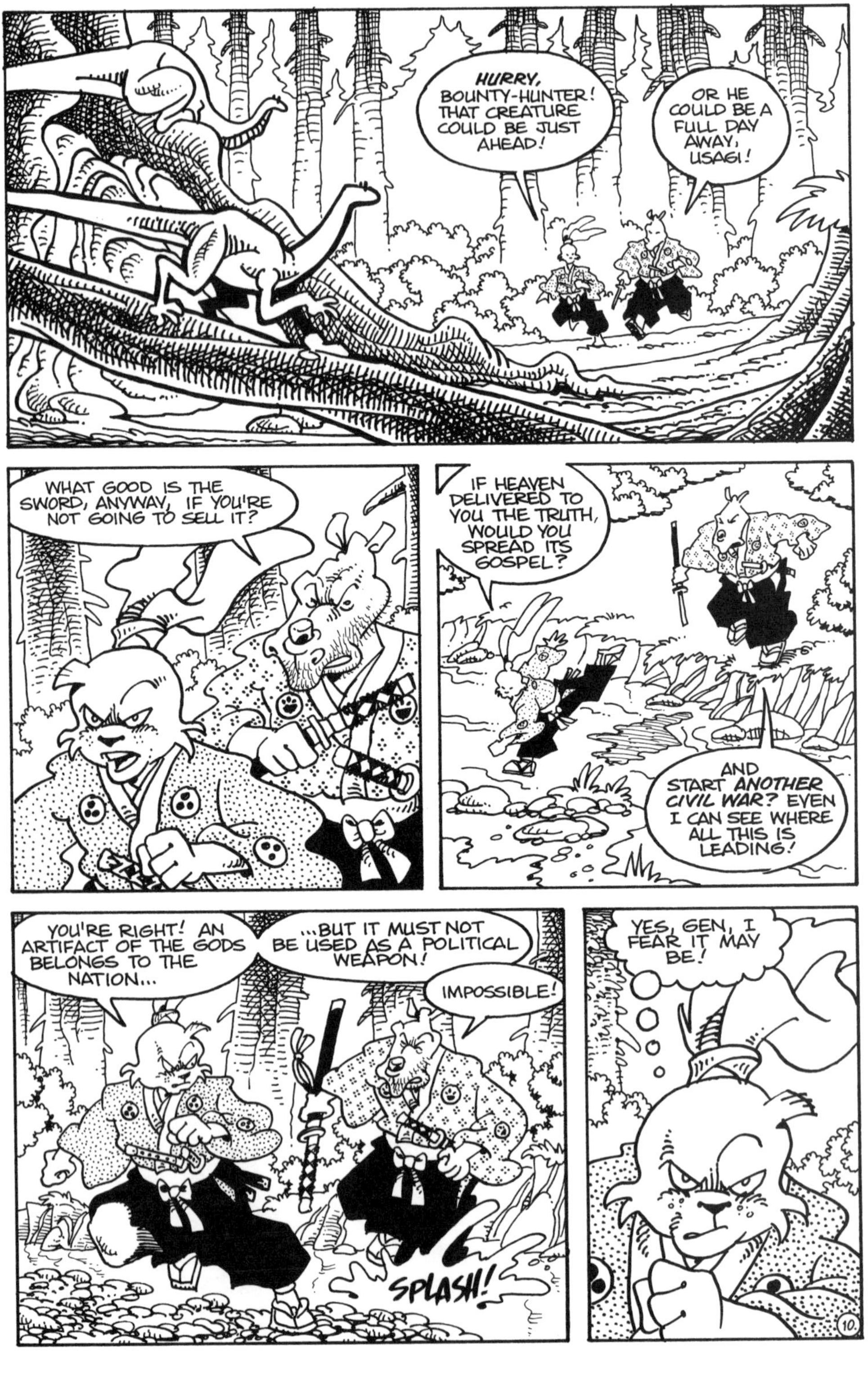
HURRY, BOUNTY-HUNTER! THAT CREATURE COULD BE JUST AHEAD!
OR HE COULD BE A FULL DAY AWAY, USAGI!
WHAT GOOD IS THE SWORD, ANYWAY, IF YOU'RE NOT GOING TO SELL IT?
IF HEAVEN DELIVERED TO YOU THE TRUTH, WOULD YOU SPREAD ITS GOSPEL?
AND START ANOTHER CIVIL WAR? EVEN I CAN SEE WHERE ALL THIS IS LEADING!
YOU'RE RIGHT! AN ARTIFACT OF THE GODS BELONGS TO THE NATION...
...BUT IT MUST NOT BE USED AS A POLITICAL WEAPON!
IMPOSSIBLE!
SPLASH!
YES, GEN, I FEAR IT MAY BE!
10.

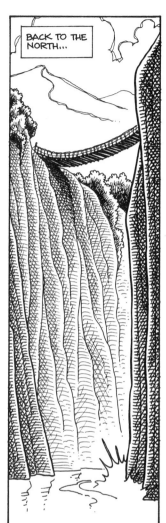

BACK TO THE NORTH...

SO, THE GORGE BRIDGE IS GUARDED.

YES, BUT WE EXPECTED THAT.

THEY DON'T LOOK LIKE THEY'RE PREPARED FOR US.

THE SAMURAI THAT ESCAPED US MUST HAVE GONE TO THEIR MAIN FORCES INSTEAD OF WARNING THESE GUARDS.

THEN WE'D BETTER CROSS QUICKLY BEFORE OTHERS ARRIVE!

STAY BACK, MOTOKAZU, LORD NORIYUKI!

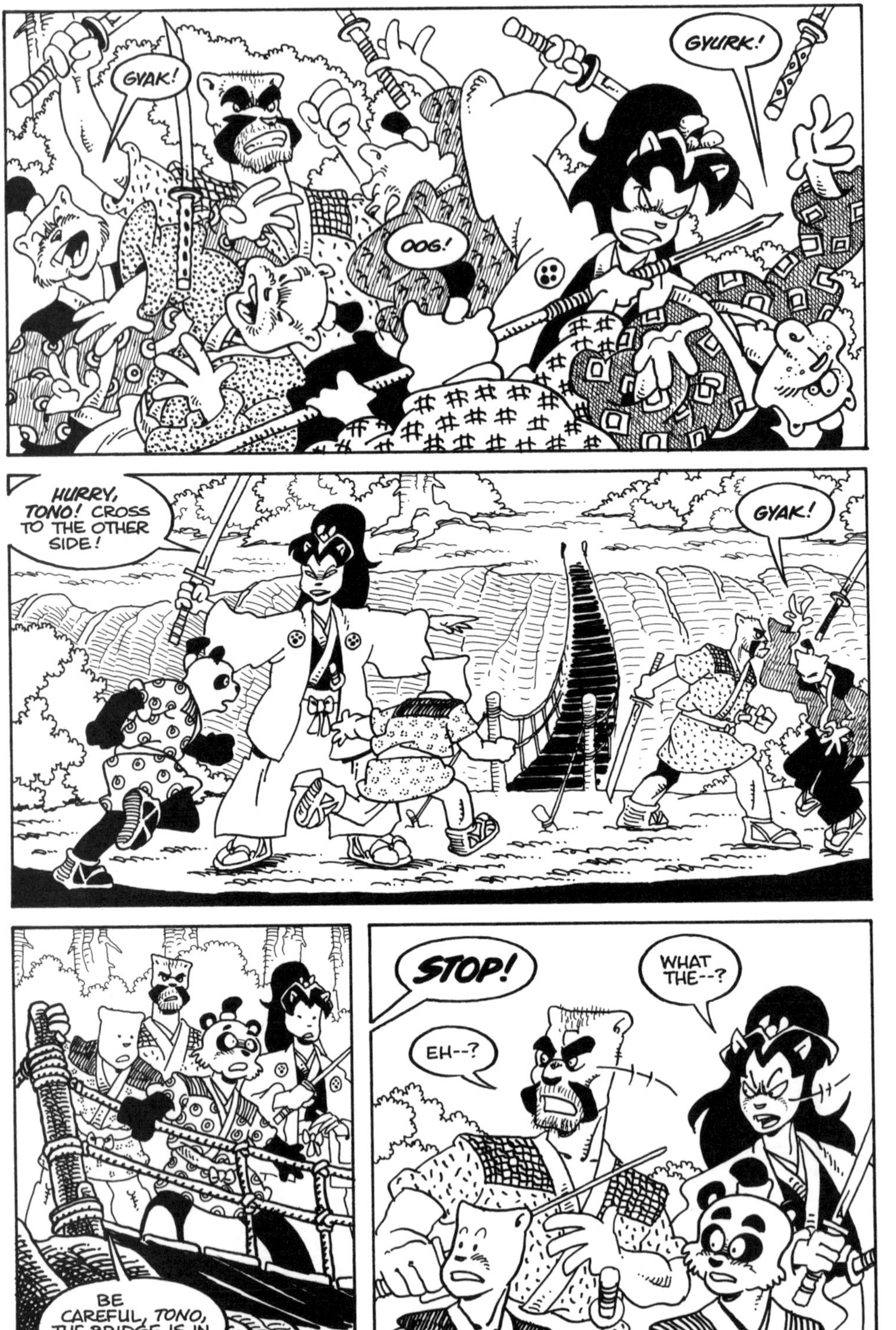
GYAK!
OOG!
GYURK!
HURRY, *TONO!* CROSS TO THE OTHER SIDE!
GYAK!
BE CAREFUL, *TONO*, THE BRIDGE IS IN DISREPAIR!
STOP!
WHAT THE--?
EH--?
12

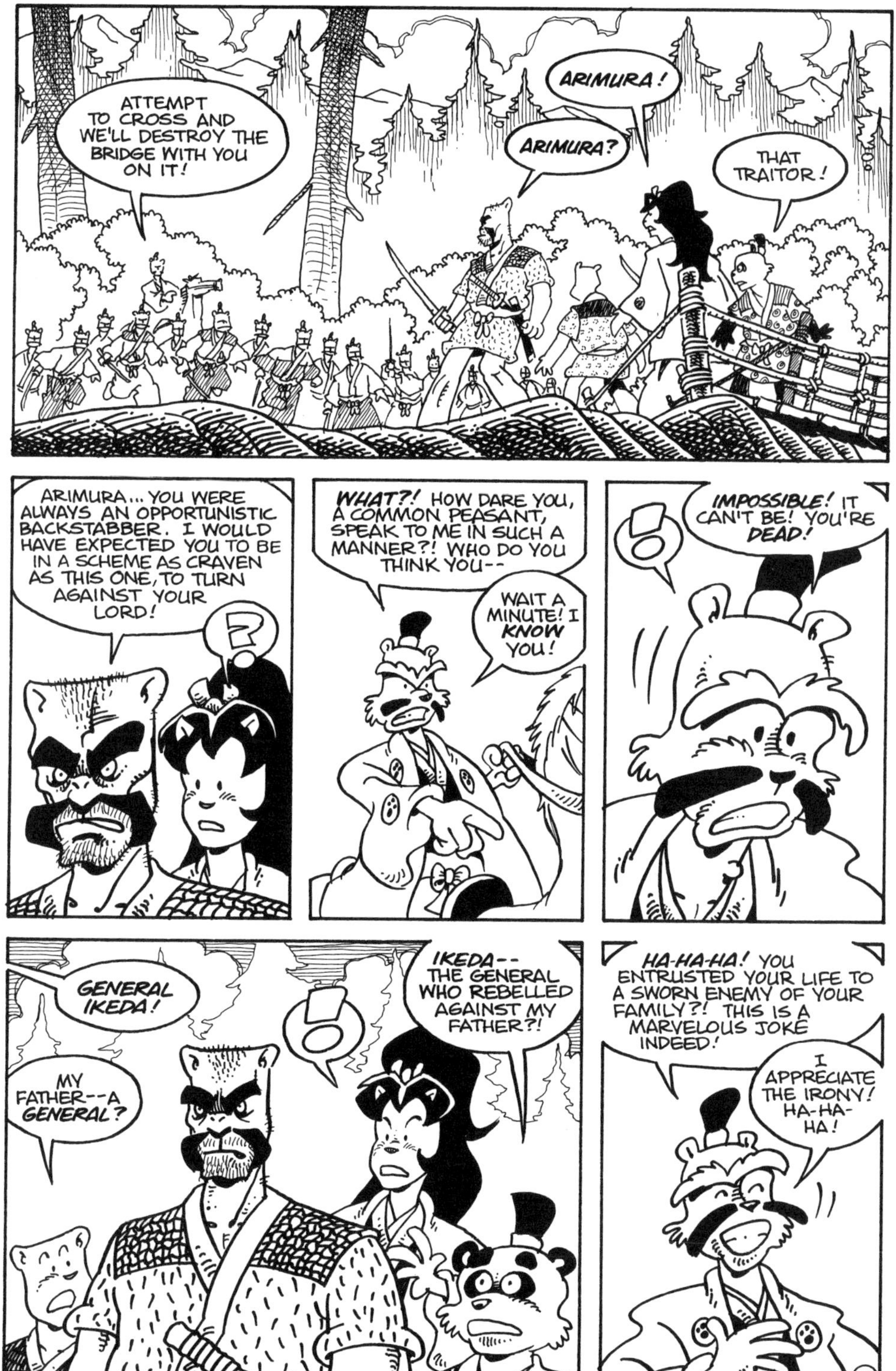
ATTEMPT TO CROSS AND WE'LL DESTROY THE BRIDGE WITH YOU ON IT!
ARIMURA?
ARIMURA!
THAT TRAITOR!
ARIMURA... YOU WERE ALWAYS AN OPPORTUNISTIC BACKSTABBER. I WOULD HAVE EXPECTED YOU TO BE IN A SCHEME AS CRAVEN AS THIS ONE, TO TURN AGAINST YOUR LORD!
?
WHAT?! HOW DARE YOU, A COMMON PEASANT, SPEAK TO ME IN SUCH A MANNER?! WHO DO YOU THINK YOU--
WAIT A MINUTE! I KNOW YOU!
!
IMPOSSIBLE! IT CAN'T BE! YOU'RE DEAD!
GENERAL IKEDA!
MY FATHER--A GENERAL?
!
IKEDA-- THE GENERAL WHO REBELLED AGAINST MY FATHER?!
HA-HA-HA! YOU ENTRUSTED YOUR LIFE TO A SWORN ENEMY OF YOUR FAMILY?! THIS IS A MARVELOUS JOKE INDEED!
I APPRECIATE THE IRONY! HA-HA-HA!
13.

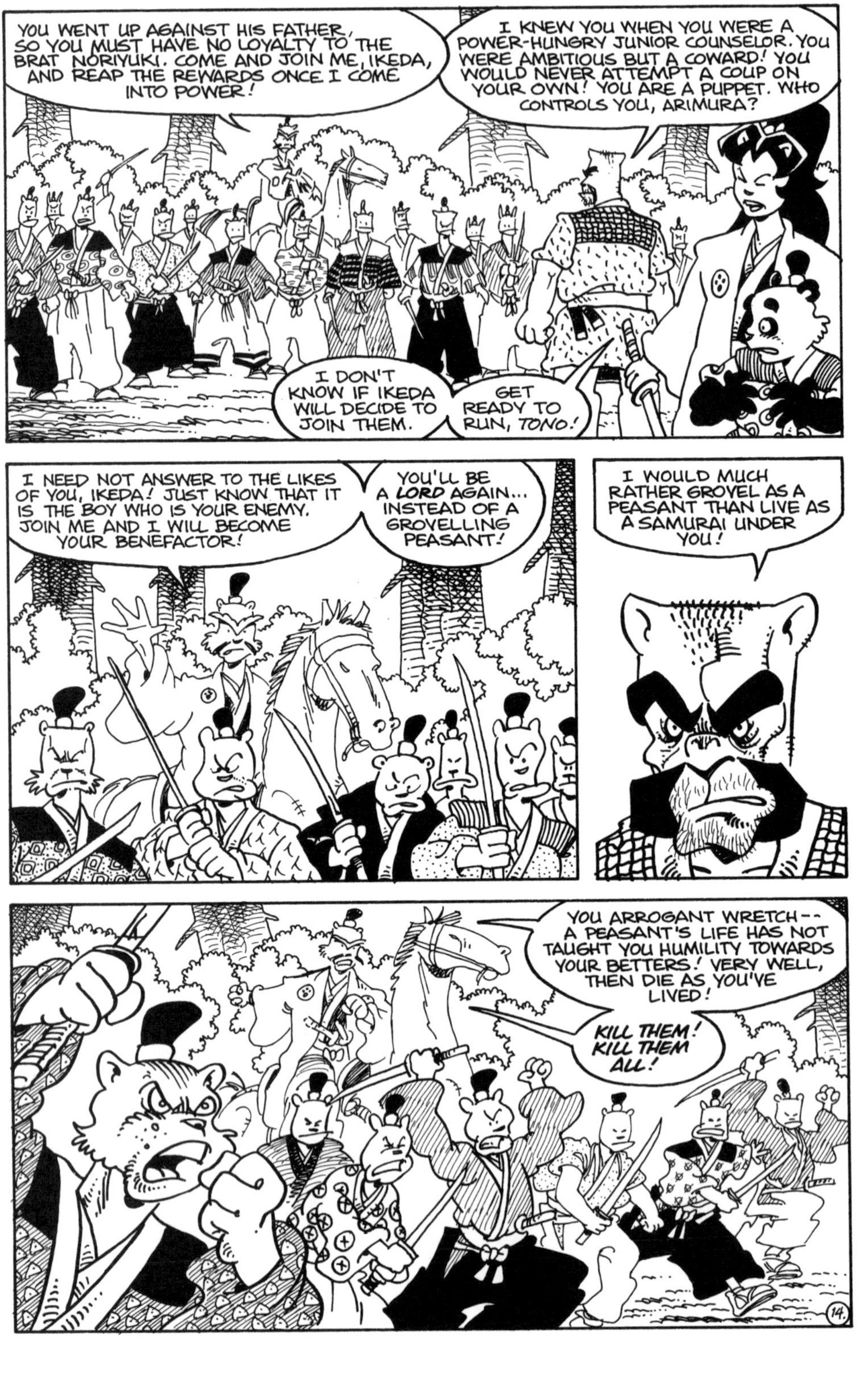
YOU WENT UP AGAINST HIS FATHER, SO YOU MUST HAVE NO LOYALTY TO THE BRAT NORIYUKI. COME AND JOIN ME, IKEDA, AND REAP THE REWARDS ONCE I COME INTO POWER!
I KNEW YOU WHEN YOU WERE A POWER-HUNGRY JUNIOR COUNSELOR. YOU WERE AMBITIOUS BUT A COWARD! YOU WOULD NEVER ATTEMPT A COUP ON YOUR OWN! YOU ARE A PUPPET. WHO CONTROLS YOU, ARIMURA?
I DON'T KNOW IF IKEDA WILL DECIDE TO JOIN THEM.
GET READY TO RUN, *TONO*!
I NEED NOT ANSWER TO THE LIKES OF YOU, IKEDA! JUST KNOW THAT IT IS THE BOY WHO IS YOUR ENEMY. JOIN ME AND I WILL BECOME YOUR BENEFACTOR!
YOU'LL BE A ***LORD*** AGAIN... INSTEAD OF A GROVELLING PEASANT!
I WOULD MUCH RATHER GROVEL AS A PEASANT THAN LIVE AS A SAMURAI UNDER YOU!
YOU ARROGANT WRETCH-- A PEASANT'S LIFE HAS NOT TAUGHT YOU HUMILITY TOWARDS YOUR BETTERS! VERY WELL, THEN DIE AS YOU'VE LIVED!
KILL THEM! KILL THEM ALL!
14.

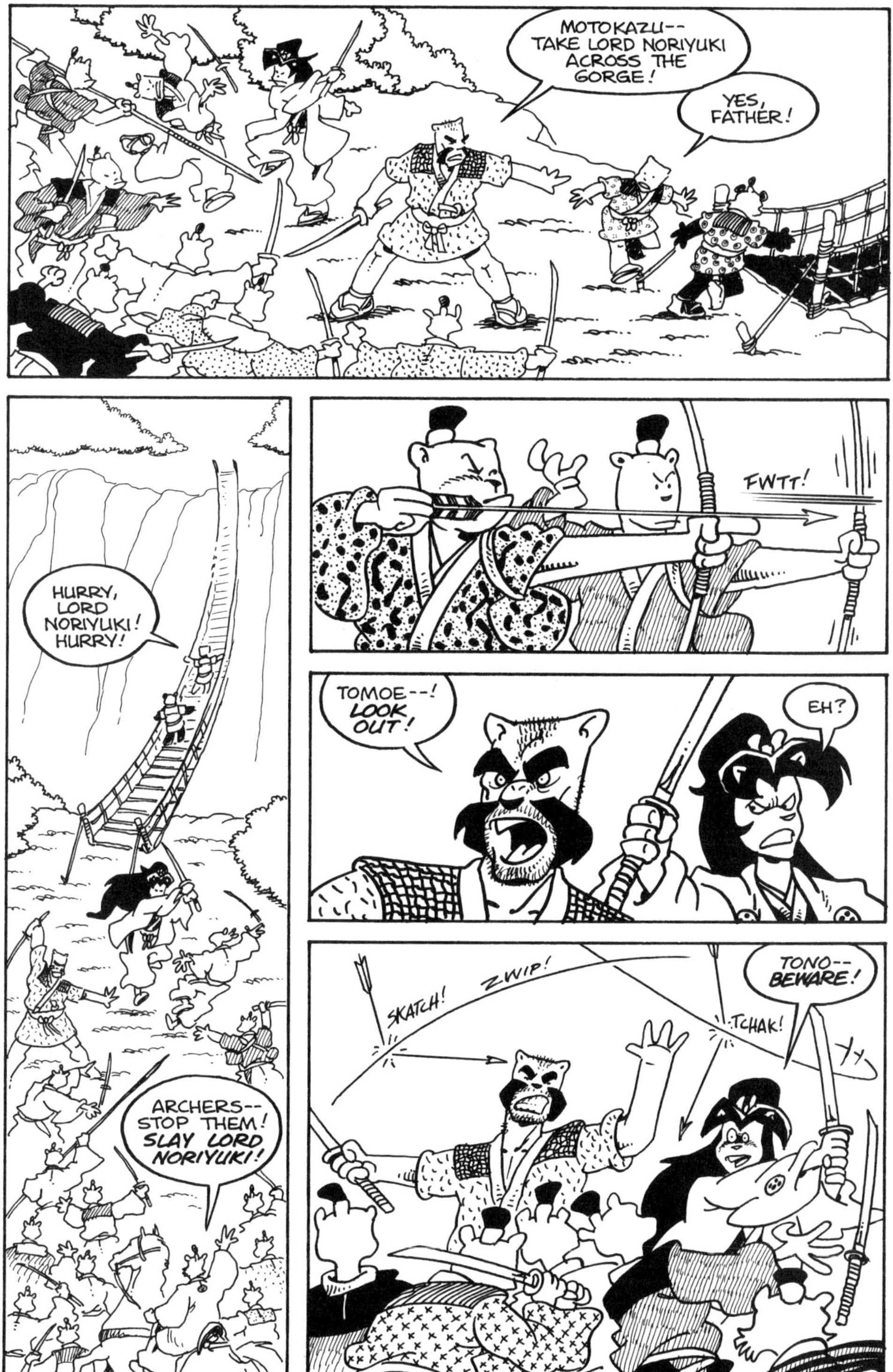
MOTOKAZU-- TAKE LORD NORIYUKI ACROSS THE GORGE!
YES, FATHER!
HURRY, LORD NORIYUKI! HURRY!
ARCHERS-- STOP THEM! SLAY LORD NORIYUKI!
FWTT!
TOMOE--! LOOK OUT!
EH?
SKATCH!
ZWIP!
TCHAK!
TONO-- BEWARE!
15.

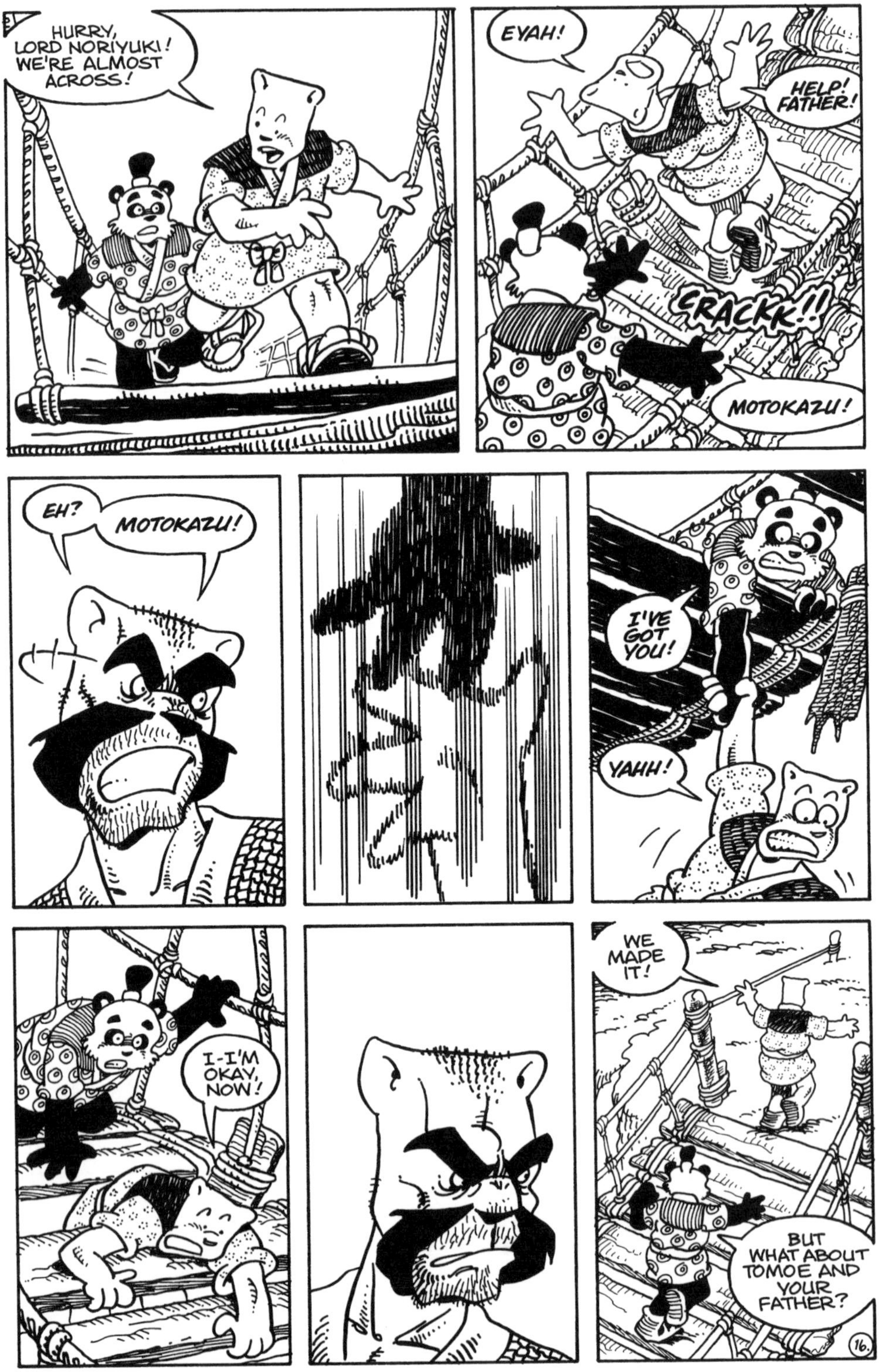
HURRY, LORD NORIYUKI! WE'RE ALMOST ACROSS!
EYAH!
HELP! FATHER!
CRACKK!!
MOTOKAZU!
EH?
MOTOKAZU!
I'VE GOT YOU!
YAHH!
I-I'M OKAY, NOW!
WE MADE IT!
BUT WHAT ABOUT TOMOE AND YOUR FATHER?
16.

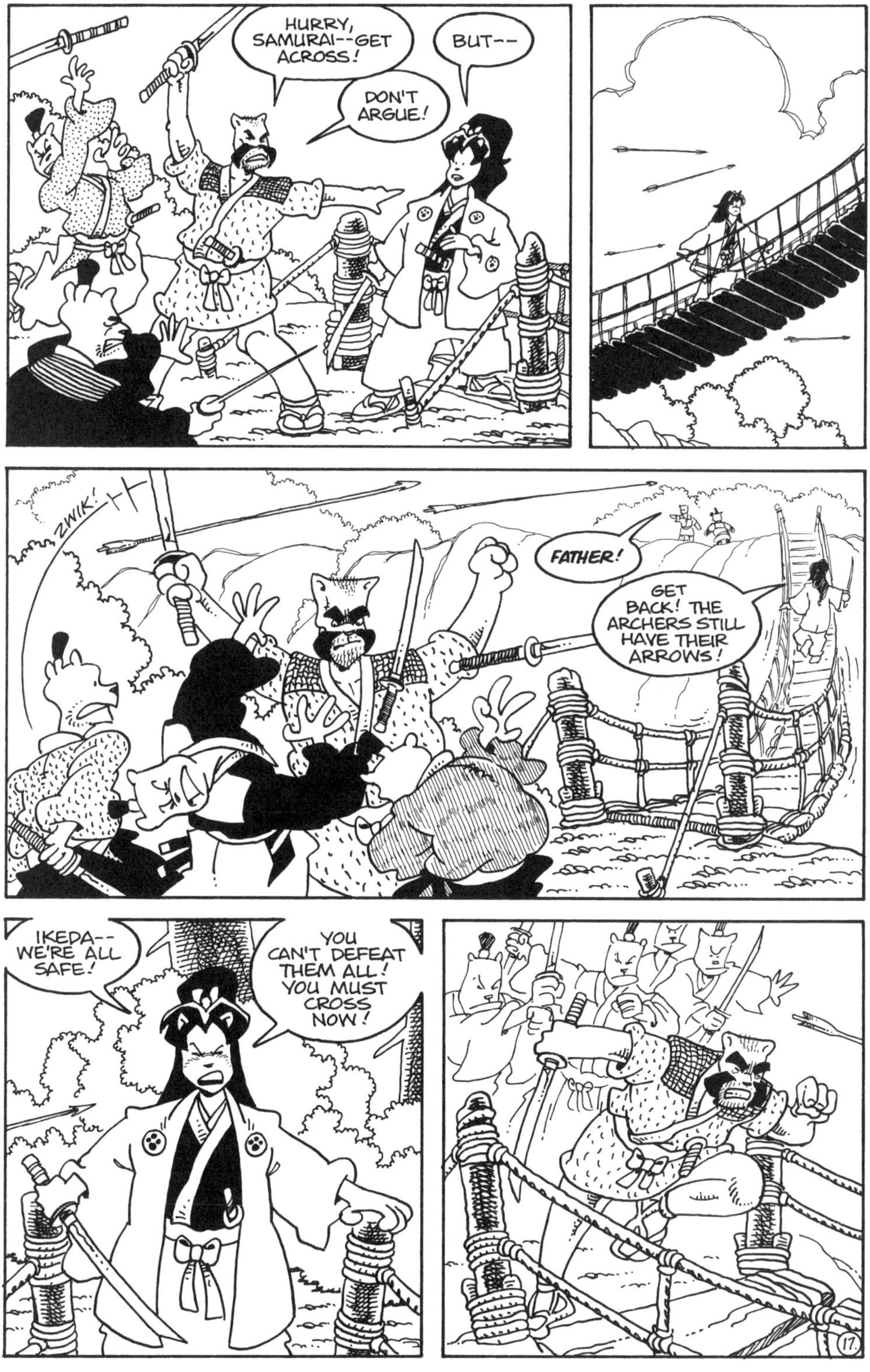
HURRY, SAMURAI--GET ACROSS!
BUT--
DON'T ARGUE!
ZWIK!
FATHER!
GET BACK! THE ARCHERS STILL HAVE THEIR ARROWS!
IKEDA--WE'RE ALL SAFE!
YOU CAN'T DEFEAT THEM ALL! YOU MUST CROSS NOW!
17.

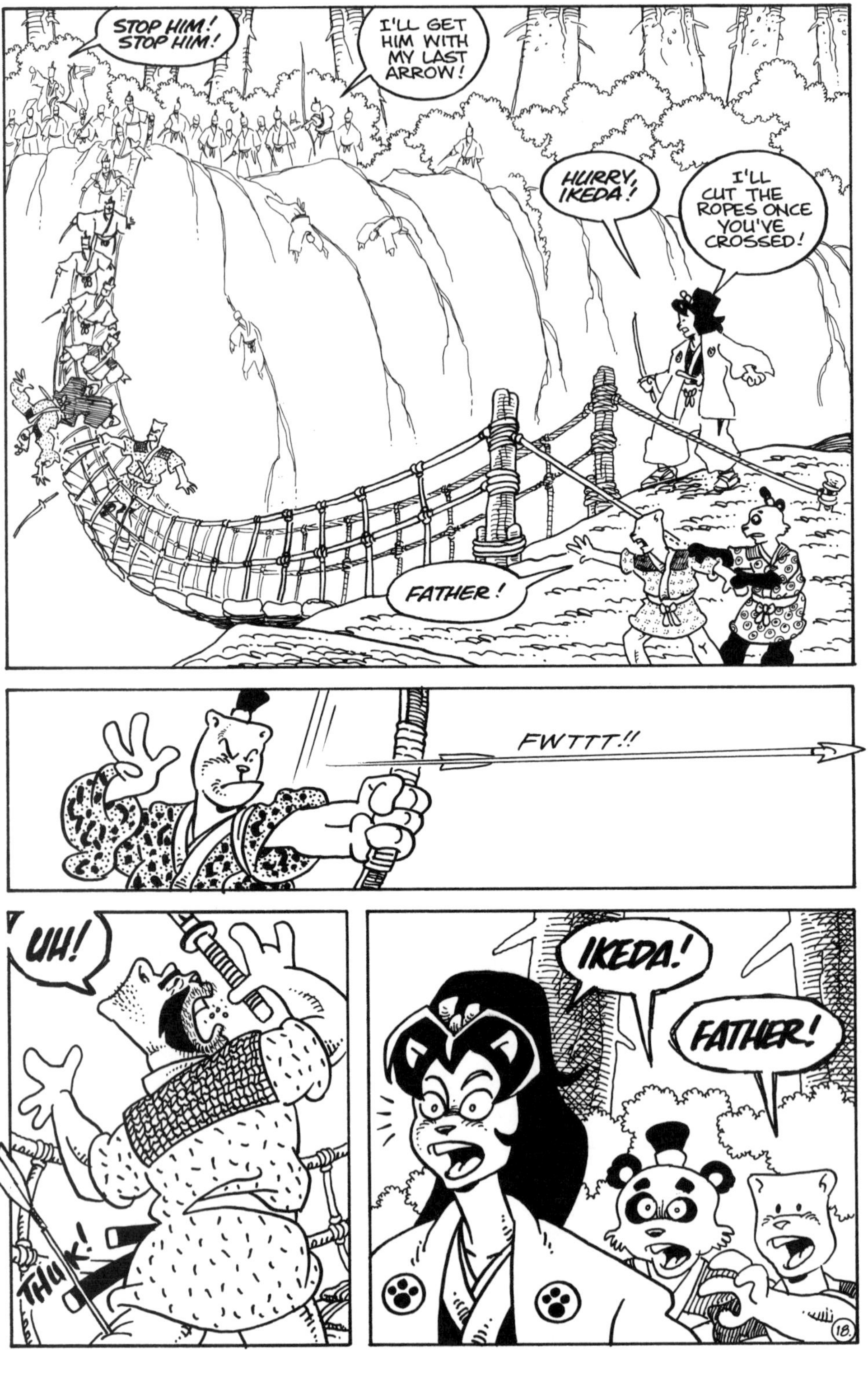
STOP HIM! STOP HIM!
I'LL GET HIM WITH MY LAST ARROW!
HURRY, IKEDA!
I'LL CUT THE ROPES ONCE YOU'VE CROSSED!
FATHER!
FWTTT!!
UH!
THUK!
IKEDA!
FATHER!
18.

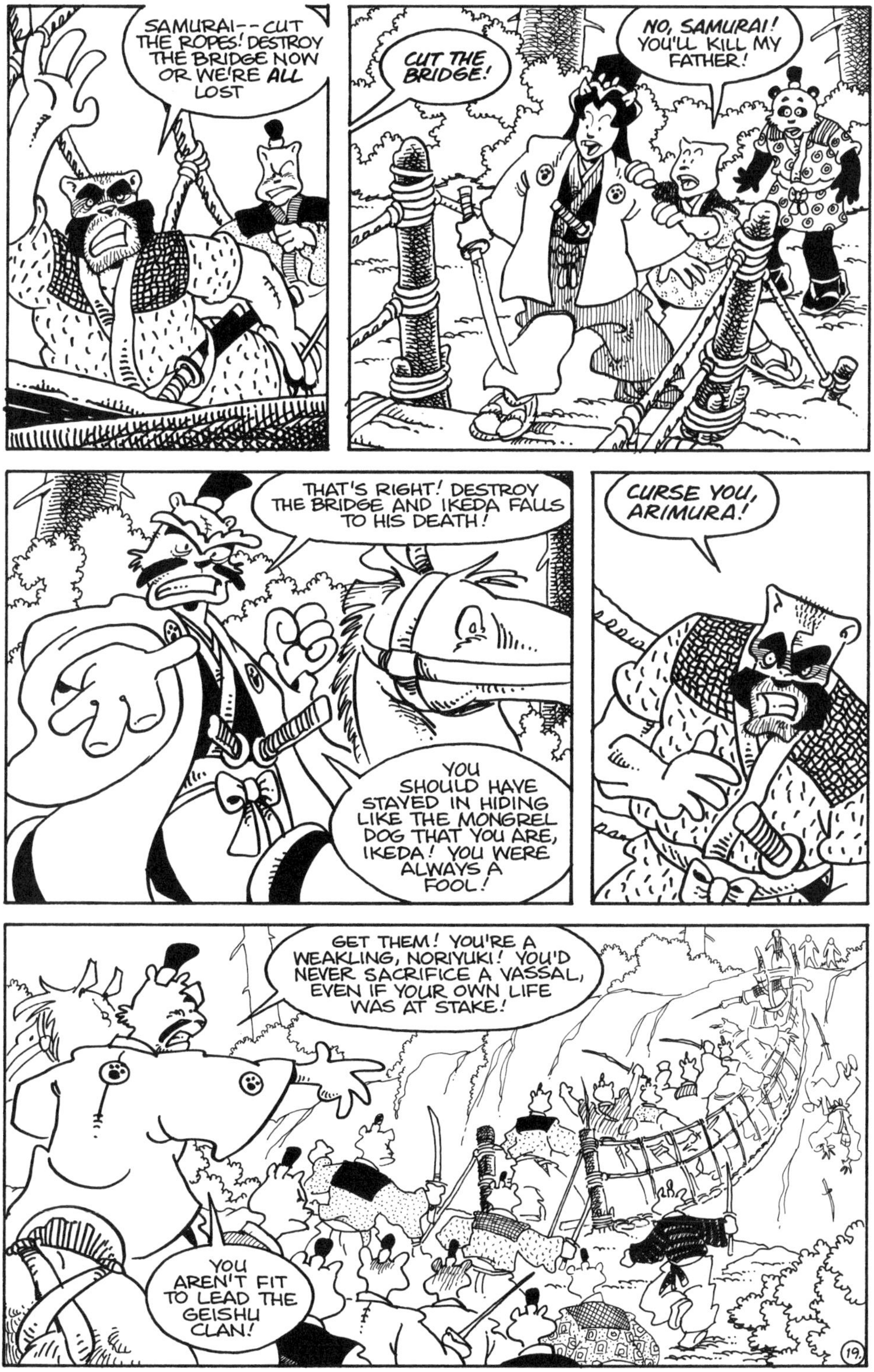
SAMURAI--CUT THE ROPES! DESTROY THE BRIDGE NOW OR WE'RE **ALL** LOST
CUT THE BRIDGE!
NO, SAMURAI! YOU'LL KILL MY FATHER!
THAT'S RIGHT! DESTROY THE BRIDGE AND IKEDA FALLS TO HIS DEATH!
YOU SHOULD HAVE STAYED IN HIDING LIKE THE MONGREL DOG THAT YOU ARE, IKEDA! YOU WERE ALWAYS A FOOL!
CURSE YOU, ARIMURA!
GET THEM! YOU'RE A WEAKLING, NORIYUKI! YOU'D NEVER SACRIFICE A VASSAL, EVEN IF YOUR OWN LIFE WAS AT STAKE!
YOU AREN'T FIT TO LEAD THE GEISHU CLAN!
19.

WE LEARN VALUABLE LESSONS AS WE FACE DEATH, LORD NORIYUKI.

I WAS WRONG.

YOU ARE A TRUE LORD!

THANK YOU FOR MY SON'S LIFE!

I GLADLY GIVE *MY* LIFE TO REGAIN LOST HONOR

NO!

FWWT!

TCK!

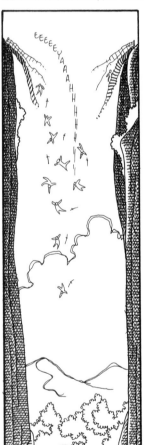

EEEEEYAAAHHHHHH

NNNG6!

THEY'RE LEAVING!

FATHER! OH, FATHER!

20.

YOUR FATHER WAS A GOOD WARRIOR.
HE WILL BE GIVEN A HERO'S MEMORIAL.
F-FATHER! SOB!
!
HMM...?
TONO! MOTOKAZU!
WELL?!
ARE YOU GOING TO HELP ME UP OR JUST LEAVE ME DANGLING HERE?!
ARIMURA WILL BE CIRCLING AROUND TO INTERCEPT US AGAIN, AND WE WON'T BE ABLE TO TRAVEL AS FAST WITH AN ARROW IN MY LEG!
21.

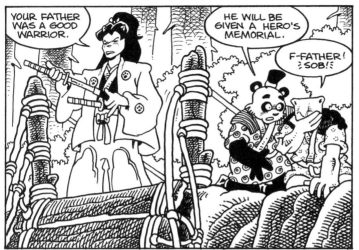

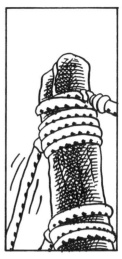

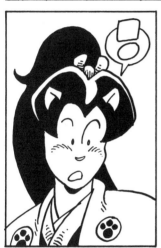

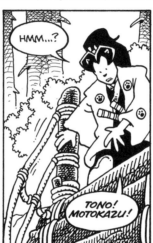

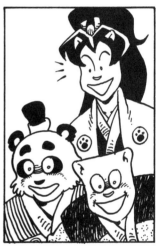

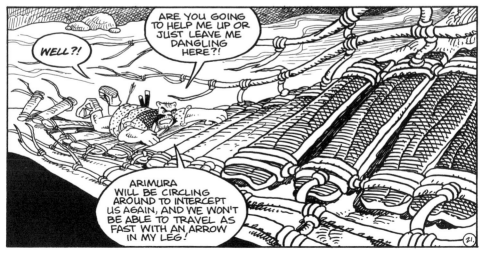

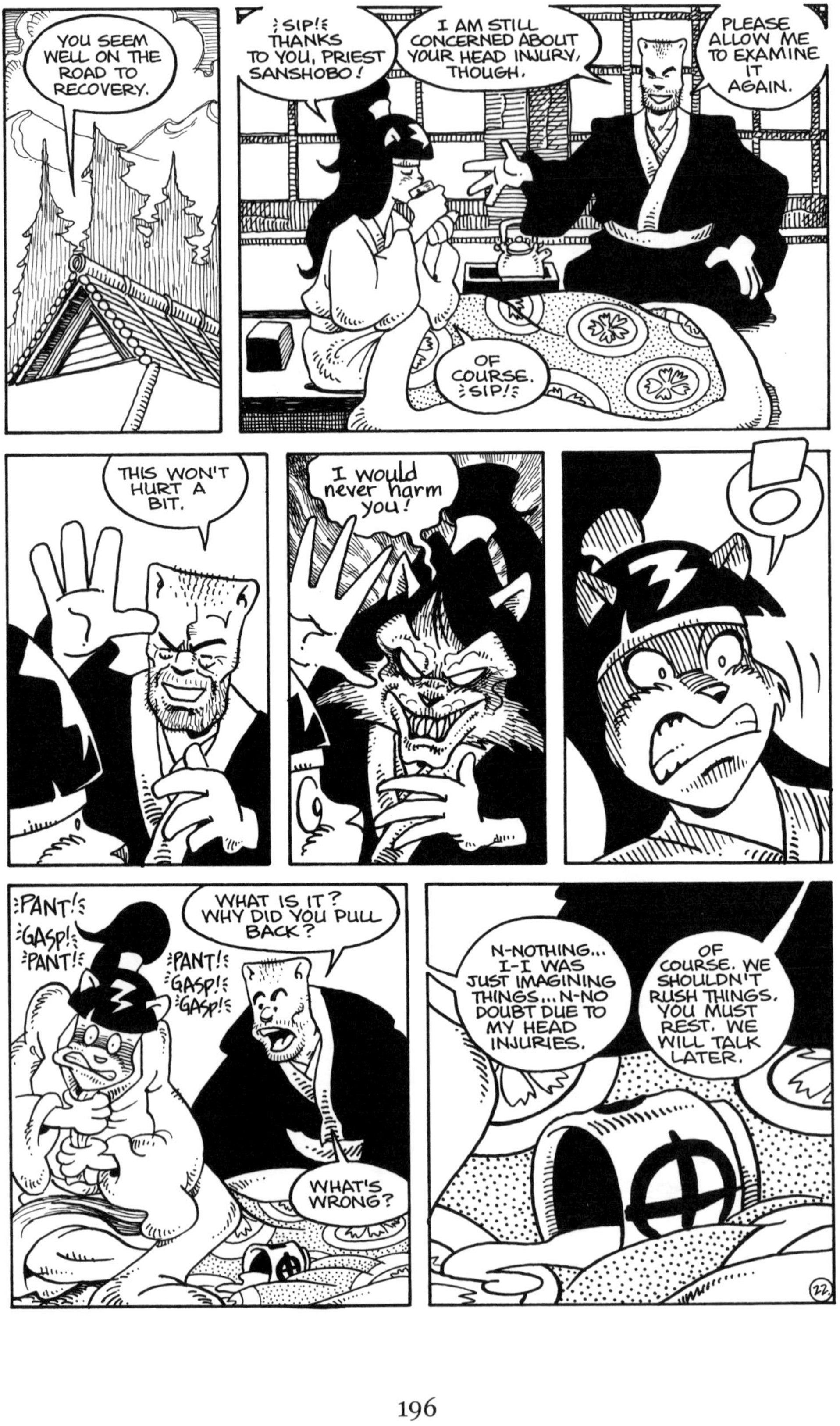
YOU SEEM WELL ON THE ROAD TO RECOVERY.
SIP! THANKS TO YOU, PRIEST SANSHOBO!
I AM STILL CONCERNED ABOUT YOUR HEAD INJURY, THOUGH.
PLEASE ALLOW ME TO EXAMINE IT AGAIN.
OF COURSE. SIP!
THIS WON'T HURT A BIT.
I would never harm you!
!
PANT! GASP! PANT!
WHAT IS IT? WHY DID YOU PULL BACK?
PANT! GASP! GASP!
WHAT'S WRONG?
N-NOTHING... I-I WAS JUST IMAGINING THINGS... N-NO DOUBT DUE TO MY HEAD INJURIES.
OF COURSE. WE SHOULDN'T RUSH THINGS. YOU MUST REST. WE WILL TALK LATER.
22.

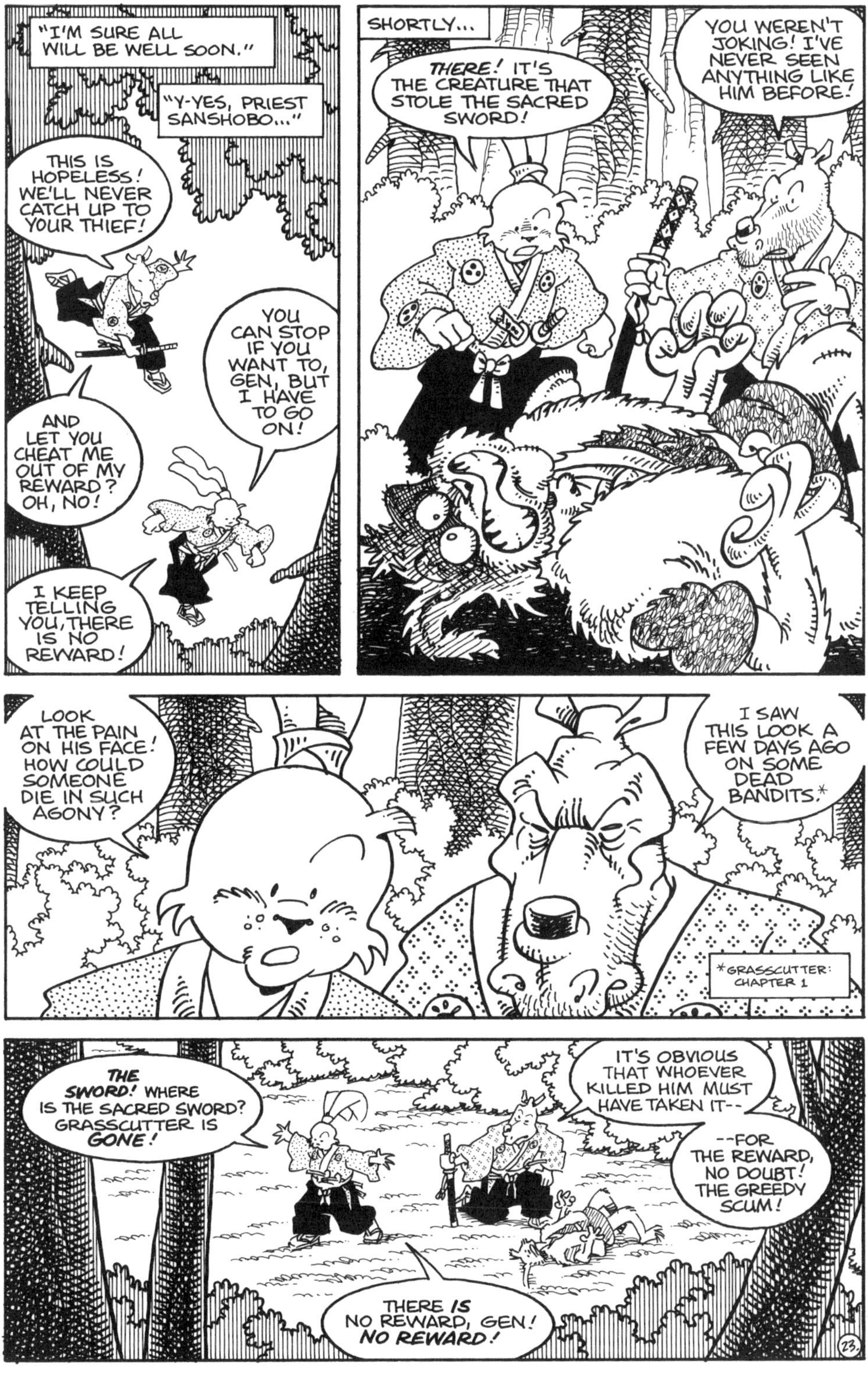
"I'M SURE ALL WILL BE WELL SOON."
"Y-YES, PRIEST SANSHOBO..."
THIS IS HOPELESS! WE'LL NEVER CATCH UP TO YOUR THIEF!
YOU CAN STOP IF YOU WANT TO, GEN, BUT I HAVE TO GO ON!
AND LET YOU CHEAT ME OUT OF MY REWARD? OH, NO!
I KEEP TELLING YOU, THERE IS NO REWARD!
SHORTLY...
THERE! IT'S THE CREATURE THAT STOLE THE SACRED SWORD!
YOU WEREN'T JOKING! I'VE NEVER SEEN ANYTHING LIKE HIM BEFORE!
LOOK AT THE PAIN ON HIS FACE! HOW COULD SOMEONE DIE IN SUCH AGONY?
I SAW THIS LOOK A FEW DAYS AGO ON SOME DEAD BANDITS.*
*GRASSCUTTER: CHAPTER 1
THE SWORD! WHERE IS THE SACRED SWORD? GRASSCUTTER IS GONE!
IT'S OBVIOUS THAT WHOEVER KILLED HIM MUST HAVE TAKEN IT--
--FOR THE REWARD, NO DOUBT! THE GREEDY SCUM!
THERE IS NO REWARD, GEN! NO REWARD!
23.

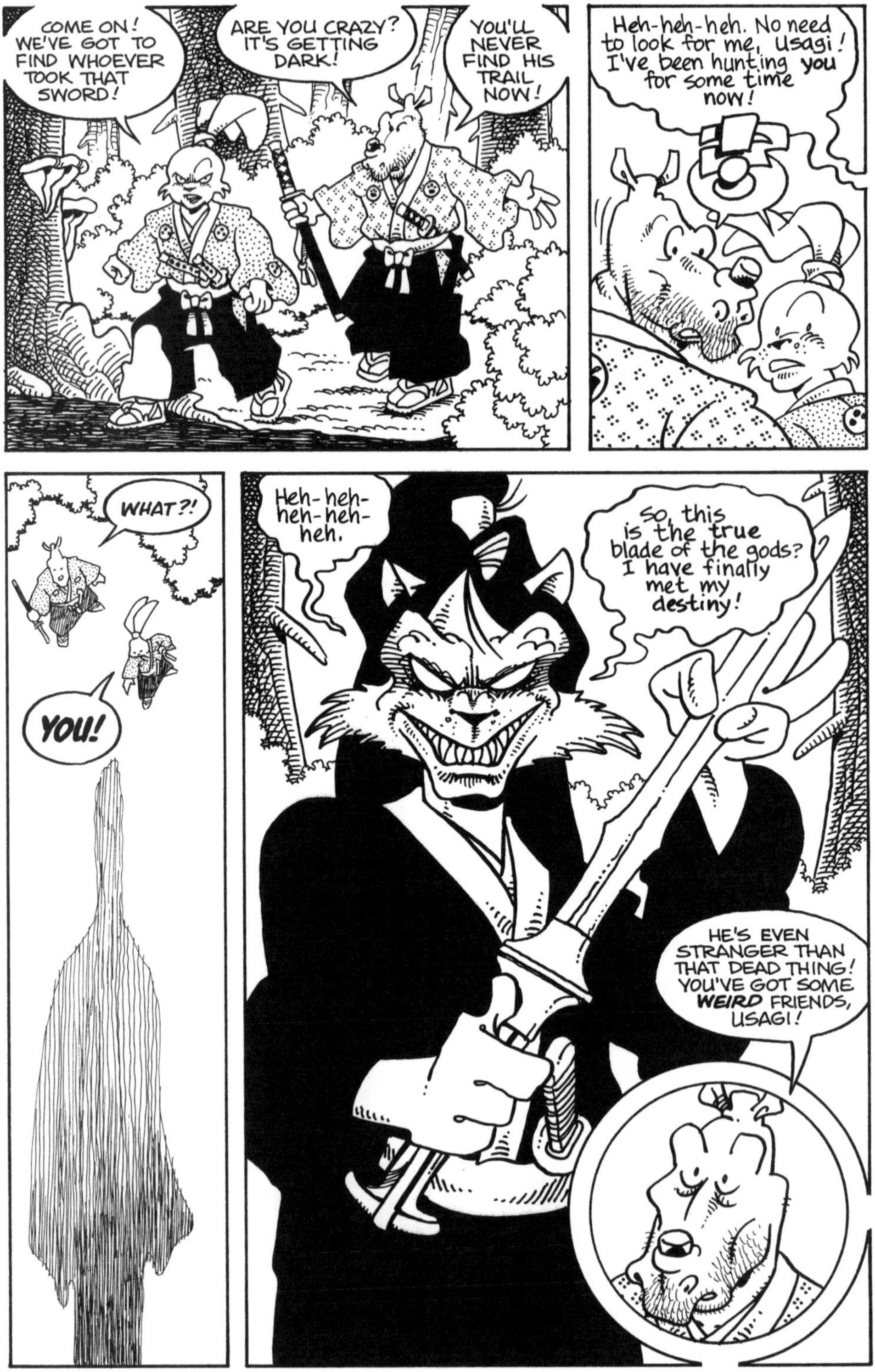
COME ON! WE'VE GOT TO FIND WHOEVER TOOK THAT SWORD!
ARE YOU CRAZY? IT'S GETTING DARK!
YOU'LL NEVER FIND HIS TRAIL NOW!
Heh-heh-heh. No need to look for me, Usagi! I've been hunting you for some time now!
WHAT?!
YOU!
Heh-heh-heh-heh-heh.
So, this is the true blade of the gods? I have finally met my destiny!
HE'S EVEN STRANGER THAN THAT DEAD THING! YOU'VE GOT SOME WEIRD FRIENDS, USAGI!

END OF CHAPTER 6

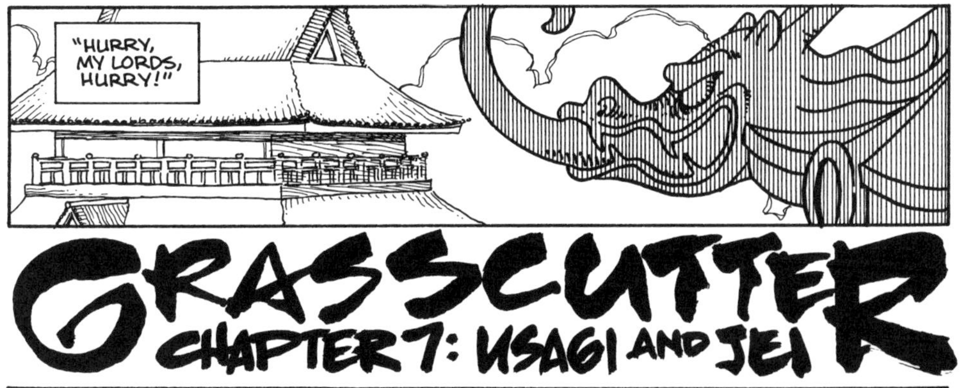
"HURRY, MY LORDS, HURRY!"

GRASSCUTTER
CHAPTER 7: USAGI AND JEI

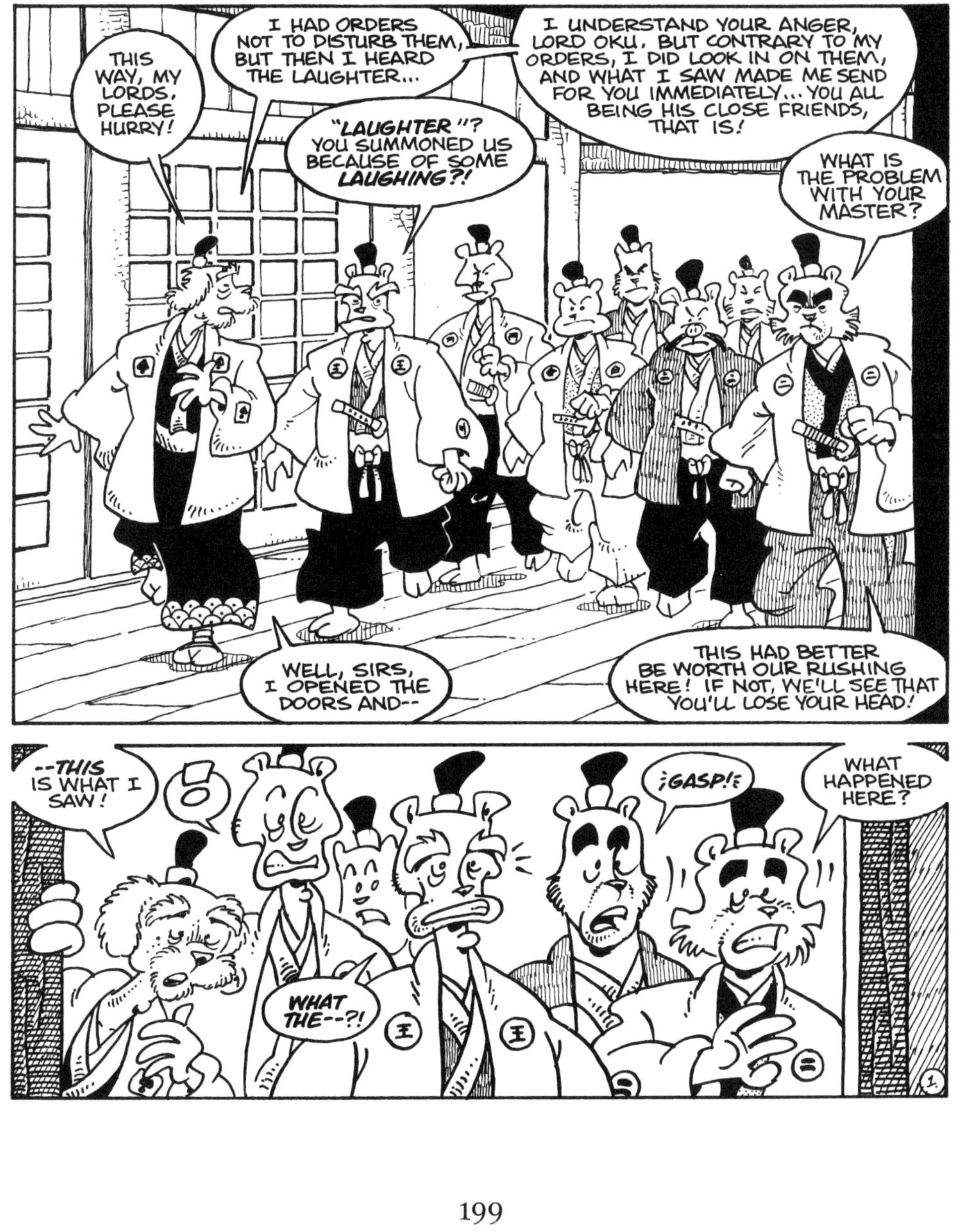
THIS WAY, MY LORDS, PLEASE HURRY!
I HAD ORDERS NOT TO DISTURB THEM, BUT THEN I HEARD THE LAUGHTER...
"LAUGHTER"? YOU SUMMONED US BECAUSE OF SOME LAUGHING?!
I UNDERSTAND YOUR ANGER, LORD OKU. BUT CONTRARY TO MY ORDERS, I DID LOOK IN ON THEM, AND WHAT I SAW MADE ME SEND FOR YOU IMMEDIATELY... YOU ALL BEING HIS CLOSE FRIENDS, THAT IS!
WHAT IS THE PROBLEM WITH YOUR MASTER?
THIS HAD BETTER BE WORTH OUR RUSHING HERE! IF NOT, WE'LL SEE THAT YOU'LL LOSE YOUR HEAD!
WELL, SIRS, I OPENED THE DOORS AND--
--THIS IS WHAT I SAW!
!
WHAT THE--?!
¡GASP!¡
WHAT HAPPENED HERE?
1.

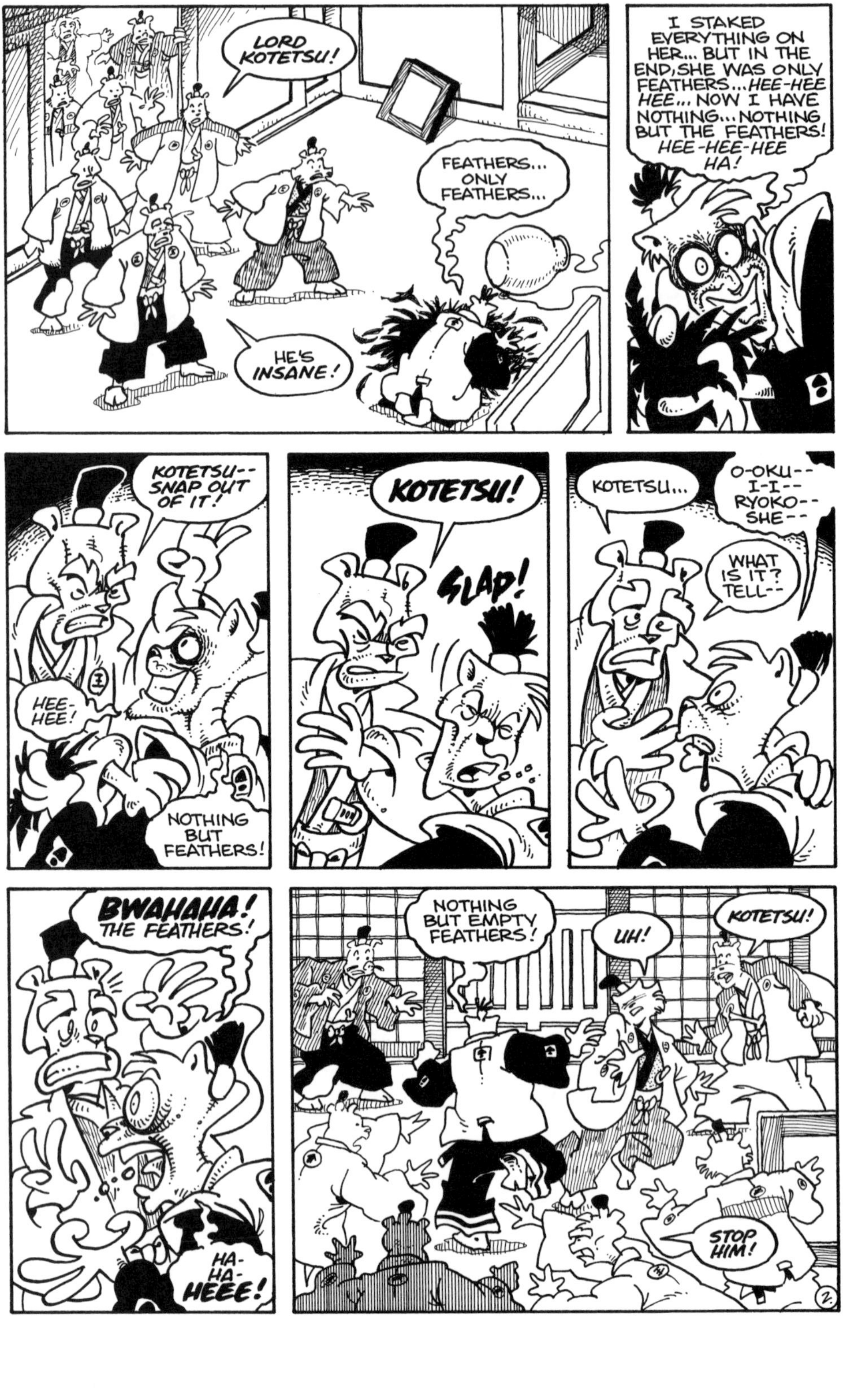
LORD KOTETSU!
FEATHERS... ONLY FEATHERS...
HE'S INSANE!
I STAKED EVERYTHING ON HER... BUT IN THE END, SHE WAS ONLY FEATHERS... HEE-HEE HEE... NOW I HAVE NOTHING... NOTHING BUT THE FEATHERS! HEE-HEE-HEE HA!
KOTETSU-- SNAP OUT OF IT!
HEE-HEE!
NOTHING BUT FEATHERS!
KOTETSU!
SLAP!
KOTETSU...
O-OKU-- I-I-- RYOKO-- SHE--
WHAT IS IT? TELL--
BWAHAHA! THE FEATHERS!
HA-HA-HEEE!
NOTHING BUT EMPTY FEATHERS!
UH!
KOTETSU!
STOP HIM!
2.

KOTETSU--
HA-HA-HA!
DO YOU HEAR IT? THE SOUND OF WINGS!
HER WINGS!
KOTETSU!
COME BACK HERE!
YES, YES! I HEAR YOU--I HEAR YOUR WINGS BEATING!
MY WINGS! HA-HA-HA!
KOTETSU!
MY WINGS! HA-HA!
HA-HA-HA-HEEEEEEEEEEEEEEEEEEEEEEEEE
HEE-HEE--
EYAHHH!
NO--IT WAS JUST FEATHERS! JUST EMPTY FEATHERS!
WHAT DO WE DO NOW?
EYAHH··:
THUD!
3.

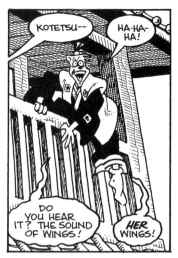

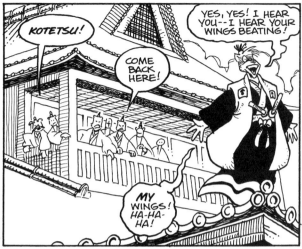

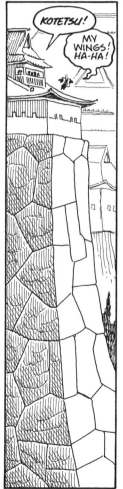

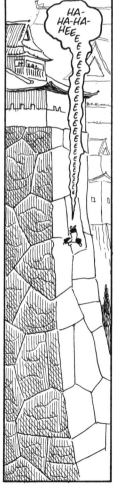

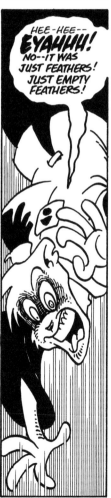

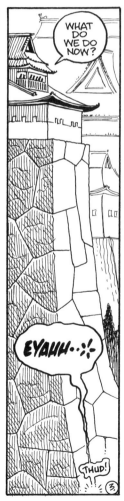

HURRY! THEY COULD BE RIGHT BEHIND US!
UHH...
ARE YOU ALL RIGHT, LORD NORIYUKI?
LADY TOMOE!
.....
TONO!
HE'S BURNING WITH FEVER! THE ARROW WOUND MUST BE INFECTED, AND ALL THIS RUNNING HAS LEFT HIM EXHAUSTED! WE'VE GOT TO GET HIM TO A DOCTOR!
T-TOMOE...
SHH... REST NOW.
THERE'S A VILLAGE NOT FAR AWAY. WE CAN GET SOME HELP THERE.
WE'LL MAKE BETTER TIME IF WE TRAVEL THE MAIN ROAD.
WE'LL ALSO BE MORE VULNERABLE OUT IN THE OPEN...
...BUT IT CAN'T BE HELPED.
.....
THE ROAD LIES TO THE EAST.
4

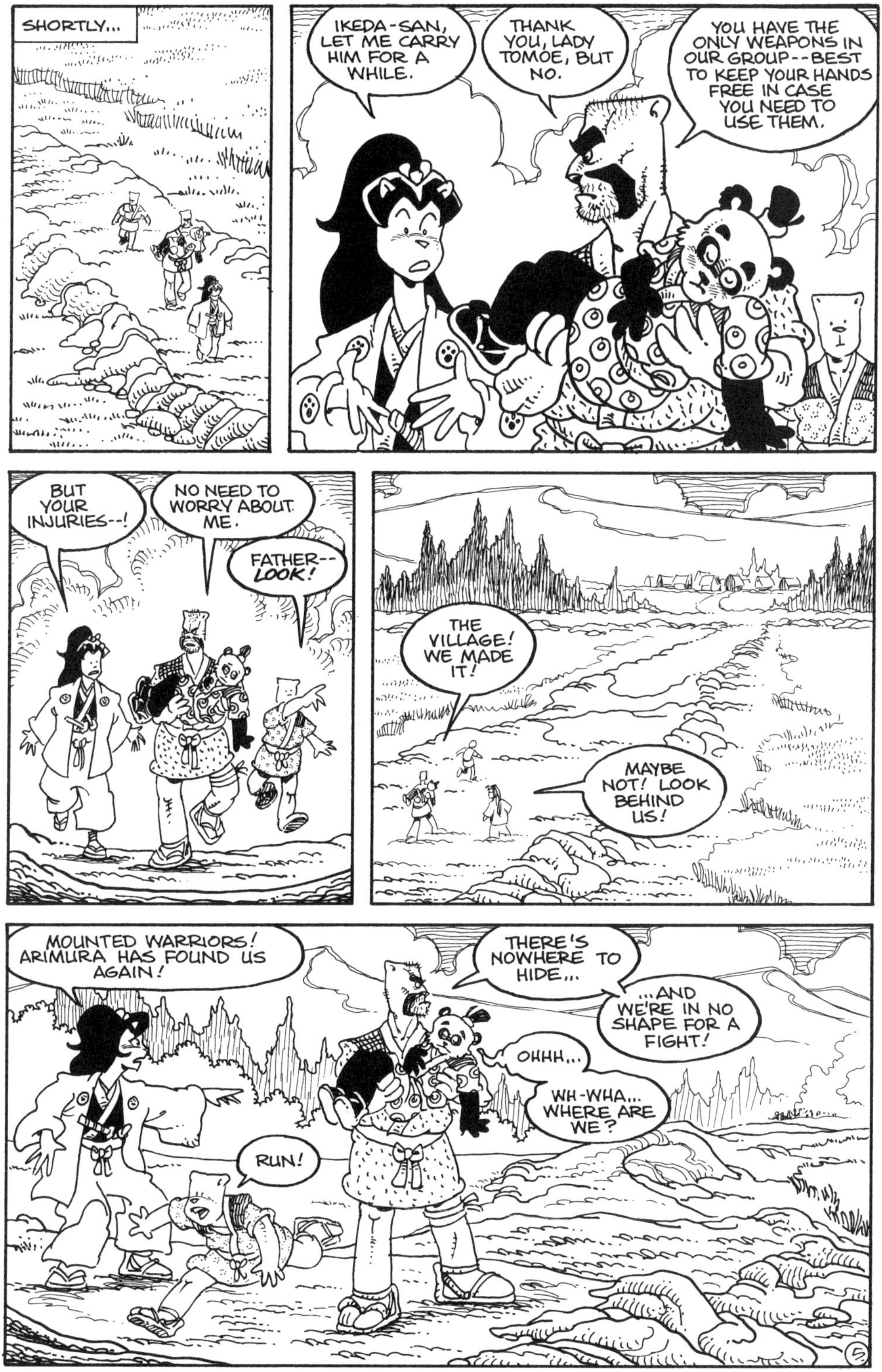
SHORTLY...
IKEDA-SAN, LET ME CARRY HIM FOR A WHILE.
THANK YOU, LADY TOMOE, BUT NO.
YOU HAVE THE ONLY WEAPONS IN OUR GROUP--BEST TO KEEP YOUR HANDS FREE IN CASE YOU NEED TO USE THEM.
BUT YOUR INJURIES--!
NO NEED TO WORRY ABOUT ME.
FATHER--LOOK!
THE VILLAGE! WE MADE IT!
MAYBE NOT! LOOK BEHIND US!
MOUNTED WARRIORS! ARIMURA HAS FOUND US AGAIN!
RUN!
THERE'S NOWHERE TO HIDE...
...AND WE'RE IN NO SHAPE FOR A FIGHT!
OHHH...
WH-WHA... WHERE ARE WE?
5

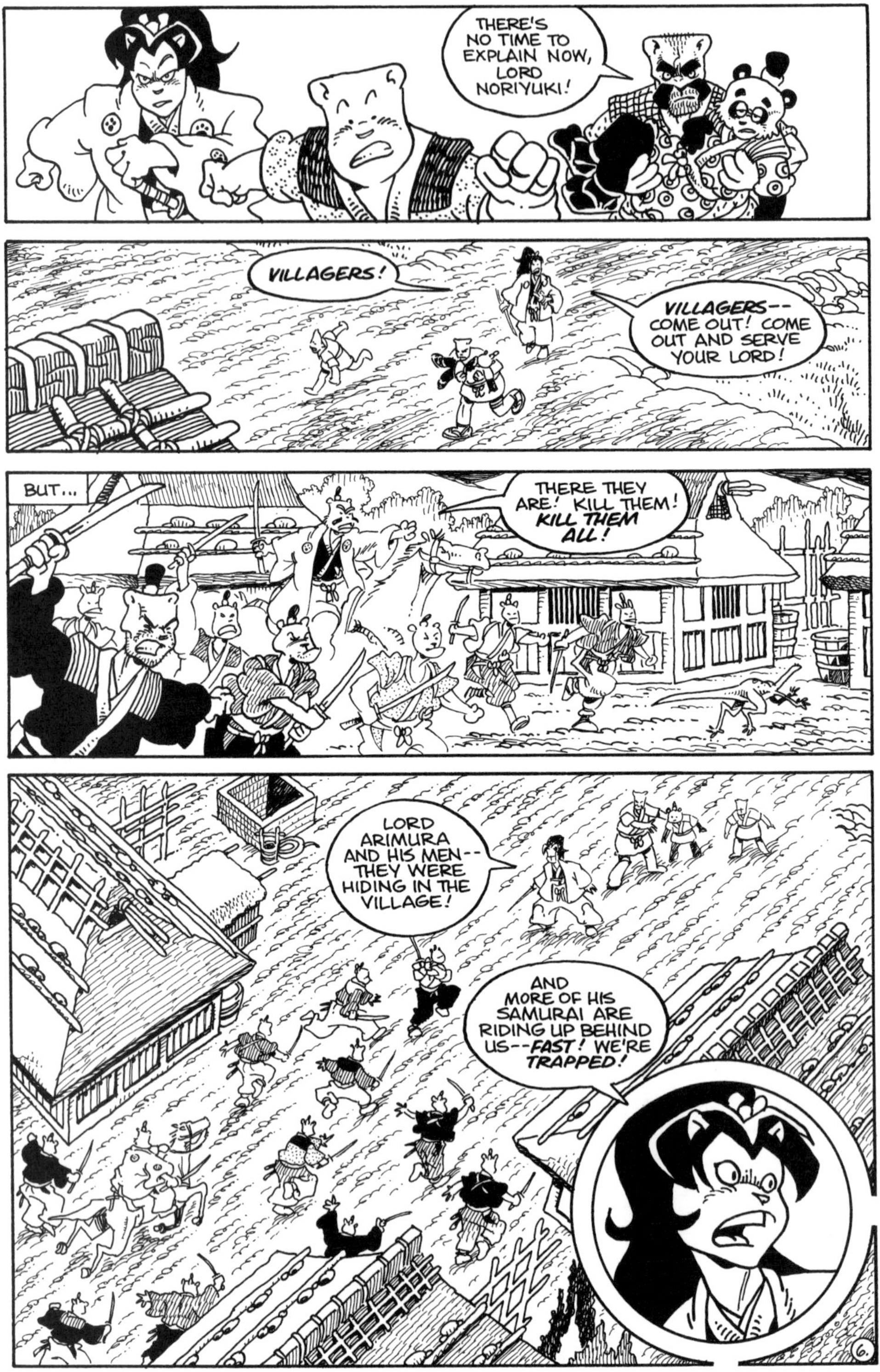
THERE'S NO TIME TO EXPLAIN NOW, LORD NORIYUKI!
VILLAGERS!
VILLAGERS-- COME OUT! COME OUT AND SERVE YOUR LORD!
BUT...
THERE THEY ARE! KILL THEM! KILL THEM ALL!
LORD ARIMURA AND HIS MEN-- THEY WERE HIDING IN THE VILLAGE!
AND MORE OF HIS SAMURAI ARE RIDING UP BEHIND US--FAST! WE'RE TRAPPED!
6.

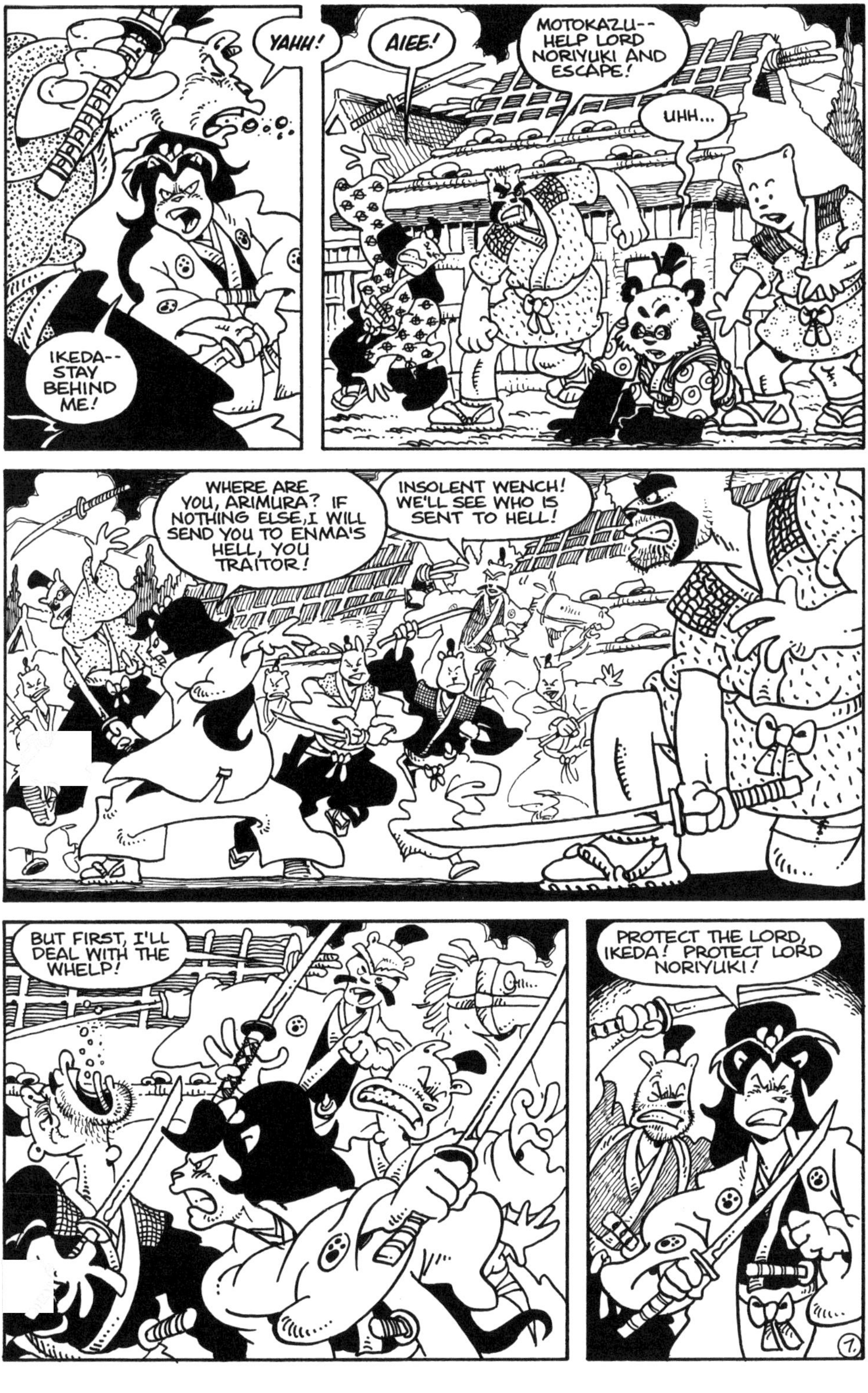

YAHH!
IKEDA-- STAY BEHIND ME!
AIEE!
MOTOKAZU-- HELP LORD NORIYUKI AND ESCAPE!
UHH...
WHERE ARE YOU, ARIMURA? IF NOTHING ELSE, I WILL SEND YOU TO ENMA'S HELL, YOU TRAITOR!
INSOLENT WENCH! WE'LL SEE WHO IS SENT TO HELL!
BUT FIRST, I'LL DEAL WITH THE WHELP!
PROTECT THE LORD, IKEDA! PROTECT LORD NORIYUKI!
7.

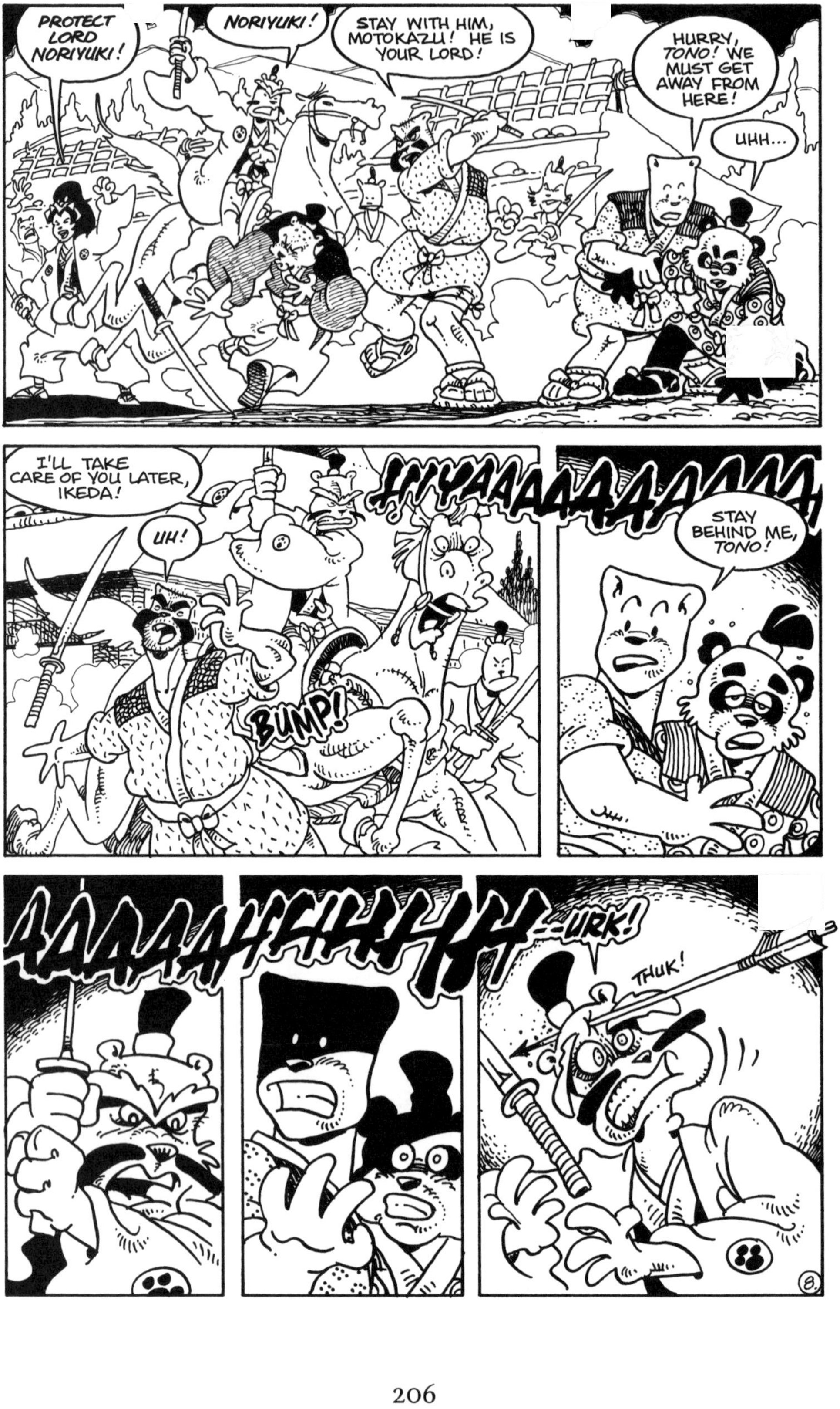

PROTECT LORD NORIYUKI!
NORIYUKI!
STAY WITH HIM, MOTOKAZU! HE IS YOUR LORD!
HURRY, TONO! WE MUST GET AWAY FROM HERE!
UHH...
I'LL TAKE CARE OF YOU LATER, IKEDA!
UH!
BUMP!
HIYAAAAAAAAAAAA
STAY BEHIND ME, TONO!
AAAAAHHHHHHH
-URK!
THUK!
8

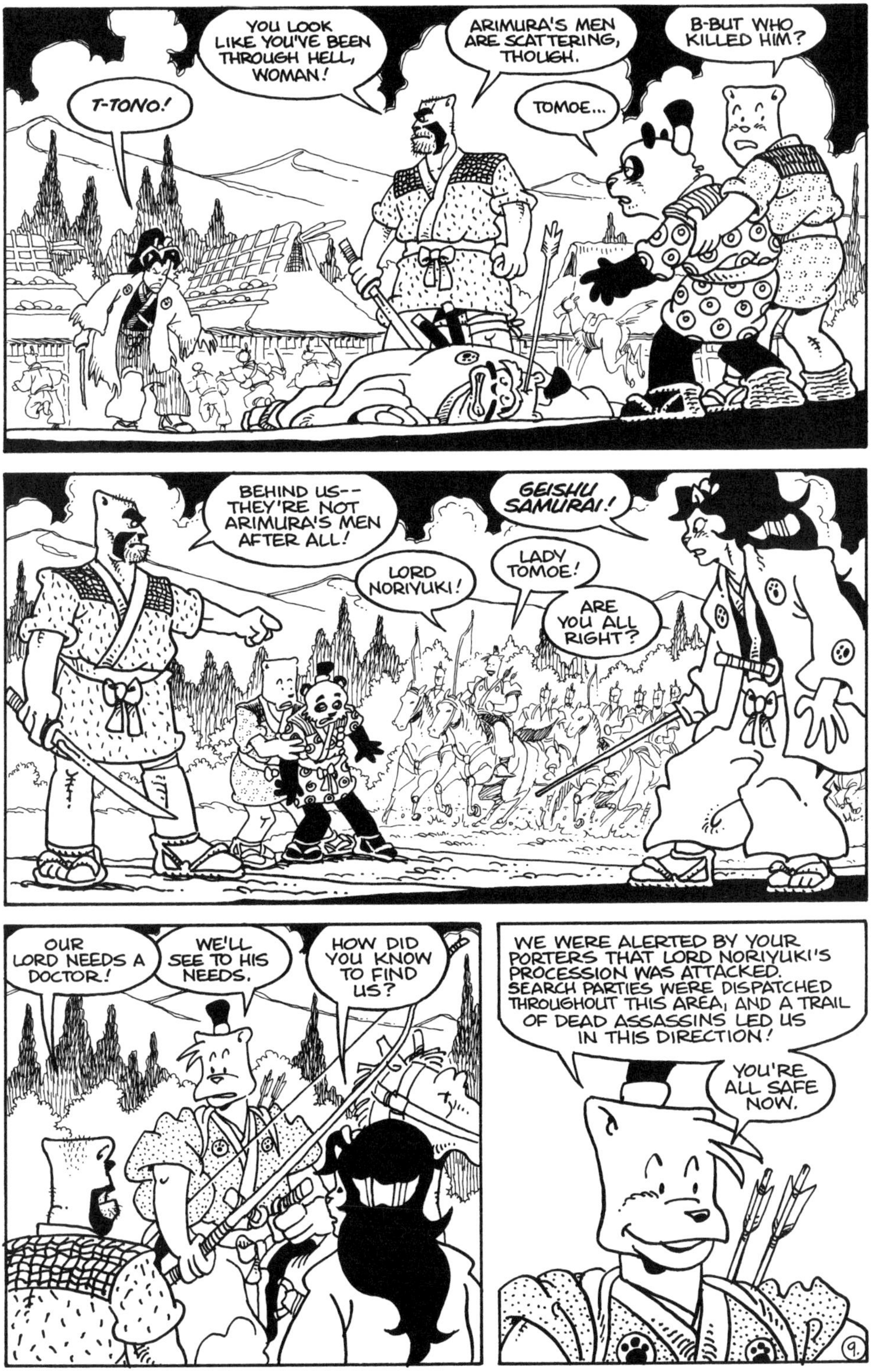
T-TONO!
YOU LOOK LIKE YOU'VE BEEN THROUGH HELL, WOMAN!
ARIMURA'S MEN ARE SCATTERING, THOUGH.
TOMOE...
B-BUT WHO KILLED HIM?
BEHIND US-- THEY'RE NOT ARIMURA'S MEN AFTER ALL!
GEISHU SAMURAI!
LORD NORIYUKI!
LADY TOMOE!
ARE YOU ALL RIGHT?
OUR LORD NEEDS A DOCTOR!
WE'LL SEE TO HIS NEEDS.
HOW DID YOU KNOW TO FIND US?
WE WERE ALERTED BY YOUR PORTERS THAT LORD NORIYUKI'S PROCESSION WAS ATTACKED. SEARCH PARTIES WERE DISPATCHED THROUGHOUT THIS AREA, AND A TRAIL OF DEAD ASSASSINS LED US IN THIS DIRECTION!
YOU'RE ALL SAFE NOW.
9.

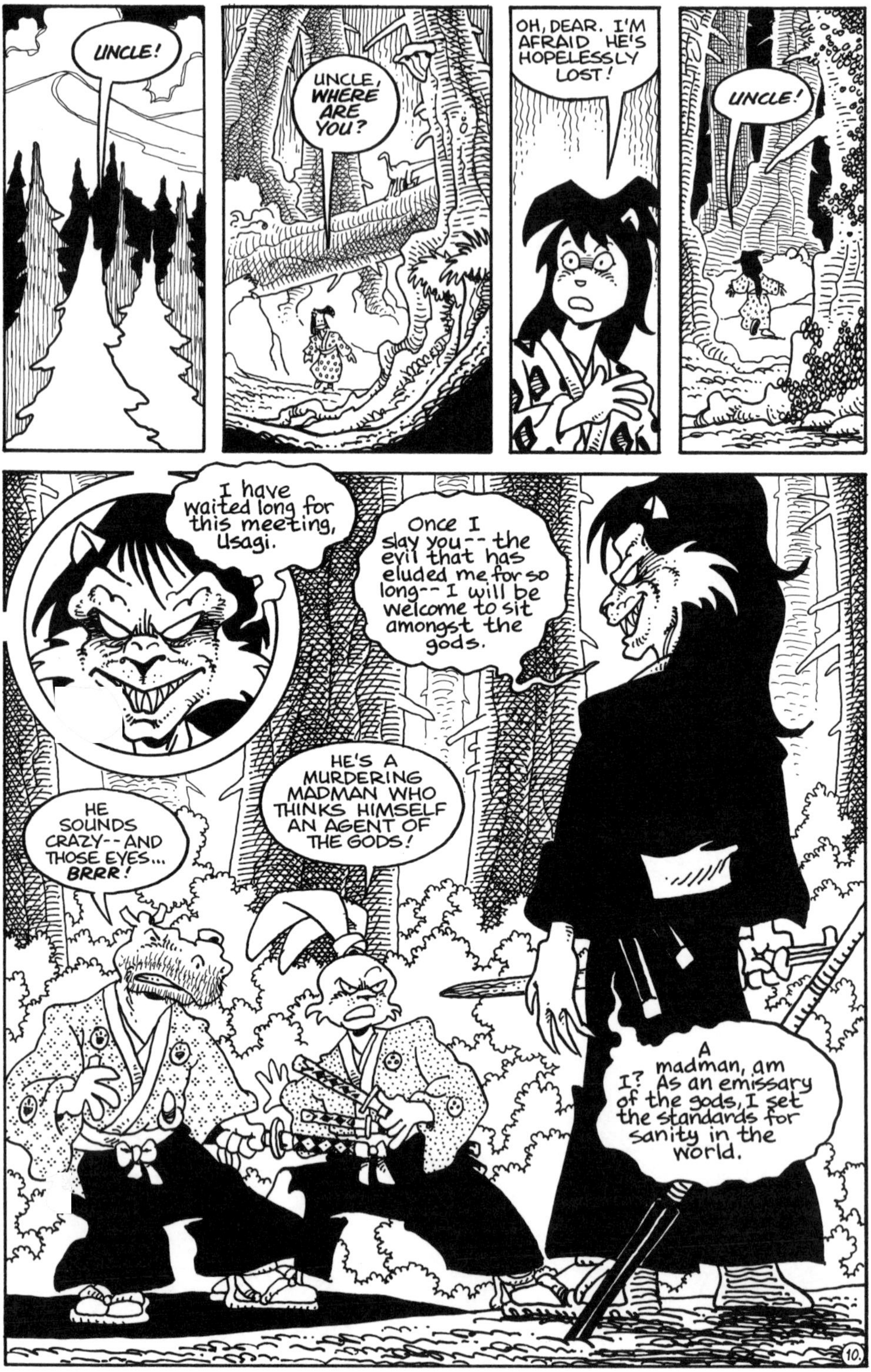
UNCLE!
UNCLE, WHERE ARE YOU?
OH, DEAR. I'M AFRAID HE'S HOPELESSLY LOST!
UNCLE!
I have waited long for this meeting, Usagi.
Once I slay you-- the evil that has eluded me for so long-- I will be welcome to sit amongst the gods.
HE SOUNDS CRAZY-- AND THOSE EYES... BRRR!
HE'S A MURDERING MADMAN WHO THINKS HIMSELF AN AGENT OF THE GODS!
A madman, am I? As an emissary of the gods, I set the standards for sanity in the world.
10.

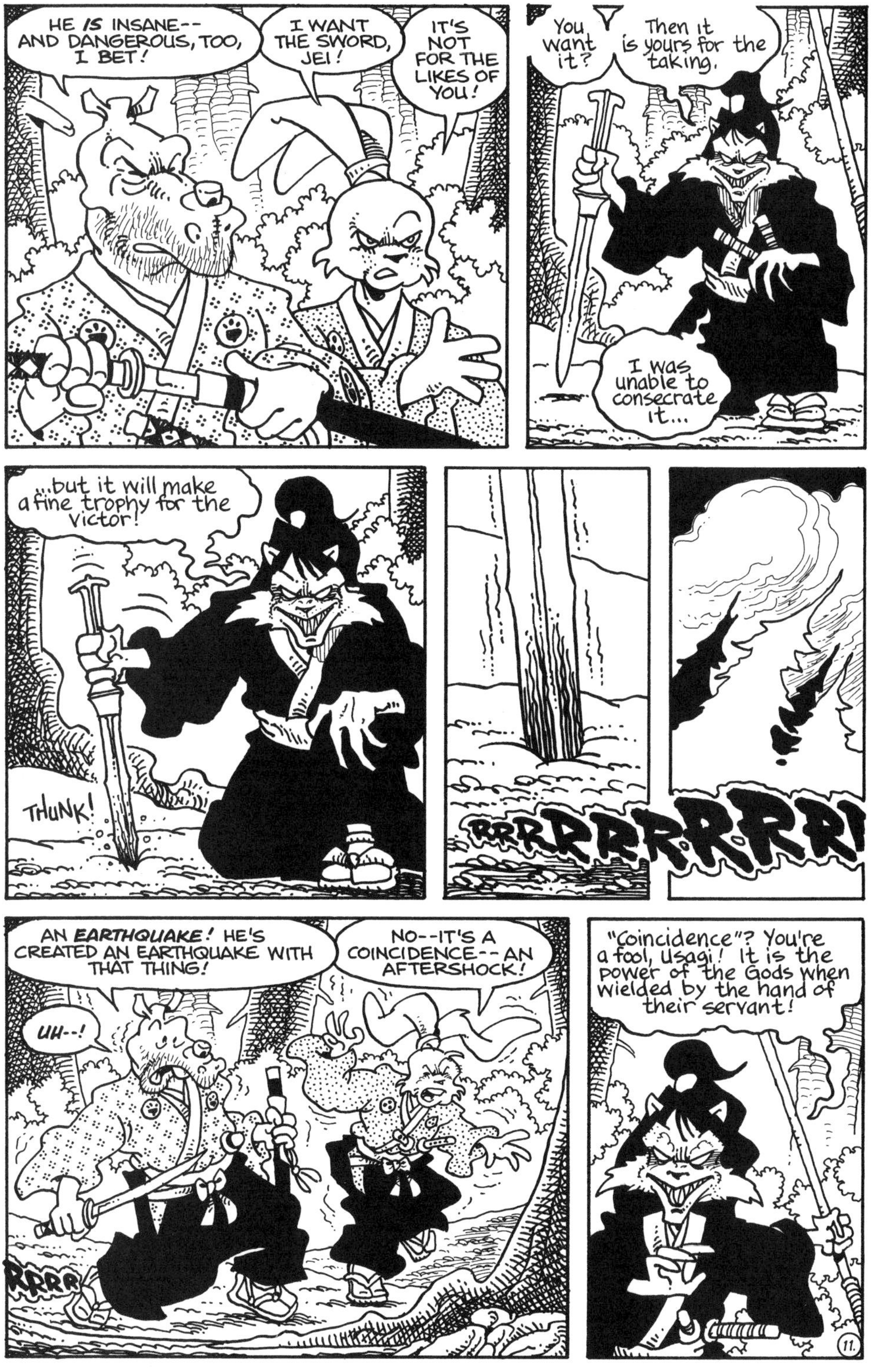
HE IS INSANE-- AND DANGEROUS, TOO, I BET!
I WANT THE SWORD, JEI!
IT'S NOT FOR THE LIKES OF YOU!
You want it?
Then it is yours for the taking.
I was unable to consecrate it...
...but it will make a fine trophy for the victor!
THUNK!
RRRRRRRRRR
AN EARTHQUAKE! HE'S CREATED AN EARTHQUAKE WITH THAT THING!
NO--IT'S A COINCIDENCE--AN AFTERSHOCK!
UH--!
RRRR
"Coincidence"? You're a fool, Usagi! It is the power of the Gods when wielded by the hand of their servant!
11.

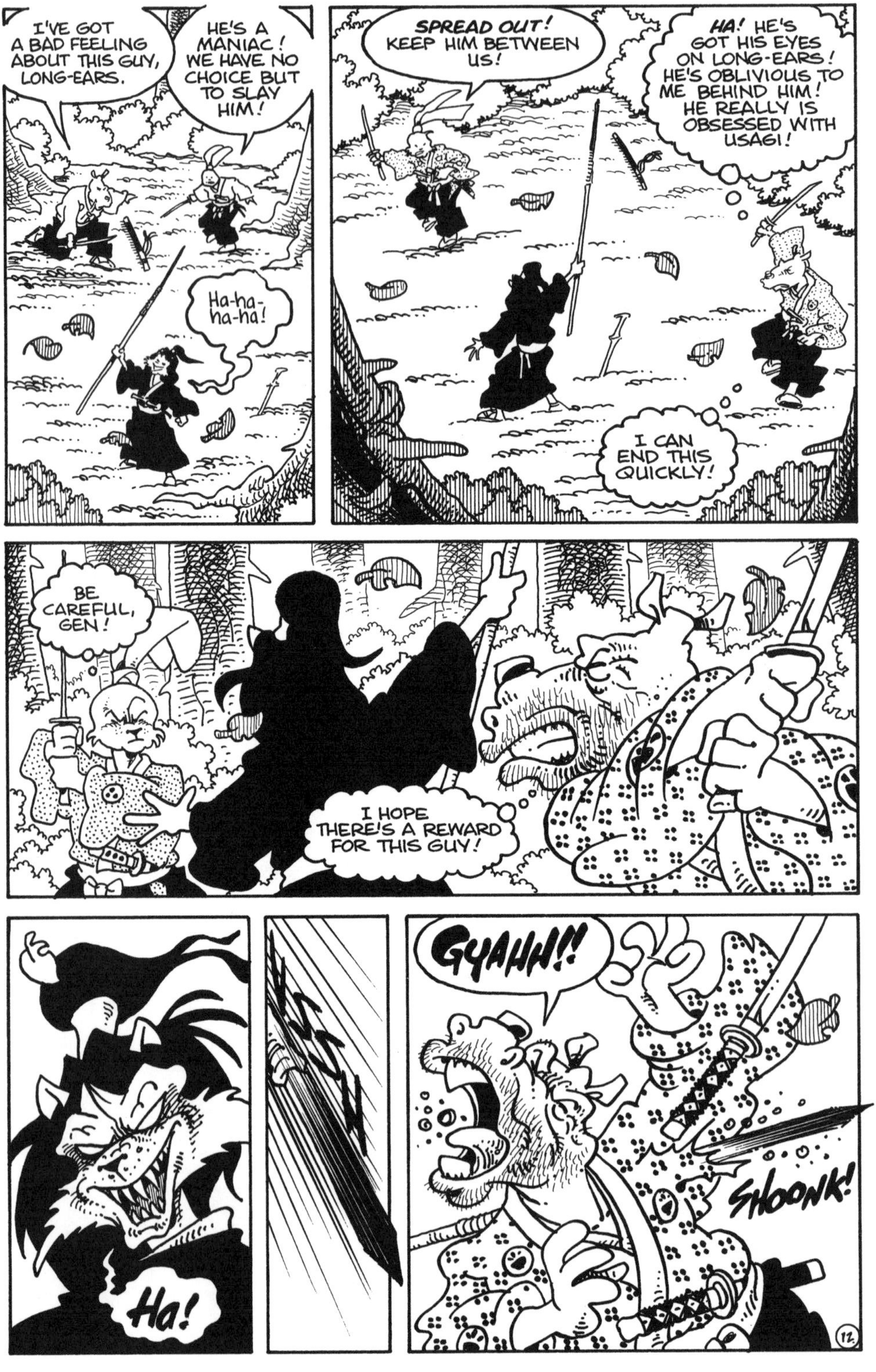
I'VE GOT A BAD FEELING ABOUT THIS GUY, LONG-EARS.
HE'S A MANIAC! WE HAVE NO CHOICE BUT TO SLAY HIM!
Ha-ha-ha-ha!
SPREAD OUT! KEEP HIM BETWEEN US!
HA! HE'S GOT HIS EYES ON LONG-EARS! HE'S OBLIVIOUS TO ME BEHIND HIM! HE REALLY IS OBSESSED WITH USAGI!
I CAN END THIS QUICKLY!
BE CAREFUL, GEN!
I HOPE THERE'S A REWARD FOR THIS GUY!
Ha!
GYAHH!!
SHOONK!
12.

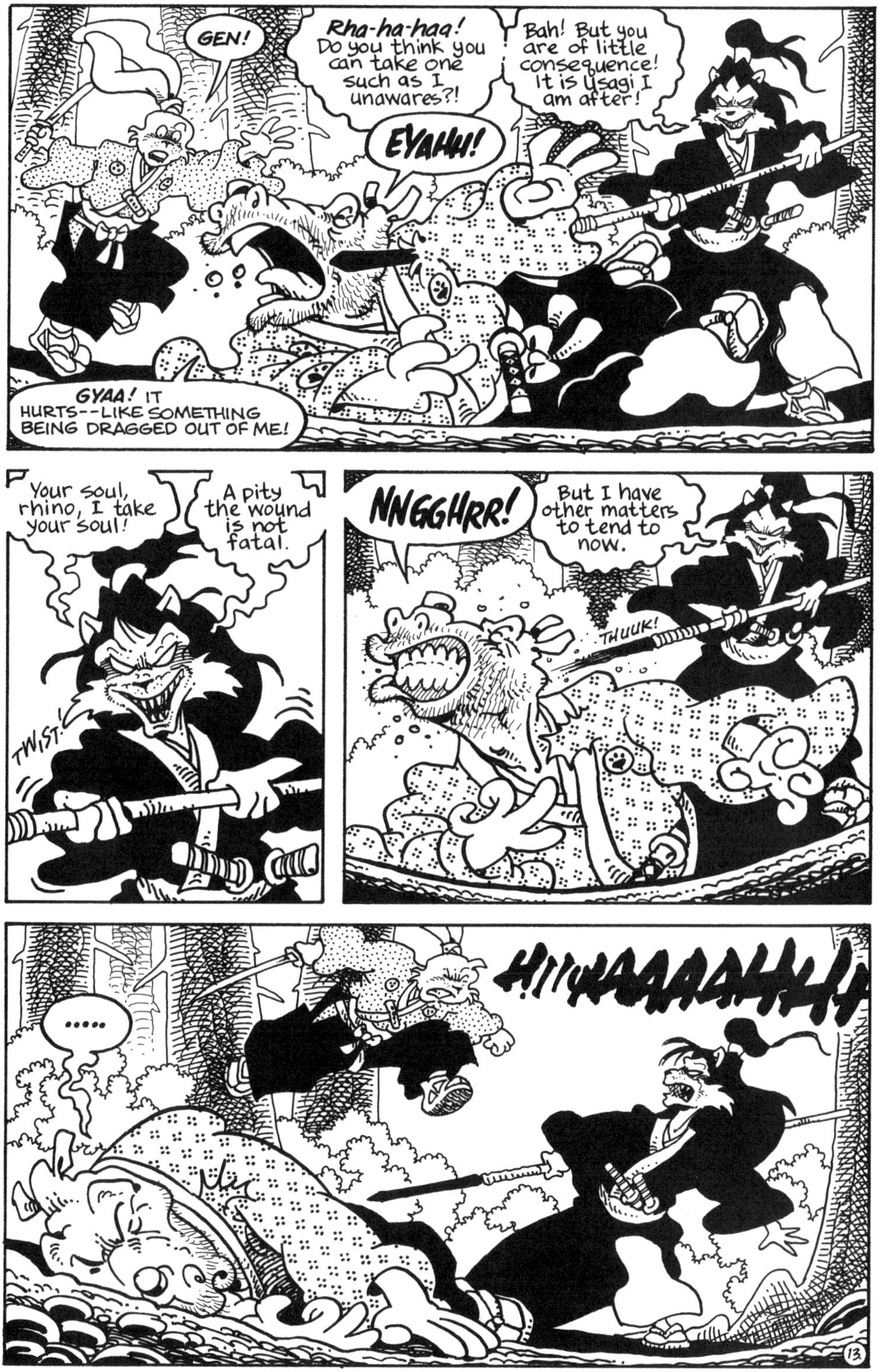
GEN!
Rha-ha-haa! Do you think you can take one such as I unawares?!
Bah! But you are of little consequence! It is Usagi I am after!
EYAHH!
GYAA! IT HURTS--LIKE SOMETHING BEING DRAGGED OUT OF ME!
Your soul, rhino, I take your soul!
A pity the wound is not fatal.
TWIST!
NNGGHRR!
But I have other matters to tend to now.
THUUK!
.....
HIIYAAAAAHHH
13

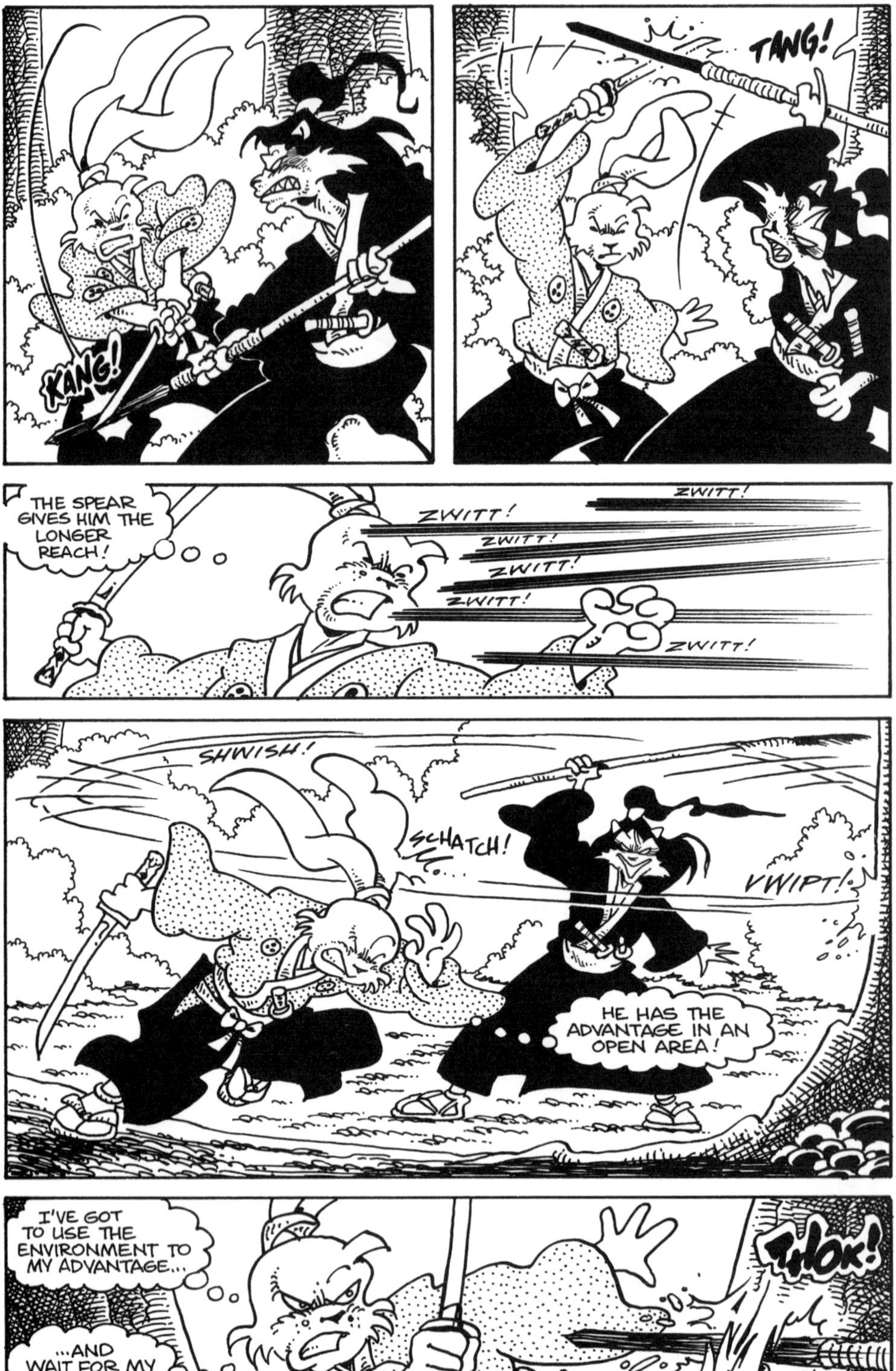
KANG!
TANG!
THE SPEAR GIVES HIM THE LONGER REACH!
ZWITT!
ZWITT!
ZWITT!
ZWITT!
ZWITT!
ZWITT!
SHWISH!
SCHATCH!
VWIPT!
HE HAS THE ADVANTAGE IN AN OPEN AREA!
I'VE GOT TO USE THE ENVIRONMENT TO MY ADVANTAGE...
...AND WAIT FOR MY TIME!
THOK!
14.

TUG! TUG!
NOW!
HI'YAHH!
SHUK!
CHOK!
UH--!
Ha ha!
THAT LAUGH--?
UNCLE!
HERE I COME, UNCLE!
15.

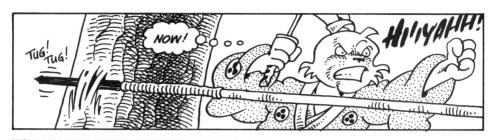

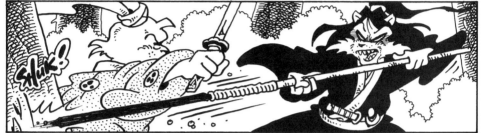

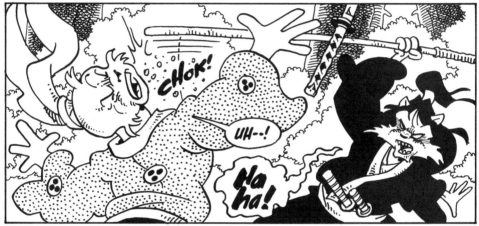

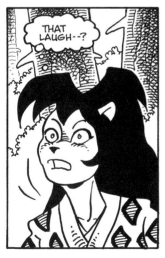

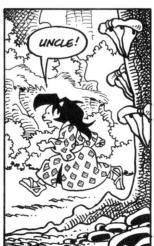

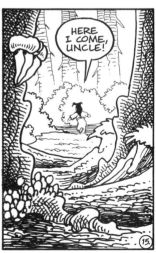

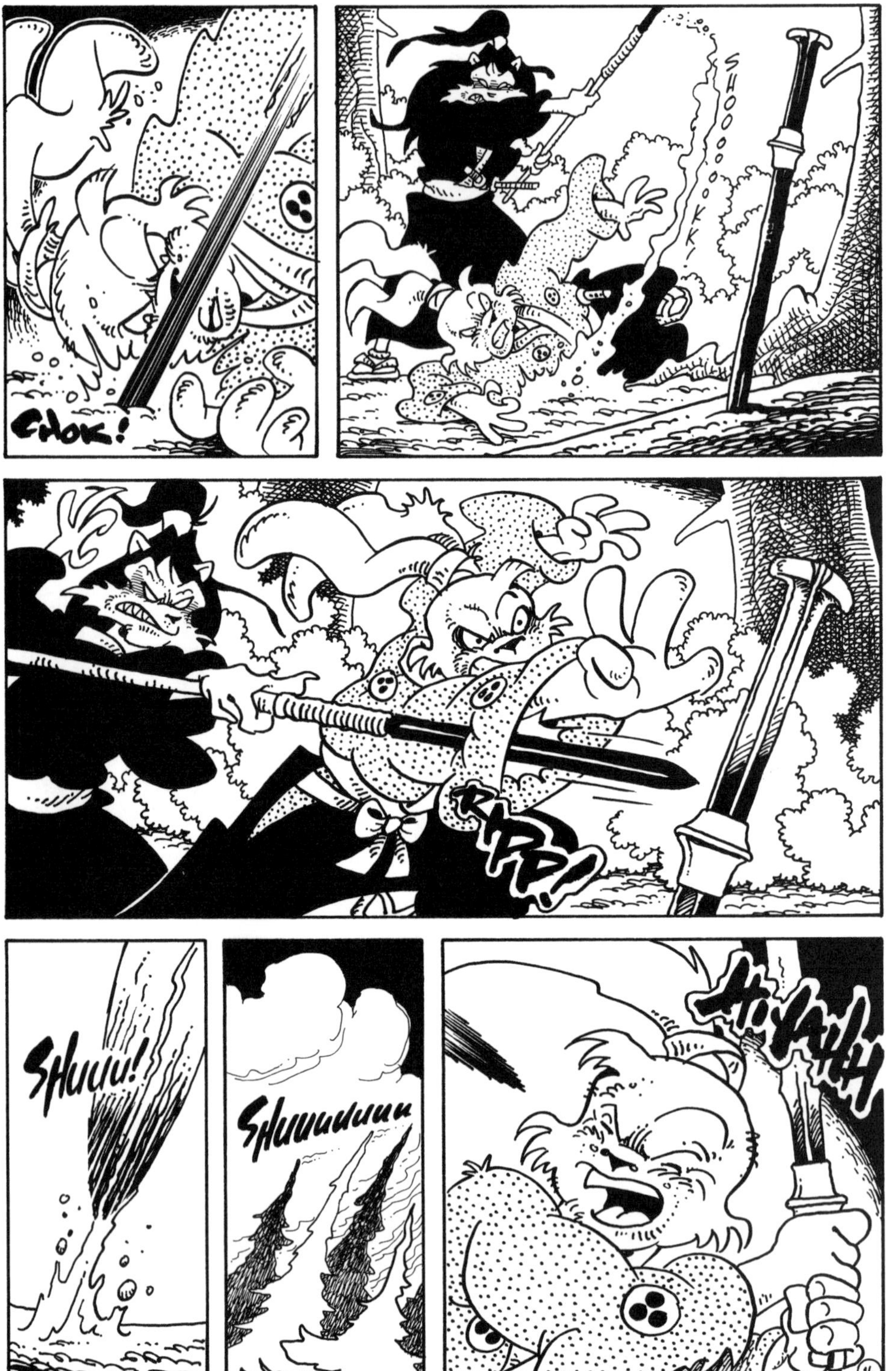
CHOK!
SHOOOOOOOKK!
RIPP!
SHUUU!
SHUUUUUUU
HI-YAAH
16.

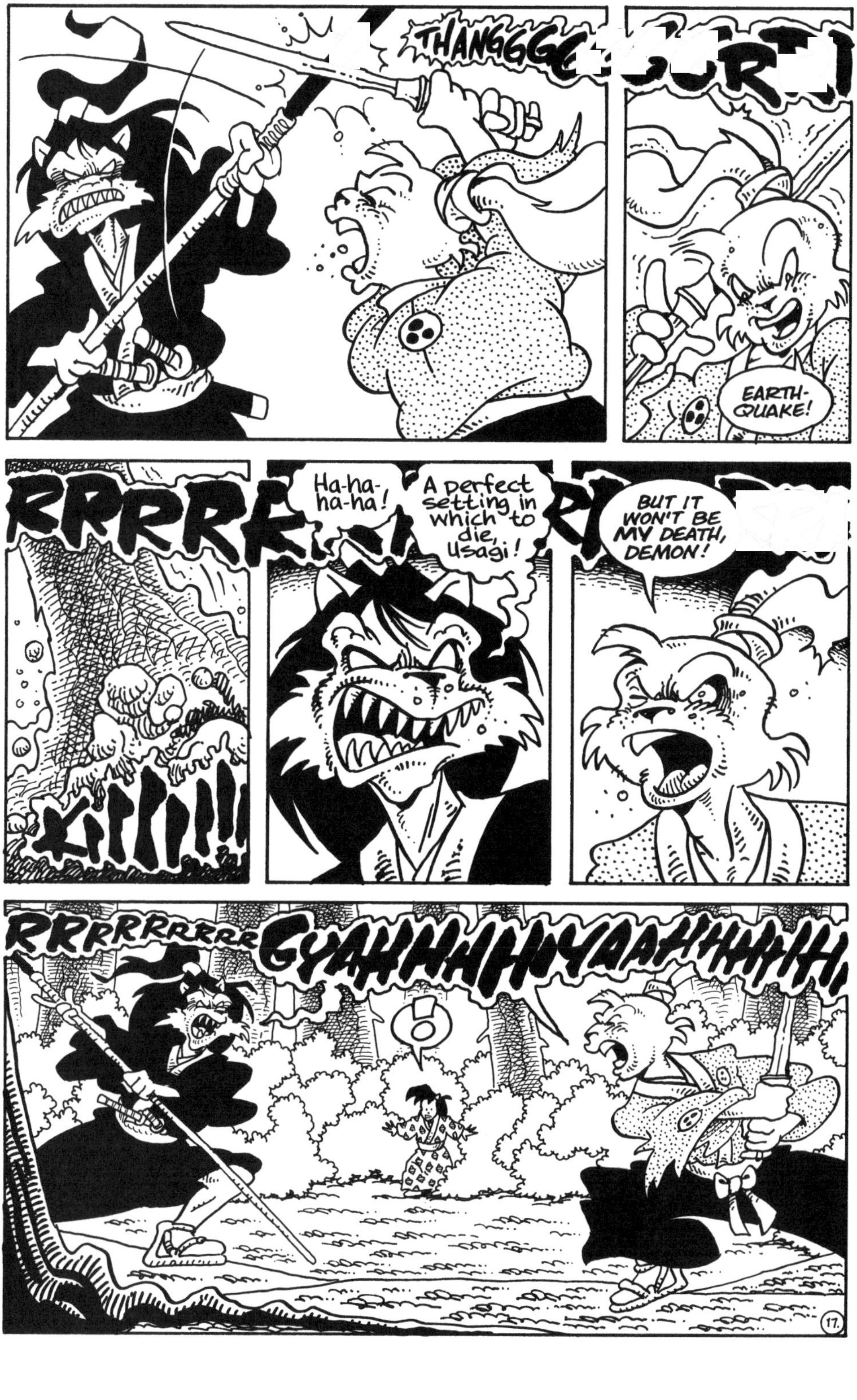
THANGGG
EARTH-QUAKE!
RRRRR
Ha-ha-ha-ha!
A perfect setting in which to die, Usagi!
BUT IT WON'T BE MY DEATH, DEMON!
RRRRRRRRRR
GYAHHHHHYAAHHHHHH
!
17.

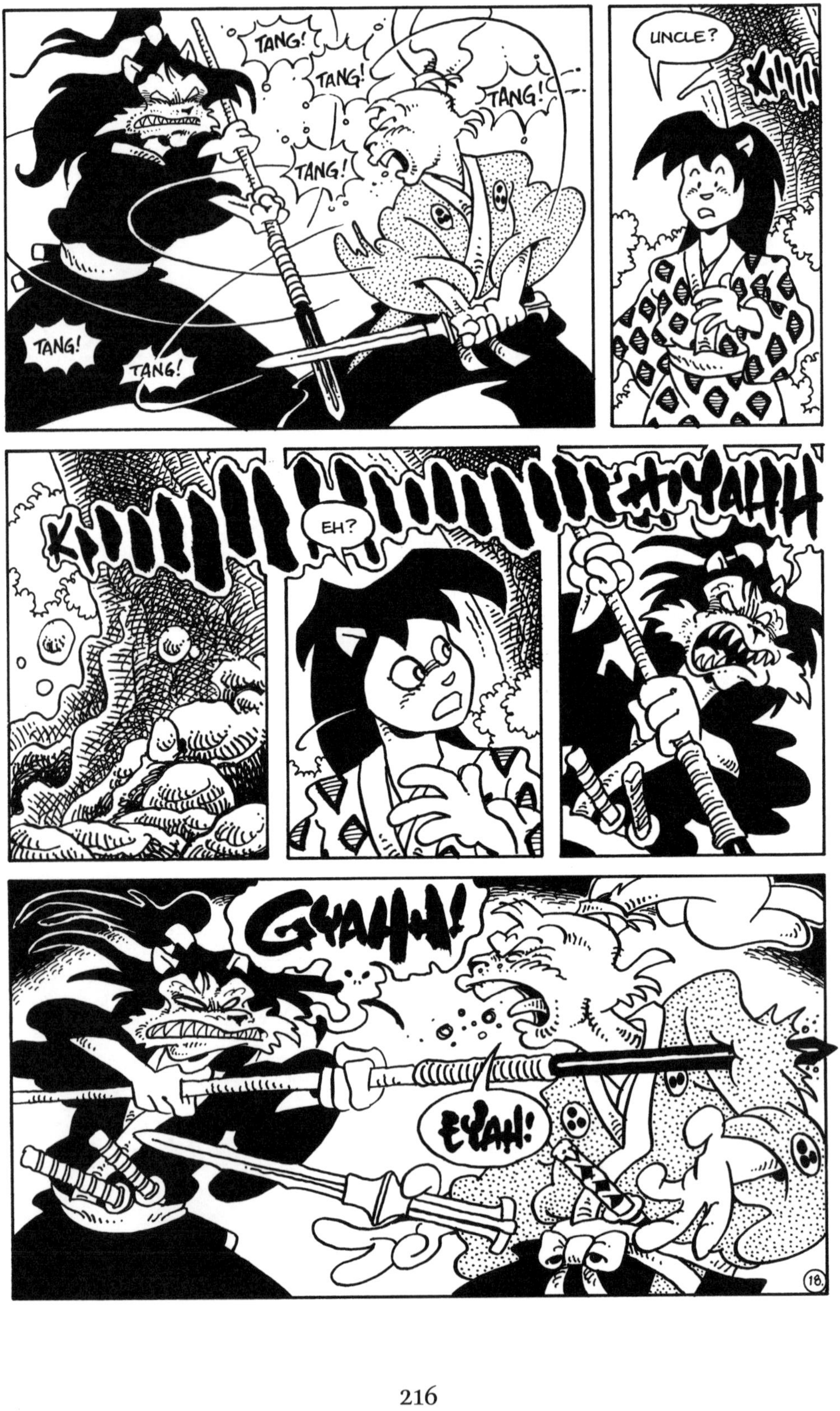
TANG!
TANG!
TANG!
TANG!
TANG!
TANG!
UNCLE?
KIIII
KIIIIIIIIIIIIIIIIIIIIIIEHIYAHH
EH?
GYAHH!
EYAH!
18

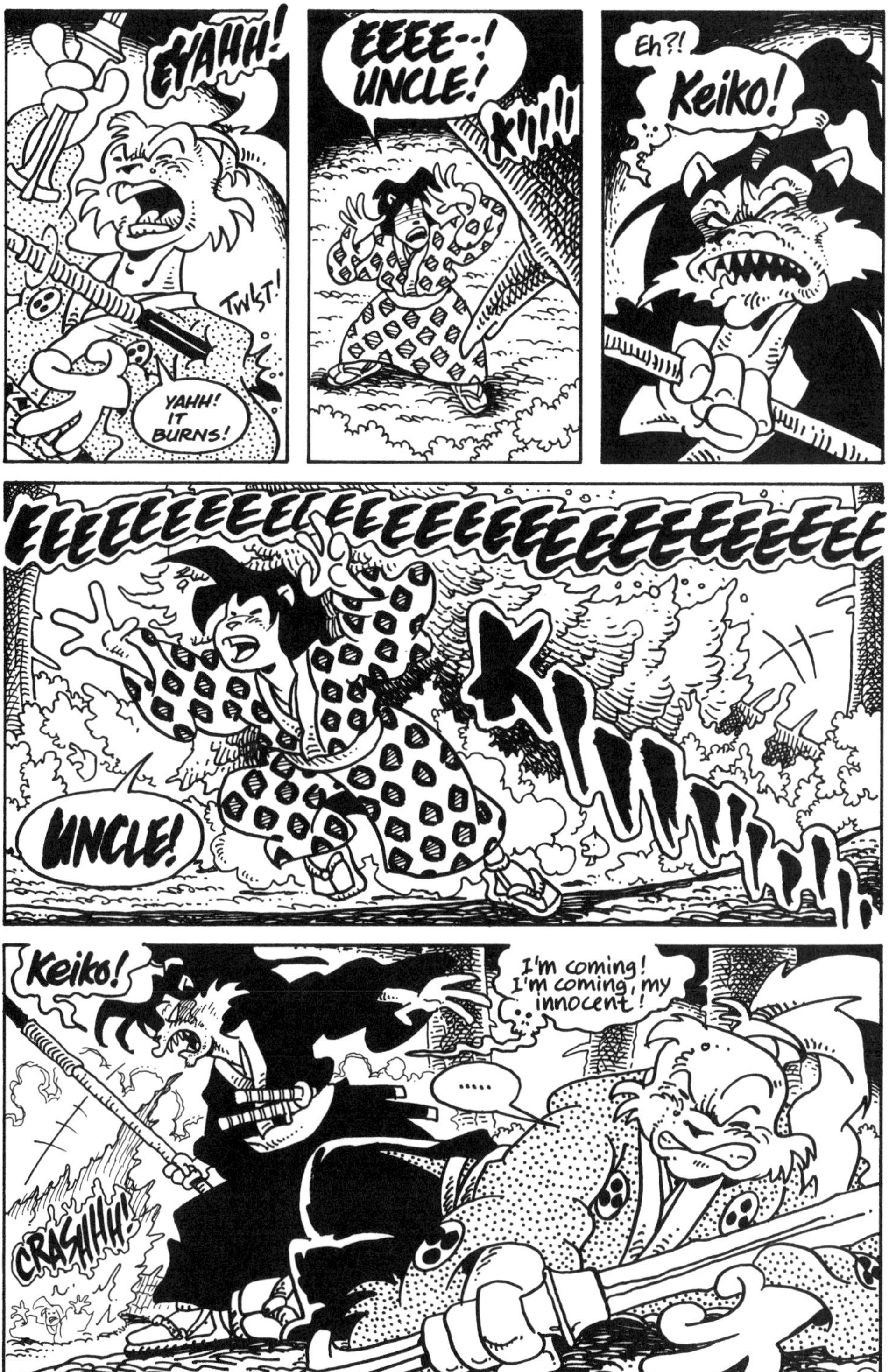
EYAHH!
TWIST!
YAHH! IT BURNS!
EEEE--! UNCLE!
K'I!!!
Eh?!
Keiko!
EEEEEEEEEEEEEEEEEEEEEEEEEEEEEEEE
UNCLE!
Keiko!
I'm coming! I'm coming, my innocent!
.....
CRASHHH!
19.

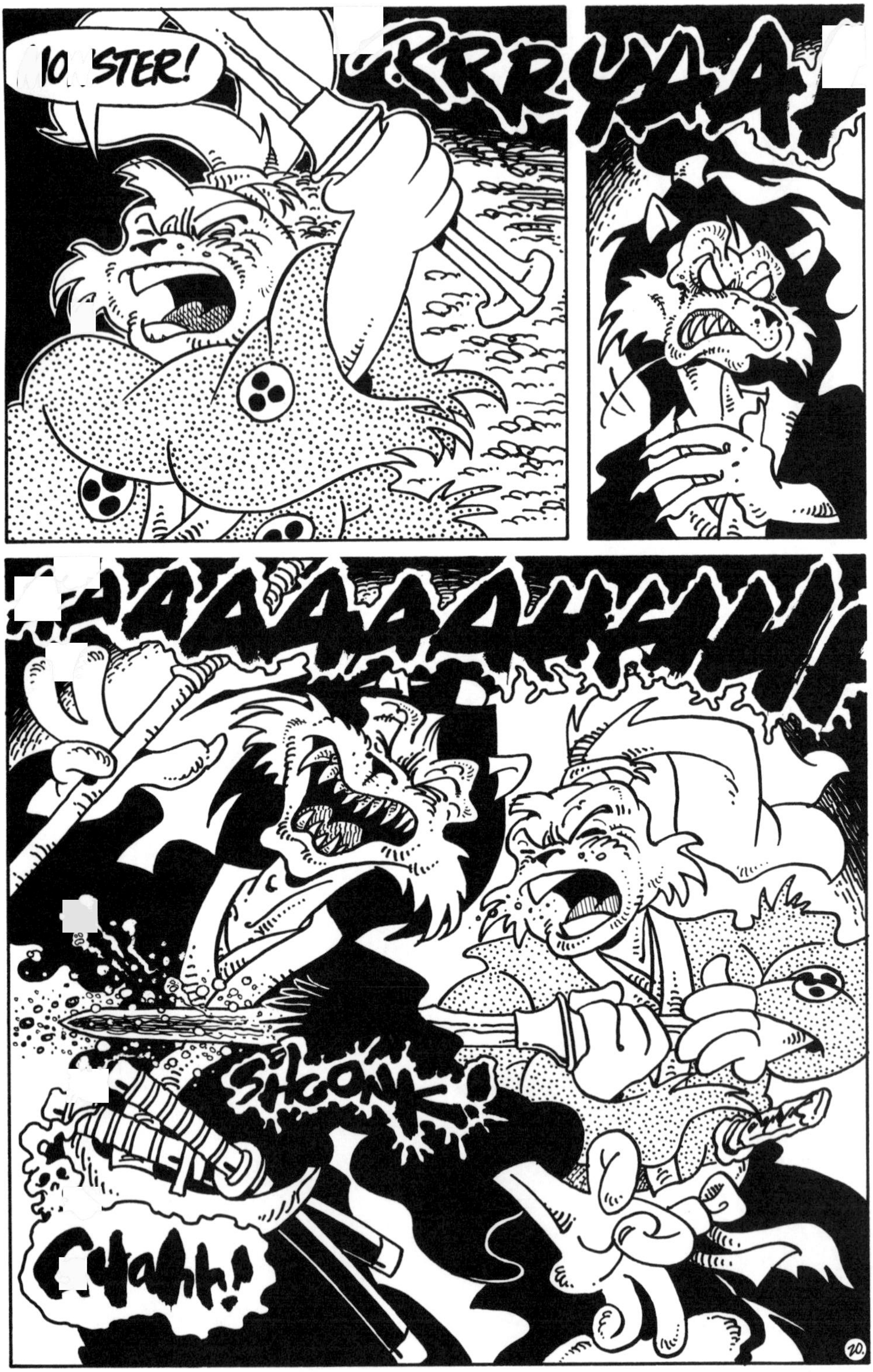
STER!
RRRYAA
AAAAAHHH
SHGONK!
yahh!
20.

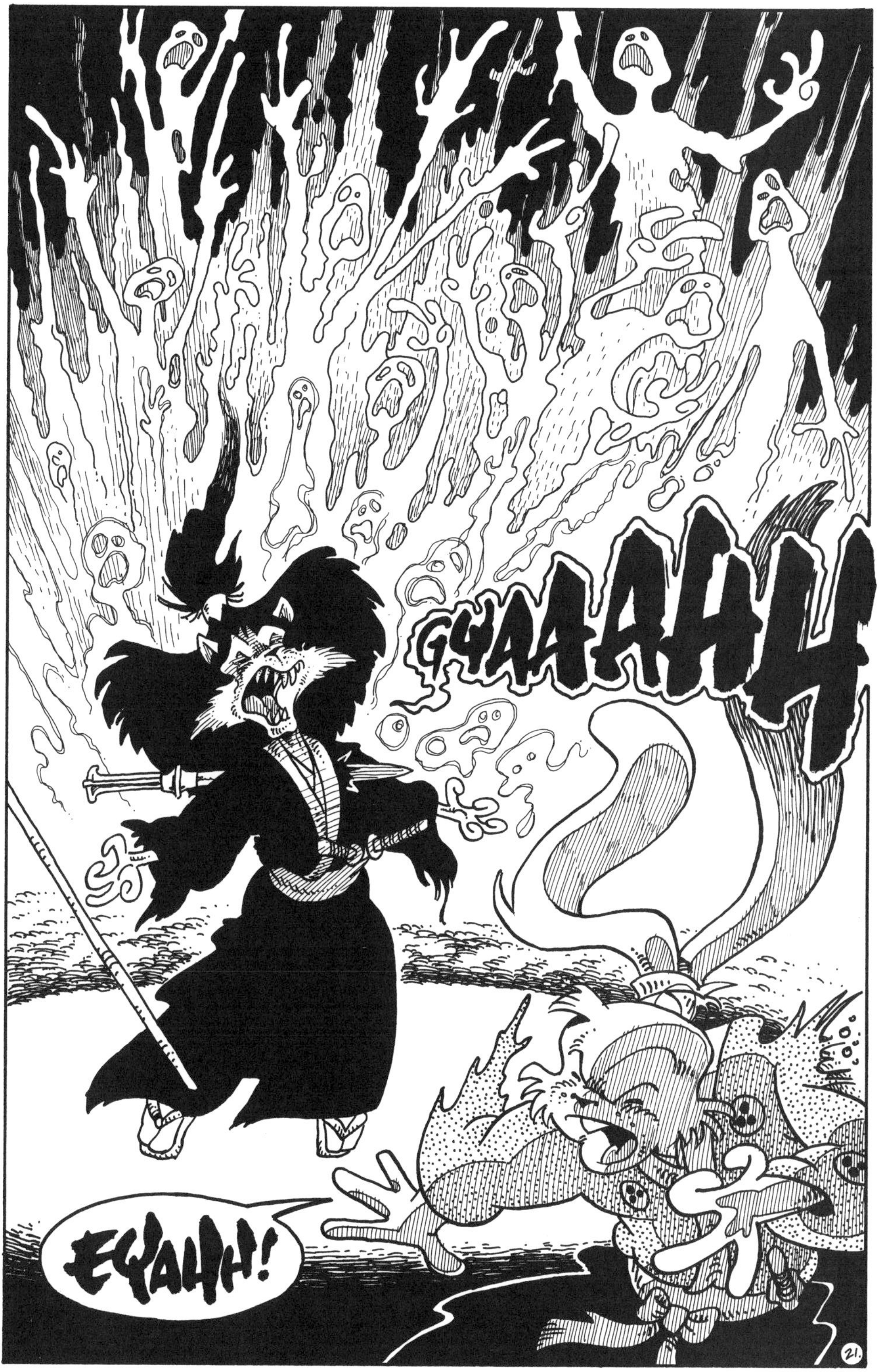
GYAAAAHH
EYAHH!
21.

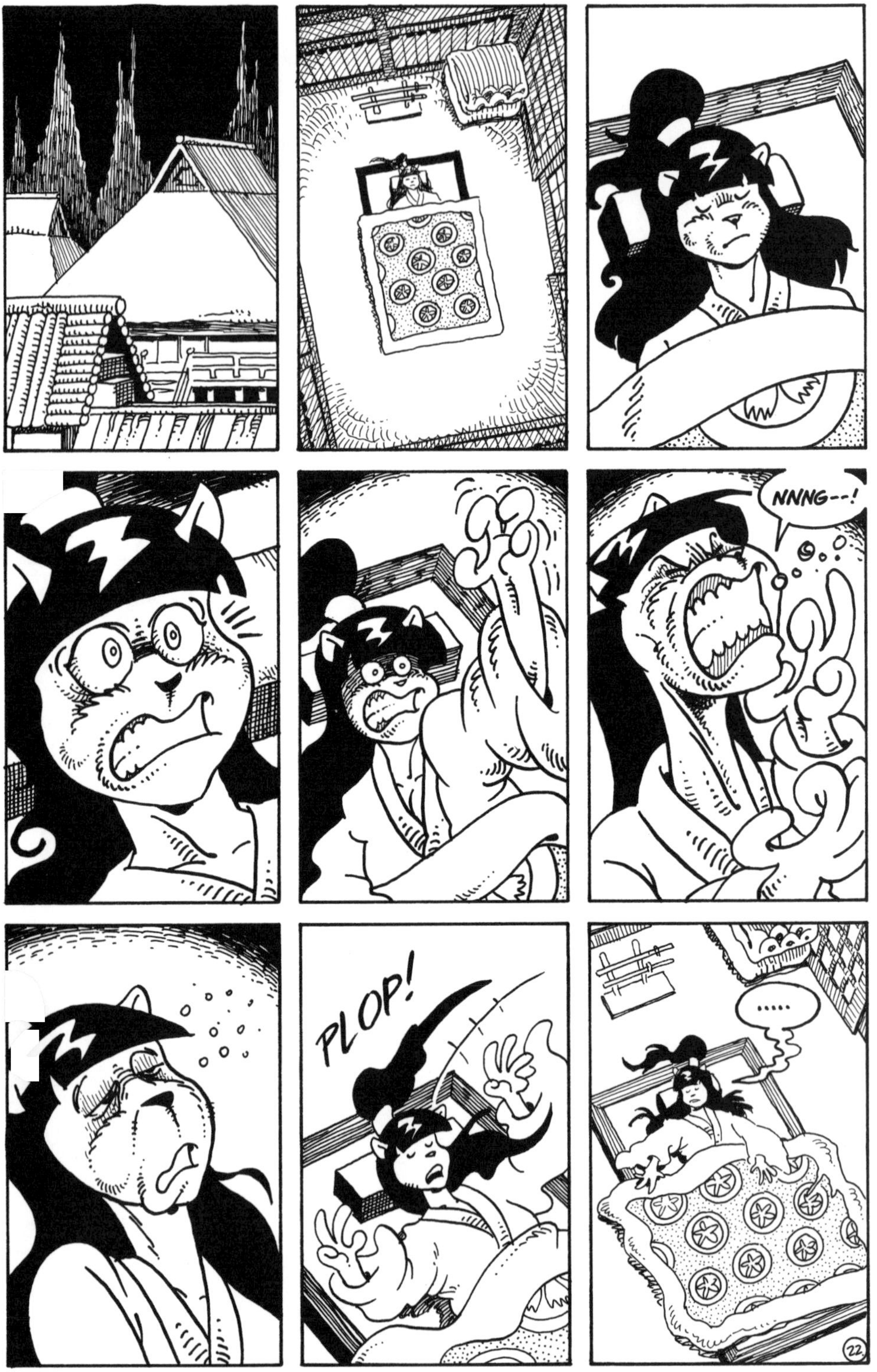
NNNG--!
PLOP!
.....
22

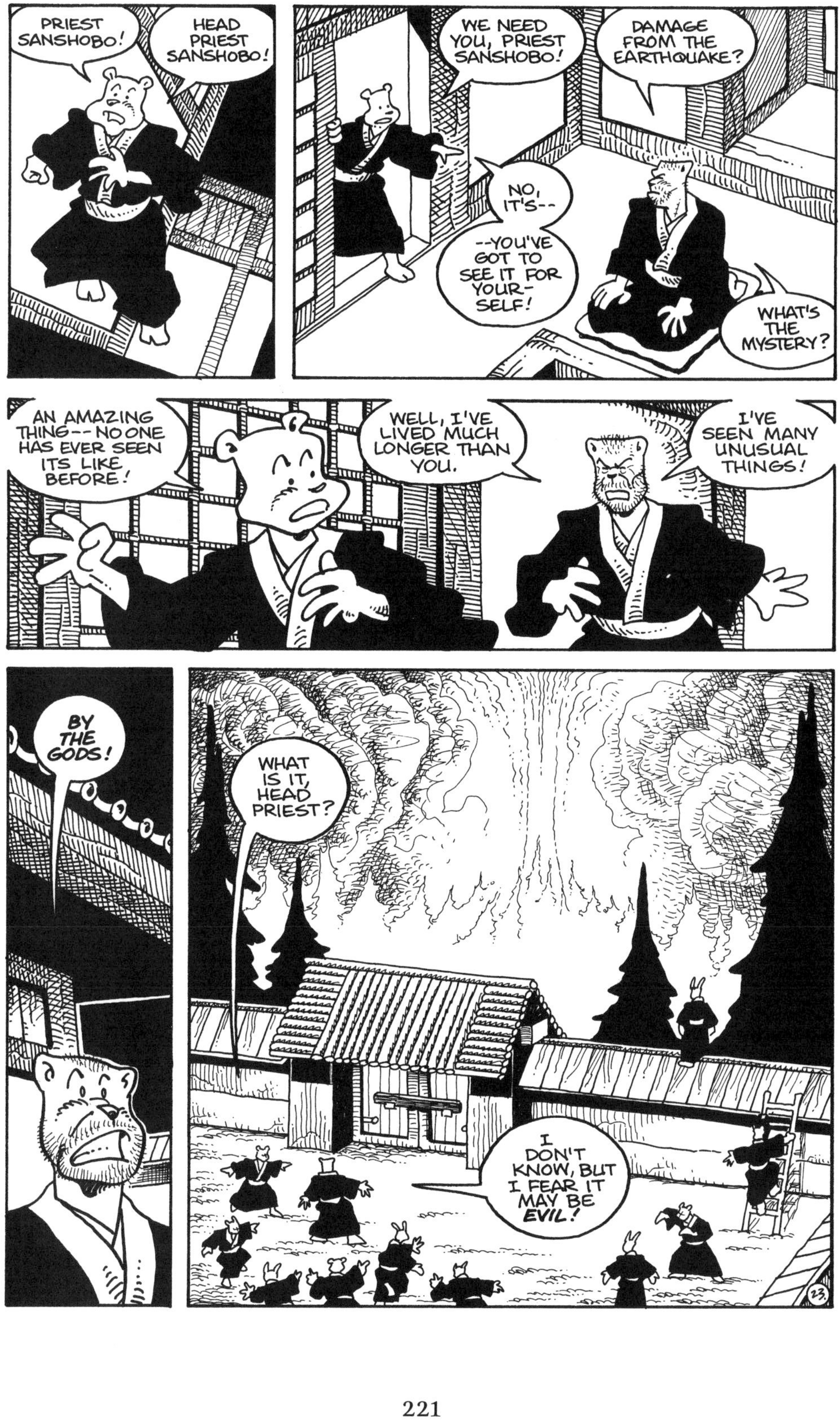
PRIEST SANSHOBO!
HEAD PRIEST SANSHOBO!
WE NEED YOU, PRIEST SANSHOBO!
DAMAGE FROM THE EARTHQUAKE?
NO, IT'S--
--YOU'VE GOT TO SEE IT FOR YOUR-SELF!
WHAT'S THE MYSTERY?
AN AMAZING THING--NO ONE HAS EVER SEEN ITS LIKE BEFORE!
WELL, I'VE LIVED MUCH LONGER THAN YOU.
I'VE SEEN MANY UNUSUAL THINGS!
BY THE GODS!
WHAT IS IT, HEAD PRIEST?
I DON'T KNOW, BUT I FEAR IT MAY BE EVIL!
23.

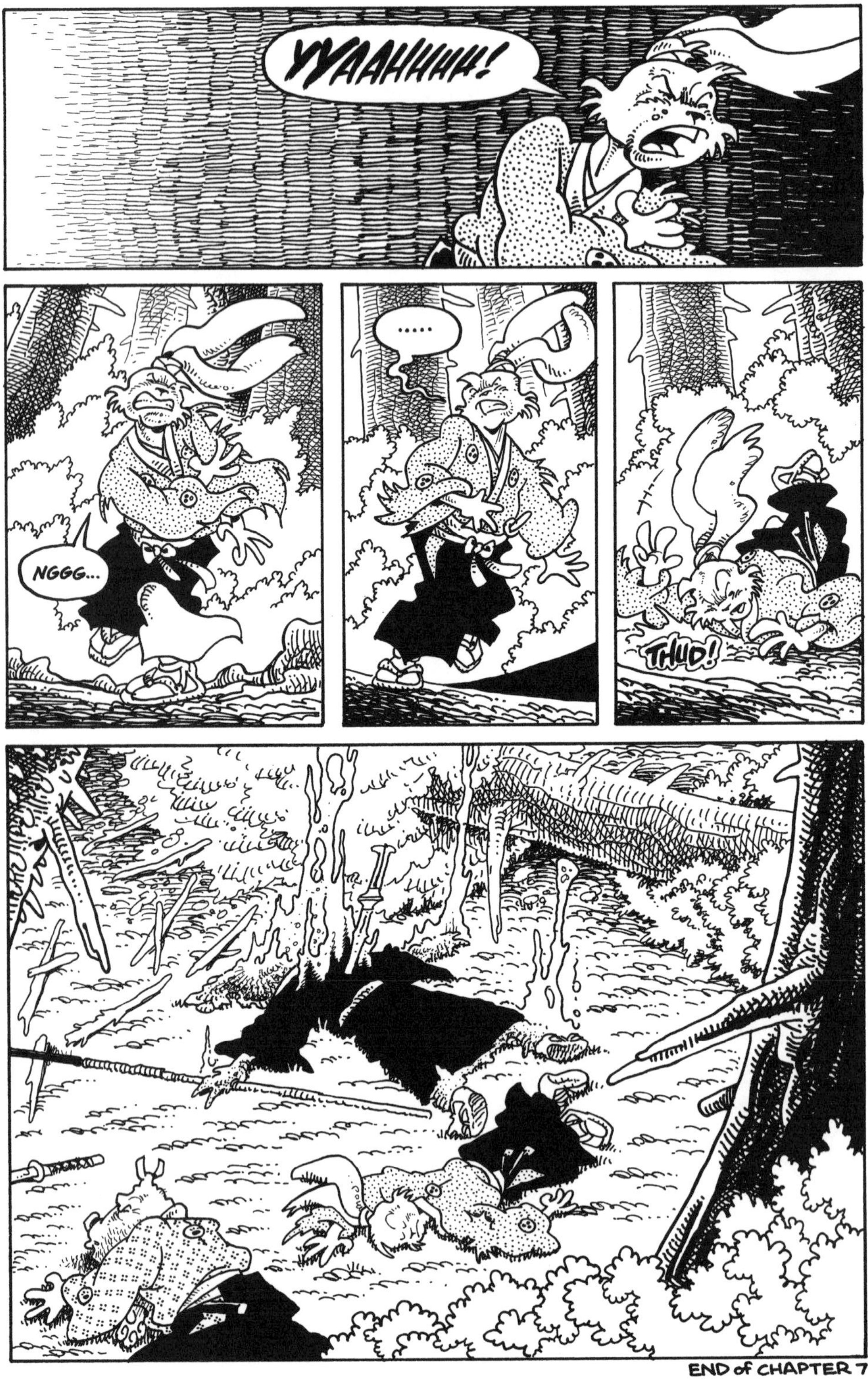
YYAAHHHH!
NGGG...
.....
THUD!

END of CHAPTER 7

GRASSCUTTER

CHAPTER 8
SANSHOBO

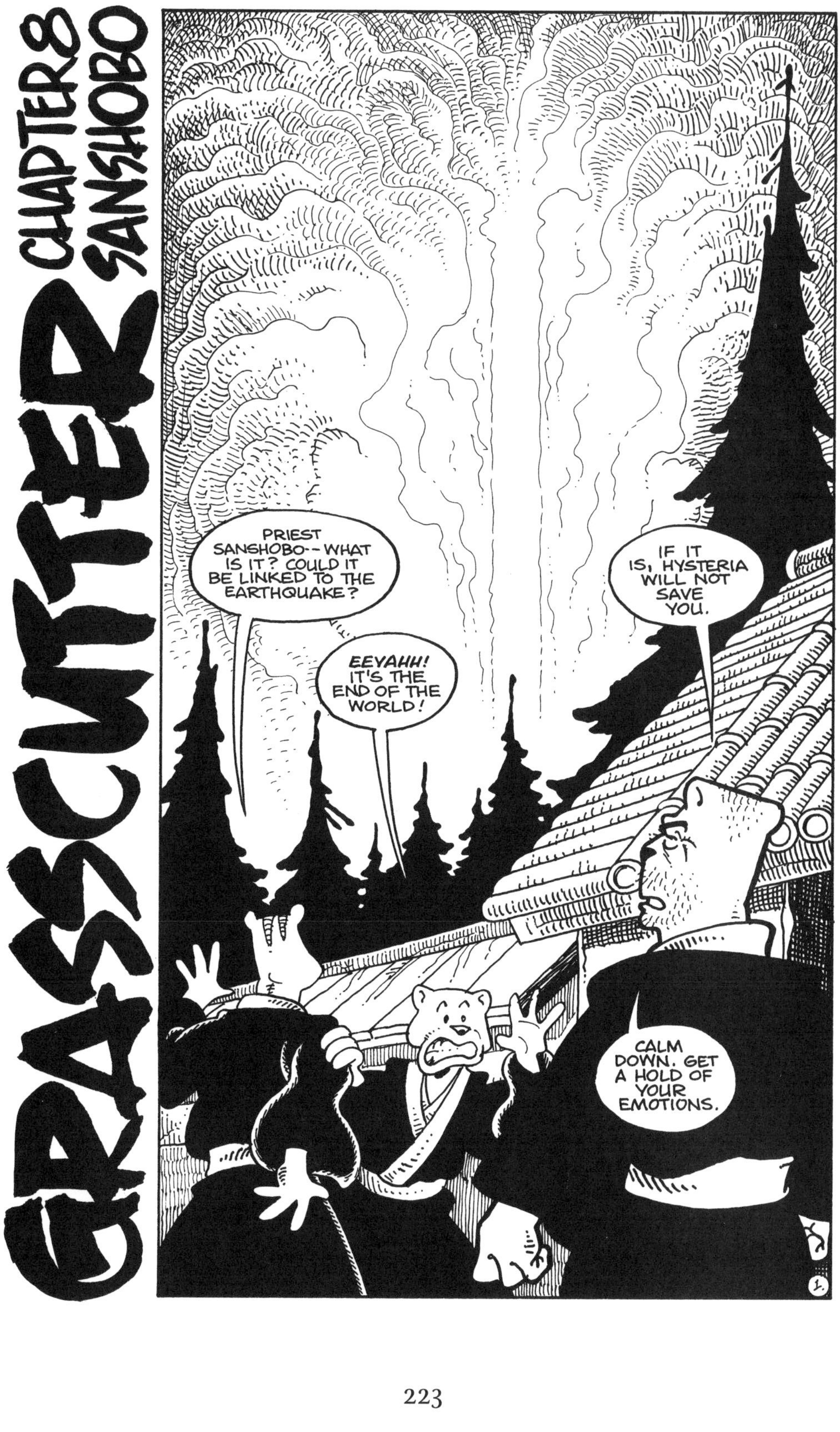
PRIEST SANSHOBO--WHAT IS IT? COULD IT BE LINKED TO THE EARTHQUAKE?
EEYAHH! IT'S THE END OF THE WORLD!
IF IT IS, HYSTERIA WILL NOT SAVE YOU.
CALM DOWN. GET A HOLD OF YOUR EMOTIONS.

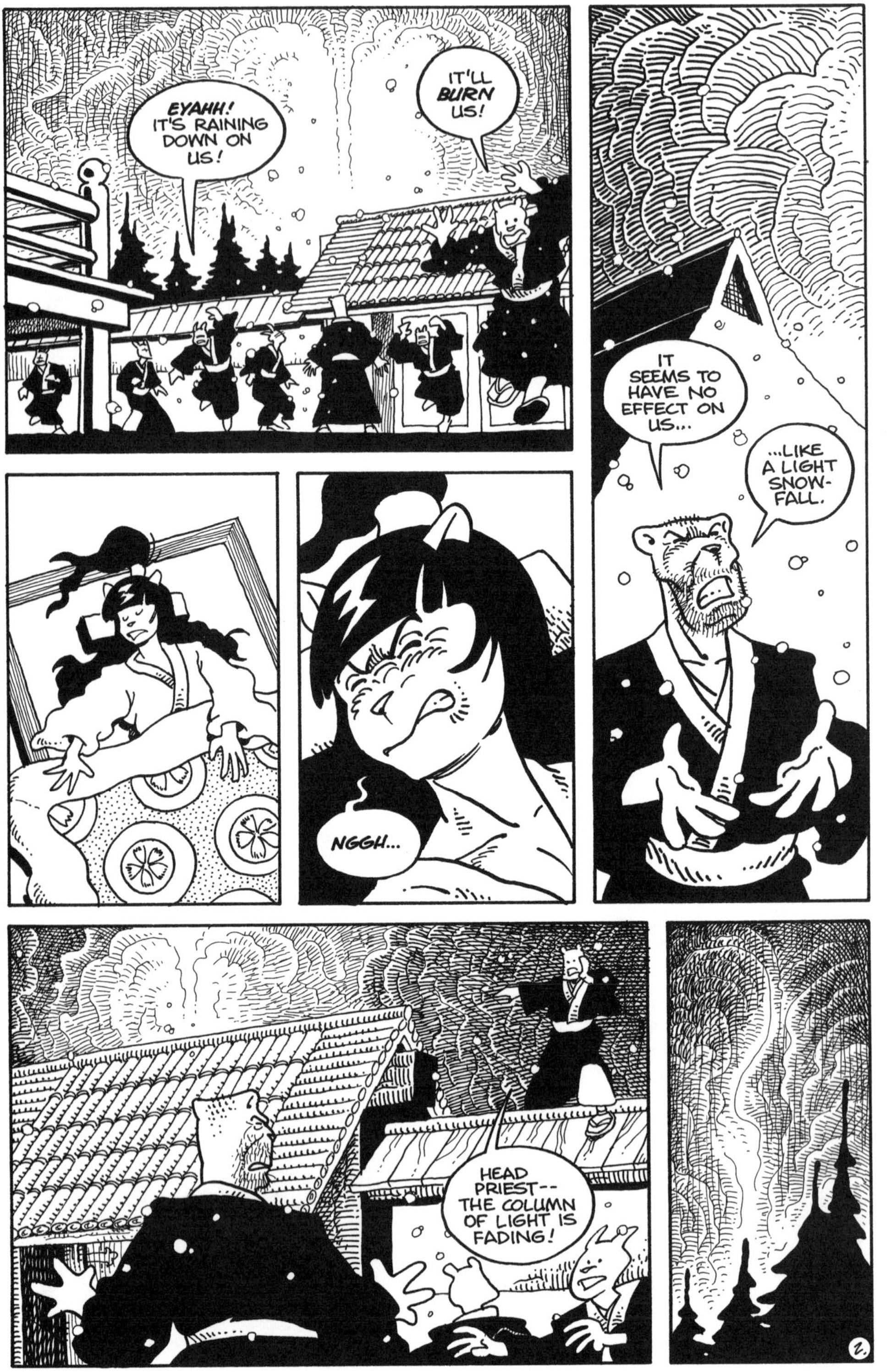
EYAHH! IT'S RAINING DOWN ON US!
IT'LL BURN US!
IT SEEMS TO HAVE NO EFFECT ON US...
...LIKE A LIGHT SNOW-FALL.
NGGH...
HEAD PRIEST-- THE COLUMN OF LIGHT IS FADING!
2.

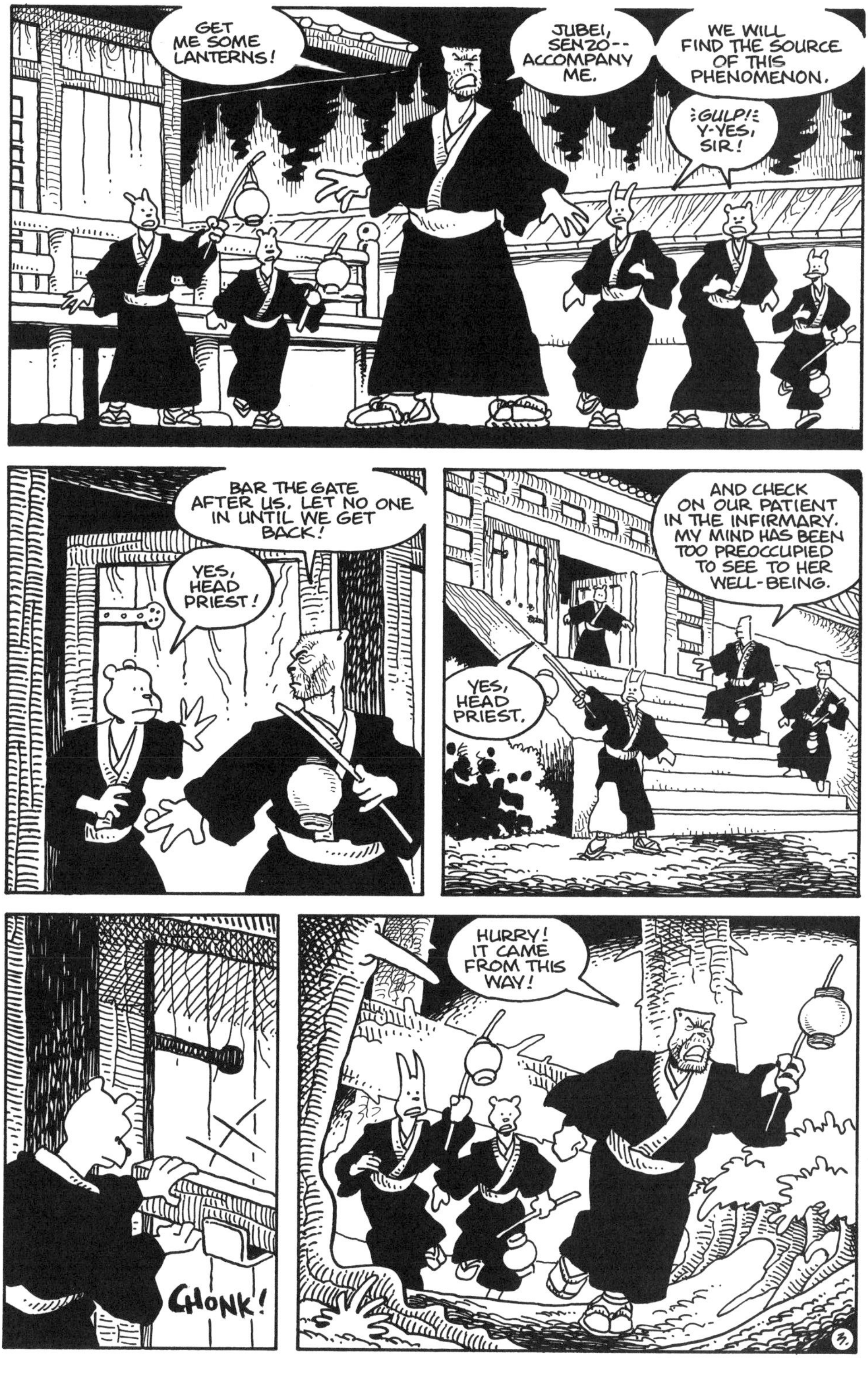
GET ME SOME LANTERNS!
JUBEI, SENZO-- ACCOMPANY ME.
WE WILL FIND THE SOURCE OF THIS PHENOMENON.
GULP! Y-YES, SIR!
BAR THE GATE AFTER US. LET NO ONE IN UNTIL WE GET BACK!
YES, HEAD PRIEST!
AND CHECK ON OUR PATIENT IN THE INFIRMARY. MY MIND HAS BEEN TOO PREOCCUPIED TO SEE TO HER WELL-BEING.
YES, HEAD PRIEST.
CHONK!
HURRY! IT CAME FROM THIS WAY!
3.

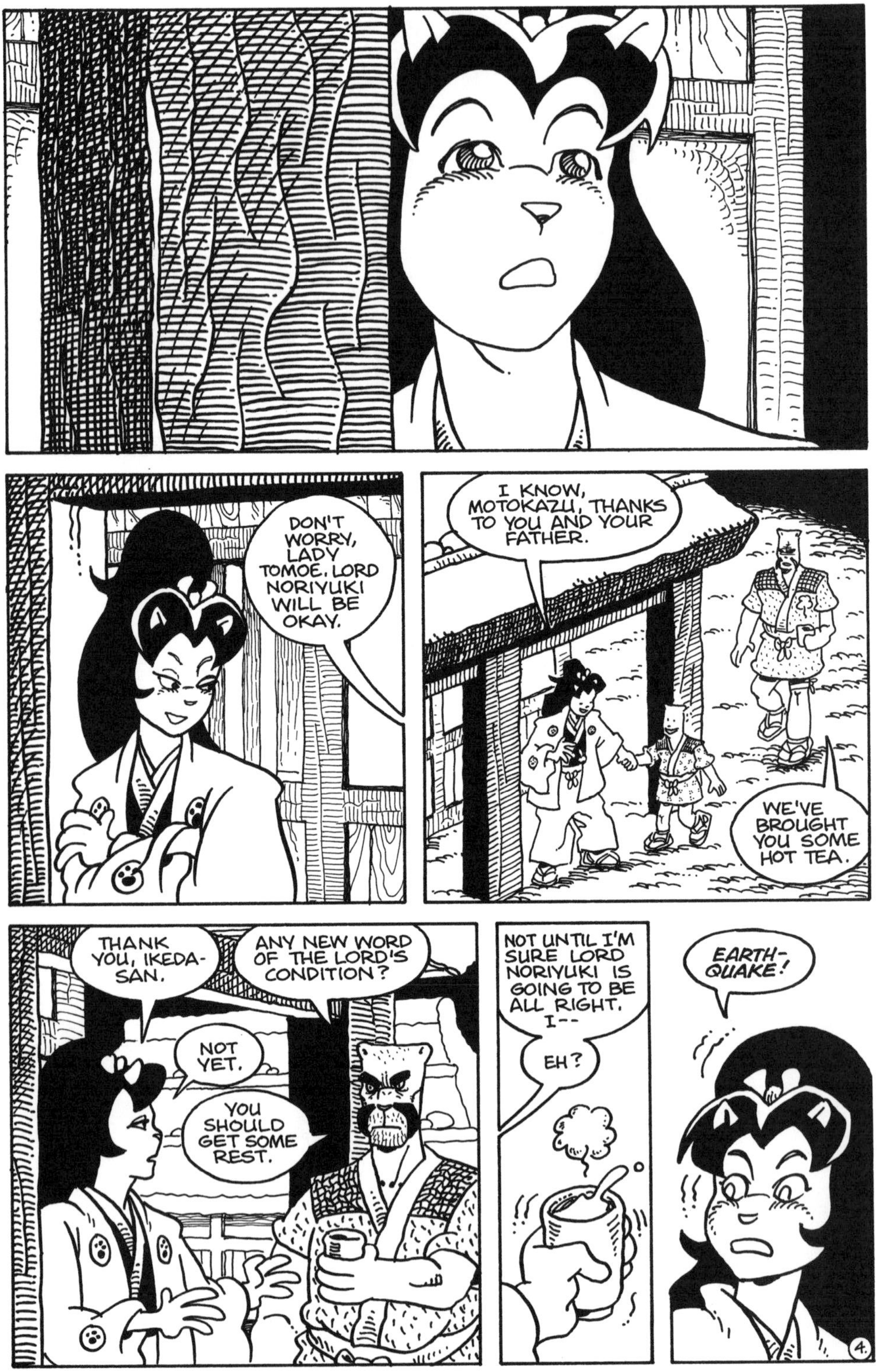
DON'T WORRY, LADY TOMOE. LORD NORIYUKI WILL BE OKAY.
I KNOW, MOTOKAZU, THANKS TO YOU AND YOUR FATHER.
WE'VE BROUGHT YOU SOME HOT TEA.
THANK YOU, IKEDA-SAN.
ANY NEW WORD OF THE LORD'S CONDITION?
NOT YET.
YOU SHOULD GET SOME REST.
NOT UNTIL I'M SURE LORD NORIYUKI IS GOING TO BE ALL RIGHT. I--
EH?
EARTH-QUAKE!
4.

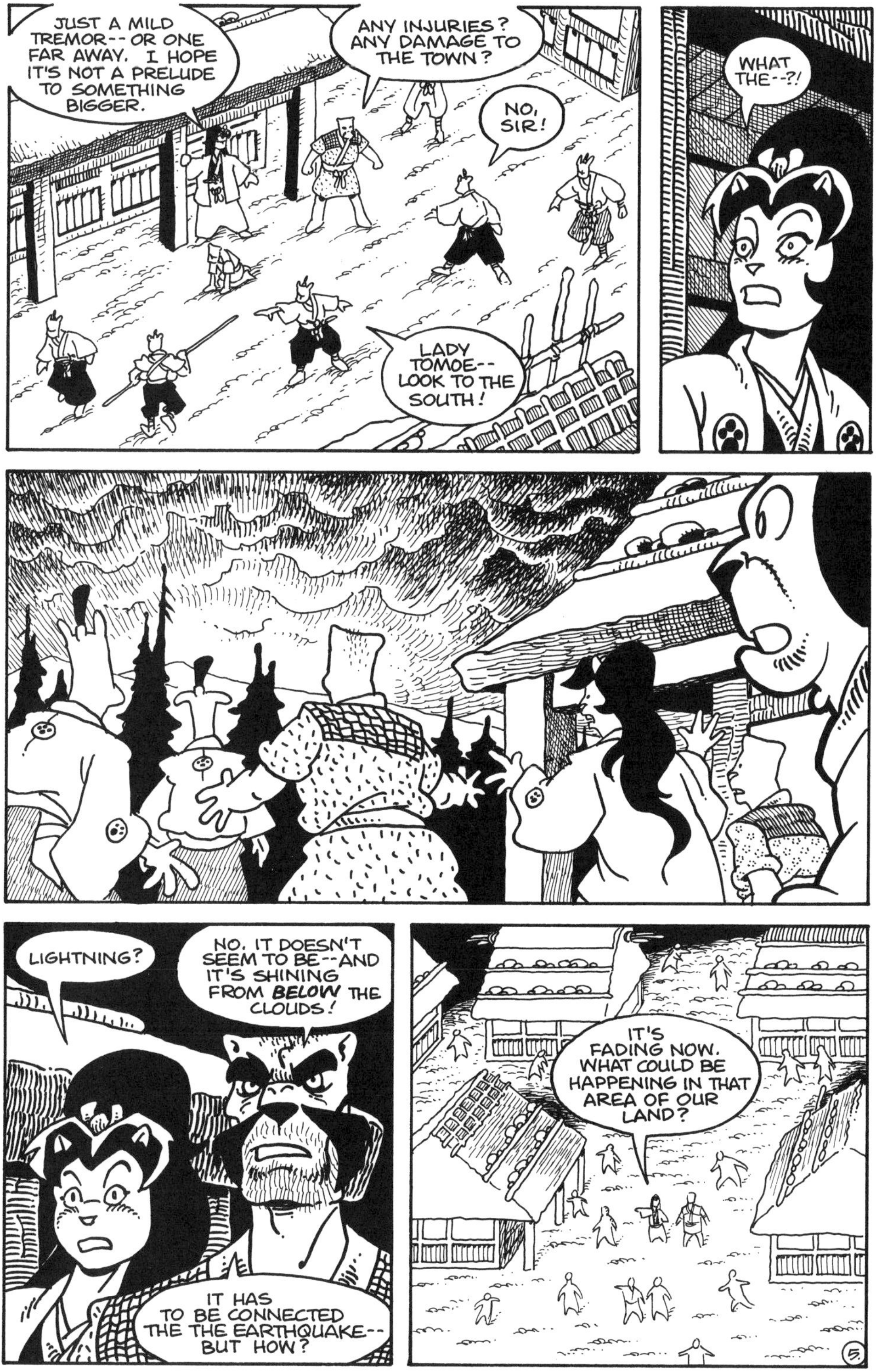
JUST A MILD TREMOR-- OR ONE FAR AWAY. I HOPE IT'S NOT A PRELUDE TO SOMETHING BIGGER.
ANY INJURIES? ANY DAMAGE TO THE TOWN?
NO, SIR!
LADY TOMOE-- LOOK TO THE SOUTH!
WHAT THE--?!
LIGHTNING?
NO. IT DOESN'T SEEM TO BE--AND IT'S SHINING FROM **BELOW** THE CLOUDS!
IT HAS TO BE CONNECTED THE THE EARTHQUAKE-- BUT HOW?
IT'S FADING NOW. WHAT COULD BE HAPPENING IN THAT AREA OF OUR LAND?
5

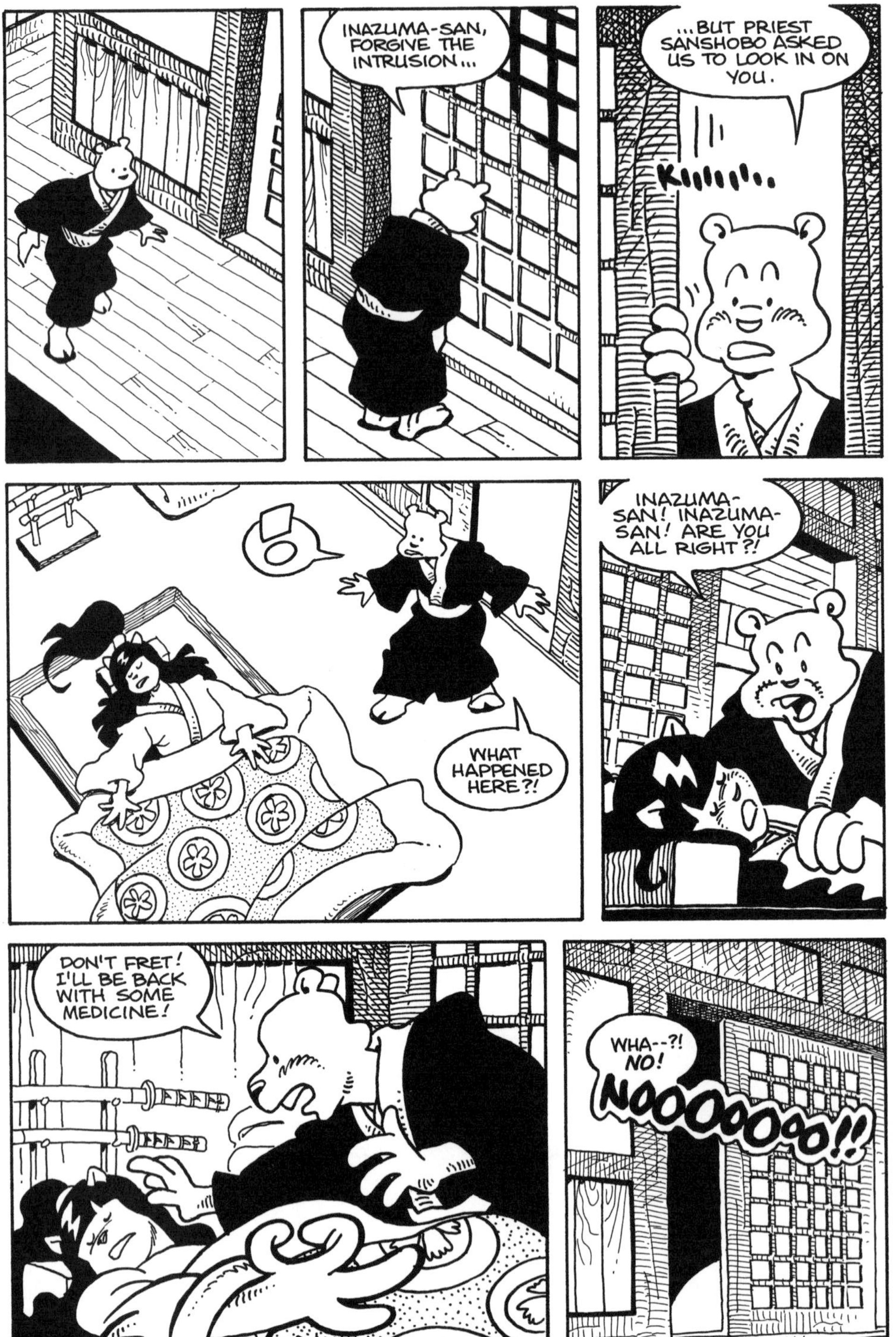
INAZUMA-SAN, FORGIVE THE INTRUSION...
...BUT PRIEST SANSHOBO ASKED US TO LOOK IN ON YOU.
WHAT HAPPENED HERE?!
INAZUMA-SAN! INAZUMA-SAN! ARE YOU ALL RIGHT?!
DON'T FRET! I'LL BE BACK WITH SOME MEDICINE!
WHA--?! NO!
NOOOOOOO!!
6.

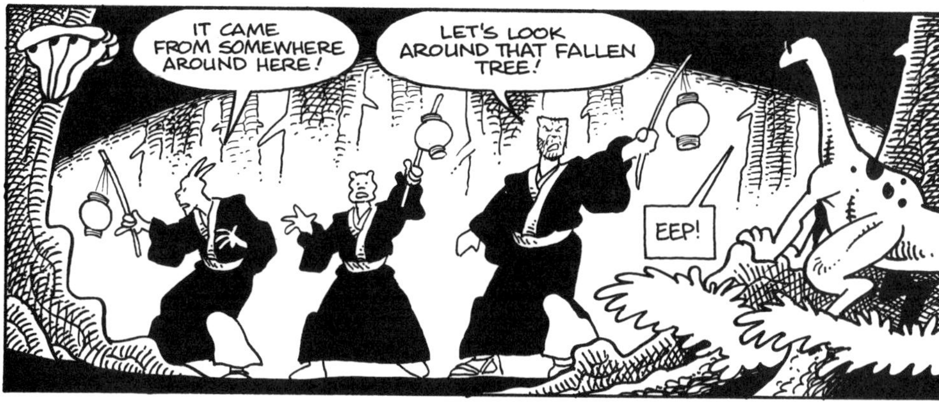
IT CAME FROM SOMEWHERE AROUND HERE!
LET'S LOOK AROUND THAT FALLEN TREE!
EEP!

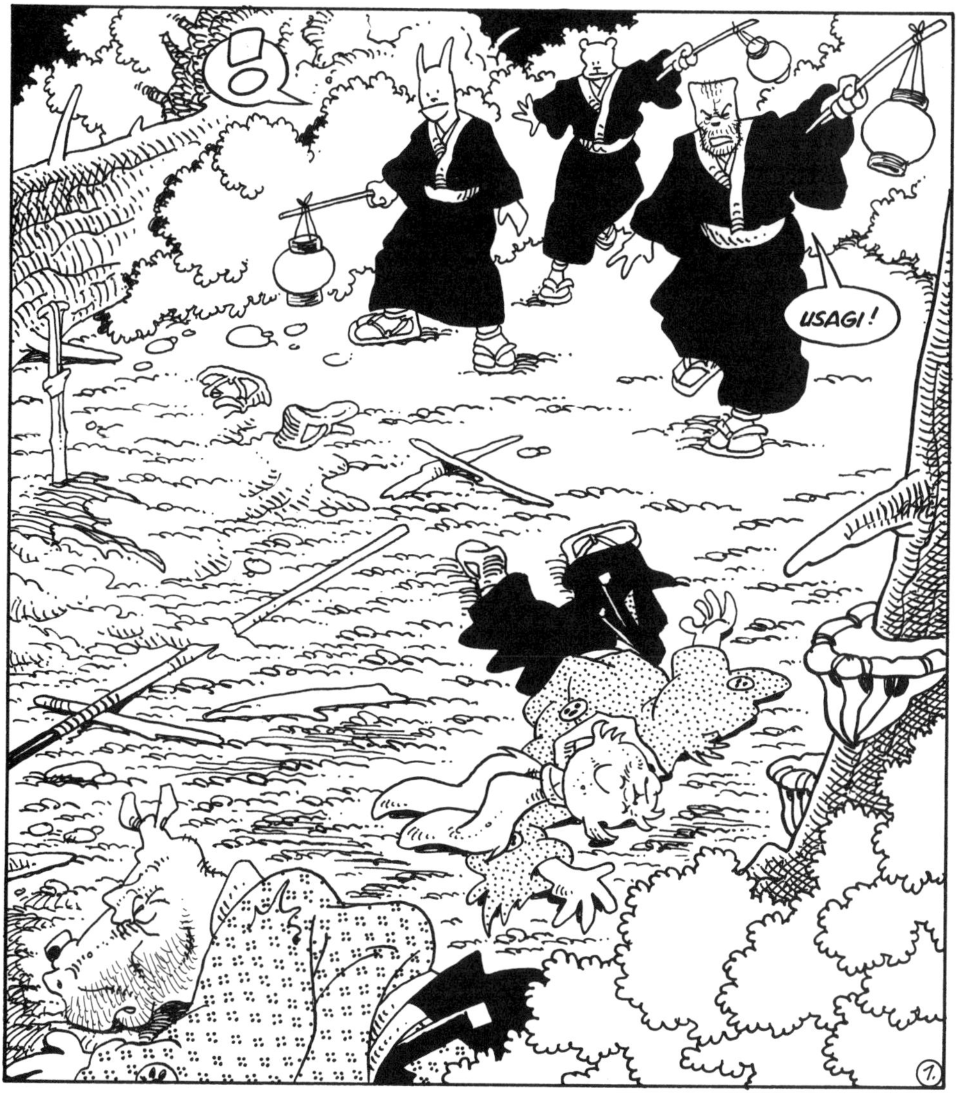
!
USAGI!
7.

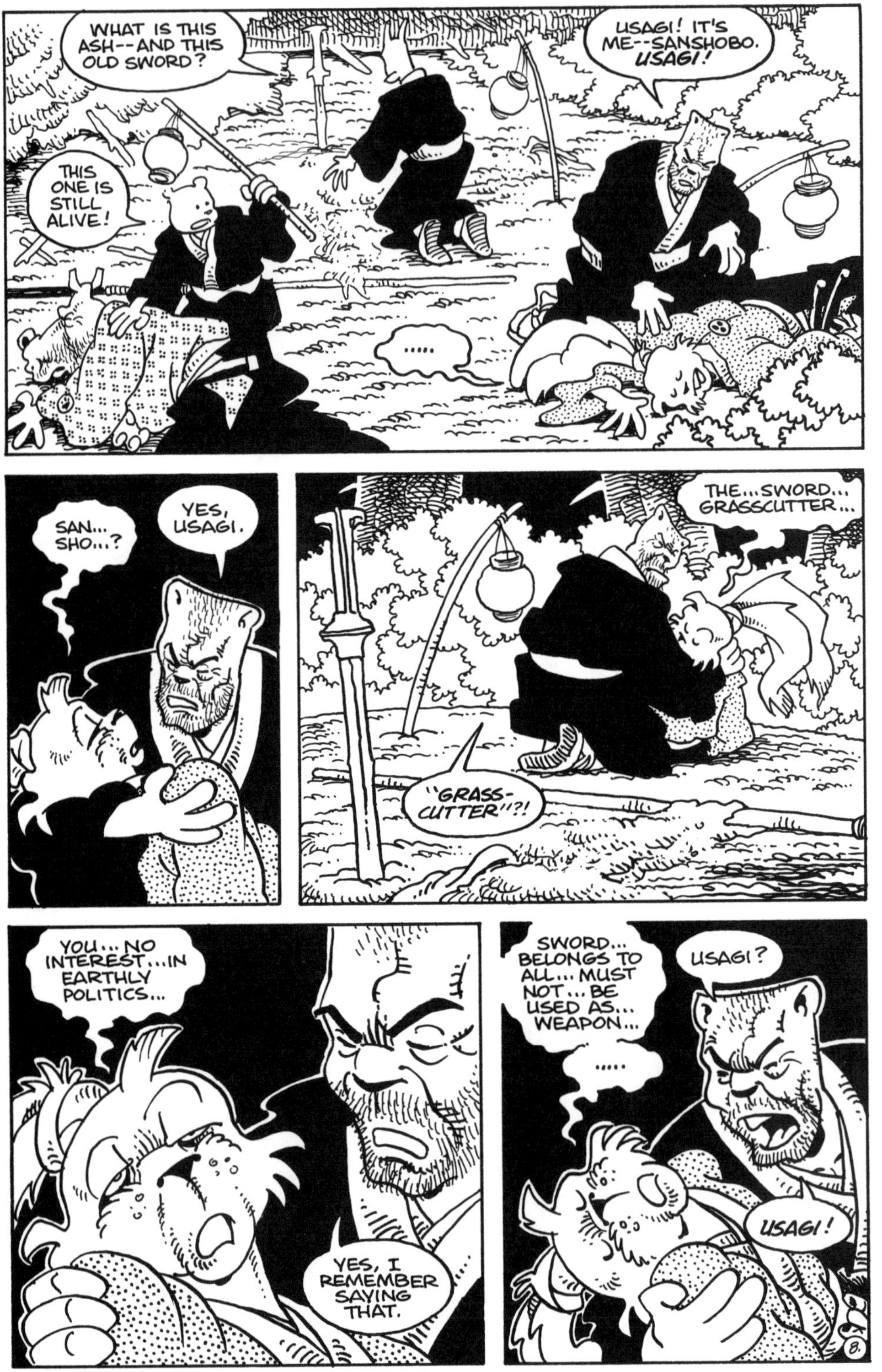
WHAT IS THIS ASH--AND THIS OLD SWORD?
USAGI! IT'S ME--SANSHOBO. USAGI!
THIS ONE IS STILL ALIVE!
.....
SAN... SHO...?
YES, USAGI.
THE...SWORD... GRASSCUTTER...
"GRASS-CUTTER"?!
YOU...NO INTEREST...IN EARTHLY POLITICS...
YES, I REMEMBER SAYING THAT.
SWORD... BELONGS TO ALL... MUST NOT... BE USED AS... WEAPON...
USAGI?
.....
USAGI!
8.

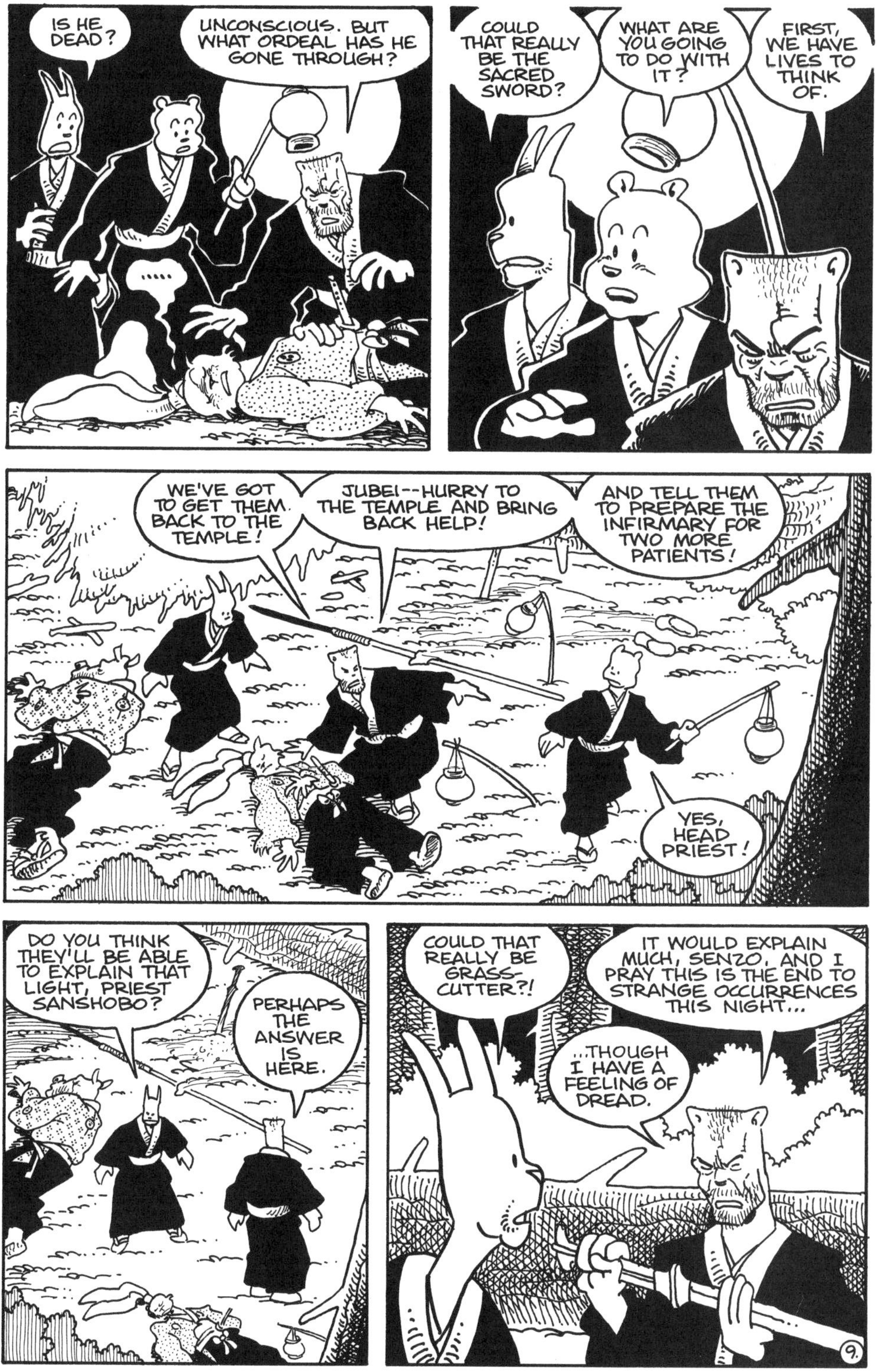
IS HE DEAD?
UNCONSCIOUS. BUT WHAT ORDEAL HAS HE GONE THROUGH?
......
COULD THAT REALLY BE THE SACRED SWORD?
WHAT ARE YOU GOING TO DO WITH IT?
FIRST, WE HAVE LIVES TO THINK OF.
WE'VE GOT TO GET THEM BACK TO THE TEMPLE!
JUBEI--HURRY TO THE TEMPLE AND BRING BACK HELP!
AND TELL THEM TO PREPARE THE INFIRMARY FOR TWO MORE PATIENTS!
YES, HEAD PRIEST!
DO YOU THINK THEY'LL BE ABLE TO EXPLAIN THAT LIGHT, PRIEST SANSHOBO?
PERHAPS THE ANSWER IS HERE.
COULD THAT REALLY BE GRASS-CUTTER?!
IT WOULD EXPLAIN MUCH, SENZO, AND I PRAY THIS IS THE END TO STRANGE OCCURRENCES THIS NIGHT...
...THOUGH I HAVE A FEELING OF DREAD.
9.

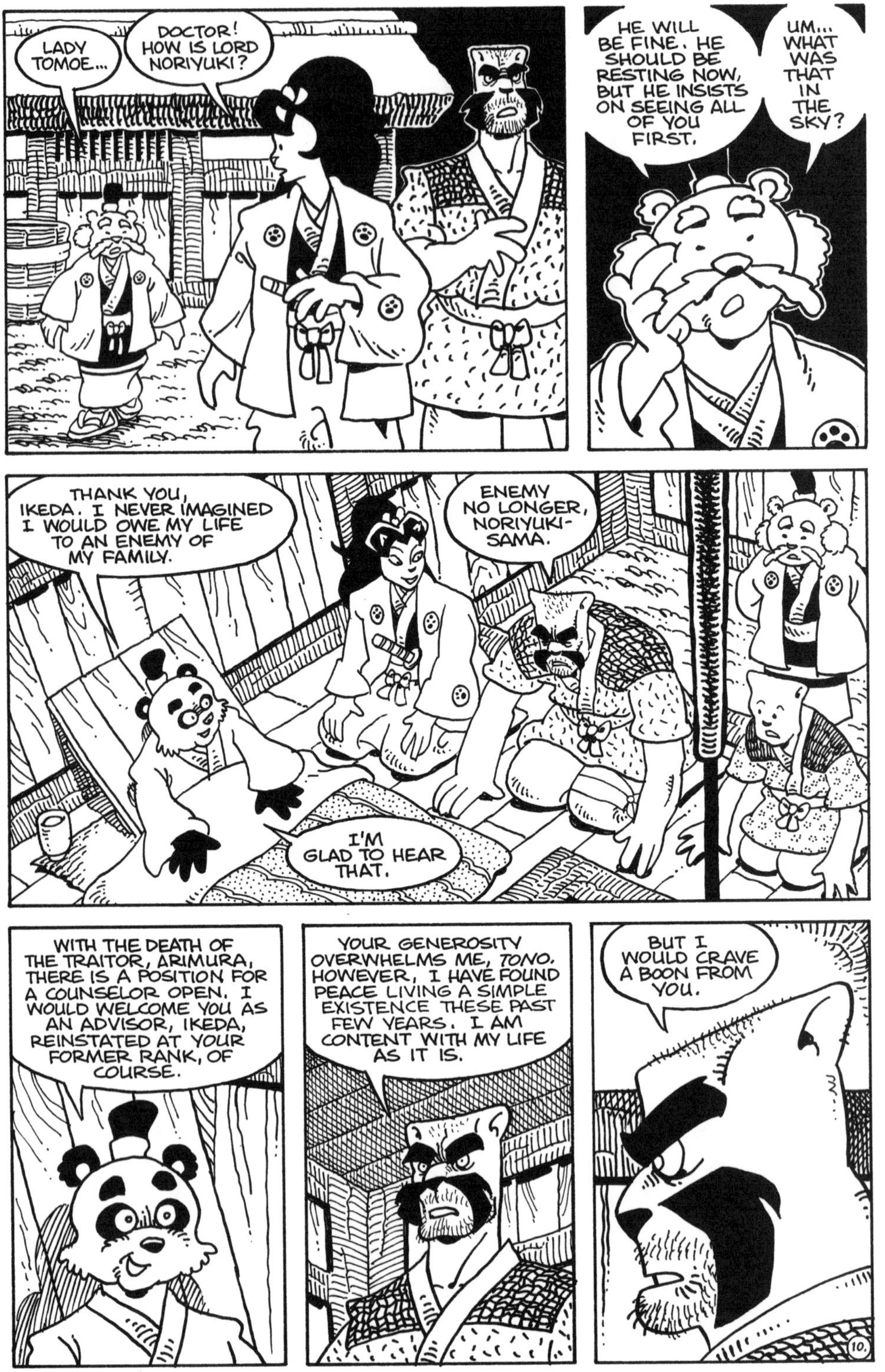
LADY TOMOE...
DOCTOR! HOW IS LORD NORIYUKI?
HE WILL BE FINE. HE SHOULD BE RESTING NOW, BUT HE INSISTS ON SEEING ALL OF YOU FIRST.
UM... WHAT WAS THAT IN THE SKY?
THANK YOU, IKEDA. I NEVER IMAGINED I WOULD OWE MY LIFE TO AN ENEMY OF MY FAMILY.
ENEMY NO LONGER, NORIYUKI-SAMA.
I'M GLAD TO HEAR THAT.
WITH THE DEATH OF THE TRAITOR, ARIMURA, THERE IS A POSITION FOR A COUNSELOR OPEN. I WOULD WELCOME YOU AS AN ADVISOR, IKEDA, REINSTATED AT YOUR FORMER RANK, OF COURSE.
YOUR GENEROSITY OVERWHELMS ME, *TONO*. HOWEVER, I HAVE FOUND PEACE LIVING A SIMPLE EXISTENCE THESE PAST FEW YEARS. I AM CONTENT WITH MY LIFE AS IT IS.
BUT I WOULD CRAVE A BOON FROM YOU.
10.

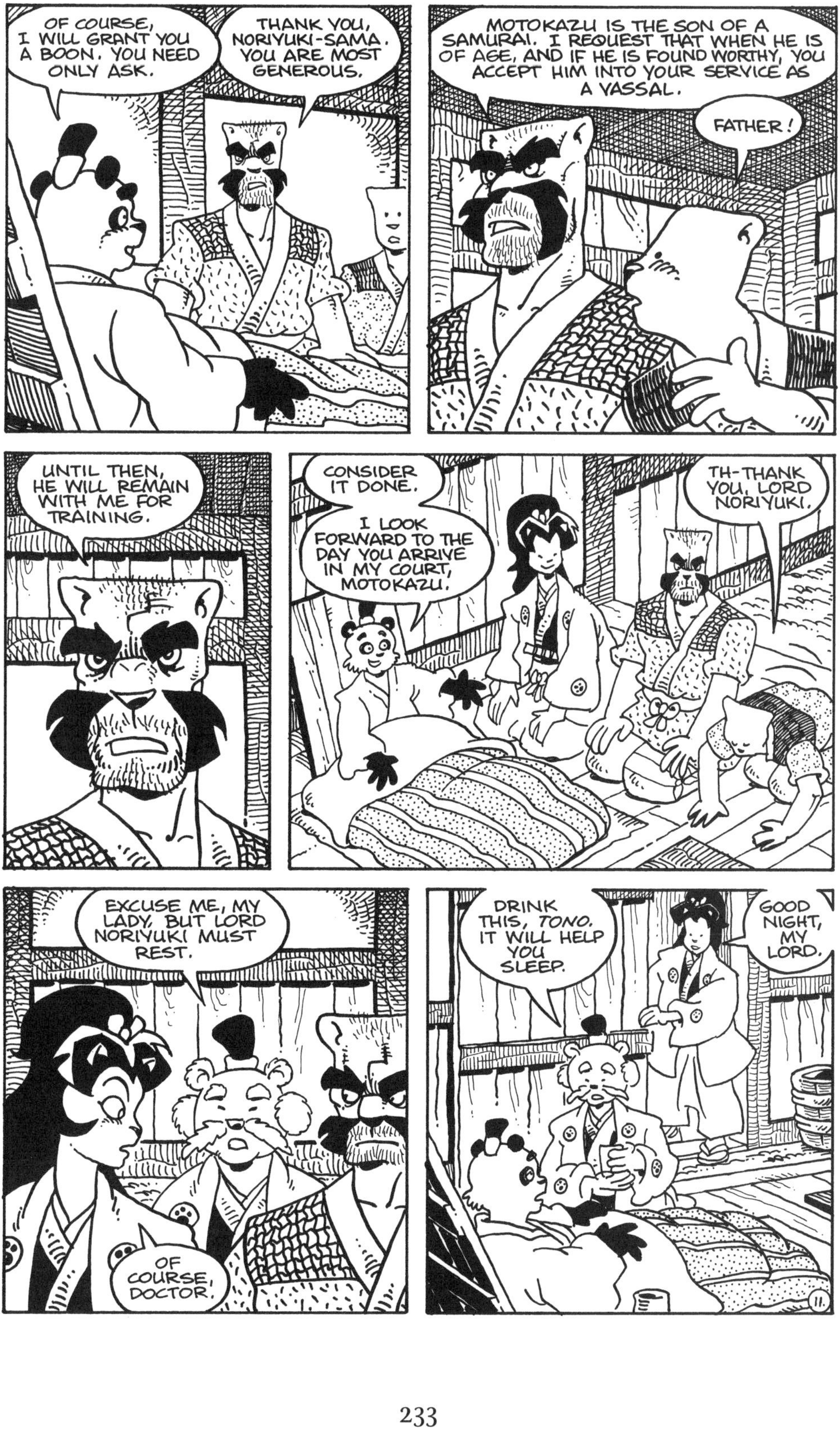
OF COURSE, I WILL GRANT YOU A BOON. YOU NEED ONLY ASK.
THANK YOU, NORIYUKI-SAMA. YOU ARE MOST GENEROUS.
MOTOKAZU IS THE SON OF A SAMURAI. I REQUEST THAT WHEN HE IS OF AGE, AND IF HE IS FOUND WORTHY, YOU ACCEPT HIM INTO YOUR SERVICE AS A VASSAL.
FATHER!
UNTIL THEN, HE WILL REMAIN WITH ME FOR TRAINING.
CONSIDER IT DONE.
I LOOK FORWARD TO THE DAY YOU ARRIVE IN MY COURT, MOTOKAZU.
TH-THANK YOU, LORD NORIYUKI.
EXCUSE ME, MY LADY, BUT LORD NORIYUKI MUST REST.
OF COURSE, DOCTOR.
DRINK THIS, *TONO*. IT WILL HELP YOU SLEEP.
GOOD NIGHT, MY LORD.
11.

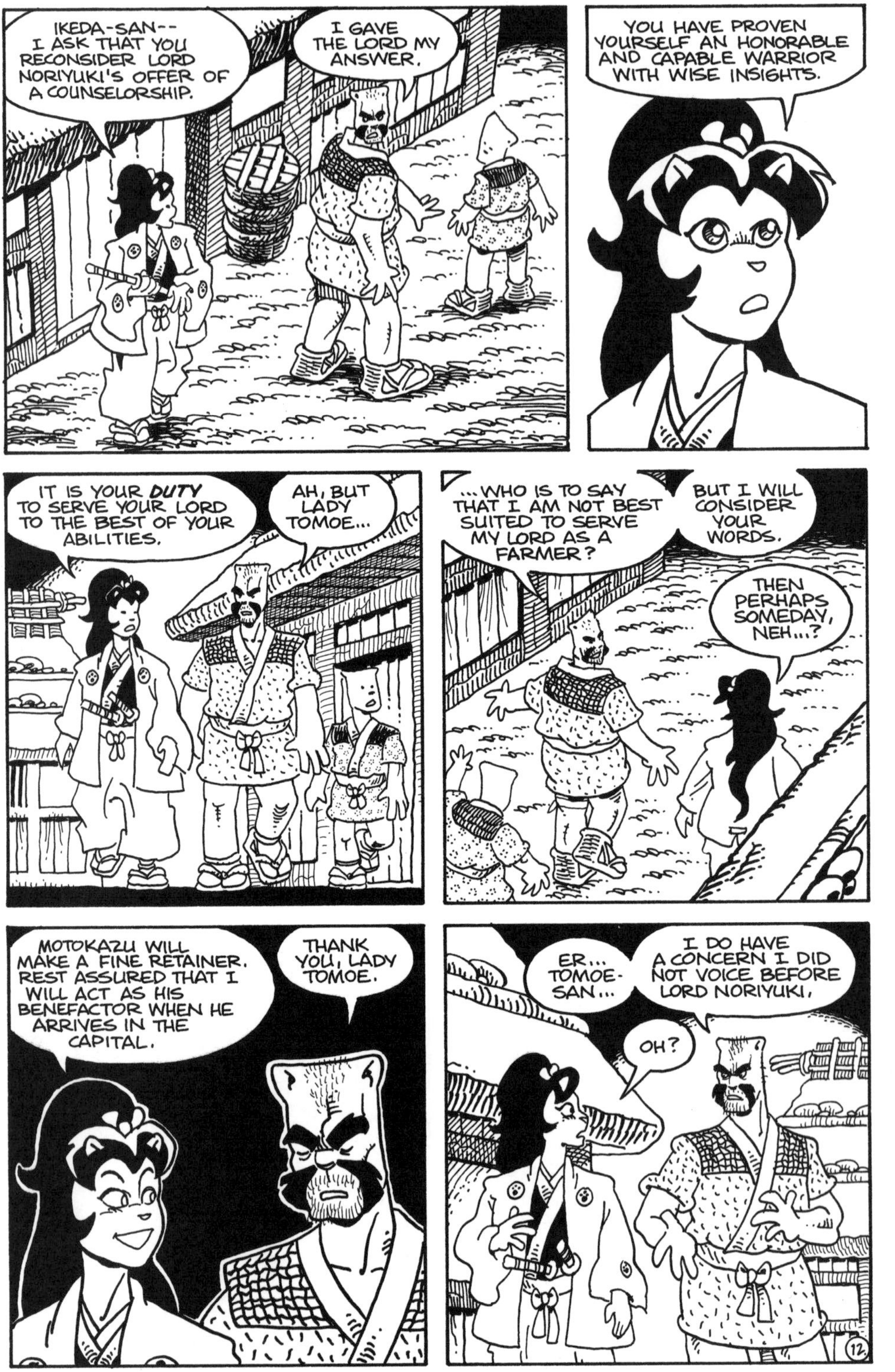
IKEDA-SAN-- I ASK THAT YOU RECONSIDER LORD NORIYUKI'S OFFER OF A COUNSELORSHIP.
I GAVE THE LORD MY ANSWER.
YOU HAVE PROVEN YOURSELF AN HONORABLE AND CAPABLE WARRIOR WITH WISE INSIGHTS.
IT IS YOUR *DUTY* TO SERVE YOUR LORD TO THE BEST OF YOUR ABILITIES.
AH, BUT LADY TOMOE...
...WHO IS TO SAY THAT I AM NOT BEST SUITED TO SERVE MY LORD AS A FARMER?
BUT I WILL CONSIDER YOUR WORDS.
THEN PERHAPS SOMEDAY, NEH...?
MOTOKAZU WILL MAKE A FINE RETAINER. REST ASSURED THAT I WILL ACT AS HIS BENEFACTOR WHEN HE ARRIVES IN THE CAPITAL.
THANK YOU, LADY TOMOE.
ER... TOMOE-SAN...
I DO HAVE A CONCERN I DID NOT VOICE BEFORE LORD NORIYUKI,
OH?
12

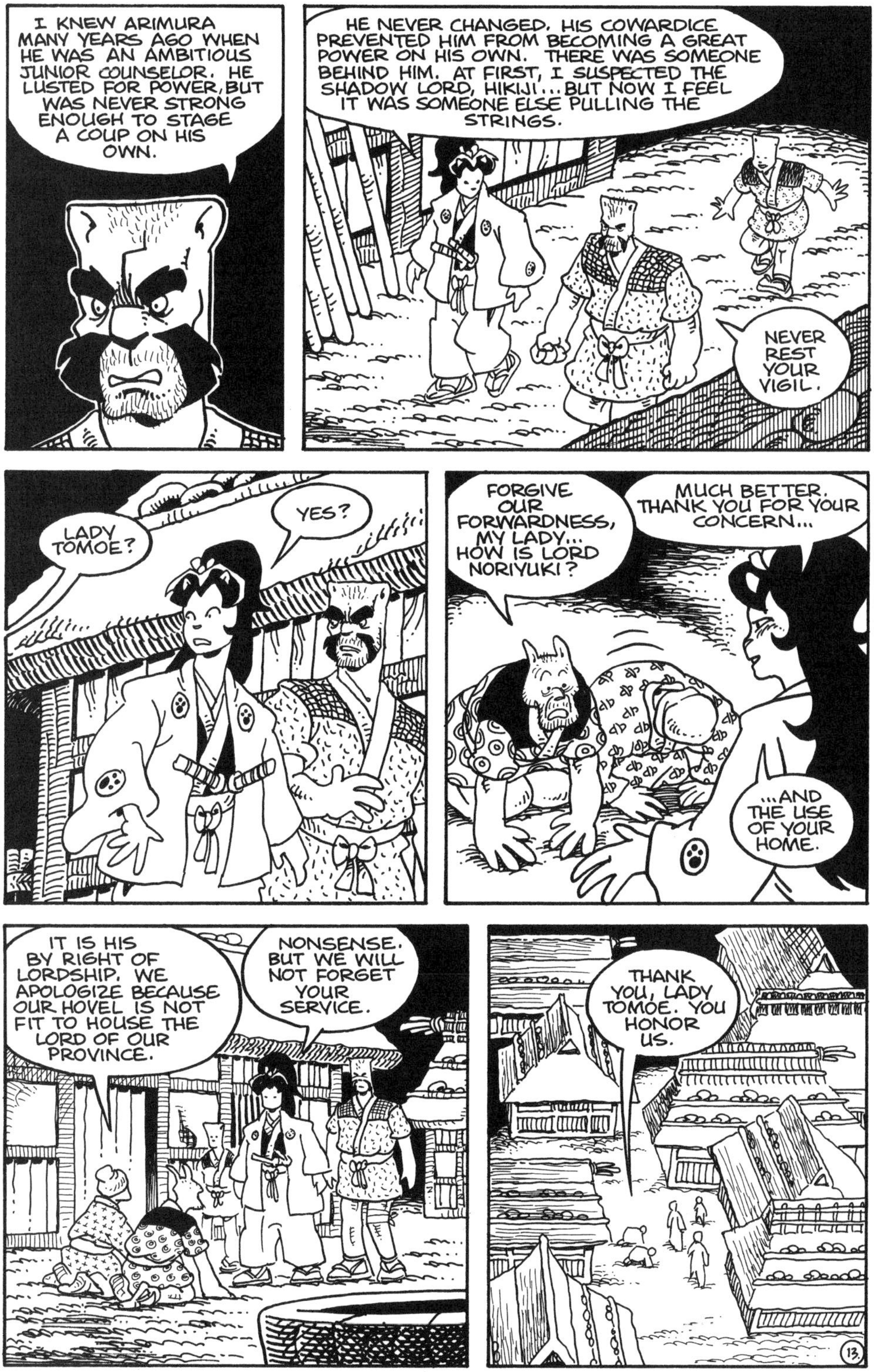
I KNEW ARIMURA MANY YEARS AGO WHEN HE WAS AN AMBITIOUS JUNIOR COUNSELOR. HE LUSTED FOR POWER, BUT WAS NEVER STRONG ENOUGH TO STAGE A COUP ON HIS OWN.
HE NEVER CHANGED. HIS COWARDICE PREVENTED HIM FROM BECOMING A GREAT POWER ON HIS OWN. THERE WAS SOMEONE BEHIND HIM. AT FIRST, I SUSPECTED THE SHADOW LORD, HIKIJI... BUT NOW I FEEL IT WAS SOMEONE ELSE PULLING THE STRINGS.
NEVER REST YOUR VIGIL.
LADY TOMOE?
YES?
FORGIVE OUR FORWARDNESS, MY LADY... HOW IS LORD NORIYUKI?
MUCH BETTER. THANK YOU FOR YOUR CONCERN...
...AND THE USE OF YOUR HOME.
IT IS HIS BY RIGHT OF LORDSHIP. WE APOLOGIZE BECAUSE OUR HOVEL IS NOT FIT TO HOUSE THE LORD OF OUR PROVINCE.
NONSENSE. BUT WE WILL NOT FORGET YOUR SERVICE.
THANK YOU, LADY TOMOE. YOU HONOR US.
13.

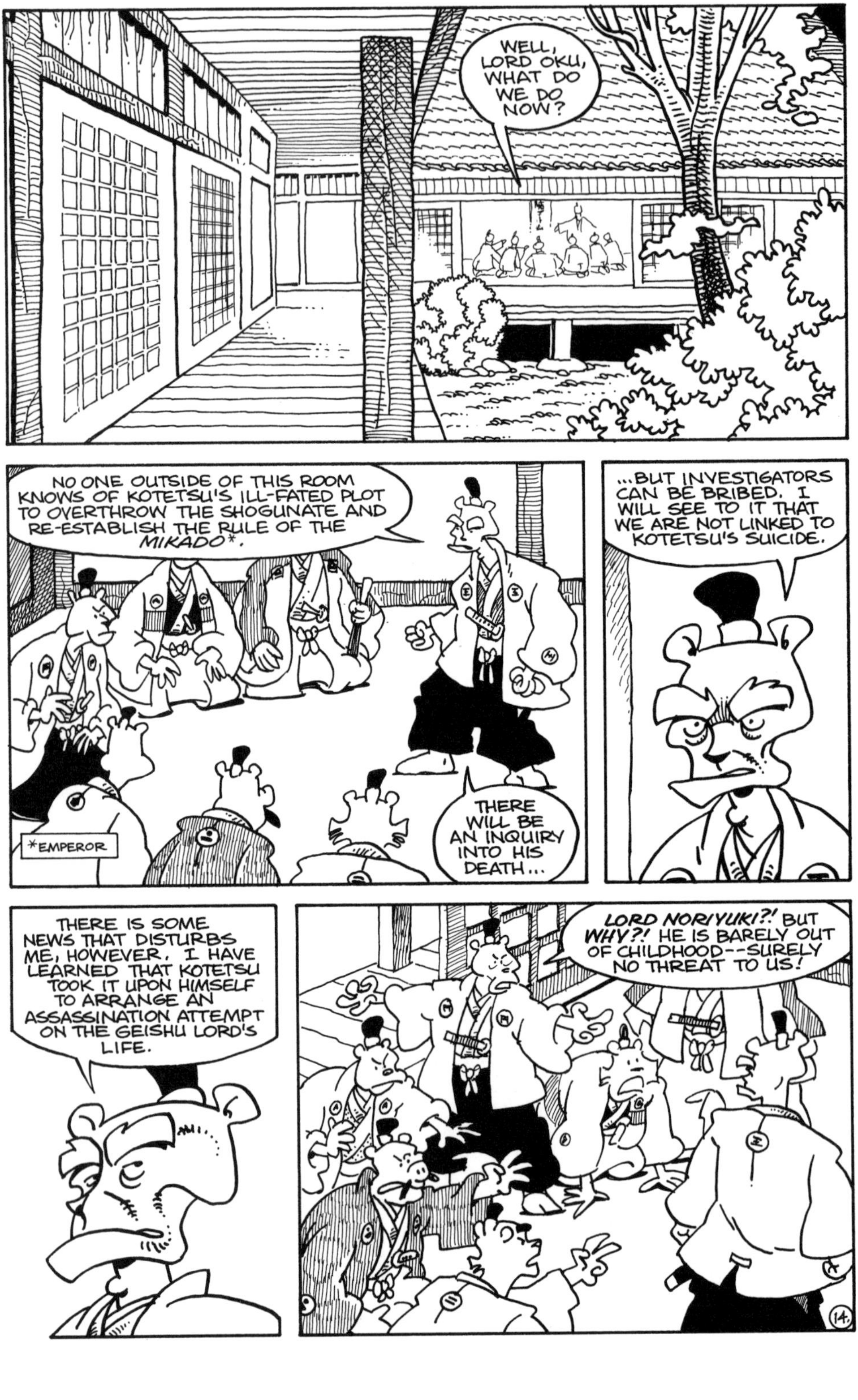
WELL, LORD OKU, WHAT DO WE DO NOW?
NO ONE OUTSIDE OF THIS ROOM KNOWS OF KOTETSU'S ILL-FATED PLOT TO OVERTHROW THE SHOGUNATE AND RE-ESTABLISH THE RULE OF THE *MIKADO**.
*EMPEROR
THERE WILL BE AN INQUIRY INTO HIS DEATH...
...BUT INVESTIGATORS CAN BE BRIBED. I WILL SEE TO IT THAT WE ARE NOT LINKED TO KOTETSU'S SUICIDE.
THERE IS SOME NEWS THAT DISTURBS ME, HOWEVER. I HAVE LEARNED THAT KOTETSU TOOK IT UPON HIMSELF TO ARRANGE AN ASSASSINATION ATTEMPT ON THE GEISHU LORD'S LIFE.
LORD NORIYUKI?! BUT *WHY?!* HE IS BARELY OUT OF CHILDHOOD--SURELY NO THREAT TO US!
14.

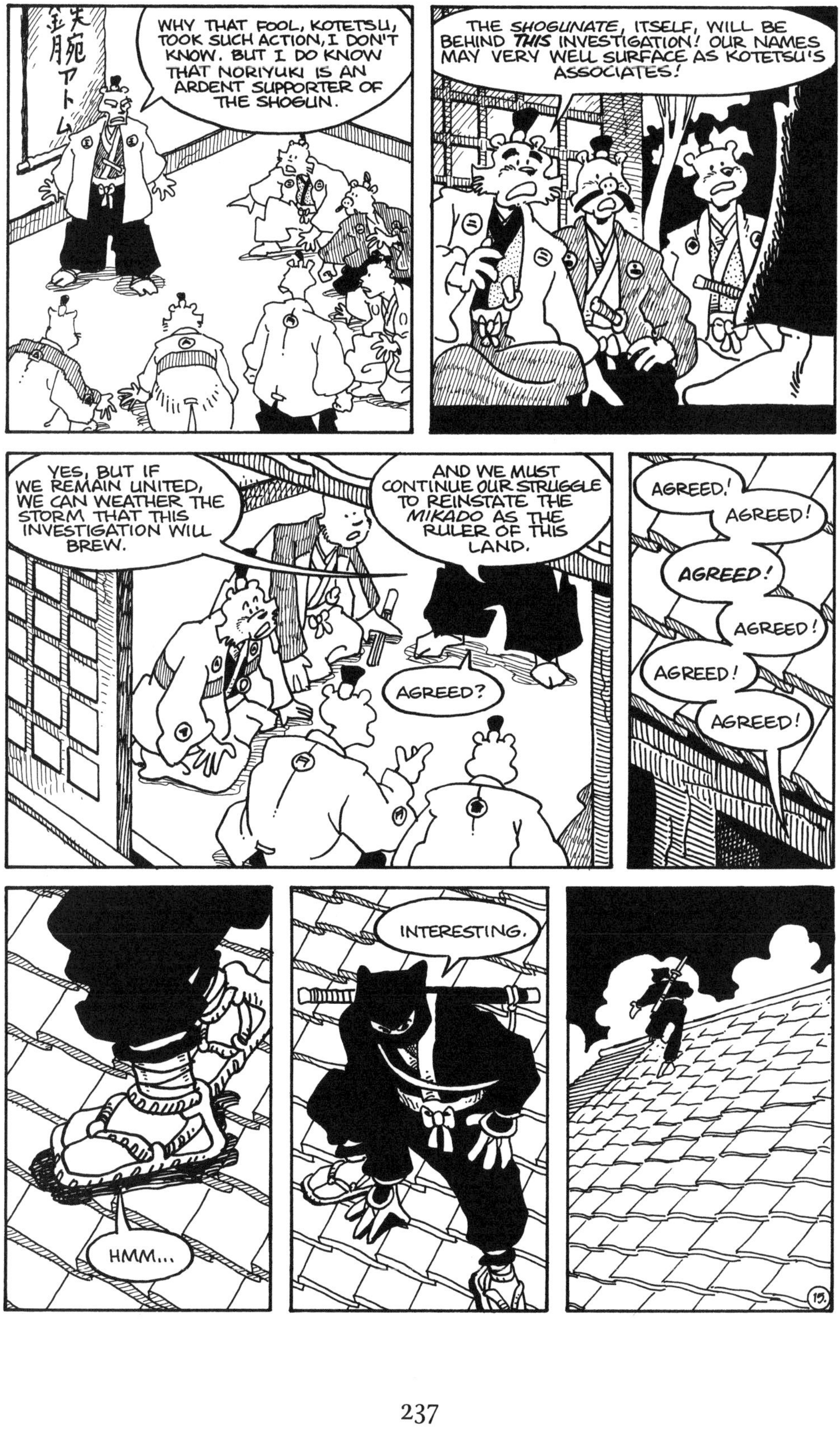
WHY THAT FOOL, KOTETSU, TOOK SUCH ACTION, I DON'T KNOW. BUT I DO KNOW THAT NORIYUKI IS AN ARDENT SUPPORTER OF THE SHOGUN.
THE *SHOGUNATE*, ITSELF, WILL BE BEHIND ***THIS*** INVESTIGATION! OUR NAMES MAY VERY WELL SURFACE AS KOTETSU'S ASSOCIATES!
YES, BUT IF WE REMAIN UNITED, WE CAN WEATHER THE STORM THAT THIS INVESTIGATION WILL BREW.
AND WE MUST CONTINUE OUR STRUGGLE TO REINSTATE THE *MIKADO* AS THE RULER OF THIS LAND.
AGREED?
AGREED!
AGREED!
AGREED!
AGREED!
AGREED!
AGREED!
HMM...
INTERESTING.
13.

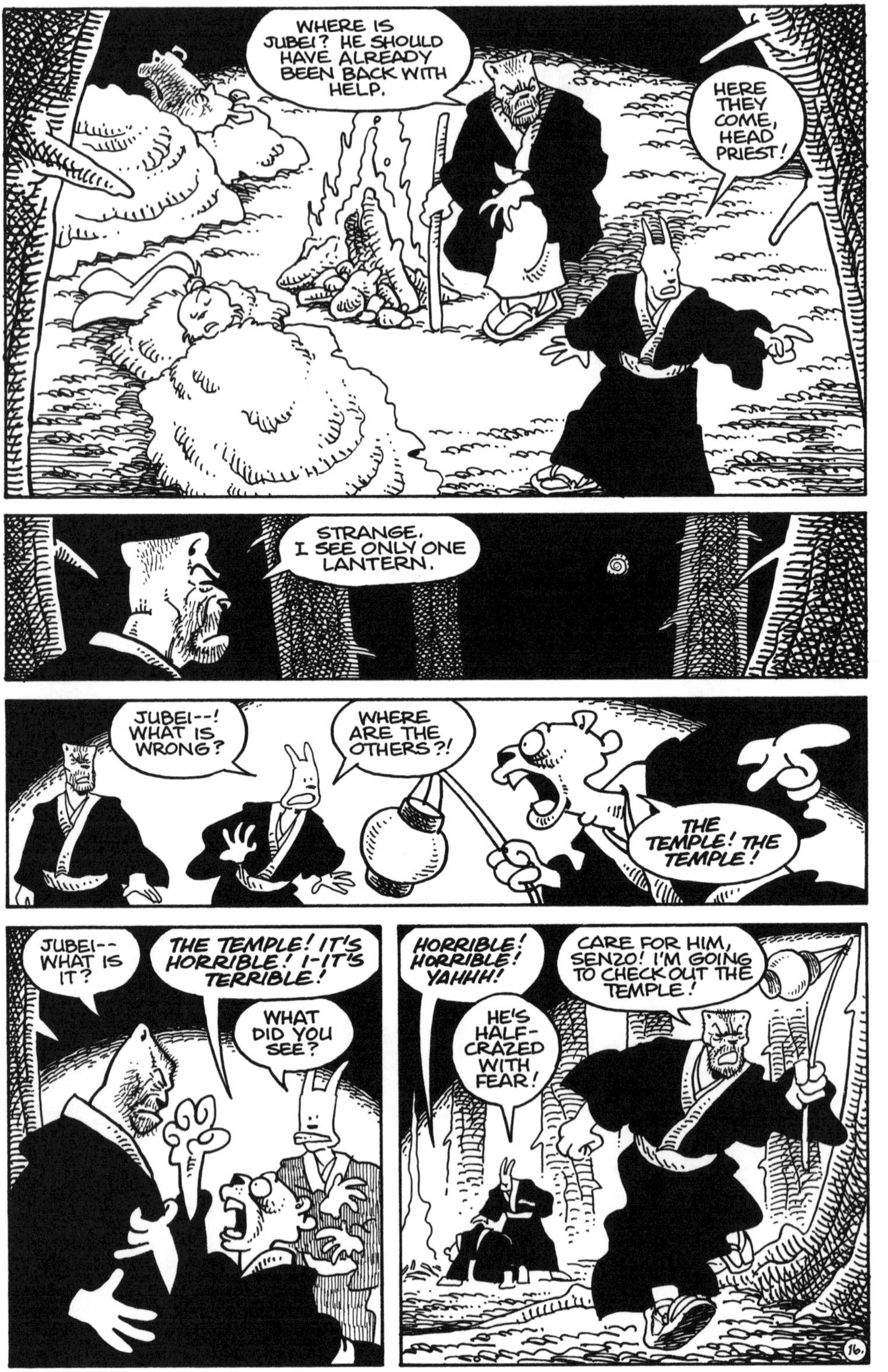
WHERE IS JUBEI? HE SHOULD HAVE ALREADY BEEN BACK WITH HELP.
HERE THEY COME, HEAD PRIEST!
STRANGE. I SEE ONLY ONE LANTERN.
JUBEI--! WHAT IS WRONG?
WHERE ARE THE OTHERS?!
THE TEMPLE! THE TEMPLE!
JUBEI-- WHAT IS IT?
THE TEMPLE! IT'S HORRIBLE! I-IT'S TERRIBLE!
WHAT DID YOU SEE?
HORRIBLE! HORRIBLE! YAHHH!
CARE FOR HIM, SENZO! I'M GOING TO CHECK OUT THE TEMPLE!
HE'S HALF-CRAZED WITH FEAR!
16.

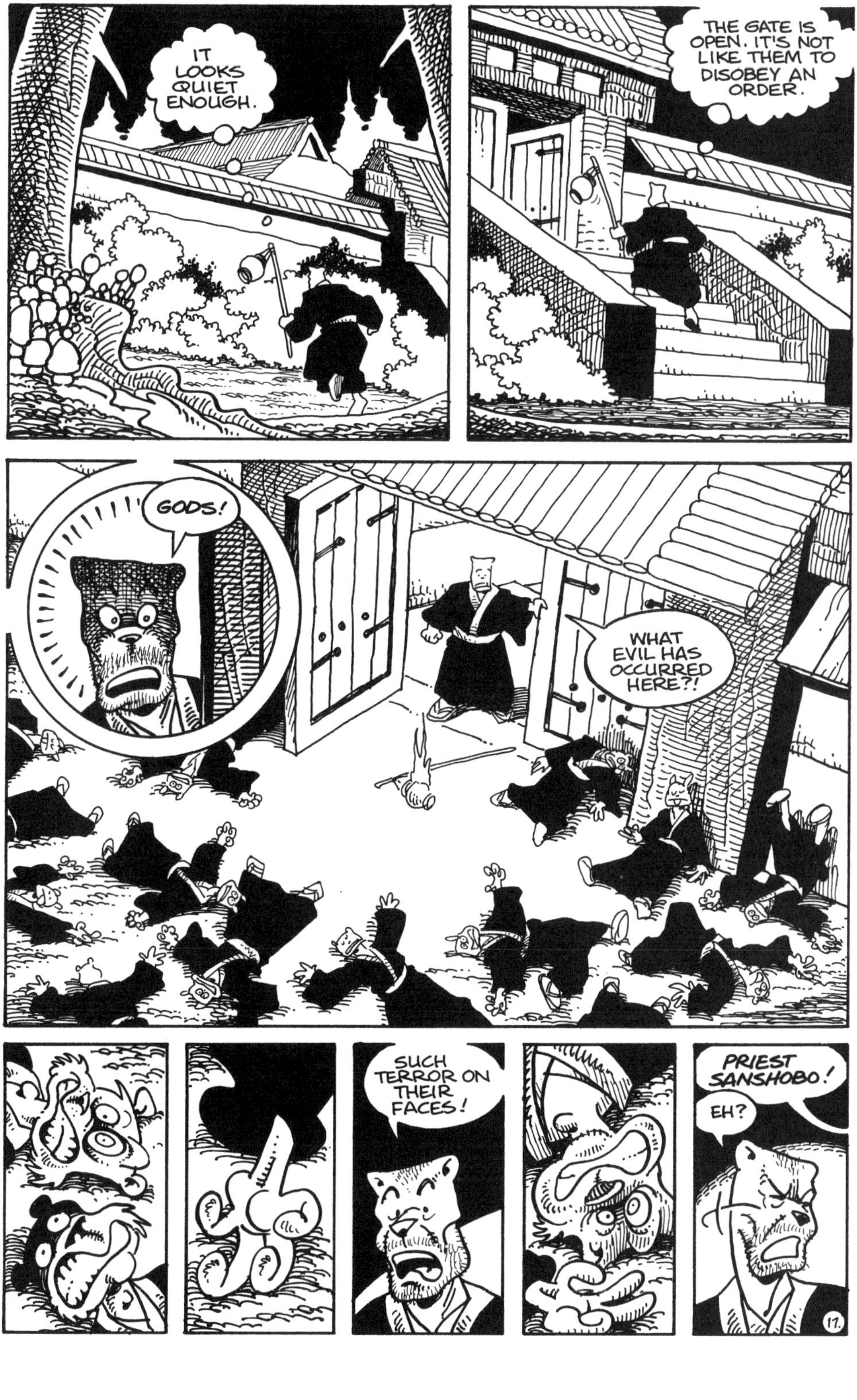
IT LOOKS QUIET ENOUGH.
THE GATE IS OPEN. IT'S NOT LIKE THEM TO DISOBEY AN ORDER.
GODS!
WHAT EVIL HAS OCCURRED HERE?!
SUCH TERROR ON THEIR FACES!
PRIEST SANSHOBO!
EH?
17.

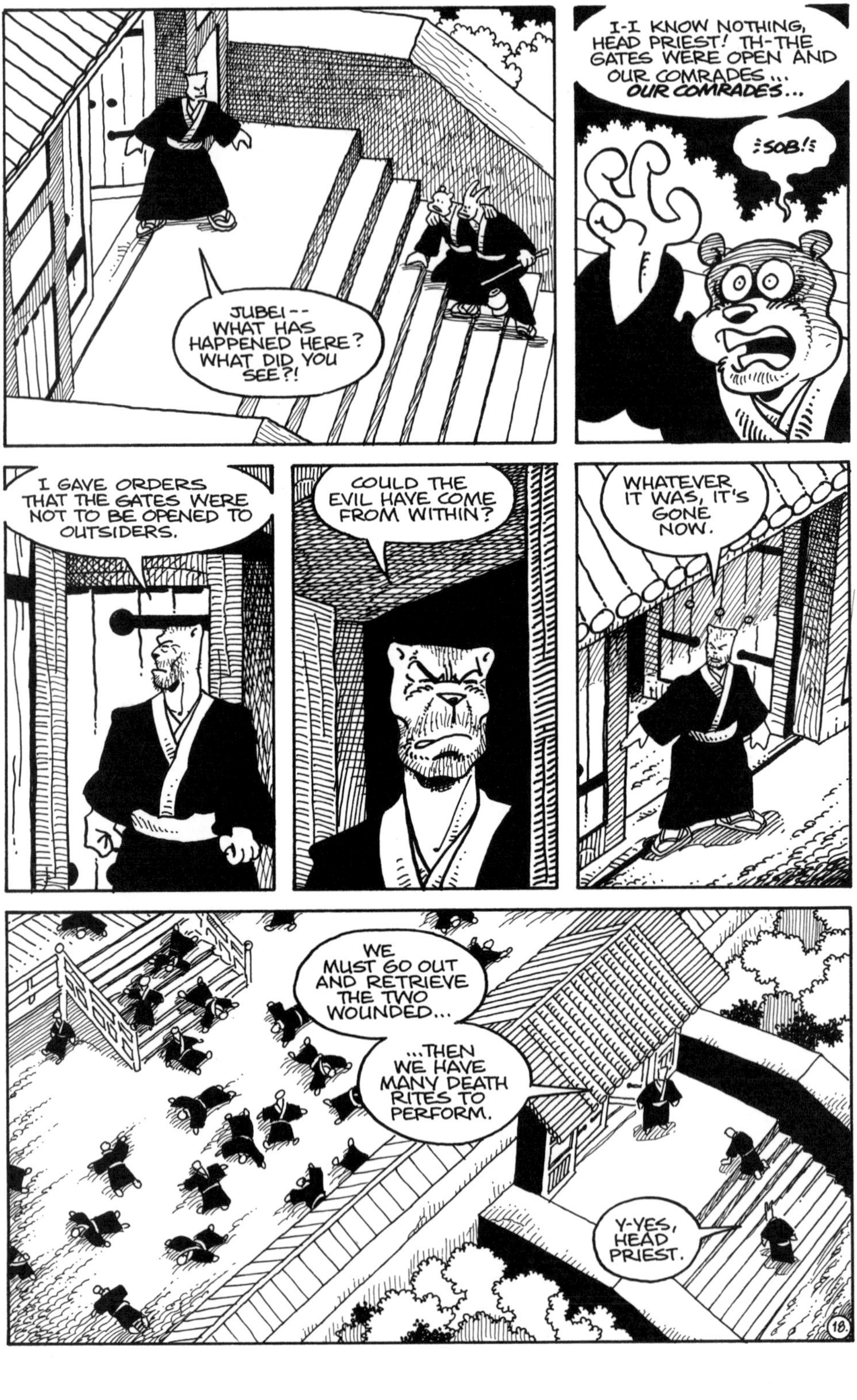
JUBEI-- WHAT HAS HAPPENED HERE? WHAT DID YOU SEE?!
I-I KNOW NOTHING, HEAD PRIEST! TH-THE GATES WERE OPEN AND OUR COMRADES... OUR COMRADES...
SOB!
I GAVE ORDERS THAT THE GATES WERE NOT TO BE OPENED TO OUTSIDERS.
COULD THE EVIL HAVE COME FROM WITHIN?
WHATEVER IT WAS, IT'S GONE NOW.
WE MUST GO OUT AND RETRIEVE THE TWO WOUNDED...
...THEN WE HAVE MANY DEATH RITES TO PERFORM.
Y-YES, HEAD PRIEST.
18.

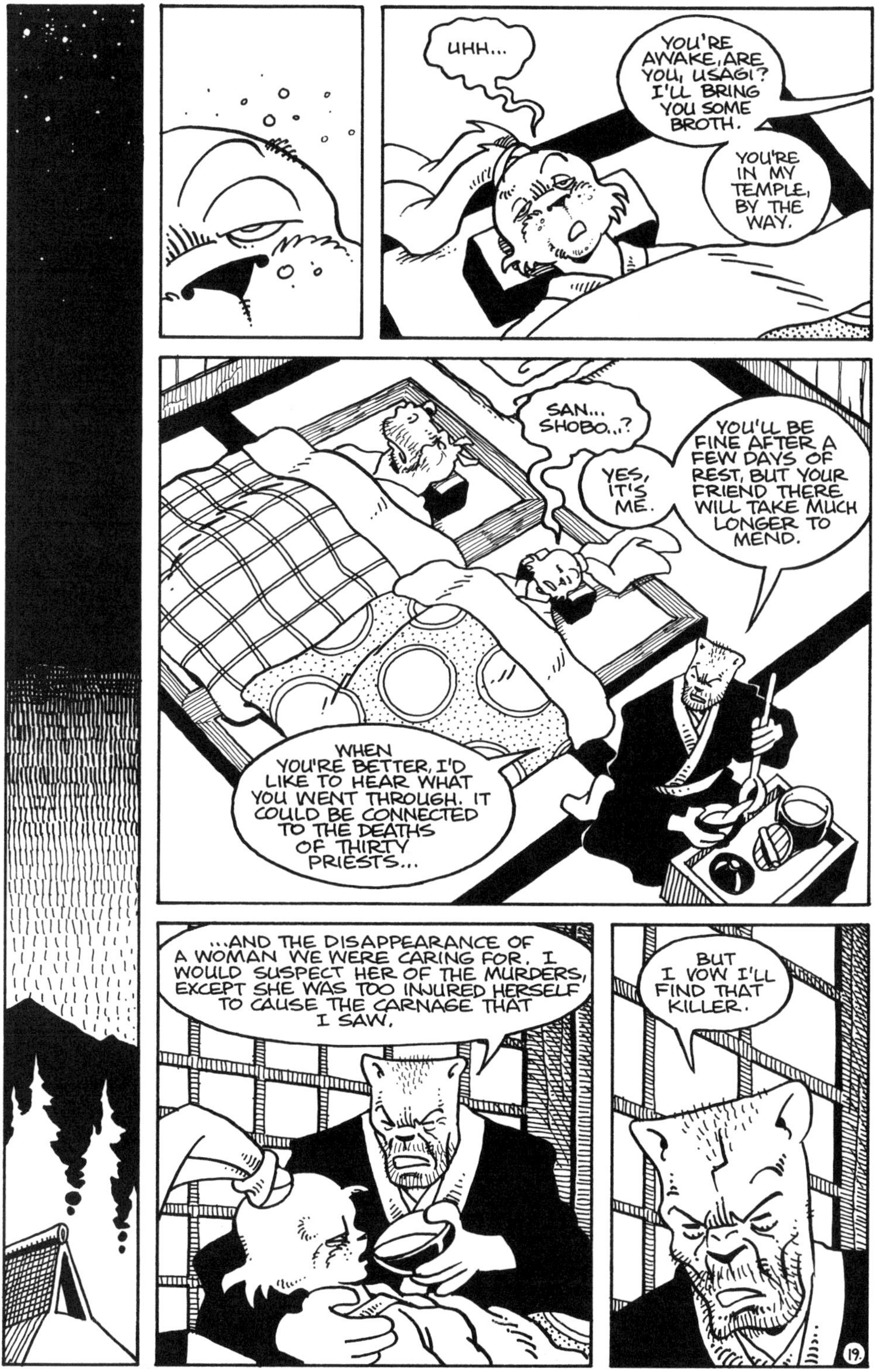
UHH...
YOU'RE AWAKE, ARE YOU, USAGI? I'LL BRING YOU SOME BROTH.
YOU'RE IN MY TEMPLE, BY THE WAY.
SAN... SHOBO...?
YES, IT'S ME.
YOU'LL BE FINE AFTER A FEW DAYS OF REST, BUT YOUR FRIEND THERE WILL TAKE MUCH LONGER TO MEND.
WHEN YOU'RE BETTER, I'D LIKE TO HEAR WHAT YOU WENT THROUGH. IT COULD BE CONNECTED TO THE DEATHS OF THIRTY PRIESTS...
...AND THE DISAPPEARANCE OF A WOMAN WE WERE CARING FOR. I WOULD SUSPECT HER OF THE MURDERS, EXCEPT SHE WAS TOO INJURED HERSELF TO CAUSE THE CARNAGE THAT I SAW.
BUT I VOW I'LL FIND THAT KILLER.
19.

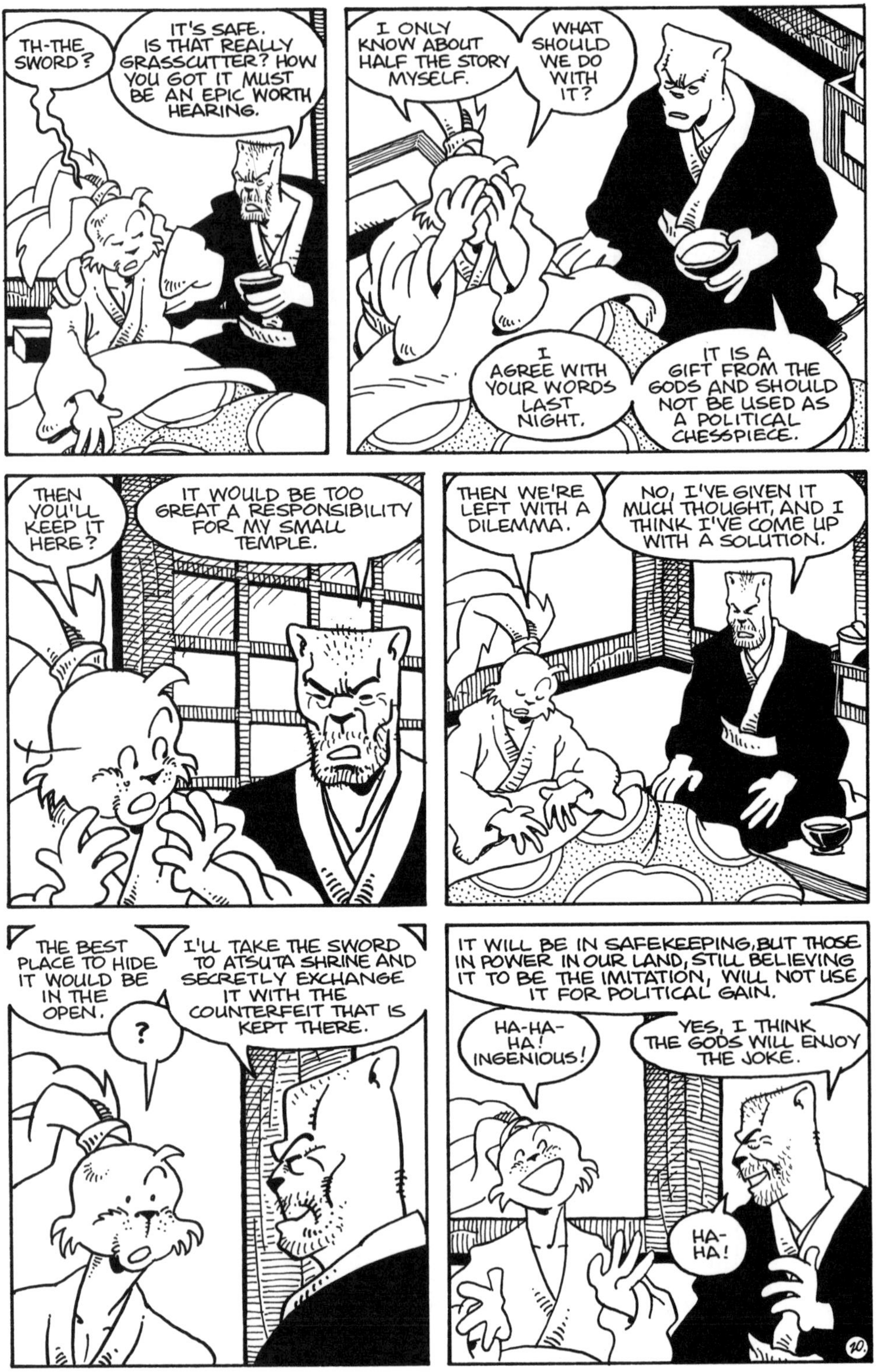
TH-THE SWORD?
IT'S SAFE. IS THAT REALLY GRASSCUTTER? HOW YOU GOT IT MUST BE AN EPIC WORTH HEARING.
I ONLY KNOW ABOUT HALF THE STORY MYSELF.
WHAT SHOULD WE DO WITH IT?
I AGREE WITH YOUR WORDS LAST NIGHT.
IT IS A GIFT FROM THE GODS AND SHOULD NOT BE USED AS A POLITICAL CHESSPIECE.
THEN YOU'LL KEEP IT HERE?
IT WOULD BE TOO GREAT A RESPONSIBILITY FOR MY SMALL TEMPLE.
THEN WE'RE LEFT WITH A DILEMMA.
NO, I'VE GIVEN IT MUCH THOUGHT, AND I THINK I'VE COME UP WITH A SOLUTION.
THE BEST PLACE TO HIDE IT WOULD BE IN THE OPEN.
?
I'LL TAKE THE SWORD TO ATSUTA SHRINE AND SECRETLY EXCHANGE IT WITH THE COUNTERFEIT THAT IS KEPT THERE.
IT WILL BE IN SAFEKEEPING, BUT THOSE IN POWER IN OUR LAND, STILL BELIEVING IT TO BE THE IMITATION, WILL NOT USE IT FOR POLITICAL GAIN.
HA-HA-HA! INGENIOUS!
YES, I THINK THE GODS WILL ENJOY THE JOKE.
HA-HA!
20.

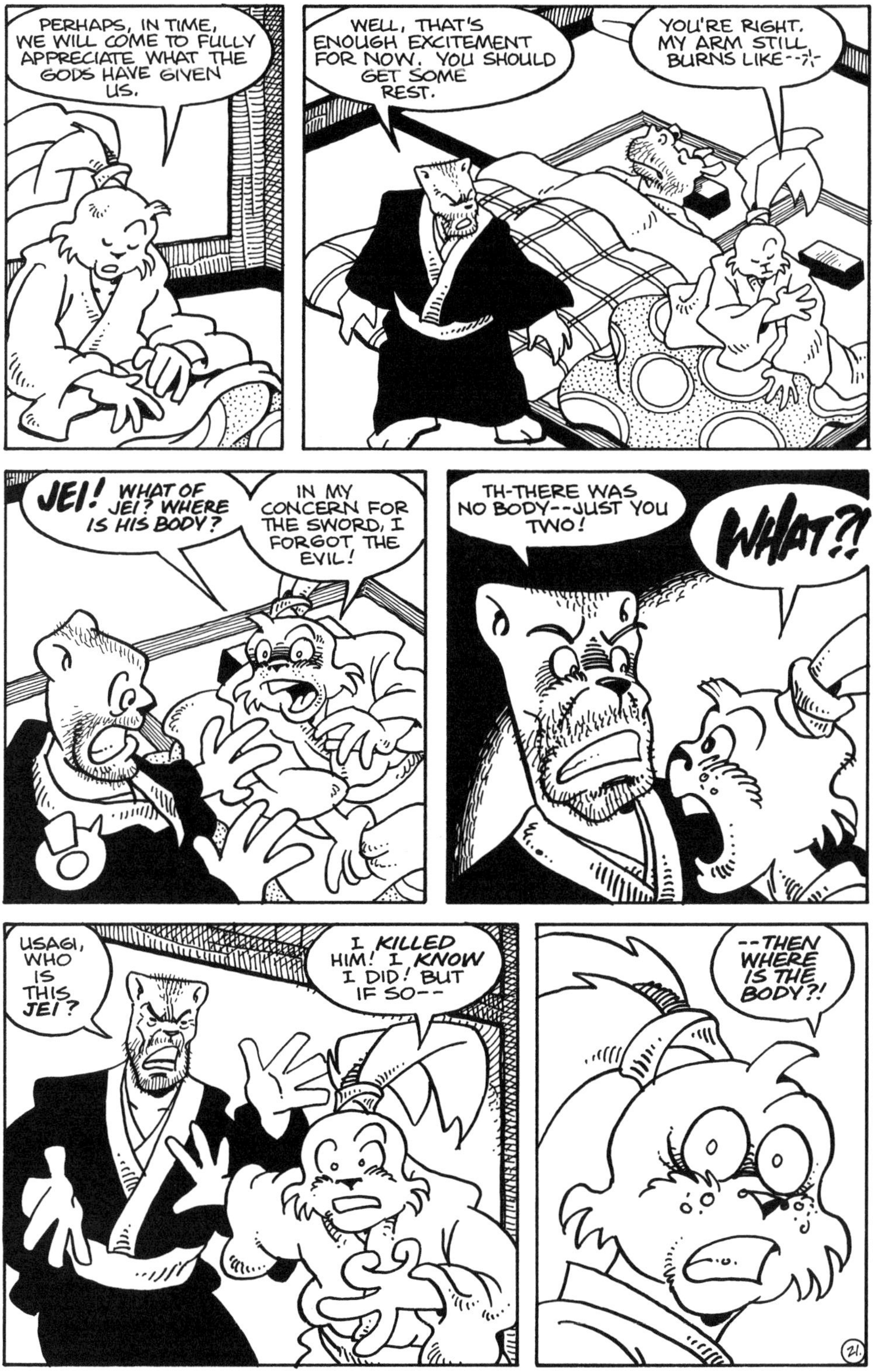
PERHAPS, IN TIME, WE WILL COME TO FULLY APPRECIATE WHAT THE GODS HAVE GIVEN US.
WELL, THAT'S ENOUGH EXCITEMENT FOR NOW. YOU SHOULD GET SOME REST.
YOU'RE RIGHT. MY ARM STILL BURNS LIKE--
JEI! WHAT OF JEI? WHERE IS HIS BODY?
IN MY CONCERN FOR THE SWORD, I FORGOT THE EVIL!
TH-THERE WAS NO BODY--JUST YOU TWO!
WHAT?!
USAGI, WHO IS THIS JEI?
I KILLED HIM! I KNOW I DID! BUT IF SO--
--THEN WHERE IS THE BODY?!
21.

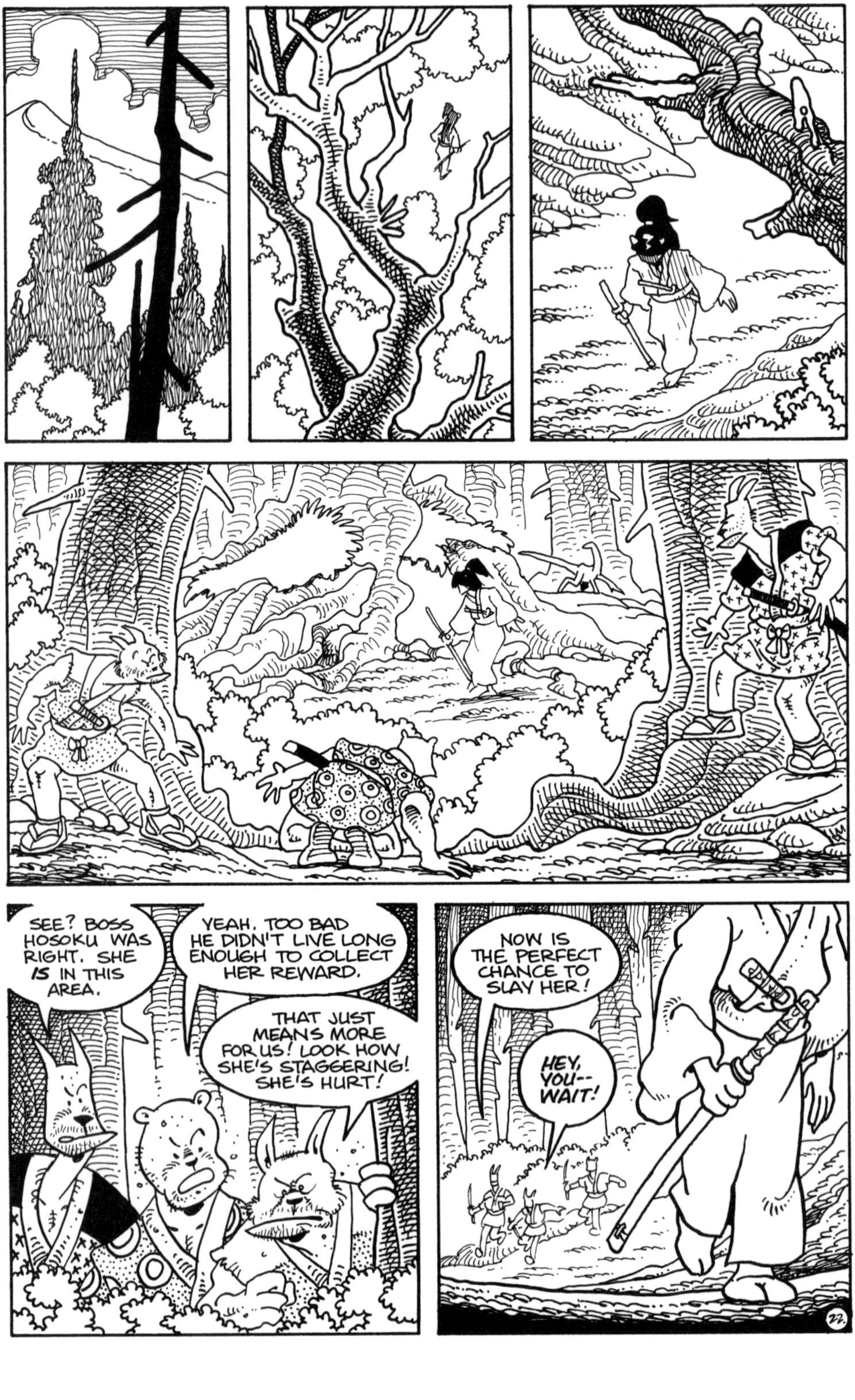
SEE? BOSS HOSOKU WAS RIGHT. SHE *IS* IN THIS AREA.
YEAH. TOO BAD HE DIDN'T LIVE LONG ENOUGH TO COLLECT HER REWARD.
THAT JUST MEANS MORE FOR US! LOOK HOW SHE'S STAGGERING! SHE'S HURT!
NOW IS THE PERFECT CHANCE TO SLAY HER!
HEY, YOU-- WAIT!
22.

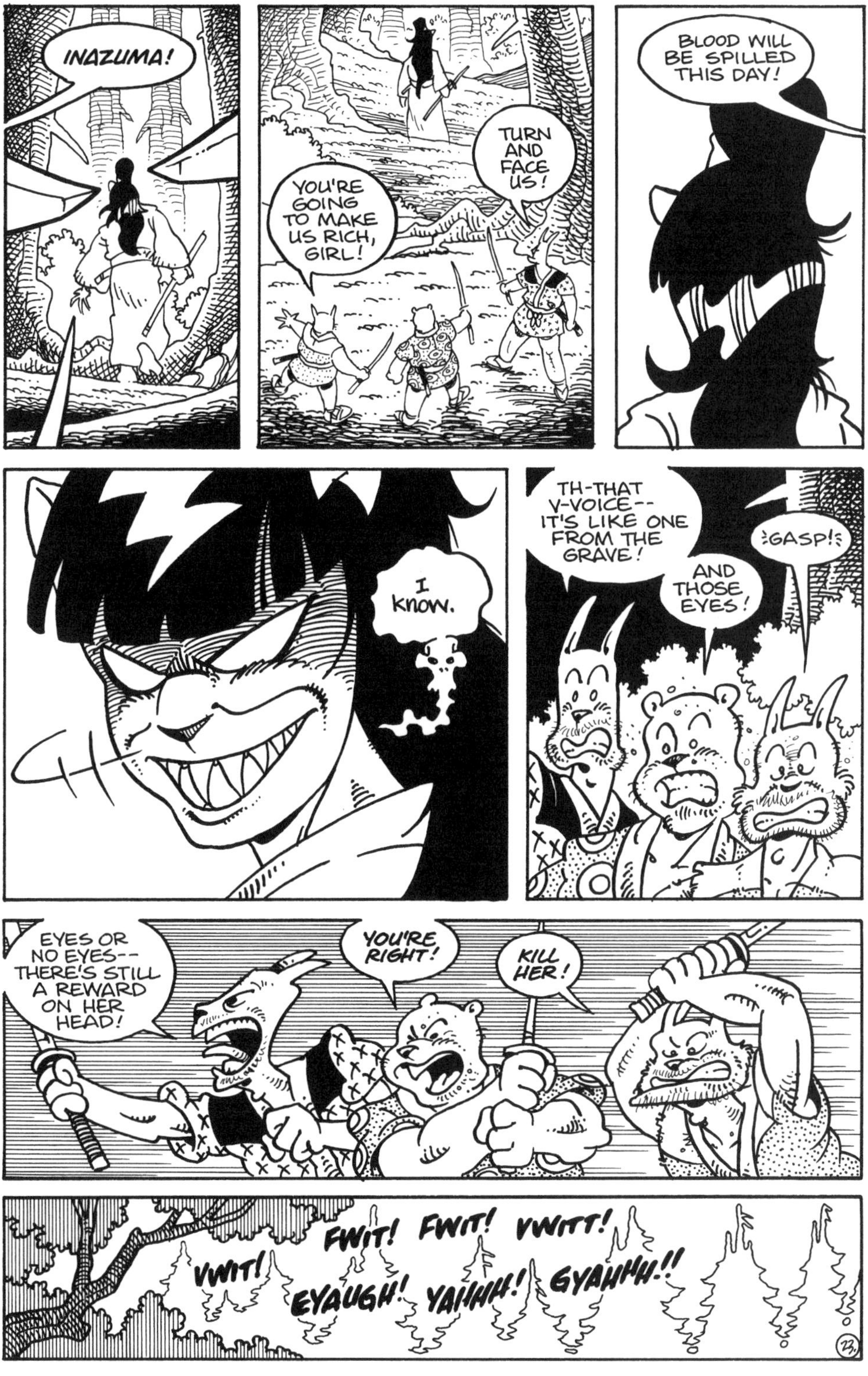
INAZUMA!
YOU'RE GOING TO MAKE US RICH, GIRL!
TURN AND FACE US!
BLOOD WILL BE SPILLED THIS DAY!
I KNOW.
TH-THAT V-VOICE-- IT'S LIKE ONE FROM THE GRAVE!
AND THOSE EYES!
GASP!
EYES OR NO EYES-- THERE'S STILL A REWARD ON HER HEAD!
YOU'RE RIGHT!
KILL HER!
FWIT! FWIT! VWITT!
VWIT!
EYAUGH! YAIHHH! GYAHHH!!
23

RUSTLE! RUSTLE!

THERE YOU ARE. I'VE BEEN LOOKING ALL OVER FOR YOU...

...AUNTY.

WHERE DO WE GO TO NOW?

To hell, my innocent, to hell.

USAGI YOJIMBO

Grasscutter Story Notes

MY APOLOGIES. I am not doing my reference materials justice. I can blame this on the restrictions placed by the comic-book medium, conflicting sources, and my own inadequacies as a storyteller. I have skirted over a lot of important events, choosing to tell only those that directly pertain to the plot. I have even made up scenes to enhance the story. But, hopefully, these more detailed story notes will resolve at least some of the problems.

Dates in Japanese history (especially pre-history) are very confusing at times because they are established in reference to the ruler of that period. For example: *The Kojiki: Records of Ancient Matters* states that the eighth emperor, Kogen, died at age fifty-seven; however, according to *The Nihongi: Chronicles of Japan from the Earliest Times to A.D. 697*, he ascended the throne at age fifty-nine and ruled for fifty-six years. One source places the story of Yamato-Dake as occurring in 110 B.C., while another has his father's reign as A.D. 71-130, having ascended the throne at the age of eighty-three.

There is no exact English equivalent to the word *kami*. Sometimes it's been translated as "god." However, ancestors can also be *kami*, and the government was once known as *okami*. I chose to translate it as "deity" or "divinity," though this is still inaccurate. According to *The Kojiki*, Japan has eight million good *kami* and ten million evil spirits.

A note of interest is that the number *eight* is sacred to the Japanese and is a recurring theme, much like how *seven* or *forty* bears significance to Christians.

PROLOGUE 1—IZANAGI & IZANAMI

There are seven generations of deities leading up to the creation of the Japanese islands. I skipped over the earlier ones as they had nothing to do with the story. Indeed, they seemed to do little except come into being and pass on (die). However, if you're interested in a complete genealogy, I suggest *The Kojiki* or *The Nihongi*.

The Bridge of Heaven is located at Miyazu Bay on the west coast of Honshu, Japan's main island. A pine-covered bar, about two miles long and sixty-six feet wide, is the remnant of the heavenly bridge.

Izanagi and Izanami learned the art of lovemaking from watching a pair of wagtails. These waterbirds are still associated with this couple. Even the *kami* of scarecrows cannot frighten wagtails, a result of a blessing given to them.

Izanagi and Izanami's first child was a leech-like creature, who at the age of three, could not stand upright and was set adrift in a reed boat. Again, for a detailed account of their children, I recommend the aforementioned books.

As Izanagi was being pursued by the Hags of Yomi, he stalled them by tearing off a vine wreath from his head and dropping it behind him. It turned into a bunch of grapes, which the hags stopped to devour. He next cast his comb away and it turned into a grove of bamboo shoots which the hags ate. He fought the "eight thunders and fifteen-hundred warriors" with his sword until he reached the entrance to Yomi. He plucked three peaches from a tree and hurled them at his enemies, driving them back. The peach was rewarded with the title of "Great Divine Fruit." Izanagi emerged at Himuka on the island of Kyushu. He blocked the path to Yomi with a rock that would take a thousand men to move.

When Izanagi washed himself after his escape, he inaugurated the Shinto rite of purification practiced to this day.

PROLOGUE 2—SUSANO-O

Some sources refer to Susano-o as "The God of Storms," others as "The God of the Ocean" or as "The God of Force." He is associated with the province of Izumo on the coast of the Sea of Japan on Honshu Island. It is from there that he forested the coasts of Korea, taking hairs from his beard and turning them into trees.

He is often mischievous and, at times, downright evil.

On one rampage, he destroyed fields, filled irrigation ditches, tore out dikes, and spread excrement about the temples where the Festival of the First Fruits was being held. He then flayed a horse and threw it through the roof into the room where Amaterasu and her attendants were weaving. This so frightened the maids that they committed suicide by stabbing themselves with their shuttles. The terrified Sun Deity hid herself in a cave, blocking the entrance with a great boulder. Everything was plunged in darkness and the deities of pestilence overran the world. The Eight Hundred Deities made an eight-span mirror, strings of jewels, and cloth streamers and hung them from a *sakaki* tree. They had a riotous celebration outside the cave, and when the curious Amaterasu emerged to investigate the noise, she was dazzled by her reflection in the mirror. One of the *kami* seized her arm and drew her out of the cave, while others stretched a straw rope across the cave entrance, preventing her retreat. She was then escorted to a new palace and light was restored to the world.

As punishment, the deities cut off Susano-o's mustache and beard and pulled out his fingernails and toenails. He was then expelled from Heaven.

Before he had gone too far, he met up with the Deity of Food and begged for something to eat. She offered a grand feast, but taken from her mouth, nose, and other parts of her body. Susano-o was outraged because he thought she was offering him filth and slew her. From her body was born rice, barley, millet, and bean seeds, as well as farm animals and grasses.

The scene in which Susano-o went off to look at the serpent himself was created from my own imagination, as I felt it was important that he see it with his own eyes, and it made for a stronger story. In legend, Susano-o merely asks the couple the serpent's description:

> His eyes are fiery and red like the winter cherry. He has but one body, with eight heads and eight scaly tails. Moreover, on his body grows moss, together with the fir and cryptomeria of the forest. In his going, he covers eight valleys and eight hills, and upon his underside he is red and gory —*Green Willow and Other Japanese Fairy Tales*

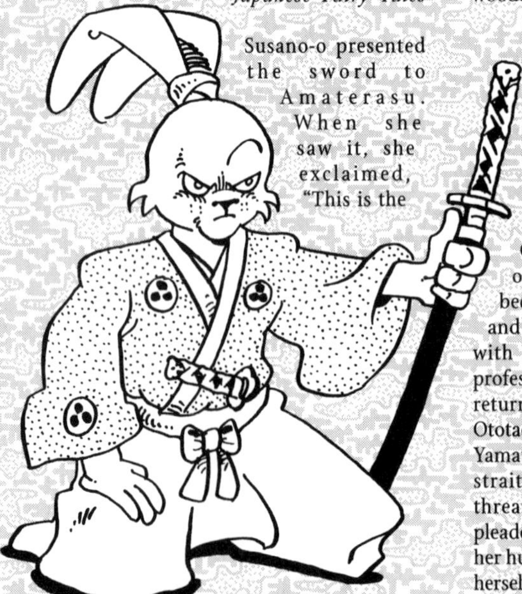

Susano-o presented the sword to Amaterasu. When she saw it, she exclaimed, "This is the sword that I lost at Takama-ga-hara ["Plain of the High Sky," a home of the heavenly deities] long ago!" [*The Tale of the Heike*]. The blade became lodged in the serpent's tail and huge clouds would billow above the village, hence the name "Sword of the Village of the Clustering Clouds."

Prologue 3—Yamato-Dake

Amaterasu's grandson, Ninigi, was sent to Earth with three treasures: a mirror, a jewel, and the sword. He fell in love with Ko-No-Hana, the princess who makes trees blossom. Her father had an elder daughter, Iha-Naga (Princess-Long-as-the-Rocks). Ninigi was given the choice of either daughter in marriage, but he remained true to the flower princess. Iha-Naga said, had he chosen her, their offspring would have lived as long as the rocks, but now his children would bloom and fade as do blossoms. Ninigi's great grandson was Jimmu Tenno, the first emperor of Japan.

The Temple of Amaterasu in Ise is one of the oldest religious sites in Japan, but it is not more than twenty years old. It has been rebuilt every two decades, with a few exceptions, since about 4 B.C., using traditional methods. It is built of *hinoki* cypress (*chamaecyparis obtusa*). Early carpenters' tools did not include the cross-cut saw or plane, and these fragrant trees with their grain that runs straight along the length of the timber were ideal for their limited technology. There was also a great abundance of these trees. Ise is located on the southern coast of the island of Honshu.

Yamato-Dake was the youngest son of Emperor Keiko and the hero of numerous campaigns. Many of his victories, though, were the result of cunning, as well as strength—such as disguising himself as a beautiful woman to get close to the brigands of Kumaso or replacing the sword of the outlaw, Takeru, with a wooden imitation, then challenging him to a duel.

"Wo-Usu" was the birth name of this hero. He was given the name Yamato-Dake ("Bravest of the Yamato") by one of the Kumaso bandits soon before the prince "ripped him up like a ripe melon and slew him."

Yamato-Dake was married to Princess Ototachibana, a faithful wife who followed him on all his campaigns. As a result, her skin became deeply tanned and her garments soiled and tattered. He met Princess Miyazu, a beauty with skin as delicate as cherry blossoms, and professed his love for her. He promised to one day return and make her his bride. Then he noticed Ototachibana had seen and heard everything. When Yamato-Dake and his entourage were crossing the straits of Kazusu, a great storm arose which threatened to capsize the boats. Ototachibana pleaded to the sea king to accept her life and deliver her husband safely to shore. Whereupon, she threw herself into the water. No sooner had she gone under when the storm abated and the clouds dispersed. Too late, Yamato-Dake realized what a treasure he had lost. Years later he stood on the mountains from which he could gaze upon the distant sea where Ototachibana had given her life for him. He stretched out his arms, sighed three times, and said, "My wife!" To this day that area is called Azuma, "my wife."

The *Yemishi* that Yamato-Dake was to subjugate are the ancestors of the modern *Ainu* of Hokkaido Island. In earlier times, the Yemishi extended from the north down the eastern section of Japan, as far south as present-day Tokyo. The Yemishi appeared to have been a peaceful people and offered no resistance. In *The Nihongi*, they were called "*kami* of the country" and so were held in some respect by the Japanese. It should be noted that the people of Suruga were not Yemishi.

There are two versions of the story of how the hero was tricked onto the moors. In the first, the Suruga lord suggests a deer hunt. In the other, he invites Yamato-Dake to see an unusually violent lake *kami*. I chose to incorporate both versions in my story. The area this incident took place in is now called Yakizu, or "The Port of Burning."

Yamato-Dake died in the seventh month of his thirtieth year at Atsuta in Owari Province. It is unclear whether he died from fatigue and exposure or from poison. His spirit ascended to heaven in the form of a white bird.

Kusanagi is a *ken* or *tsurugi*-type sword. These swords are about two-and-a-half to three feet long, straight, double-edged, and very heavy. The scabbards were generally made of wood bound with metal bands.

Kusanagi was given to Atsuta Shrine. In the seventh year of the reign of Emperor Tenchi (A.D. 668), a Korean named Dogyo stole the sword, hoping to make it a treasure of his own country. During the voyage to his homeland, a terrible storm appeared. Dogyo begged forgiveness and returned the sword to the shrine. In 686, Emperor Temmu placed the sacred sword in his court.

Prologue 4 — Dan-no-Ura

The Genpei War, the great civil war of Japan (1180-1185), gets its name from the Chinese readings of the names of the two rival clans, the Genji (Minamoto) and the Heike (Taira).

The Taira controlled the west and the imperial court while the Minamoto were dominant in the east. In 1156, the Minamoto declared a revolt against the Taira which was soon crushed. As a result, the Minamoto family was almost exterminated. A few boys escaped, however, and when they grew to manhood, set out to avenge their clan. In 1180, minor outbreaks developed into a full-scale civil war. The leader of the Minamoto clan was Yoritomo. The Taira

leader, Imperial Grandfather Kiyomori, died of a fever in 1181 and was succeeded by his son, Munemori, an incompetent whose own mother revealed that he was not a true Taira but the son of an umbrella merchant.

In 1182, Yoritomo's cousin, Minamoto Kiso no Yoshinaka, conquered Kyoto and set himself as *Shogun* or military ruler. This enraged Yoritomo, who sent his younger half-brother, Yoshitsune, to retake the capital. After his defeat, Yoshinaka escaped with his wife, Tomoe Gozen, and a few retainers. They were ambushed and legend has it that Yoshinaka took his own life but refused to let Tomoe die with him. She killed some of the attackers and fled to a temple to become a nun.

While their enemies were fighting amongst themselves, the Taira fled south, taking the eight-year-old emperor Antoku. Yoshitsune hounded them until they made their final stand at Dan-no-Ura.

Again, I've taken a lot of liberties for the sake of the story. I have depicted a few events out of sequence and, for the sake of space, combined the actions of several people into one character. There are also many conflicting accounts of the battle, such as its date and time and the age of the emperor. In the case of conflicting resources, I've either chosen that which was best for the narrative or that which is agreed upon by most scholars.

Seagoing warfare was very similar to fighting on land in that there was no maneuvering or much naval strategy involved. Ships were, for the most part, commandeered ferry or fishing boats whose main purpose was to get the armies into bow range and then sword reach. The number of boats actually involved in this battle varies greatly with researchers; anywhere from less than fourteen hundred to more than four thousand.

Keiko or Kei-Chan is fictitious as is her early-morning conversation with the emperor's grandmother. This sequence was invented to reveal a bit of the backstory.

Taira Munemori was the younger "son" of Kiyomori, but upon the death of his older, more capable brother, Shigemori, became the Taira heir. He and his son, Kiyomune, were captured at Dan-no-Ura and were later put to death at Shinowara.

My depiction of Taira Tomomori is a conglomeration of personages. True, he was a great general who defeated the Minamoto in three separate battles, but it was the imperial diviner Harenobu who accompanied Munemori and forecast the omen of the dolphins. I suggested that Tomomori, disgusted with his lord's cowardice, forced Munemori overboard; however, it was the fault of some unnamed soldiers who "accidentally" pushed him as he stood in shock and fear, at a loss as to what to do.

Tomomori fought bravely, but after hearing of his lord's capture, donned a double set of armor and, with his uncle, jumped into the sea.

The defection of Lord Taguchi Shigeyoshi was not unexpected. His loyalty fell under suspicion after his son, who was captured by the Minamoto, came to side with them and urged his father to do so also. Shigeyoshi not only took his son's advice but chose the time most disastrous to the Taira to do so.

Emperor Antoku's age at the time of his death was somewhere between six and ten. I showed him as eight years because that seems to be the most consistent among researchers and eight is a significant number to the Japanese. As stated in *The Tale of the Heike*—

> THE GREAT SERPENT THAT WAS KILLED BY SUSANO-O-NO-MIKOTO LONG AGO AT THE UPPER PART OF THE HIGAWA RIVER MUST HAVE BORNE A GRUDGE BECAUSE OF THE LOSS OF THE SWORD. THEREFORE WITH HIS EIGHT HEADS AND EIGHT TAILS, HE HAS ENTERED INTO THE EIGHT-YEAR-OLD EMPEROR AFTER EIGHTY GENERATIONS, AND HAS TAKEN THE SWORD BACK TO THE DEPTHS OF THE SEA.

Antoku was succeeded by Emperor Go-Toba, his younger brother.

Yoshitsune is the most popular and most tragic of all the Japanese heroes. Always at his side was the warrior-monk Benkei, whom he had defeated in a duel and who had pledged eternal loyalty. Yoshitsune was twenty-one when he joined Yoritomo's rebellion, but his half-brother became increasingly jealous and wary of Yoshitsune, especially in light of the traitorous actions of their cousin, Yoshinaka. Soon after the triumph over the Taira, Yoshitsune became a hunted man and was forced to flee Yoritomo's assassins. He was finally cornered in the northern province, and, as Benkei gave his life to defend the stronghold, Yoshitsune killed his wife and children before committing suicide. He was thirty-one years old. However, according to legend, Yoshitsune did not die then. He escaped further north and is now honored by the aboriginal Ainu under the name "Gikyo-daimyo-jin." Others say that he made his way to Mongolia where Minamoto Yoshitsune (or "Genji-Kyo" in the Chinese reading) became Genghis Khan (1157-1226).

In 1192, Yoritomo was proclaimed *Shogun* and set about to form his own government. The Heian Period had ended and the Kamakura Era had begun. Military dominance of Japan would continue until the Meiji Restoration in 1868.

CHAPTER 1—JEI

Usagi's adventures take place at the turn of 17th century Japan.

I've deliberately kept exact dates vague to give myself more latitude in storytelling; however, I'm making an exception in this story with the retirement of *Shogun* Tokugawa Ieyasu.

In 1603, Ieyasu (1542-1616), the first of the Tokugawa *Shogun*, received the title *Sei-i-tai Shogun*, or "supreme military dictator," from Emperor Go-Yozei. Two years later, he abdicated in favor of his son, Hidetada, then twenty-six years old. He did this to guarantee the succession of the position to his family. Ieyasu retired to Shizuoka but still maintained an active role in politics. And, after almost a lifetime on the battle-field, he now devoted his leisure time to literature and poetry.

Hidetada ruled until 1622 when he abdicated in favor of his son, Iemitsu.

The Tokugawa Shogunate endured for fifteen successions and came to an end in 1868 with the Meiji Restoration, which gave power back to the emperor.

Jishin-Uwo (pg. 71) is a giant catfish that lives under Shimofusa and Hitachi Provinces. Its movements are responsible for Japan's many earthquakes. A stone in the temple of Kashima is the exposed part of a sword that the gods used to pin the fish in place.

The *Kanji* characters on page one read "Kusanagi-no-Tsurugi," literally "The Grasscutting Sword."

CHAPTER 2—HEIKE GANI

The *Heike gani* or Heike crab (*Heikea Japonica*) has, on its carapace (shell), the image of a scowling human face. According to legend, these crabs are the ghosts of the Heike warriors who died during the sea battle at Dan-no-ura.

These small crabs reach a maximum size of 1.2 inches (31 mm) across their backs. The rear two legs on each side are much smaller and claw-like for carrying objects. Their red coloration further reinforced their connection to the Heike clan whose banners were also red. There are actually two varieties of "face crabs" along Dan-no-Ura. I've drawn the smaller *Heike gani*, which are the spirits of the common warriors. The slightly larger, more ornate *taisho gani* (chieftain crab), or *tatsugashira* (dragon helmet), were animated by the ghosts of the clan leaders.

The shell-images are not merely decorative but serve a specific purpose. They are the external grooves of support ridges, called apodemes, inside the carapace that are the sites where muscles are attached. These grooves occur in almost all species of crabs. There are other varieties of "face crabs" —the *Kuei Lien Hsieh* (ghost crabs) of China and the *paradorippe granulata*, a northwestern Pacific species, to name two.

BIBLIOGRAPHY

My ultimate references for Japanese pre-history are: *The Kojiki: Records of Ancient Matters*, trans. Basil Hall Chamberlain (Boston: C. E. Tuttle & co., 1981), and *The Nihongi: Chronicles of Japan from the Earliest Times to A.D. 697*, trans. William George Aston (Boston: C. E. Tuttle & Co., 1971).

Also used for the prologues: *The Japanese: People of the Three Treasures* by Robert Newman (?: Atheneum, 1964); *History of the Japanese from the Earlist Times to the End of the Meiji Era* by Capt. F. Brinkley, R. A. (New York: The Encyclopedia Britannica C., 1915) contained both records of prehistory and the Genpei Wars, as well as a photo of the Shrine at Ise and a statue of Emperor Jimmu, upon which I based the visuals of Susano-o); *Japanese Mythology* by Juliet Piggot (New York: Hamlyn Publishing Group, 1969); *Ancient Tales and Folklore of Japan* by Richard Gordon Smith (New York: Studio Editions, 1995); *Gods of Myth and Stone* by Michael Czaja (New York: John Weatherhill, Inc., 1974) went into detail on the creation myth and Susano-o with an analysis of each act and artifact; *Green Willow and Other Japanese Fairy Tales* by Grace James (New York: Avenel Books, 1987) contains stories on Susano-o and the land of Yomi; *The Book of the Samurai: The Warrior Class of Japan* by Stephen T. Turnbull (New York: Arco, 1982) has woodcut prints of Yamato-Dake using Kusanagi, as well as Emperor Antoku and his grandmother; *Myths and Legends of Japan* by F. Hadlands Davis (New York: Dover Books, 1992); *Myths & Legends Series: China and Japan* Donald A. Mackenzie (London: Bracken Books, 1985) is part of their myths and legends series; and *Vanishing Peoples of the Earth* (Washington: National Geographic Society, 1969) contains a section entitled "Mysterious Sky People: Japan's Dwindling Ainu" by Sister Mary Inez Hilger.

Photos of the Temple of Ise can be found in : *The Lessons of Japanese Architecture* by Hiro Harada (New York: Dover Books, 1985) and *Japanese Folkhouses* by Norman F. Carver, Jr. (Kalamazoo: Documan Press, 1984) *The Creators: A History of the Imagination*, chronicles the Japanese use of wood in building, particularly in the Temple of Ise.

The visuals for Yamato-Hime were based upon Shinto temple maidens found in *Festivals of Japan* and *A Look into Japan*, both published in 1985 by Japan Travel Bureau, Inc.

The History of the Genpei War: *The Tale of the Heike*, trans. Hiroshi Kitagawa and Bruce T. Tsuchida (Japan: University of Tokyo Press, 1975); *The Ten Foot Square Hut and Tales of the Heike*, trans. A. L. Sadler (Boston: C. E. Tuttle & Co.,1985); *Genpei* by Hideo Takeda is an art book chronicling the history of the war; *Of Nightingales That Weep* by Katherine Paterson (New York: Harper Trophy, 1989) is a very

enjoyable, well researched, young-adults novel; *Yoshitsune* is a Japanese television docu-drama chronicling the life of this hero and helped with the visuals of my story.

Books that contain chapters on the war: *The Samurai: A Military History* by Stephen R. Turnbull (New York: Macmillan Publishing, 1977) devotes chapters to the rivalry between the Minamoto and the Taira clans in detail; *Samurai Warriors* by Turnbull (New York: Blandford Press, 1987); *The Samurai: Warriors of Medieval Japan 940-1600* by Anthony J. Bryant (London: Osprey Press, 1989) also has many photographs and paintings, including Yoshitsune's and Benkei's armor; and *Arms and Armor of the Samurai: The History of Weaponry in Ancient Japan* by I. Bottomley and A. P. Hopson (New York: Crescent Books, 1988).

Additional war-related sources: *Historical and Geographical Dictionary of Japan* by E. Papinot (Boston: C. E. Tuttle & Co., 1984); *Dictionary of Japanese Culture* by Setsuko Kojima and Gene A. Crane (Torrance: Heian International, 1991); *Bushido, The Way of the Warrior: A New Perspective on the Japanese Military Tradition* by John Newman (Leicester: Magna Books, 1989); *Battles of the Samurai* by Turnbull (New York: Arms and Armor Press, 1987) has a chapter on the Battle of Kurikara during the early days of the war; and *Samurai Warfare* by Turnbull (New York: Arms and Armor Press, 1996) has a section on naval warfare.

Research on the *Heike gani* crabs came from: the periodical *Terra*, vol. 31, no. 4 (Los Angeles: Natural History Museum of Los Angeles County, September 1993); *Kotto* by Lafcadio Hearn (Rutland, VT/Tokyo: Charles E. Tuttle Co., Inc., 1971) contains a chapter and drawings of these unusual crustaceans; and *Japan Day by Day 1877-1883* by Edward Morse (Boston: Houghton Mifflin Co., 1945) has drawings and a brief history of the crabs.

Usagi Yojimbo

Stan Sakai's cover art from issues thirteen through twenty-two of Dark Horse's Usagi Yojimbo™ Volume Three *series.*

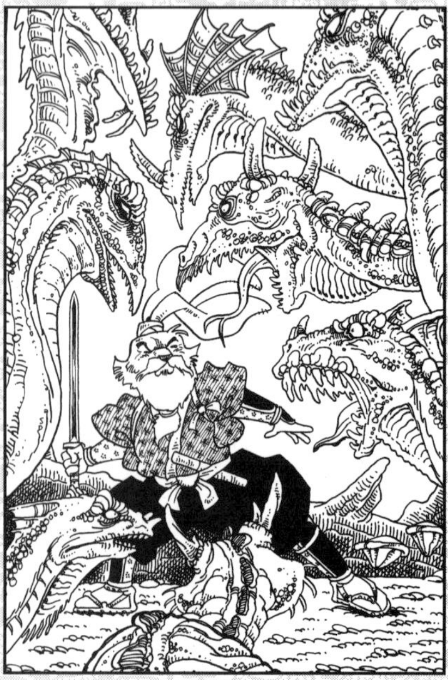

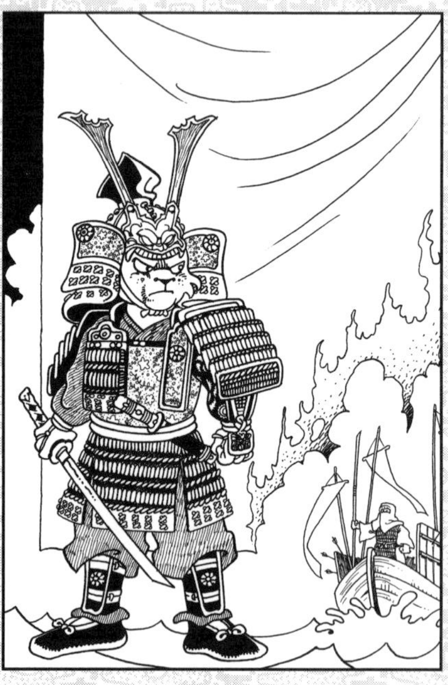

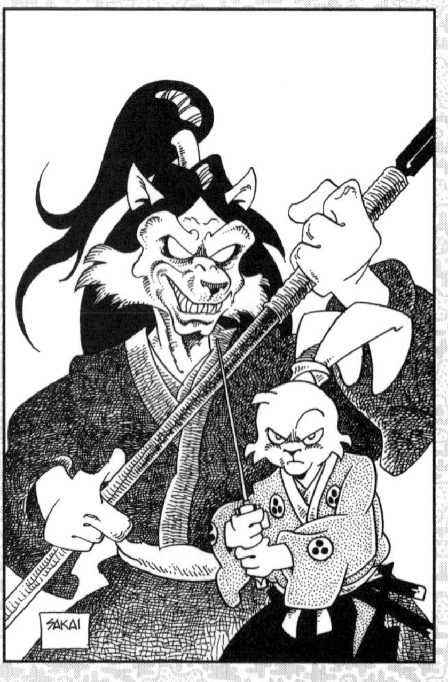
SAKAI

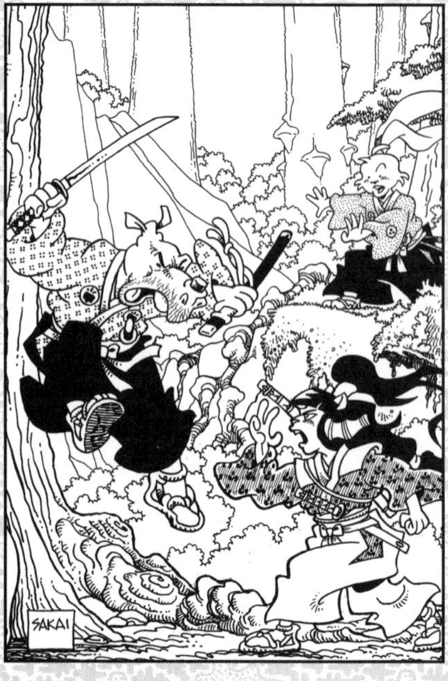
SAKAI

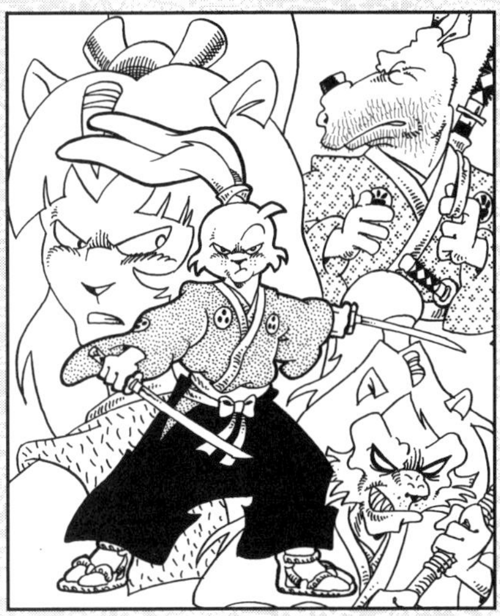
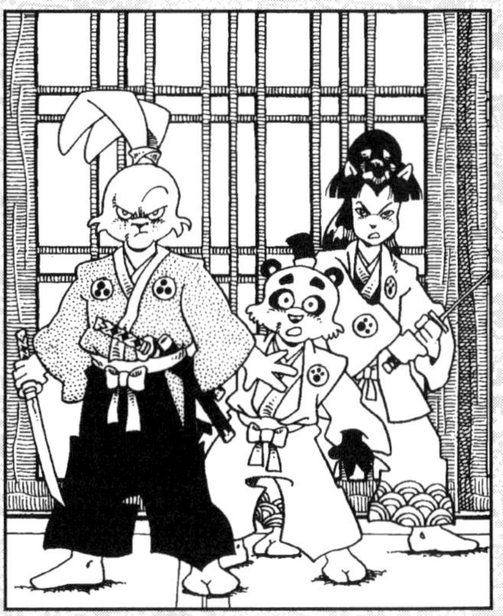
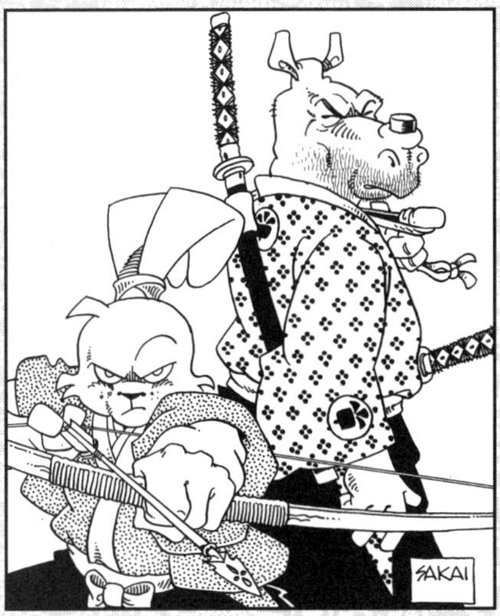
SAKAI
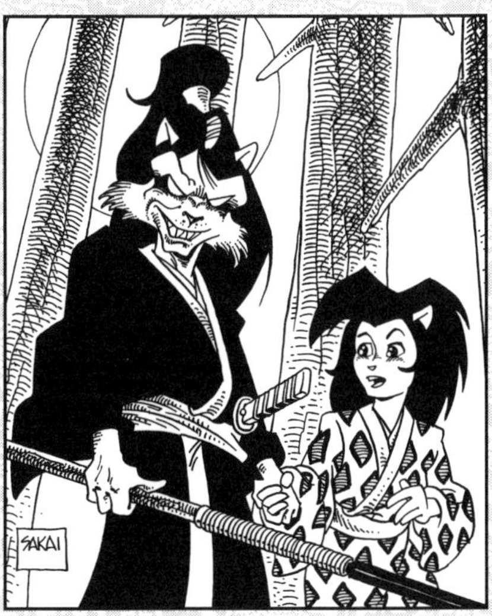
SAKAI
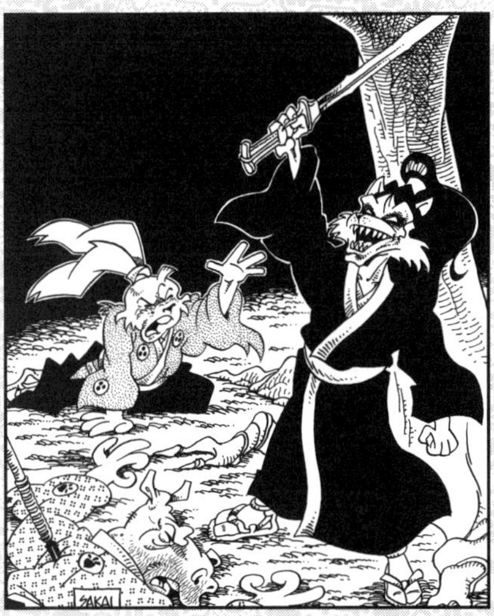
SAKAI
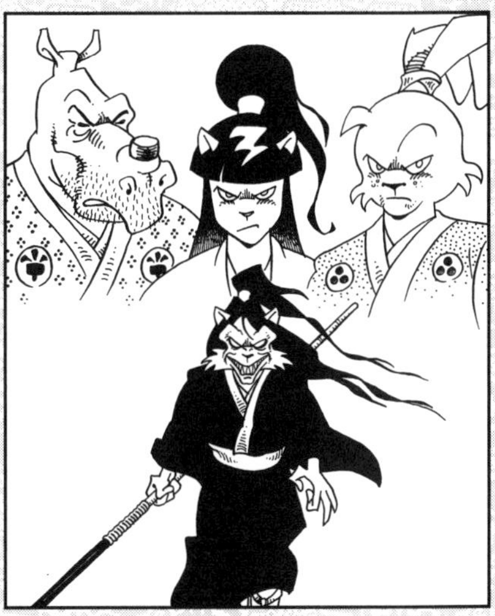

BIOGRAPHY
Stan Sakai

STAN SAKAI WAS BORN in Kyoto, Japan, grew up in Hawaii, and now lives in California with his wife, Sharon, and children, Hannah and Matthew. He received a Fine Arts degree from the University of Hawaii and furthered his studies at Art Center College of Design in Pasadena, California.

His creation, Usagi Yojimbo, first appeared in comics in 1984. Since then, Usagi has been on television as a guest of the Teenage Mutant Ninja Turtles and has been made into toys, seen on clothing, and featured in a series of trade-paperback collections.

In 1991, Stan created *Space Usagi*, a series about the adventures of a descendant of the original Usagi that dealt with samurai in a futuristic setting.

Stan is also an award-winning letterer for his work on Sergio Aragonés' *Groo the Wanderer*, the "Spider-Man" Sunday newspaper strips, and *Usagi Yojimbo*.

Stan is a recipient of a Parents' Choice Award, an Inkpot Award, and multiple Eisner Awards.

Usagi Yojimbo

*Trade paperbacks, limited-edition hardcover collections,
and merchandise available from Dark Horse Comics*

Shades of Death
200-page black-and-white paperback
ISBN: 1-56971-259-X $14.95
limited-edition hardcover
ISBN: 1-56971-279-4 $49.95

Daisho
200-page black-and-white paperback
ISBN: 1-56971-292-1 $14.95
limited-edition hardcover
ISBN: 1-56971-293-X $49.95

The Brink of Life and Death
200-page black-and-white paperback
ISBN: 1-56971-297-2 $14.95
limited-edition hardcover
ISBN: 1-56971-298-0 $55.00

Seasons
200-page black-and-white paperback
ISBN: 1-56971-375-8 $14.95
limited-edition hardcover
ISBN: 1-56971-376-6 $55.00

Grasscutter
254-page black-and-white paperback
ISBN: 1-56971-413-4 $16.95

Grey Shadows
200-page black-and-white paperback
ISBN: 1-56971-459-2 $14.95

Demon Mask
224-page black-and-white paperback
ISBN: 1-56971-523-8 $15.95
limited-edition hardcover
ISBN: 1-56971-524-6 $56.95

Space Usagi
296-page black-and-white paperback
ISBN: 1-56971-290-5 $17.95
limited-edition hardcover
ISBN: 1-56971-291-3 $59.95

Usagi Yojimbo Cold-Cast Resin Statues
*Each statue stands 8" tall, fully-painted. Includes a mini-sketchbook and
nine exclusive Usagi trading cards; one signed by Stan Sakai.
Usagi Yojimbo #19-179 $79.95 • Young Usagi & Katsuichi #19-289 $79.95*

Usagi Yojimbo Wristwatch
*Limited edition of 1,000. Packaged in a collectible,
wooden box. Includes certificate of authenticity.
#10-011 $49.99*

AVAILABLE AT YOUR LOCAL COMICS SHOP OR BOOKSTORE.
To find a comics shop in your area, call 1-888-266-4226. For more information or to
order direct: E-mail: mailorder@darkhorse.com On the web: www.darkhorse.com
Phone: 1-800-862-0052 or (503) 652-9701 Mon.-Sat. 9 a.m. to 5 p.m. Pacific Time